Disney
Tangled
The Series

Also From Joe Books

Disney Princess Comics Treasury
Disney Frozen Cinestory Comic
Disney Cinderella Cinestory Comic
Disney Descendants Wicked World Cinestory Comic Volume One
Disney Descendants Wicked World Cinestory Comic Volume Two
Disney Descendants Wicked World Cinestory Comic Volume Three
Disney Descendants Wicked World Cinestory Comic Volume Four
Disney Alice in Wonderland Cinestory Comic
Disney Princess Comic Strips Collection Volume One
Disney Princess Comic Strips Collection Volume Two
Disney Tangled Cinestory Comic
Disney Beauty and the Beast Cinestory Comic
Disney Tangled Before Ever After Cinestory Comic

Disney Tangled The Series

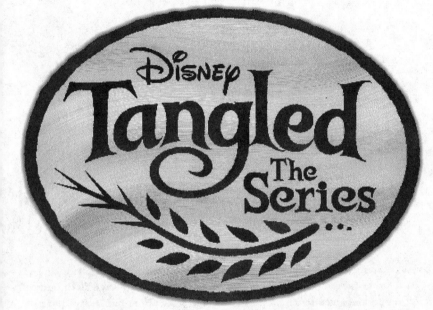

Take on the World

Cinestory Comic

JOE BOOKS LTD

Published simultaneously in the United States and Canada
by Joe Books Ltd, 489 College Street, Suite 203, Toronto, ON M6G 1A5

www.joebooks.com

First Joe Books edition: September 2017

Print ISBN: 978-1-77275-497-1
ebook ISBN: 978-1-77275-555-8

Library and Archives Canada Cataloguing in Publication
information is available upon request

Printed and bound in Canada
1 3 5 7 9 10 8 6 4 2

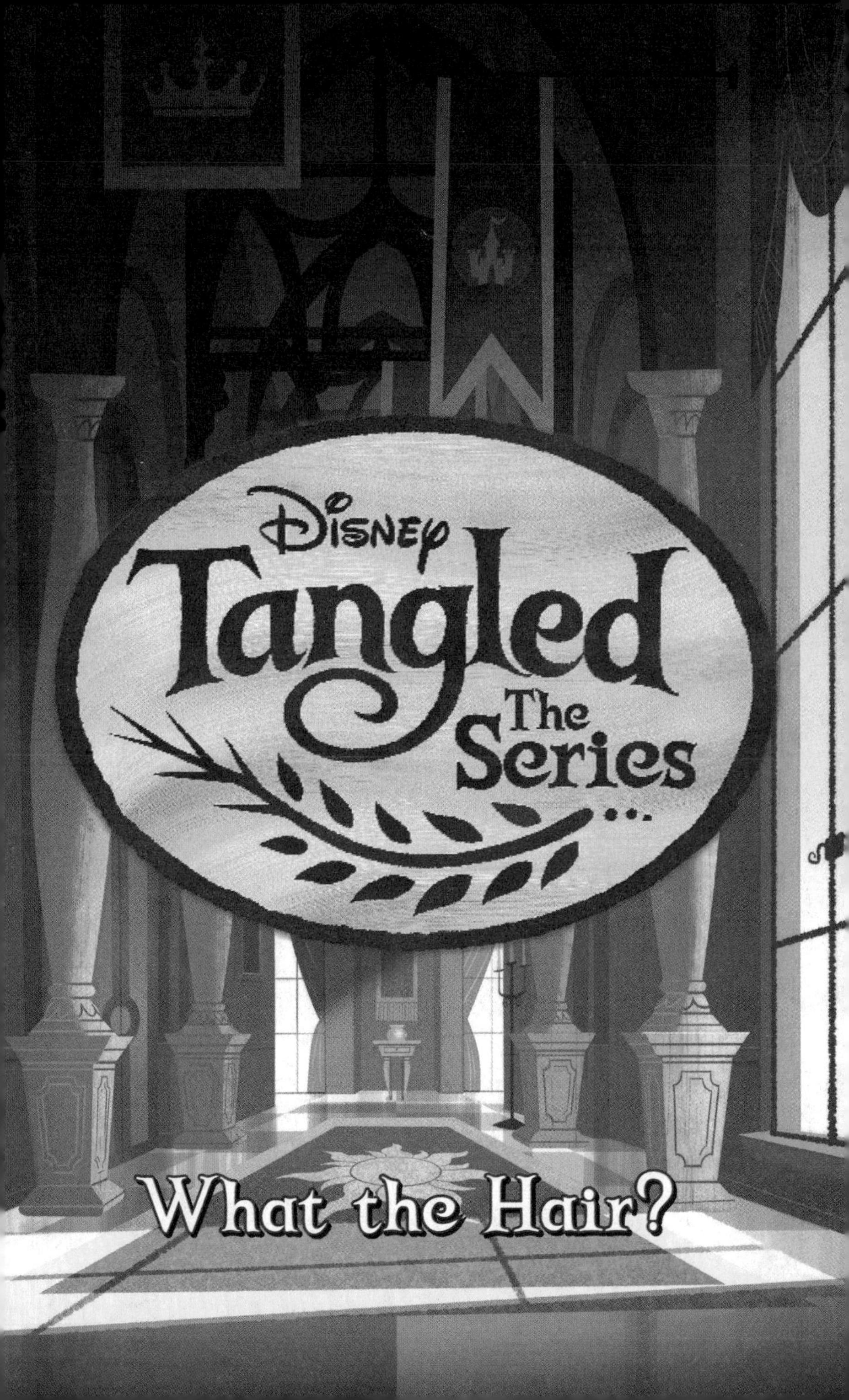
Disney
Tangled
The Series
What the Hair?

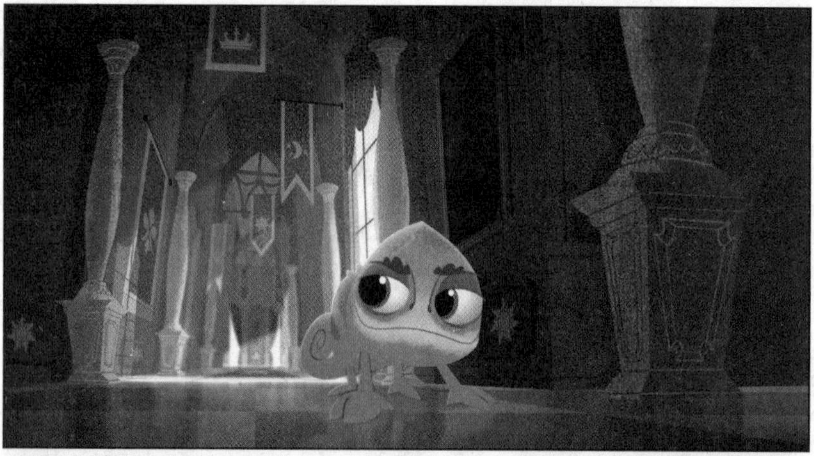
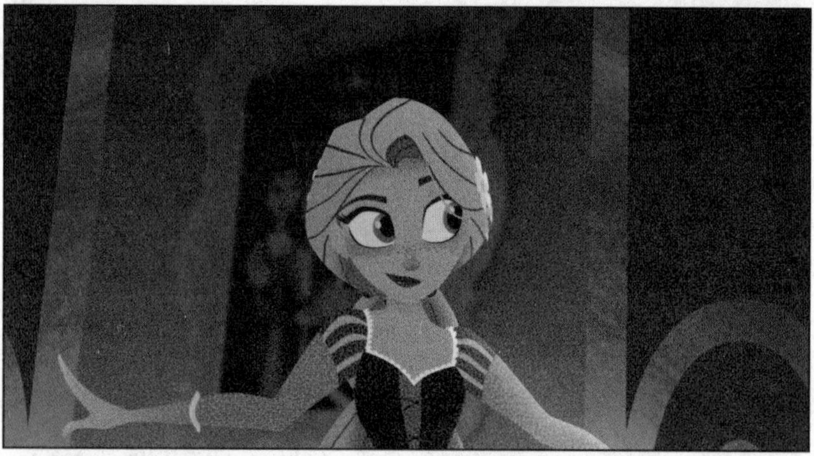
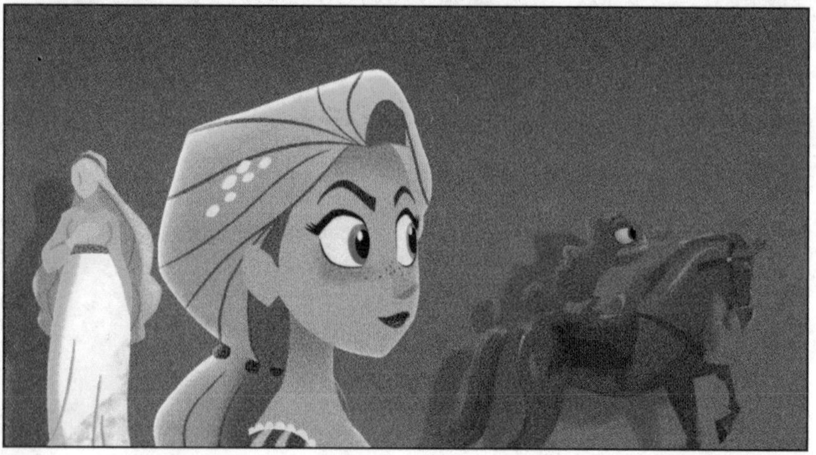

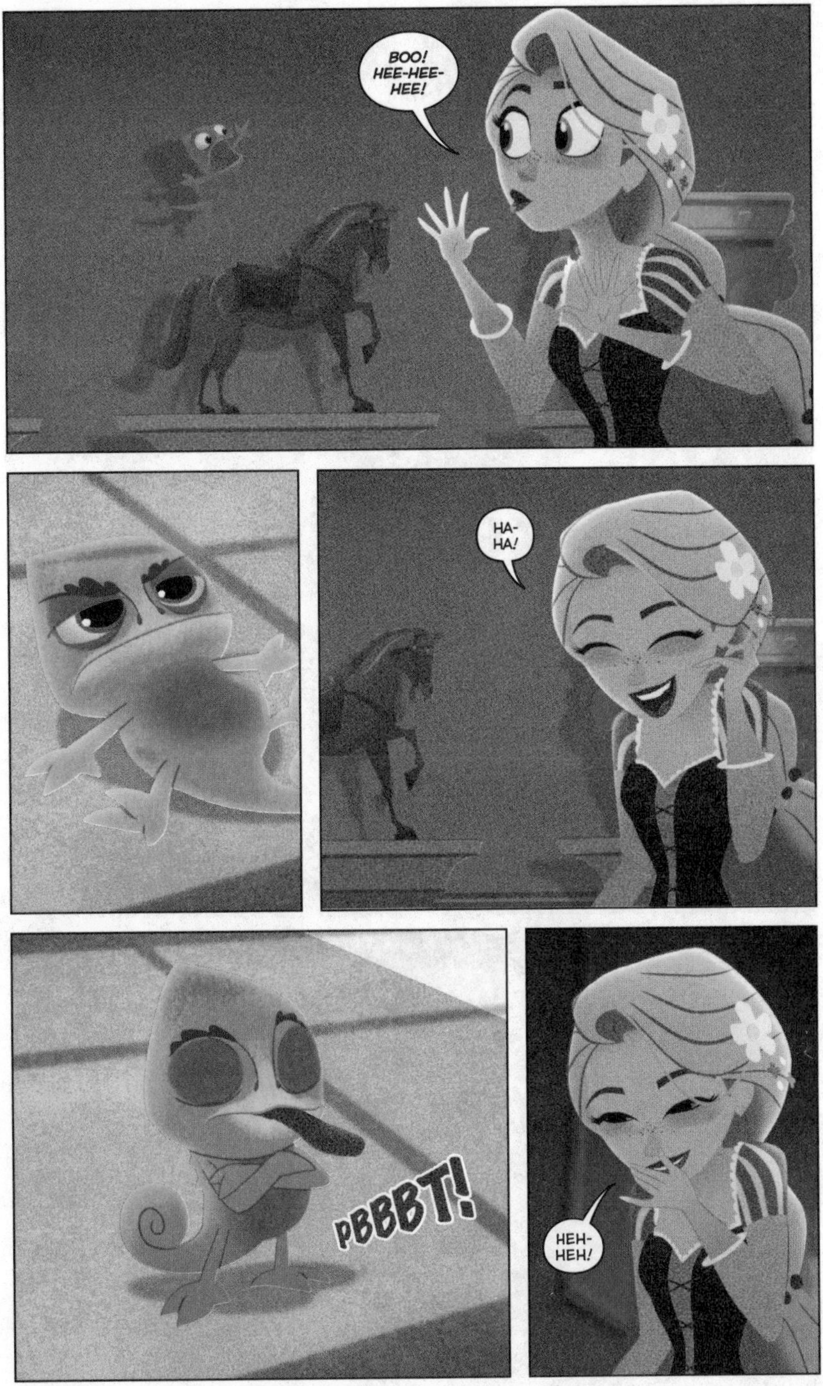
BOO! HEE-HEE-HEE!
HA-HA!
PBBBT!
HEH-HEH!

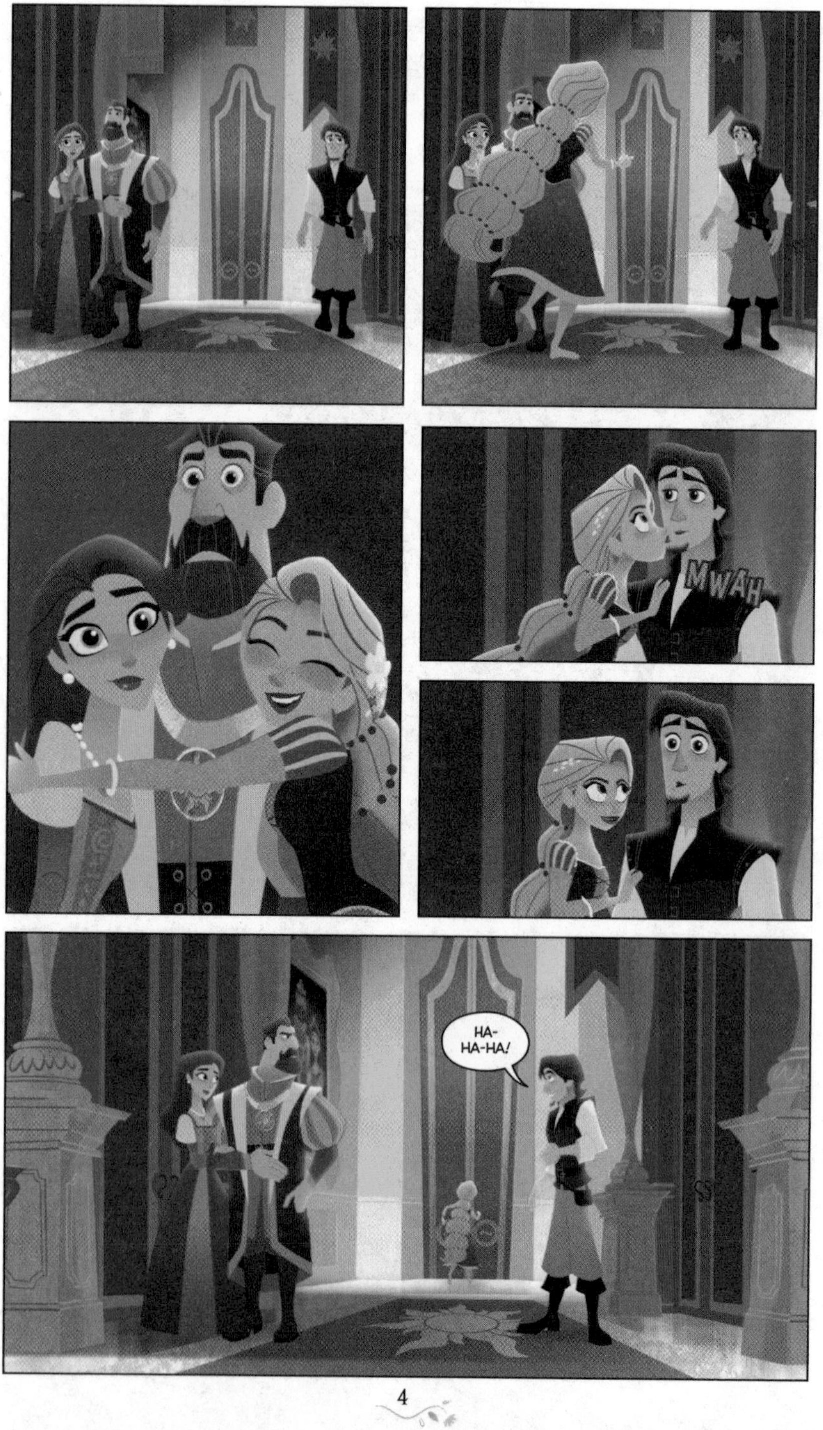
MWAH
HA-
HA-HA!

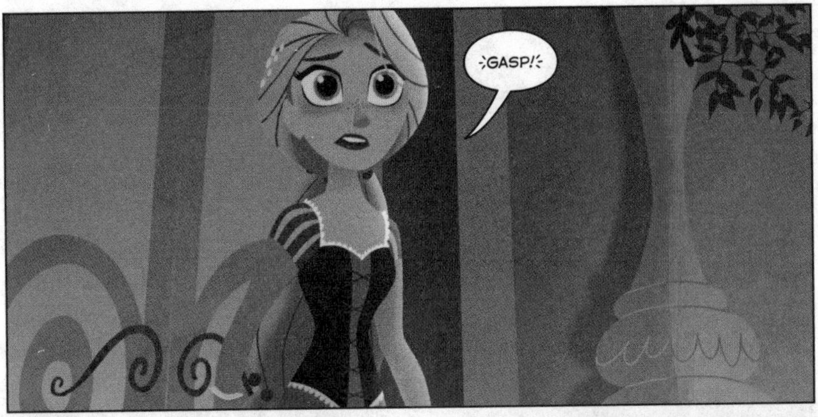
GASP!

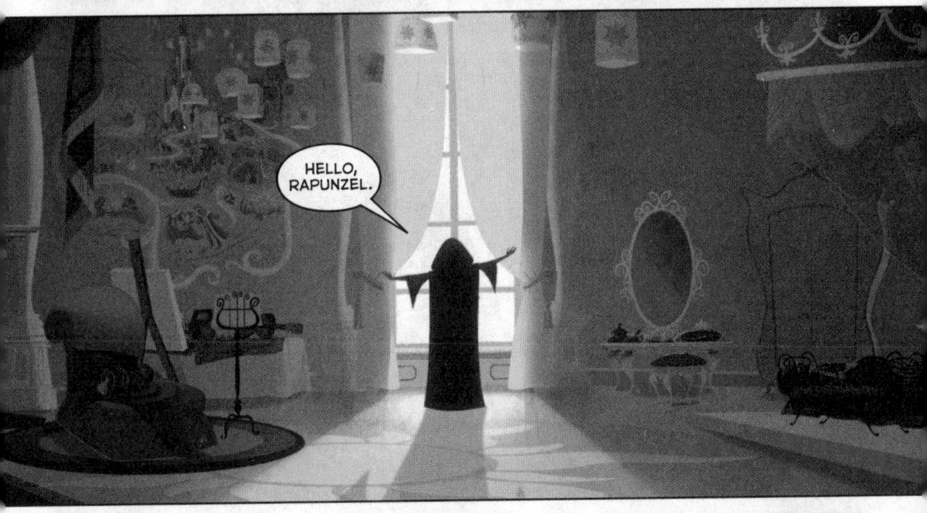
HELLO, RAPUNZEL.

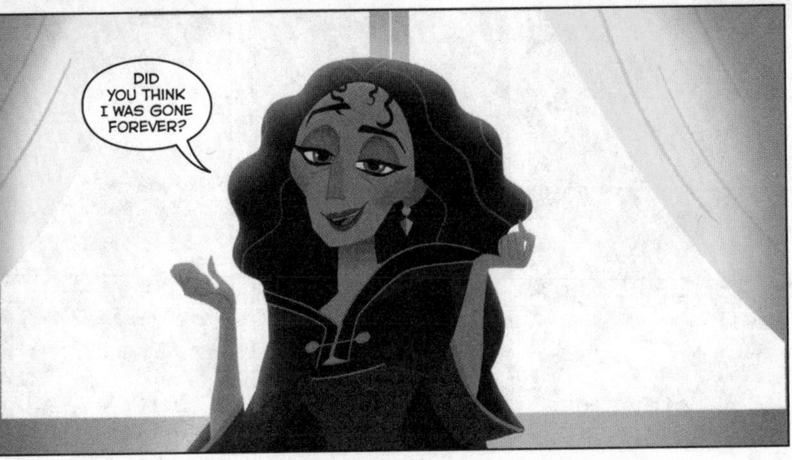
DID YOU THINK I WAS GONE FOREVER?

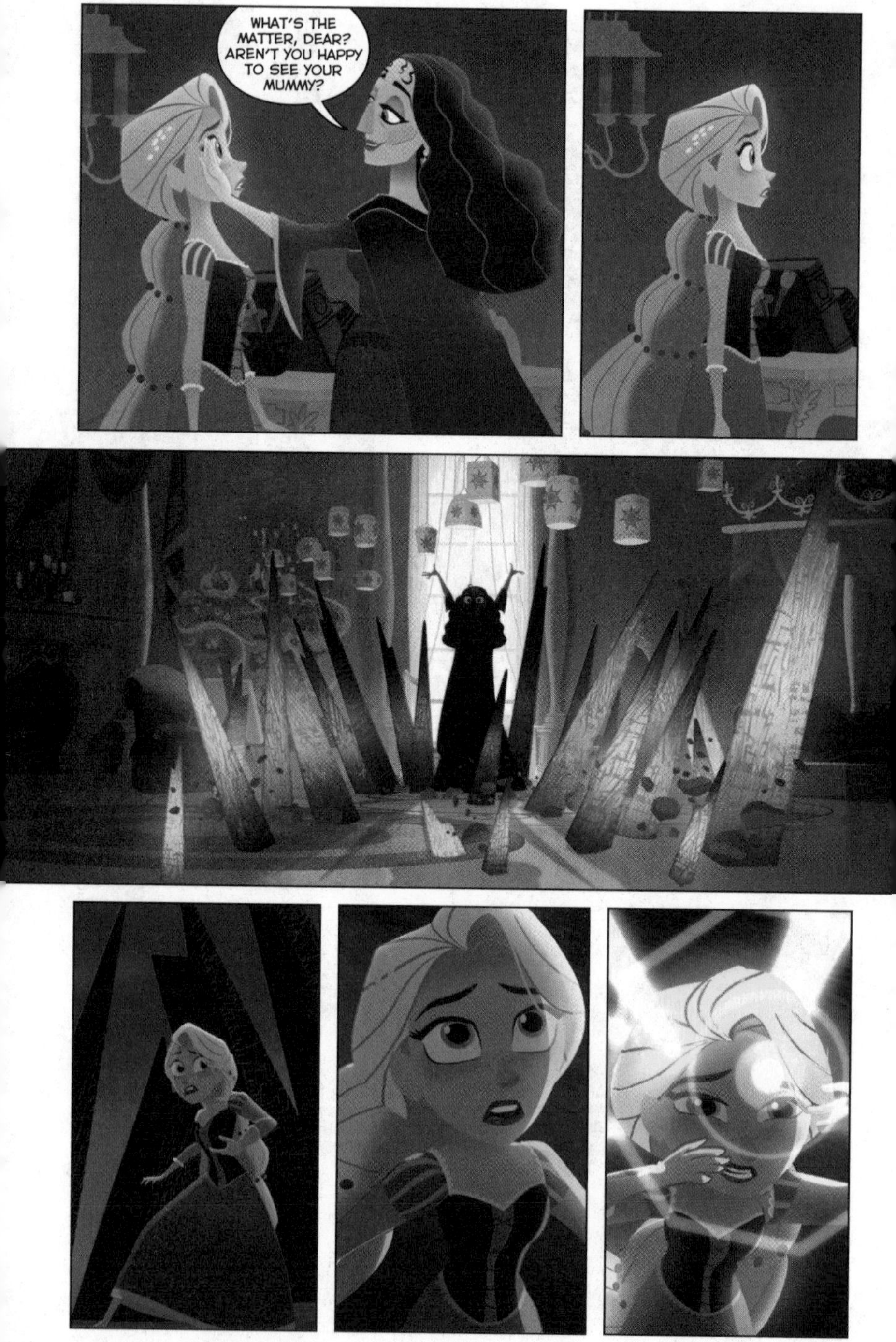
WHAT'S THE MATTER, DEAR? AREN'T YOU HAPPY TO SEE YOUR MUMMY?

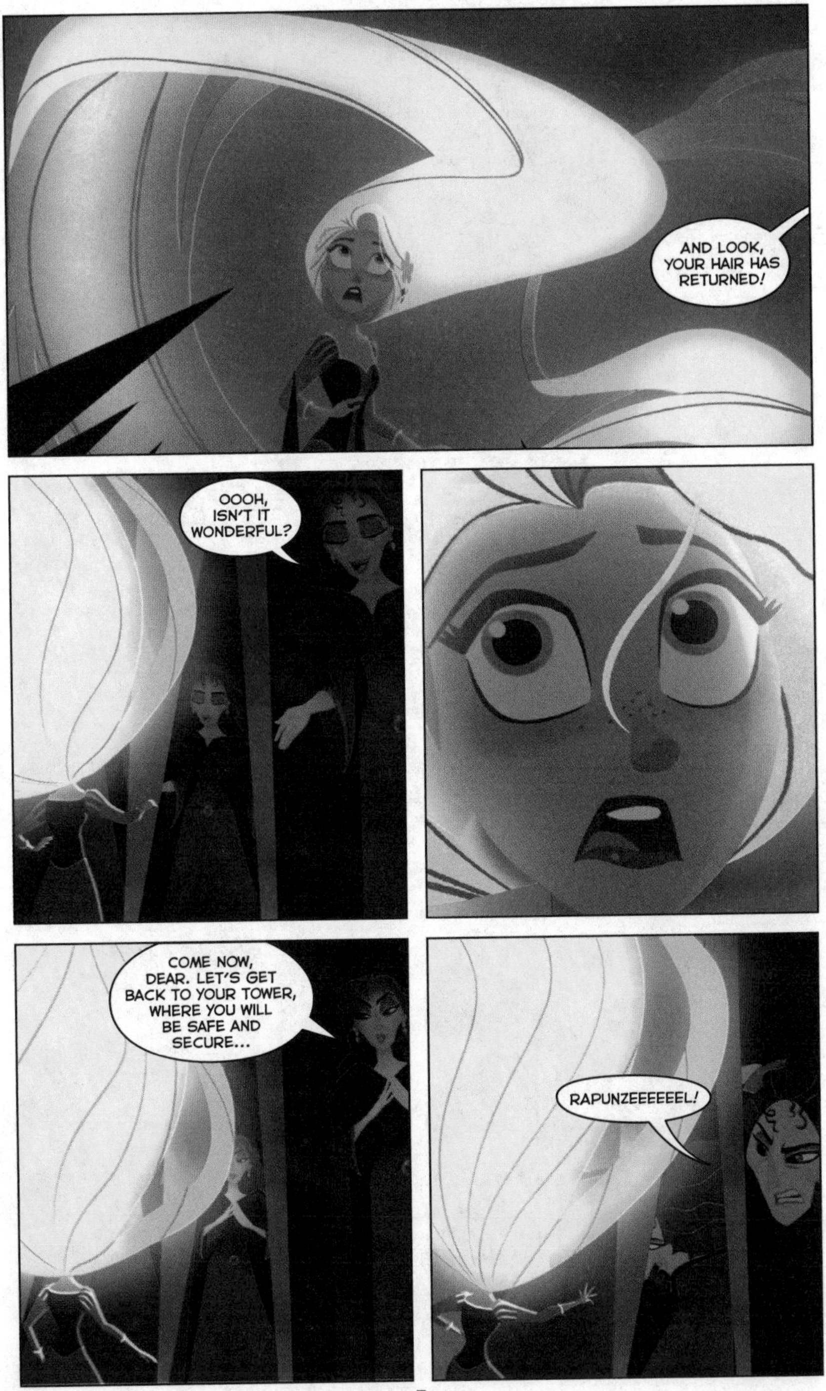
AND LOOK, YOUR HAIR HAS RETURNED!
OOOH, ISN'T IT WONDERFUL?
COME NOW, DEAR. LET'S GET BACK TO YOUR TOWER, WHERE YOU WILL BE SAFE AND SECURE...
RAPUNZEEEEEEL!

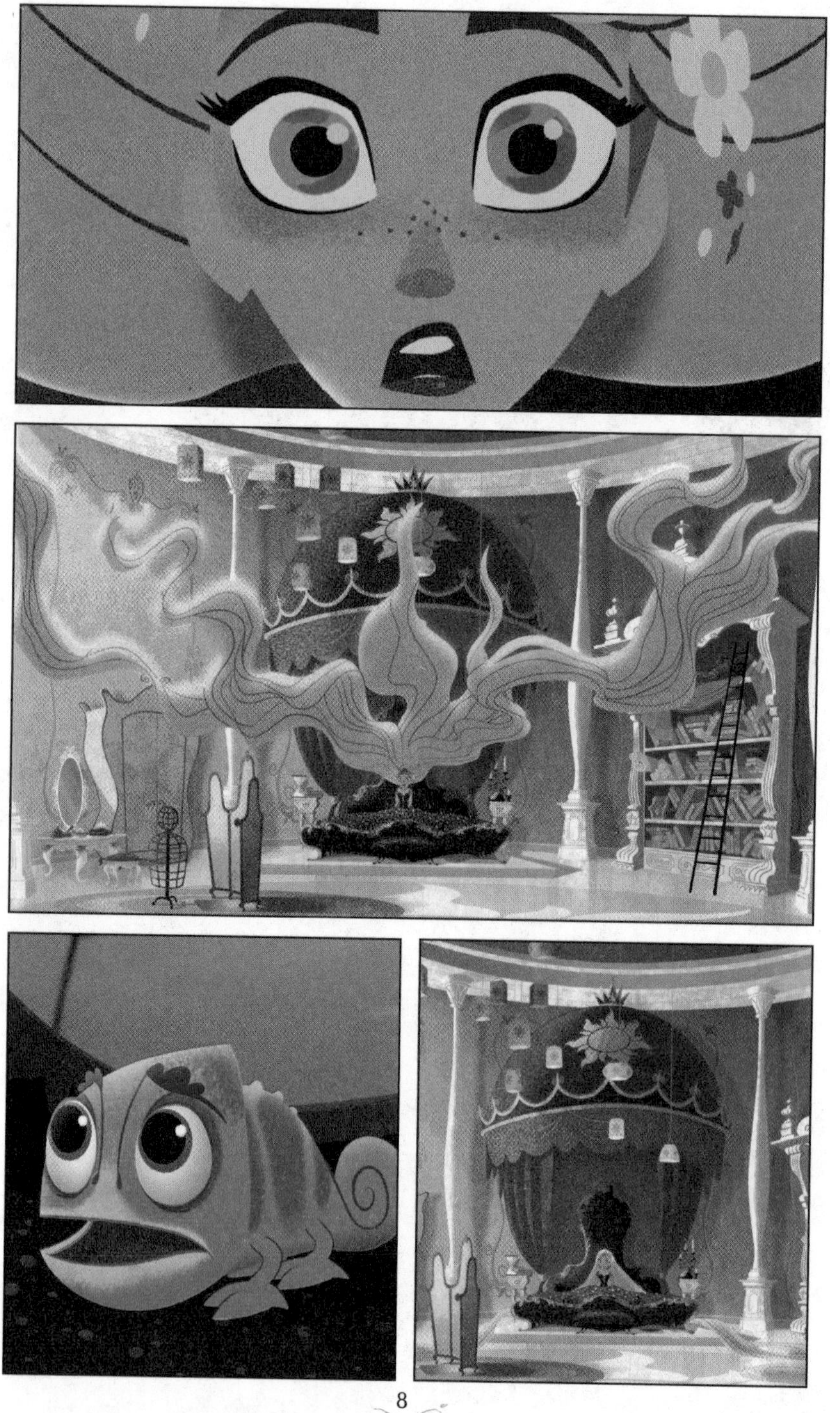

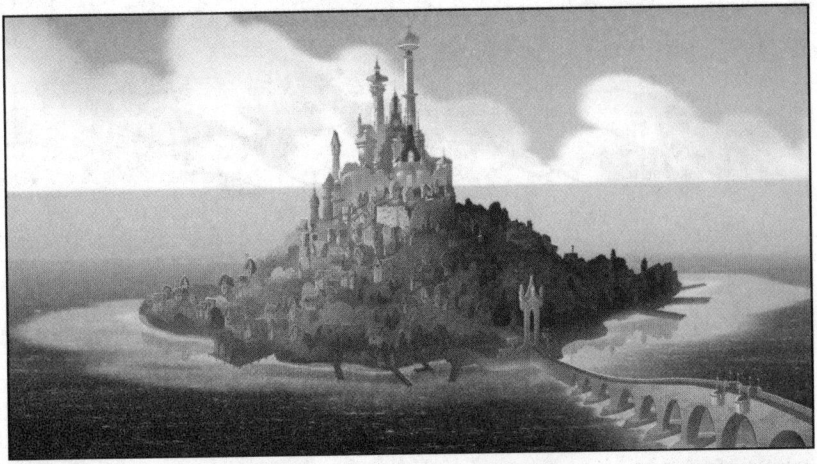

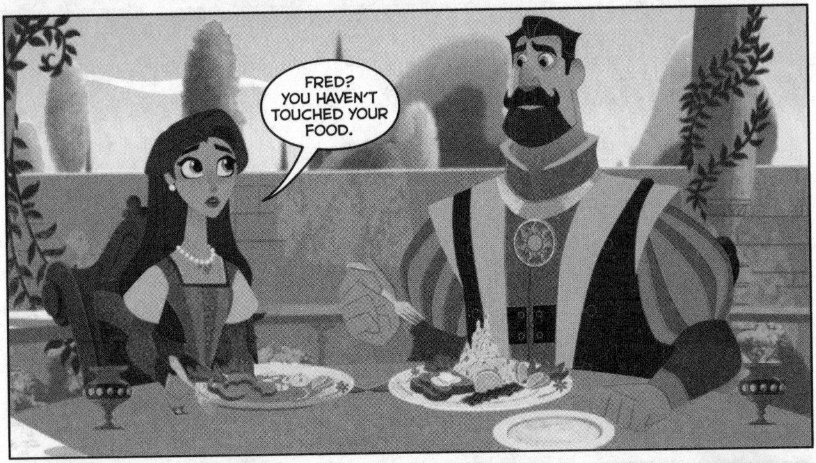
FRED? YOU HAVEN'T TOUCHED YOUR FOOD.

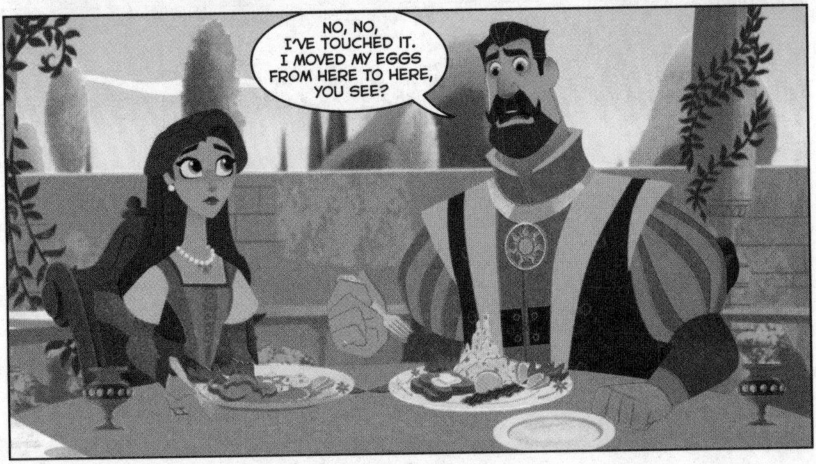
NO, NO, I'VE TOUCHED IT. I MOVED MY EGGS FROM HERE TO HERE, YOU SEE?

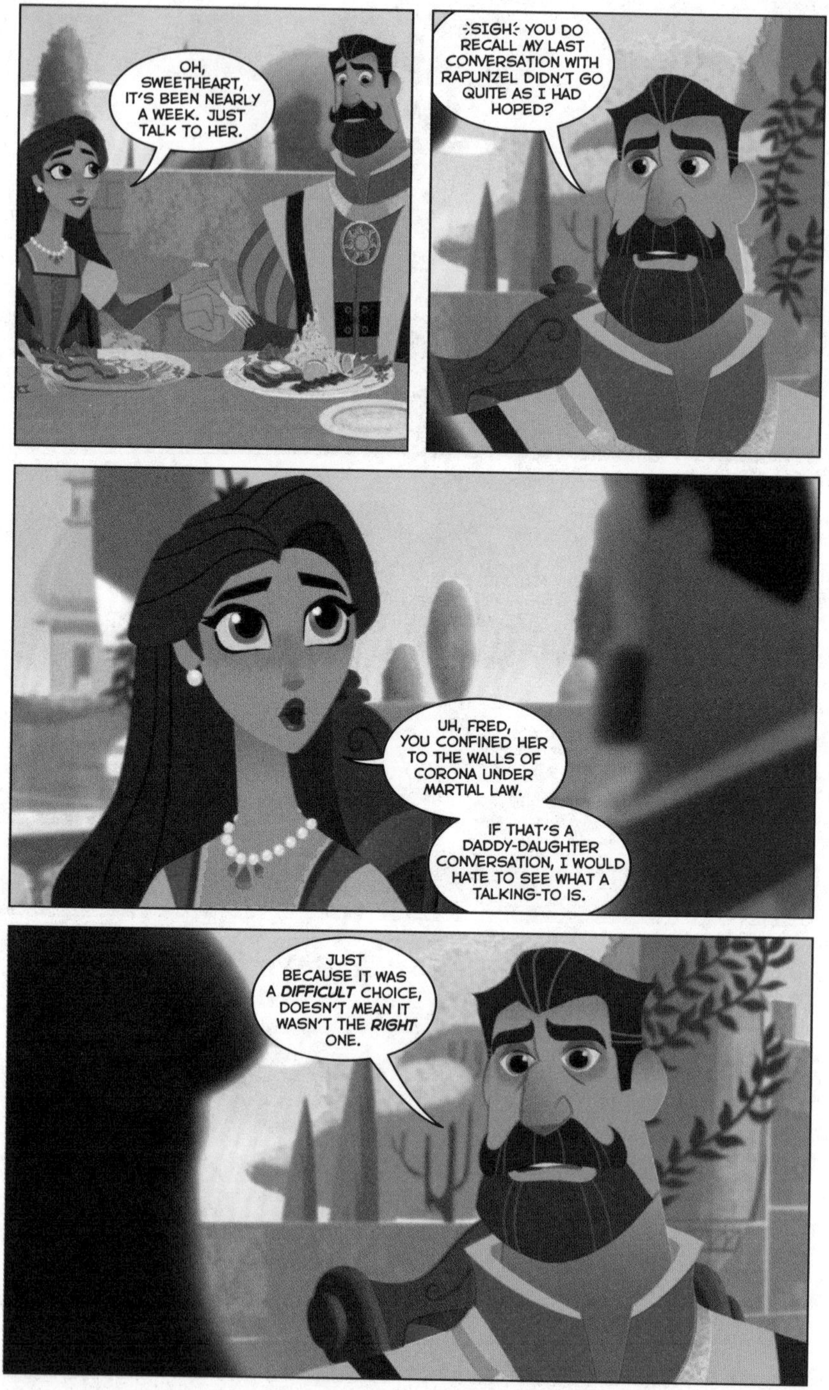
OH, SWEETHEART, IT'S BEEN NEARLY A WEEK. JUST TALK TO HER.
-SIGH- YOU DO RECALL MY LAST CONVERSATION WITH RAPUNZEL DIDN'T GO QUITE AS I HAD HOPED?
UH, FRED, YOU CONFINED HER TO THE WALLS OF CORONA UNDER MARTIAL LAW.
IF THAT'S A DADDY-DAUGHTER CONVERSATION, I WOULD HATE TO SEE WHAT A TALKING-TO IS.
JUST BECAUSE IT WAS A *DIFFICULT* CHOICE, DOESN'T MEAN IT WASN'T THE *RIGHT* ONE.

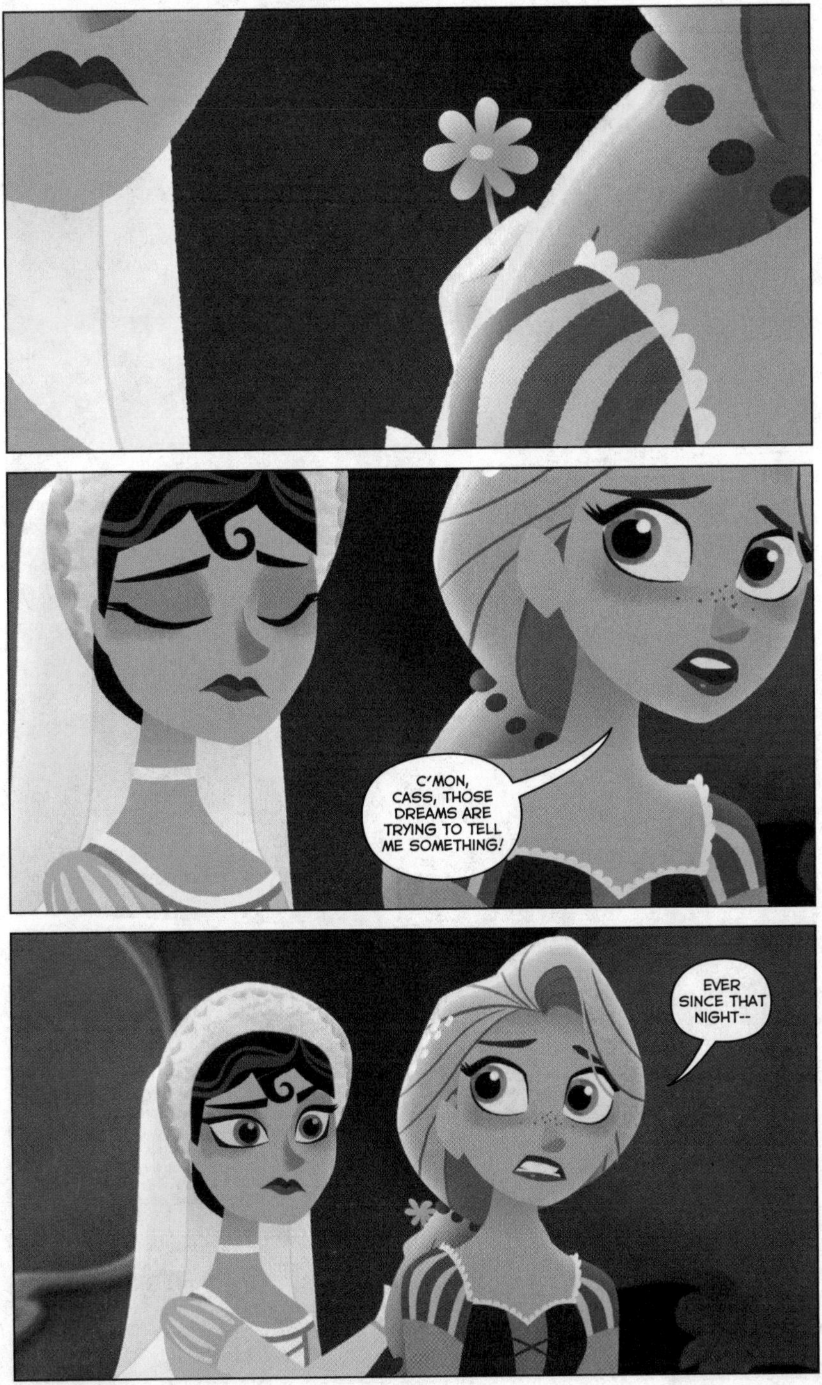
C'MON, CASS, THOSE DREAMS ARE TRYING TO TELL ME SOMETHING!
EVER SINCE THAT NIGHT--

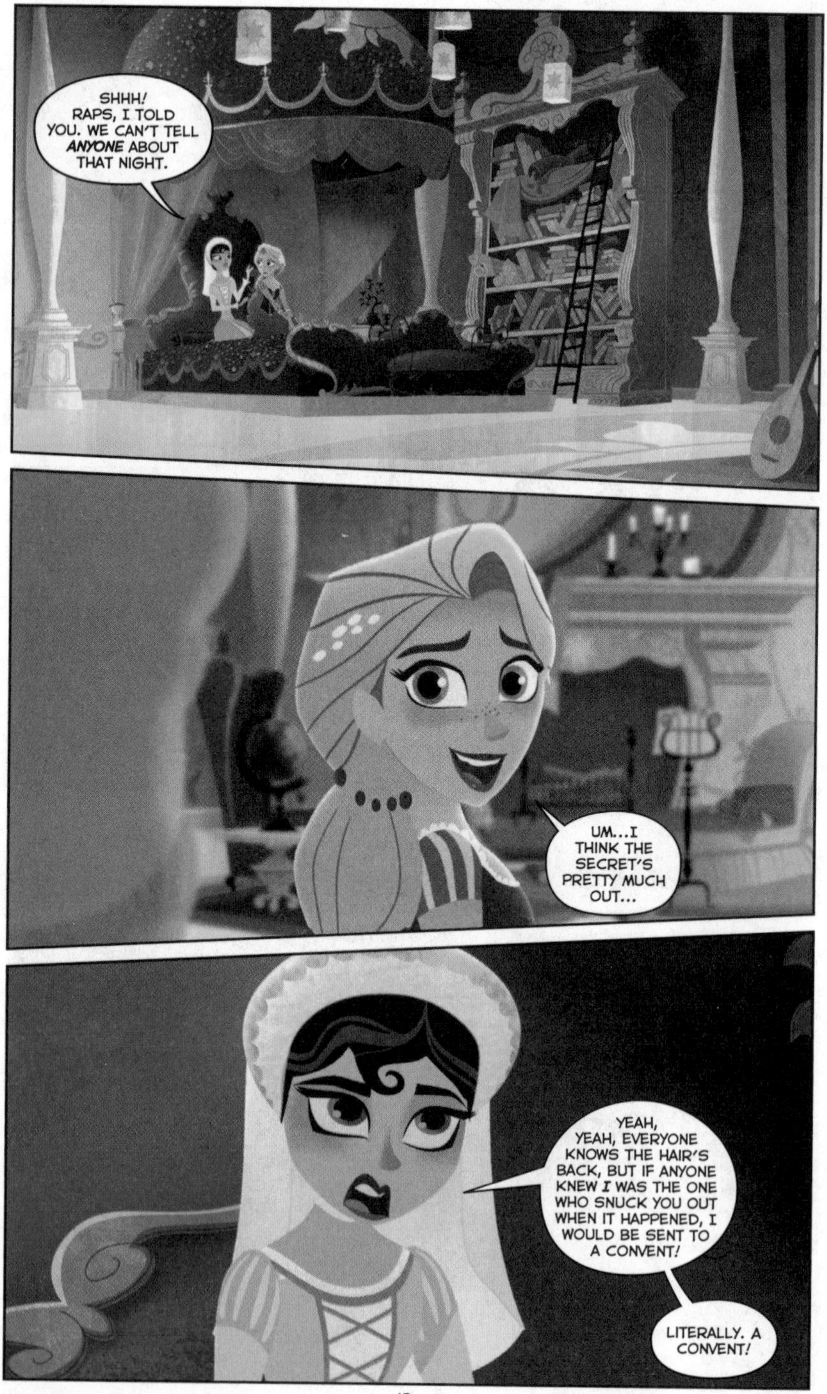
SHHH! RAPS, I TOLD YOU. WE CAN'T TELL *ANYONE* ABOUT THAT NIGHT.
UM...I THINK THE SECRET'S PRETTY MUCH OUT...
YEAH, YEAH, EVERYONE KNOWS THE HAIR'S BACK, BUT IF ANYONE KNEW *I* WAS THE ONE WHO SNUCK YOU OUT WHEN IT HAPPENED, I WOULD BE SENT TO A CONVENT!
LITERALLY. A CONVENT!

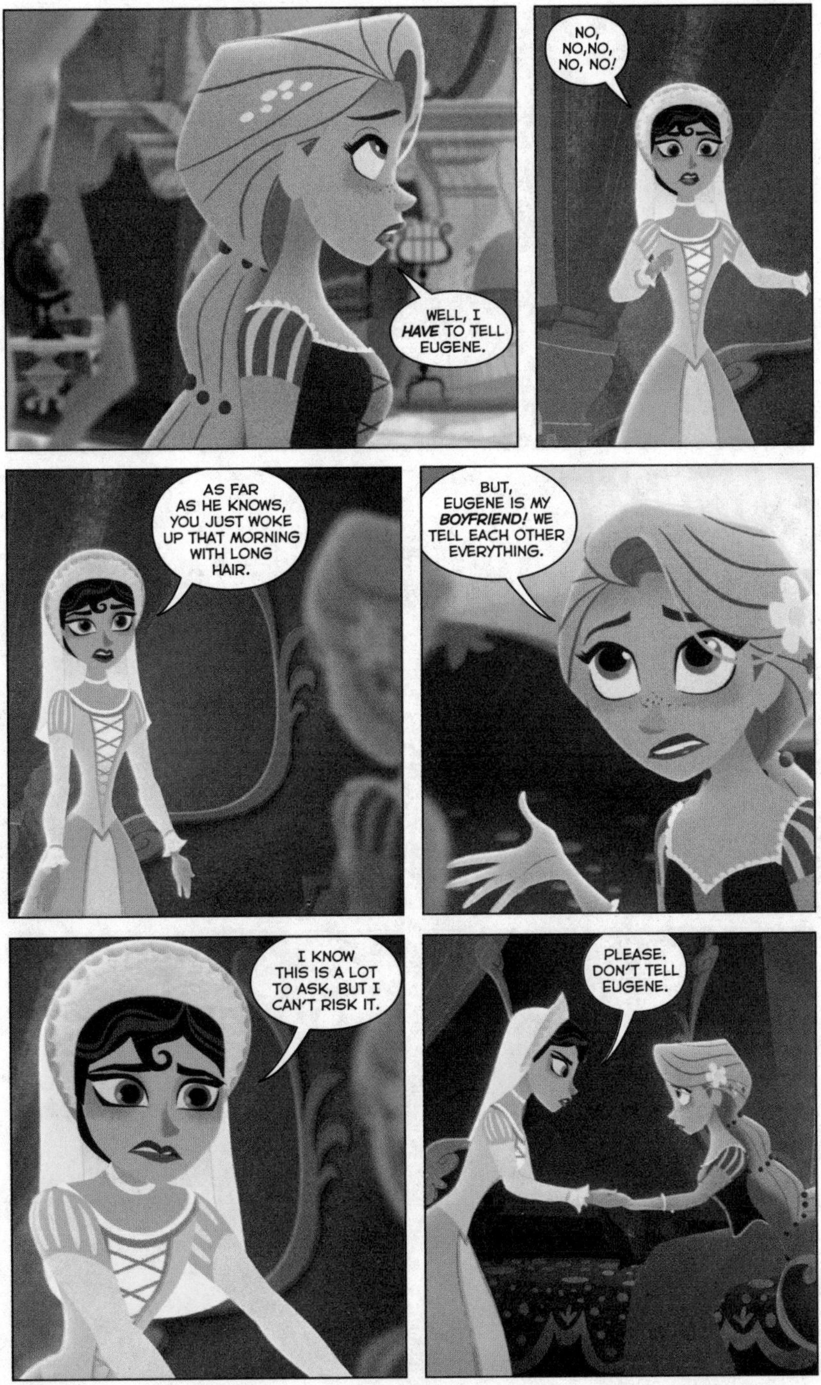
WELL, I *HAVE* TO TELL EUGENE.
NO, NO,NO, NO, NO!
AS FAR AS HE KNOWS, YOU JUST WOKE UP THAT MORNING WITH LONG HAIR.
BUT, EUGENE IS MY *BOYFRIEND!* WE TELL EACH OTHER EVERYTHING.
I KNOW THIS IS A LOT TO ASK, BUT I CAN'T RISK IT.
PLEASE. DON'T TELL EUGENE.

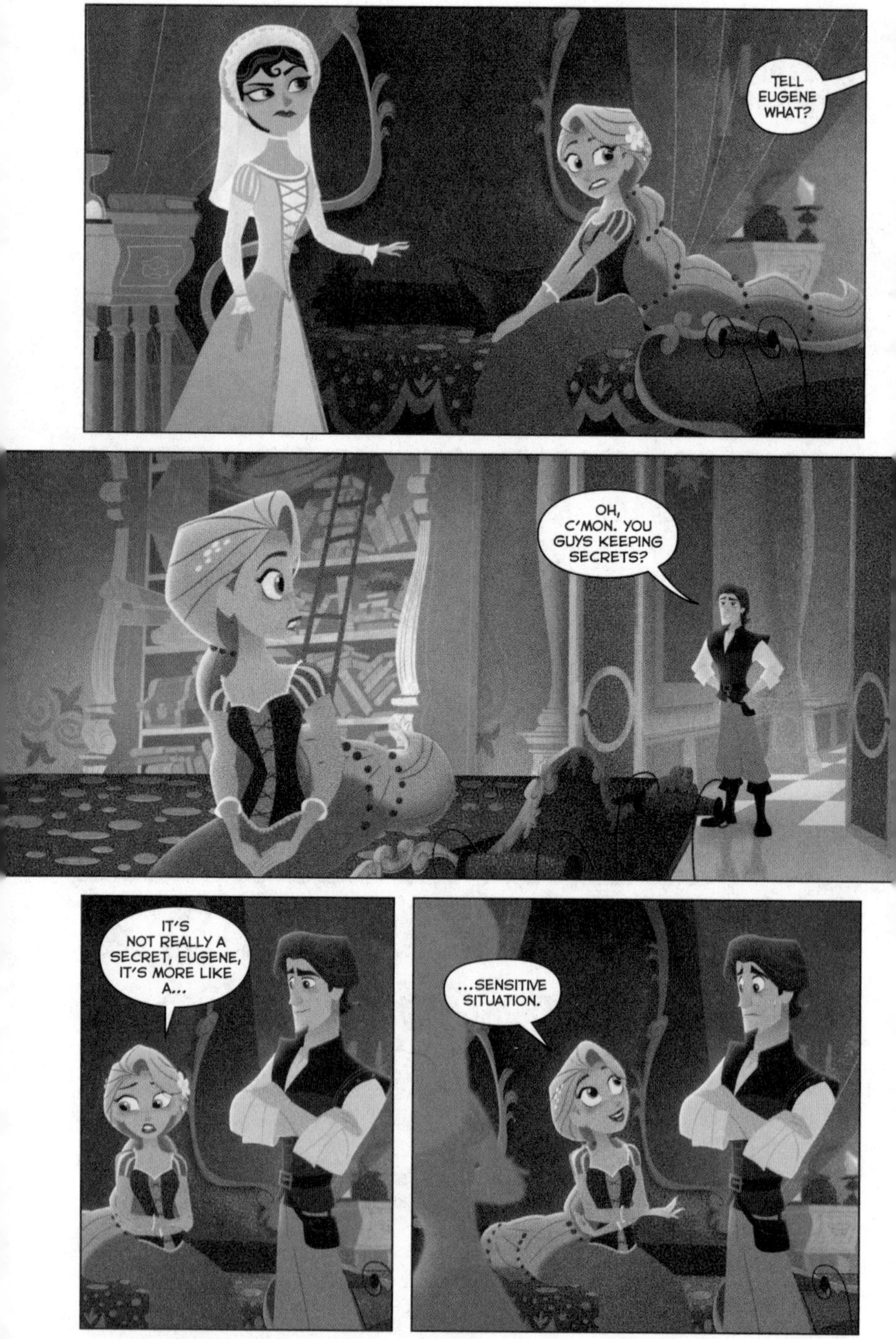
TELL EUGENE WHAT?
OH, C'MON. YOU GUYS KEEPING SECRETS?
IT'S NOT REALLY A SECRET, EUGENE, IT'S MORE LIKE A...
...SENSITIVE SITUATION.

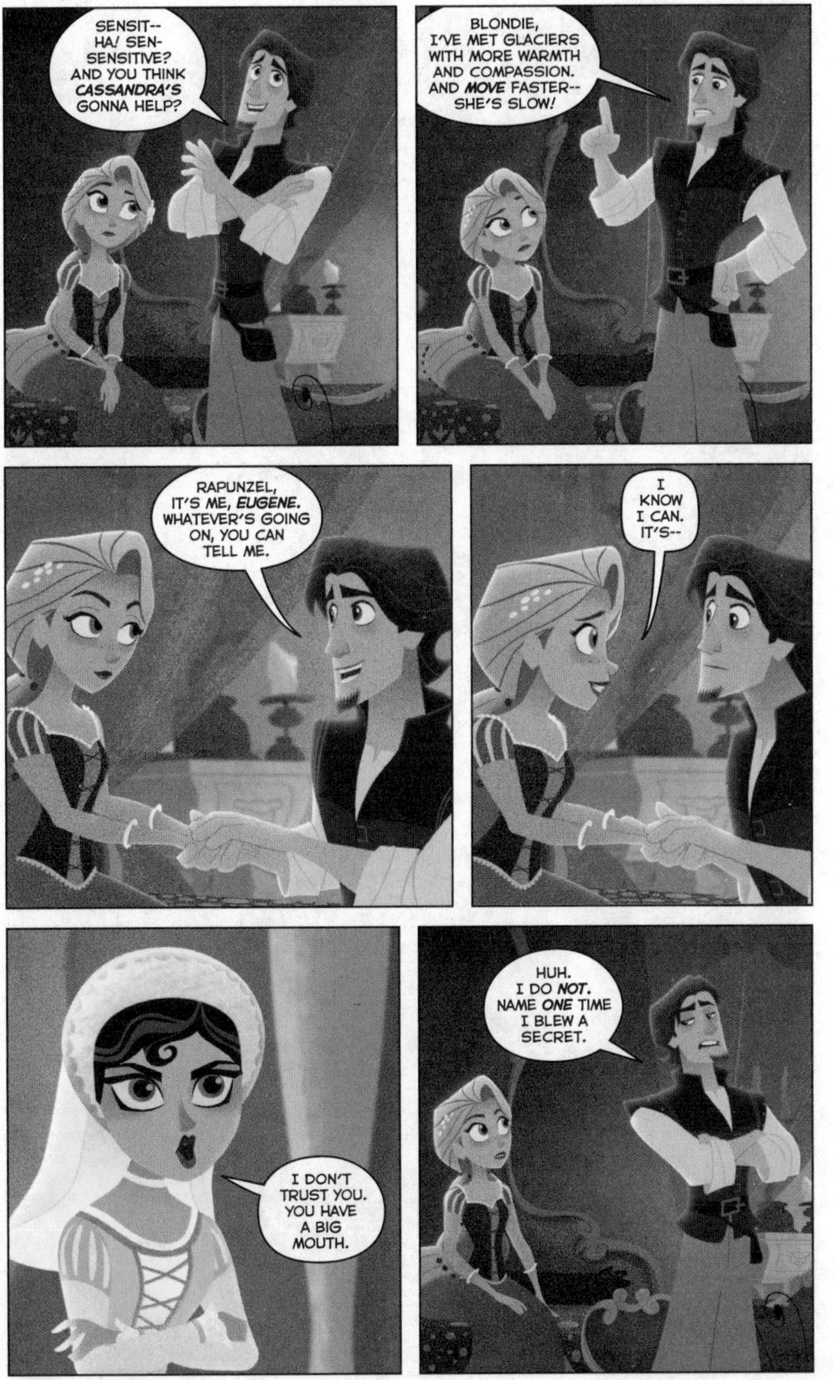
SENSIT-- HA! SEN-SENSITIVE? AND YOU THINK CASSANDRA'S GONNA HELP?
BLONDIE, I'VE MET GLACIERS WITH MORE WARMTH AND COMPASSION. AND MOVE FASTER-- SHE'S SLOW!
RAPUNZEL, IT'S ME, EUGENE. WHATEVER'S GOING ON, YOU CAN TELL ME.
I KNOW I CAN. IT'S--
I DON'T TRUST YOU. YOU HAVE A BIG MOUTH.
HUH. I DO NOT. NAME ONE TIME I BLEW A SECRET.

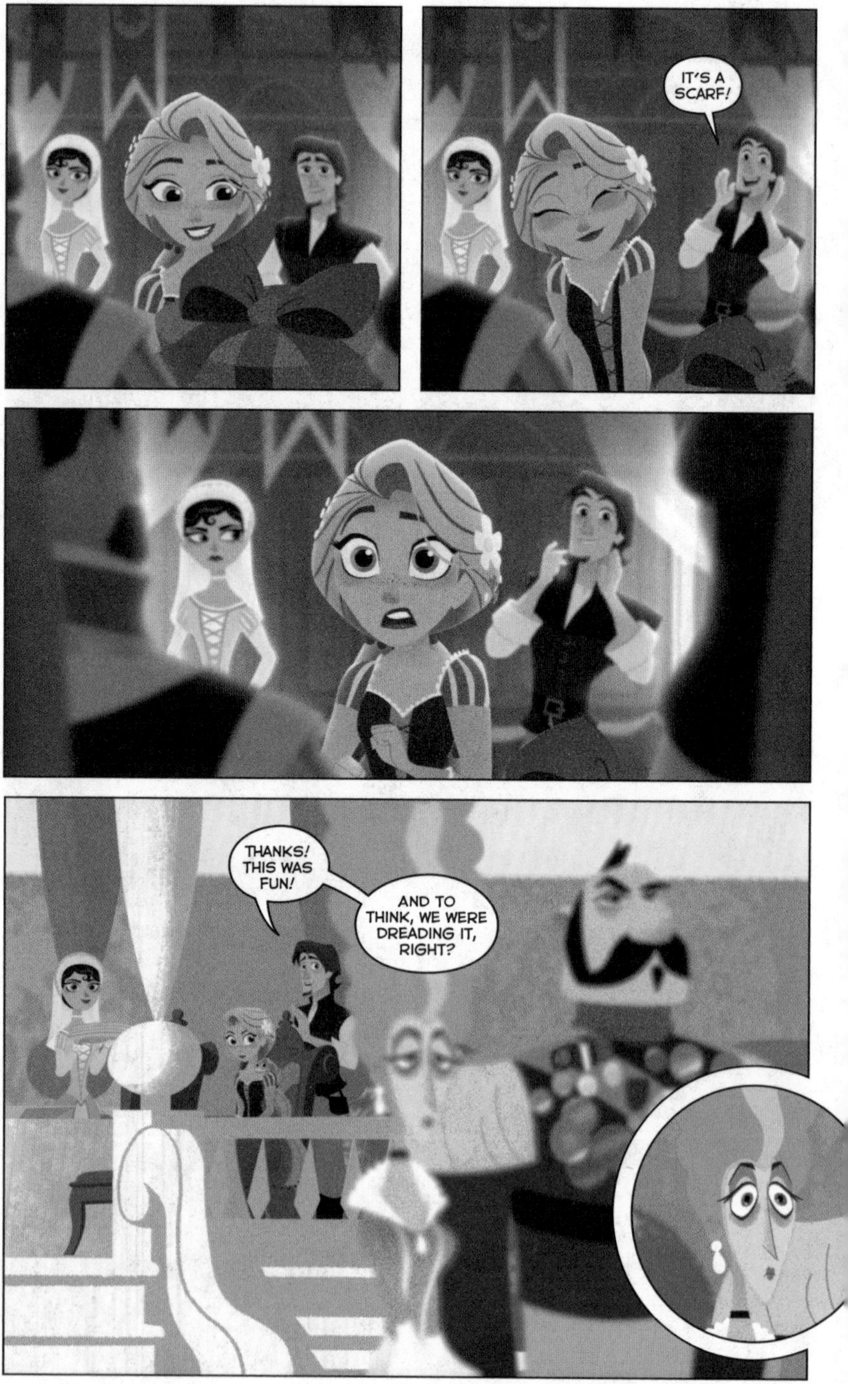
IT'S A SCARF!
THANKS! THIS WAS FUN!
AND TO THINK, WE WERE DREADING IT, RIGHT?

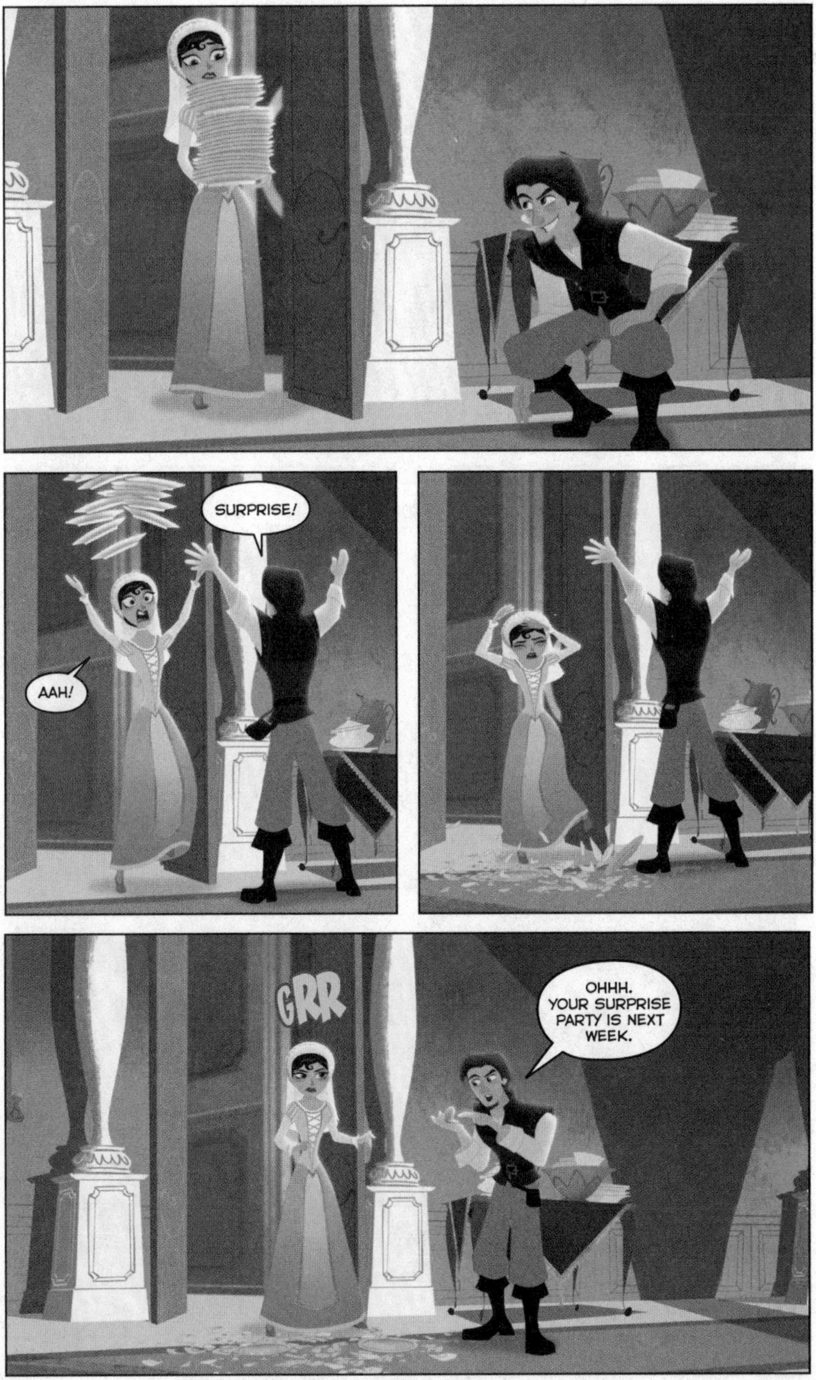
SURPRISE!
AAH!
GRR
OHHH. YOUR SURPRISE PARTY IS NEXT WEEK.

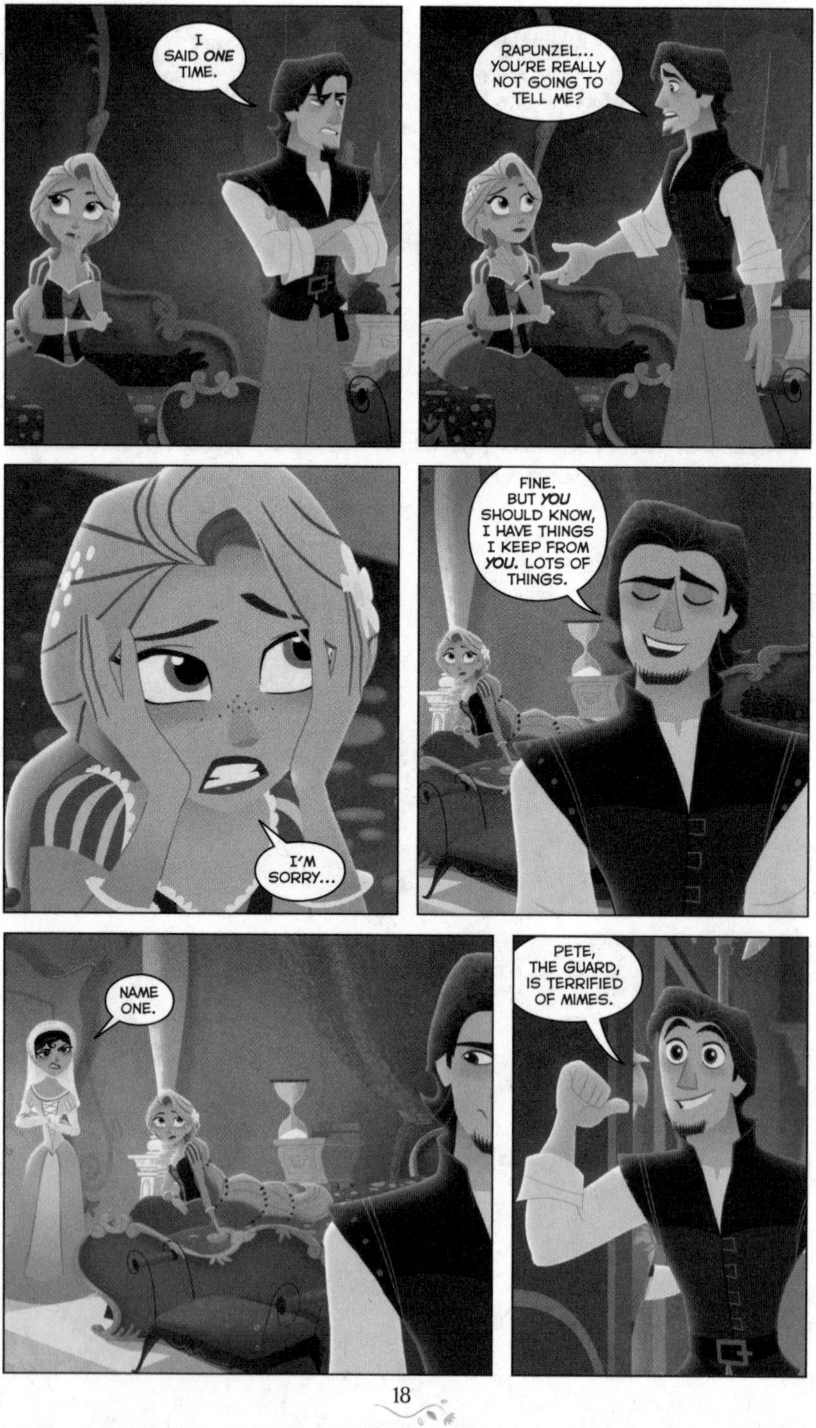
I SAID *ONE* TIME.
RAPUNZEL... YOU'RE REALLY NOT GOING TO TELL ME?
I'M SORRY...
FINE. BUT *YOU* SHOULD KNOW, I HAVE THINGS I KEEP FROM *YOU*. LOTS OF THINGS.
NAME ONE.
PETE, THE GUARD, IS TERRIFIED OF MIMES.

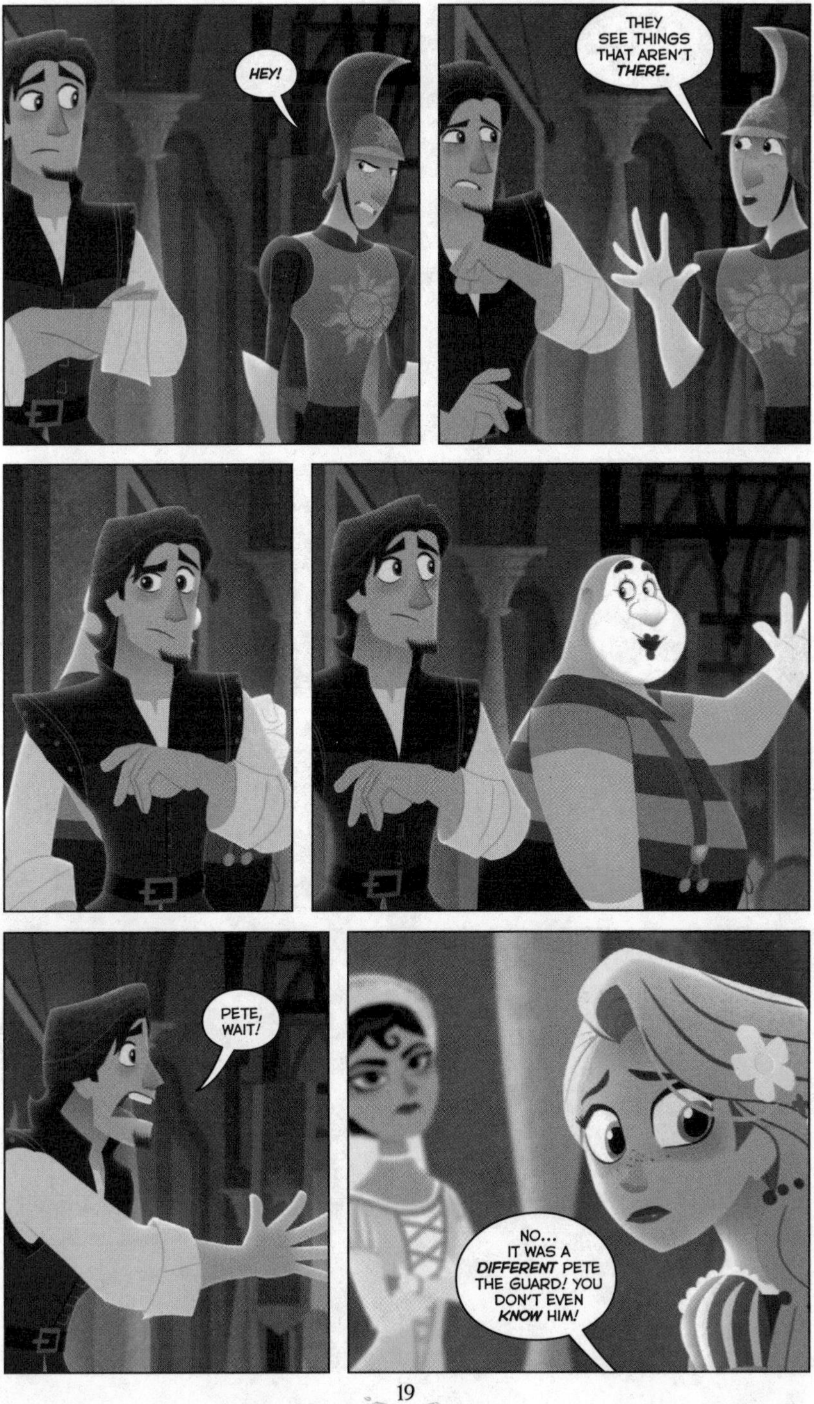
HEY!
THEY SEE THINGS THAT AREN'T *THERE.*
PETE, WAIT!
NO... IT WAS A *DIFFERENT* PETE THE GUARD! YOU DON'T EVEN *KNOW* HIM!

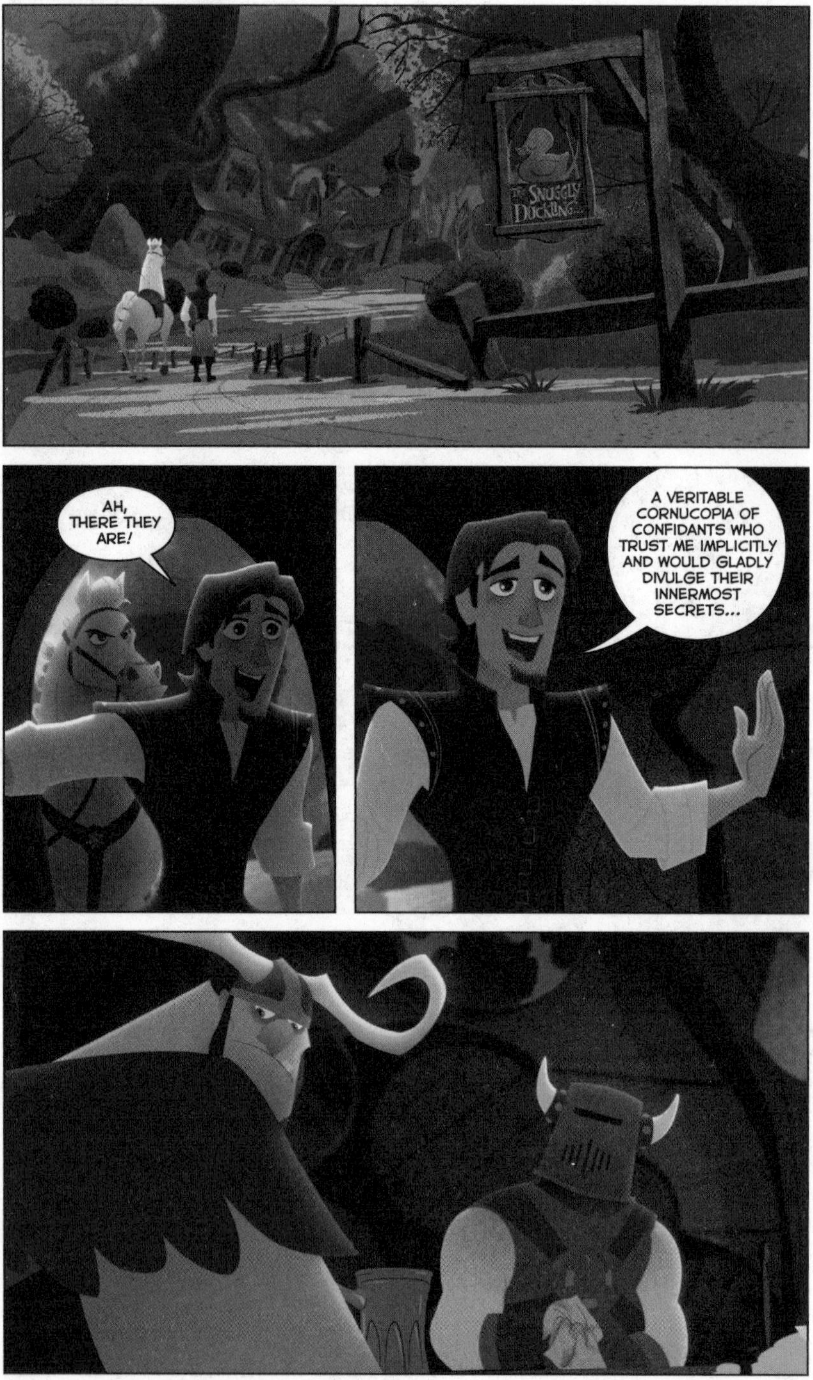
THE SNUGGLY DUCKLING
AH, THERE THEY ARE!
A VERITABLE CORNUCOPIA OF CONFIDANTS WHO TRUST ME IMPLICITLY AND WOULD GLADLY DIVULGE THEIR INNERMOST SECRETS...

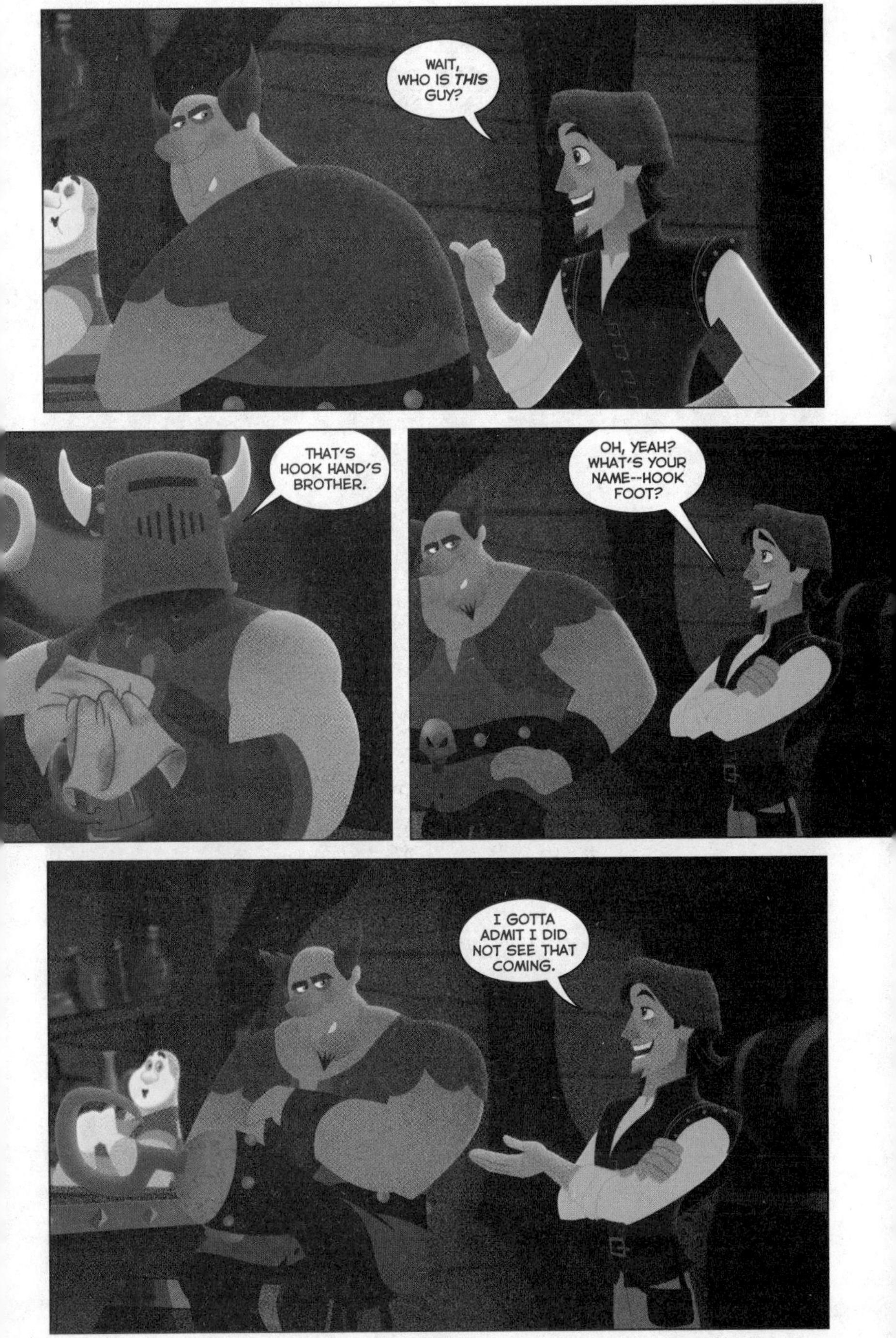
WAIT, WHO IS *THIS* GUY?
THAT'S HOOK HAND'S BROTHER.
OH, YEAH? WHAT'S YOUR NAME--HOOK FOOT?
I GOTTA ADMIT I DID NOT SEE THAT COMING.

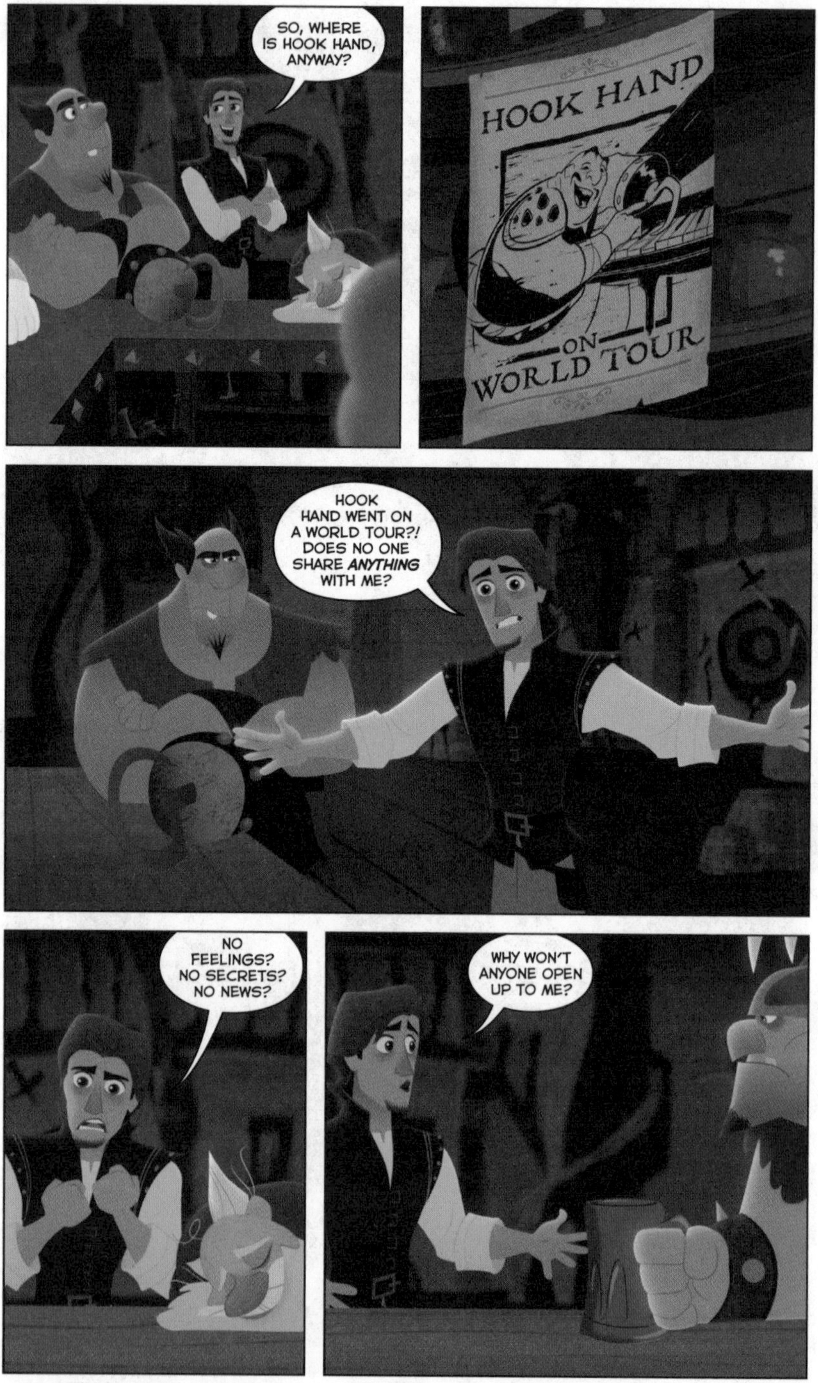

SO, WHERE IS HOOK HAND, ANYWAY?
HOOK HAND ON WORLD TOUR
HOOK HAND WENT ON A WORLD TOUR?! DOES NO ONE SHARE *ANYTHING* WITH ME?
NO FEELINGS? NO SECRETS? NO NEWS?
WHY WON'T ANYONE OPEN UP TO ME?

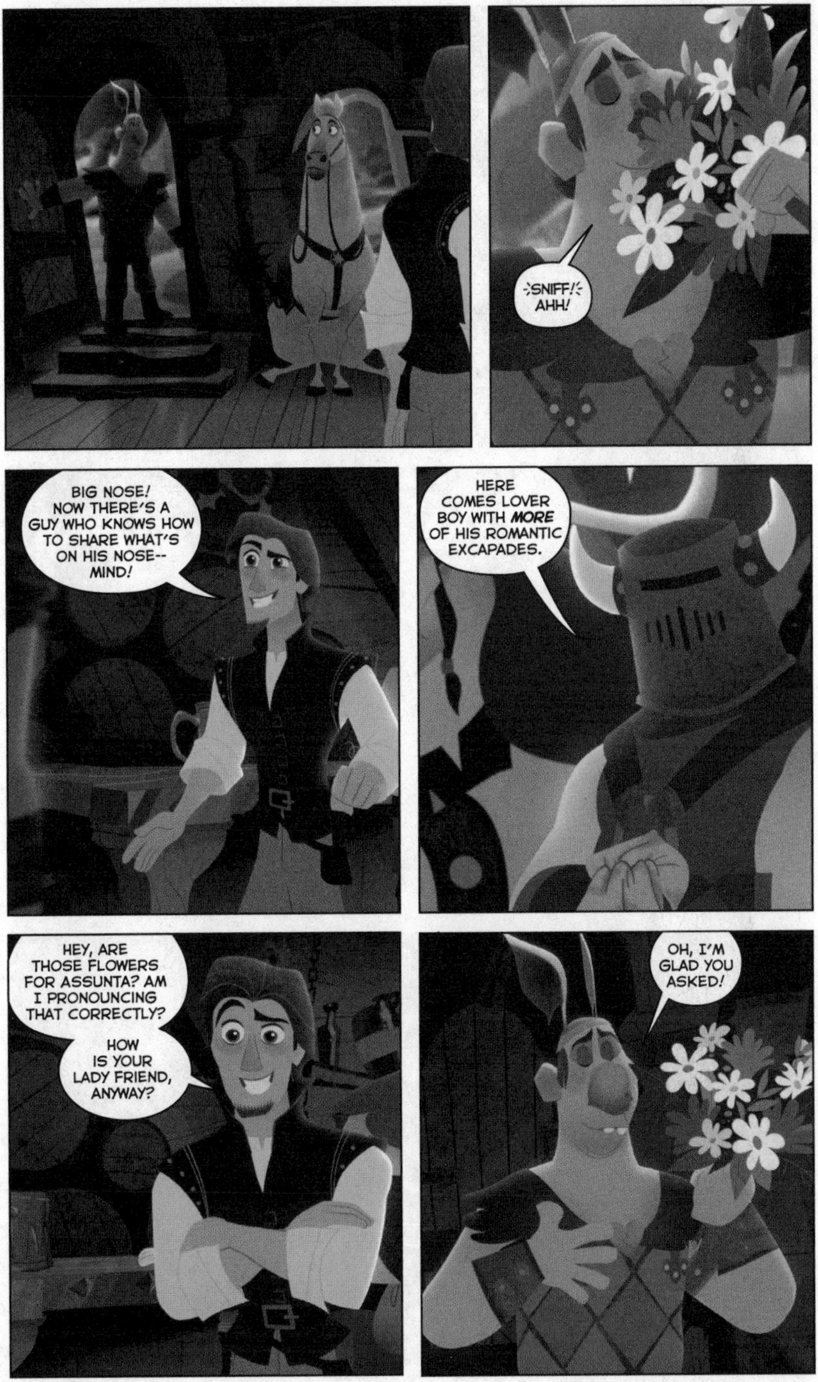
-SNIFF!- AHH!
BIG NOSE! NOW THERE'S A GUY WHO KNOWS HOW TO SHARE WHAT'S ON HIS NOSE-- MIND!
HERE COMES LOVER BOY WITH *MORE* OF HIS ROMANTIC EXCAPADES.
HEY, ARE THOSE FLOWERS FOR ASSUNTA? AM I PRONOUNCING THAT CORRECTLY?
HOW IS YOUR LADY FRIEND, ANYWAY?
OH, I'M GLAD YOU ASKED!

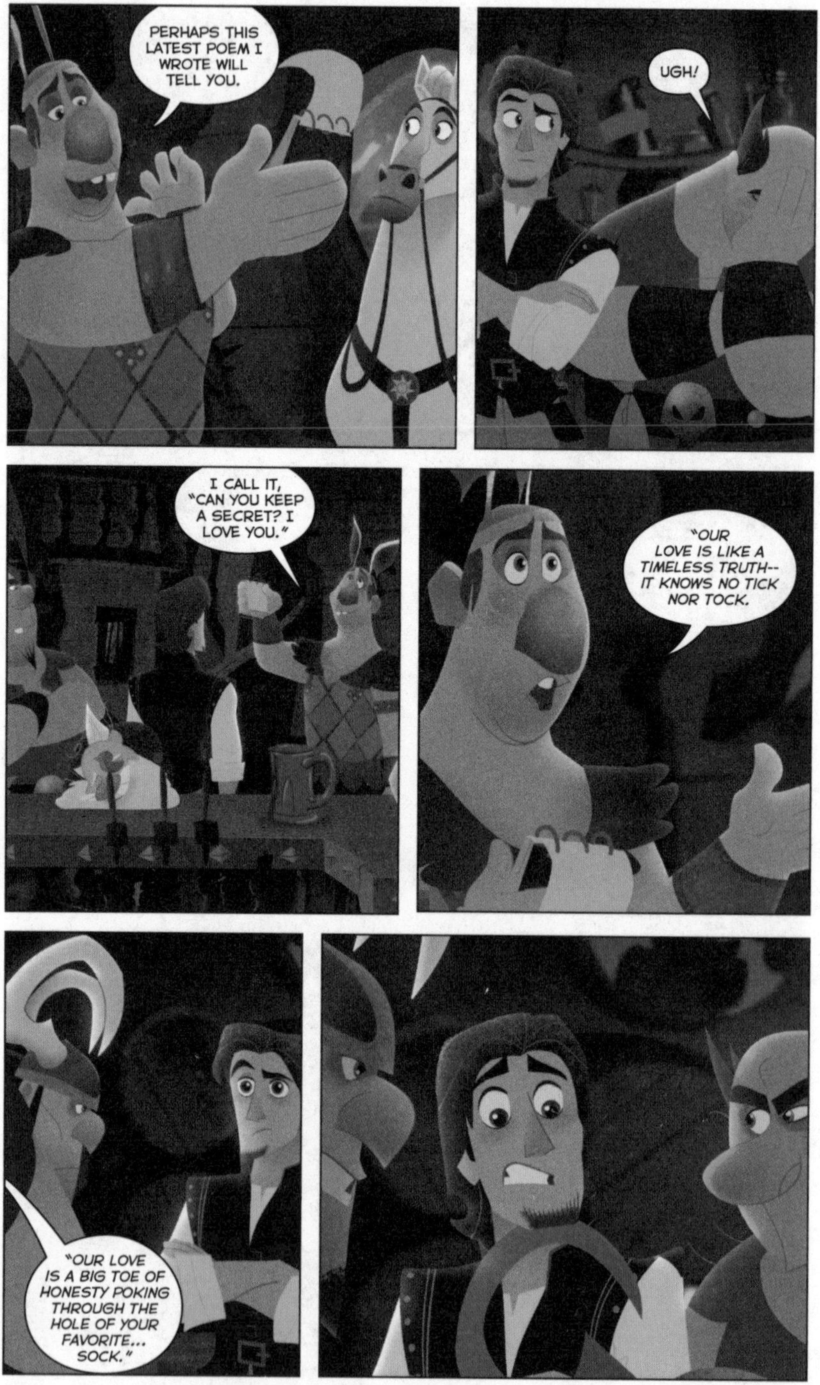
PERHAPS THIS LATEST POEM I WROTE WILL TELL YOU.
UGH!
I CALL IT, "CAN YOU KEEP A SECRET? I LOVE YOU."
"OUR LOVE IS LIKE A TIMELESS TRUTH-- IT KNOWS NO TICK NOR TOCK.
"OUR LOVE IS A BIG TOE OF HONESTY POKING THROUGH THE HOLE OF YOUR FAVORITE... SOCK."

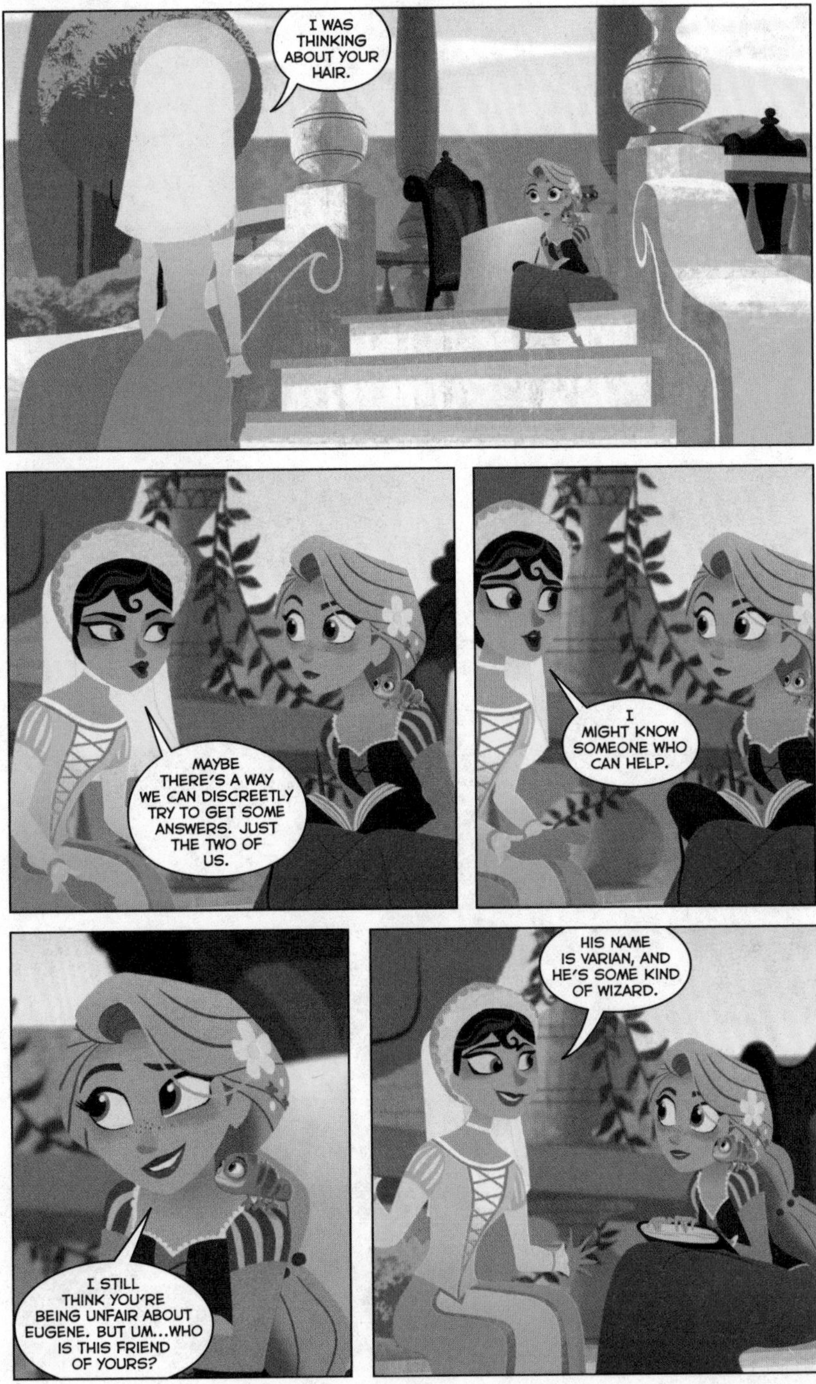
I WAS THINKING ABOUT YOUR HAIR.
MAYBE THERE'S A WAY WE CAN DISCREETLY TRY TO GET SOME ANSWERS. JUST THE TWO OF US.
I MIGHT KNOW SOMEONE WHO CAN HELP.
I STILL THINK YOU'RE BEING UNFAIR ABOUT EUGENE. BUT UM...WHO IS THIS FRIEND OF YOURS?
HIS NAME IS VARIAN, AND HE'S SOME KIND OF WIZARD.

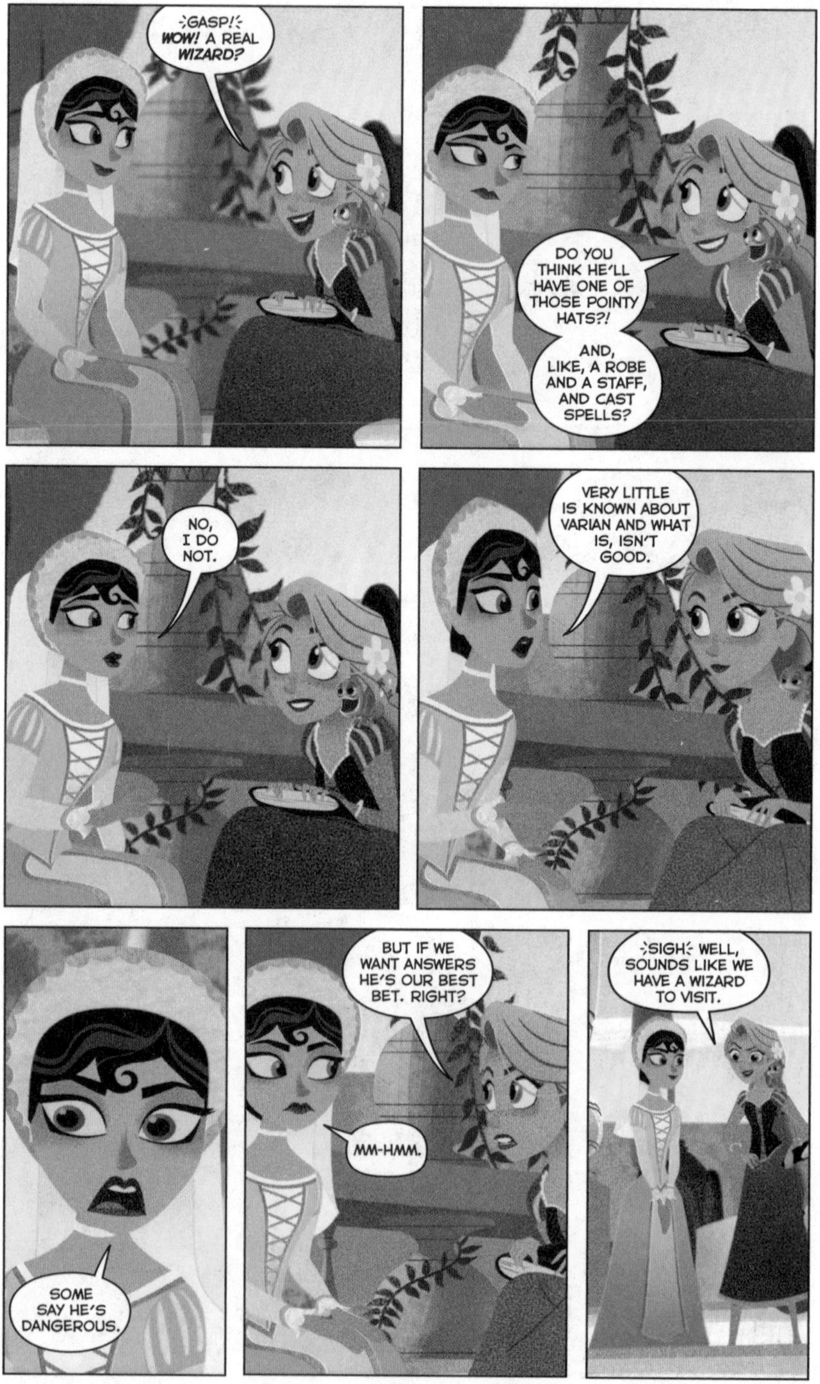
-;GASP!-; WOW! A REAL WIZARD?
DO YOU THINK HE'LL HAVE ONE OF THOSE POINTY HATS?!
AND, LIKE, A ROBE AND A STAFF, AND CAST SPELLS?
NO, I DO NOT.
VERY LITTLE IS KNOWN ABOUT VARIAN AND WHAT IS, ISN'T GOOD.
SOME SAY HE'S DANGEROUS.
BUT IF WE WANT ANSWERS HE'S OUR BEST BET. RIGHT?
MM-HMM.
-;SIGH-; WELL, SOUNDS LIKE WE HAVE A WIZARD TO VISIT.

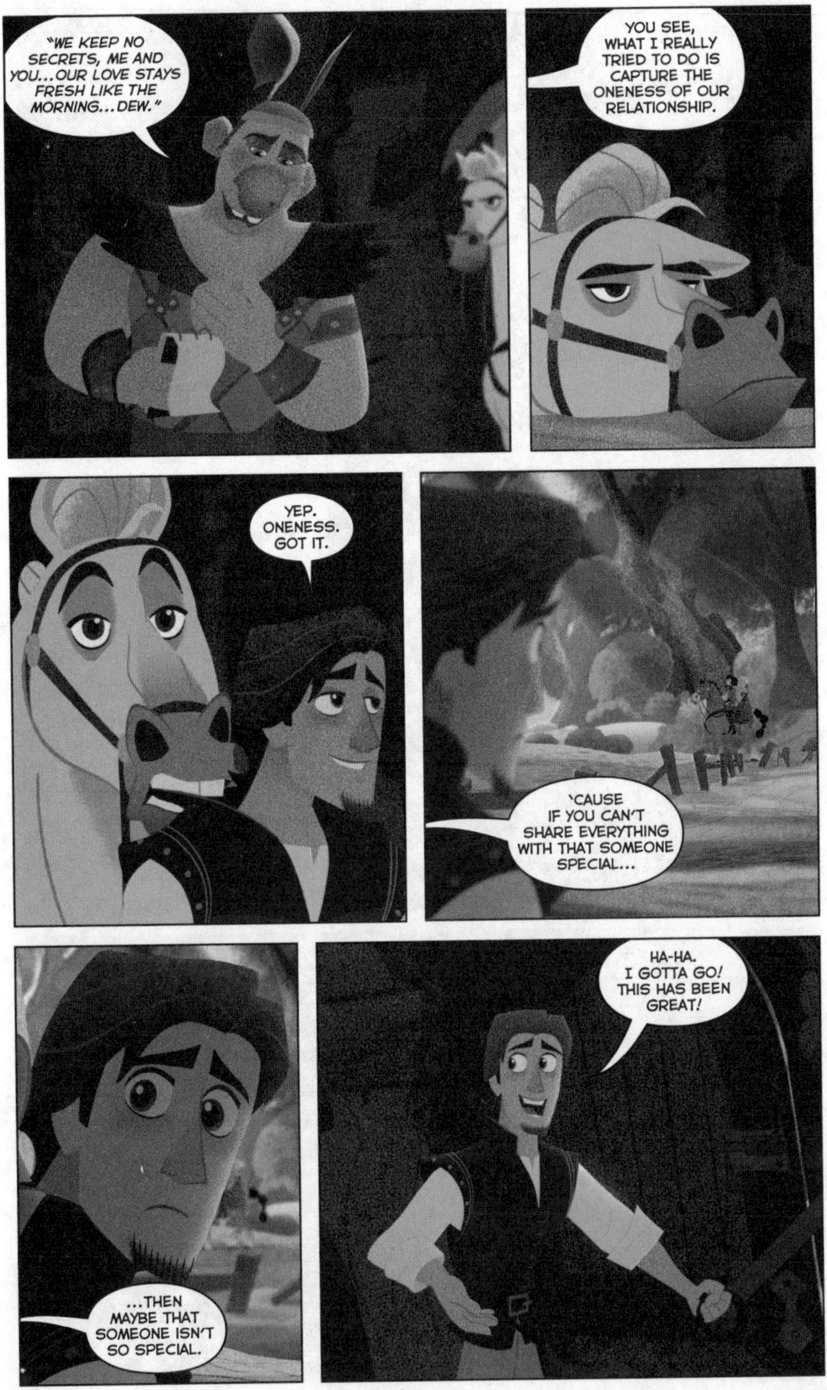
"WE KEEP NO SECRETS, ME AND YOU...OUR LOVE STAYS FRESH LIKE THE MORNING...DEW."
YOU SEE, WHAT I REALLY TRIED TO DO IS CAPTURE THE ONENESS OF OUR RELATIONSHIP.
YEP. ONENESS. GOT IT.
'CAUSE IF YOU CAN'T SHARE EVERYTHING WITH THAT SOMEONE SPECIAL...
...THEN MAYBE THAT SOMEONE ISN'T SO SPECIAL.
HA-HA. I GOTTA GO! THIS HAS BEEN GREAT!

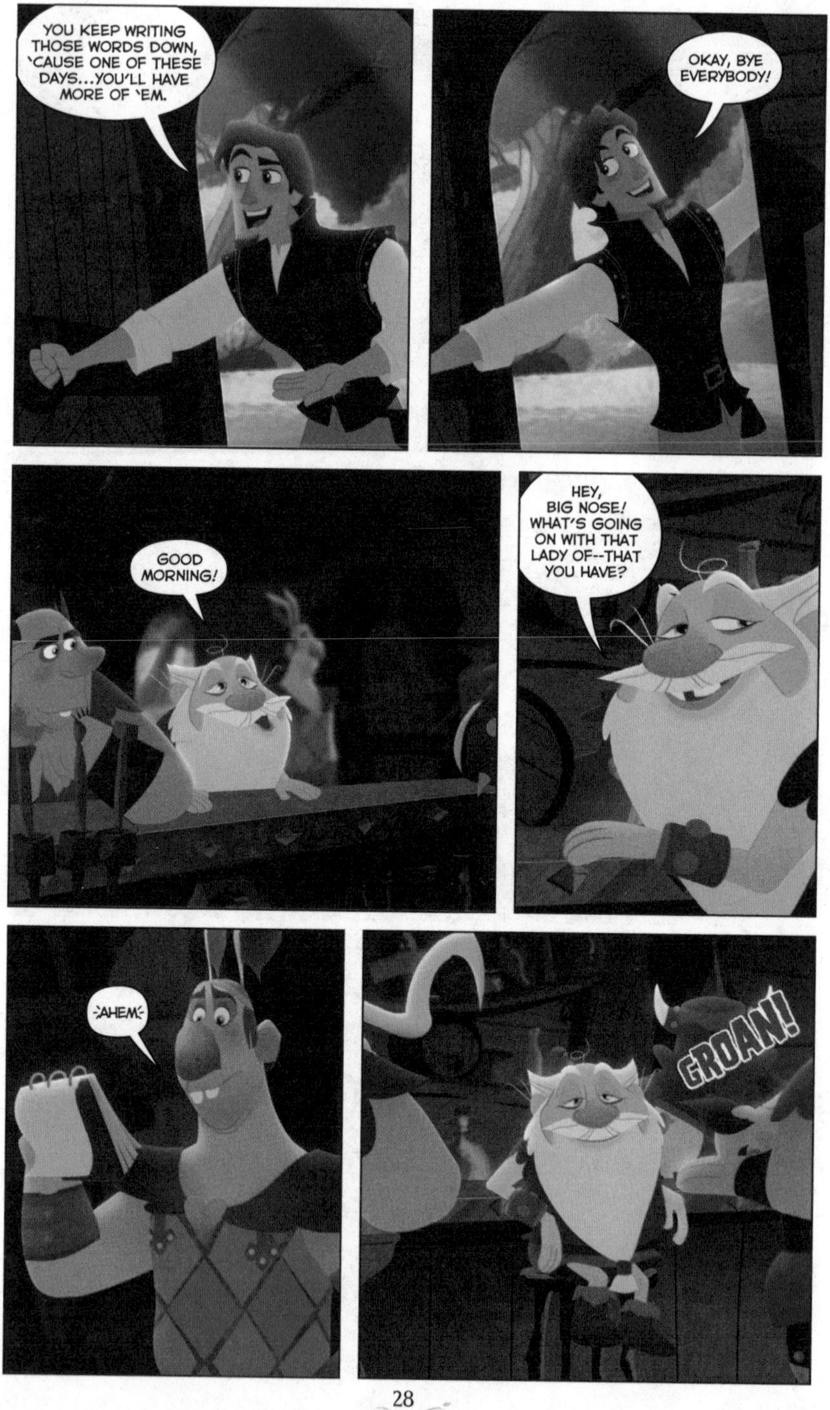
YOU KEEP WRITING THOSE WORDS DOWN, 'CAUSE ONE OF THESE DAYS...YOU'LL HAVE MORE OF 'EM.
OKAY, BYE EVERYBODY!
GOOD MORNING!
HEY, BIG NOSE! WHAT'S GOING ON WITH THAT LADY OF--THAT YOU HAVE?
AHEM
GROAN!

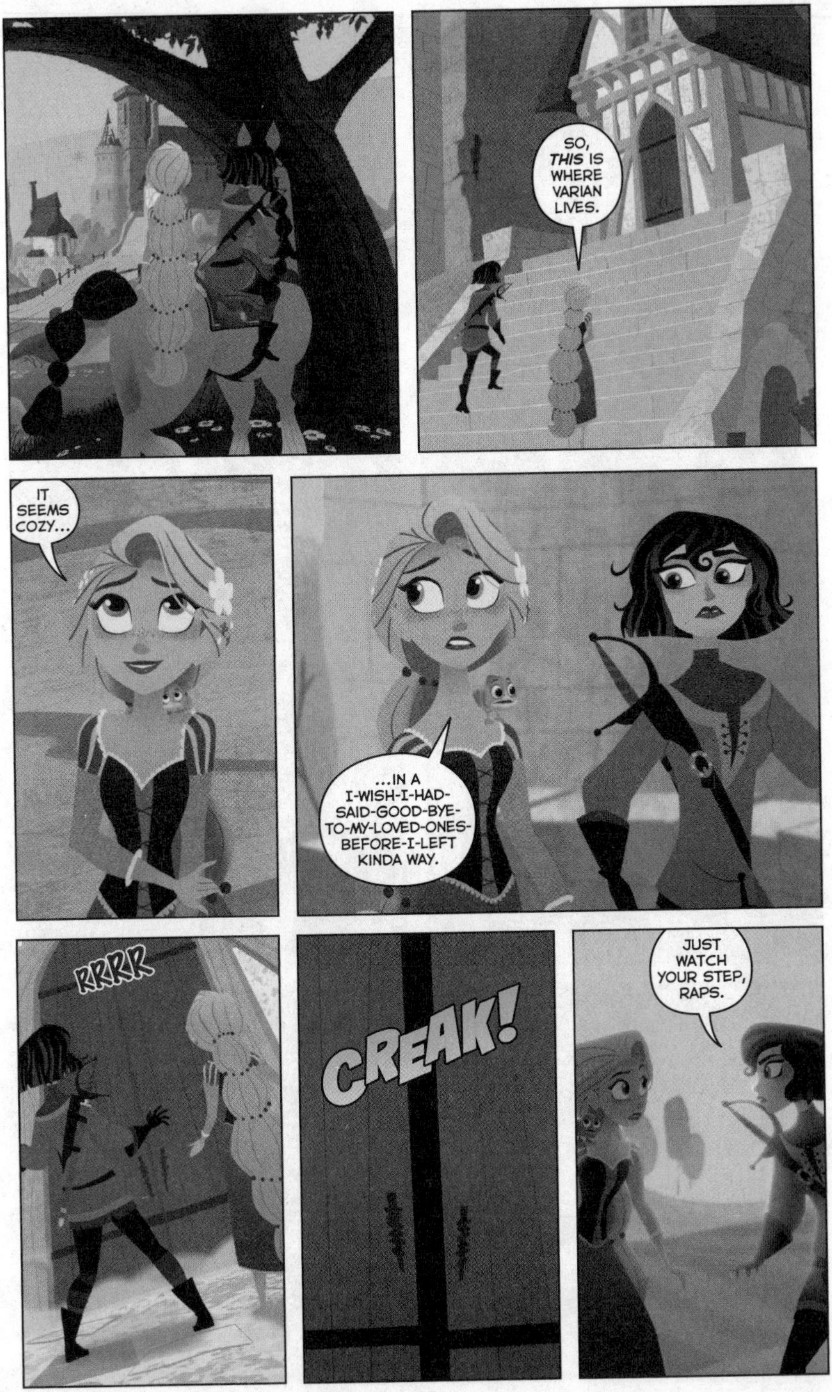
SO, THIS IS WHERE VARIAN LIVES.
IT SEEMS COZY...
...IN A I-WISH-I-HAD-SAID-GOOD-BYE-TO-MY-LOVED-ONES-BEFORE-I-LEFT KINDA WAY.
RRRR
CREAK!
JUST WATCH YOUR STEP, RAPS.

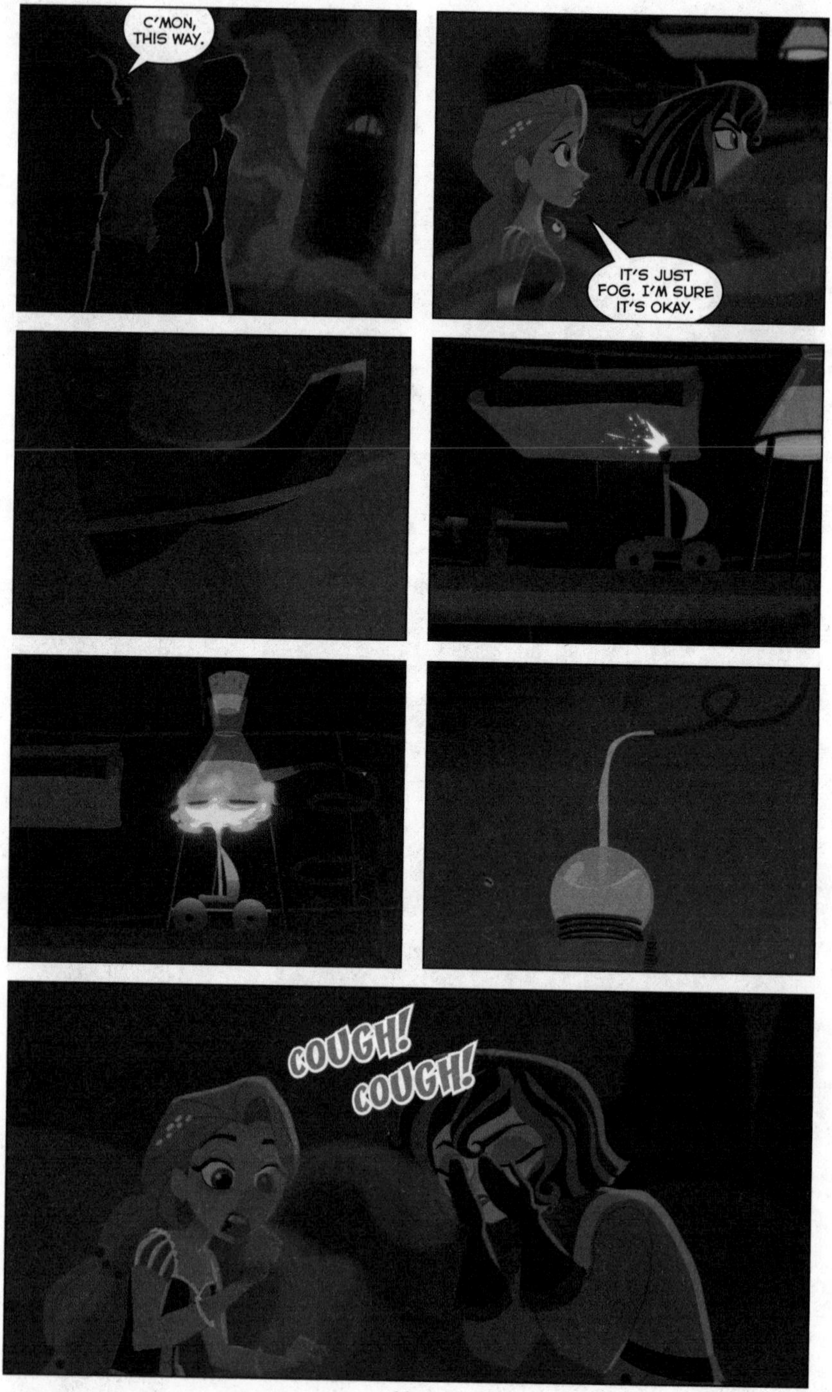
C'MON, THIS WAY.
IT'S JUST FOG. I'M SURE IT'S OKAY.
COUGH!
COUGH!

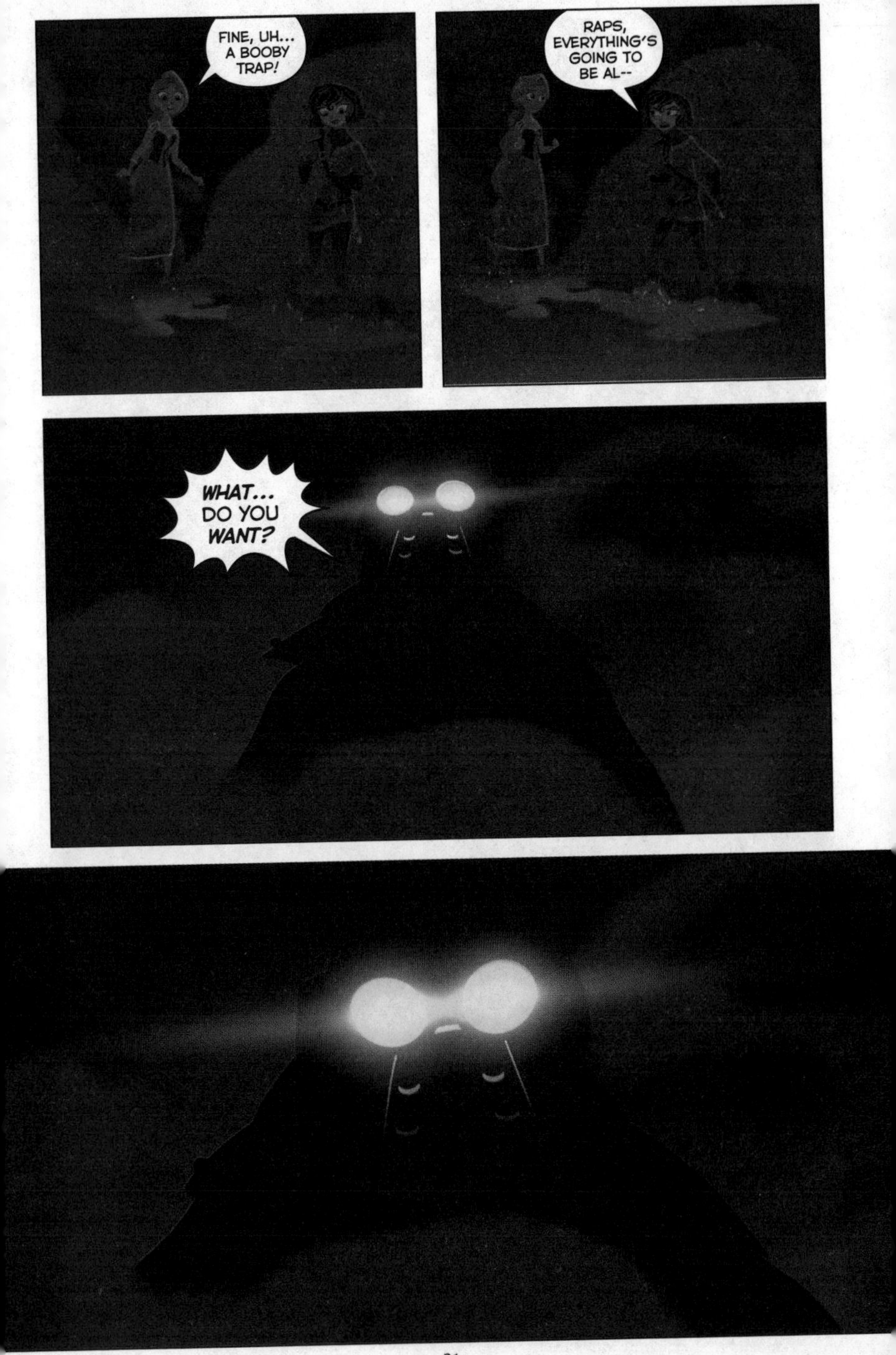
FINE, UH... A BOOBY TRAP!
RAPS, EVERYTHING'S GOING TO BE AL--
WHAT... DO YOU WANT?

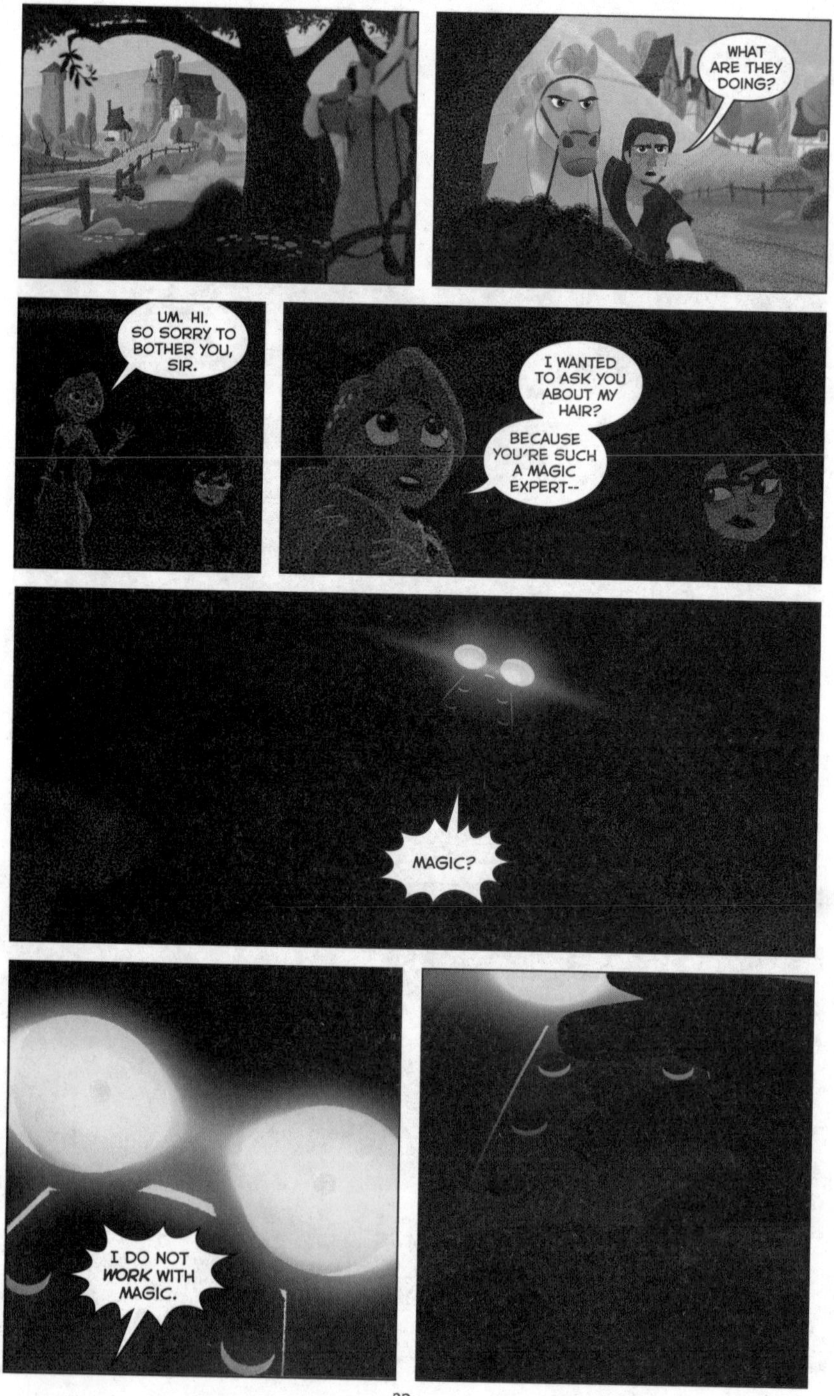

WHAT ARE THEY DOING?
UM. HI. SO SORRY TO BOTHER YOU, SIR.
I WANTED TO ASK YOU ABOUT MY HAIR?
BECAUSE YOU'RE SUCH A MAGIC EXPERT--
MAGIC?
I DO NOT *WORK* WITH MAGIC.

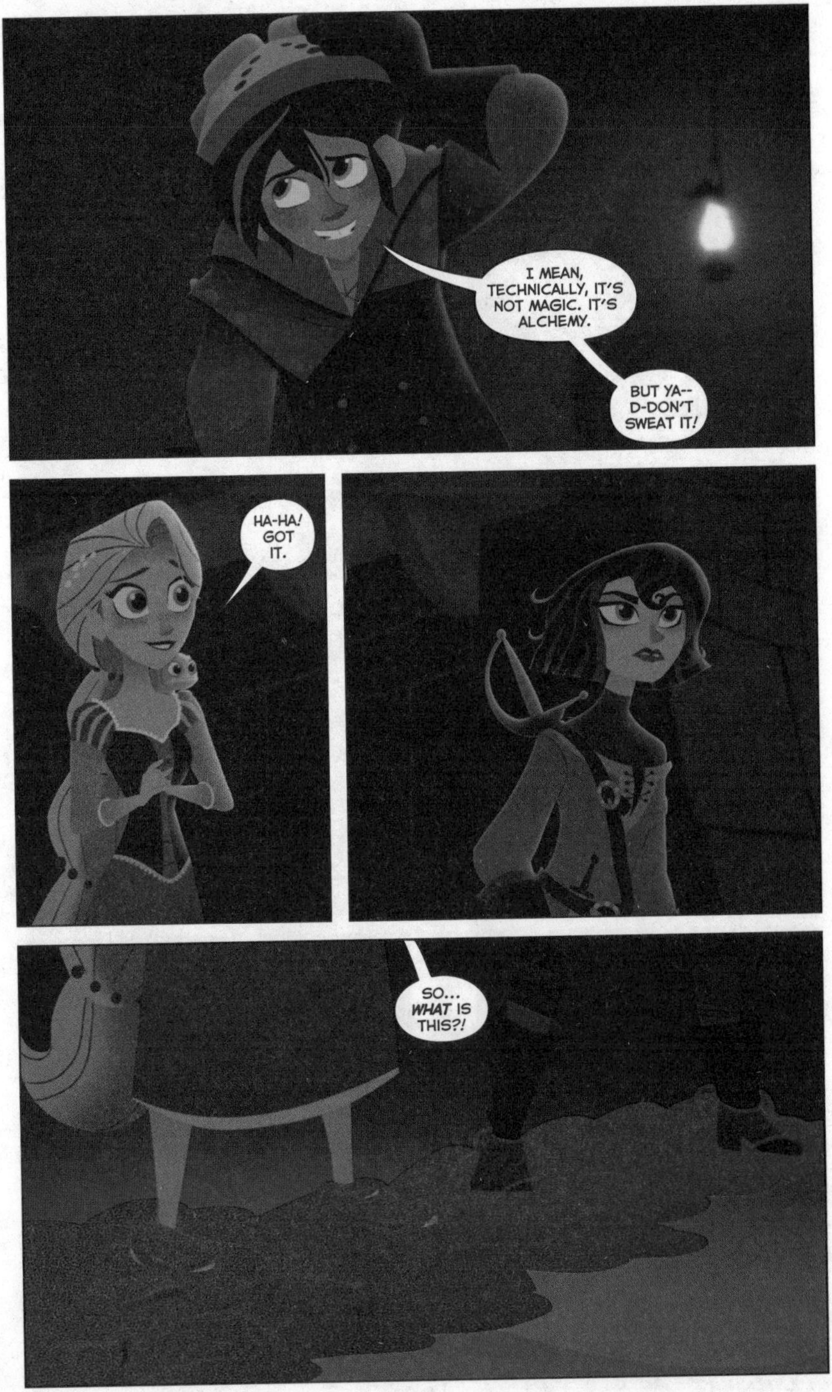
I MEAN, TECHNICALLY, IT'S NOT MAGIC. IT'S ALCHEMY.
BUT YA-- D-DON'T SWEAT IT!
HA-HA! GOT IT.
SO... *WHAT* IS THIS?!

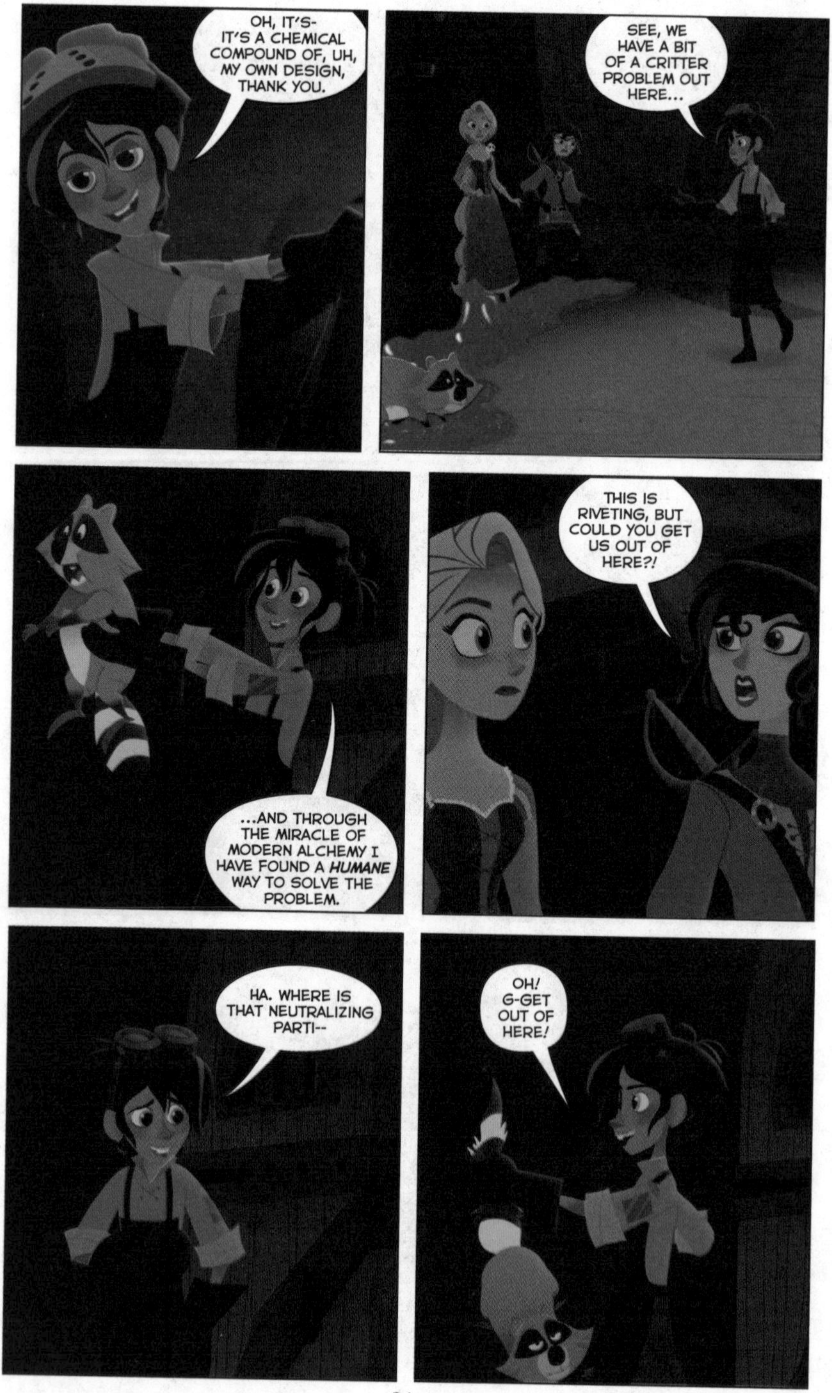
OH, IT'S- IT'S A CHEMICAL COMPOUND OF, UH, MY OWN DESIGN, THANK YOU.
SEE, WE HAVE A BIT OF A CRITTER PROBLEM OUT HERE...
...AND THROUGH THE MIRACLE OF MODERN ALCHEMY I HAVE FOUND A *HUMANE* WAY TO SOLVE THE PROBLEM.
THIS IS RIVETING, BUT COULD YOU GET US OUT OF HERE?!
HA. WHERE IS THAT NEUTRALIZING PARTI--
OH! G-GET OUT OF HERE!

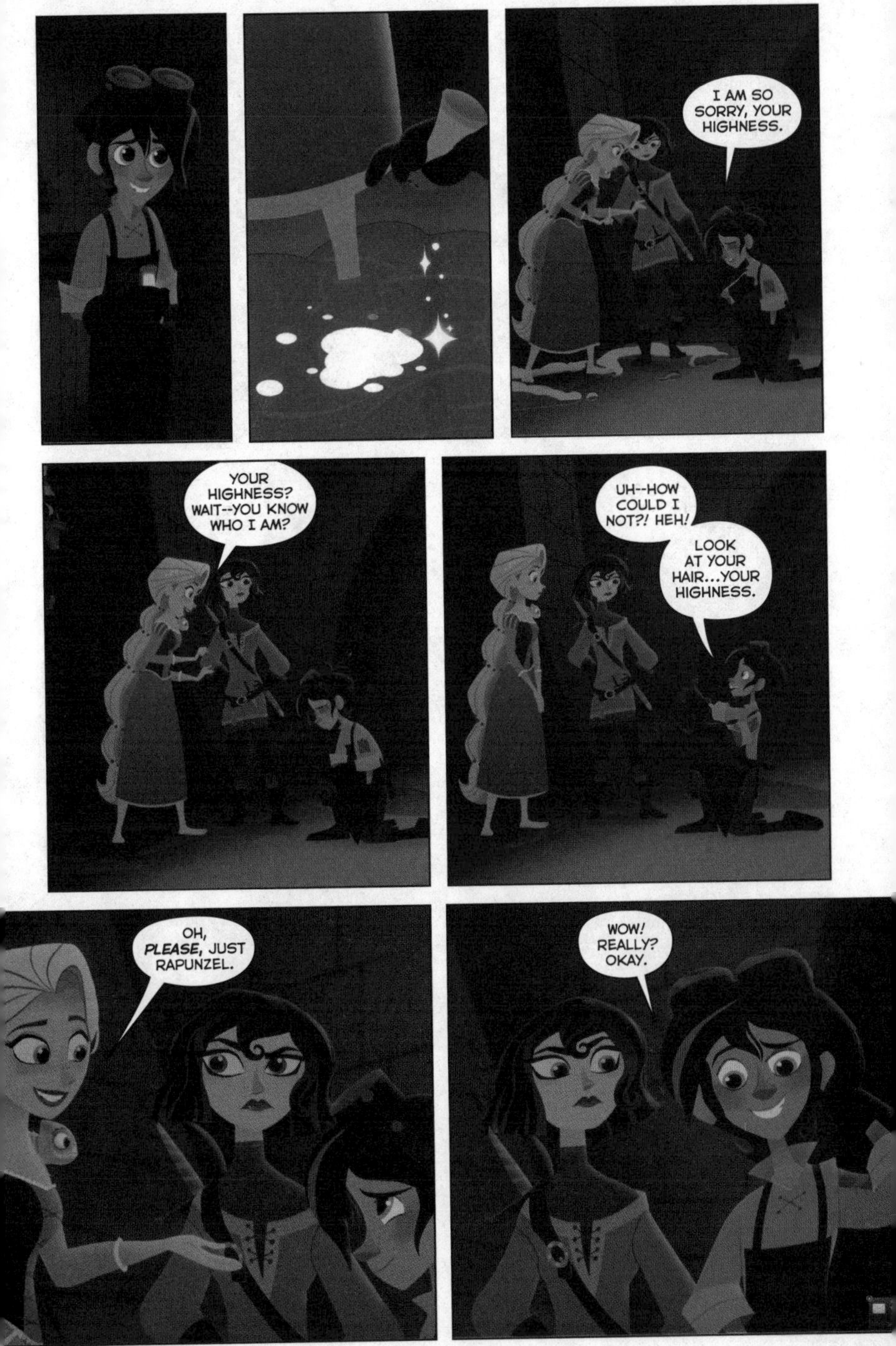
I AM SO SORRY, YOUR HIGHNESS.
YOUR HIGHNESS? WAIT--YOU KNOW WHO I AM?
UH--HOW COULD I NOT?! HEH!
LOOK AT YOUR HAIR...YOUR HIGHNESS.
OH, *PLEASE,* JUST RAPUNZEL.
WOW! REALLY? OKAY.

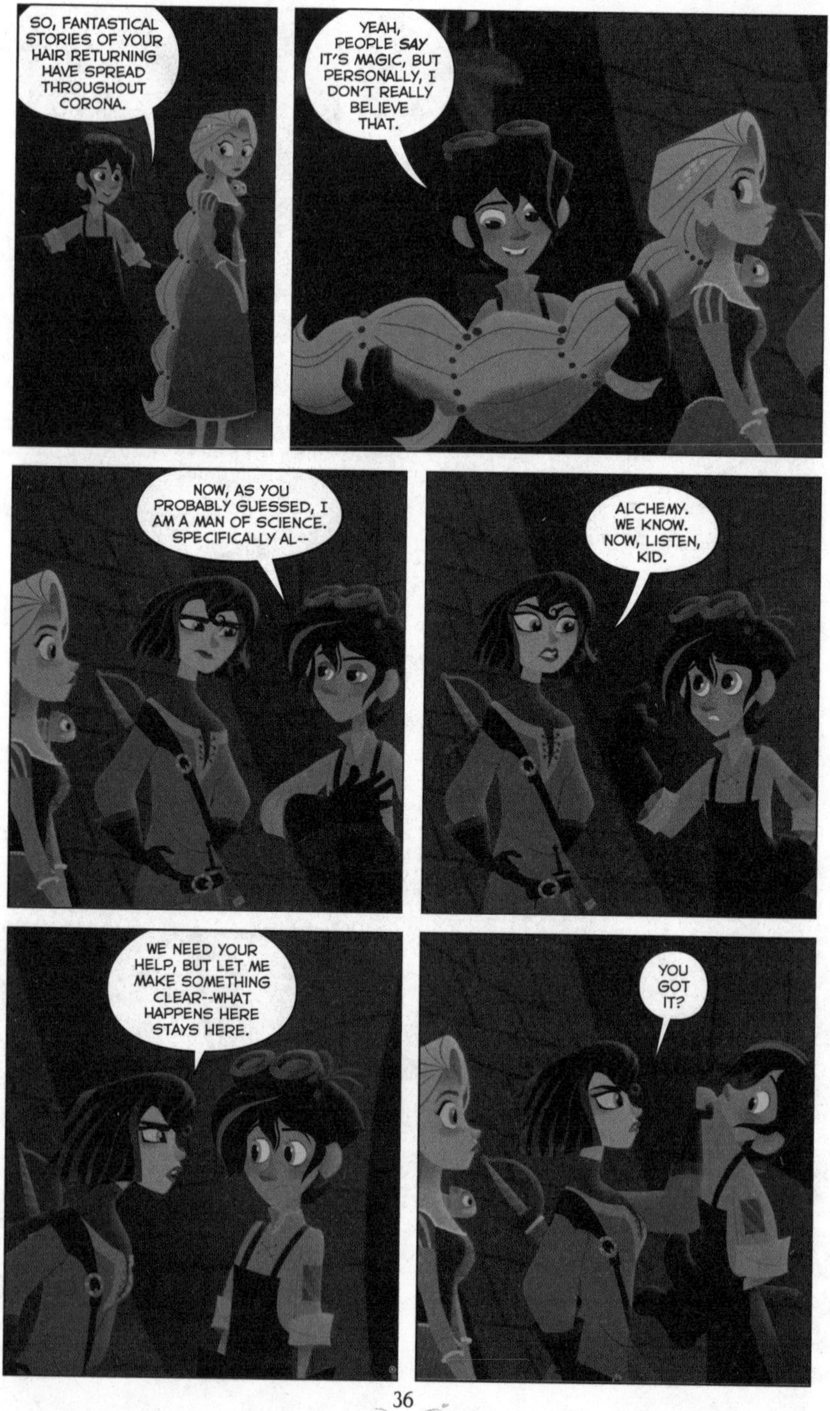
SO, FANTASTICAL STORIES OF YOUR HAIR RETURNING HAVE SPREAD THROUGHOUT CORONA.
YEAH, PEOPLE SAY IT'S MAGIC, BUT PERSONALLY, I DON'T REALLY BELIEVE THAT.
NOW, AS YOU PROBABLY GUESSED, I AM A MAN OF SCIENCE. SPECIFICALLY AL--
ALCHEMY. WE KNOW. NOW, LISTEN, KID.
WE NEED YOUR HELP, BUT LET ME MAKE SOMETHING CLEAR--WHAT HAPPENS HERE STAYS HERE.
YOU GOT IT?

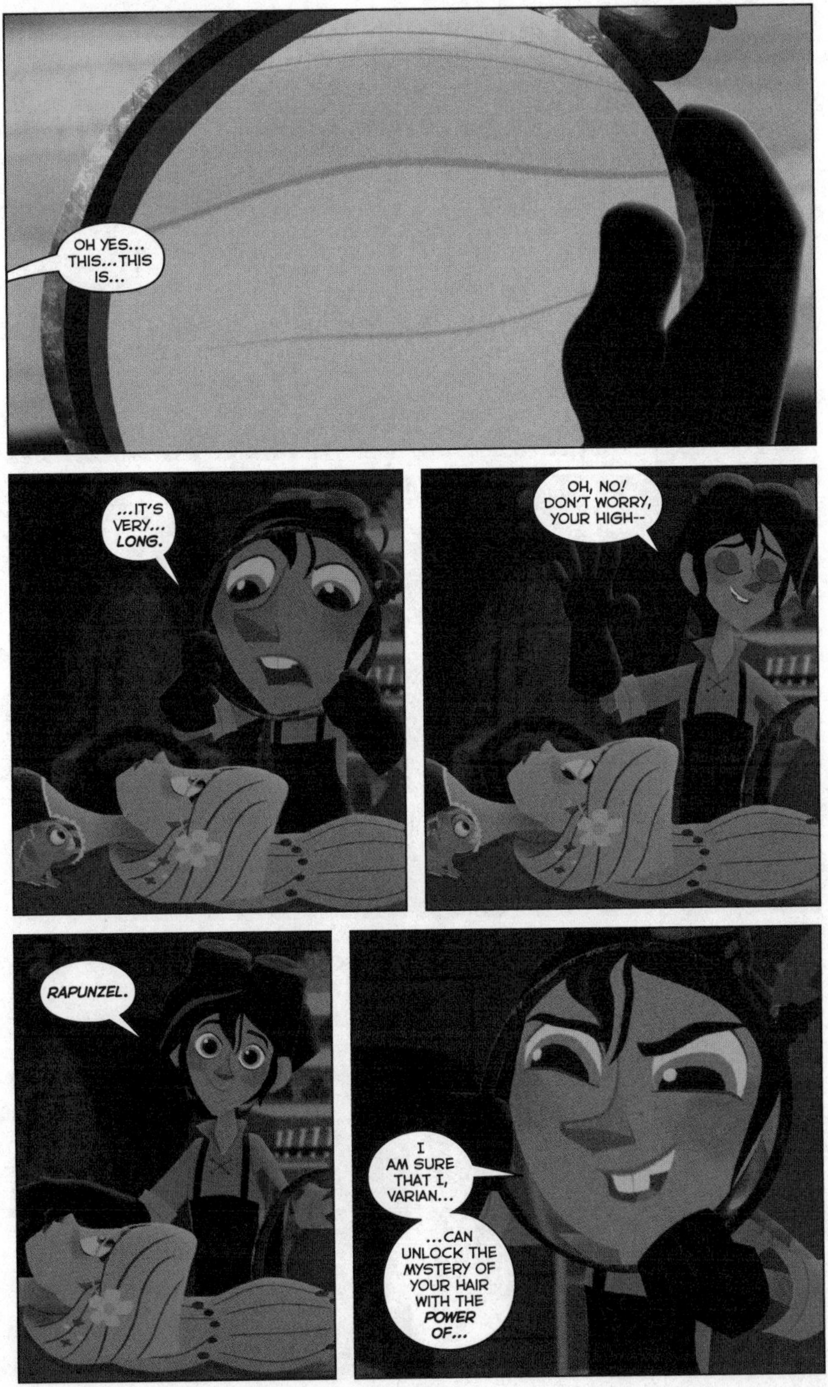

OH YES... THIS...THIS IS...
...IT'S VERY... LONG.
OH, NO! DON'T WORRY, YOUR HIGH--
RAPUNZEL.
I AM SURE THAT I, VARIAN...
...CAN UNLOCK THE MYSTERY OF YOUR HAIR WITH THE POWER OF...

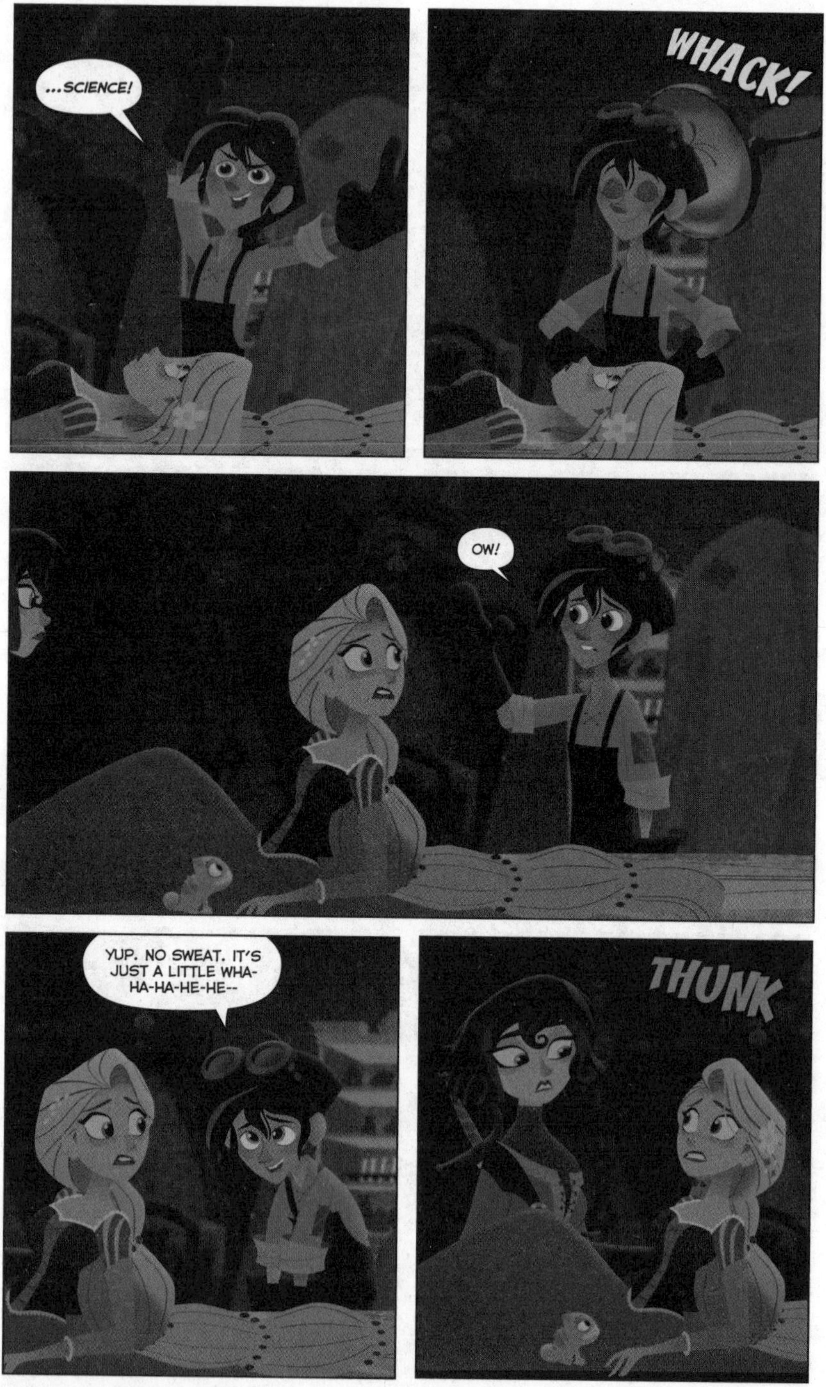
...SCIENCE!
WHACK!
OW!
YUP. NO SWEAT. IT'S JUST A LITTLE WHA-HA-HA-HE-HE--
THUNK

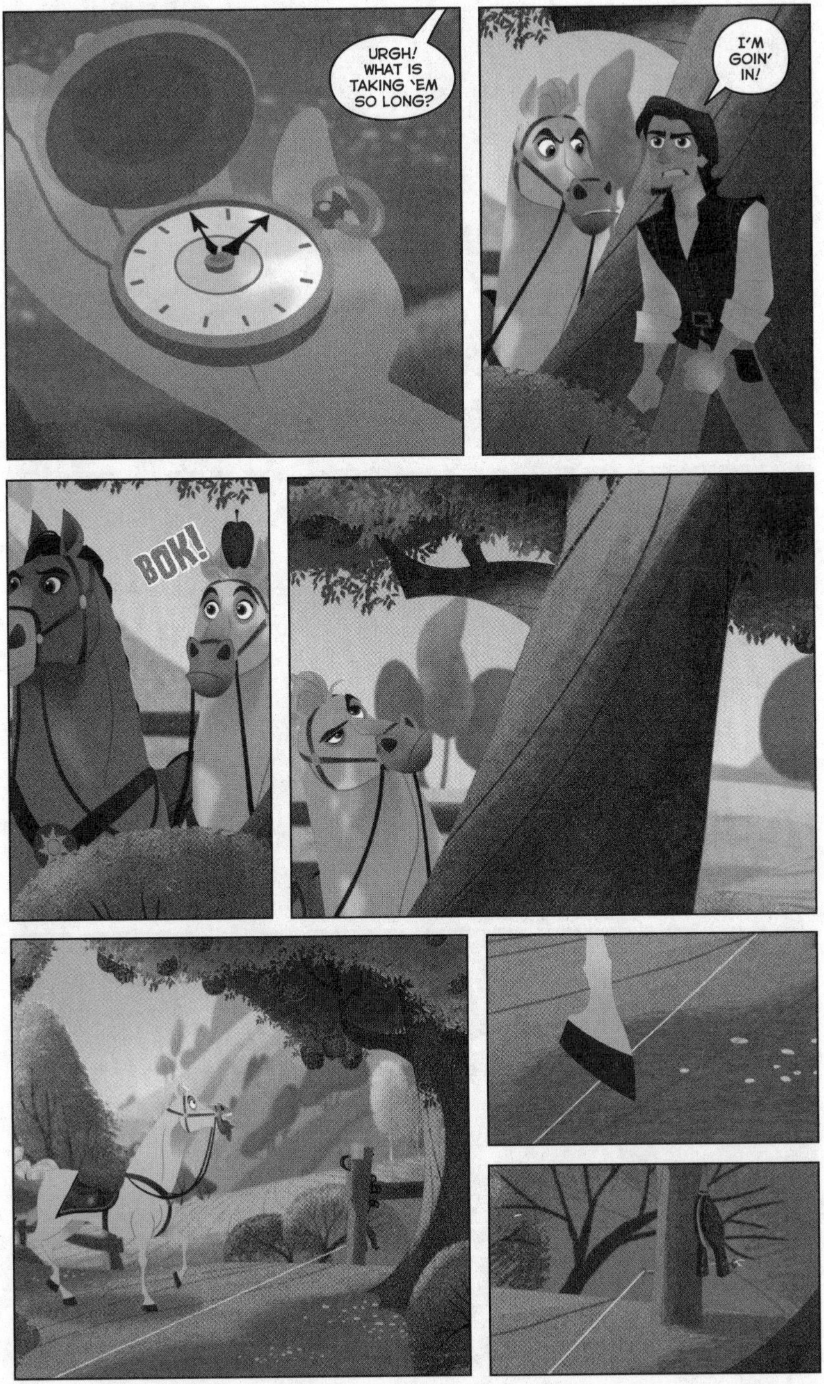
URGH! WHAT IS TAKING 'EM SO LONG?
I'M GOIN' IN!
BOK!

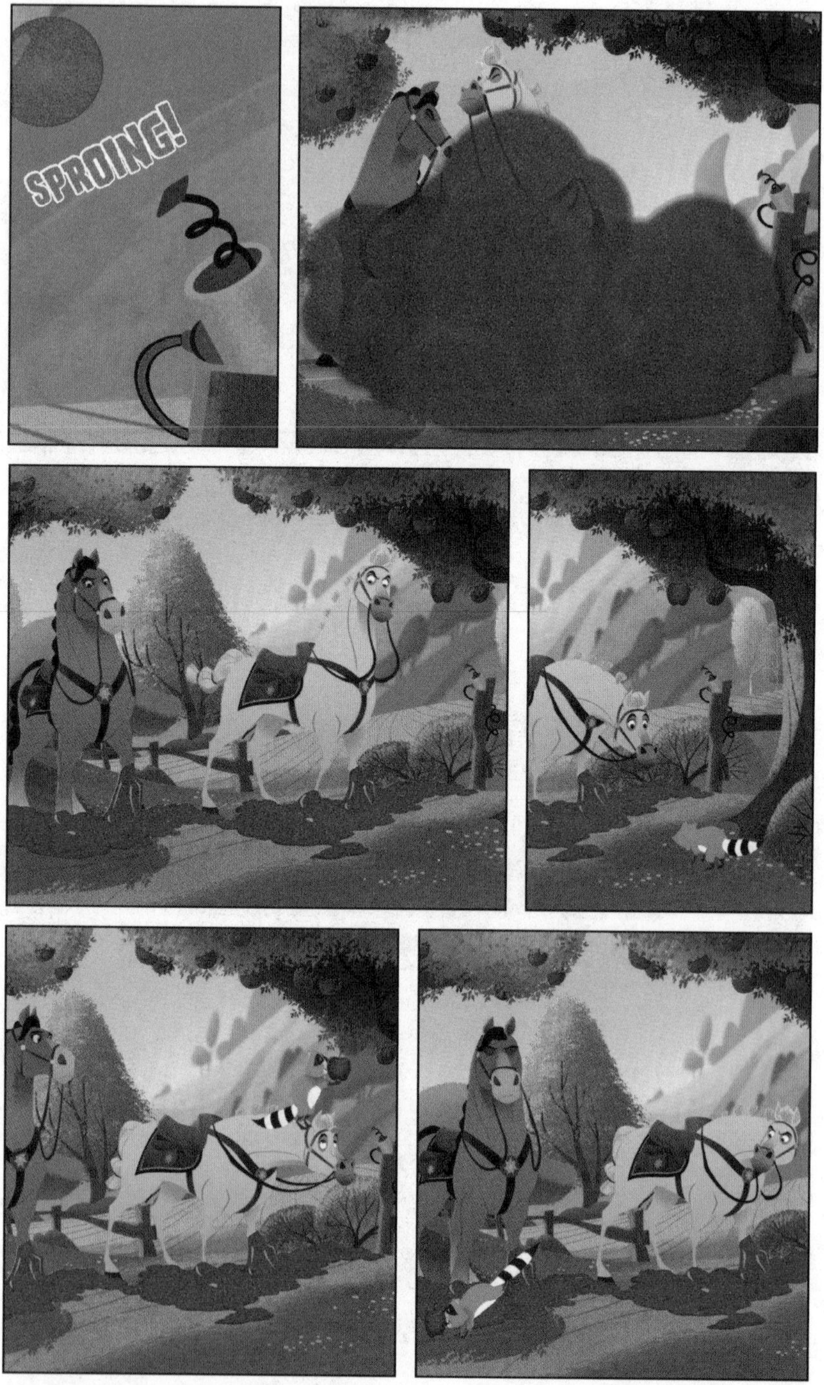
SPROING!

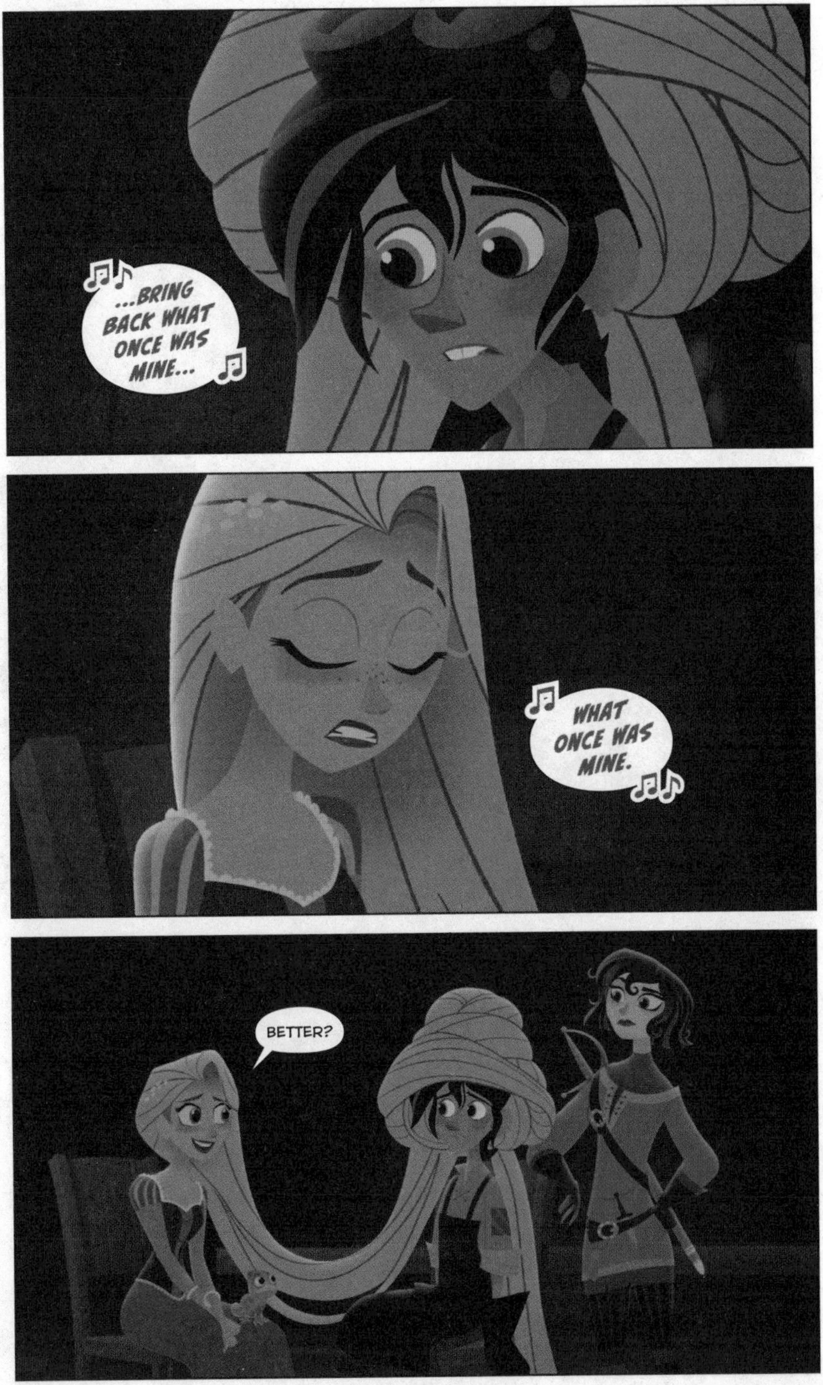
...BRING BACK WHAT ONCE WAS MINE...
WHAT ONCE WAS MINE.
BETTER?

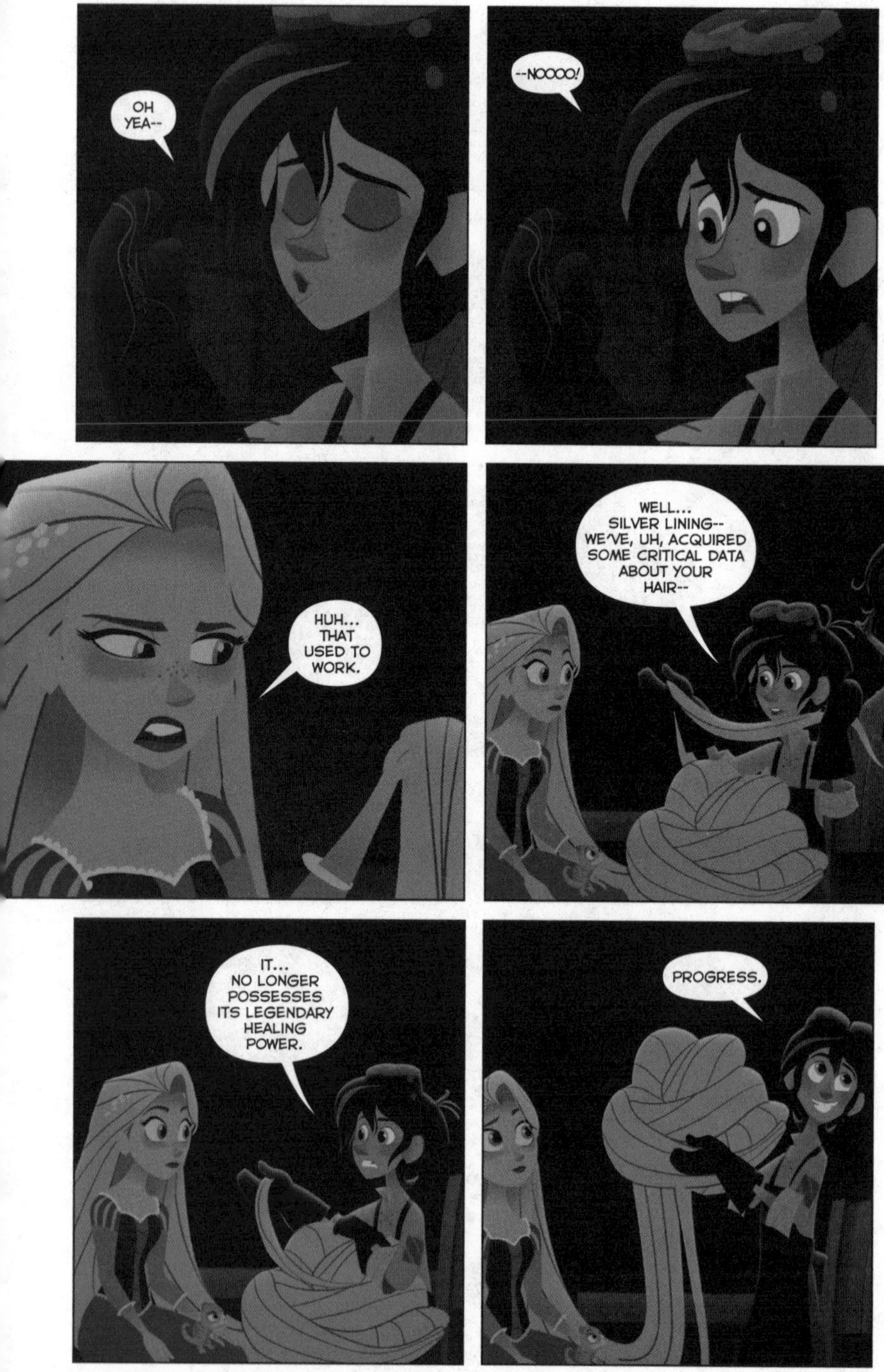
OH YEA--
--NOOOO!
HUH... THAT USED TO WORK.
WELL... SILVER LINING-- WE'VE, UH, ACQUIRED SOME CRITICAL DATA ABOUT YOUR HAIR--
IT... NO LONGER POSSESSES ITS LEGENDARY HEALING POWER.
PROGRESS.

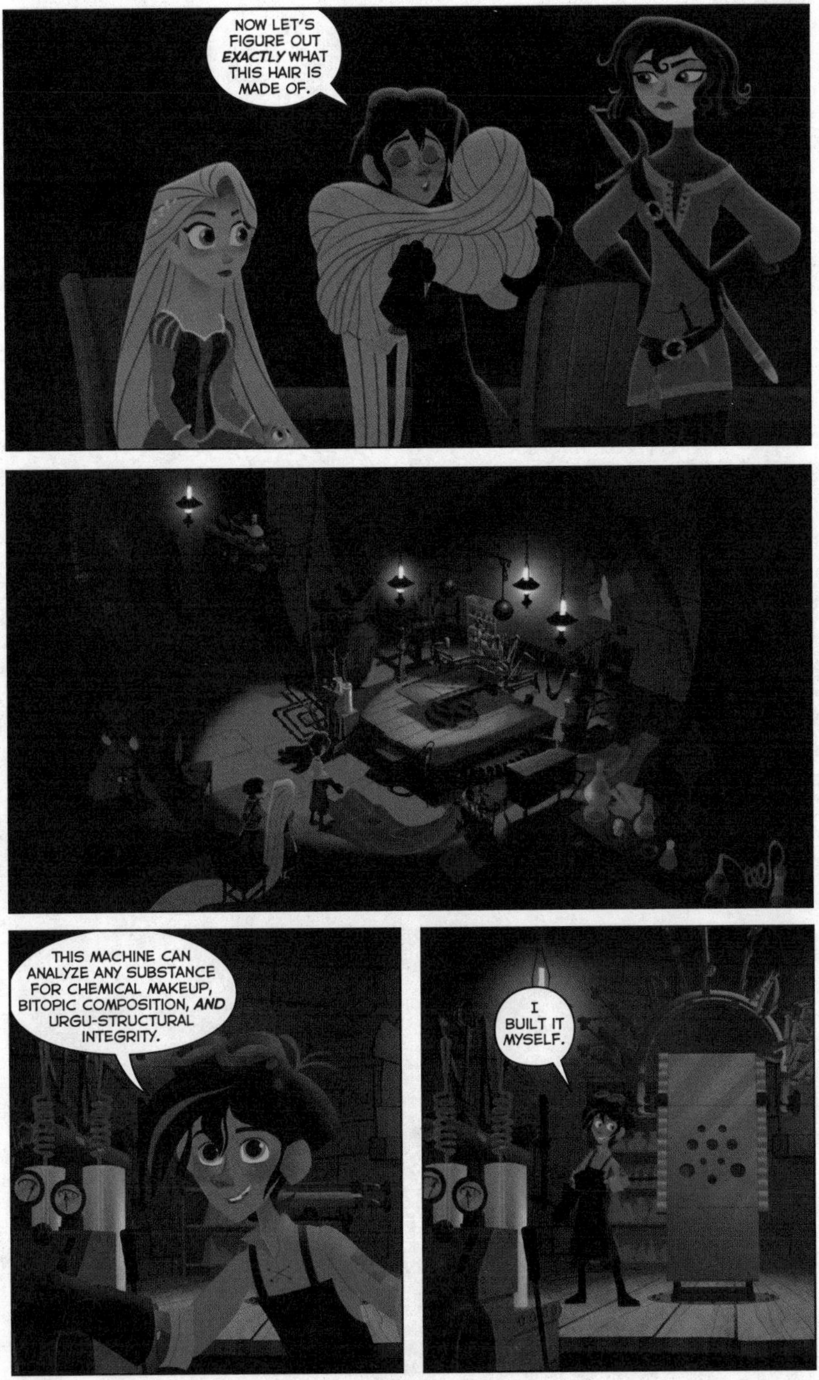
NOW LET'S FIGURE OUT *EXACTLY* WHAT THIS HAIR IS MADE OF.
THIS MACHINE CAN ANALYZE ANY SUBSTANCE FOR CHEMICAL MAKEUP, BITOPIC COMPOSITION, *AND* URGU-STRUCTURAL INTEGRITY.
I BUILT IT MYSELF.

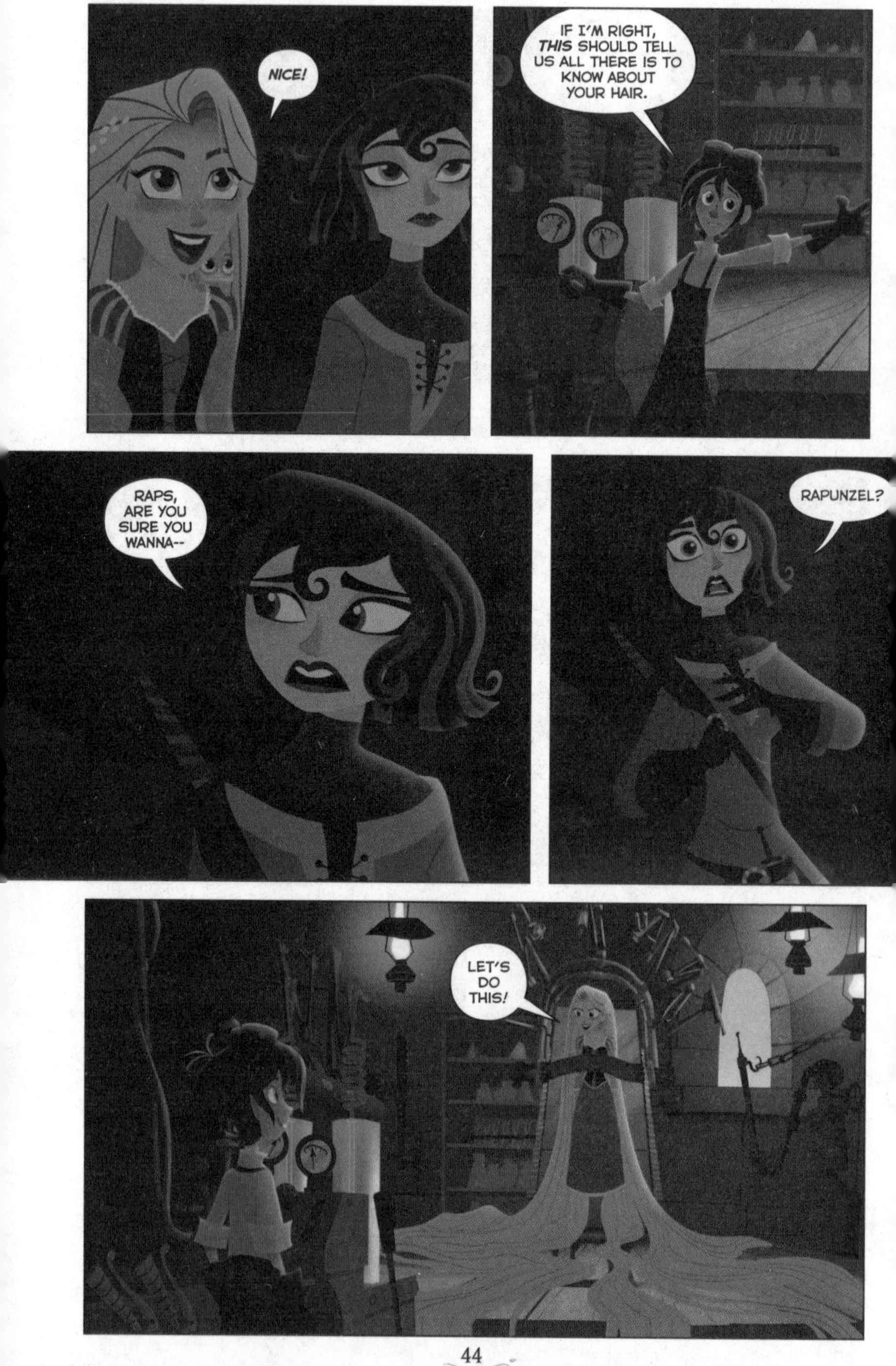
NICE!
IF I'M RIGHT, THIS SHOULD TELL US ALL THERE IS TO KNOW ABOUT YOUR HAIR.
RAPS, ARE YOU SURE YOU WANNA--
RAPUNZEL?
LET'S DO THIS!

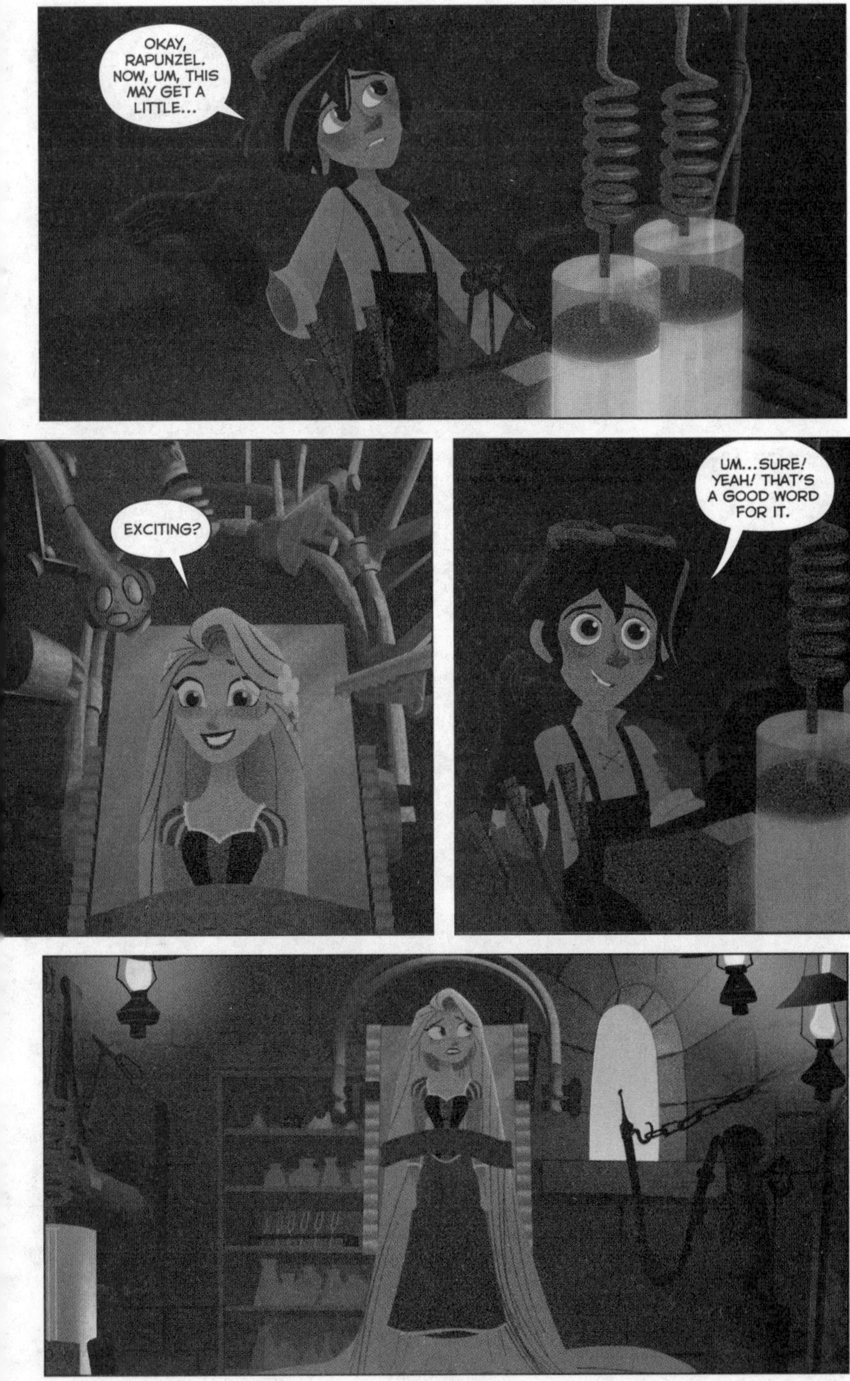

OKAY, RAPUNZEL. NOW, UM, THIS MAY GET A LITTLE...
EXCITING?
UM...SURE! YEAH! THAT'S A GOOD WORD FOR IT.

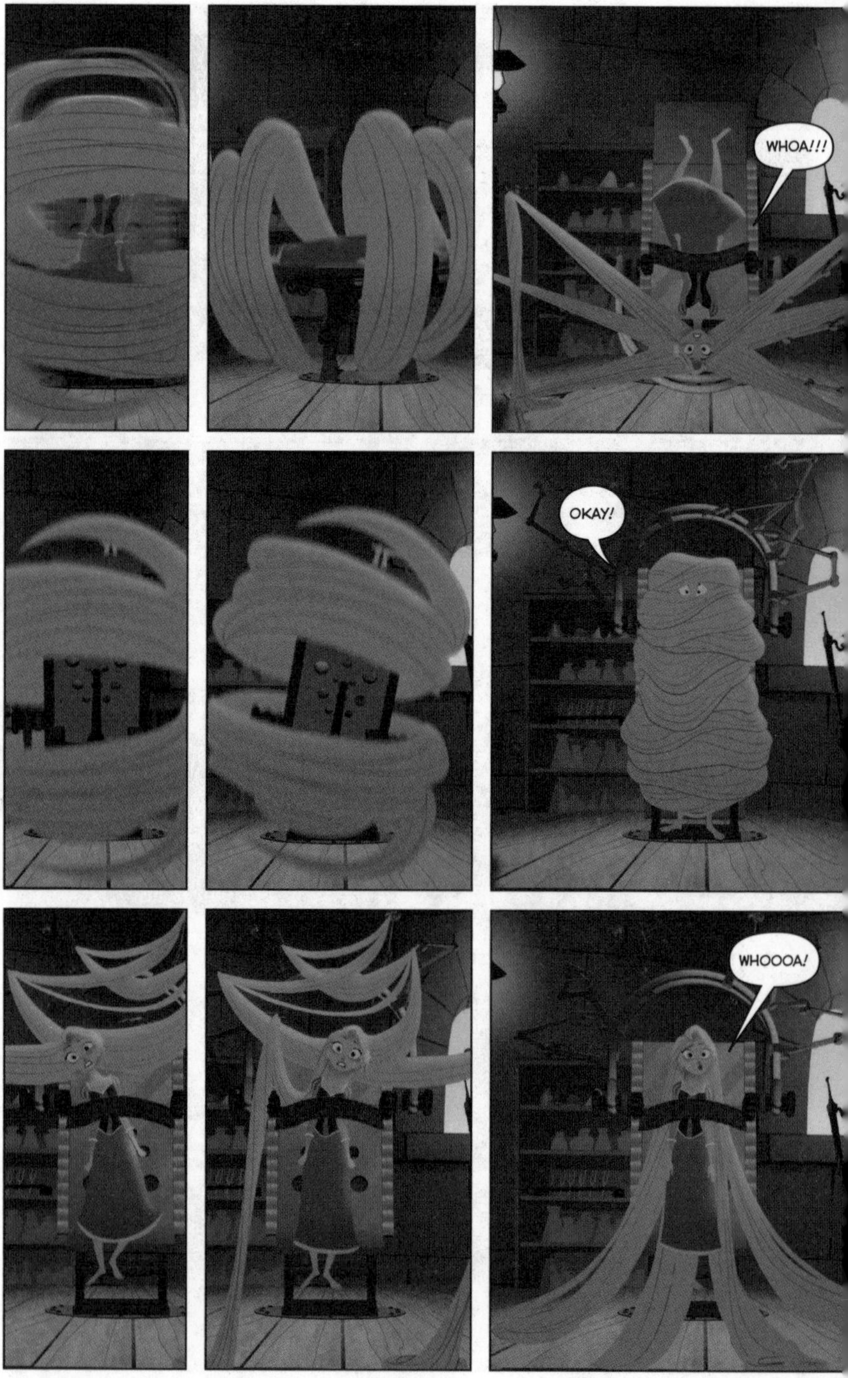
WHOA!!!
OKAY!
WHOOOA!

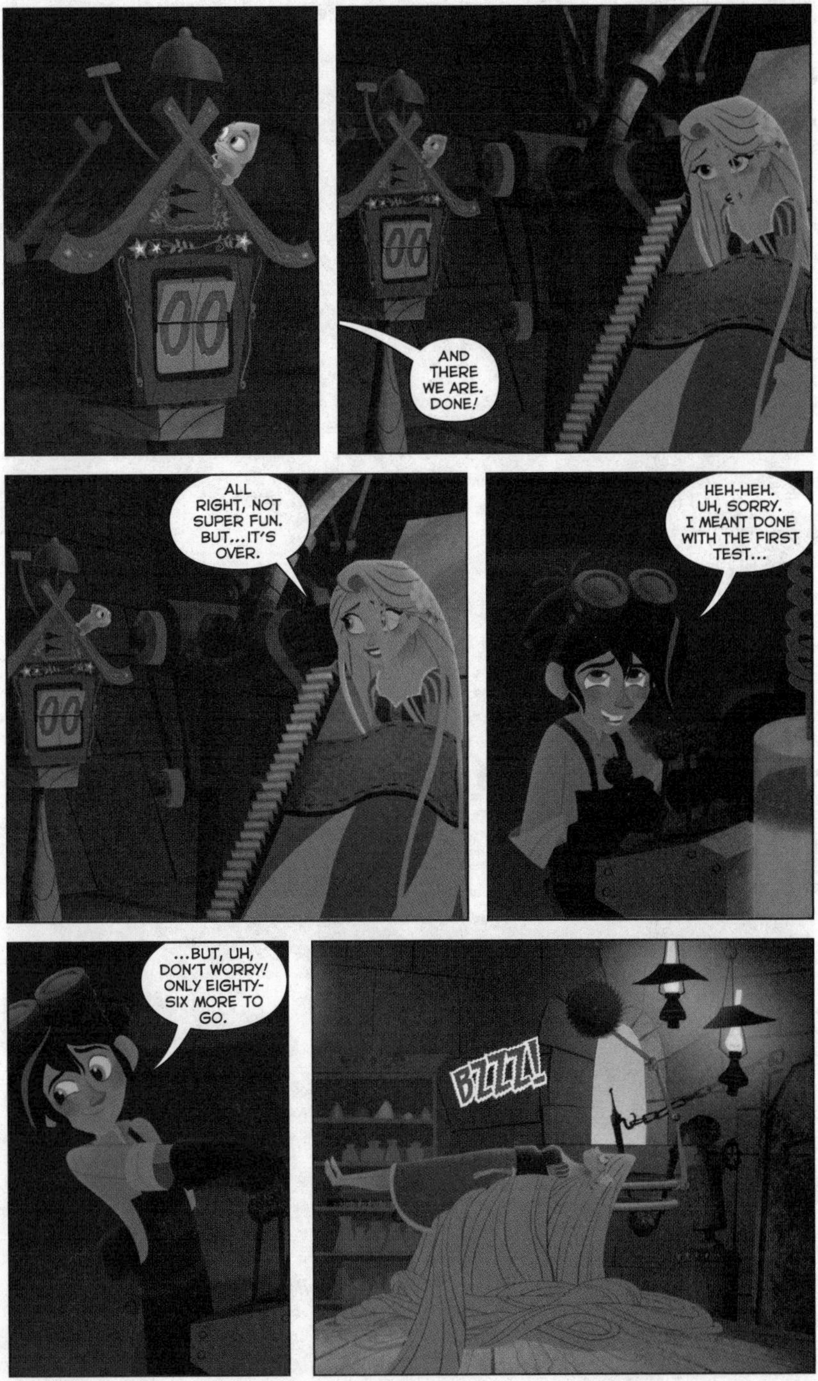
AND THERE WE ARE. DONE!
ALL RIGHT, NOT SUPER FUN. BUT...IT'S OVER.
HEH-HEH. UH, SORRY. I MEANT DONE WITH THE FIRST TEST...
...BUT, UH, DON'T WORRY! ONLY EIGHTY-SIX MORE TO GO.
BZZZA!

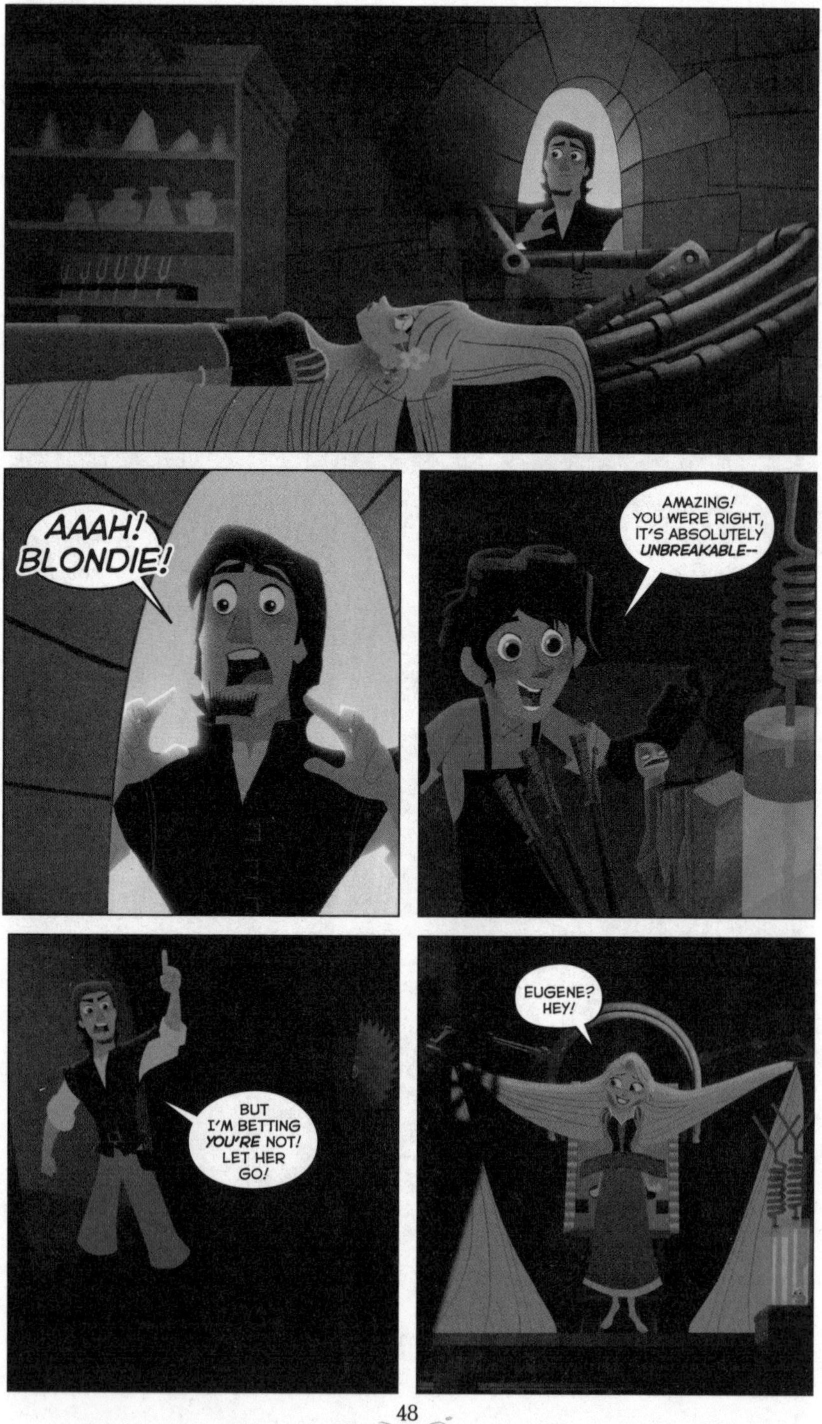
AAAH! BLONDIE!
AMAZING! YOU WERE RIGHT, IT'S ABSOLUTELY UNBREAKABLE--
BUT I'M BETTING YOU'RE NOT! LET HER GO!
EUGENE? HEY!

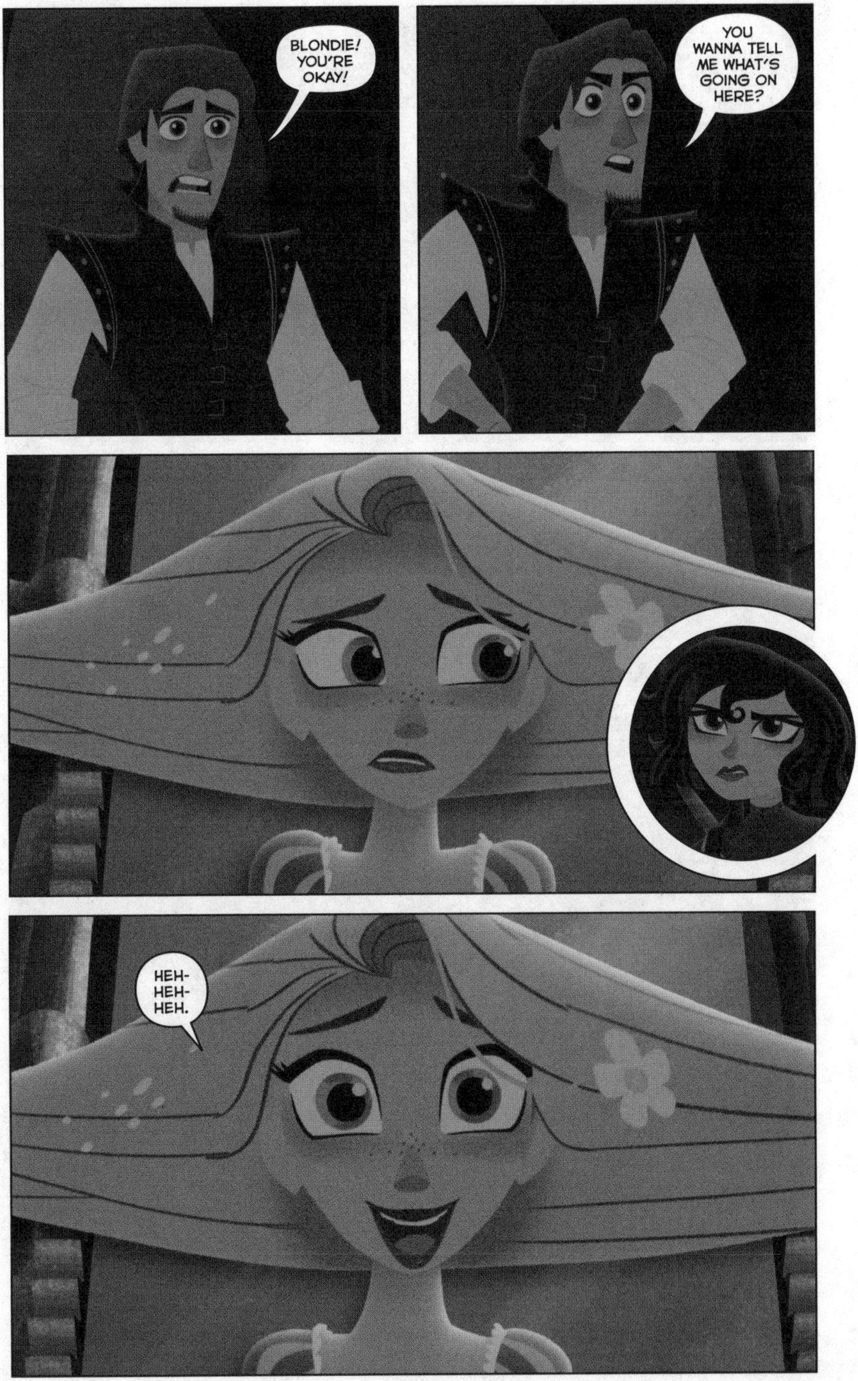
BLONDIE! YOU'RE OKAY!
YOU WANNA TELL ME WHAT'S GOING ON HERE?
HEH-HEH-HEH.

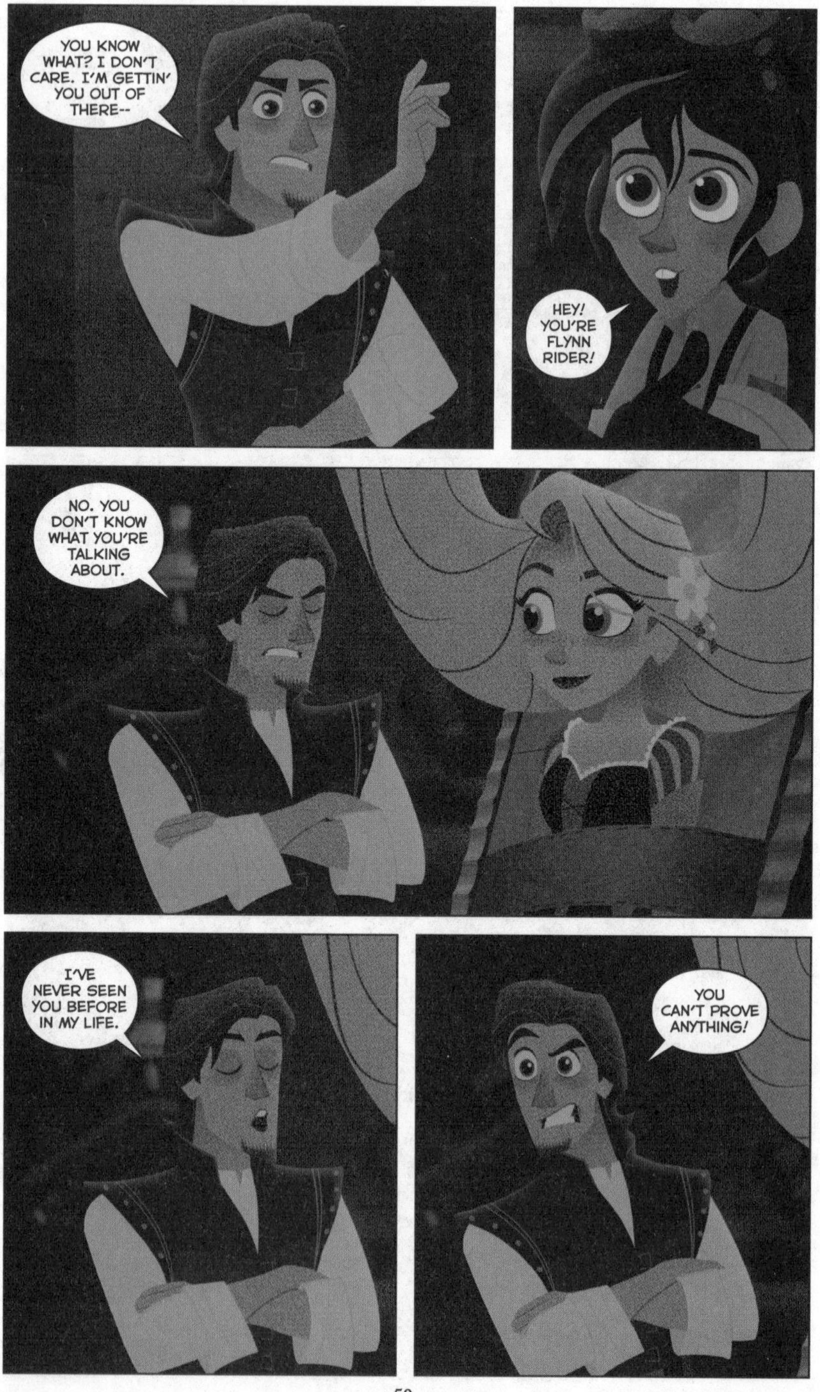
YOU KNOW WHAT? I DON'T CARE. I'M GETTIN' YOU OUT OF THERE--
HEY! YOU'RE FLYNN RIDER!
NO. YOU DON'T KNOW WHAT YOU'RE TALKING ABOUT.
I'VE NEVER SEEN YOU BEFORE IN MY LIFE.
YOU CAN'T PROVE ANYTHING!

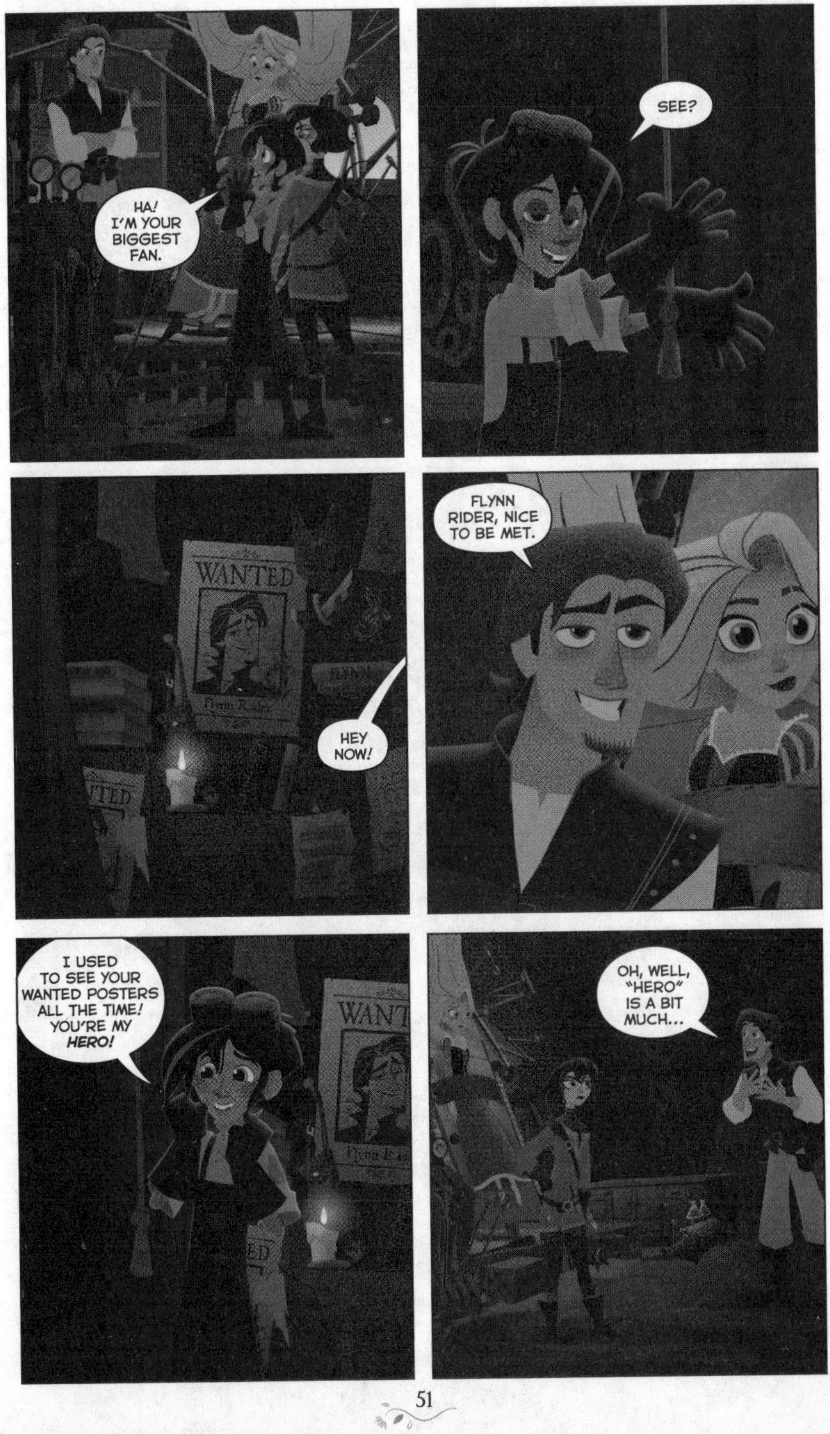
HA! I'M YOUR BIGGEST FAN.
SEE?
WANTED
HEY NOW!
FLYNN RIDER, NICE TO BE MET.
I USED TO SEE YOUR WANTED POSTERS ALL THE TIME! YOU'RE MY *HERO!*
OH, WELL, "HERO" IS A BIT MUCH...

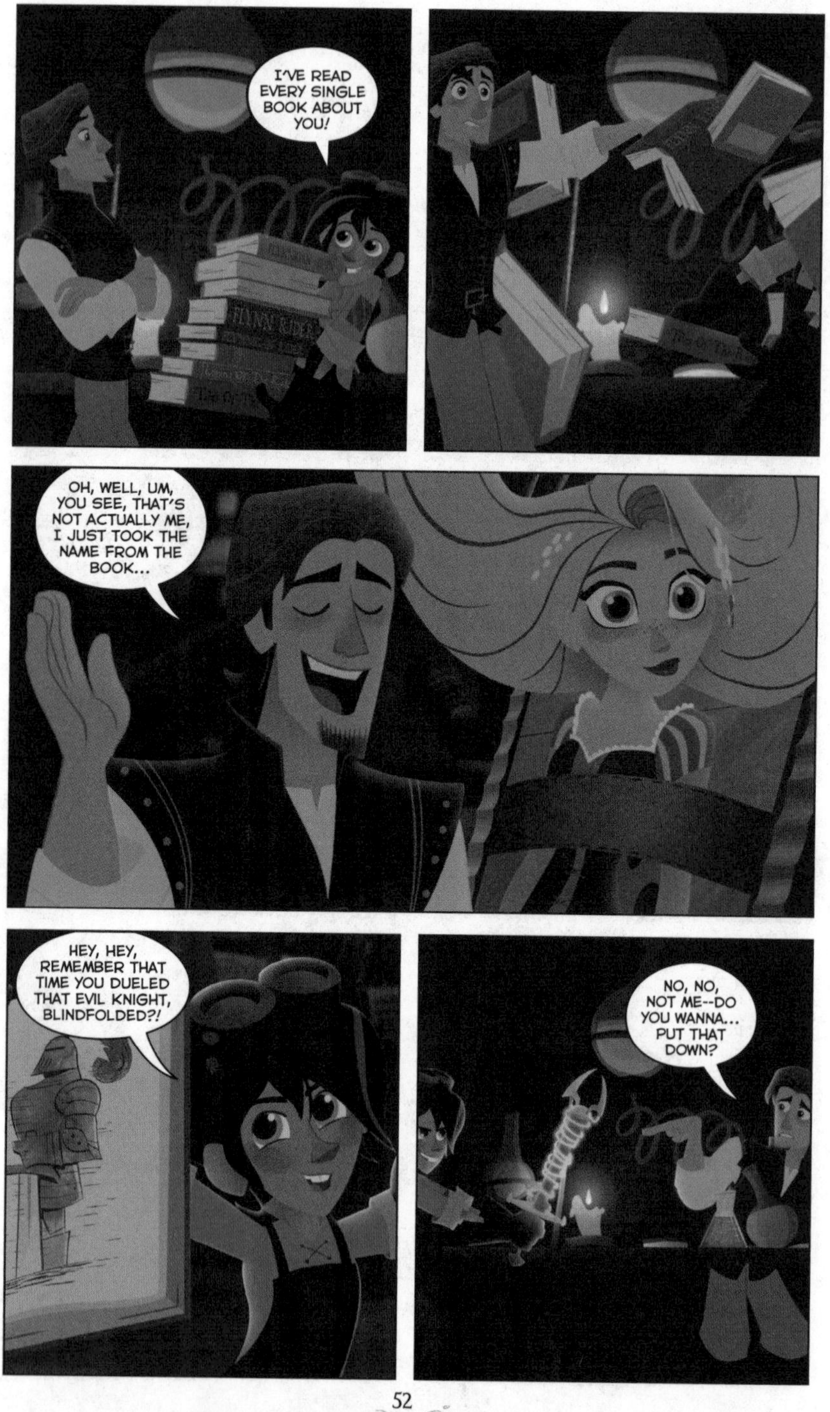
I'VE READ EVERY SINGLE BOOK ABOUT YOU!
FLYNN RIDER
OH, WELL, UM, YOU SEE, THAT'S NOT ACTUALLY ME, I JUST TOOK THE NAME FROM THE BOOK...
HEY, HEY, REMEMBER THAT TIME YOU DUELED THAT EVIL KNIGHT, BLINDFOLDED?!
NO, NO, NOT ME--DO YOU WANNA... PUT THAT DOWN?

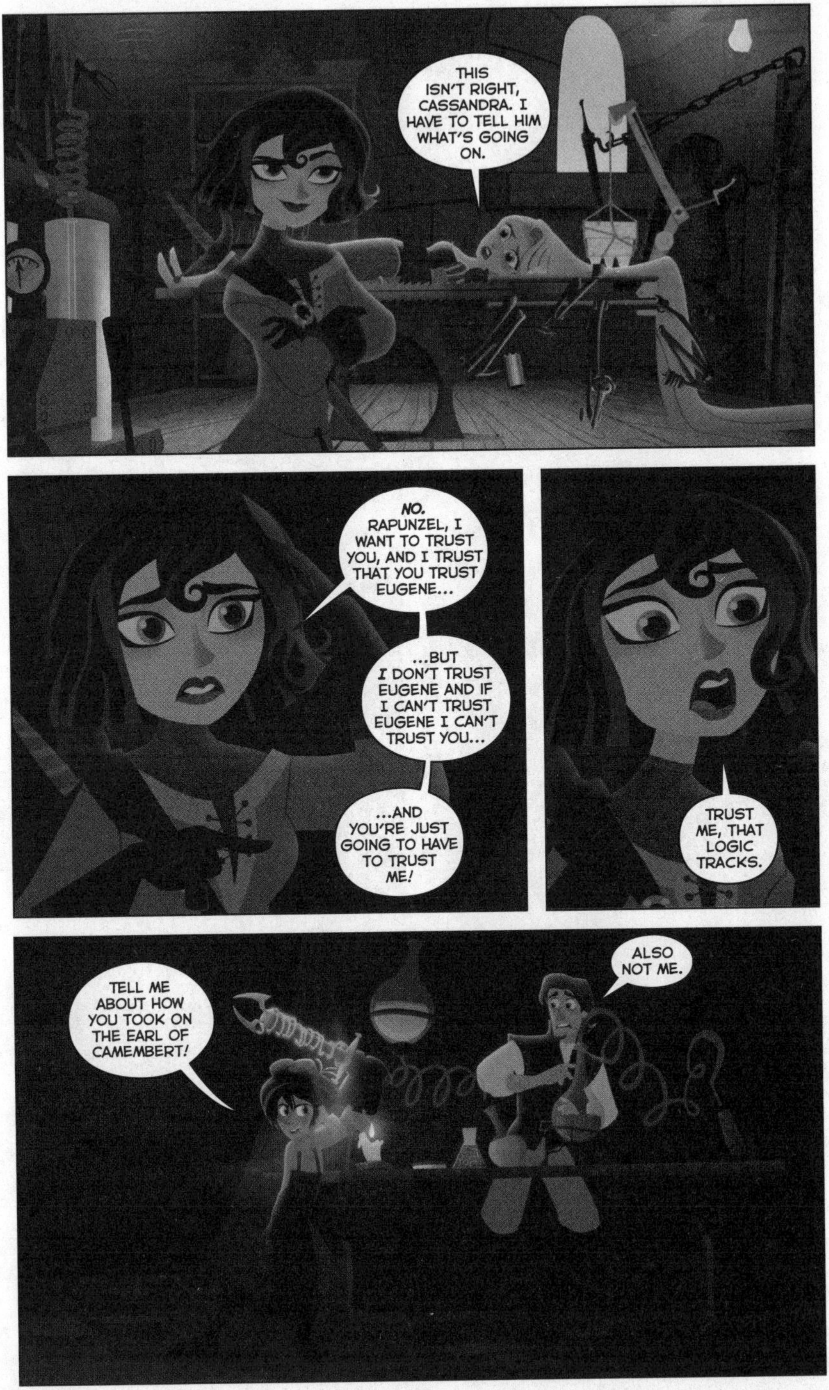
THIS ISN'T RIGHT, CASSANDRA. I HAVE TO TELL HIM WHAT'S GOING ON.
NO. RAPUNZEL, I WANT TO TRUST YOU, AND I TRUST THAT YOU TRUST EUGENE...
...BUT I DON'T TRUST EUGENE AND IF I CAN'T TRUST EUGENE I CAN'T TRUST YOU...
...AND YOU'RE JUST GOING TO HAVE TO TRUST ME!
TRUST ME, THAT LOGIC TRACKS.
TELL ME ABOUT HOW YOU TOOK ON THE EARL OF CAMEMBERT!
ALSO NOT ME.

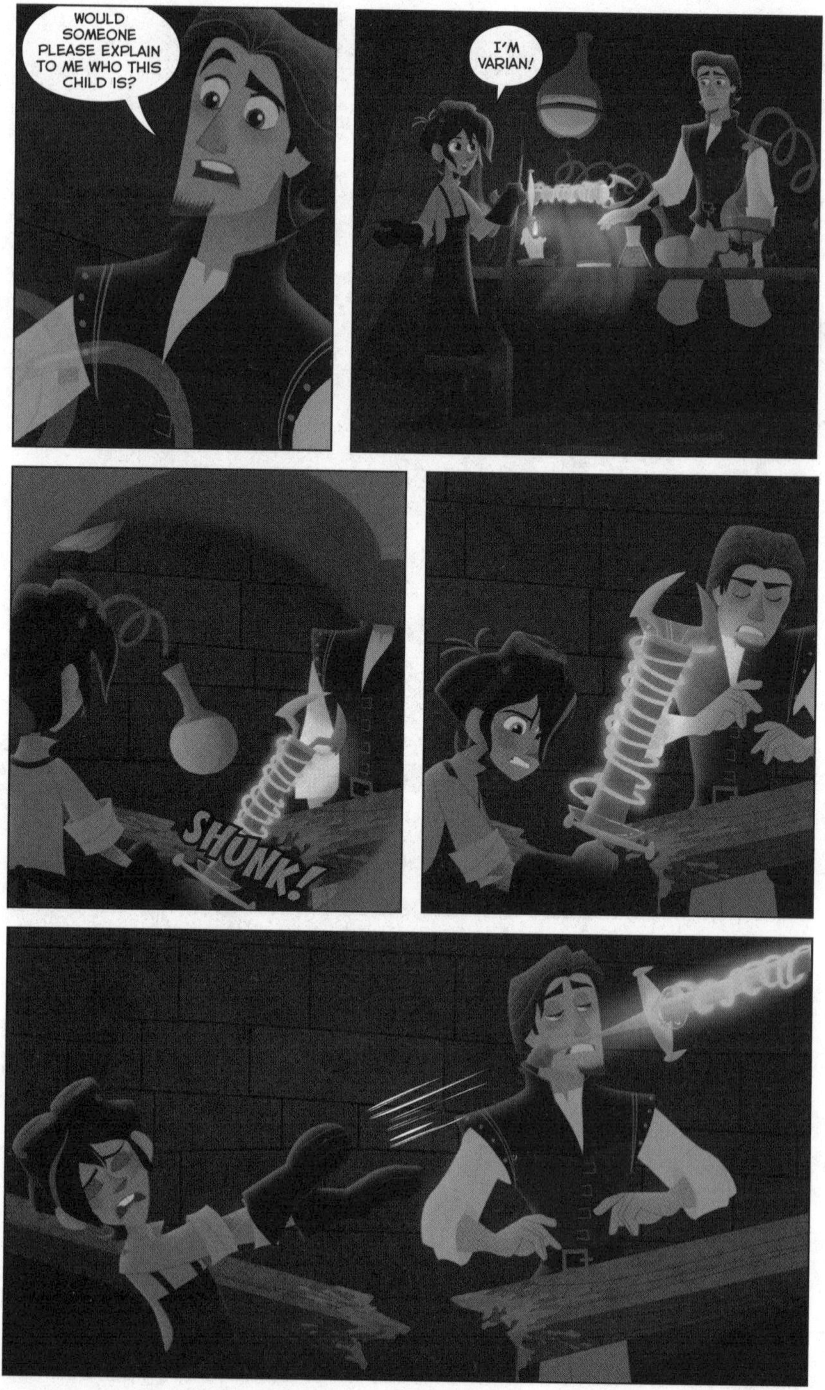
WOULD SOMEONE PLEASE EXPLAIN TO ME WHO THIS CHILD IS?
I'M VARIAN!
SHUNK!

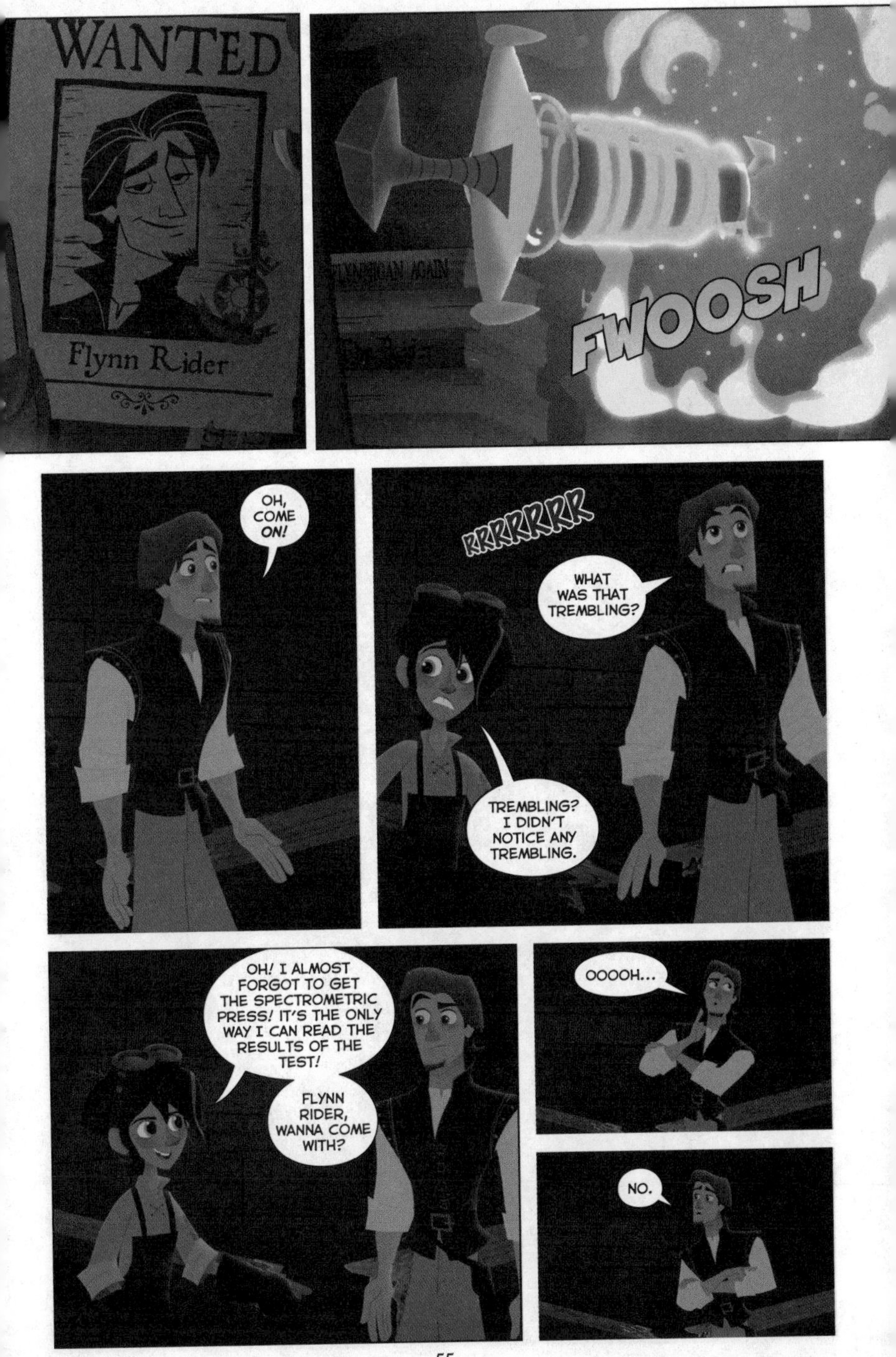
WANTED
Flynn Rider
FWOOSH
OH, COME ON!
RRRRRRR
WHAT WAS THAT TREMBLING?
TREMBLING? I DIDN'T NOTICE ANY TREMBLING.
OH! I ALMOST FORGOT TO GET THE SPECTROMETRIC PRESS! IT'S THE ONLY WAY I CAN READ THE RESULTS OF THE TEST!
FLYNN RIDER, WANNA COME WITH?
OOOOH...
NO.

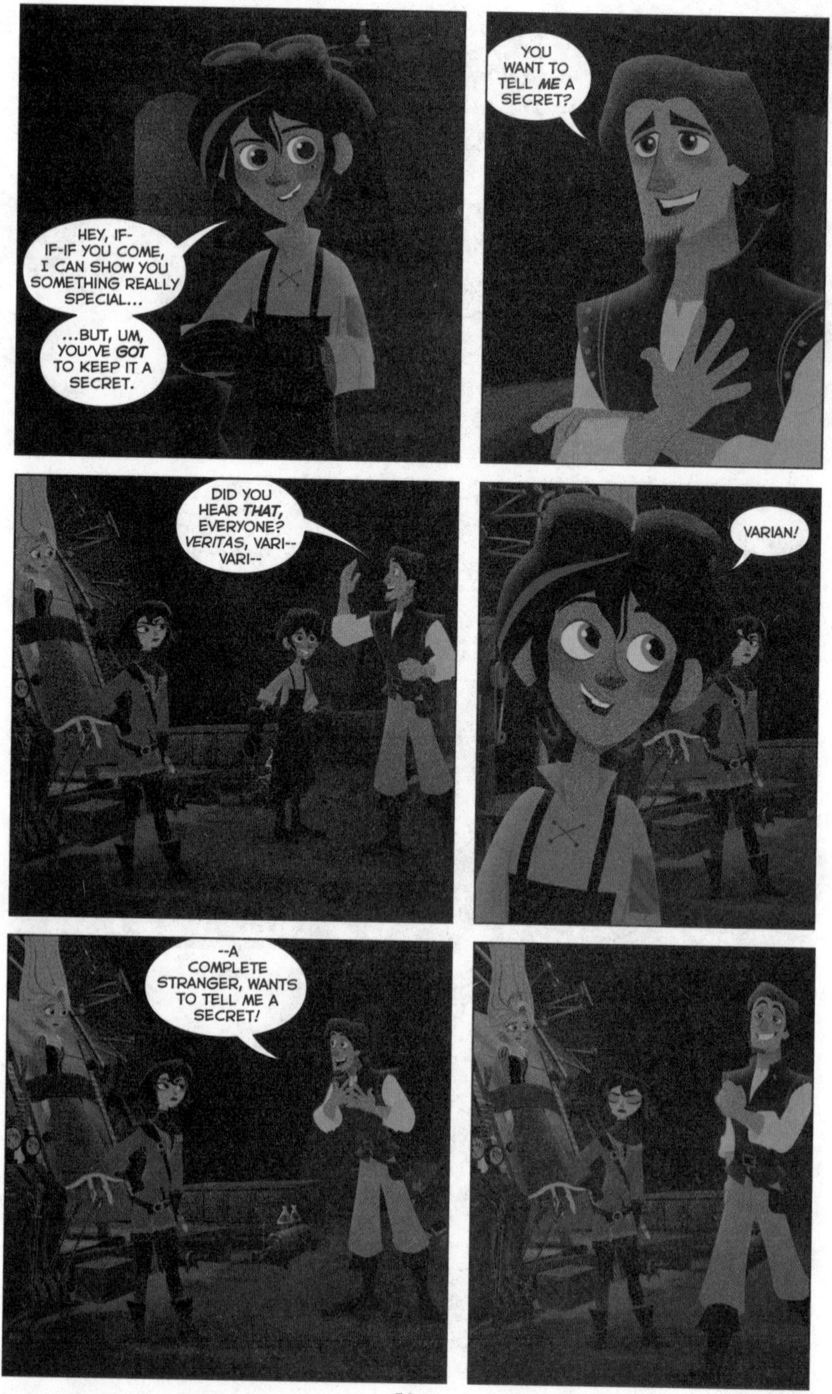
HEY, IF- IF-IF YOU COME, I CAN SHOW YOU SOMETHING REALLY SPECIAL...
...BUT, UM, YOU'VE *GOT* TO KEEP IT A SECRET.
YOU WANT TO TELL *ME* A SECRET?
DID YOU HEAR *THAT,* EVERYONE? *VERITAS,* VARI-- VARI--
VARIAN!
--A COMPLETE STRANGER, WANTS TO TELL ME A SECRET!

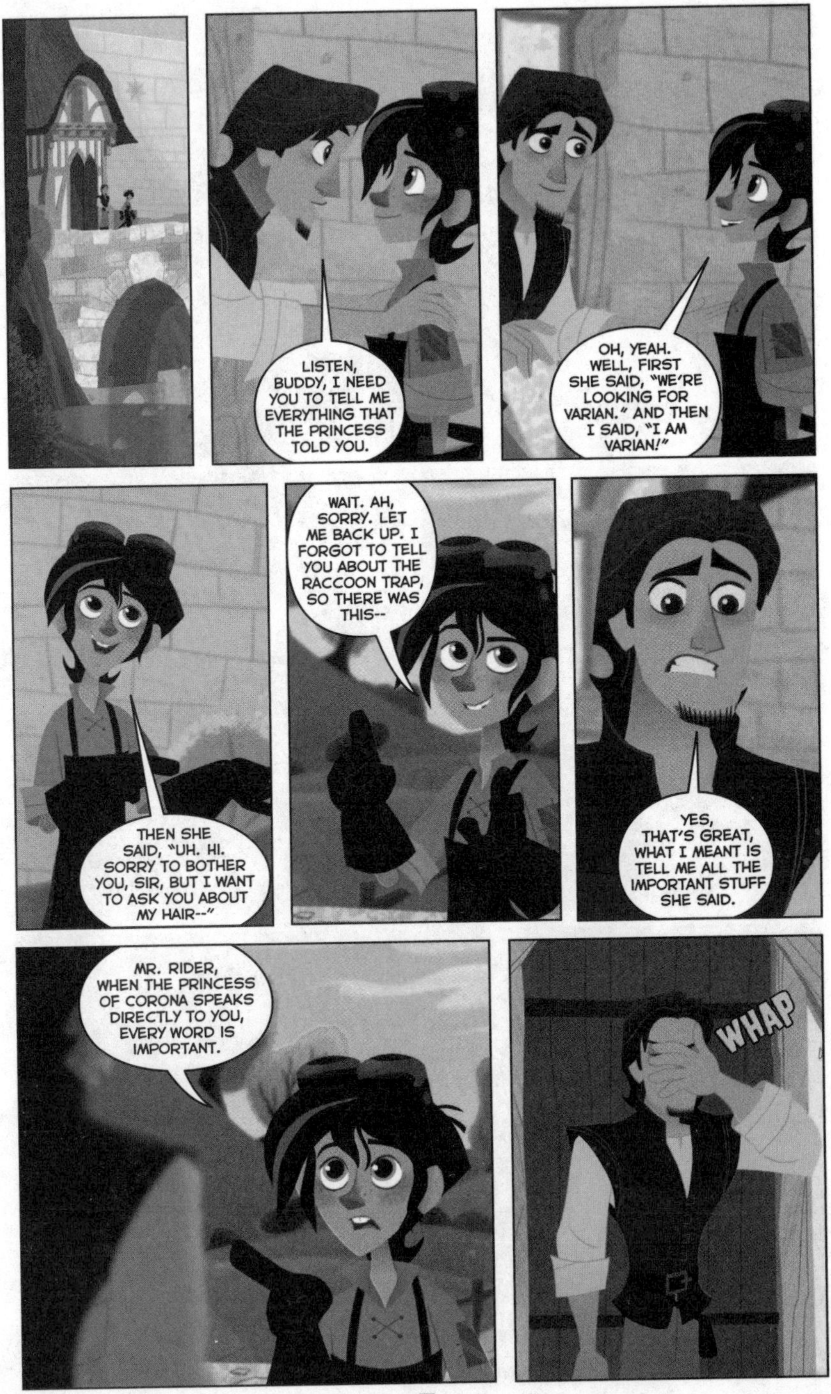

LISTEN, BUDDY, I NEED YOU TO TELL ME EVERYTHING THAT THE PRINCESS TOLD YOU.
OH, YEAH. WELL, FIRST SHE SAID, "WE'RE LOOKING FOR VARIAN." AND THEN I SAID, "I AM VARIAN!"
THEN SHE SAID, "UH. HI. SORRY TO BOTHER YOU, SIR, BUT I WANT TO ASK YOU ABOUT MY HAIR--"
WAIT. AH, SORRY. LET ME BACK UP. I FORGOT TO TELL YOU ABOUT THE RACCOON TRAP, SO THERE WAS THIS--
YES, THAT'S GREAT, WHAT I MEANT IS TELL ME ALL THE IMPORTANT STUFF SHE SAID.
MR. RIDER, WHEN THE PRINCESS OF CORONA SPEAKS DIRECTLY TO YOU, EVERY WORD IS IMPORTANT.
WHAP

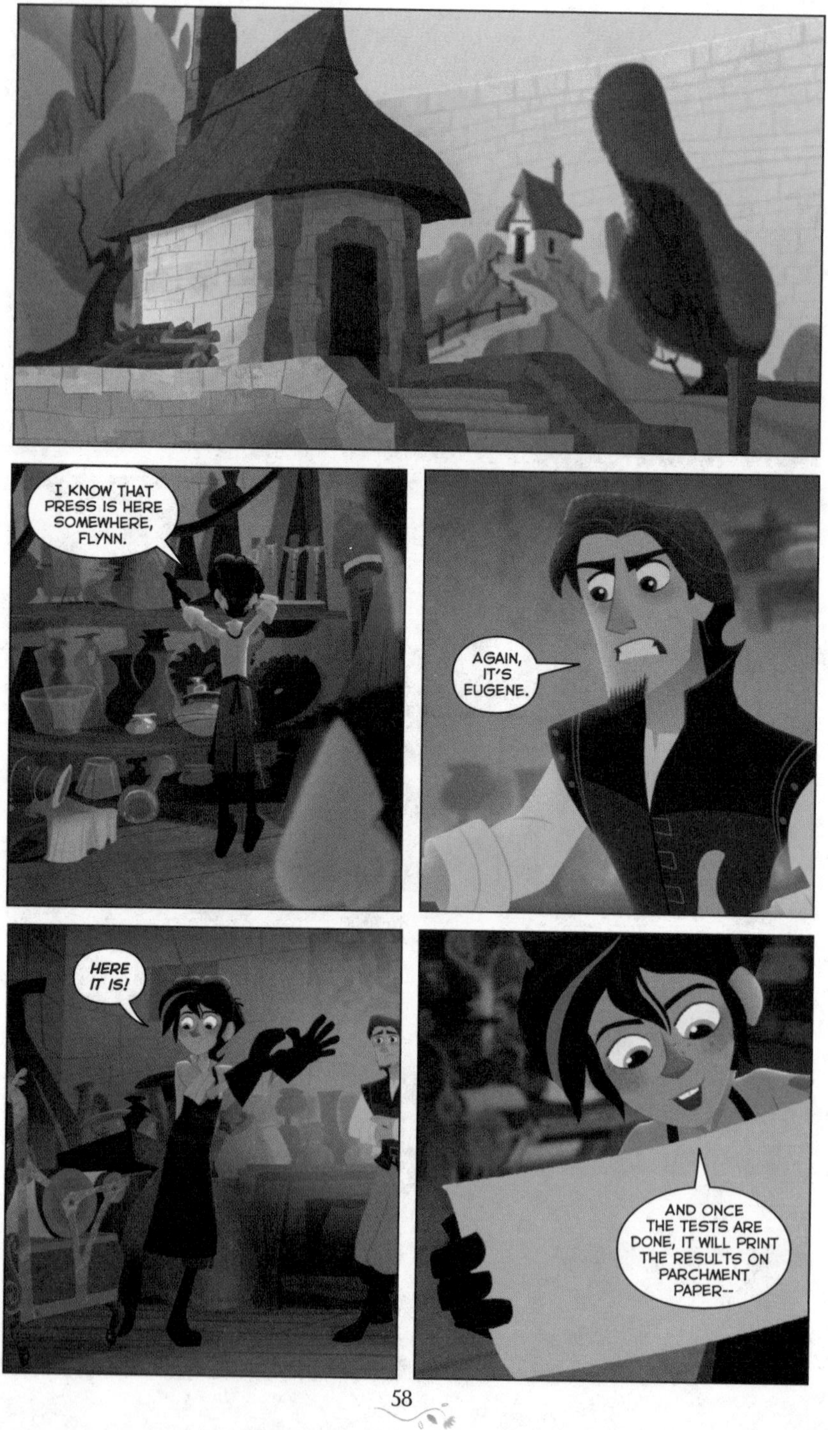
I KNOW THAT PRESS IS HERE SOMEWHERE, FLYNN.
AGAIN, IT'S EUGENE.
HERE IT IS!
AND ONCE THE TESTS ARE DONE, IT WILL PRINT THE RESULTS ON PARCHMENT PAPER--

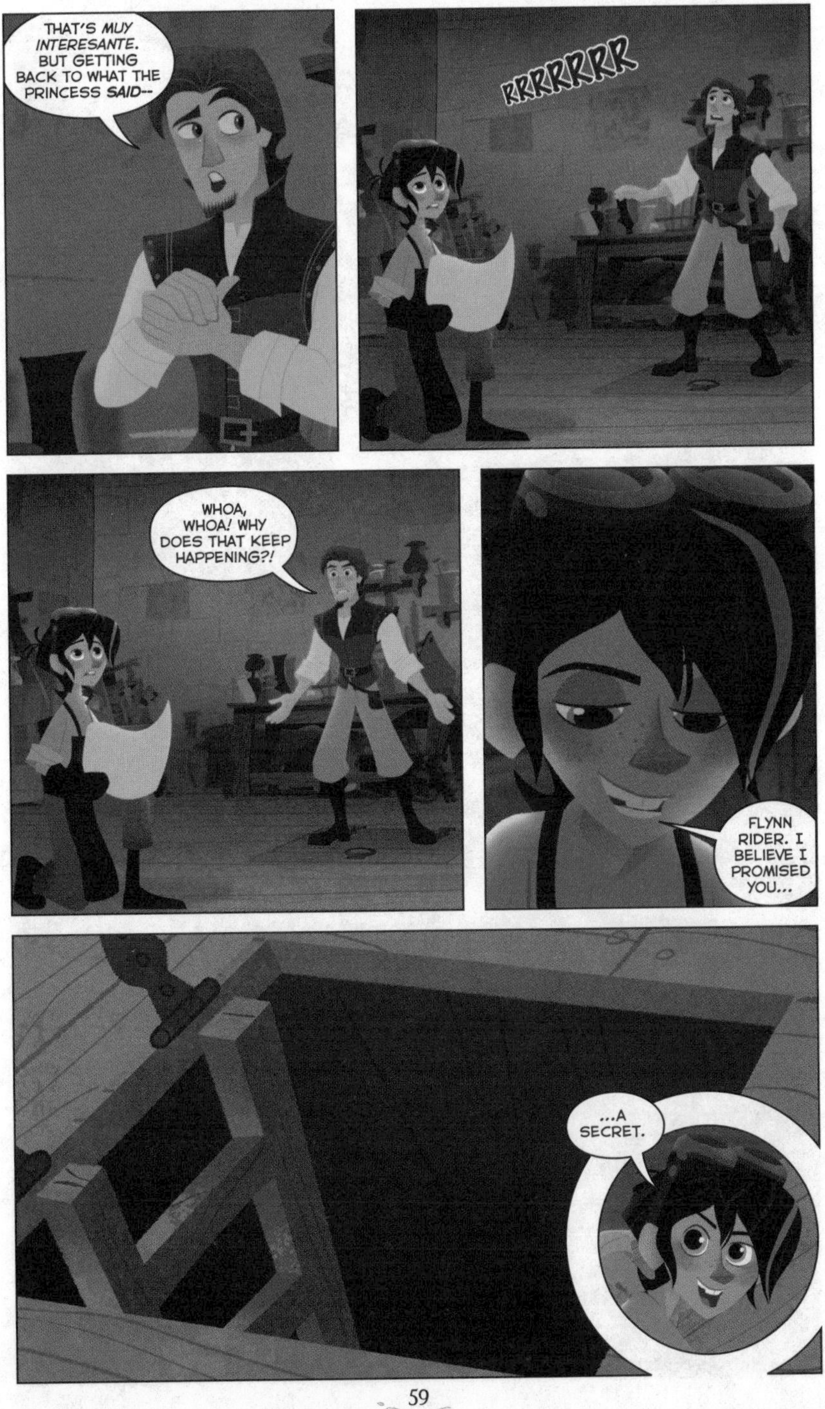
THAT'S MUY INTERESANTE. BUT GETTING BACK TO WHAT THE PRINCESS SAID--
RRRRRRR
WHOA, WHOA! WHY DOES THAT KEEP HAPPENING?!
FLYNN RIDER. I BELIEVE I PROMISED YOU...
...A SECRET.

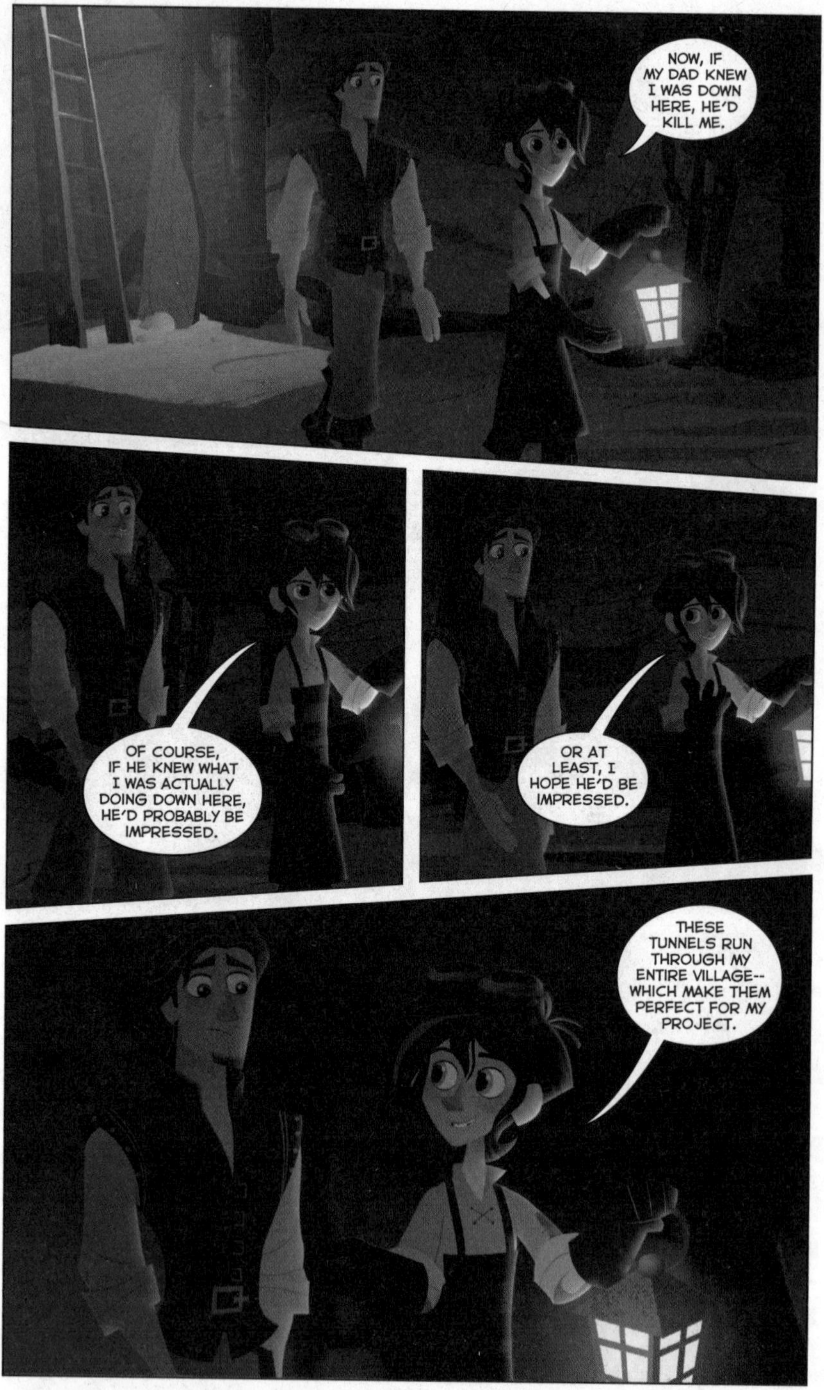
NOW, IF MY DAD KNEW I WAS DOWN HERE, HE'D KILL ME.
OF COURSE, IF HE KNEW WHAT I WAS ACTUALLY DOING DOWN HERE, HE'D PROBABLY BE IMPRESSED.
OR AT LEAST, I HOPE HE'D BE IMPRESSED.
THESE TUNNELS RUN THROUGH MY ENTIRE VILLAGE--WHICH MAKE THEM PERFECT FOR MY PROJECT.

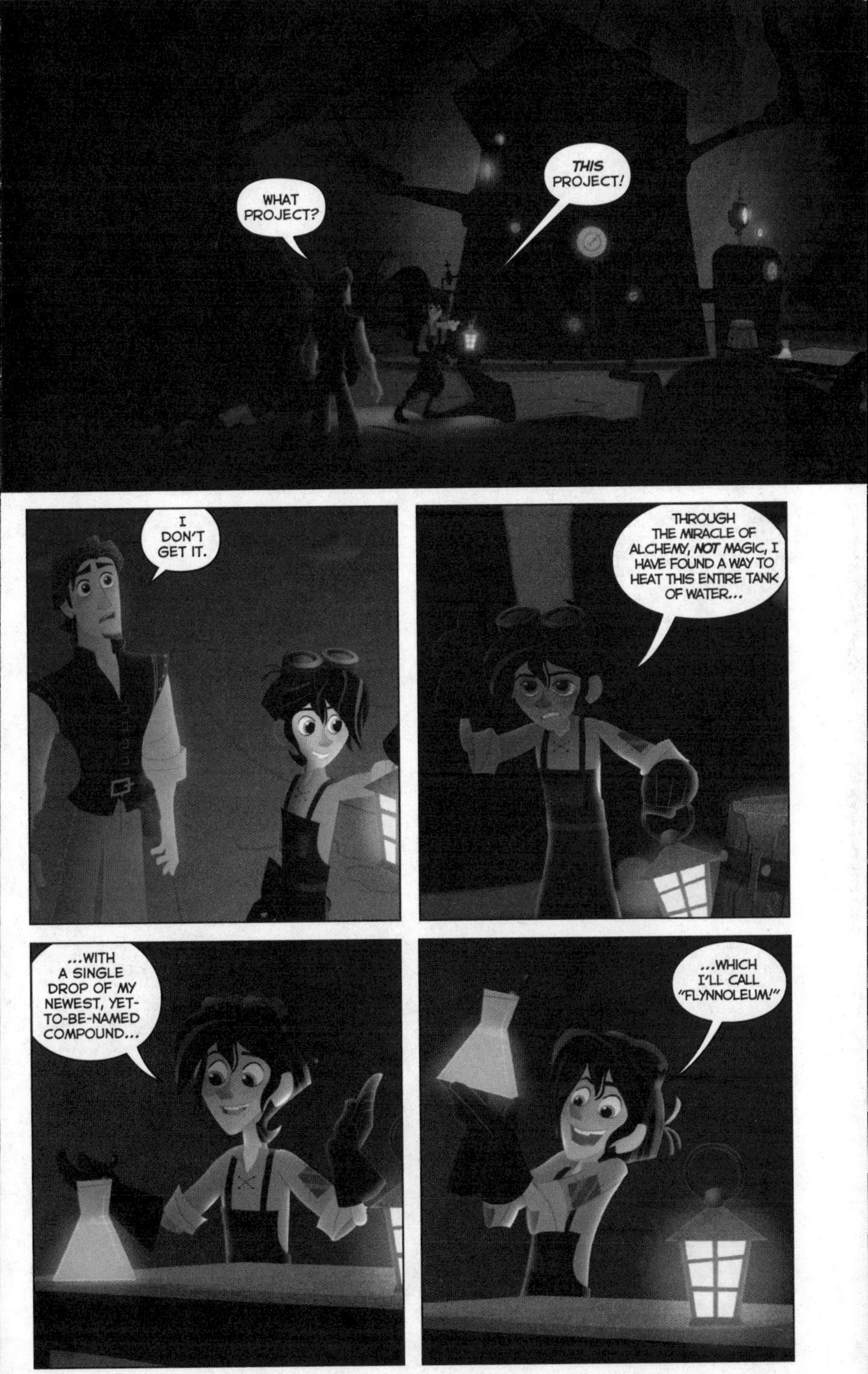
WHAT PROJECT?
THIS PROJECT!
I DON'T GET IT.
THROUGH THE MIRACLE OF ALCHEMY, NOT MAGIC, I HAVE FOUND A WAY TO HEAT THIS ENTIRE TANK OF WATER...
...WITH A SINGLE DROP OF MY NEWEST, YET-TO-BE-NAMED COMPOUND...
...WHICH I'LL CALL "FLYNNOLEUM!"

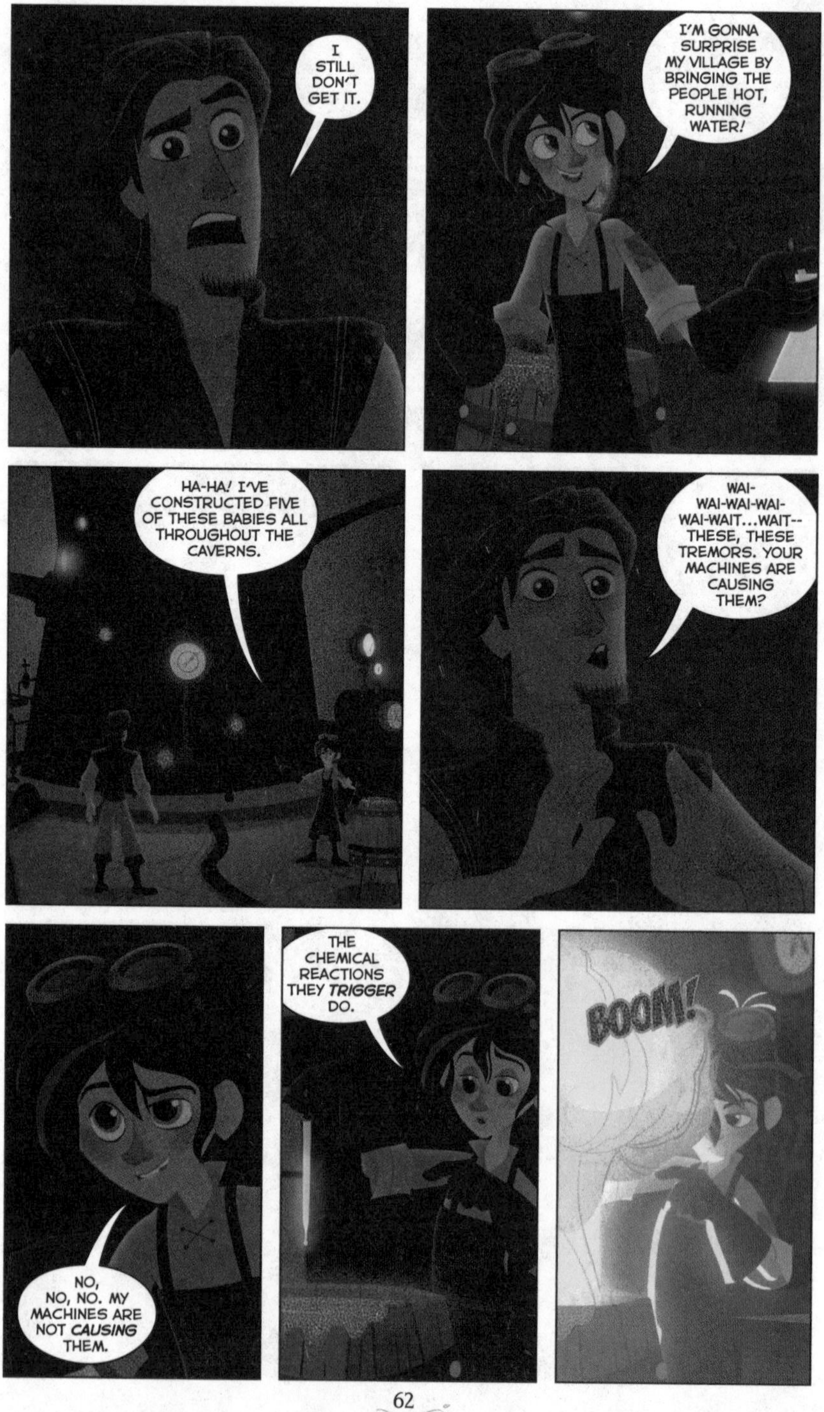
I STILL DON'T GET IT.
I'M GONNA SURPRISE MY VILLAGE BY BRINGING THE PEOPLE HOT, RUNNING WATER!
HA-HA! I'VE CONSTRUCTED FIVE OF THESE BABIES ALL THROUGHOUT THE CAVERNS.
WAI-WAI-WAI-WAI-WAI-WAIT...WAIT--THESE, THESE TREMORS. YOUR MACHINES ARE CAUSING THEM?
NO, NO, NO. MY MACHINES ARE NOT *CAUSING* THEM.
THE CHEMICAL REACTIONS THEY *TRIGGER* DO.
BOOM!

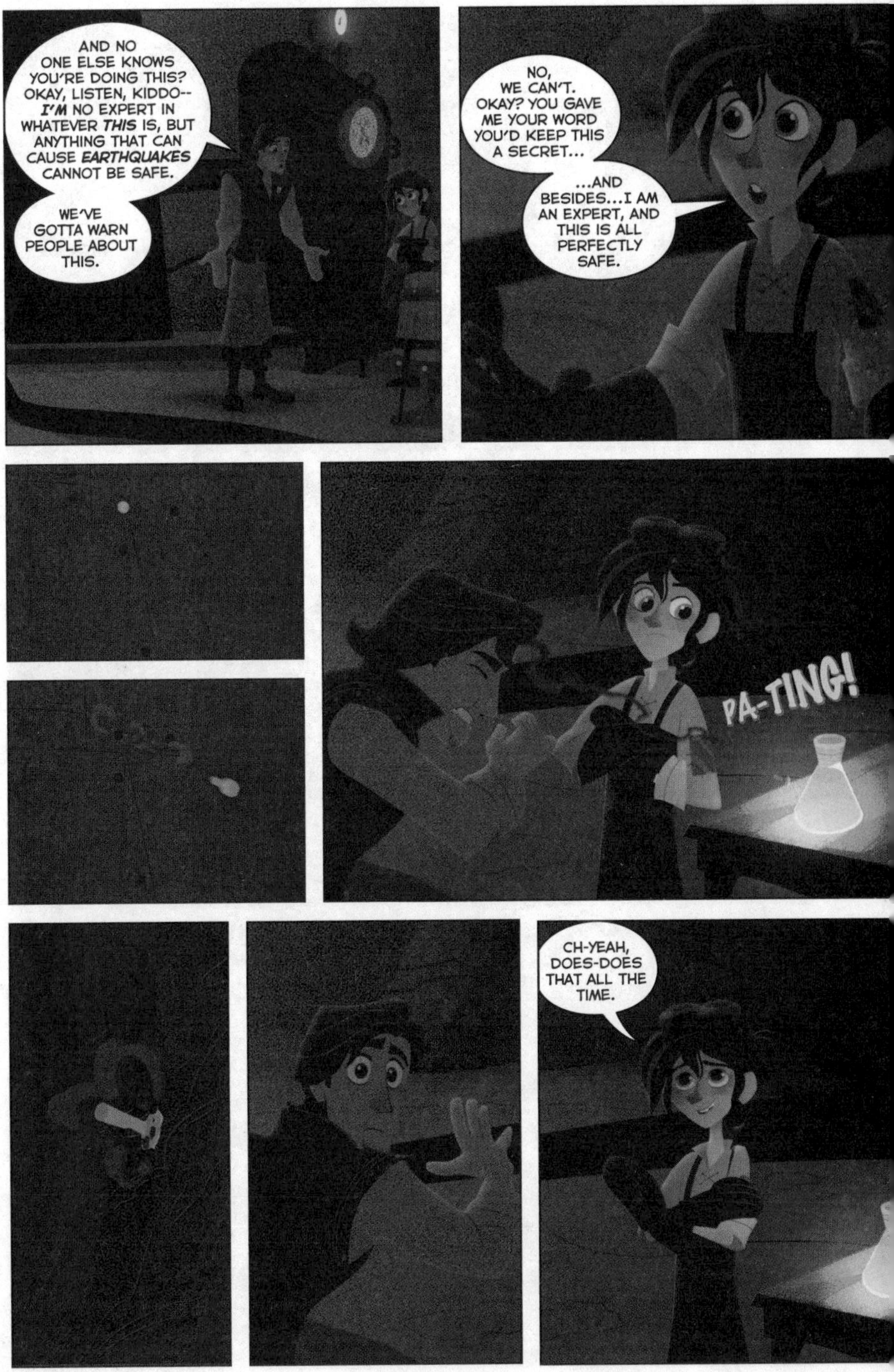
AND NO ONE ELSE KNOWS YOU'RE DOING THIS? OKAY, LISTEN, KIDDO-- I'M NO EXPERT IN WHATEVER THIS IS, BUT ANYTHING THAT CAN CAUSE EARTHQUAKES CANNOT BE SAFE.
WE'VE GOTTA WARN PEOPLE ABOUT THIS.
NO, WE CAN'T. OKAY? YOU GAVE ME YOUR WORD YOU'D KEEP THIS A SECRET...
...AND BESIDES...I AM AN EXPERT, AND THIS IS ALL PERFECTLY SAFE.
PA-TING!
CH-YEAH, DOES-DOES THAT ALL THE TIME.

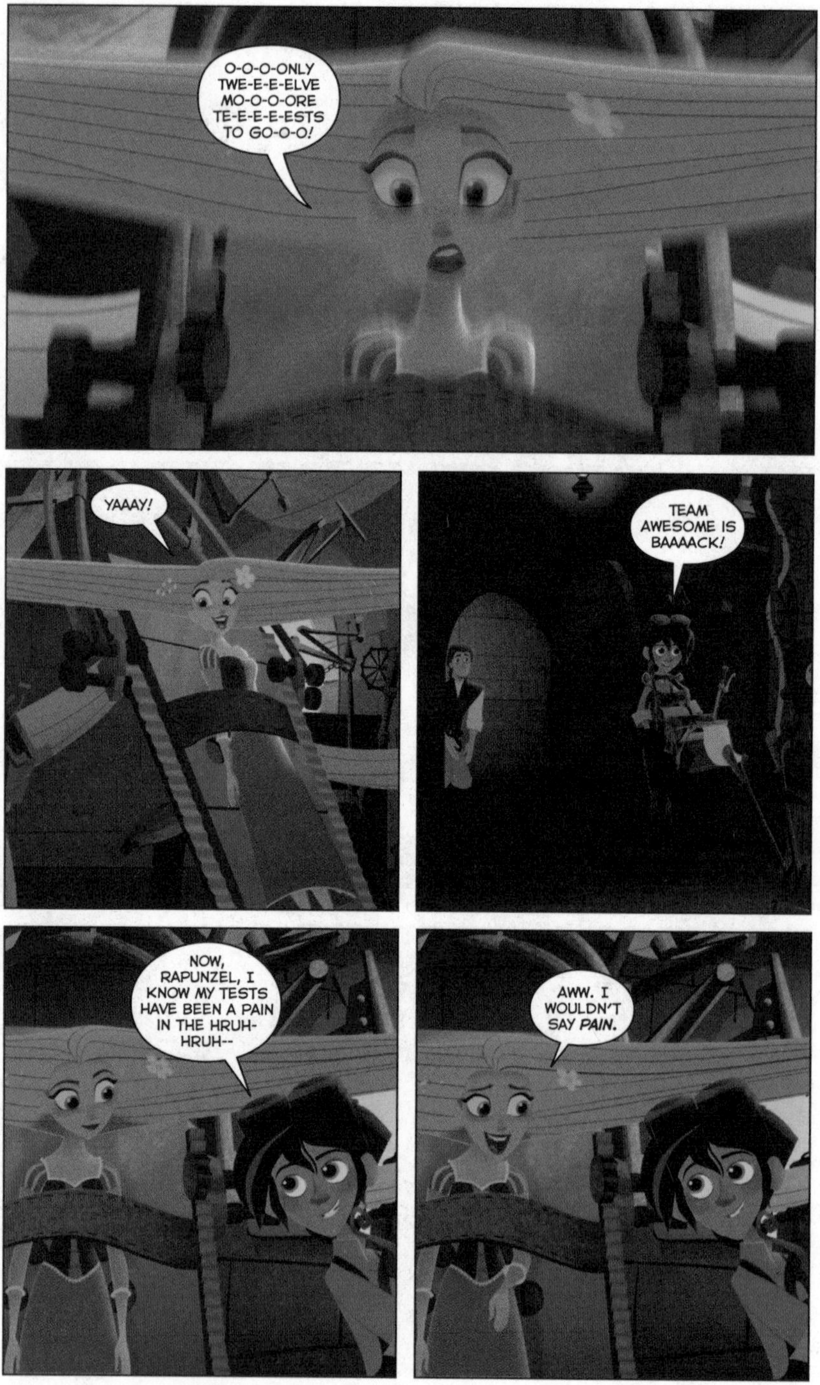
O-O-O-ONLY TWE-E-E-ELVE MO-O-O-ORE TE-E-E-E-ESTS TO GO-O-O!
YAAAY!
TEAM AWESOME IS BAAAACK!
NOW, RAPUNZEL, I KNOW MY TESTS HAVE BEEN A PAIN IN THE HRUH-HRUH--
AWW. I WOULDN'T SAY *PAIN*.

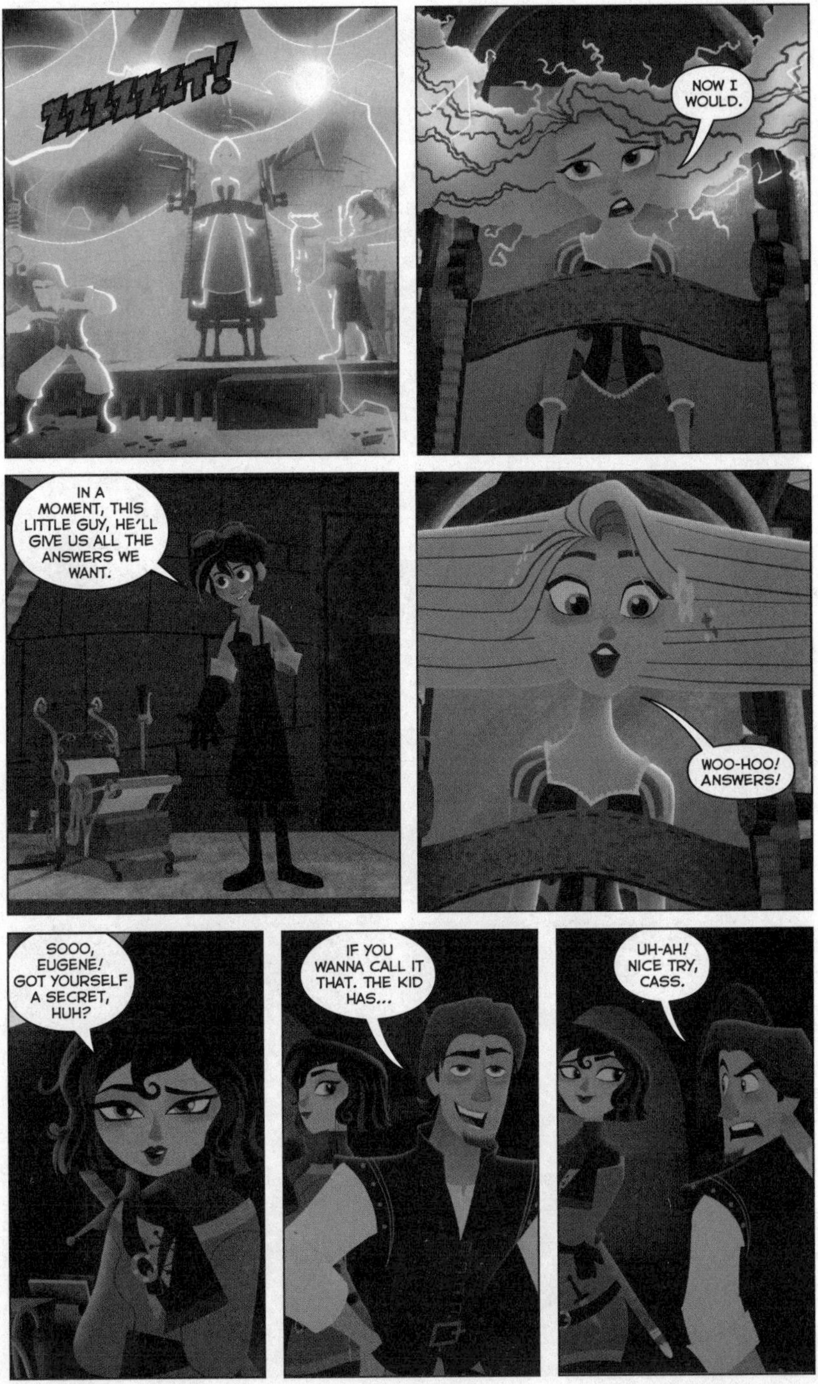
ZZZZZZZT!
NOW I WOULD.
IN A MOMENT, THIS LITTLE GUY, HE'LL GIVE US ALL THE ANSWERS WE WANT.
WOO-HOO! ANSWERS!
SOOO, EUGENE! GOT YOURSELF A SECRET, HUH?
IF YOU WANNA CALL IT THAT. THE KID HAS...
UH-AH! NICE TRY, CASS.

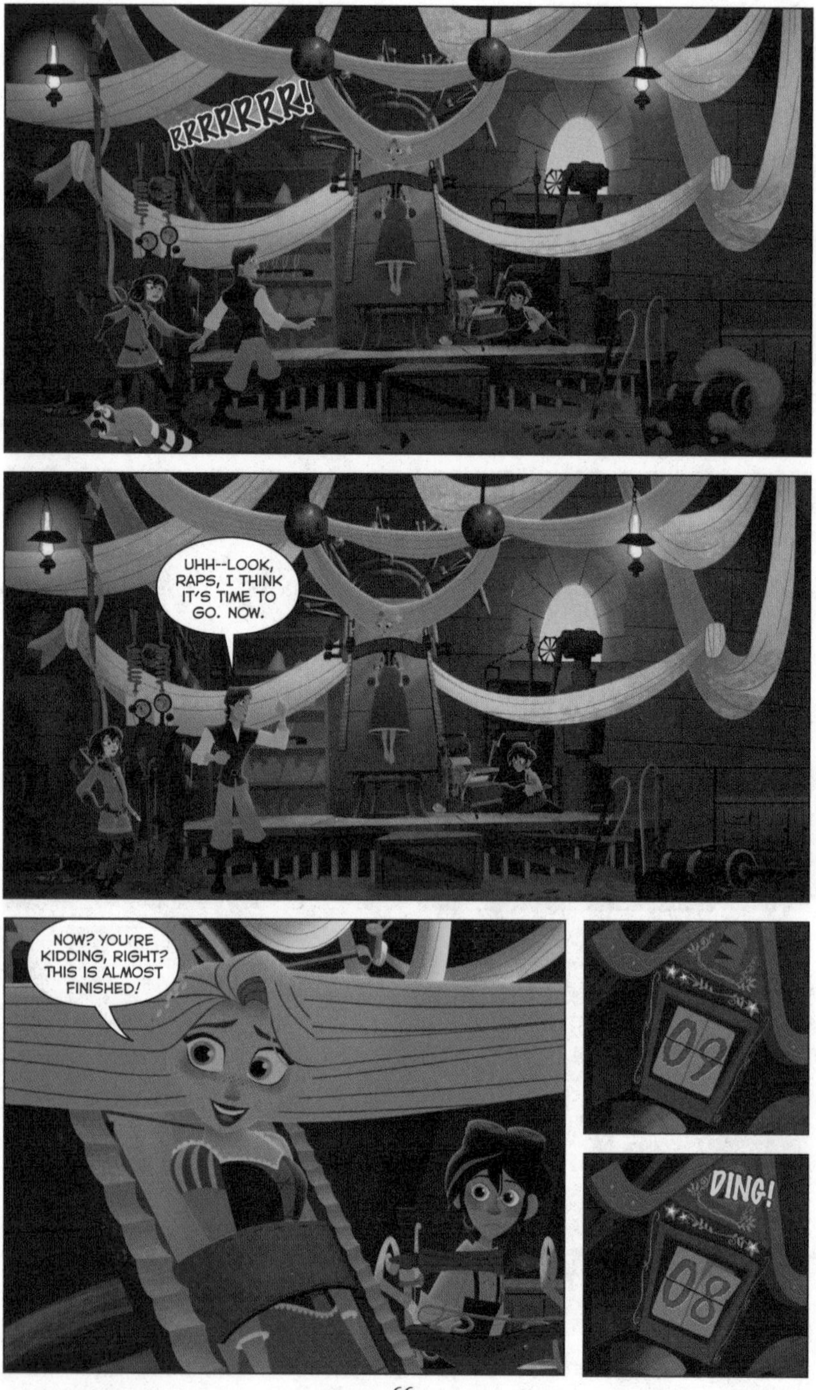
RRRRRRR!
UHH--LOOK, RAPS, I THINK IT'S TIME TO GO. NOW.
NOW? YOU'RE KIDDING, RIGHT? THIS IS ALMOST FINISHED!
09
DING!
08

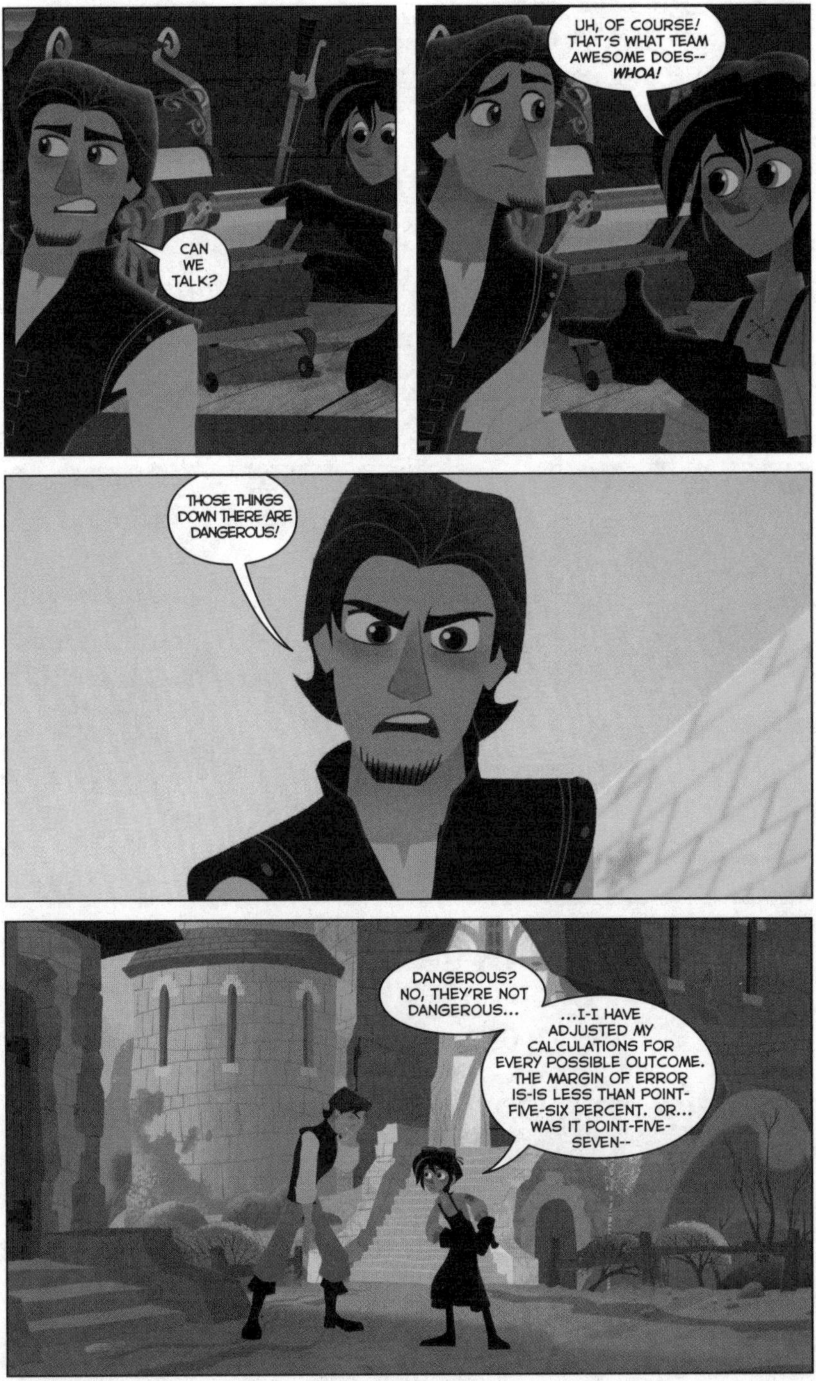
CAN WE TALK?
UH, OF COURSE! THAT'S WHAT TEAM AWESOME DOES-- *WHOA!*
THOSE THINGS DOWN THERE ARE DANGEROUS!
DANGEROUS? NO, THEY'RE NOT DANGEROUS...
...I-I HAVE ADJUSTED MY CALCULATIONS FOR EVERY POSSIBLE OUTCOME. THE MARGIN OF ERROR IS-IS LESS THAN POINT-FIVE-SIX PERCENT. OR... WAS IT POINT-FIVE-SEVEN--

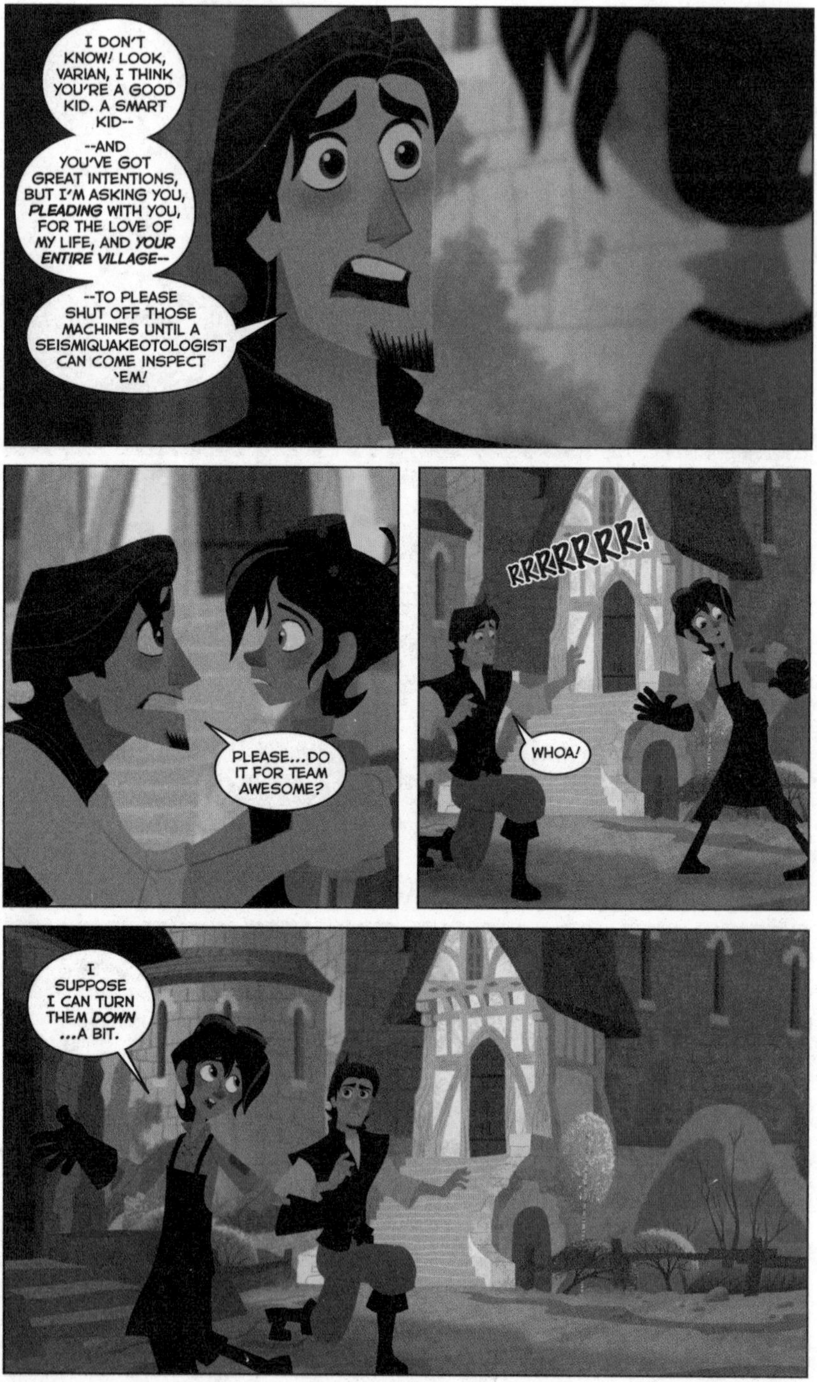
I DON'T KNOW! LOOK, VARIAN, I THINK YOU'RE A GOOD KID. A SMART KID--
--AND YOU'VE GOT GREAT INTENTIONS, BUT I'M ASKING YOU, *PLEADING* WITH YOU, FOR THE LOVE OF MY LIFE, AND *YOUR ENTIRE VILLAGE*--
--TO PLEASE SHUT OFF THOSE MACHINES UNTIL A SEISMIQUAKEOTOLOGIST CAN COME INSPECT 'EM!
PLEASE...DO IT FOR TEAM AWESOME?
RRRRRRR!
WHOA!
I SUPPOSE I CAN TURN THEM *DOWN* ...A BIT.

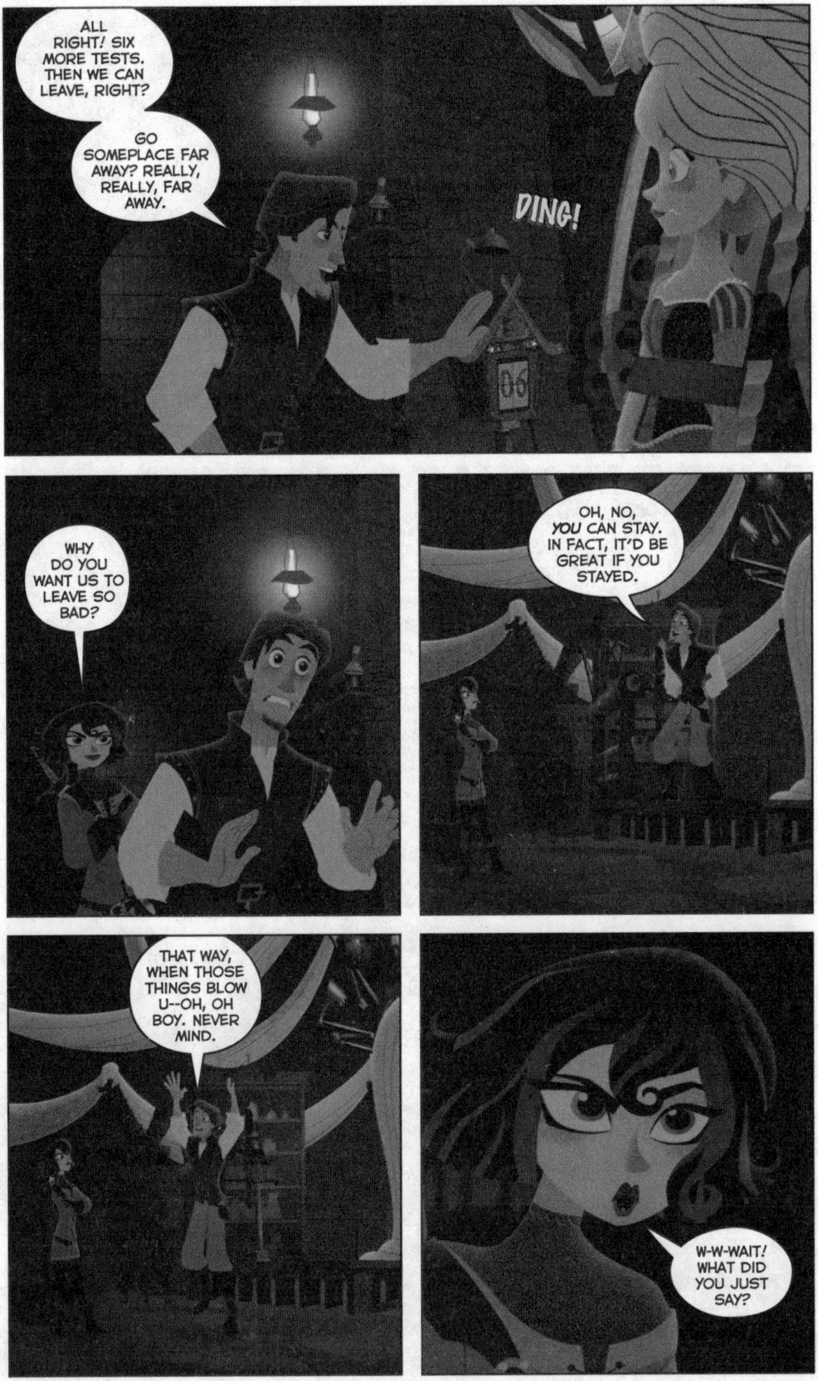
ALL RIGHT! SIX MORE TESTS. THEN WE CAN LEAVE, RIGHT?
GO SOMEPLACE FAR AWAY? REALLY, REALLY, FAR AWAY.
DING!
06
WHY DO YOU WANT US TO LEAVE SO BAD?
OH, NO, *YOU* CAN STAY. IN FACT, IT'D BE GREAT IF YOU STAYED.
THAT WAY, WHEN THOSE THINGS BLOW U--OH, OH BOY. NEVER MIND.
W-W-WAIT! WHAT DID YOU JUST SAY?

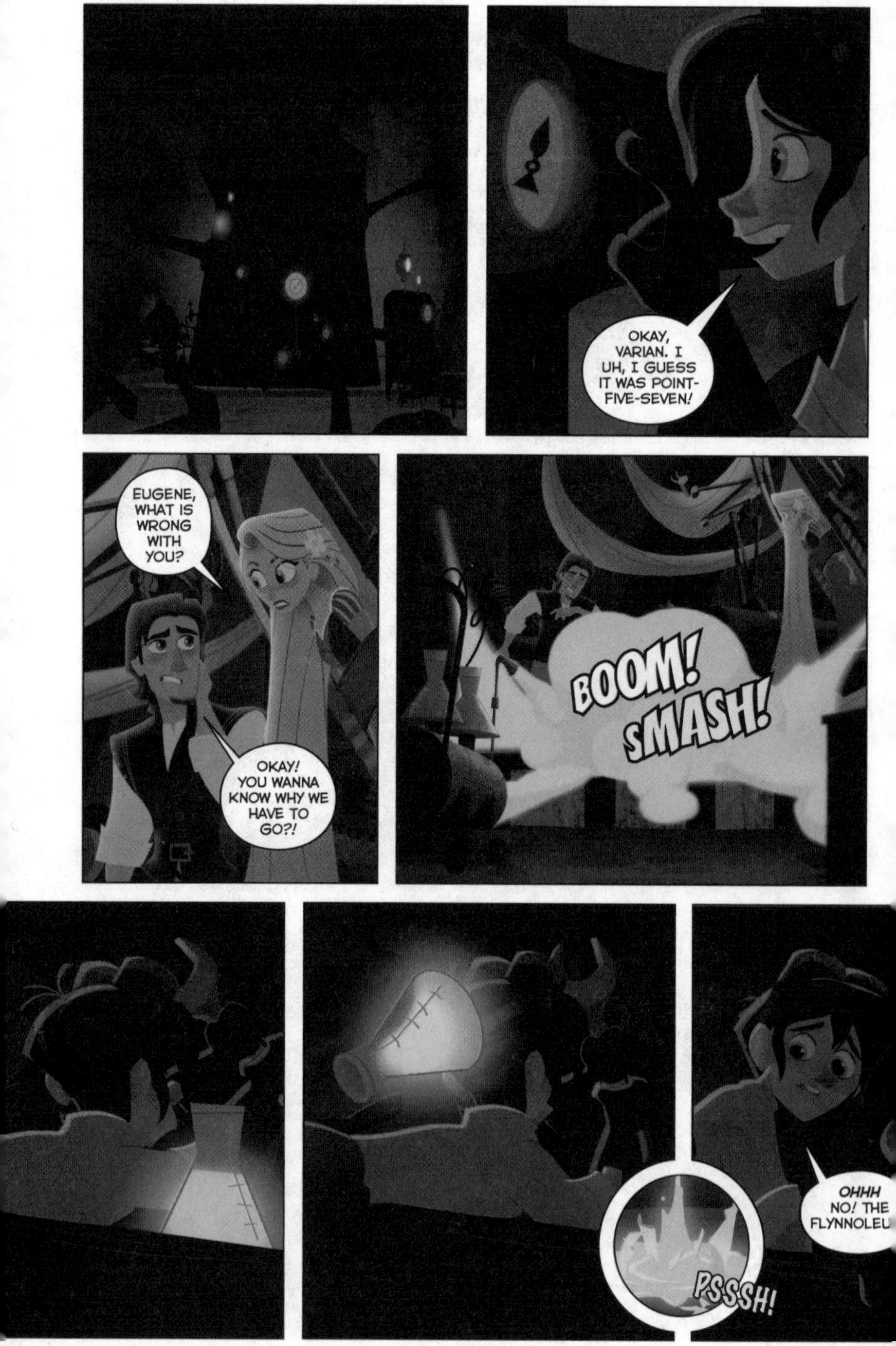
OKAY, VARIAN. I UH, I GUESS IT WAS POINT-FIVE-SEVEN!
EUGENE, WHAT IS WRONG WITH YOU?
OKAY! YOU WANNA KNOW WHY WE HAVE TO GO?!
BOOM! SMASH!
OHHH NO! THE FLYNNOLEU
PS-S-SH!

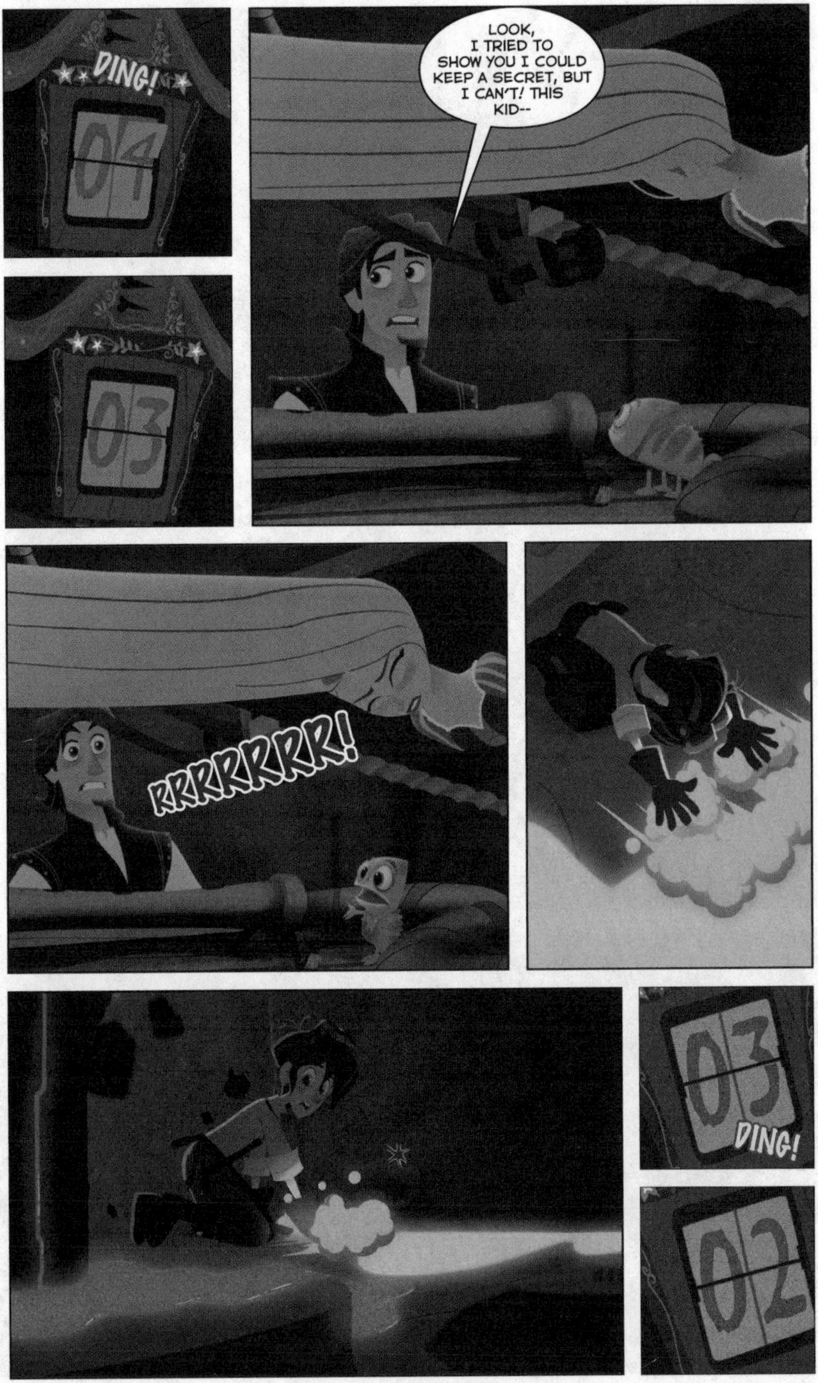
DING!
LOOK, I TRIED TO SHOW YOU I COULD KEEP A SECRET, BUT I CAN'T! THIS KID--
RRRRRRR!
DING!

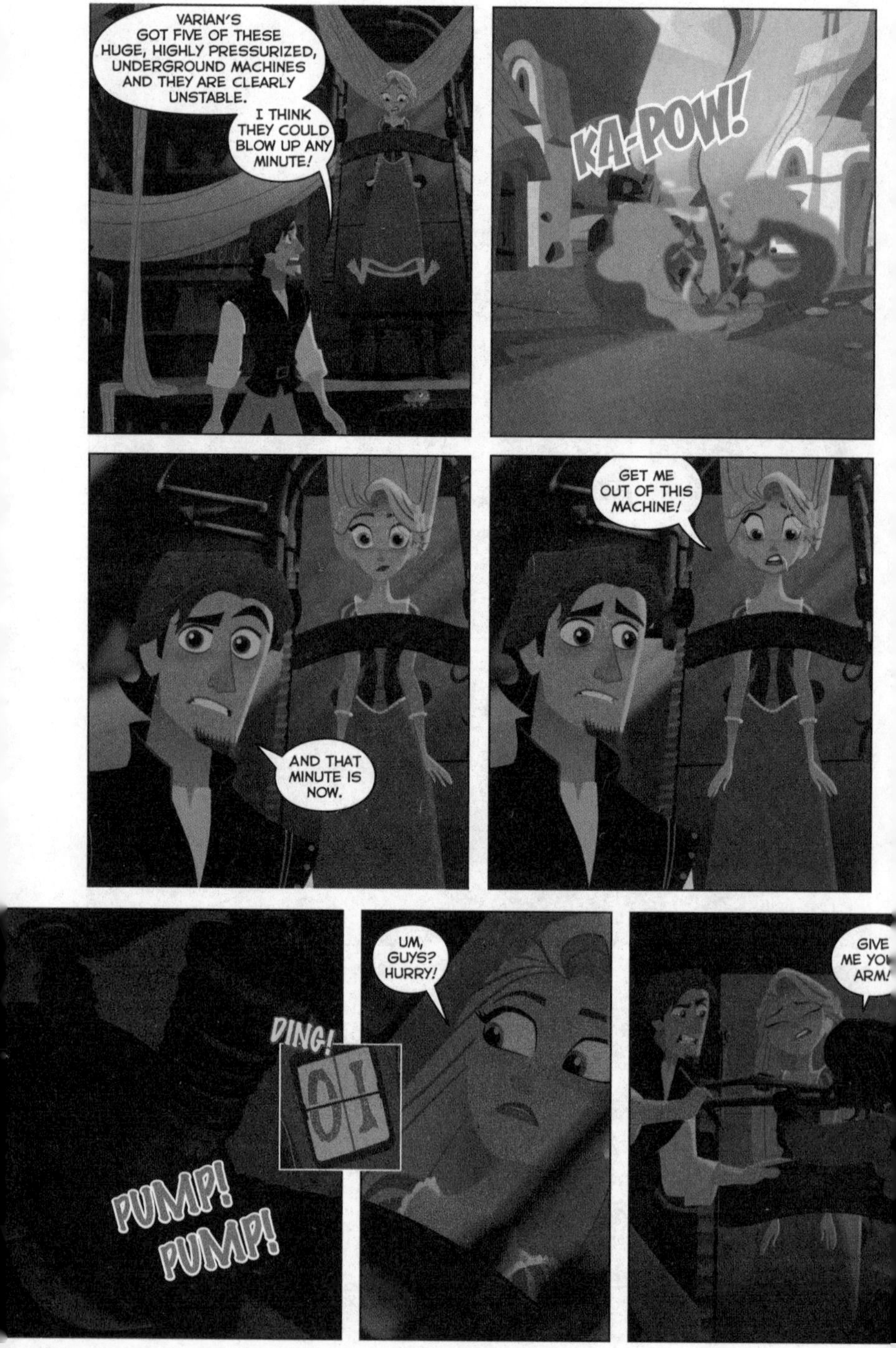
VARIAN'S GOT FIVE OF THESE HUGE, HIGHLY PRESSURIZED, UNDERGROUND MACHINES AND THEY ARE CLEARLY UNSTABLE.
I THINK THEY COULD BLOW UP ANY MINUTE!
KA-POW!
AND THAT MINUTE IS NOW.
GET ME OUT OF THIS MACHINE!
DING!
01
PUMP! PUMP!
UM, GUYS? HURRY!
GIVE ME YO
ARM!

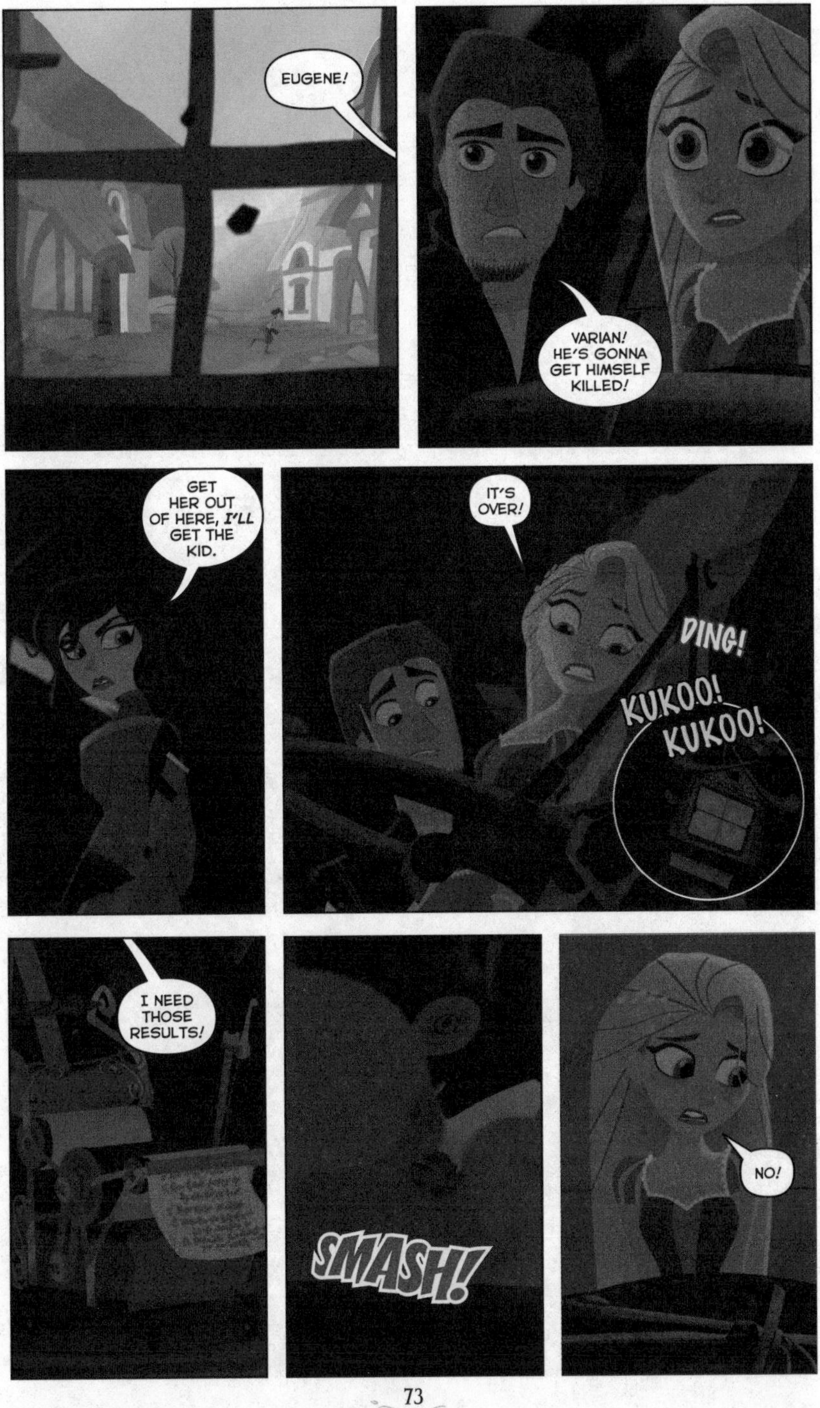
EUGENE!
VARIAN! HE'S GONNA GET HIMSELF KILLED!
GET HER OUT OF HERE, *I'LL* GET THE KID.
IT'S OVER!
DING!
KUKOO! KUKOO!
I NEED THOSE RESULTS!
SMASH!
NO!

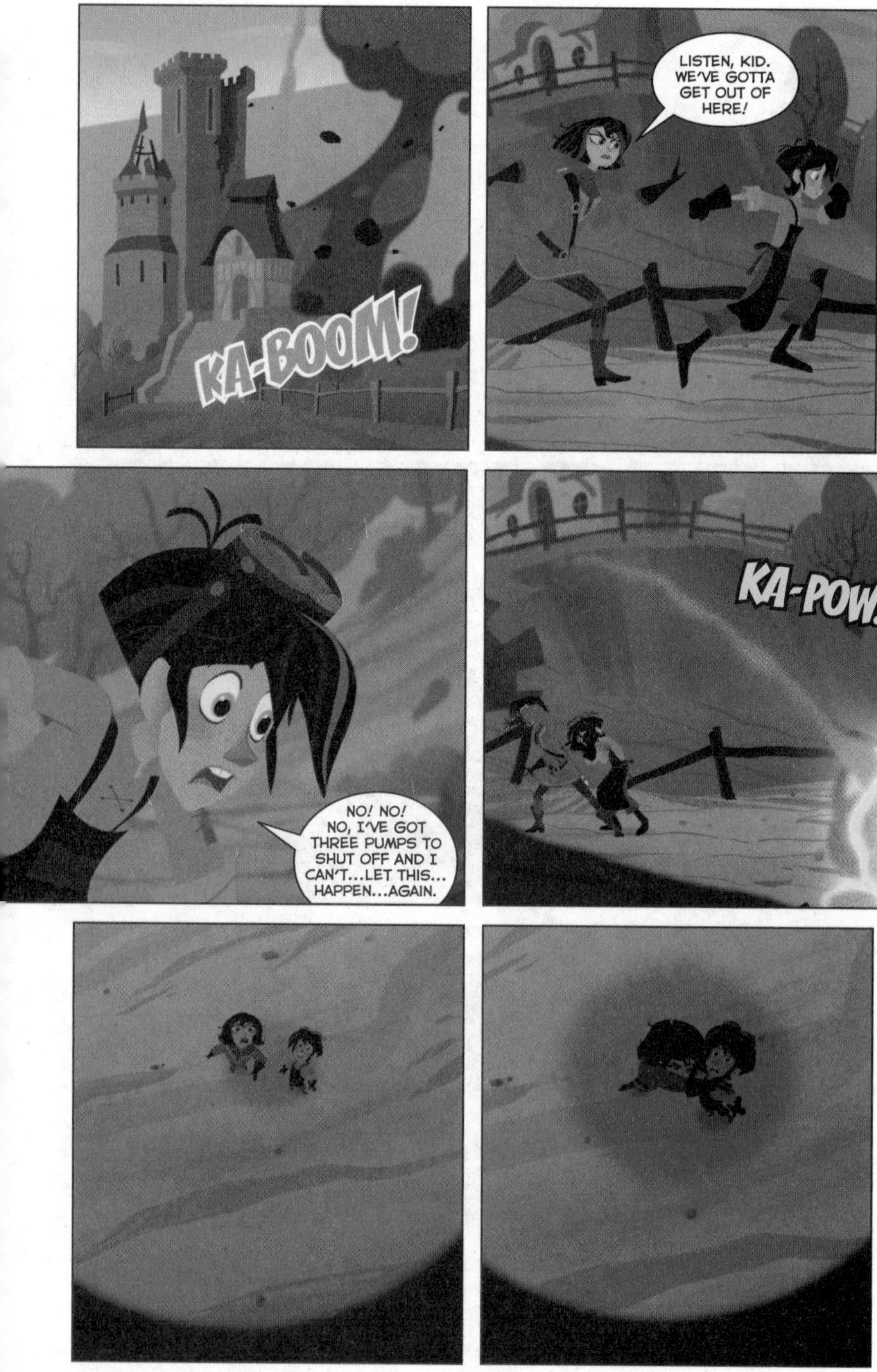
KA-BOOM!
LISTEN, KID. WE'VE GOTTA GET OUT OF HERE!
NO! NO! NO, I'VE GOT THREE PUMPS TO SHUT OFF AND I CAN'T...LET THIS... HAPPEN...AGAIN.
KA-POW!

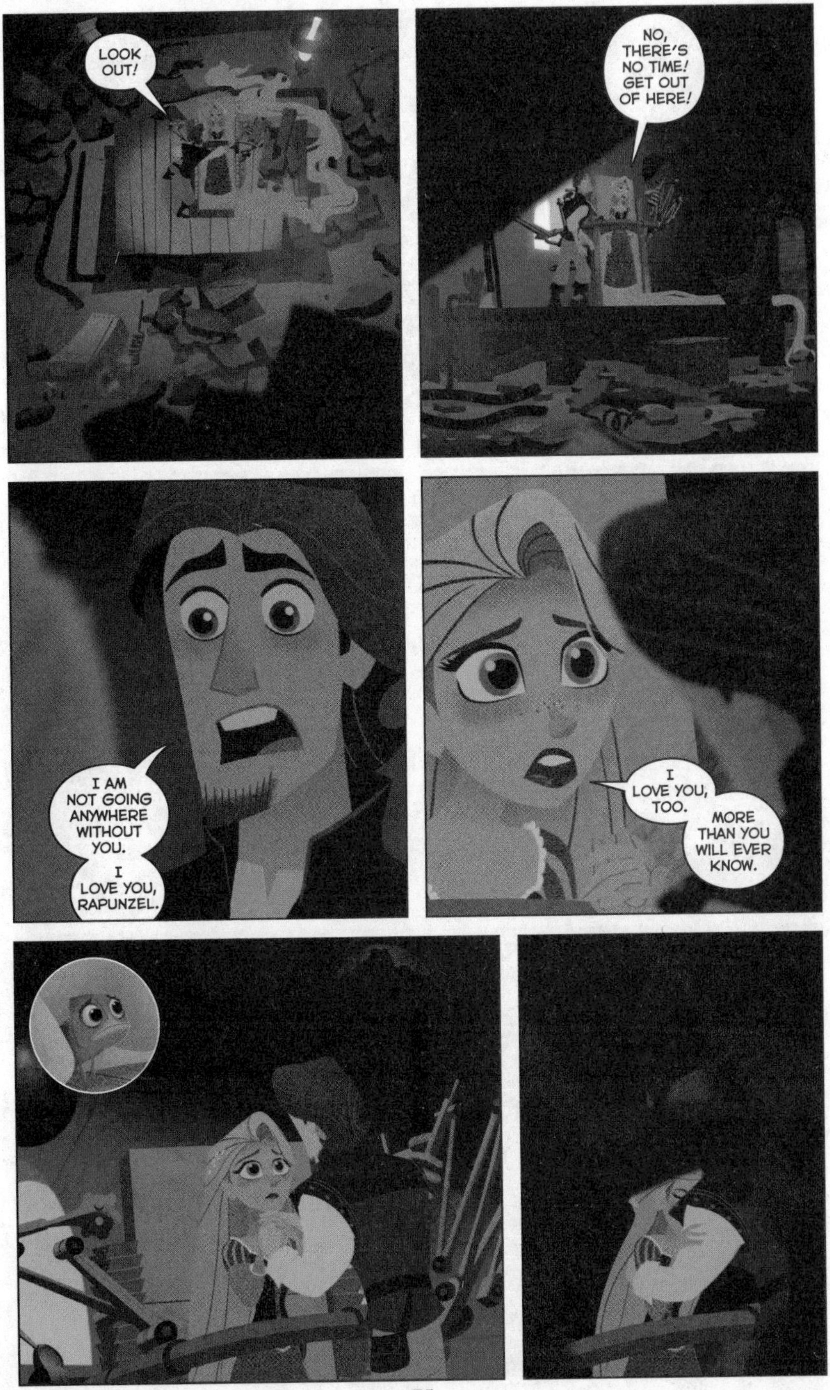
LOOK OUT!
NO, THERE'S NO TIME! GET OUT OF HERE!
I AM NOT GOING ANYWHERE WITHOUT YOU.
I LOVE YOU, RAPUNZEL.
I LOVE YOU, TOO.
MORE THAN YOU WILL EVER KNOW.

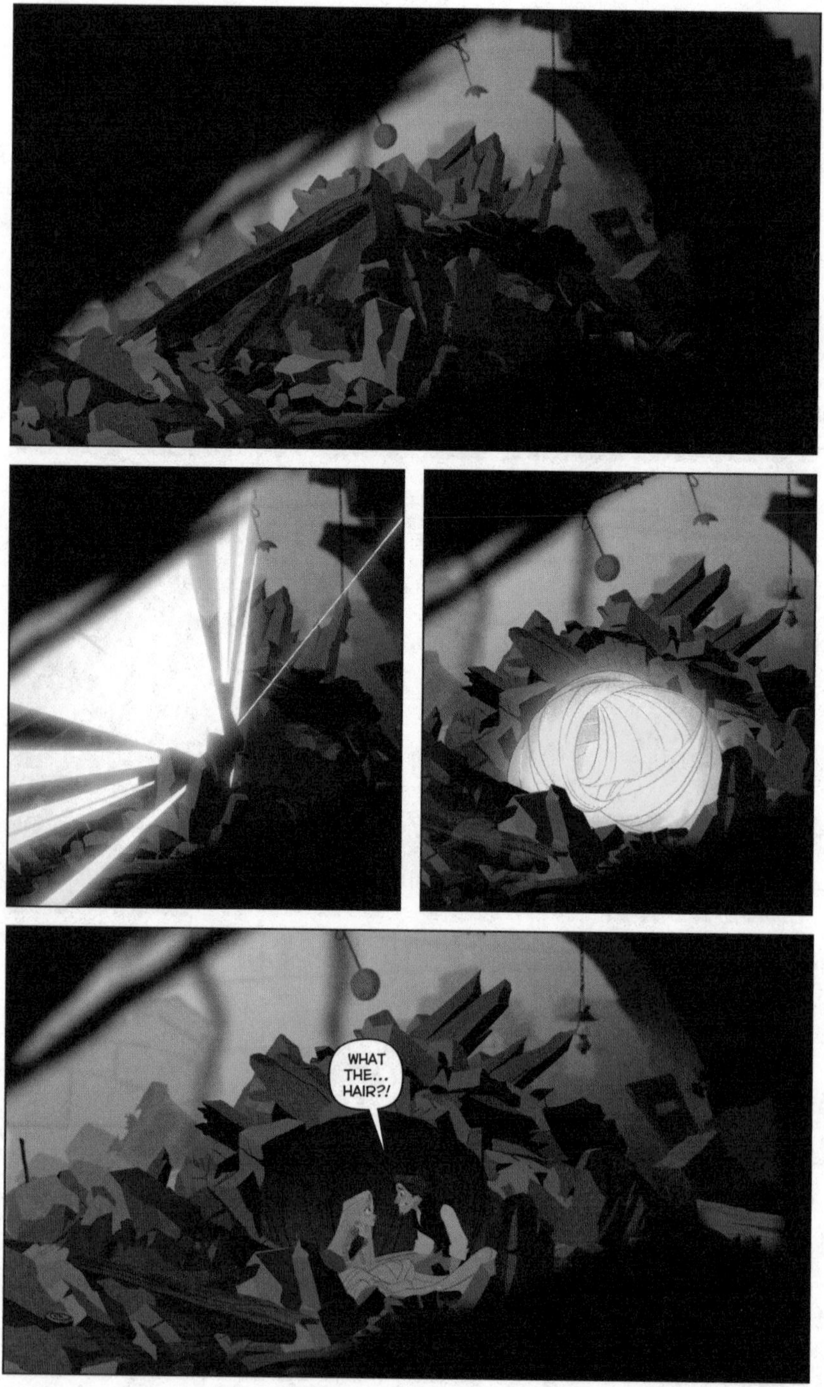
WHAT THE... HAIR?!

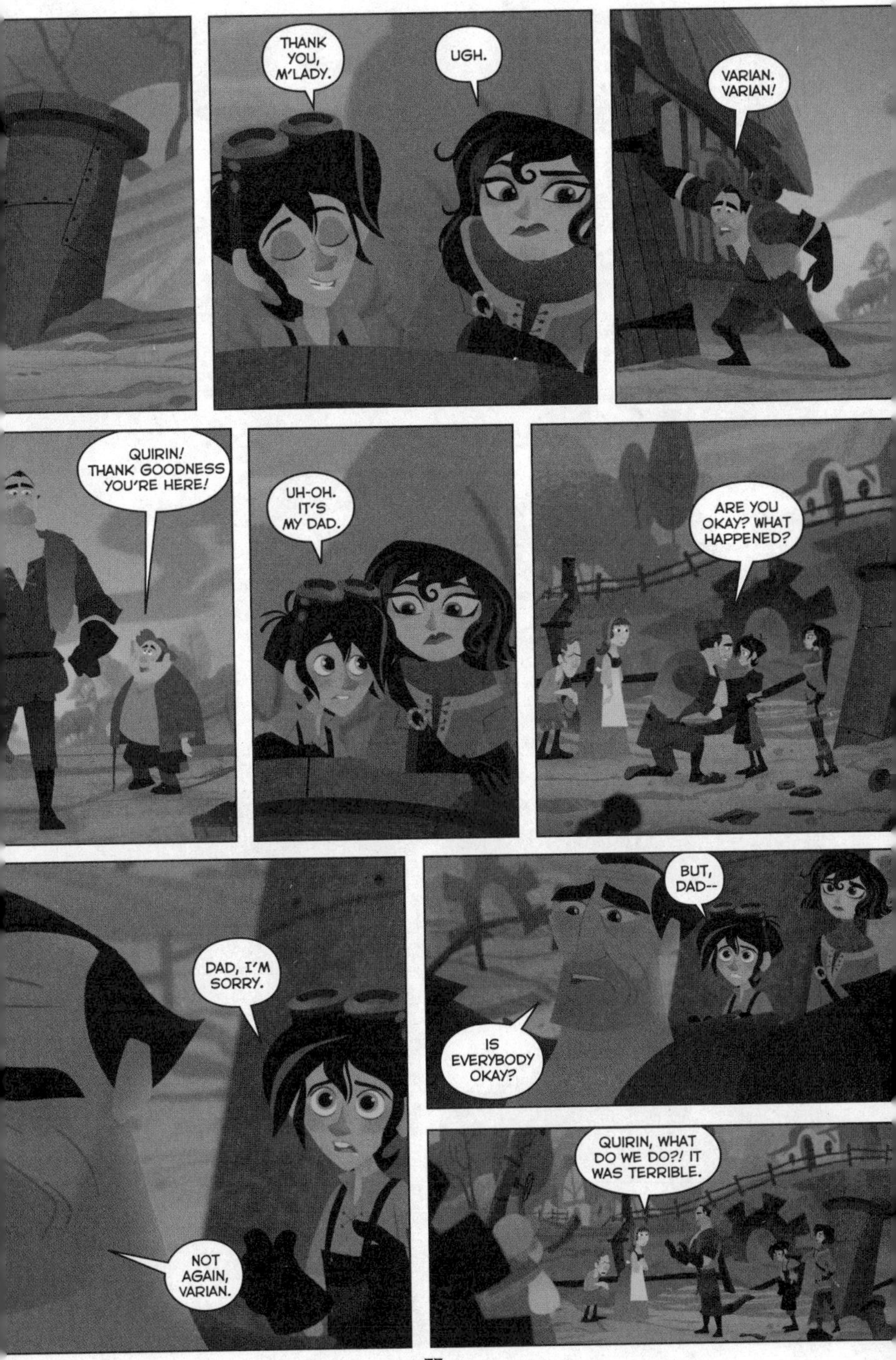
THANK YOU, M'LADY.
UGH.
VARIAN. VARIAN!
QUIRIN! THANK GOODNESS YOU'RE HERE!
UH-OH. IT'S MY DAD.
ARE YOU OKAY? WHAT HAPPENED?
DAD, I'M SORRY.
NOT AGAIN, VARIAN.
BUT, DAD--
IS EVERYBODY OKAY?
QUIRIN, WHAT DO WE DO?! IT WAS TERRIBLE.

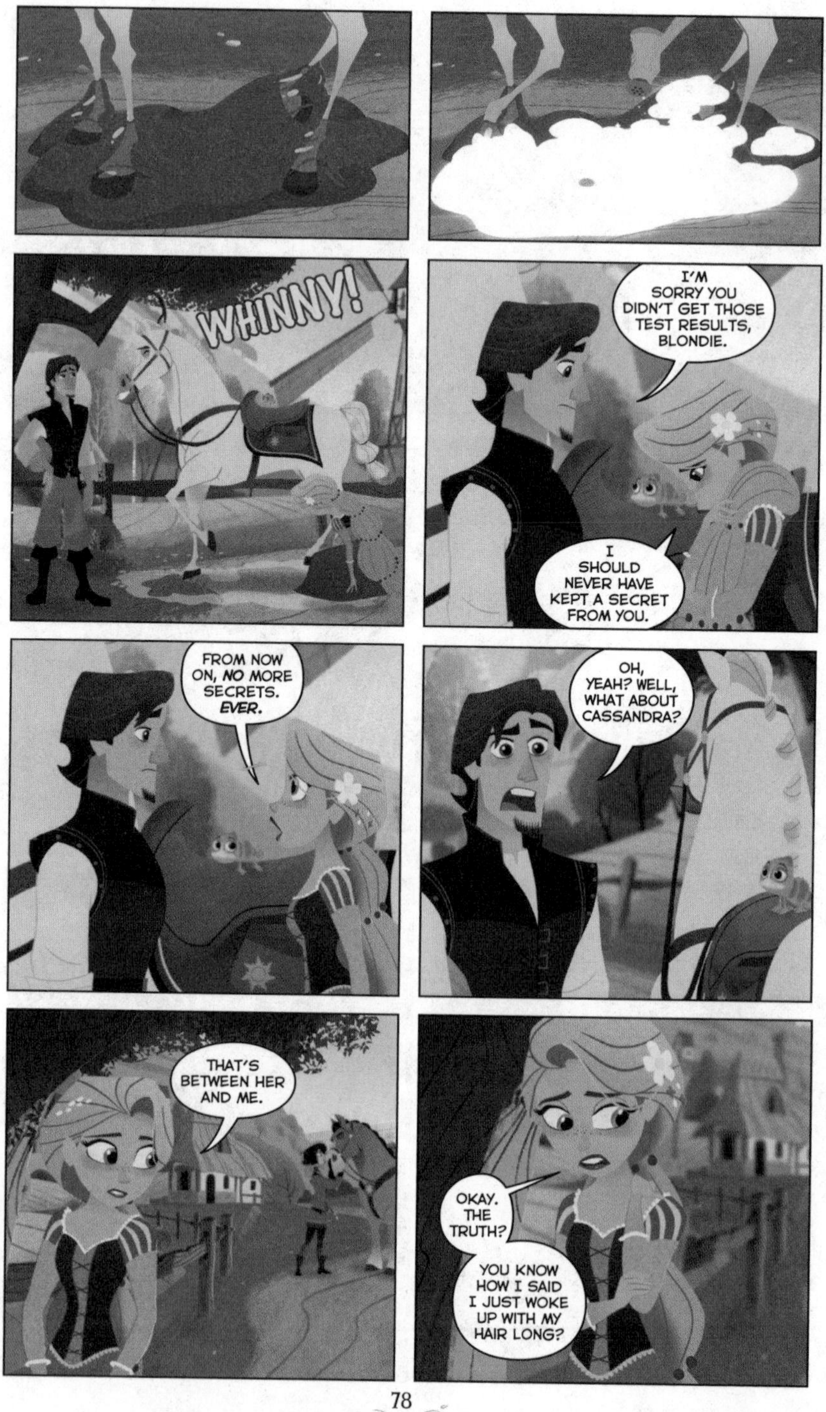
WHINNY!
I'M SORRY YOU DIDN'T GET THOSE TEST RESULTS, BLONDIE.
I SHOULD NEVER HAVE KEPT A SECRET FROM YOU.
FROM NOW ON, *NO* MORE SECRETS. ***EVER.***
OH, YEAH? WELL, WHAT ABOUT CASSANDRA?
THAT'S BETWEEN HER AND ME.
OKAY. THE TRUTH?
YOU KNOW HOW I SAID I JUST WOKE UP WITH MY HAIR LONG?

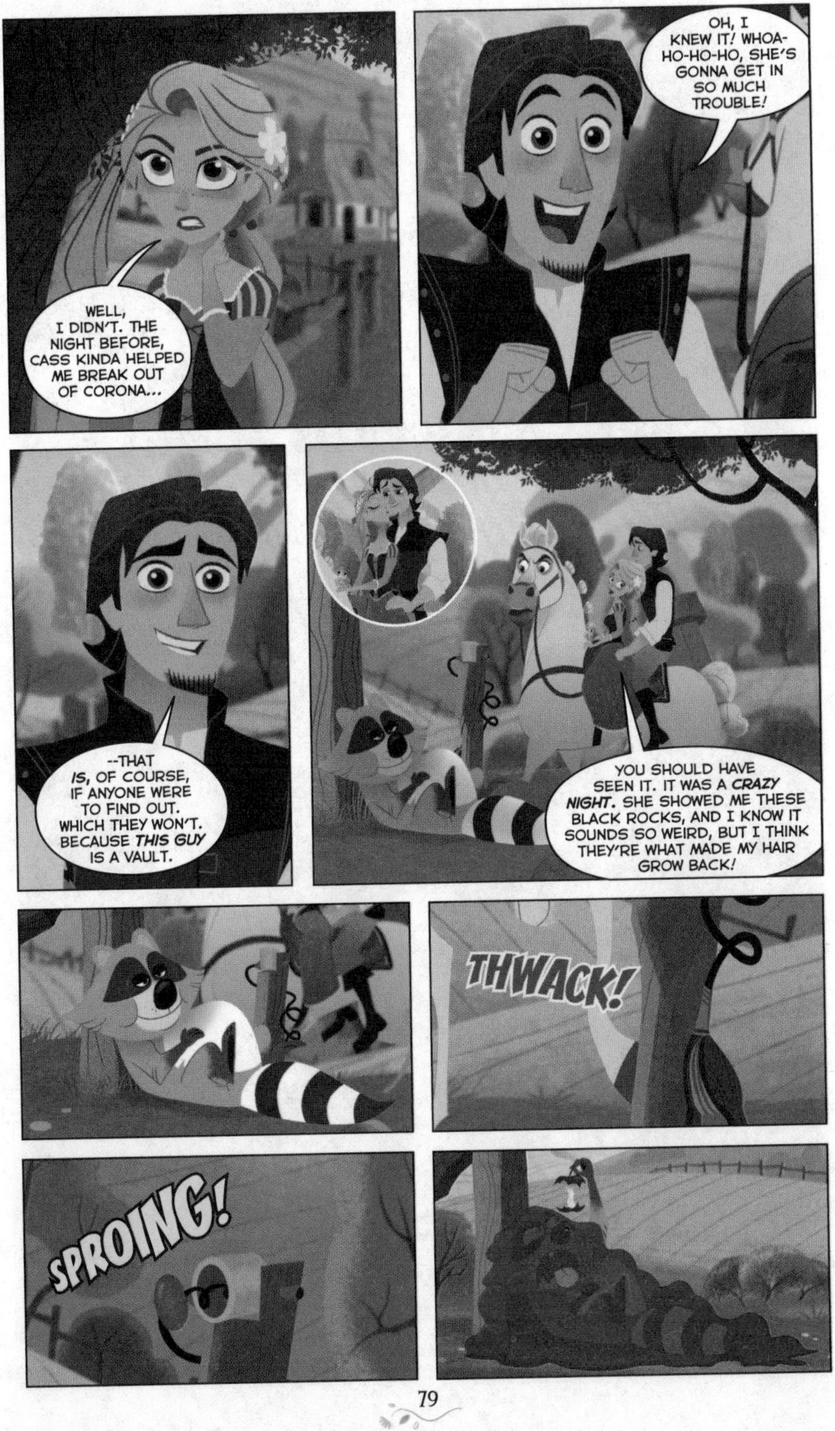
WELL, I DIDN'T. THE NIGHT BEFORE, CASS KINDA HELPED ME BREAK OUT OF CORONA...
OH, I KNEW IT! WHOA-HO-HO-HO, SHE'S GONNA GET IN SO MUCH TROUBLE!
--THAT *IS*, OF COURSE, IF ANYONE WERE TO FIND OUT. WHICH THEY WON'T. BECAUSE *THIS GUY* IS A VAULT.
YOU SHOULD HAVE SEEN IT. IT WAS A *CRAZY NIGHT*. SHE SHOWED ME THESE BLACK ROCKS, AND I KNOW IT SOUNDS SO WEIRD, BUT I THINK THEY'RE WHAT MADE MY HAIR GROW BACK!
THWACK!
SPROING!

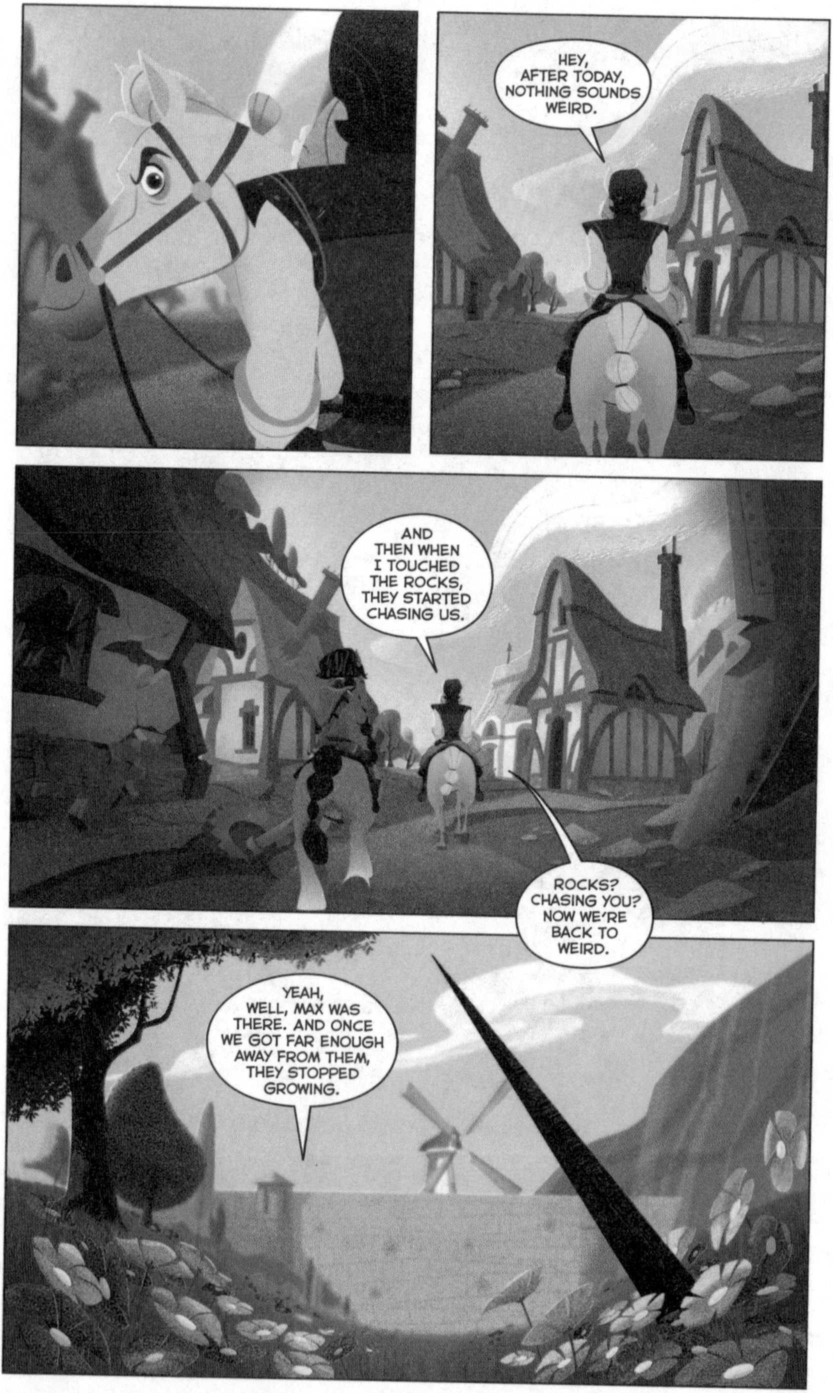
HEY, AFTER TODAY, NOTHING SOUNDS WEIRD.
AND THEN WHEN I TOUCHED THE ROCKS, THEY STARTED CHASING US.
ROCKS? CHASING YOU? NOW WE'RE BACK TO WEIRD.
YEAH, WELL, MAX WAS THERE. AND ONCE WE GOT FAR ENOUGH AWAY FROM THEM, THEY STOPPED GROWING.

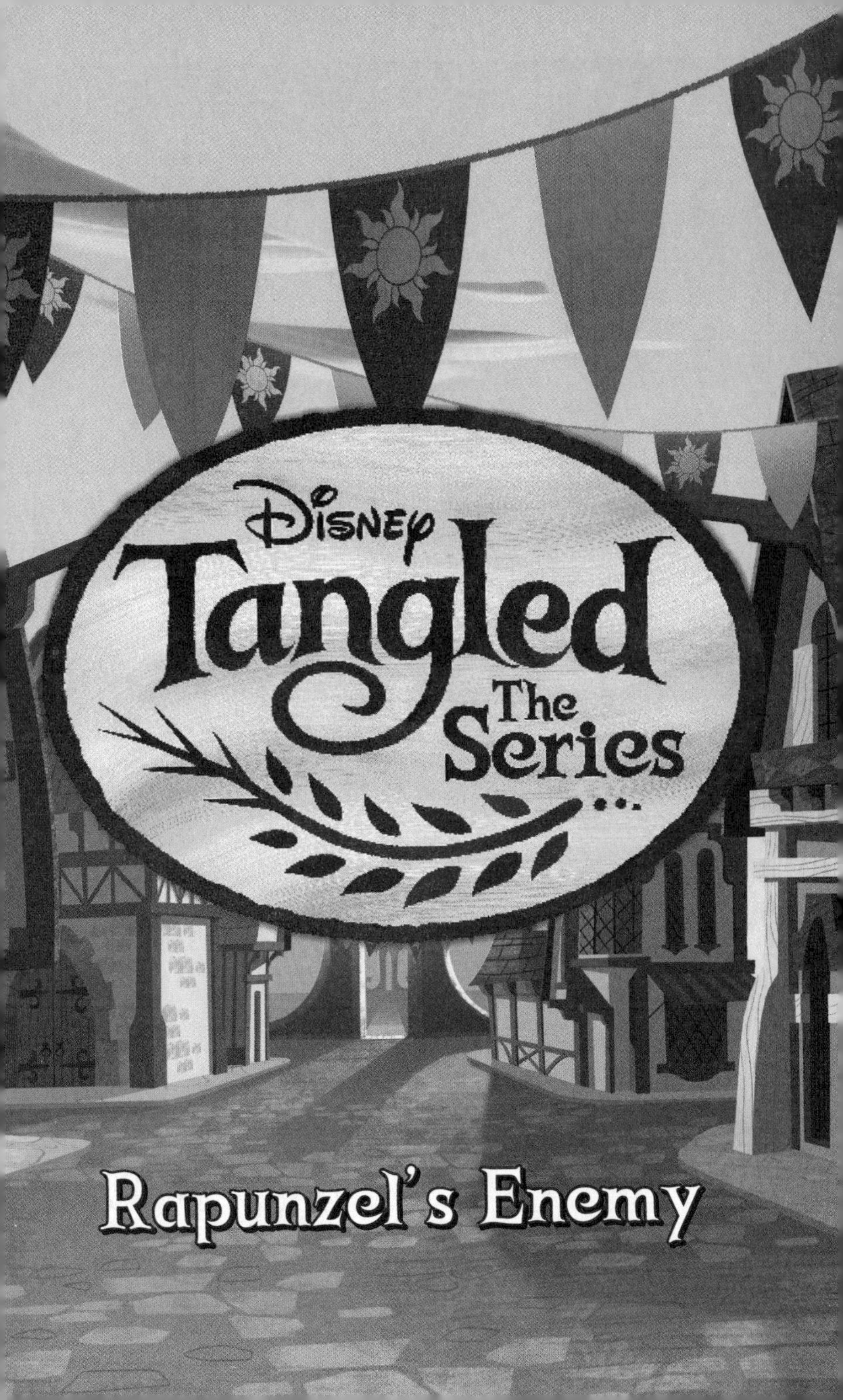
Disney
Tangled
The Series
Rapunzel's Enemy

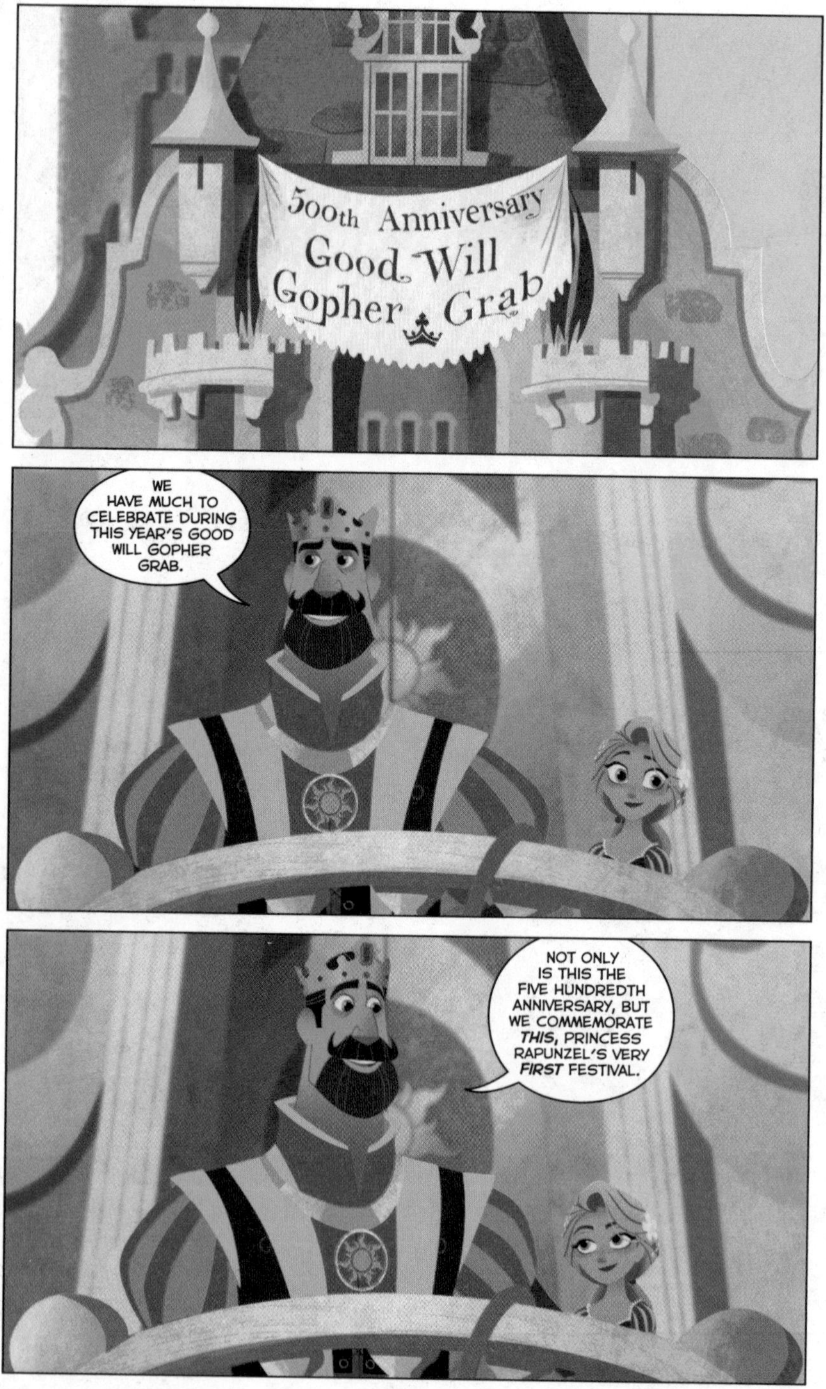
500th Anniversary
Good Will
Gopher Grab
WE HAVE MUCH TO CELEBRATE DURING THIS YEAR'S GOOD WILL GOPHER GRAB.
NOT ONLY IS THIS THE FIVE HUNDREDTH ANNIVERSARY, BUT WE COMMEMORATE *THIS*, PRINCESS RAPUNZEL'S VERY *FIRST* FESTIVAL.

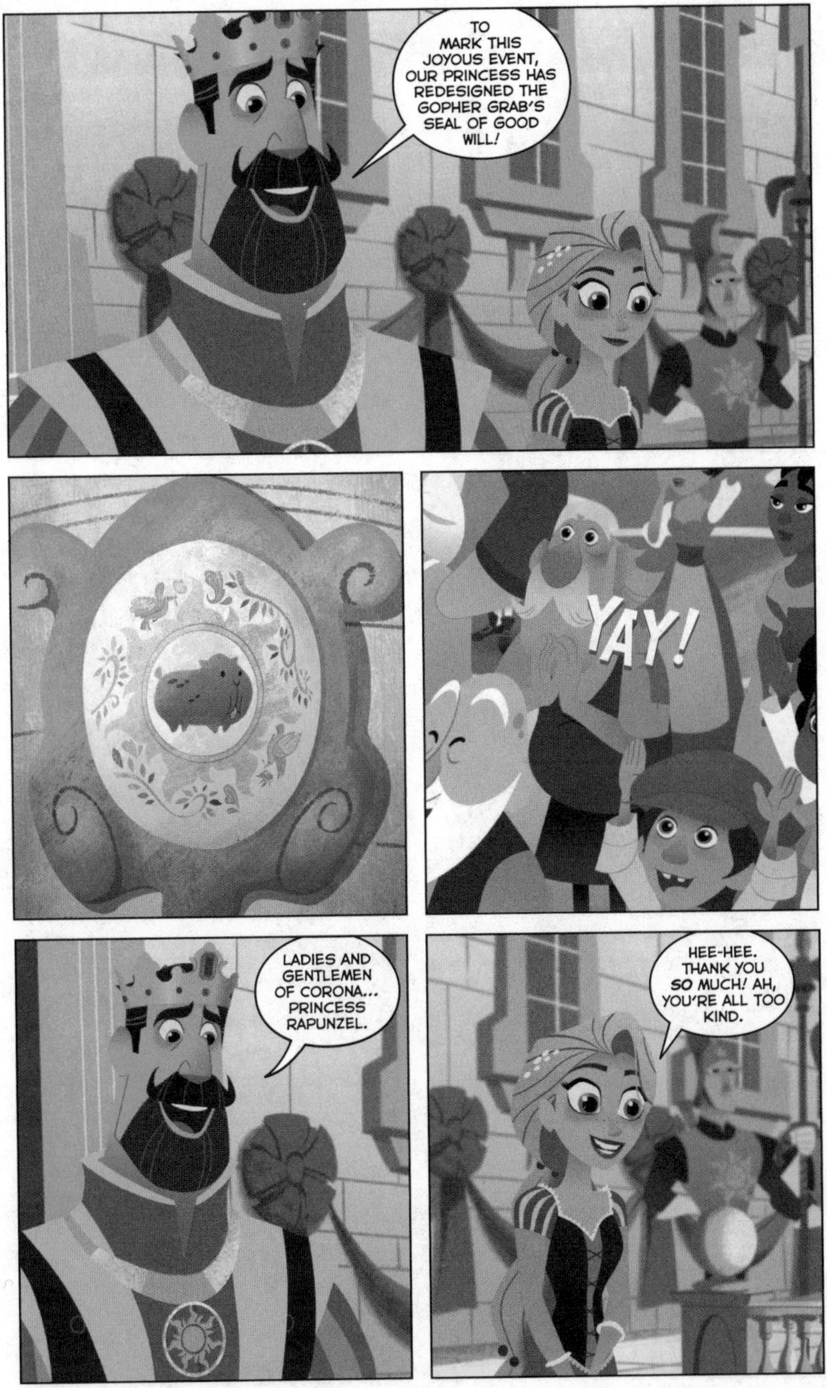
TO MARK THIS JOYOUS EVENT, OUR PRINCESS HAS REDESIGNED THE GOPHER GRAB'S SEAL OF GOOD WILL!
YAY!
LADIES AND GENTLEMEN OF CORONA... PRINCESS RAPUNZEL.
HEE-HEE. THANK YOU SO MUCH! AH, YOU'RE ALL TOO KIND.

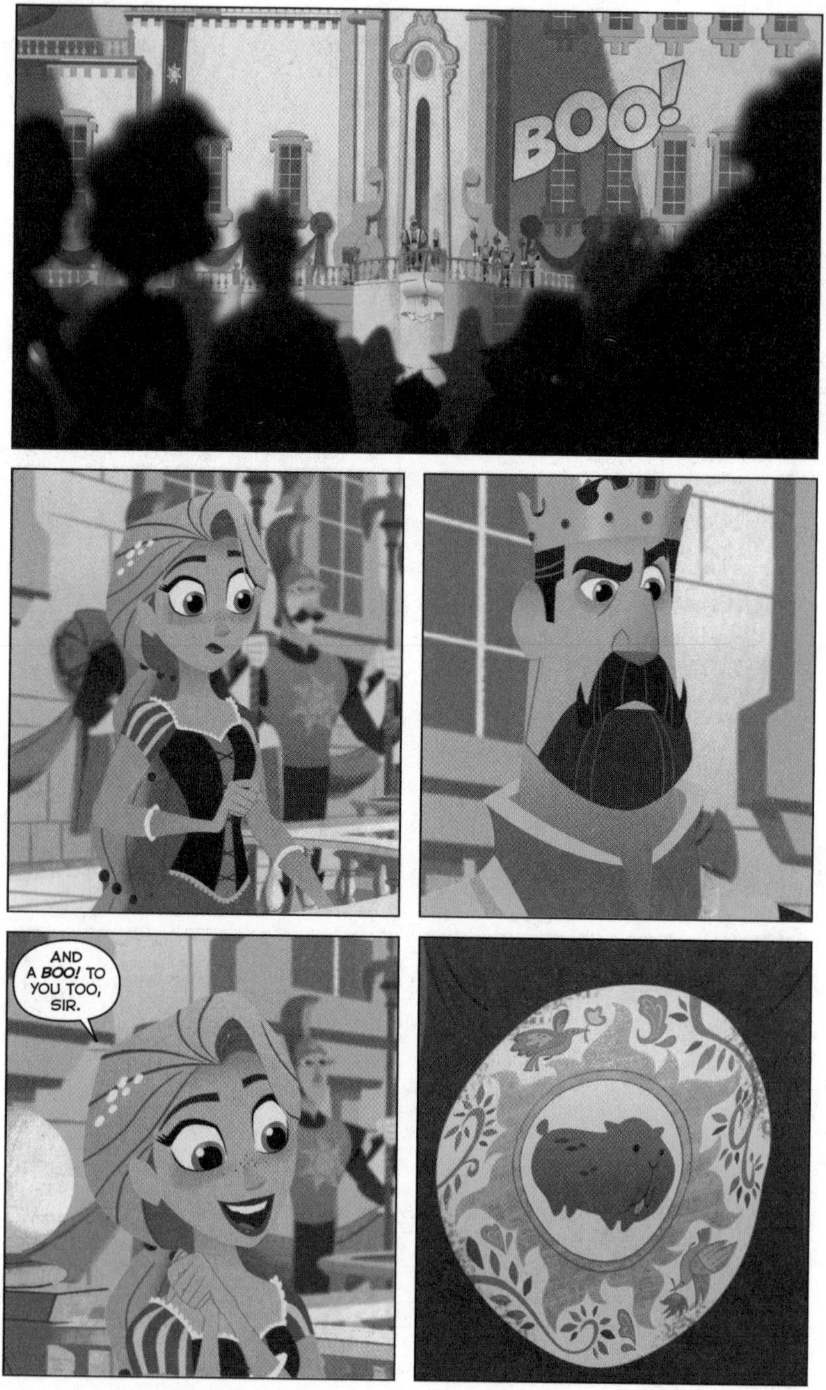
BOO!
AND A *BOO!* TO YOU TOO, SIR.

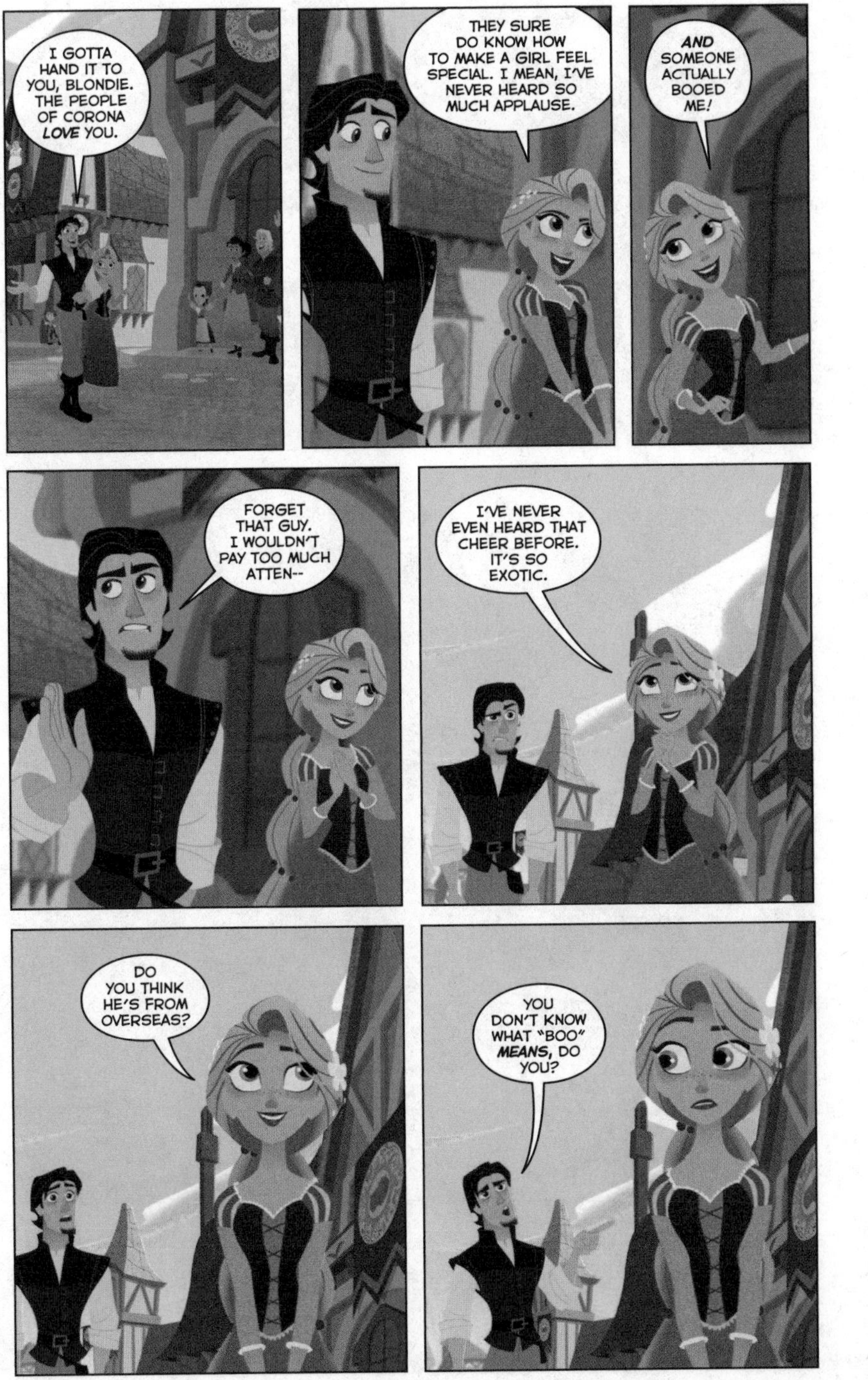
I GOTTA HAND IT TO YOU, BLONDIE. THE PEOPLE OF CORONA *LOVE* YOU.
THEY SURE DO KNOW HOW TO MAKE A GIRL FEEL SPECIAL. I MEAN, I'VE NEVER HEARD SO MUCH APPLAUSE.
AND SOMEONE ACTUALLY BOOED ME*!*
FORGET THAT GUY. I WOULDN'T PAY TOO MUCH ATTEN--
I'VE NEVER EVEN HEARD THAT CHEER BEFORE. IT'S SO EXOTIC.
DO YOU THINK HE'S FROM OVERSEAS?
YOU DON'T KNOW WHAT "BOO" *MEANS,* DO YOU?

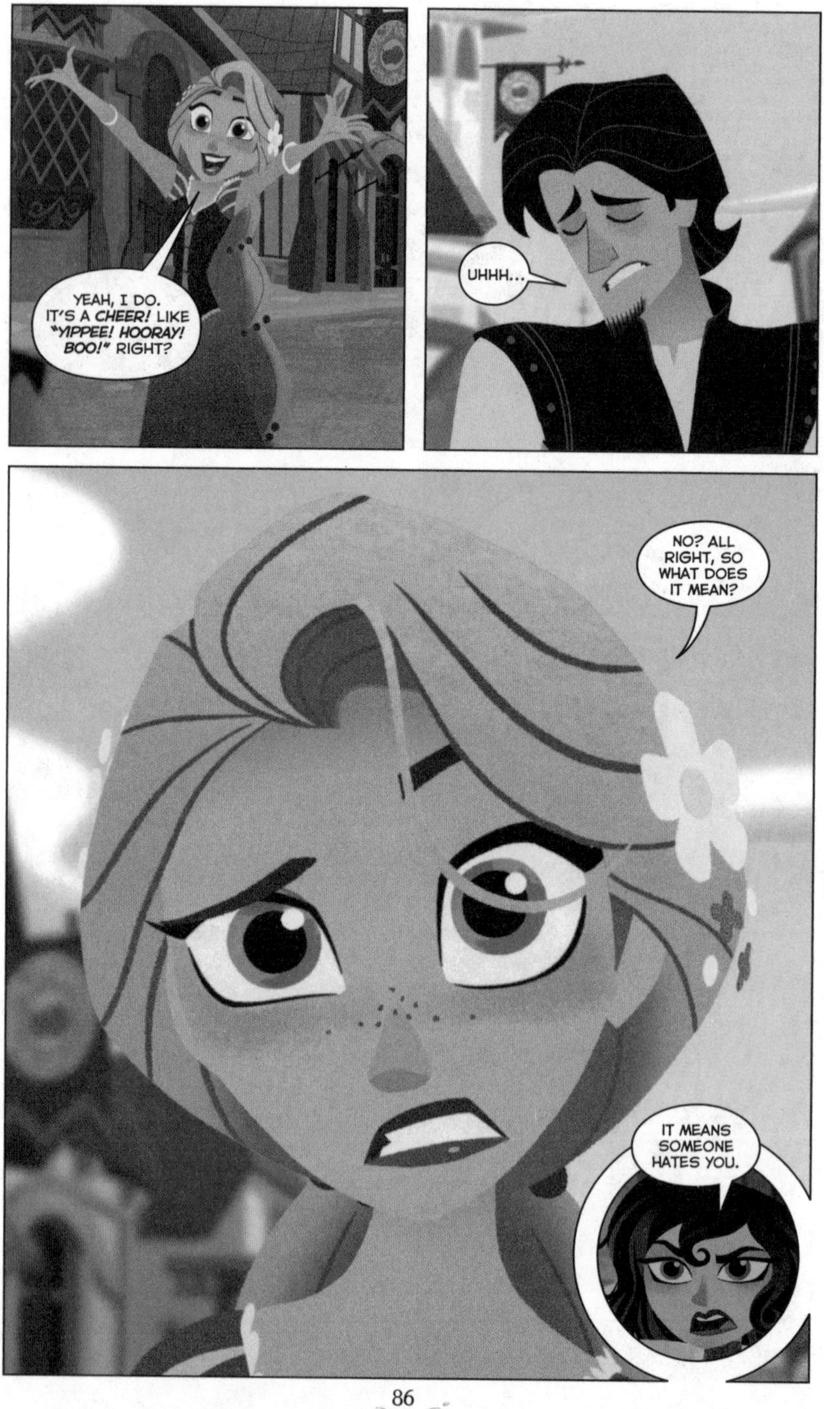
YEAH, I DO. IT'S A *CHEER!* LIKE *"YIPPEE! HOORAY! BOO!"* RIGHT?
UHHH...
NO? ALL RIGHT, SO WHAT DOES IT MEAN?
IT MEANS SOMEONE HATES YOU.

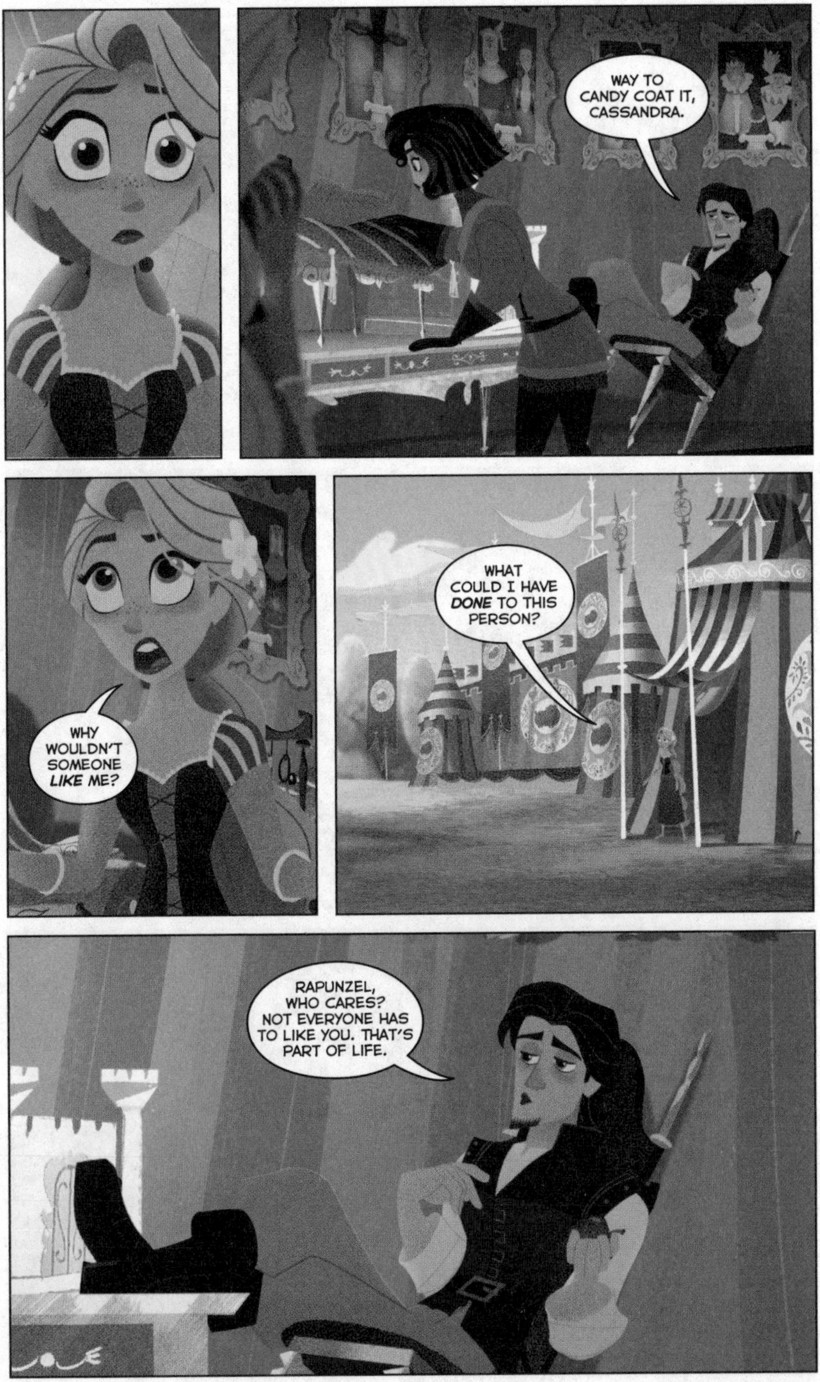
WAY TO CANDY COAT IT, CASSANDRA.
WHY WOULDN'T SOMEONE *LIKE* ME?
WHAT COULD I HAVE *DONE* TO THIS PERSON?
RAPUNZEL, WHO CARES? NOT EVERYONE HAS TO LIKE YOU. THAT'S PART OF LIFE.

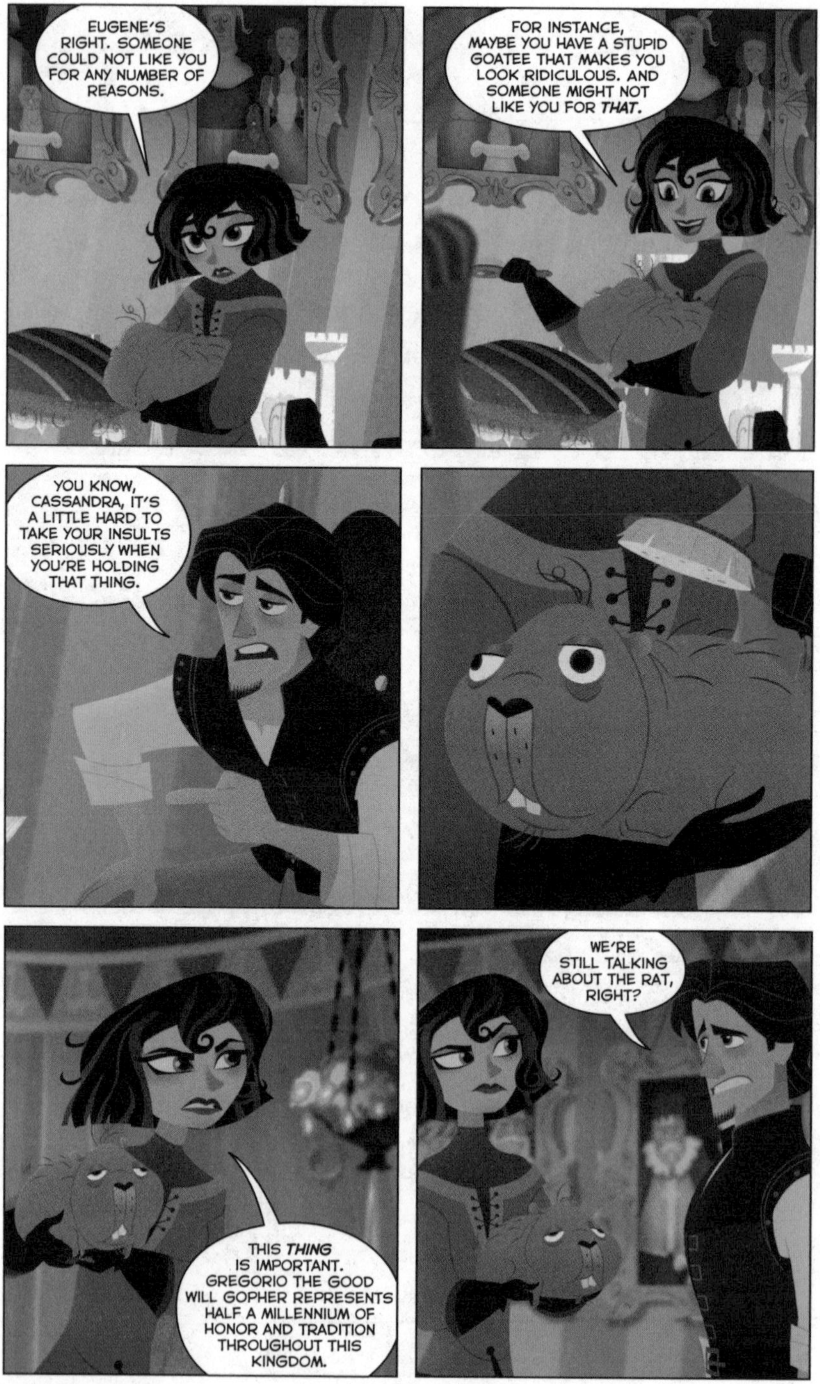
EUGENE'S RIGHT. SOMEONE COULD NOT LIKE YOU FOR ANY NUMBER OF REASONS.
FOR INSTANCE, MAYBE YOU HAVE A STUPID GOATEE THAT MAKES YOU LOOK RIDICULOUS. AND SOMEONE MIGHT NOT LIKE YOU FOR *THAT*.
YOU KNOW, CASSANDRA, IT'S A LITTLE HARD TO TAKE YOUR INSULTS SERIOUSLY WHEN YOU'RE HOLDING THAT THING.
THIS *THING* IS IMPORTANT. GREGORIO THE GOOD WILL GOPHER REPRESENTS HALF A MILLENNIUM OF HONOR AND TRADITION THROUGHOUT THIS KINGDOM.
WE'RE STILL TALKING ABOUT THE RAT, RIGHT?

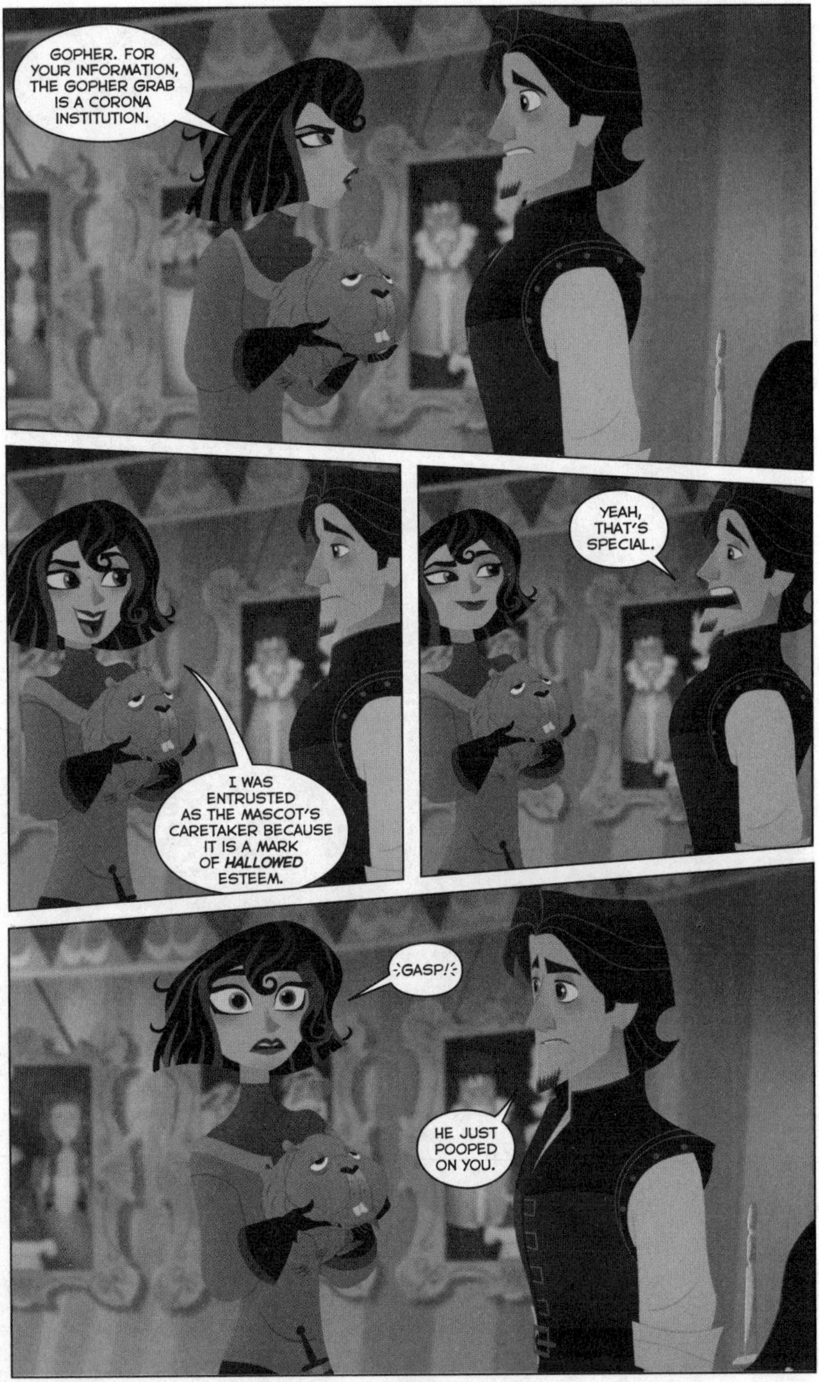
GOPHER. FOR YOUR INFORMATION, THE GOPHER GRAB IS A CORONA INSTITUTION.
I WAS ENTRUSTED AS THE MASCOT'S CARETAKER BECAUSE IT IS A MARK OF HALLOWED ESTEEM.
YEAH, THAT'S SPECIAL.
GASP!
HE JUST POOPED ON YOU.

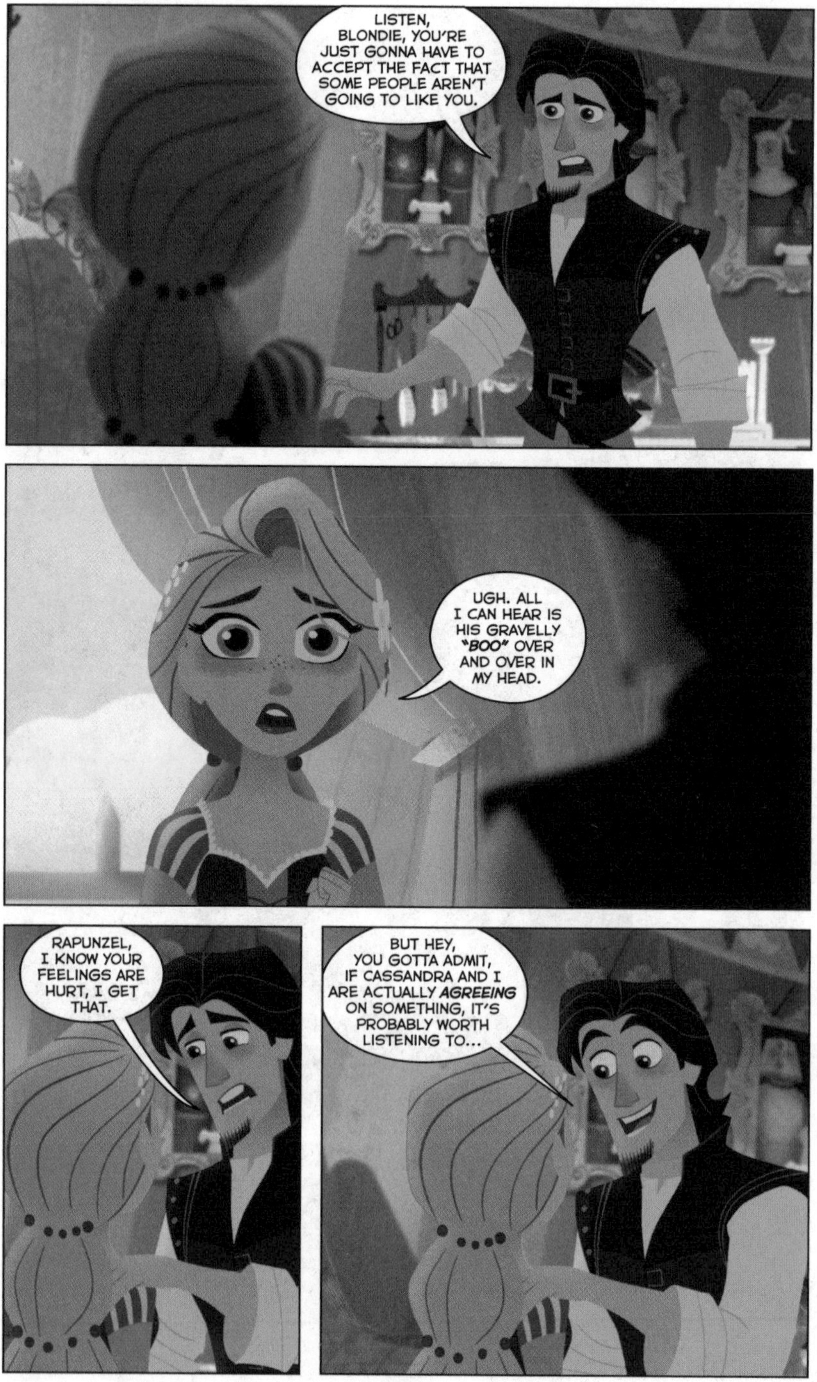
LISTEN, BLONDIE, YOU'RE JUST GONNA HAVE TO ACCEPT THE FACT THAT SOME PEOPLE AREN'T GOING TO LIKE YOU.
UGH. ALL I CAN HEAR IS HIS GRAVELLY *"BOO"* OVER AND OVER IN MY HEAD.
RAPUNZEL, I KNOW YOUR FEELINGS ARE HURT, I GET THAT.
BUT HEY, YOU GOTTA ADMIT, IF CASSANDRA AND I ARE ACTUALLY *AGREEING* ON SOMETHING, IT'S PROBABLY WORTH LISTENING TO...

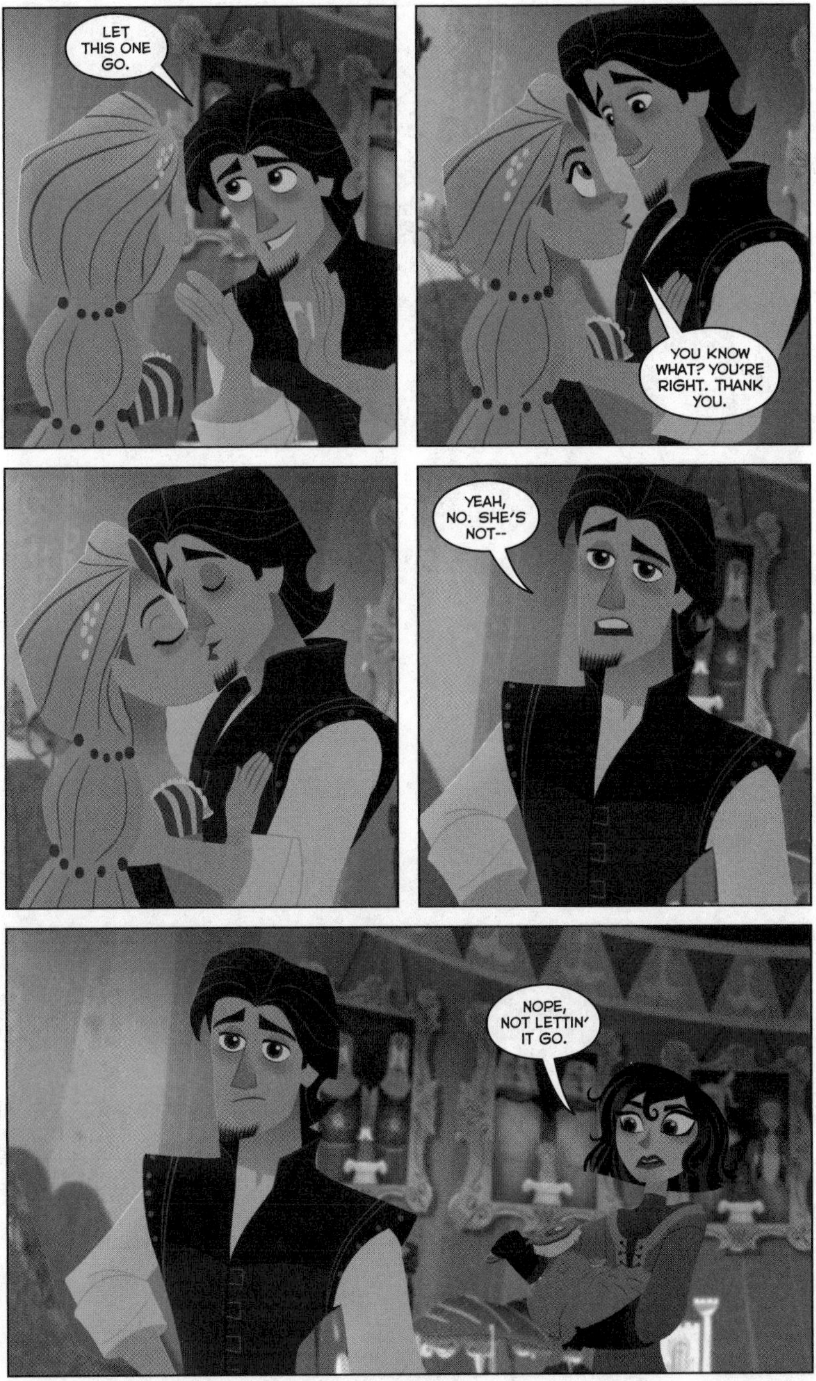
LET THIS ONE GO.
YOU KNOW WHAT? YOU'RE RIGHT. THANK YOU.
YEAH, NO. SHE'S NOT--
NOPE, NOT LETTIN' IT GO.

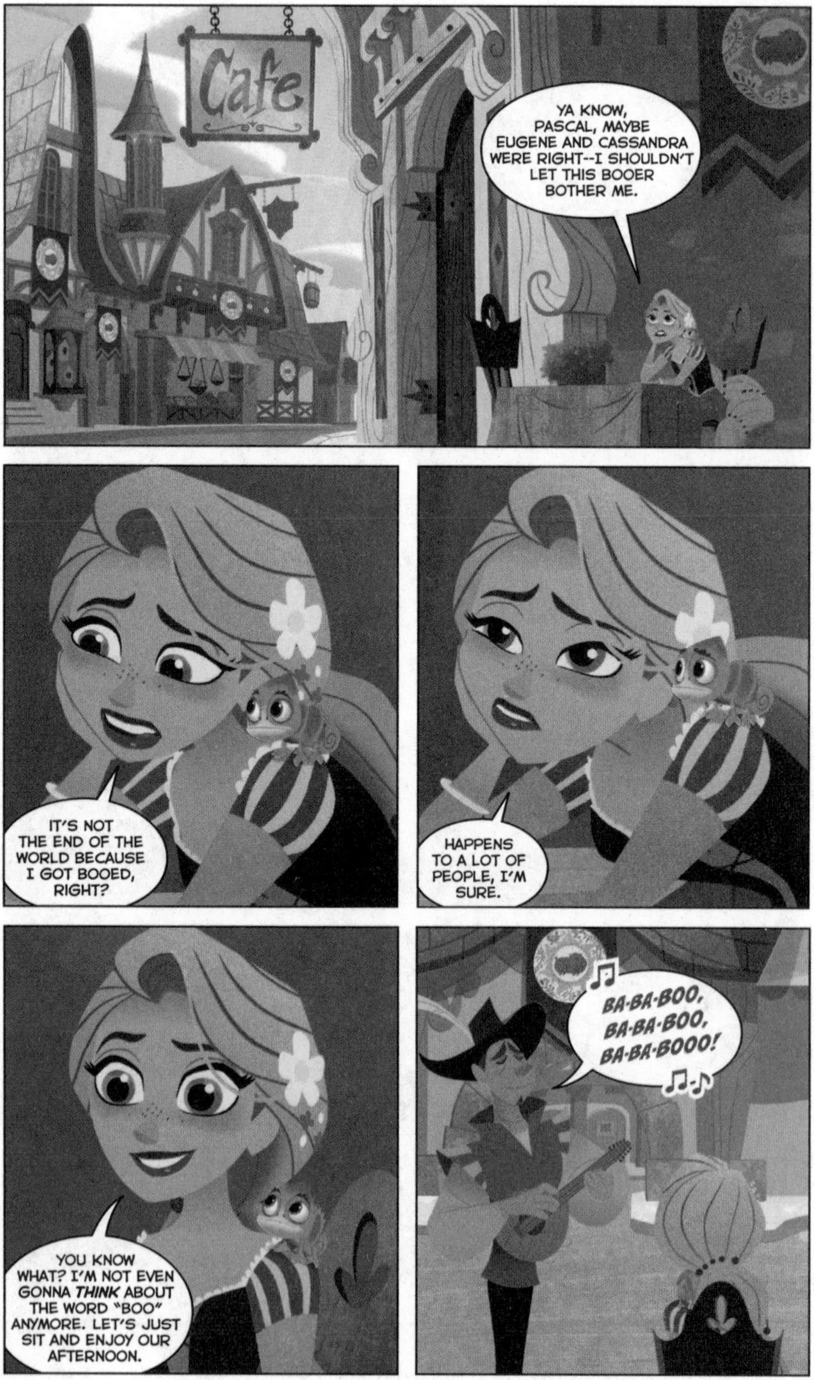
Cafe
YA KNOW, PASCAL, MAYBE EUGENE AND CASSANDRA WERE RIGHT--I SHOULDN'T LET THIS BOOER BOTHER ME.
IT'S NOT THE END OF THE WORLD BECAUSE I GOT BOOED, RIGHT?
HAPPENS TO A LOT OF PEOPLE, I'M SURE.
YOU KNOW WHAT? I'M NOT EVEN GONNA *THINK* ABOUT THE WORD "BOO" ANYMORE. LET'S JUST SIT AND ENJOY OUR AFTERNOON.
BA-BA-BOO, BA-BA-BOO, BA-BA-BOOO!

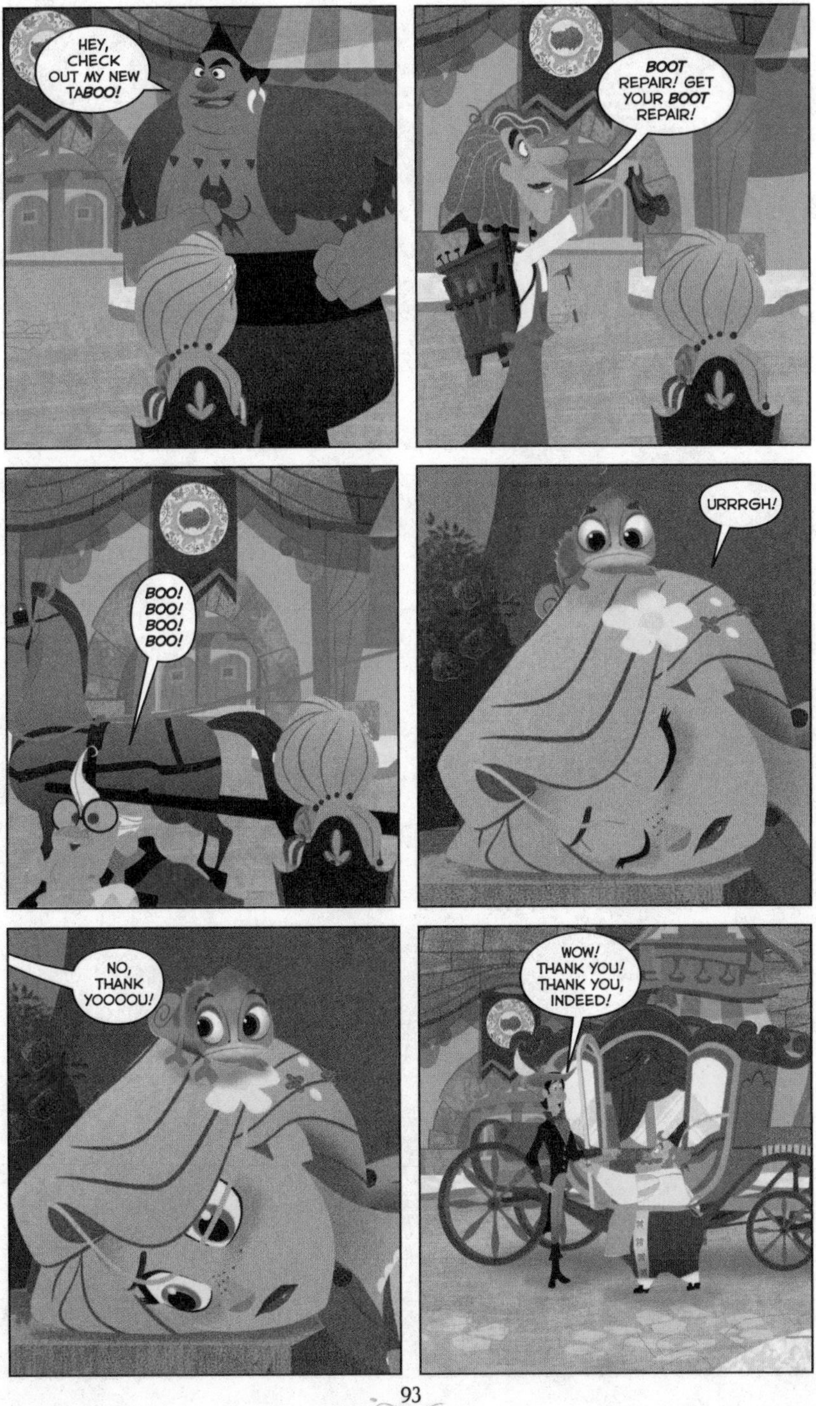
HEY, CHECK OUT MY NEW TABOO!
BOOT REPAIR! GET YOUR BOOT REPAIR!
BOO! BOO! BOO! BOO!
URRRGH!
NO, THANK YOOOOU!
WOW! THANK YOU! THANK YOU, INDEED!

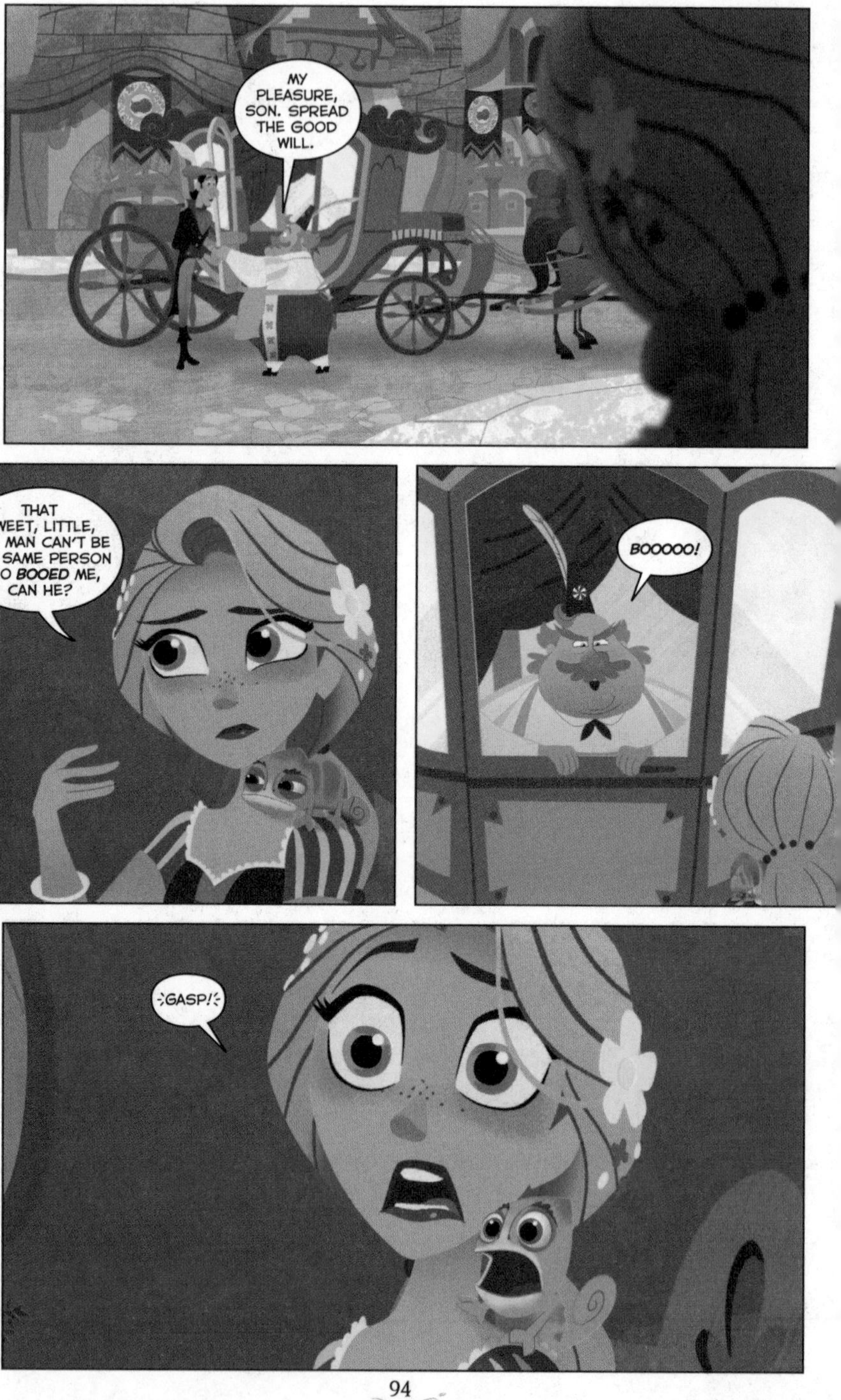
MY PLEASURE, SON. SPREAD THE GOOD WILL.
THAT SWEET, LITTLE, OLD MAN CAN'T BE THE SAME PERSON WHO *BOOED* ME, CAN HE?
BOOOOO!
GASP!

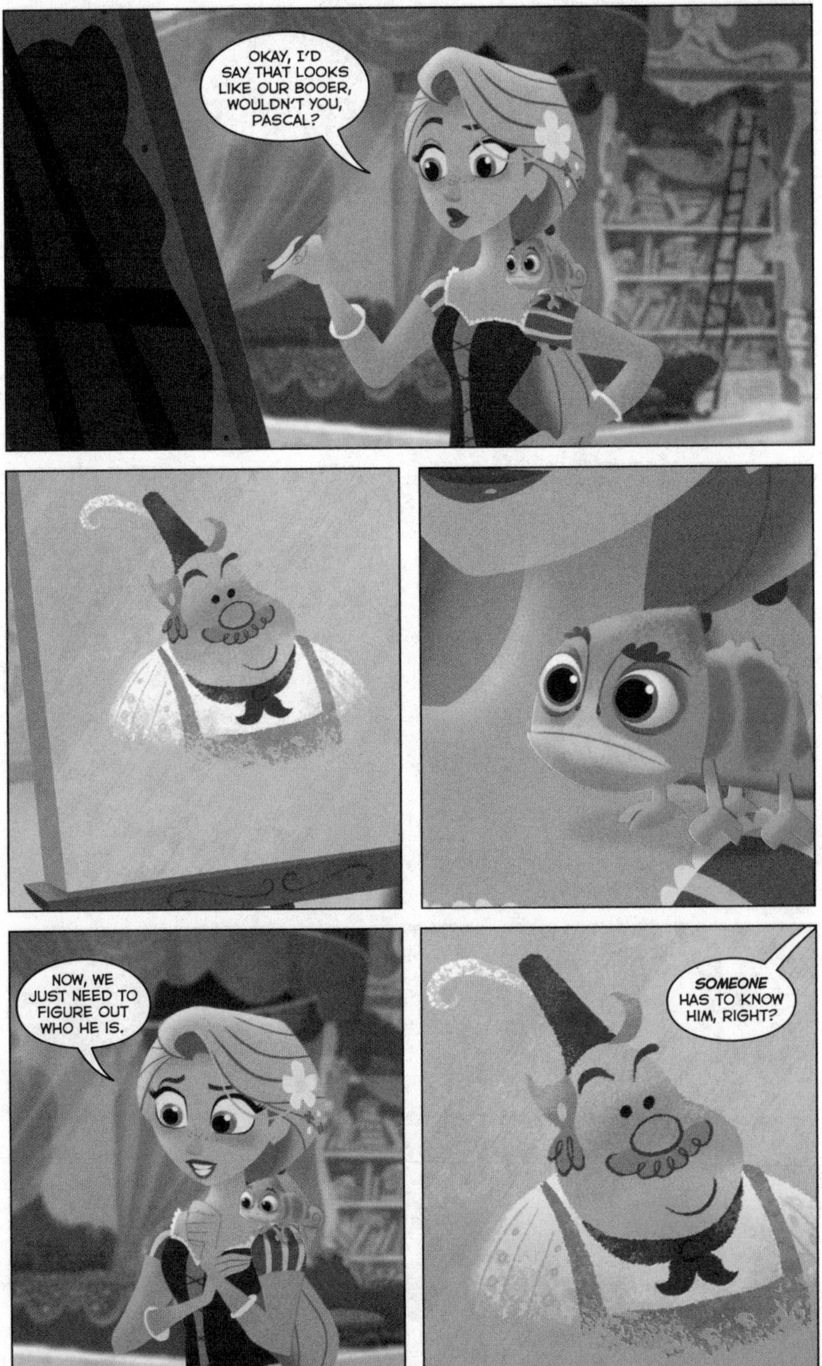
OKAY, I'D SAY THAT LOOKS LIKE OUR BOOER, WOULDN'T YOU, PASCAL?
NOW, WE JUST NEED TO FIGURE OUT WHO HE IS.
SOMEONE HAS TO KNOW HIM, RIGHT?

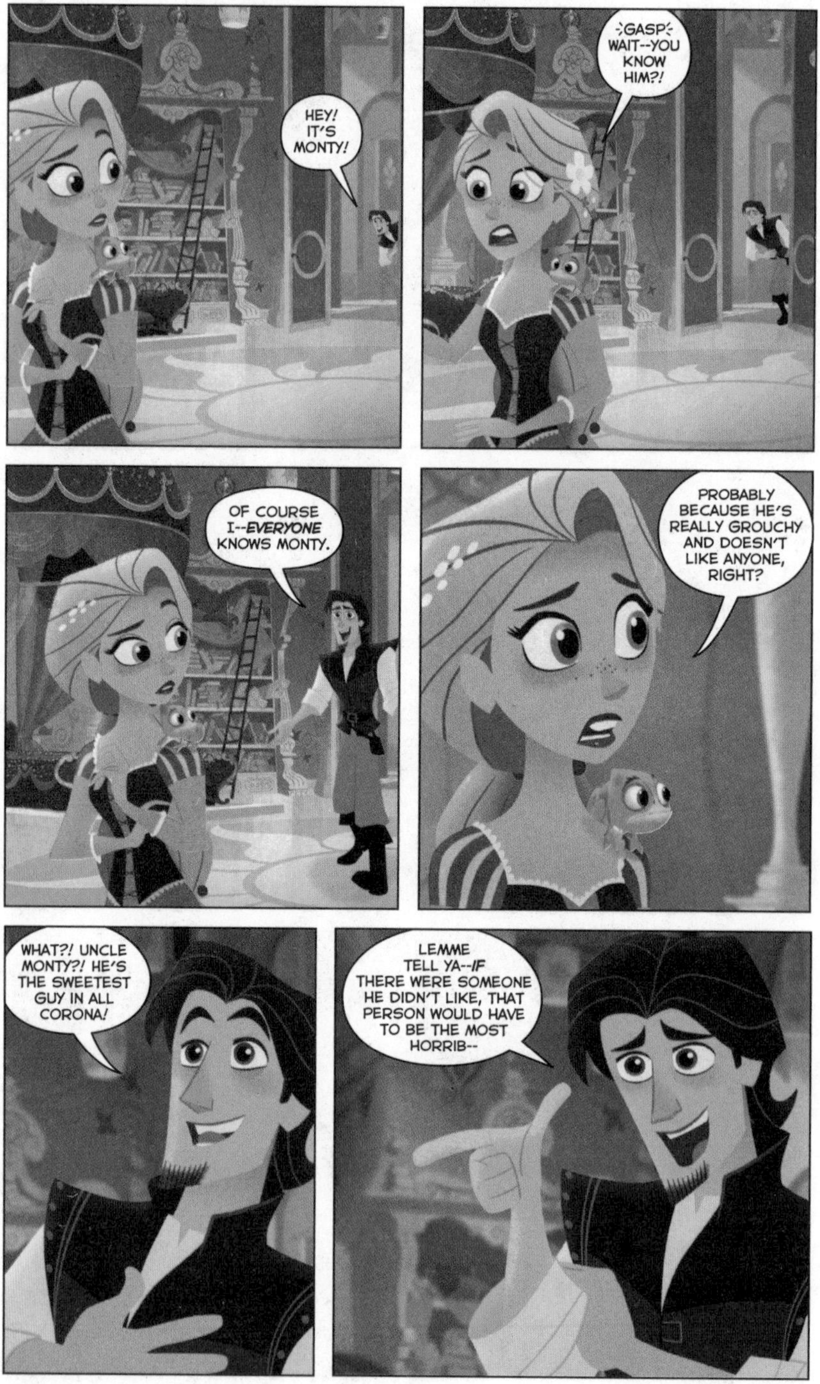
HEY! IT'S MONTY!
-GASP- WAIT--YOU KNOW HIM?!
OF COURSE I--*EVERYONE* KNOWS MONTY.
PROBABLY BECAUSE HE'S REALLY GROUCHY AND DOESN'T LIKE ANYONE, RIGHT?
WHAT?! UNCLE MONTY?! HE'S THE SWEETEST GUY IN ALL CORONA!
LEMME TELL YA--*IF* THERE WERE SOMEONE HE DIDN'T LIKE, THAT PERSON WOULD HAVE TO BE THE MOST HORRIB--

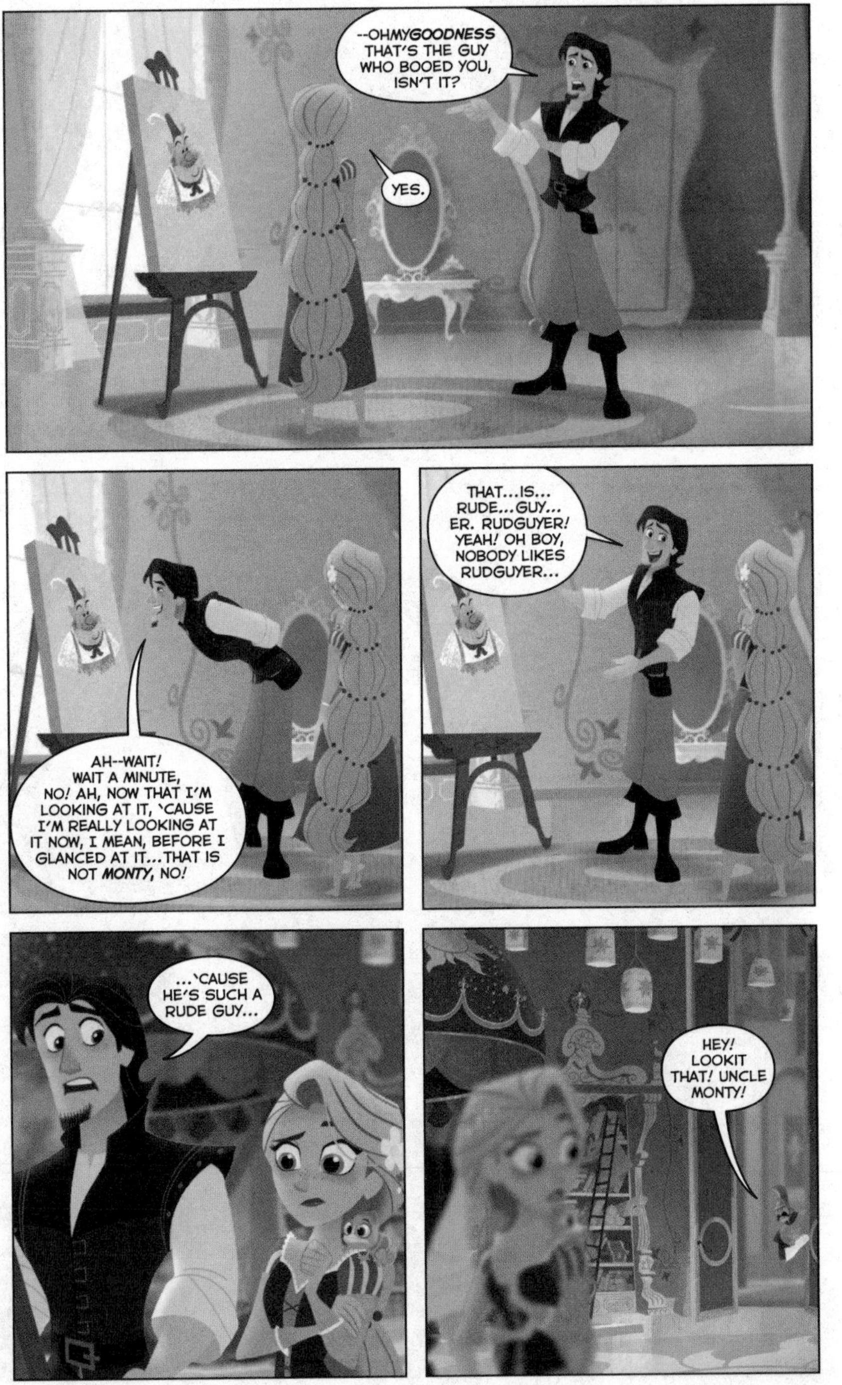

--OHMY*GOODNESS* THAT'S THE GUY WHO BOOED YOU, ISN'T IT?
YES.
AH--WAIT! WAIT A MINUTE, NO! AH, NOW THAT I'M LOOKING AT IT, 'CAUSE I'M REALLY LOOKING AT IT NOW, I MEAN, BEFORE I GLANCED AT IT...THAT IS NOT *MONTY*, NO!
THAT...IS... RUDE...GUY... ER. RUDGUYER! YEAH! OH BOY, NOBODY LIKES RUDGUYER...
...'CAUSE HE'S SUCH A RUDE GUY...
HEY! LOOKIT THAT! UNCLE MONTY!

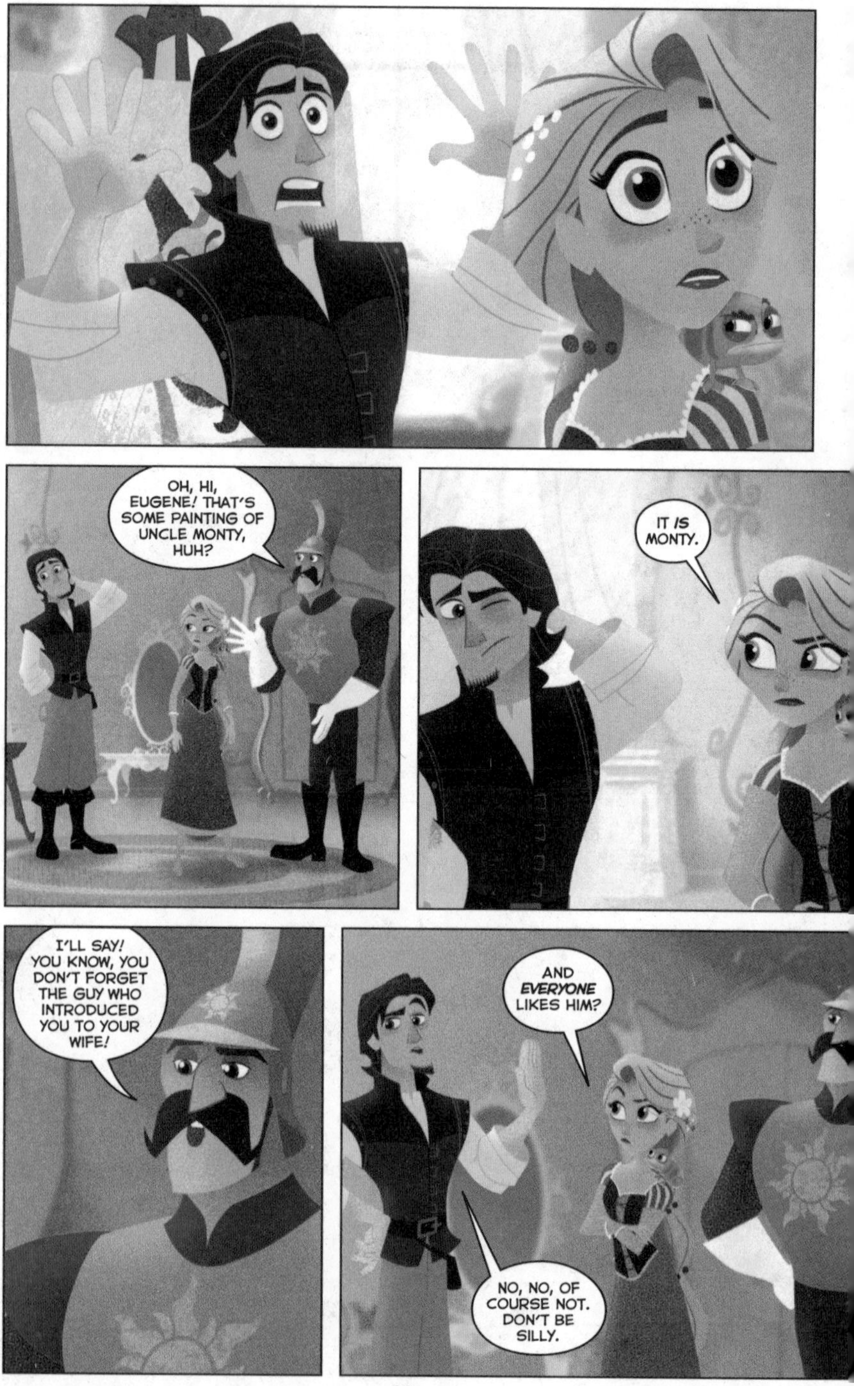
OH, HI, EUGENE! THAT'S SOME PAINTING OF UNCLE MONTY, HUH?
IT *IS* MONTY.
I'LL SAY! YOU KNOW, YOU DON'T FORGET THE GUY WHO INTRODUCED YOU TO YOUR WIFE!
AND *EVERYONE* LIKES HIM?
NO, NO, OF COURSE NOT. DON'T BE SILLY.

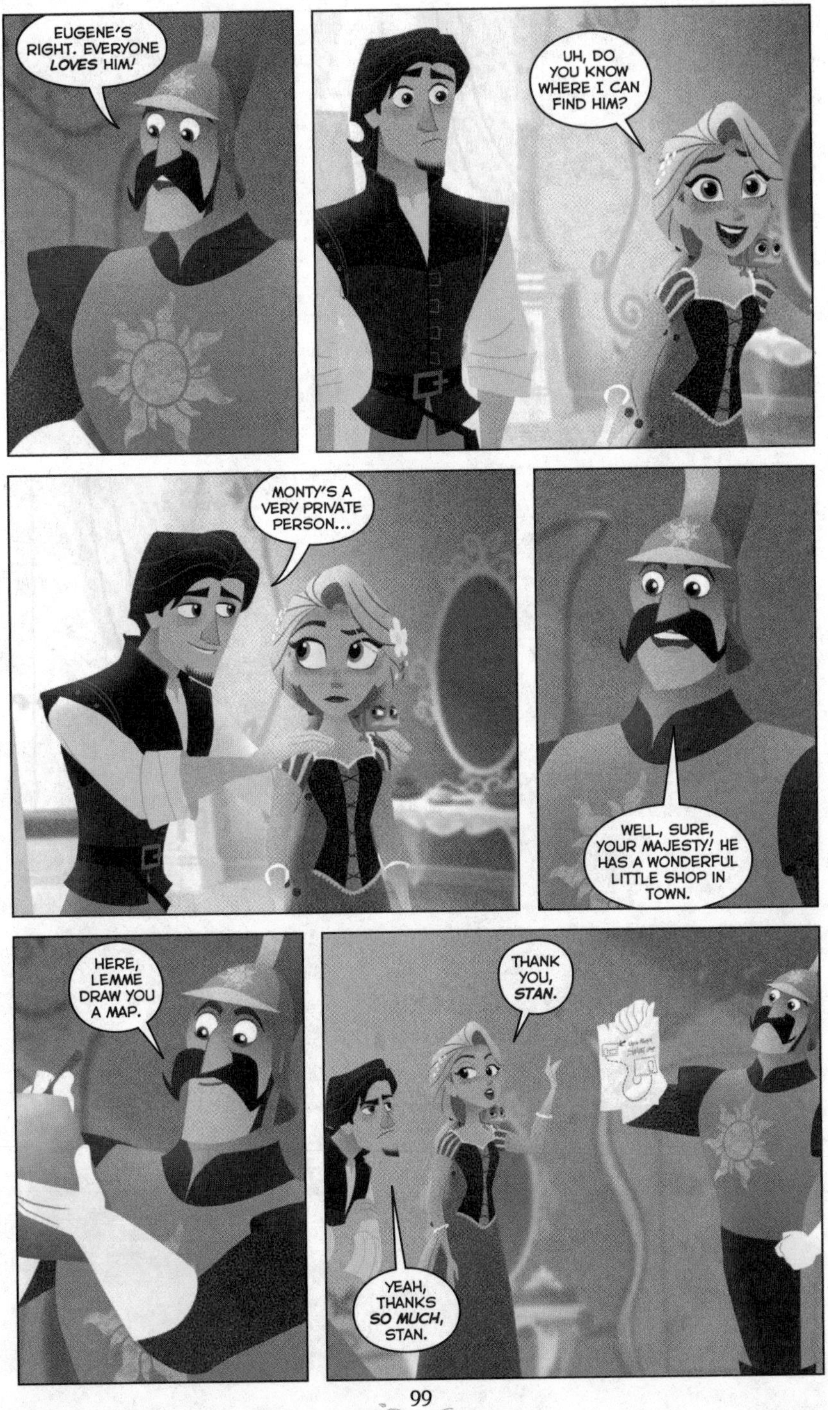
EUGENE'S RIGHT. EVERYONE *LOVES* HIM!
UH, DO YOU KNOW WHERE I CAN FIND HIM?
MONTY'S A VERY PRIVATE PERSON...
WELL, SURE, YOUR MAJESTY! HE HAS A WONDERFUL LITTLE SHOP IN TOWN.
HERE, LEMME DRAW YOU A MAP.
THANK YOU, *STAN.*
YEAH, THANKS *SO MUCH,* STAN.

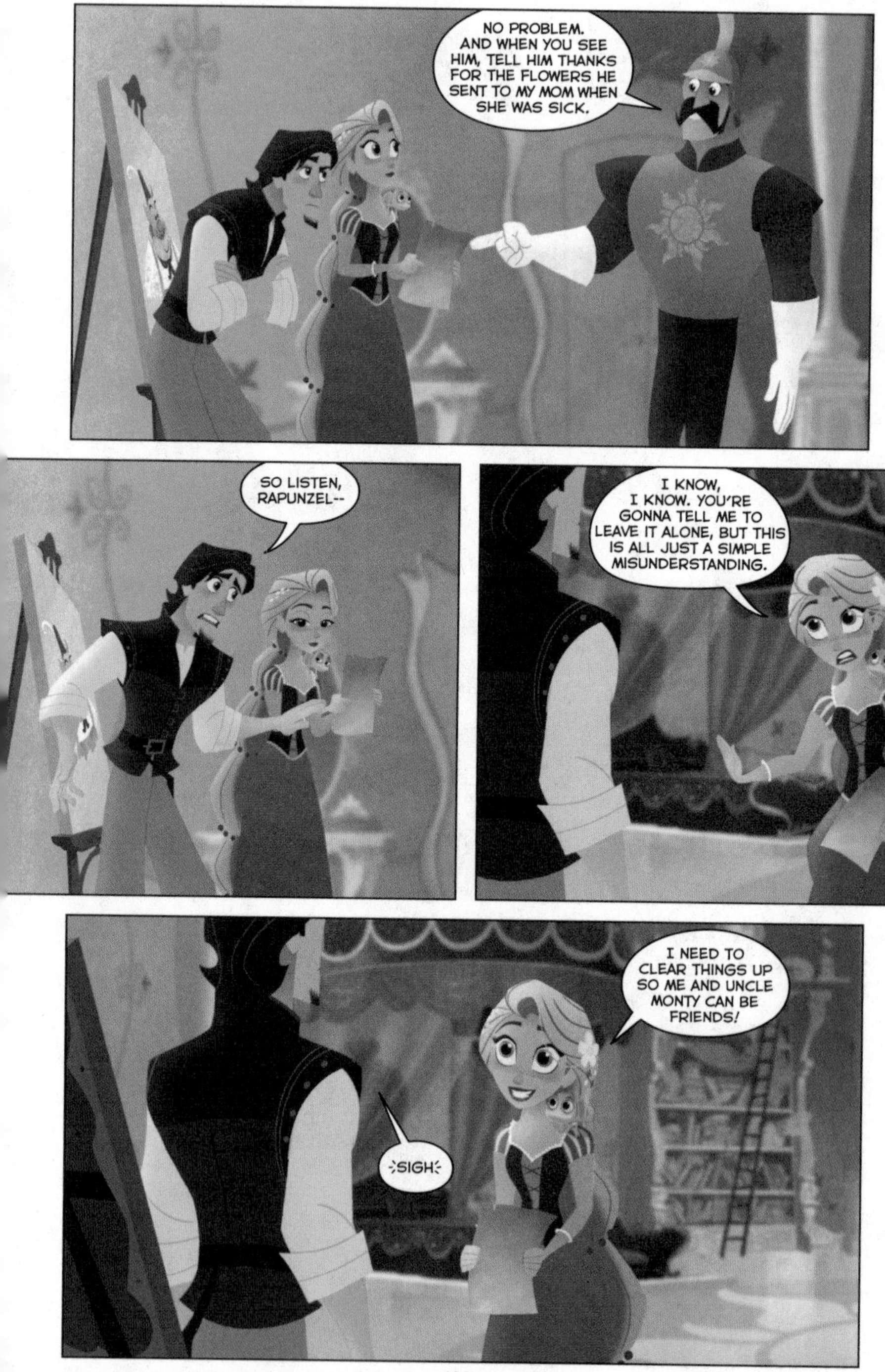
NO PROBLEM. AND WHEN YOU SEE HIM, TELL HIM THANKS FOR THE FLOWERS HE SENT TO MY MOM WHEN SHE WAS SICK.
SO LISTEN, RAPUNZEL--
I KNOW, I KNOW. YOU'RE GONNA TELL ME TO LEAVE IT ALONE, BUT THIS IS ALL JUST A SIMPLE MISUNDERSTANDING.
I NEED TO CLEAR THINGS UP SO ME AND UNCLE MONTY CAN BE FRIENDS!
SIGH

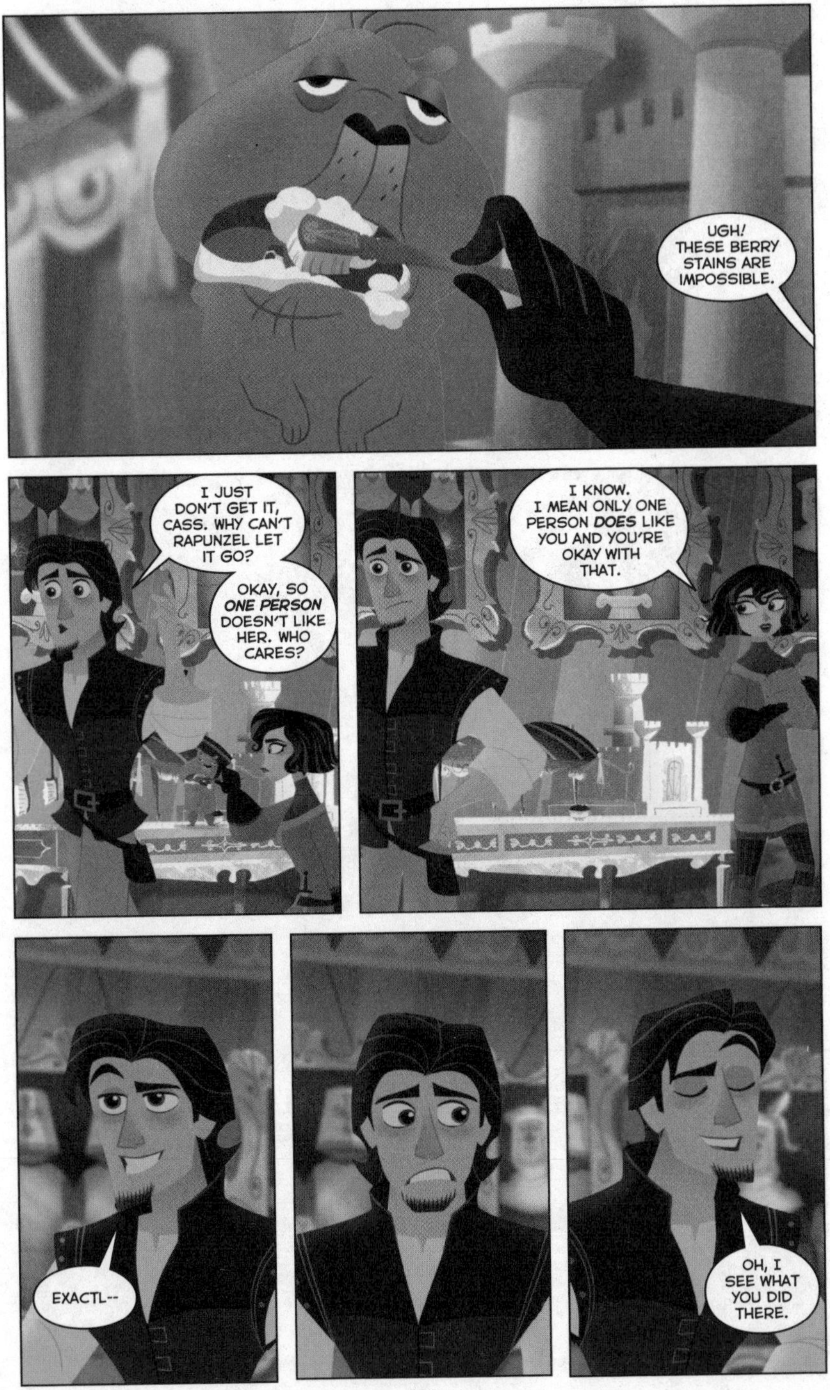
UGH! THESE BERRY STAINS ARE IMPOSSIBLE.
I JUST DON'T GET IT, CASS. WHY CAN'T RAPUNZEL LET IT GO?
OKAY, SO ONE PERSON DOESN'T LIKE HER. WHO CARES?
I KNOW. I MEAN ONLY ONE PERSON DOES LIKE YOU AND YOU'RE OKAY WITH THAT.
EXACTL--
OH, I SEE WHAT YOU DID THERE.

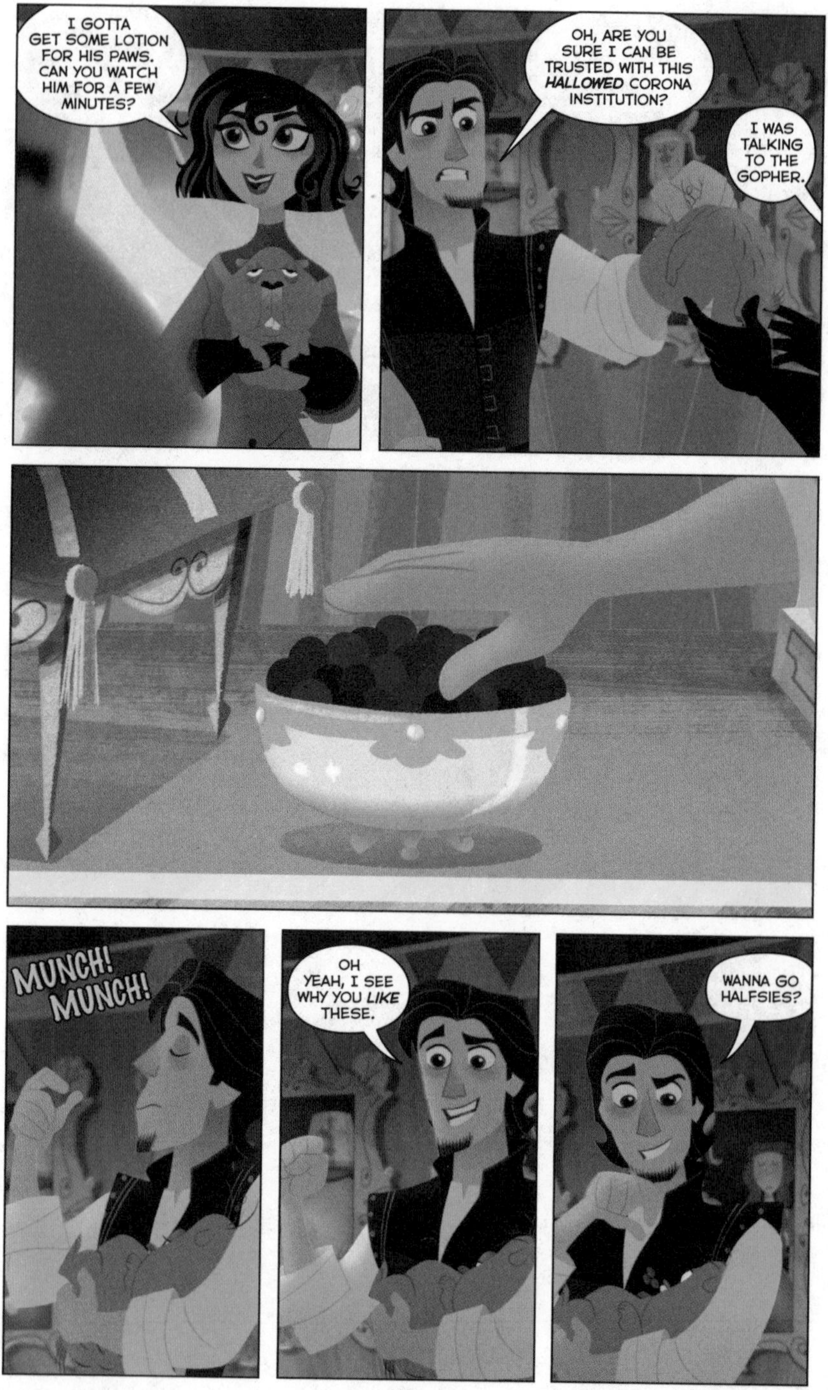
I GOTTA GET SOME LOTION FOR HIS PAWS. CAN YOU WATCH HIM FOR A FEW MINUTES?
OH, ARE YOU SURE I CAN BE TRUSTED WITH THIS HALLOWED CORONA INSTITUTION?
I WAS TALKING TO THE GOPHER.
MUNCH! MUNCH!
OH YEAH, I SEE WHY YOU LIKE THESE.
WANNA GO HALFSIES?

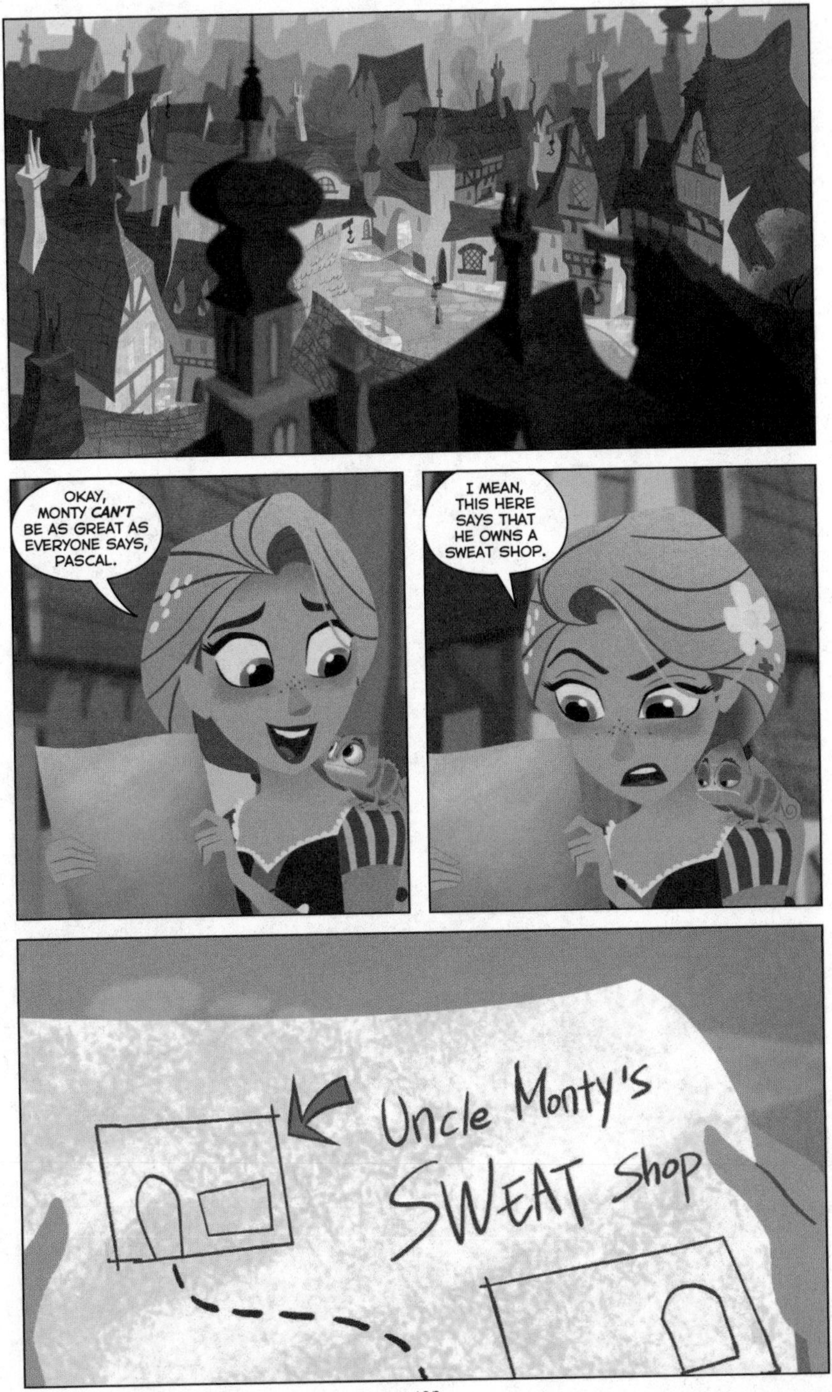
OKAY, MONTY CAN'T BE AS GREAT AS EVERYONE SAYS, PASCAL.
I MEAN, THIS HERE SAYS THAT HE OWNS A SWEAT SHOP.
Uncle Monty's SWEAT Shop

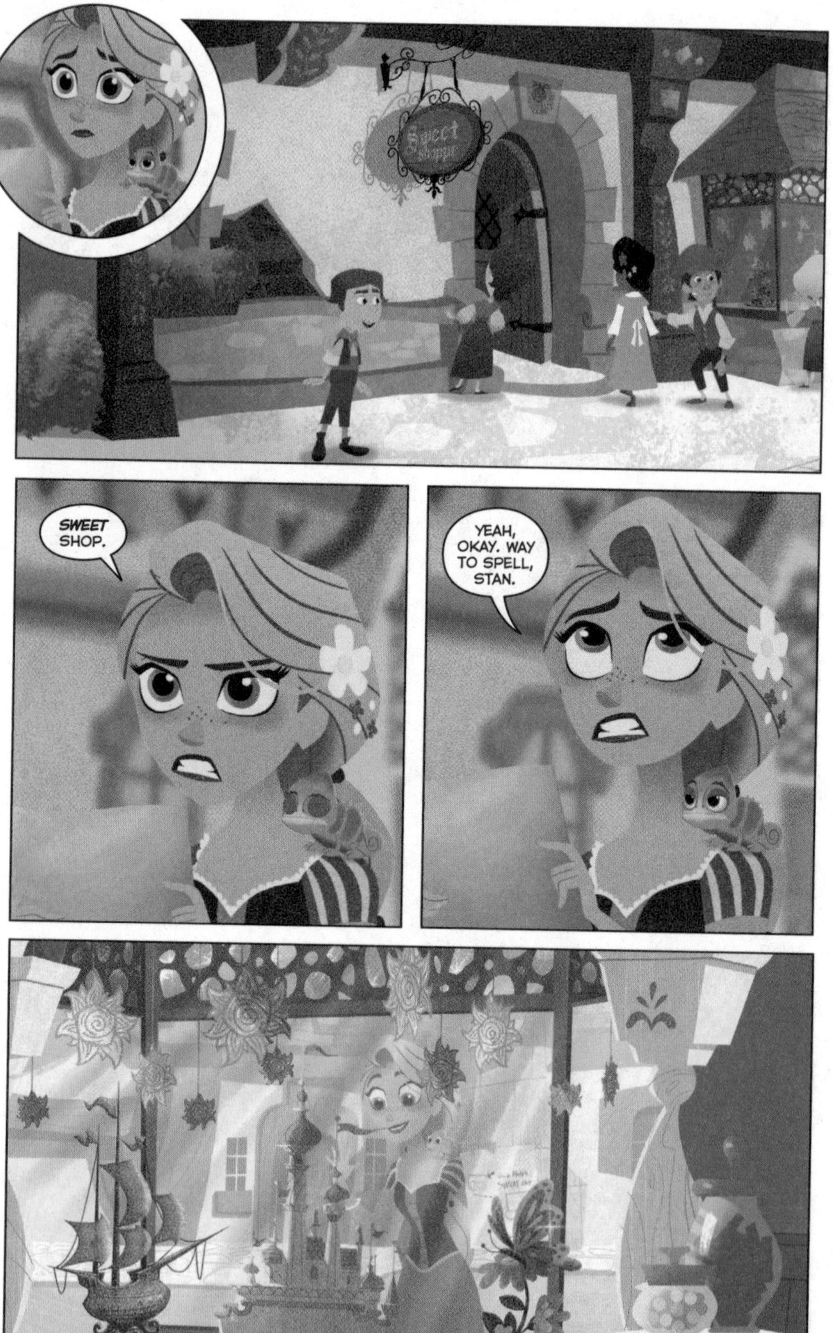
SWEET SHOP.
YEAH, OKAY. WAY TO SPELL, STAN.

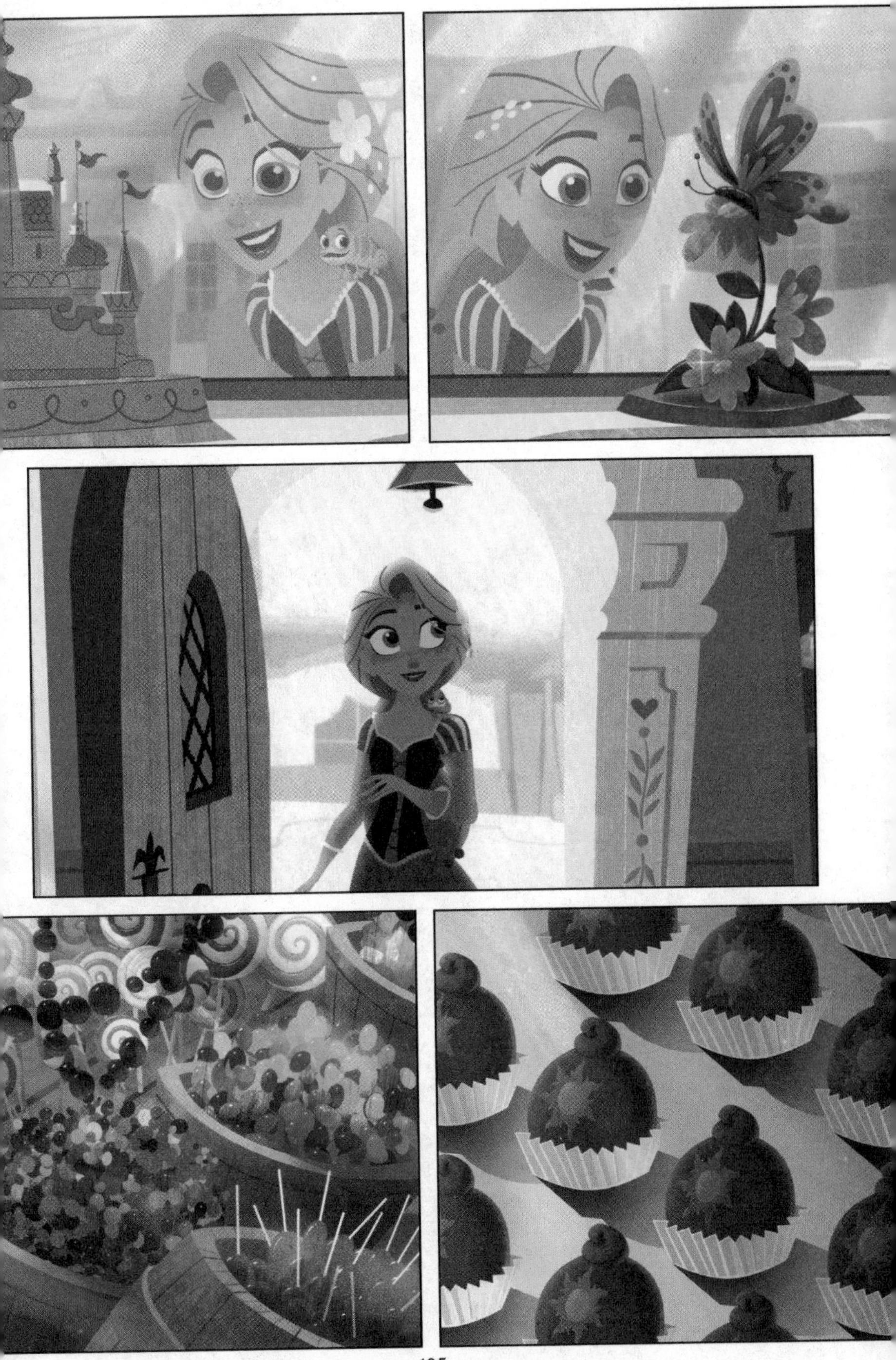

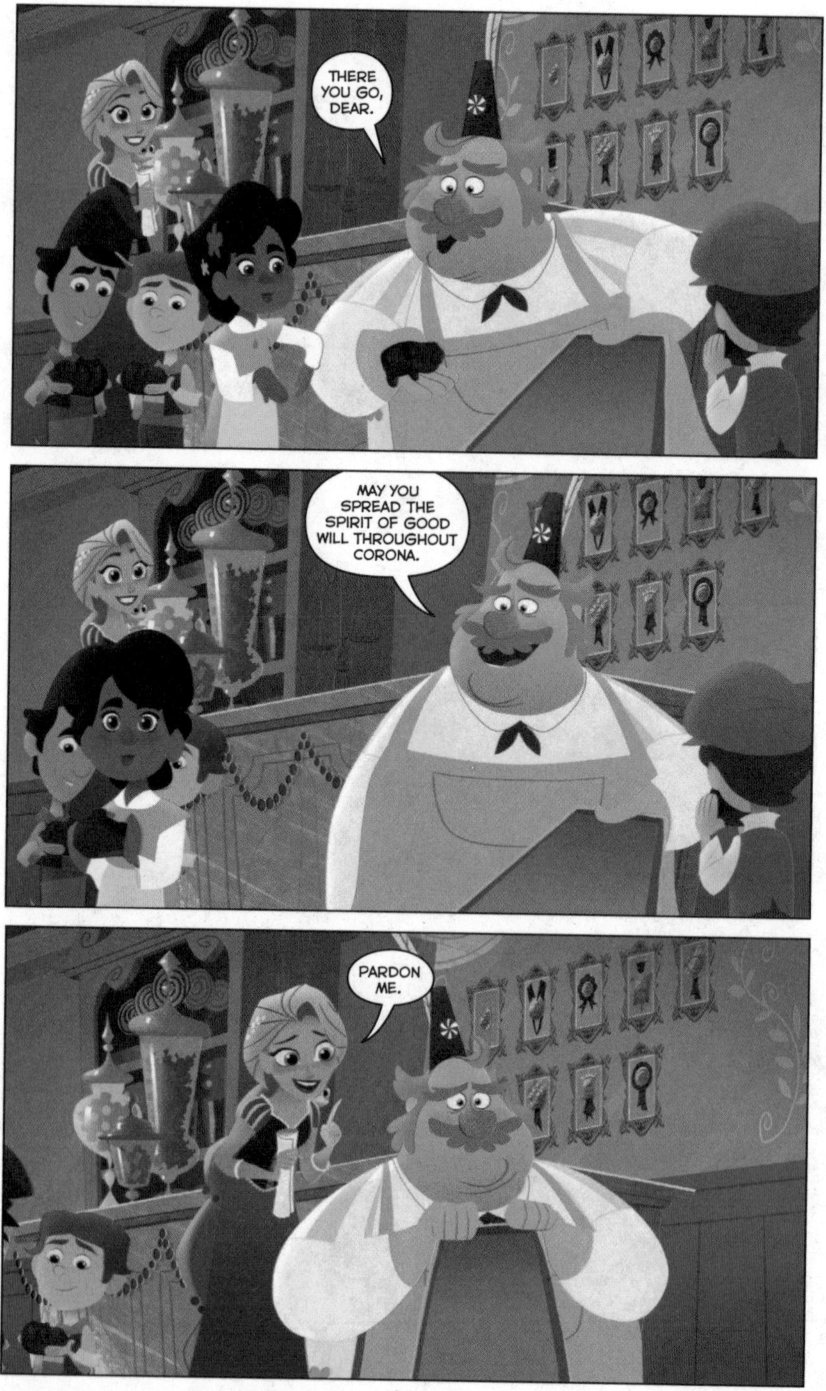
THERE YOU GO, DEAR.
MAY YOU SPREAD THE SPIRIT OF GOOD WILL THROUGHOUT CORONA.
PARDON ME.

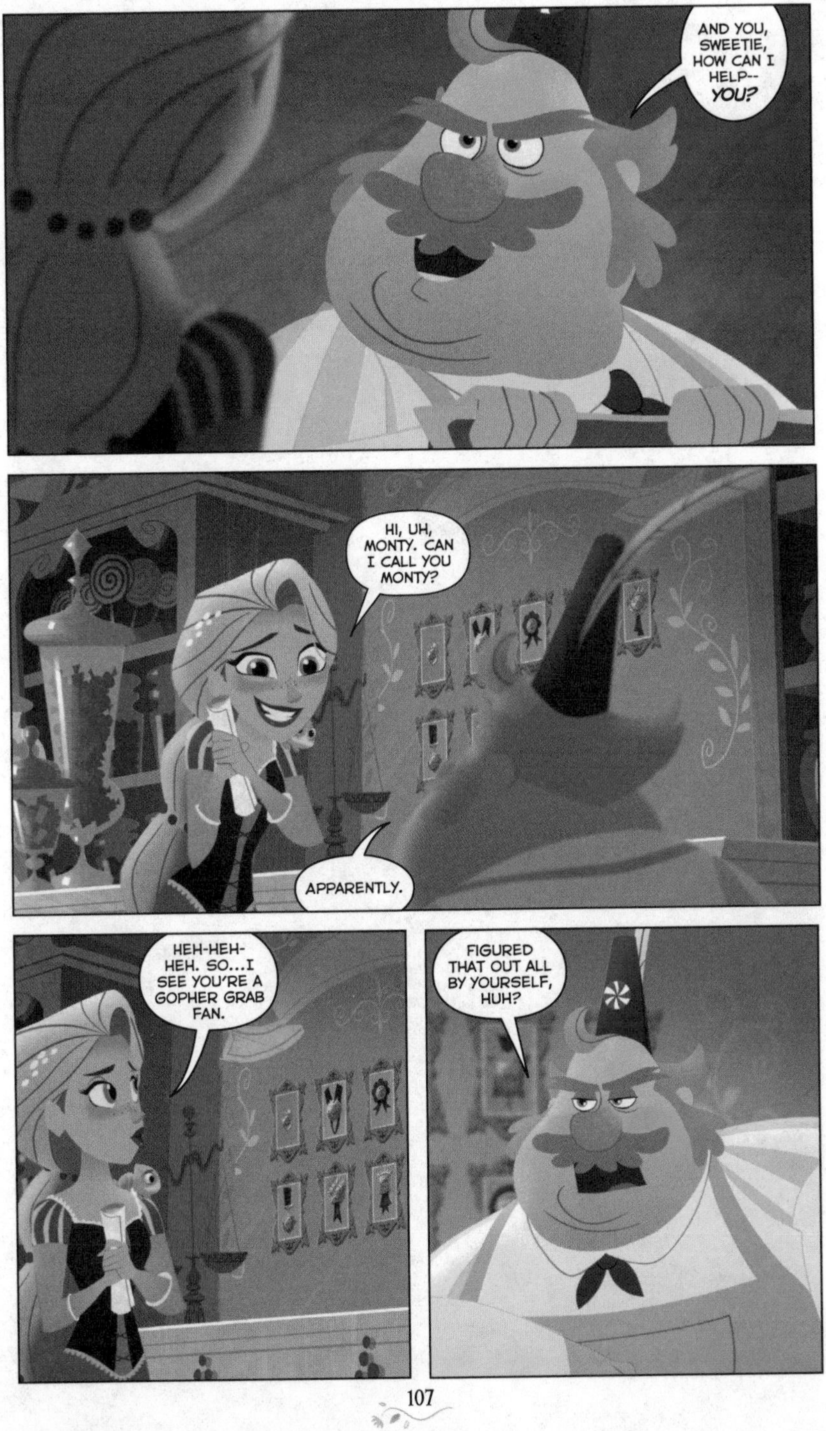
AND YOU, SWEETIE, HOW CAN I HELP-- YOU?
HI, UH, MONTY. CAN I CALL YOU MONTY?
APPARENTLY.
HEH-HEH-HEH. SO...I SEE YOU'RE A GOPHER GRAB FAN.
FIGURED THAT OUT ALL BY YOURSELF, HUH?

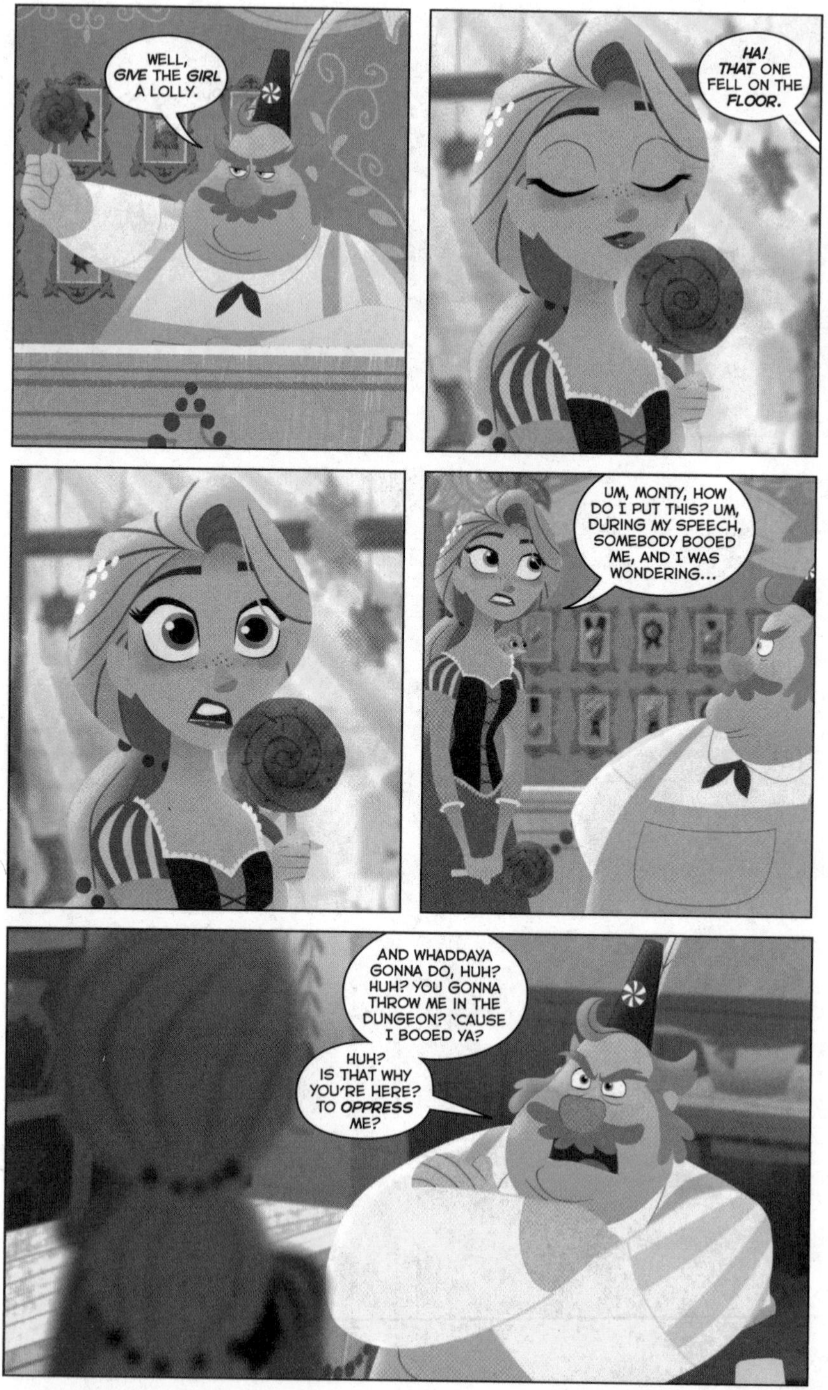
WELL, GIVE THE GIRL A LOLLY.
HA! THAT ONE FELL ON THE FLOOR.
UM, MONTY, HOW DO I PUT THIS? UM, DURING MY SPEECH, SOMEBODY BOOED ME, AND I WAS WONDERING...
AND WHADDAYA GONNA DO, HUH? HUH? YOU GONNA THROW ME IN THE DUNGEON? 'CAUSE I BOOED YA?
HUH? IS THAT WHY YOU'RE HERE? TO OPPRESS ME?

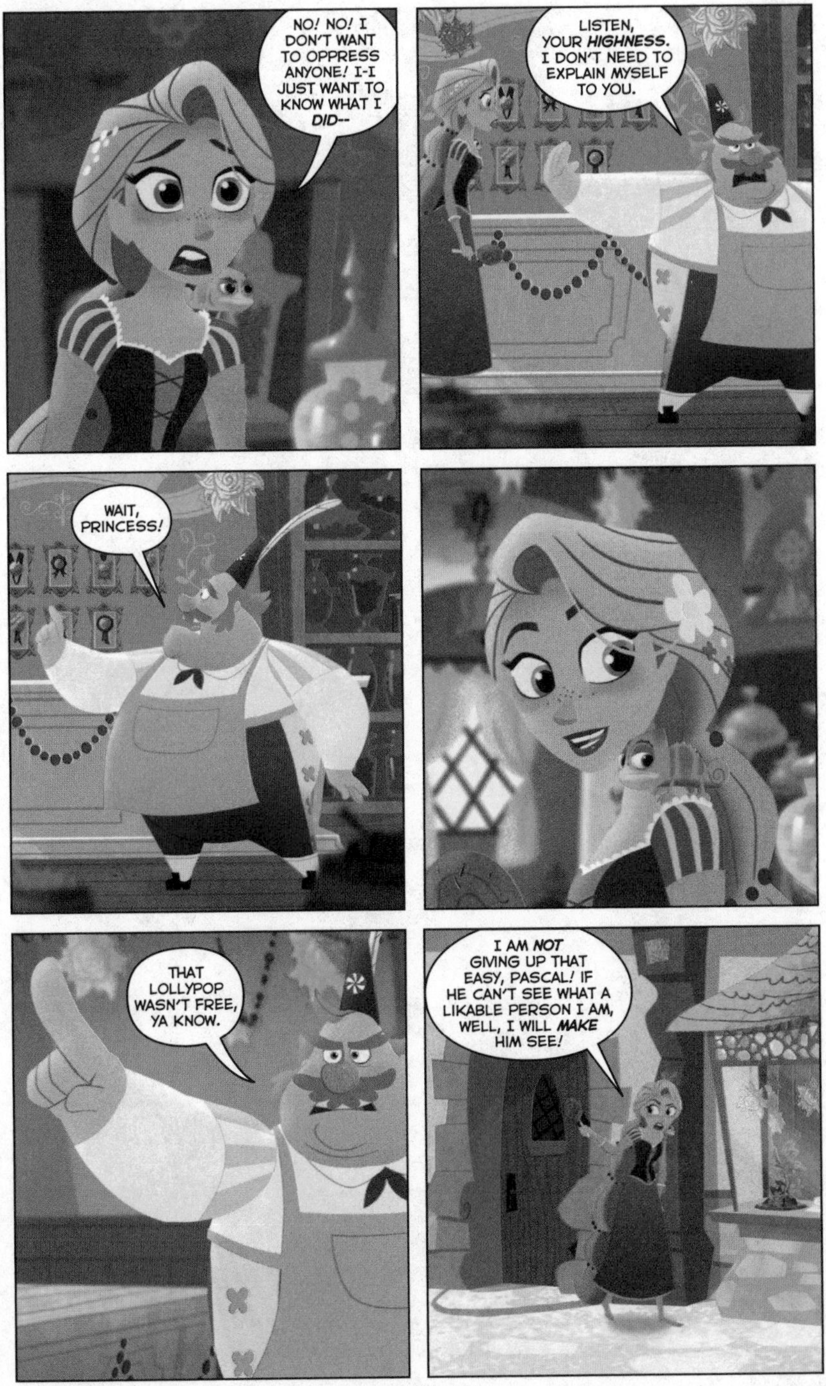
NO! NO! I DON'T WANT TO OPPRESS ANYONE! I-I JUST WANT TO KNOW WHAT I DID--
LISTEN, YOUR HIGHNESS. I DON'T NEED TO EXPLAIN MYSELF TO YOU.
WAIT, PRINCESS!
THAT LOLLYPOP WASN'T FREE, YA KNOW.
I AM NOT GIVING UP THAT EASY, PASCAL! IF HE CAN'T SEE WHAT A LIKABLE PERSON I AM, WELL, I WILL MAKE HIM SEE!

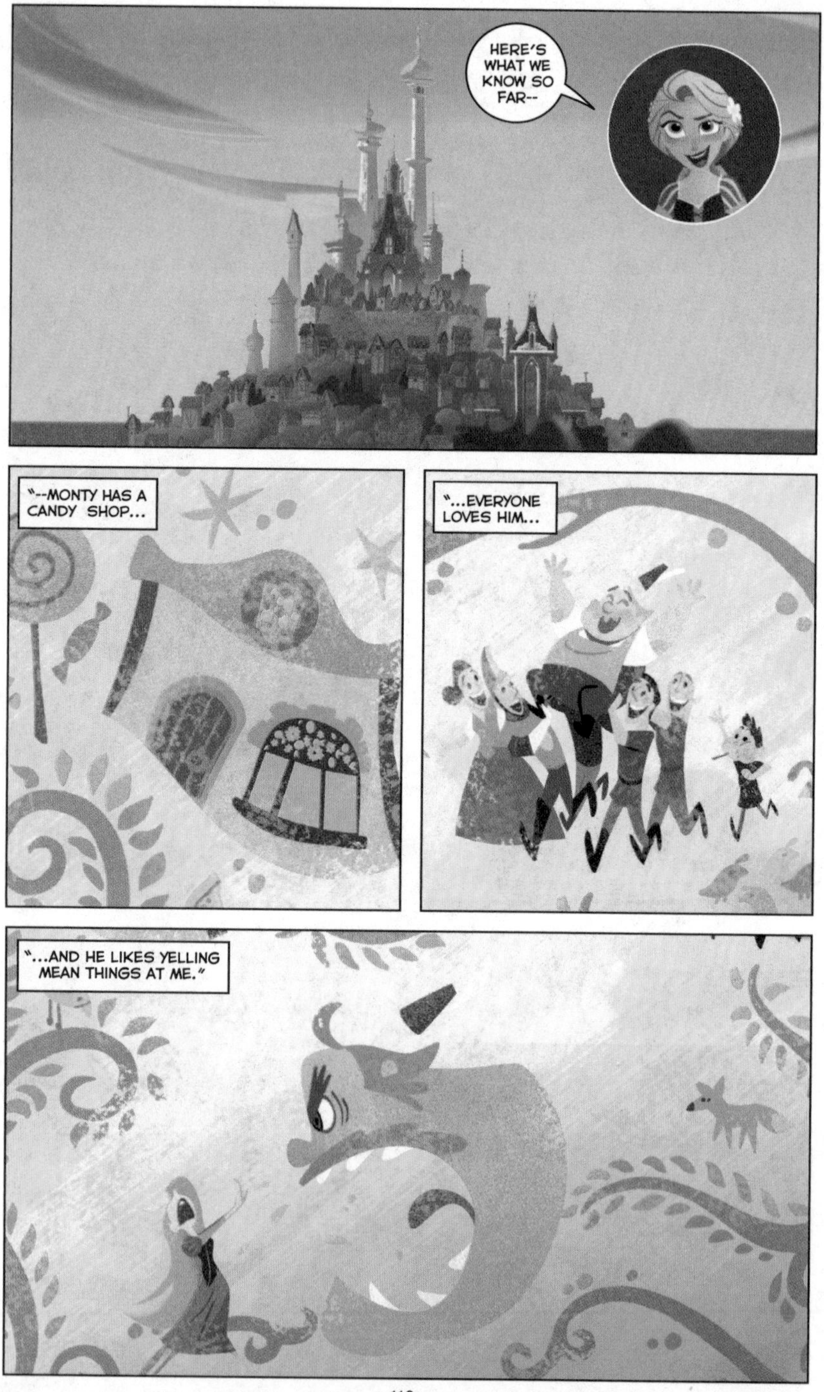
HERE'S WHAT WE KNOW SO FAR--
"--MONTY HAS A CANDY SHOP...
"...EVERYONE LOVES HIM...
"...AND HE LIKES YELLING MEAN THINGS AT ME."

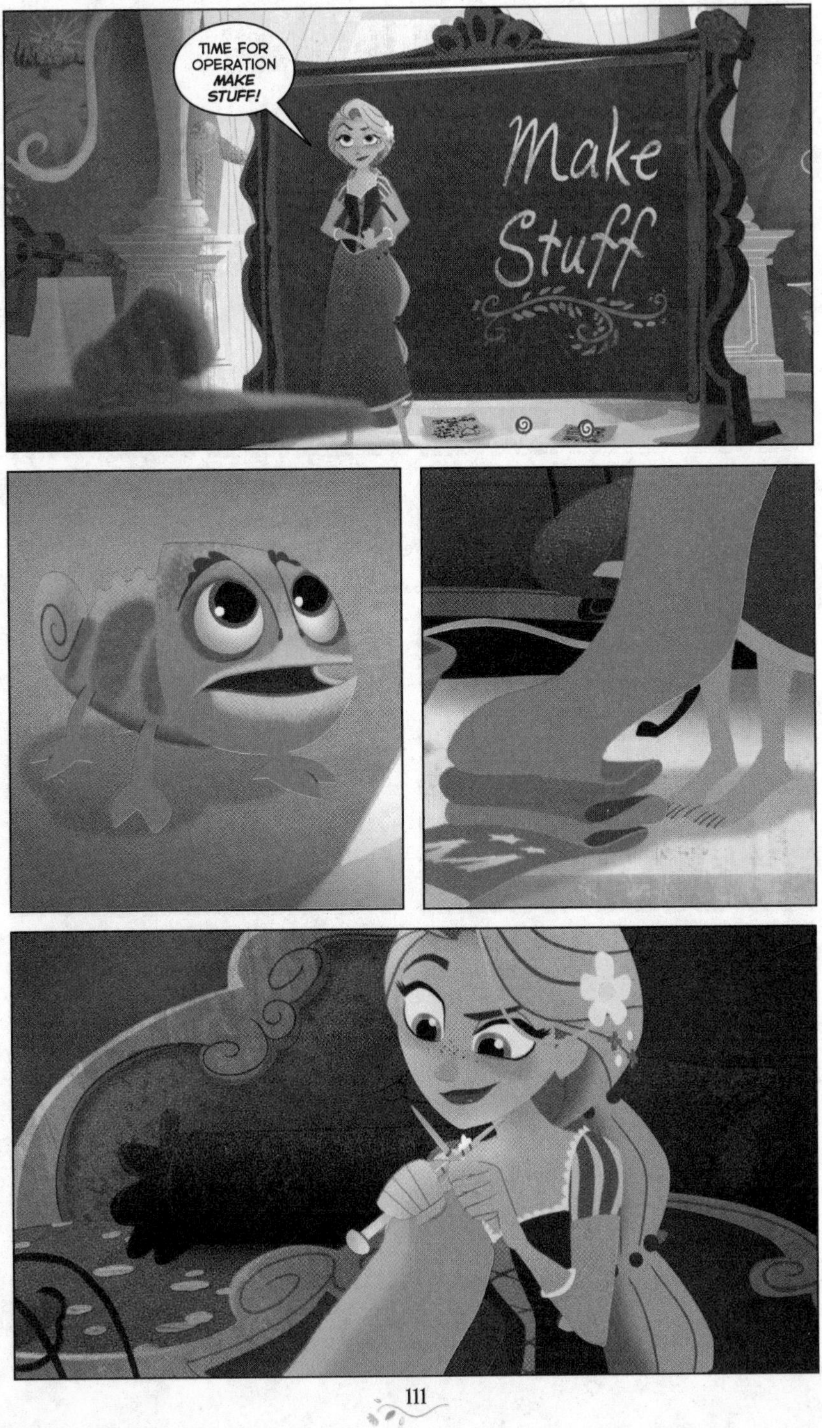
TIME FOR OPERATION MAKE STUFF!
Make Stuff

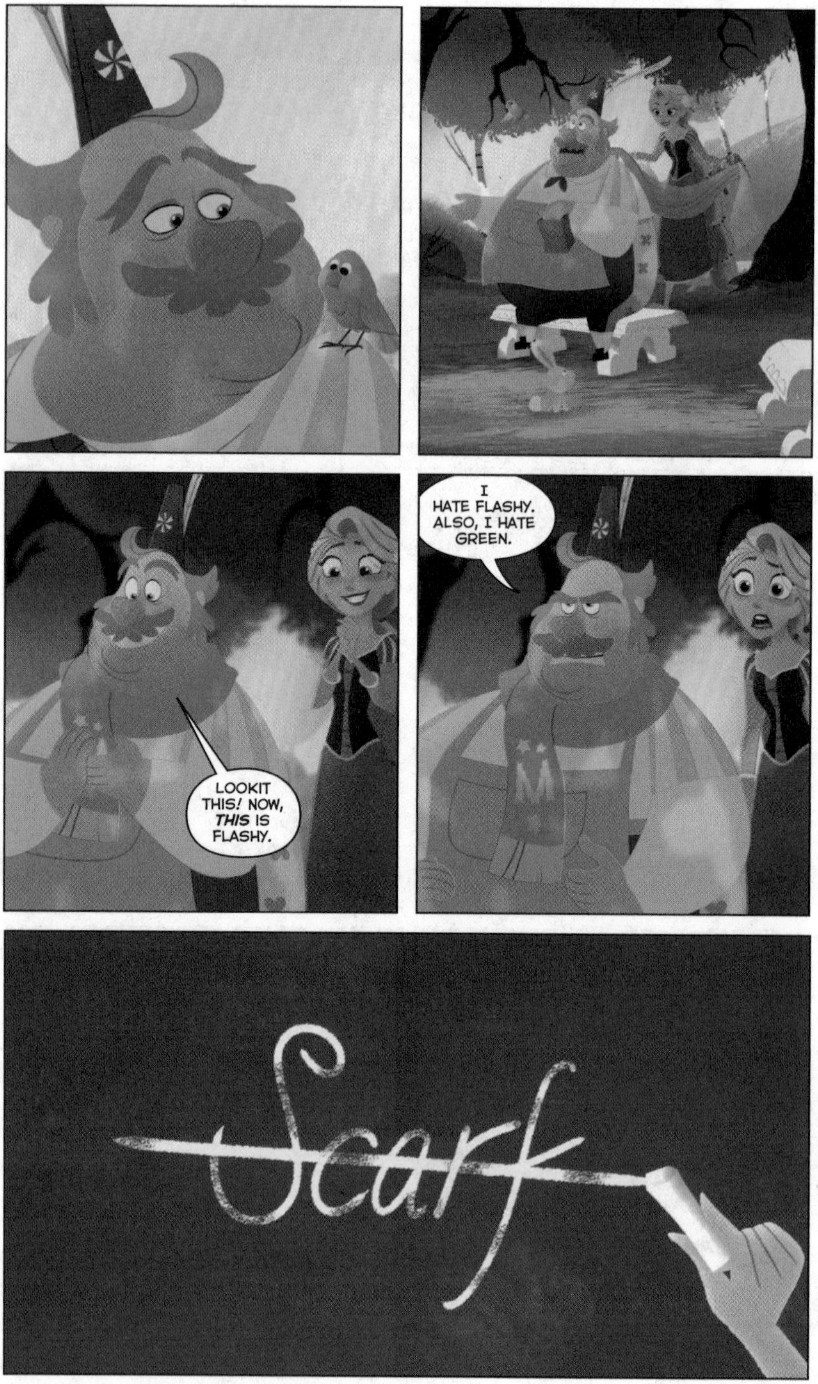
LOOKIT THIS! NOW, *THIS* IS FLASHY.
I HATE FLASHY. ALSO, I HATE GREEN.
Scarf

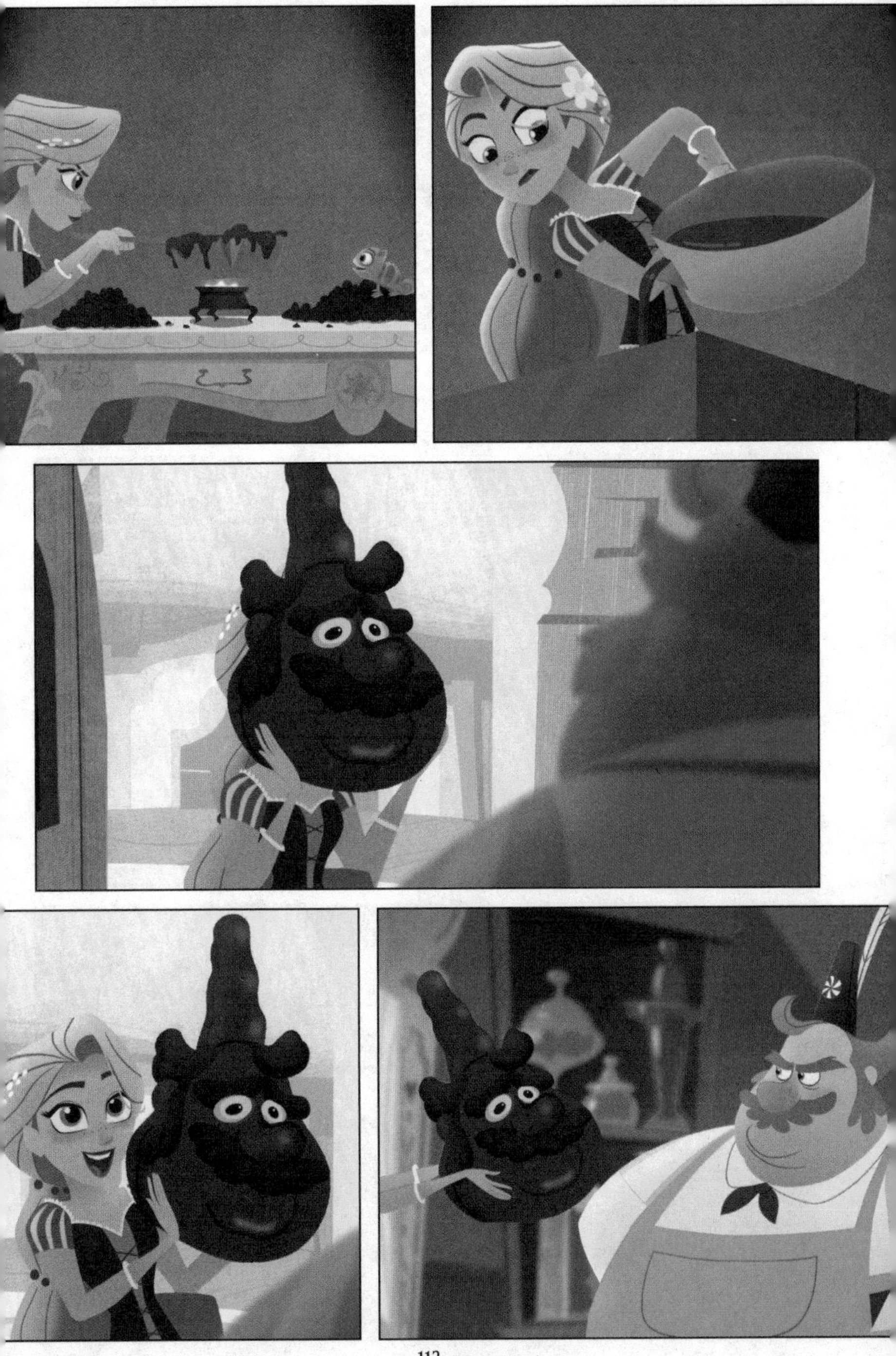

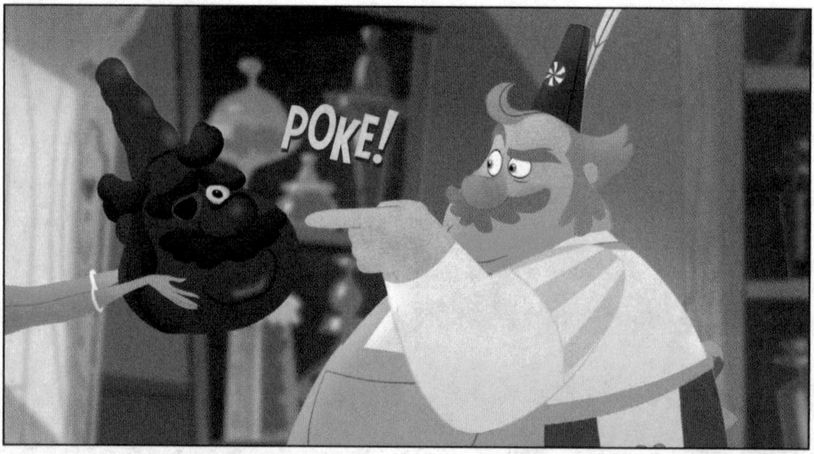
POKE!

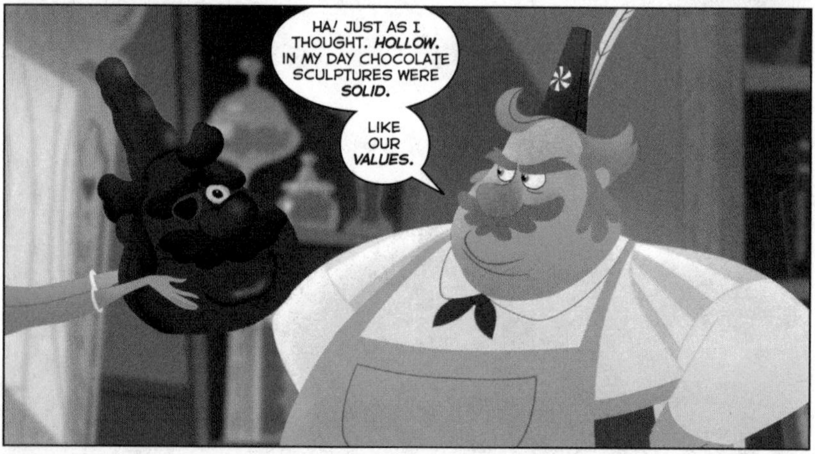
HA! JUST AS I THOUGHT. *HOLLOW.* IN MY DAY CHOCOLATE SCULPTURES WERE *SOLID.*
LIKE OUR *VALUES.*

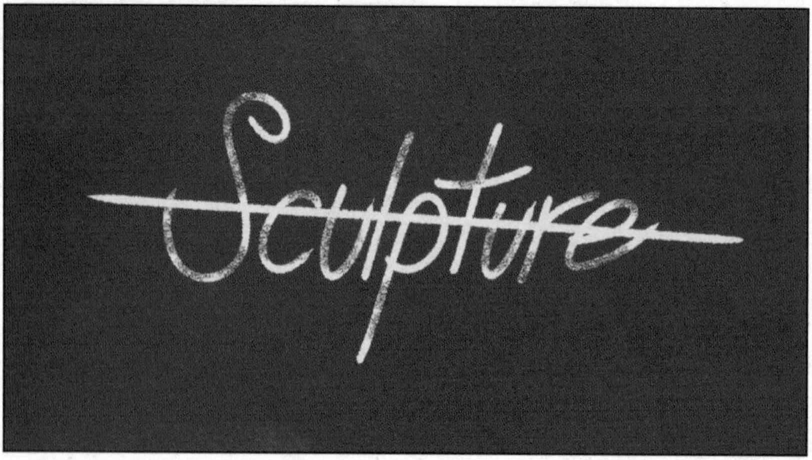
Sculpture

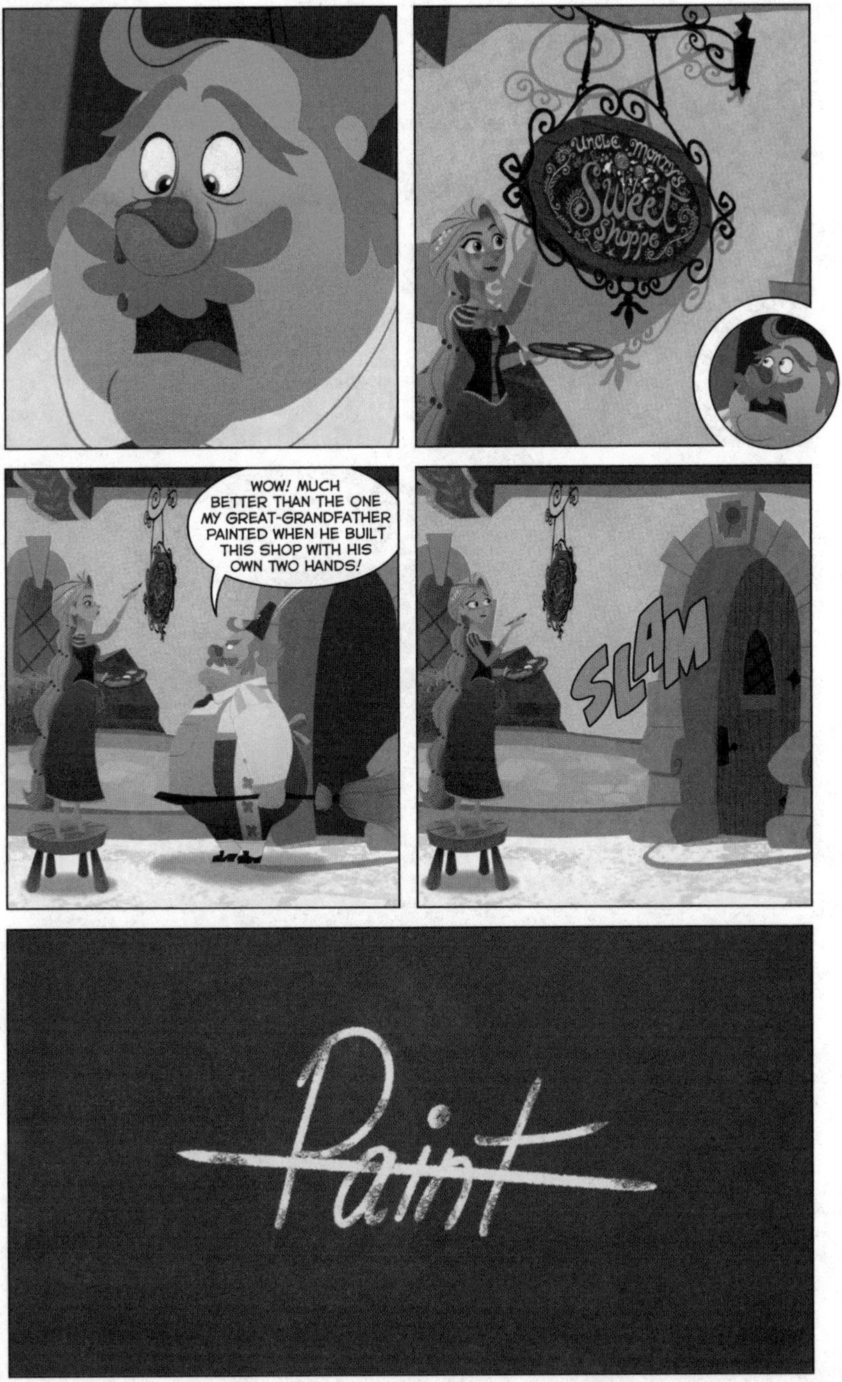
UNCLE MONTY'S
Sweet
Shoppe
WOW! MUCH BETTER THAN THE ONE MY GREAT-GRANDFATHER PAINTED WHEN HE BUILT THIS SHOP WITH HIS OWN TWO HANDS!
SLAM
Paint

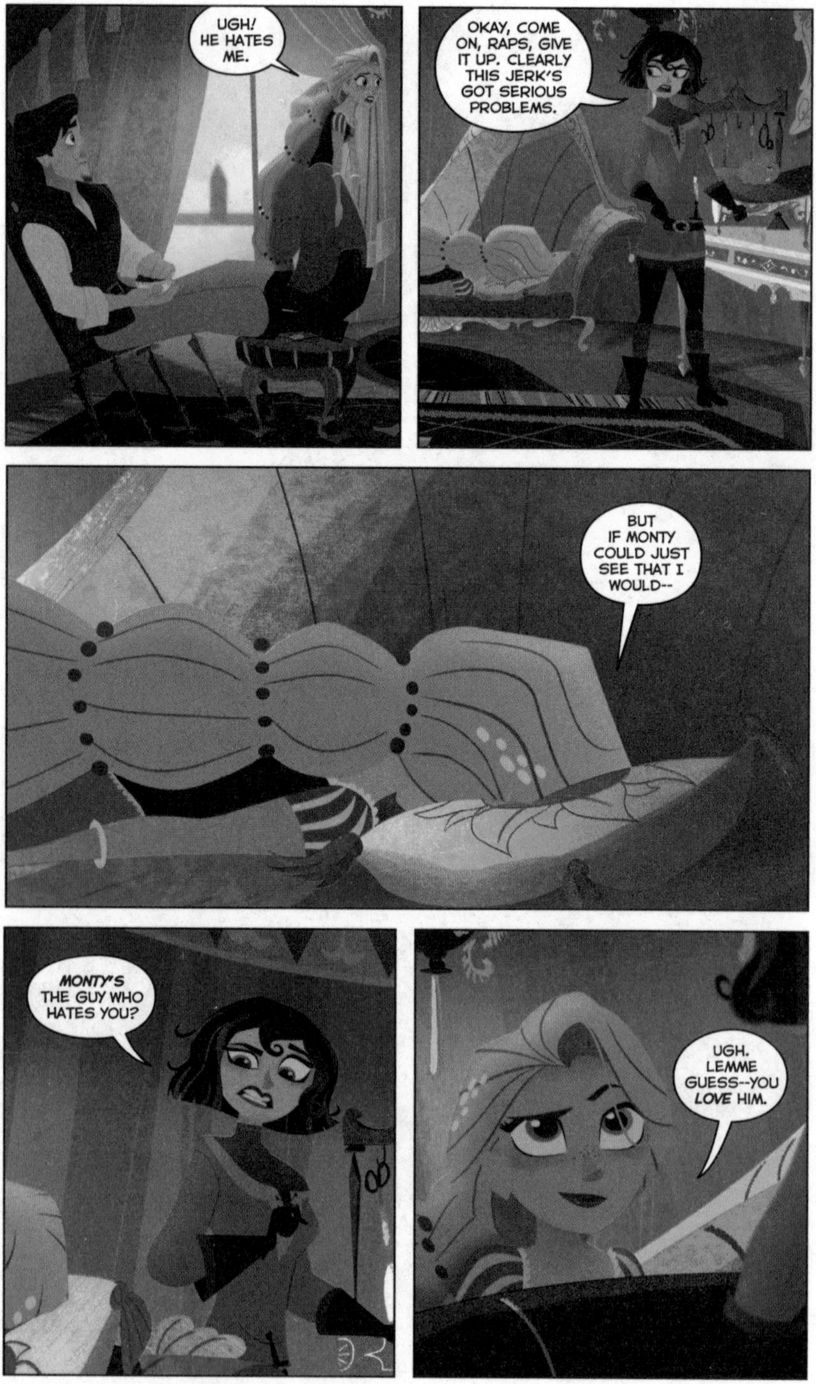
UGH! HE HATES ME.
OKAY, COME ON, RAPS, GIVE IT UP. CLEARLY THIS JERK'S GOT SERIOUS PROBLEMS.
BUT IF MONTY COULD JUST SEE THAT I WOULD--
MONTY'S THE GUY WHO HATES YOU?
UGH. LEMME GUESS--YOU *LOVE* HIM.

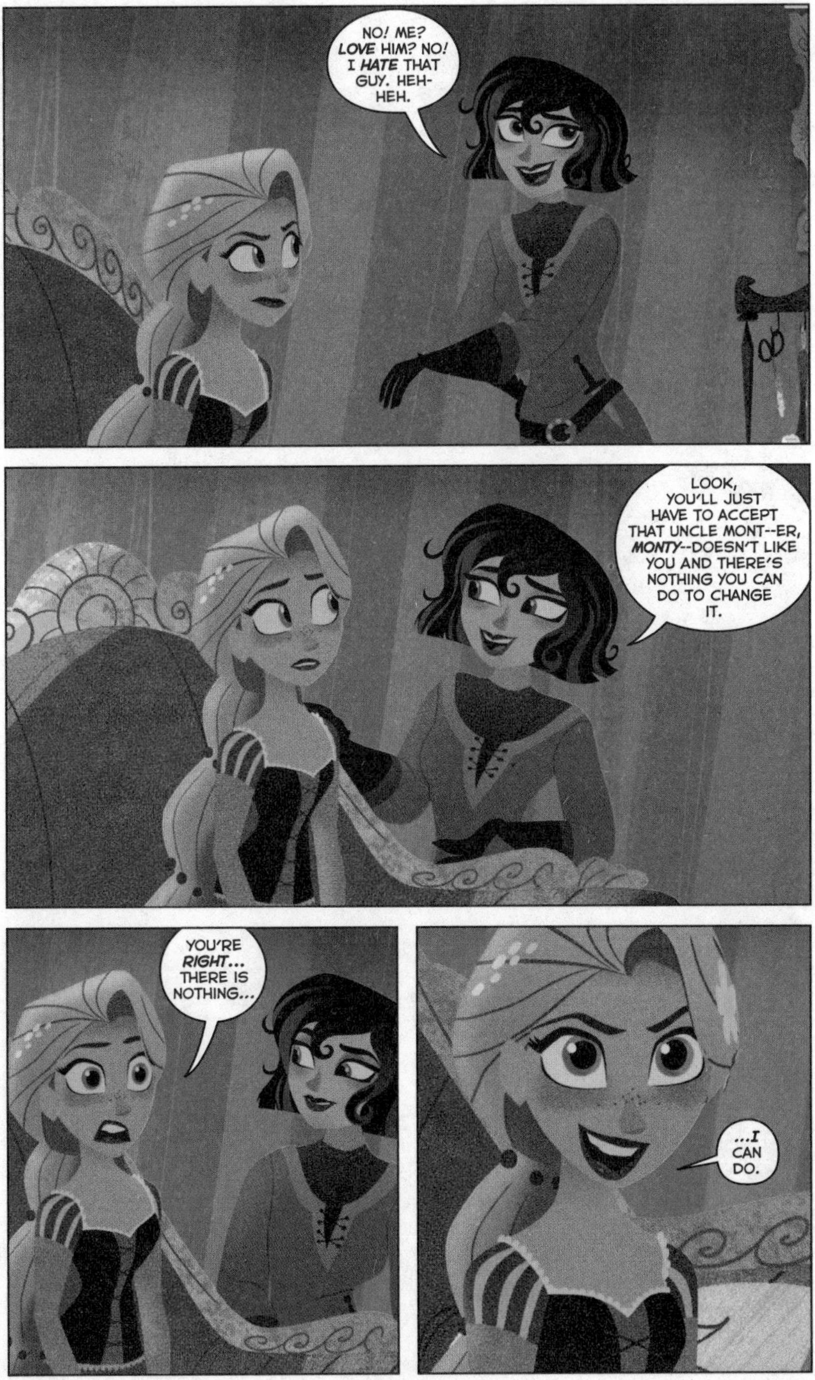
NO! ME? LOVE HIM? NO! I HATE THAT GUY. HEH-HEH.
LOOK, YOU'LL JUST HAVE TO ACCEPT THAT UNCLE MONT--ER, MONTY--DOESN'T LIKE YOU AND THERE'S NOTHING YOU CAN DO TO CHANGE IT.
YOU'RE RIGHT... THERE IS NOTHING...
...I CAN DO.

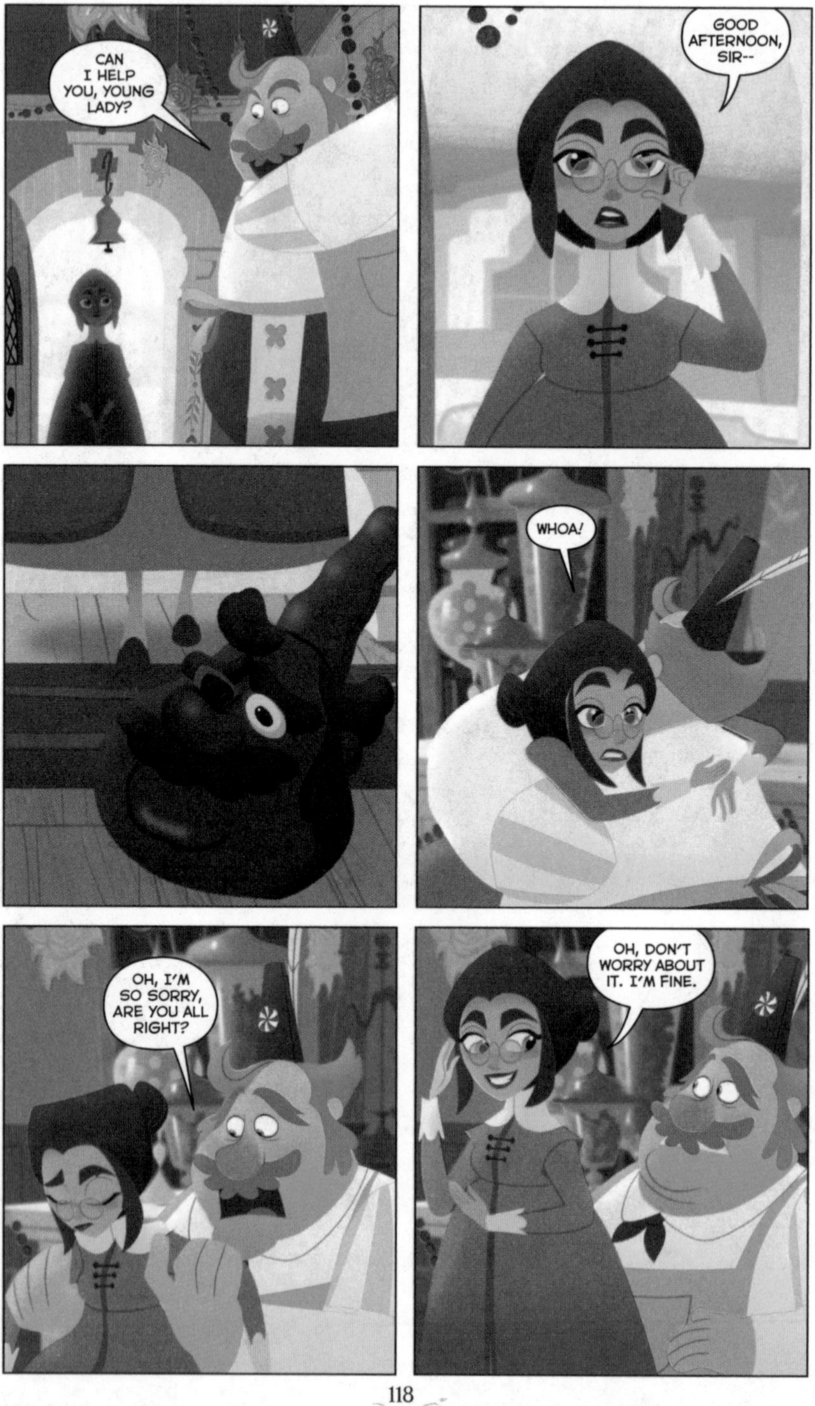
CAN I HELP YOU, YOUNG LADY?
GOOD AFTERNOON, SIR--
WHOA!
OH, I'M SO SORRY, ARE YOU ALL RIGHT?
OH, DON'T WORRY ABOUT IT. I'M FINE.

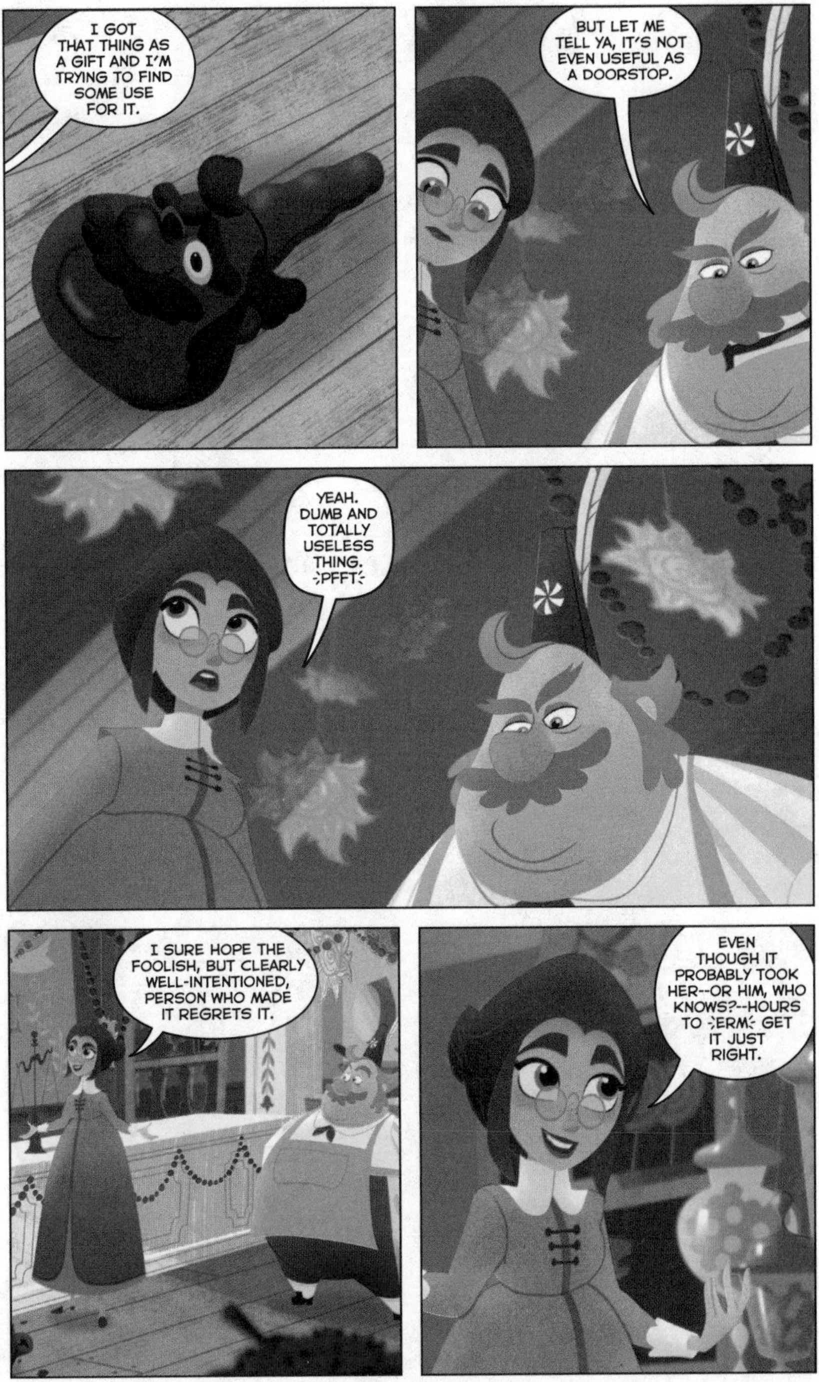
I GOT THAT THING AS A GIFT AND I'M TRYING TO FIND SOME USE FOR IT.
BUT LET ME TELL YA, IT'S NOT EVEN USEFUL AS A DOORSTOP.
YEAH. DUMB AND TOTALLY USELESS THING. PFFT
I SURE HOPE THE FOOLISH, BUT CLEARLY WELL-INTENTIONED, PERSON WHO MADE IT REGRETS IT.
EVEN THOUGH IT PROBABLY TOOK HER--OR HIM, WHO KNOWS?--HOURS TO ERM GET IT JUST RIGHT.

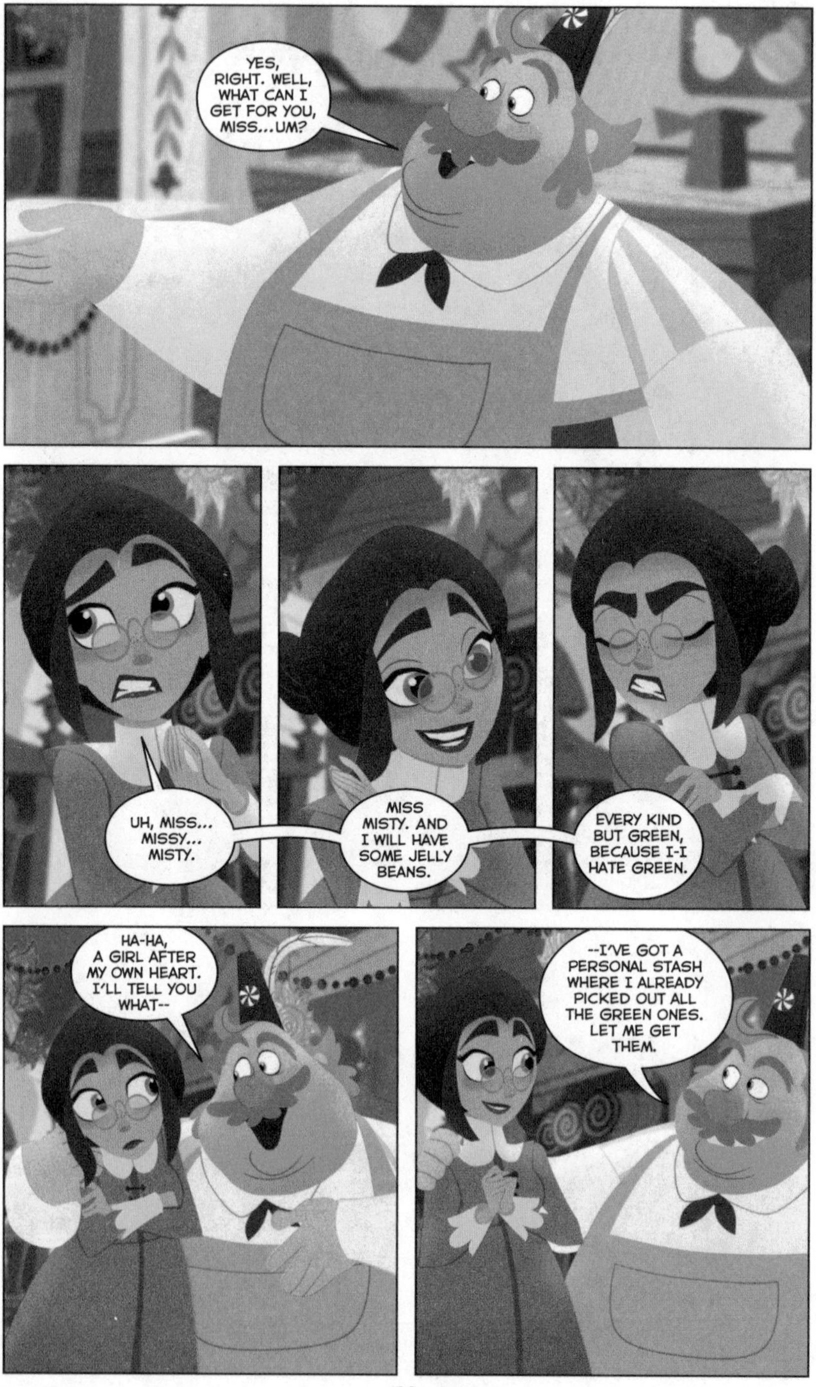
YES, RIGHT. WELL, WHAT CAN I GET FOR YOU, MISS...UM?
UH, MISS... MISSY... MISTY.
MISS MISTY. AND I WILL HAVE SOME JELLY BEANS.
EVERY KIND BUT GREEN, BECAUSE I-I HATE GREEN.
HA-HA, A GIRL AFTER MY OWN HEART. I'LL TELL YOU WHAT--
--I'VE GOT A PERSONAL STASH WHERE I ALREADY PICKED OUT ALL THE GREEN ONES. LET ME GET THEM.

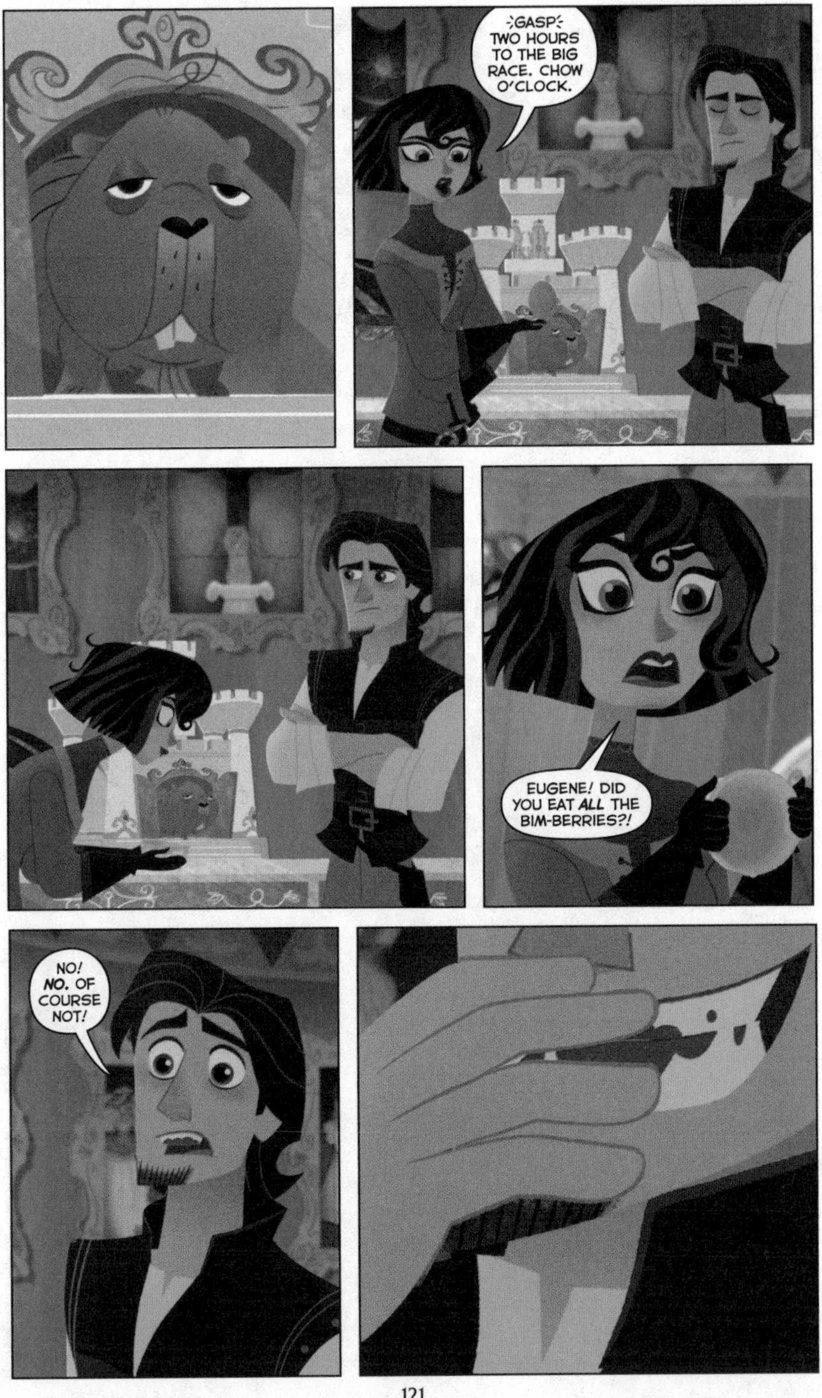

-GASP-
TWO HOURS TO THE BIG RACE. CHOW O'CLOCK.
EUGENE! DID YOU EAT *ALL* THE BIM-BERRIES?!
NO! ***NO.*** OF COURSE NOT!

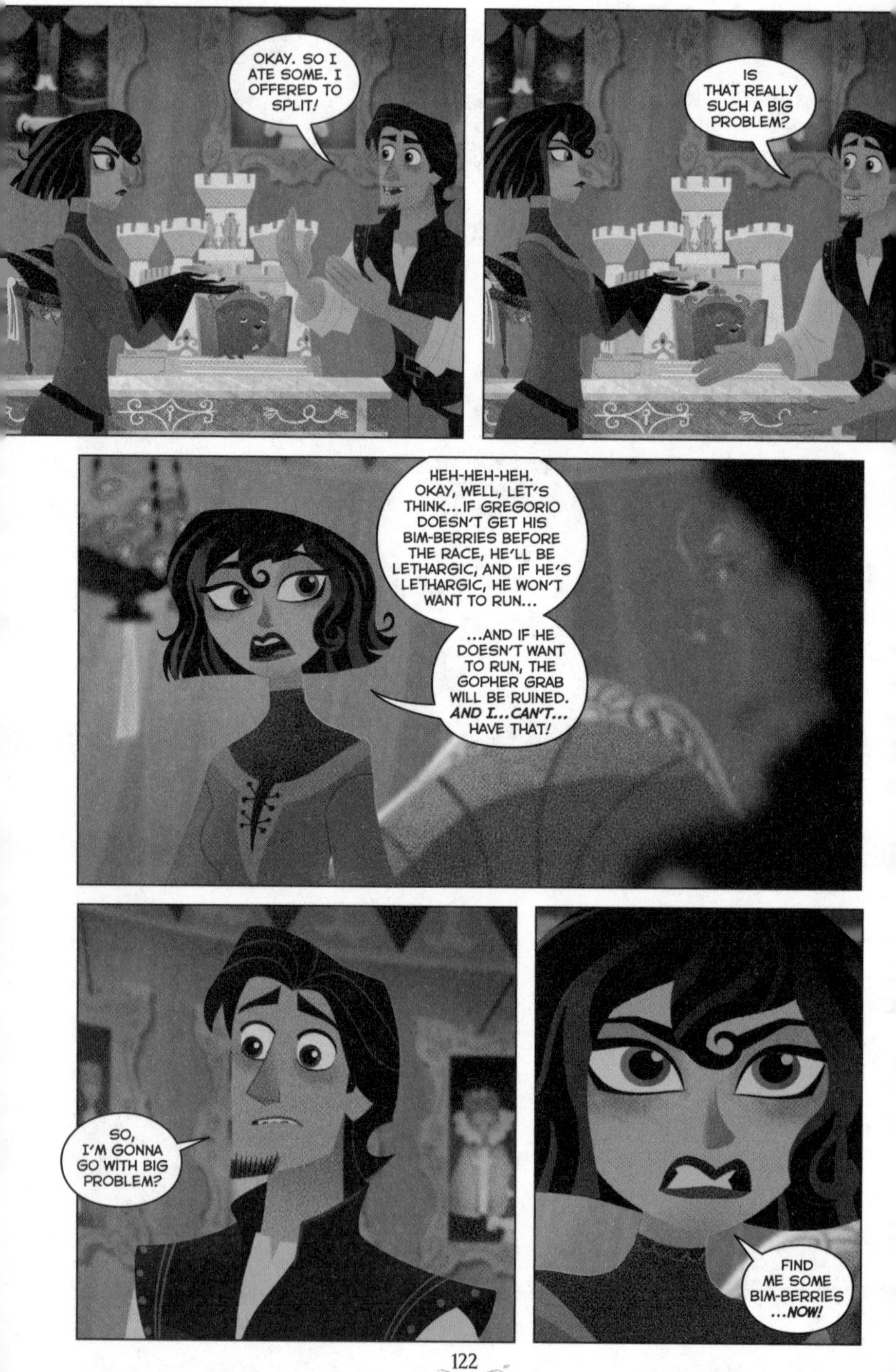

OKAY. SO I ATE SOME. I OFFERED TO SPLIT!
IS THAT REALLY SUCH A BIG PROBLEM?
HEH-HEH-HEH. OKAY, WELL, LET'S THINK...IF GREGORIO DOESN'T GET HIS BIM-BERRIES BEFORE THE RACE, HE'LL BE LETHARGIC, AND IF HE'S LETHARGIC, HE WON'T WANT TO RUN...
...AND IF HE DOESN'T WANT TO RUN, THE GOPHER GRAB WILL BE RUINED. *AND I...CAN'T...* HAVE THAT!
SO, I'M GONNA GO WITH BIG PROBLEM?
FIND ME SOME BIM-BERRIES *...NOW!*

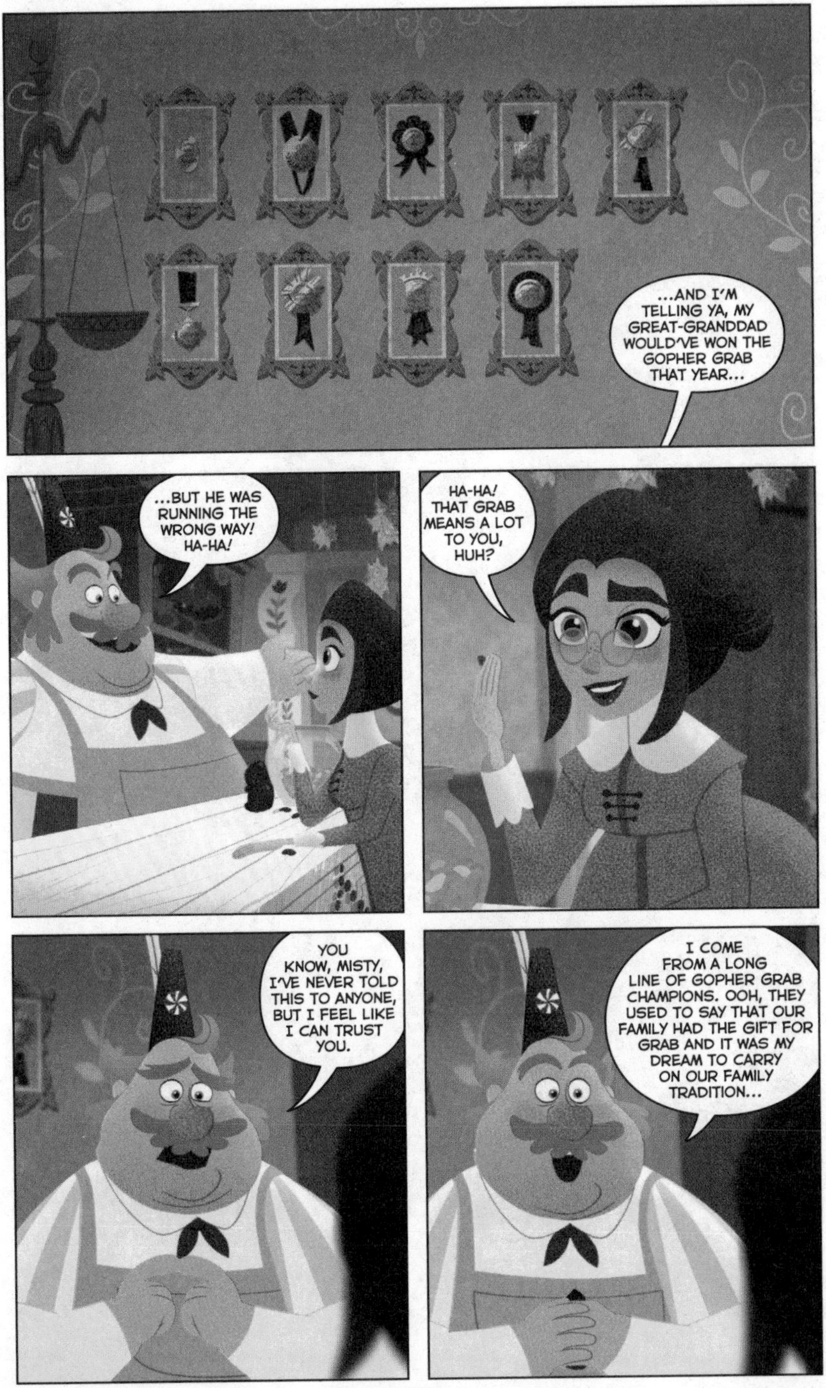
...AND I'M TELLING YA, MY GREAT-GRANDDAD WOULD'VE WON THE GOPHER GRAB THAT YEAR...
...BUT HE WAS RUNNING THE WRONG WAY! HA-HA!
HA-HA! THAT GRAB MEANS A LOT TO YOU, HUH?
YOU KNOW, MISTY, I'VE NEVER TOLD THIS TO ANYONE, BUT I FEEL LIKE I CAN TRUST YOU.
I COME FROM A LONG LINE OF GOPHER GRAB CHAMPIONS. OOH, THEY USED TO SAY THAT OUR FAMILY HAD THE GIFT FOR GRAB AND IT WAS MY DREAM TO CARRY ON OUR FAMILY TRADITION...

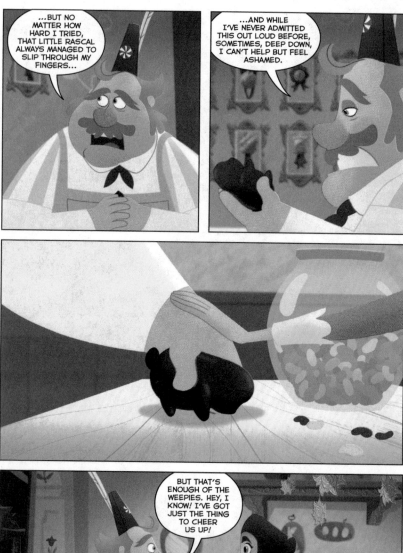

...BUT NO MATTER HOW HARD I TRIED, THAT LITTLE RASCAL ALWAYS MANAGED TO SLIP THROUGH MY FINGERS...

...AND WHILE I'VE NEVER ADMITTED THIS OUT LOUD BEFORE, SOMETIMES, DEEP DOWN, I CAN'T HELP BUT FEEL ASHAMED.

BUT THAT'S ENOUGH OF THE WEEPIES. HEY, I KNOW! I'VE GOT JUST THE THING TO CHEER US UP!

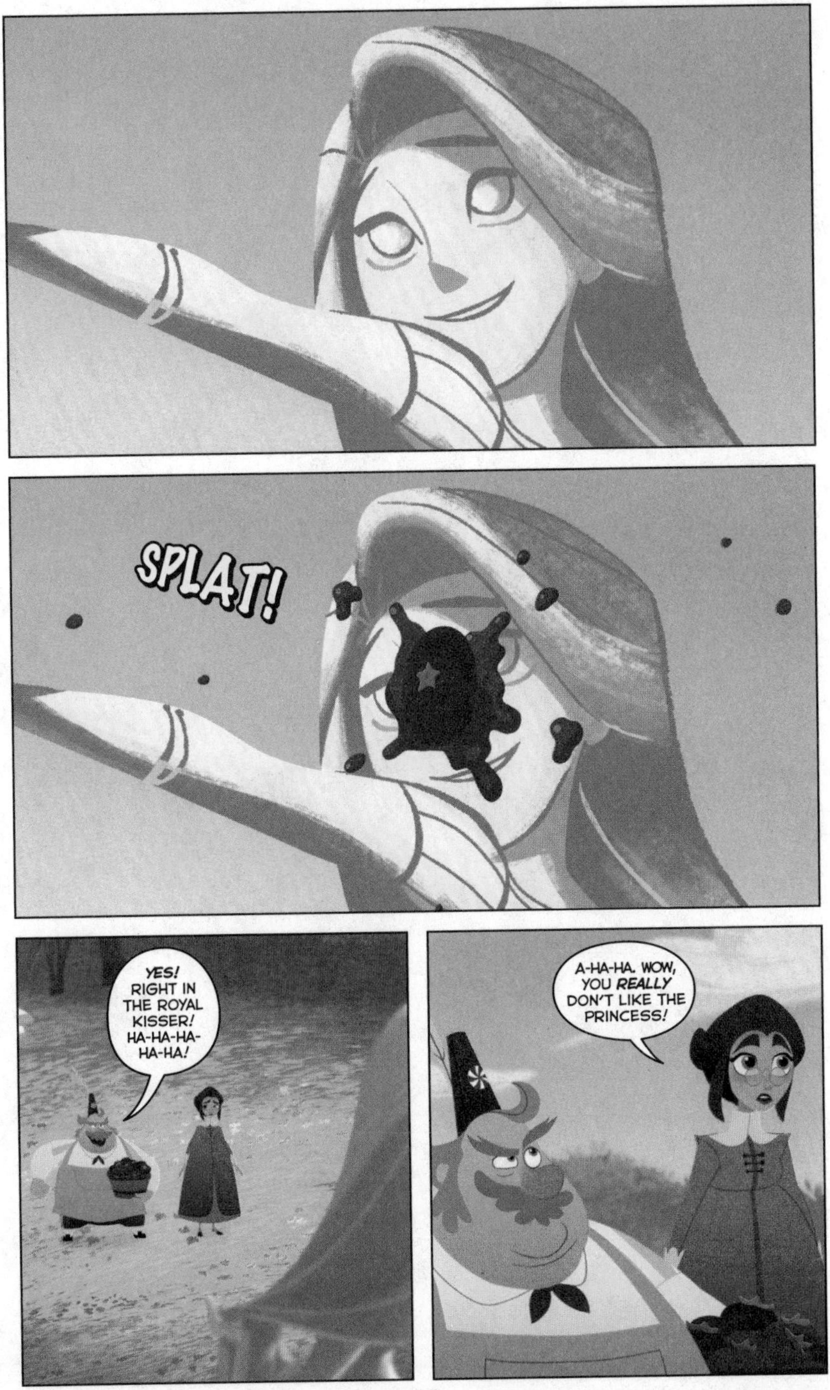
SPLAT!
YES! RIGHT IN THE ROYAL KISSER! HA-HA-HA-HA-HA!
A-HA-HA. WOW, YOU *REALLY* DON'T LIKE THE PRINCESS!

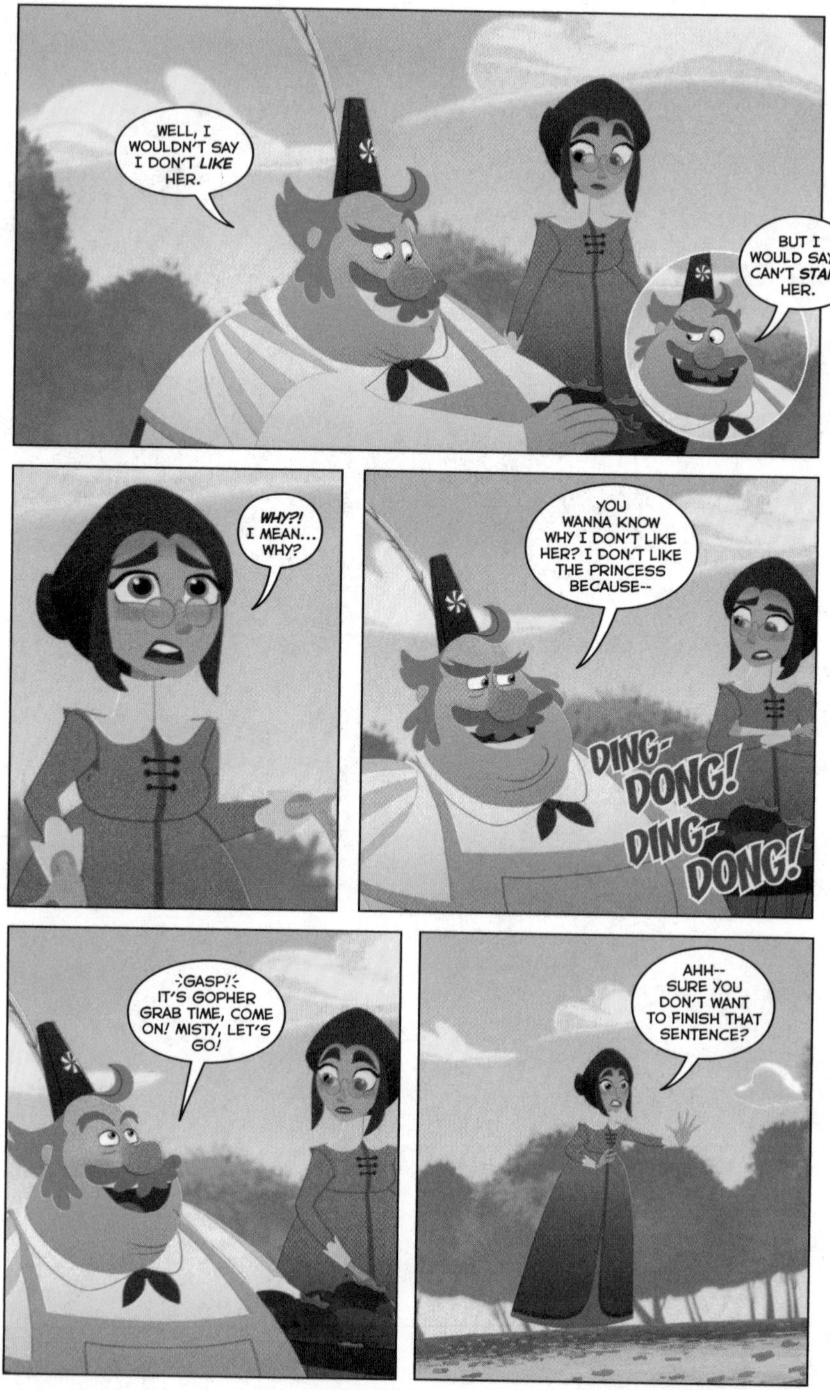
WELL, I WOULDN'T SAY I DON'T *LIKE* HER.
BUT I WOULD SAY I CAN'T *STAND* HER.
WHY?! I MEAN... WHY?
YOU WANNA KNOW WHY I DON'T LIKE HER? I DON'T LIKE THE PRINCESS BECAUSE--
DING-DONG! DING-DONG!
GASP! IT'S GOPHER GRAB TIME, COME ON! MISTY, LET'S GO!
AHH-- SURE YOU DON'T WANT TO FINISH THAT SENTENCE?

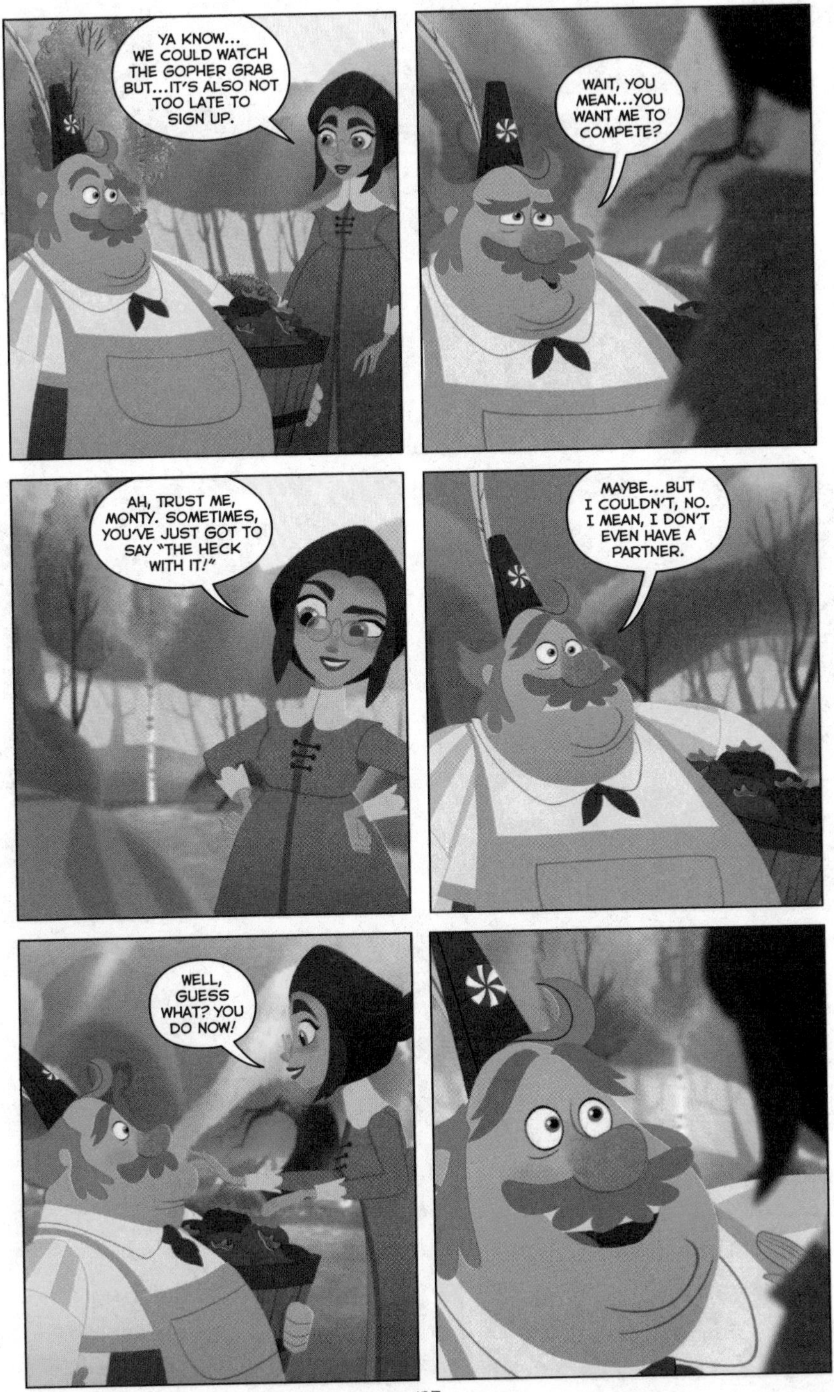
YA KNOW... WE COULD WATCH THE GOPHER GRAB BUT...IT'S ALSO NOT TOO LATE TO SIGN UP.
WAIT, YOU MEAN...YOU WANT ME TO COMPETE?
AH, TRUST ME, MONTY. SOMETIMES, YOU'VE JUST GOT TO SAY "THE HECK WITH IT!"
MAYBE...BUT I COULDN'T, NO. I MEAN, I DON'T EVEN HAVE A PARTNER.
WELL, GUESS WHAT? YOU DO NOW!

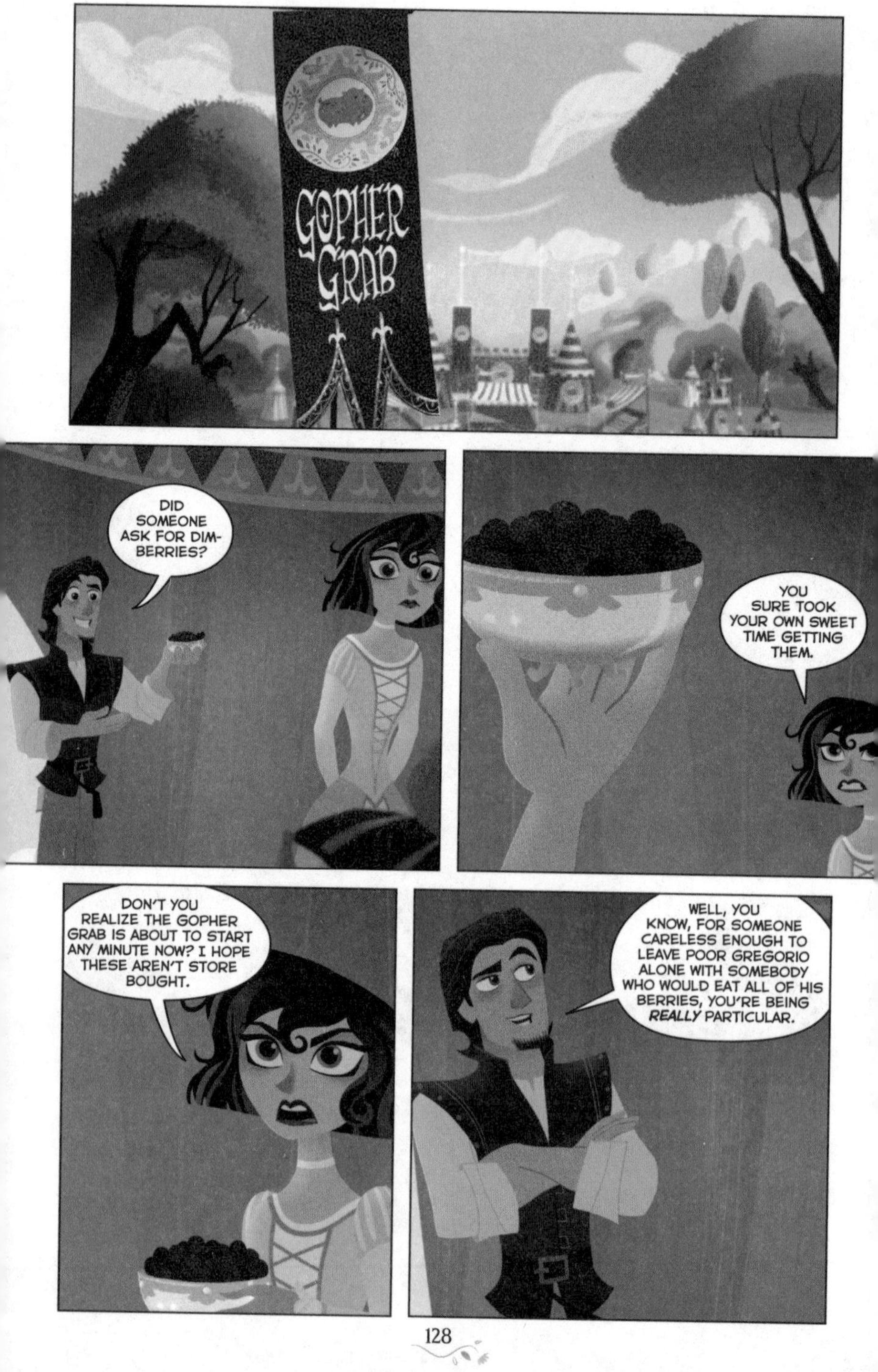
GOPHER GRAB
DID SOMEONE ASK FOR DIM-BERRIES?
YOU SURE TOOK YOUR OWN SWEET TIME GETTING THEM.
DON'T YOU REALIZE THE GOPHER GRAB IS ABOUT TO START ANY MINUTE NOW? I HOPE THESE AREN'T STORE BOUGHT.
WELL, YOU KNOW, FOR SOMEONE CARELESS ENOUGH TO LEAVE POOR GREGORIO ALONE WITH SOMEBODY WHO WOULD EAT ALL OF HIS BERRIES, YOU'RE BEING *REALLY* PARTICULAR.

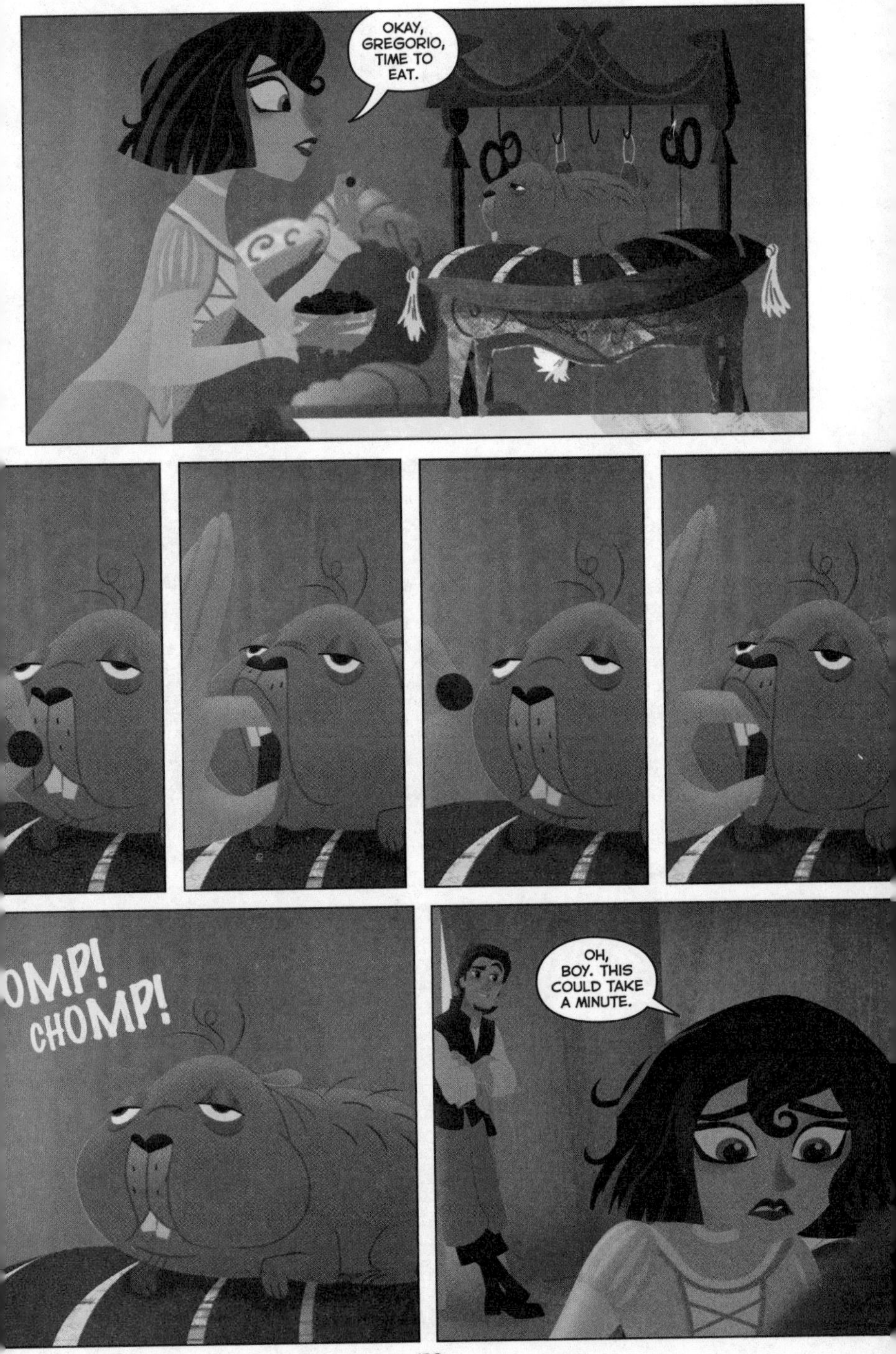
OKAY, GREGORIO, TIME TO EAT.
OMP! CHOMP!
OH, BOY. THIS COULD TAKE A MINUTE.

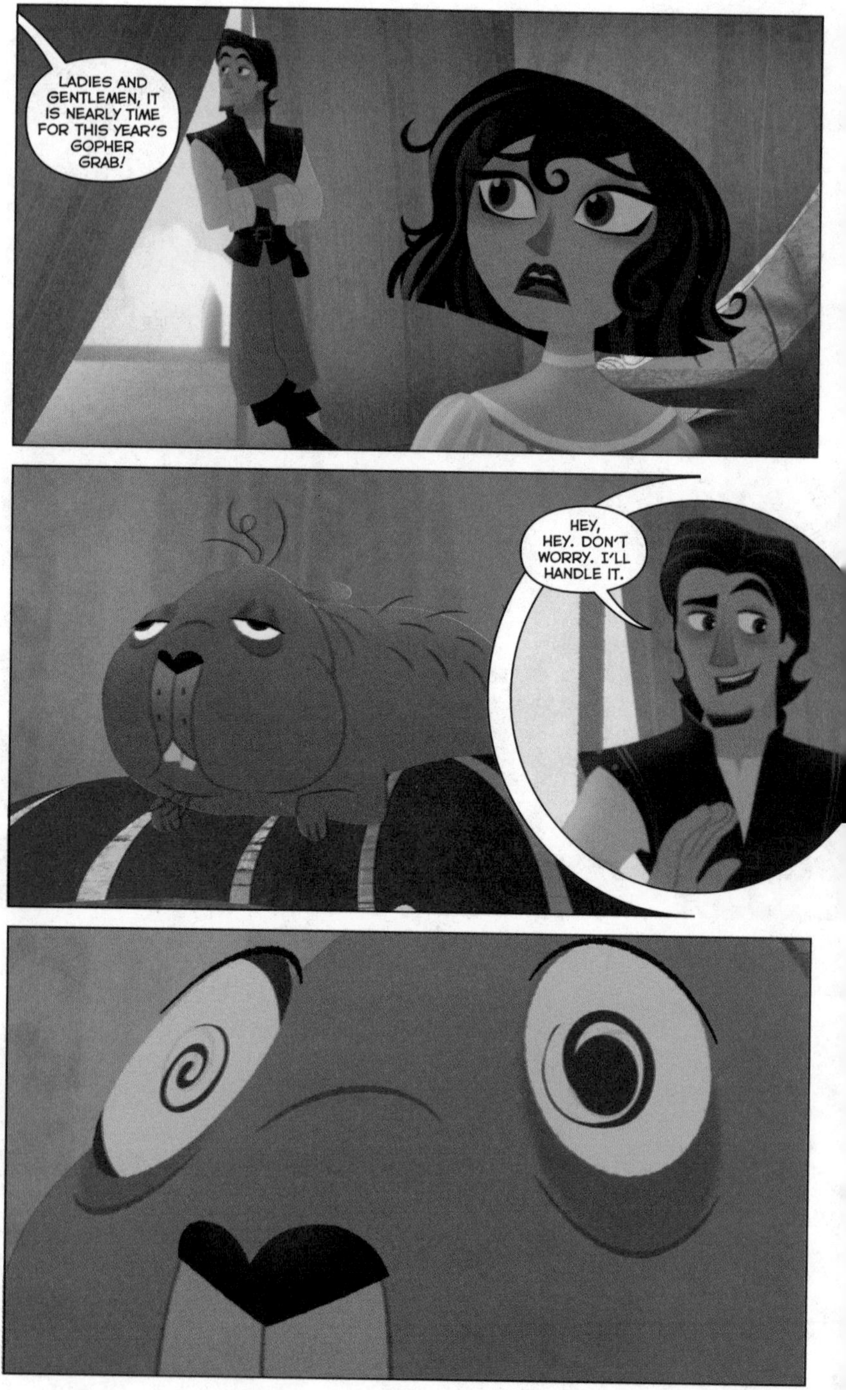
LADIES AND GENTLEMEN, IT IS NEARLY TIME FOR THIS YEAR'S GOPHER GRAB!
HEY, HEY. DON'T WORRY. I'LL HANDLE IT.

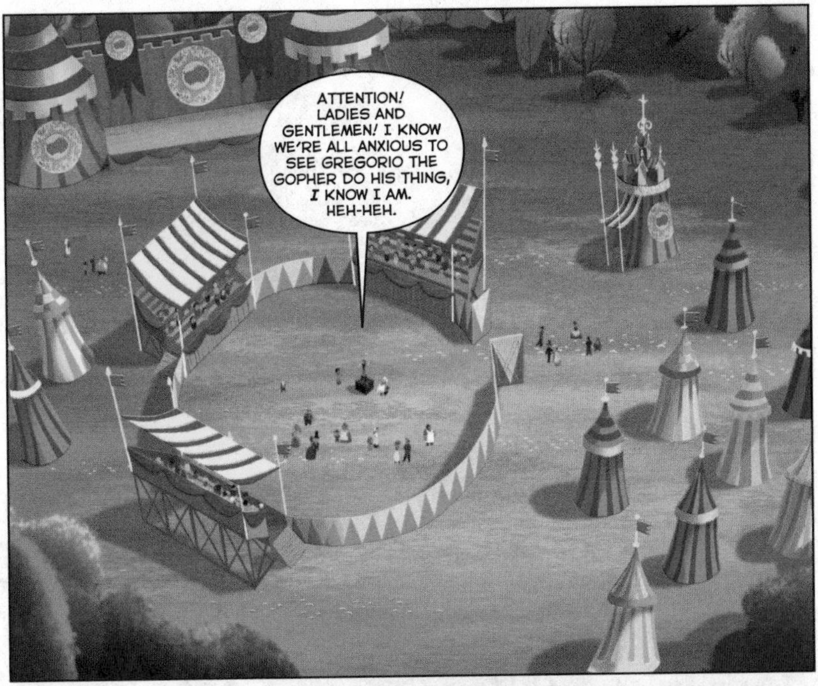
ATTENTION! LADIES AND GENTLEMEN! I KNOW WE'RE ALL ANXIOUS TO SEE GREGORIO THE GOPHER DO HIS THING, *I* KNOW I AM. HEH-HEH.

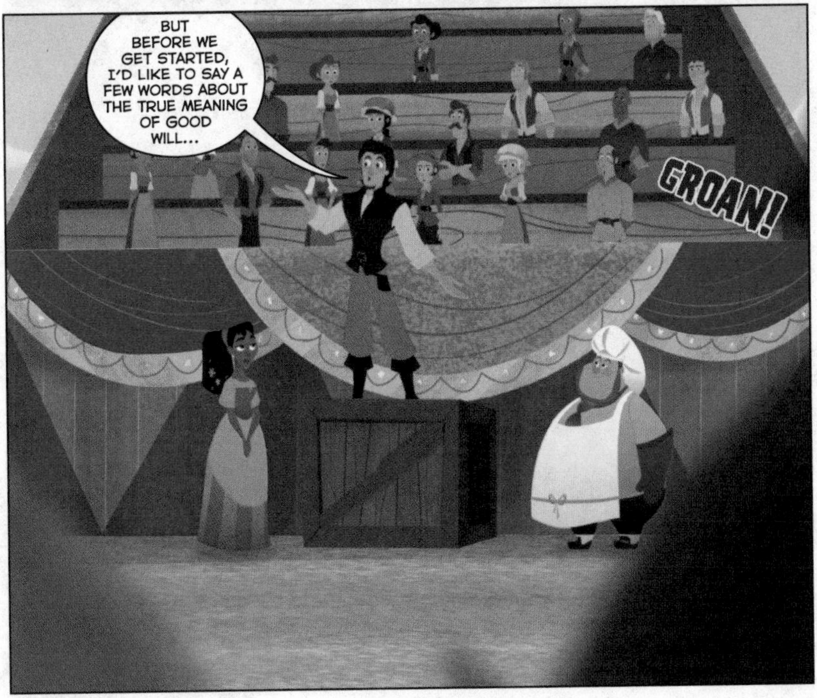
BUT BEFORE WE GET STARTED, I'D LIKE TO SAY A FEW WORDS ABOUT THE TRUE MEANING OF GOOD WILL...
GROAN!

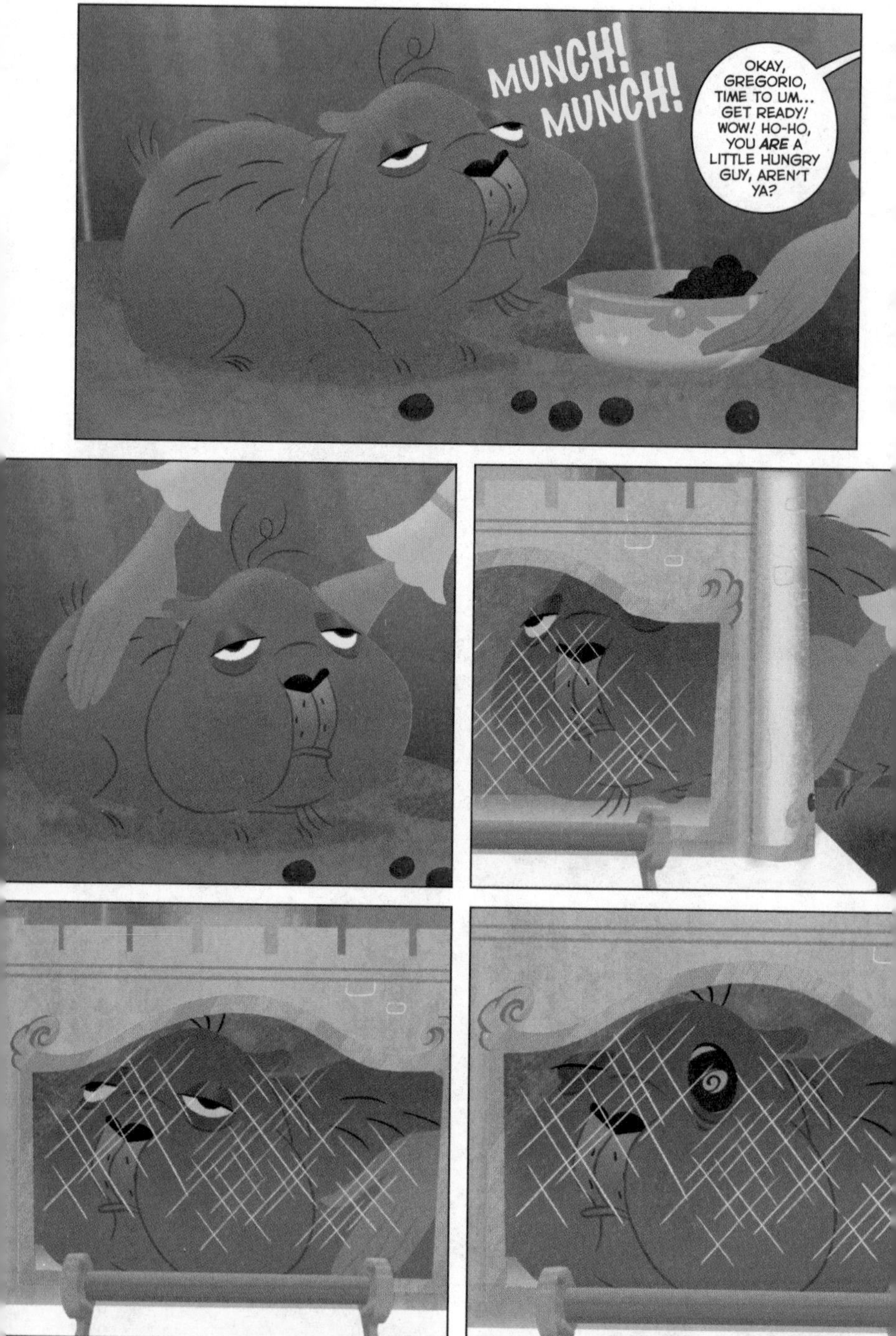
MUNCH! MUNCH!
OKAY, GREGORIO, TIME TO UM... GET READY! WOW! HO-HO, YOU *ARE* A LITTLE HUNGRY GUY, AREN'T YA?

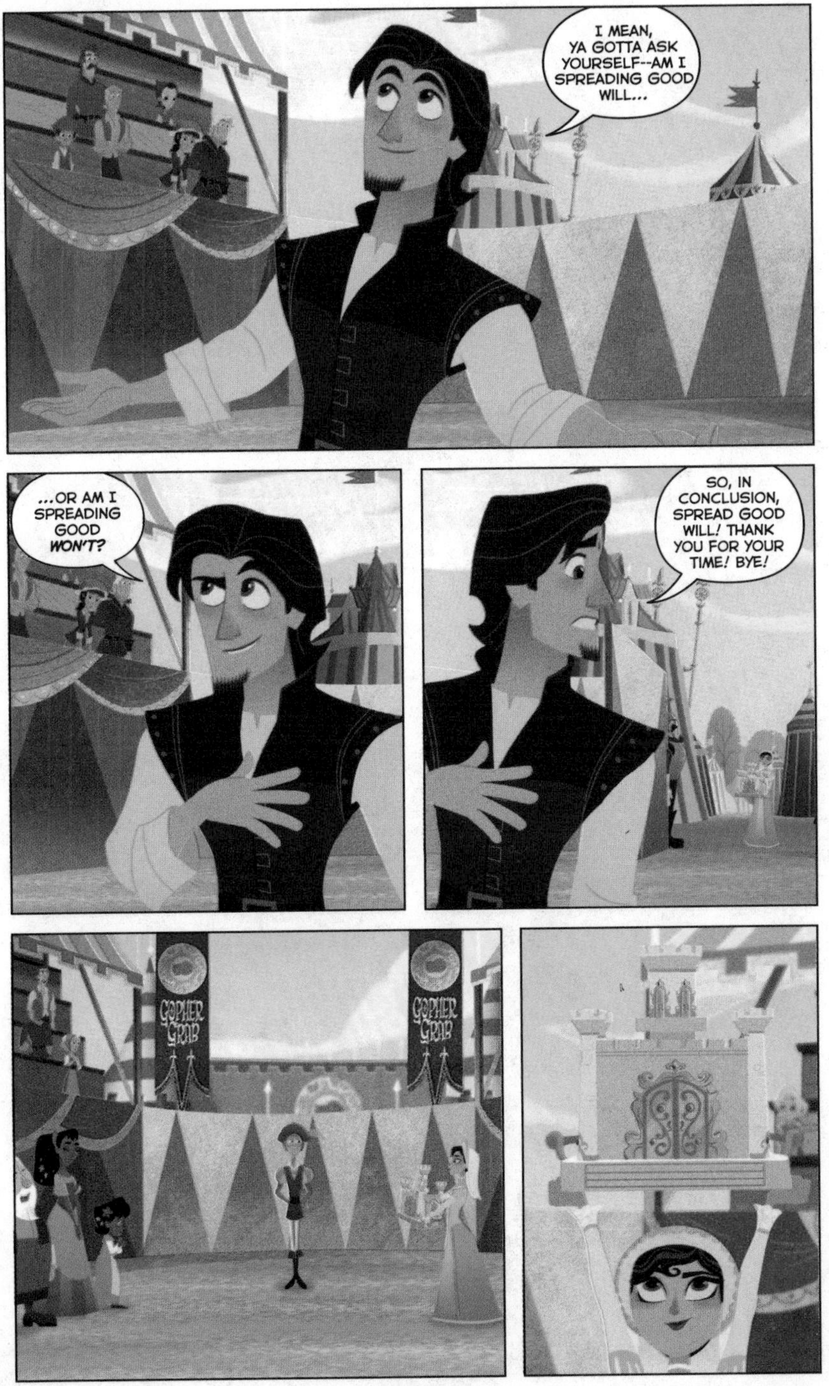
I MEAN, YA GOTTA ASK YOURSELF--AM I SPREADING GOOD WILL...
...OR AM I SPREADING GOOD *WON'T?*
SO, IN CONCLUSION, SPREAD GOOD WILL! THANK YOU FOR YOUR TIME! BYE!
GOPHER GRAB
GOPHER GRAB

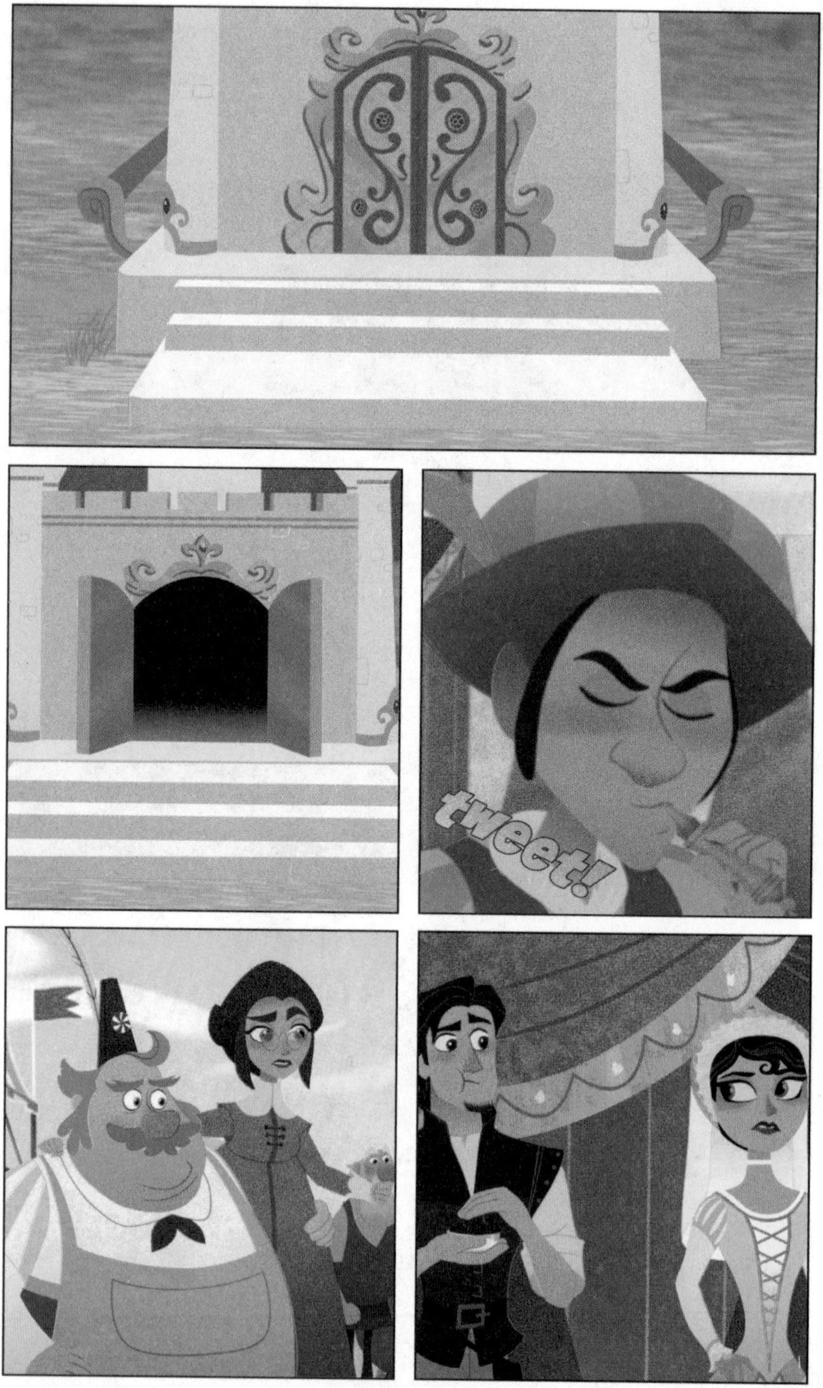
tweet!

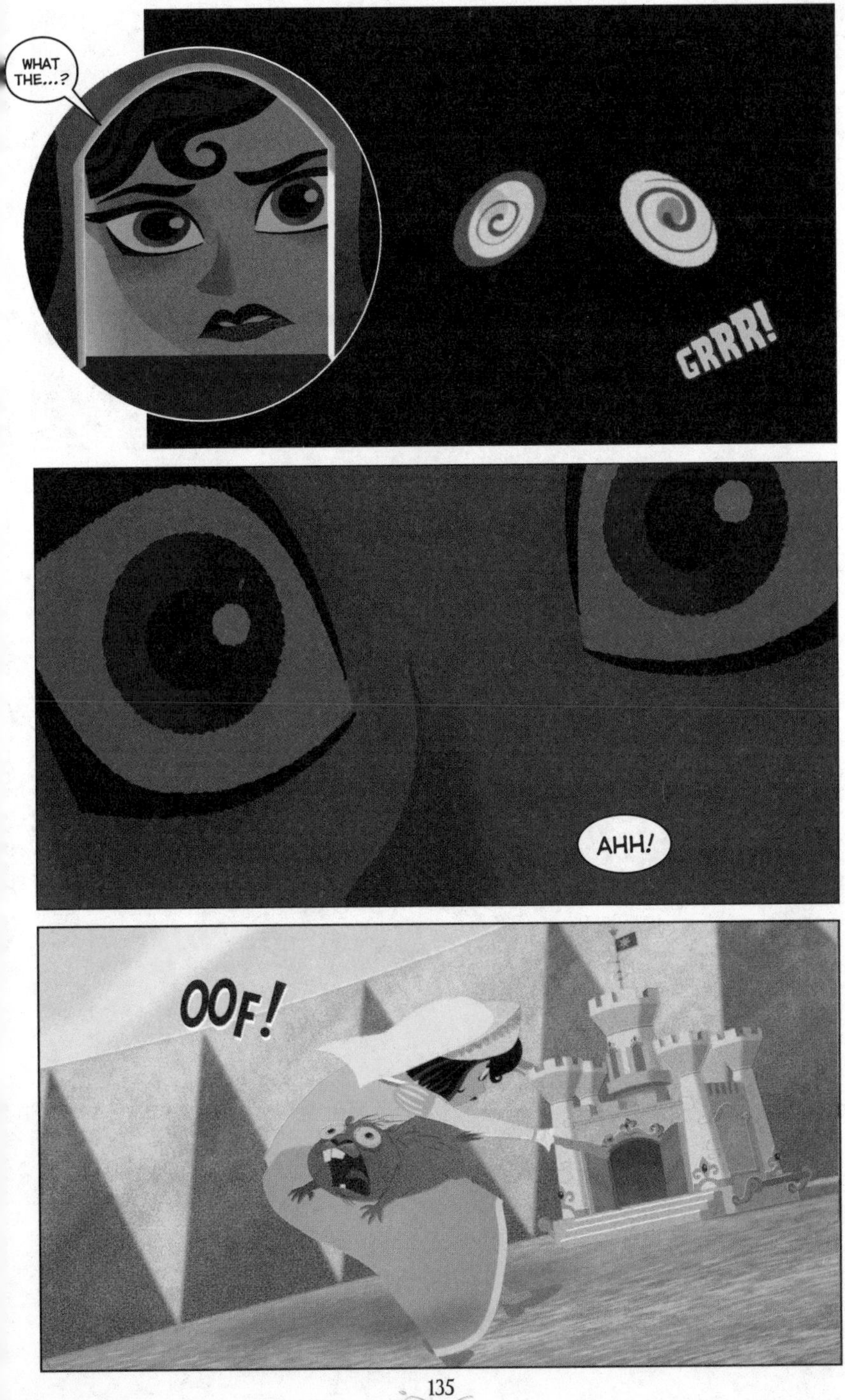
WHAT THE...?
GRRR!
AHH!
OOF!

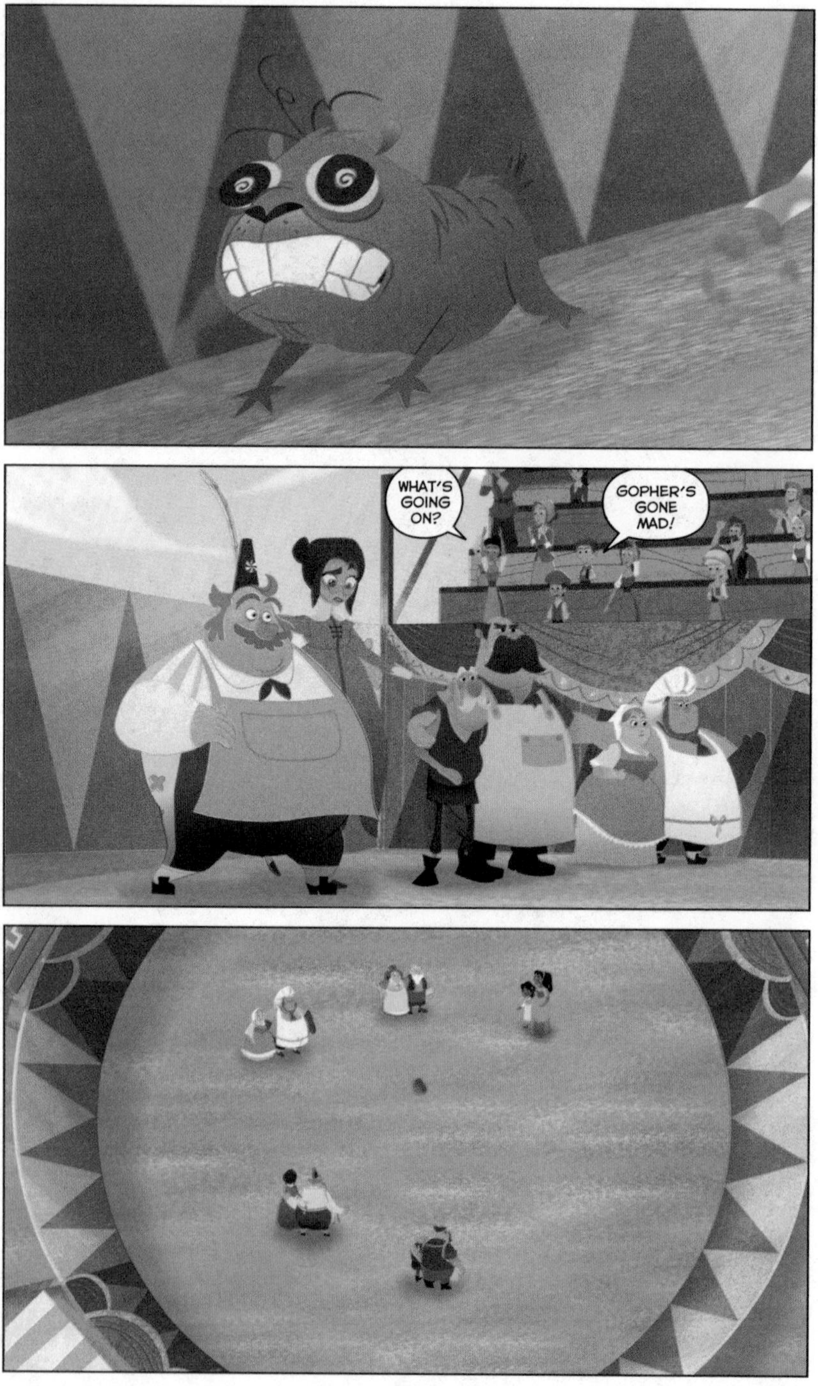
WHAT'S GOING ON?
GOPHER'S GONE MAD!

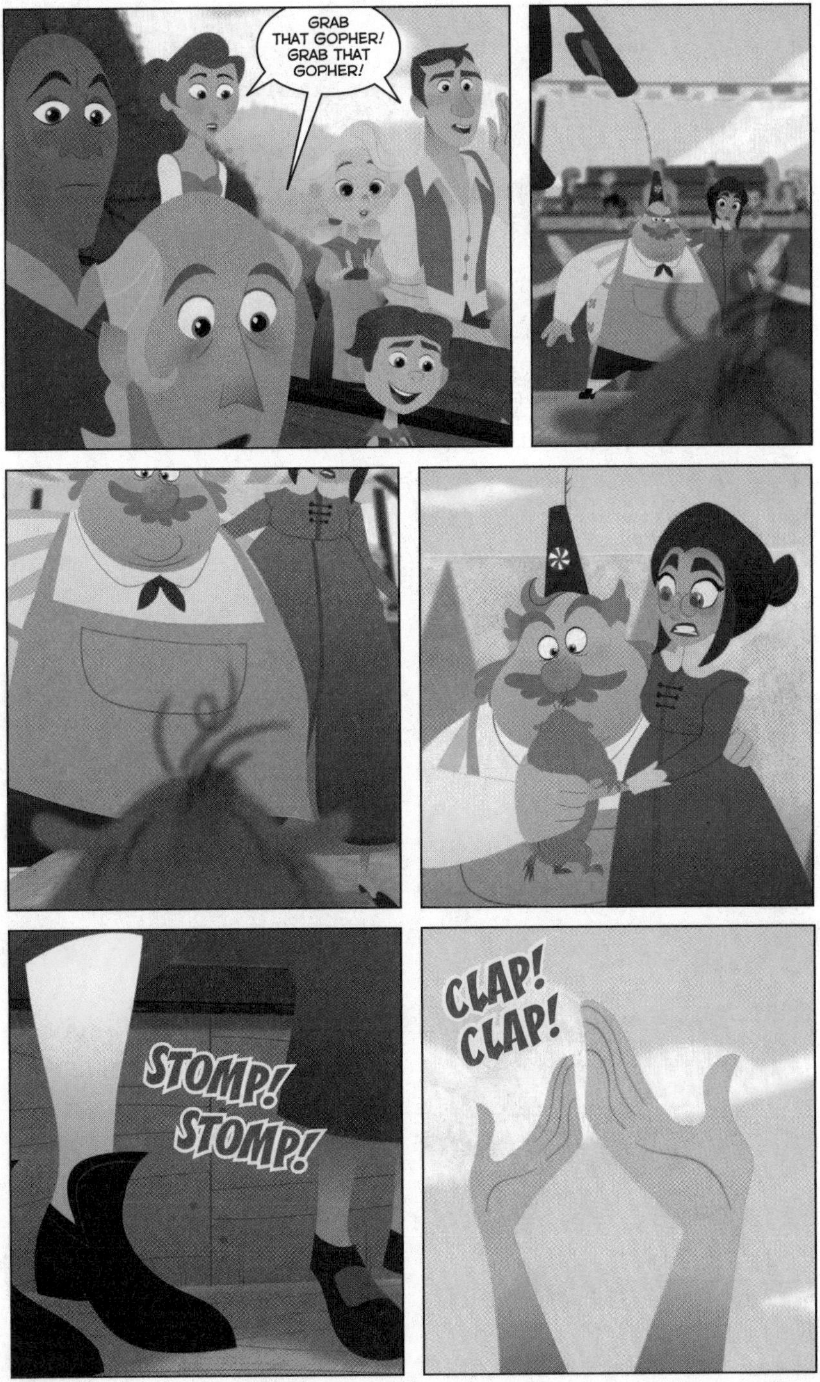
GRAB THAT GOPHER! GRAB THAT GOPHER!
STOMP! STOMP!
CLAP! CLAP!

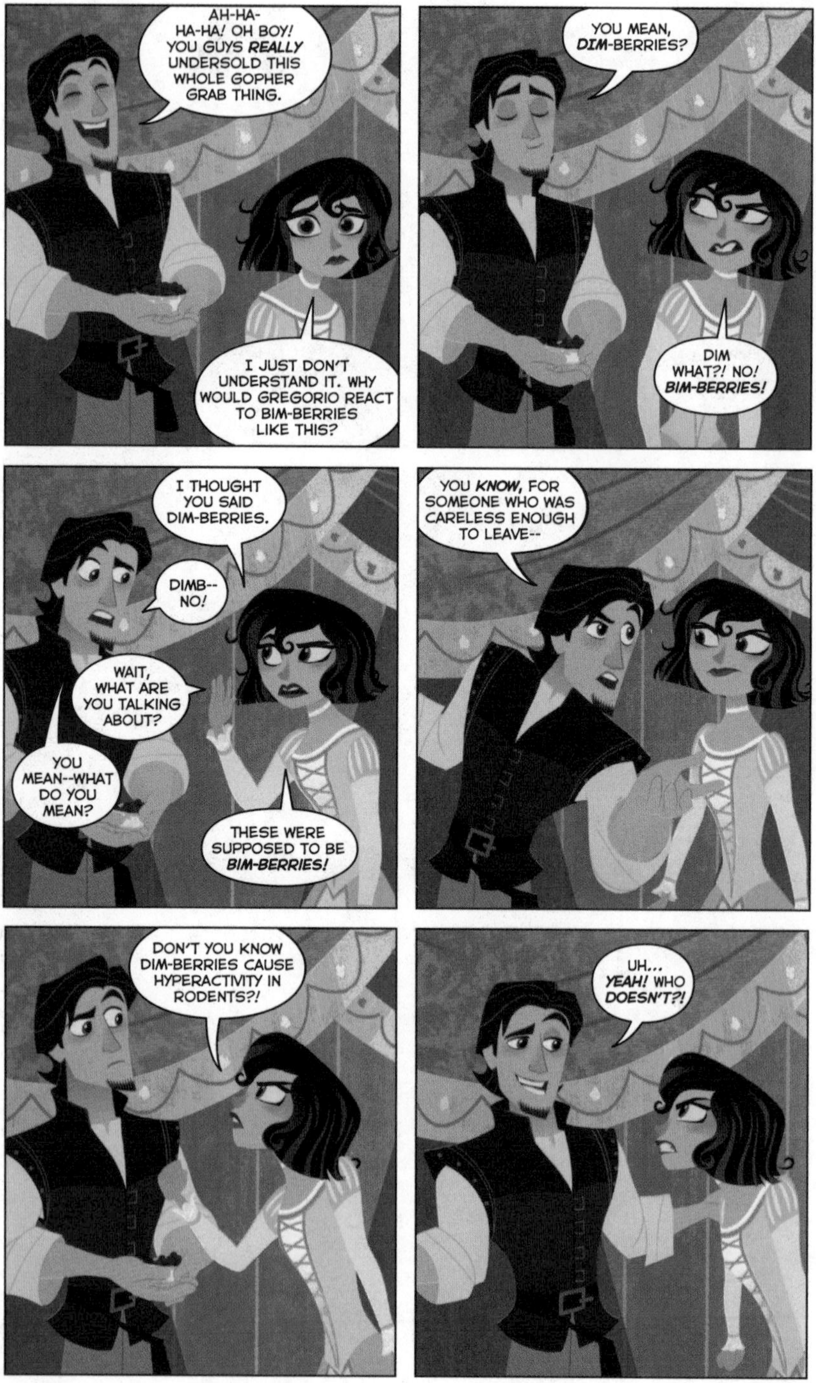
AH-HA-HA-HA! OH BOY! YOU GUYS REALLY UNDERSOLD THIS WHOLE GOPHER GRAB THING.
I JUST DON'T UNDERSTAND IT. WHY WOULD GREGORIO REACT TO BIM-BERRIES LIKE THIS?
YOU MEAN, DIM-BERRIES?
DIM WHAT?! NO! BIM-BERRIES!
I THOUGHT YOU SAID DIM-BERRIES.
DIMB-- NO!
WAIT, WHAT ARE YOU TALKING ABOUT?
YOU MEAN--WHAT DO YOU MEAN?
THESE WERE SUPPOSED TO BE BIM-BERRIES!
YOU KNOW, FOR SOMEONE WHO WAS CARELESS ENOUGH TO LEAVE--
DON'T YOU KNOW DIM-BERRIES CAUSE HYPERACTIVITY IN RODENTS?!
UH... YEAH! WHO DOESN'T?!

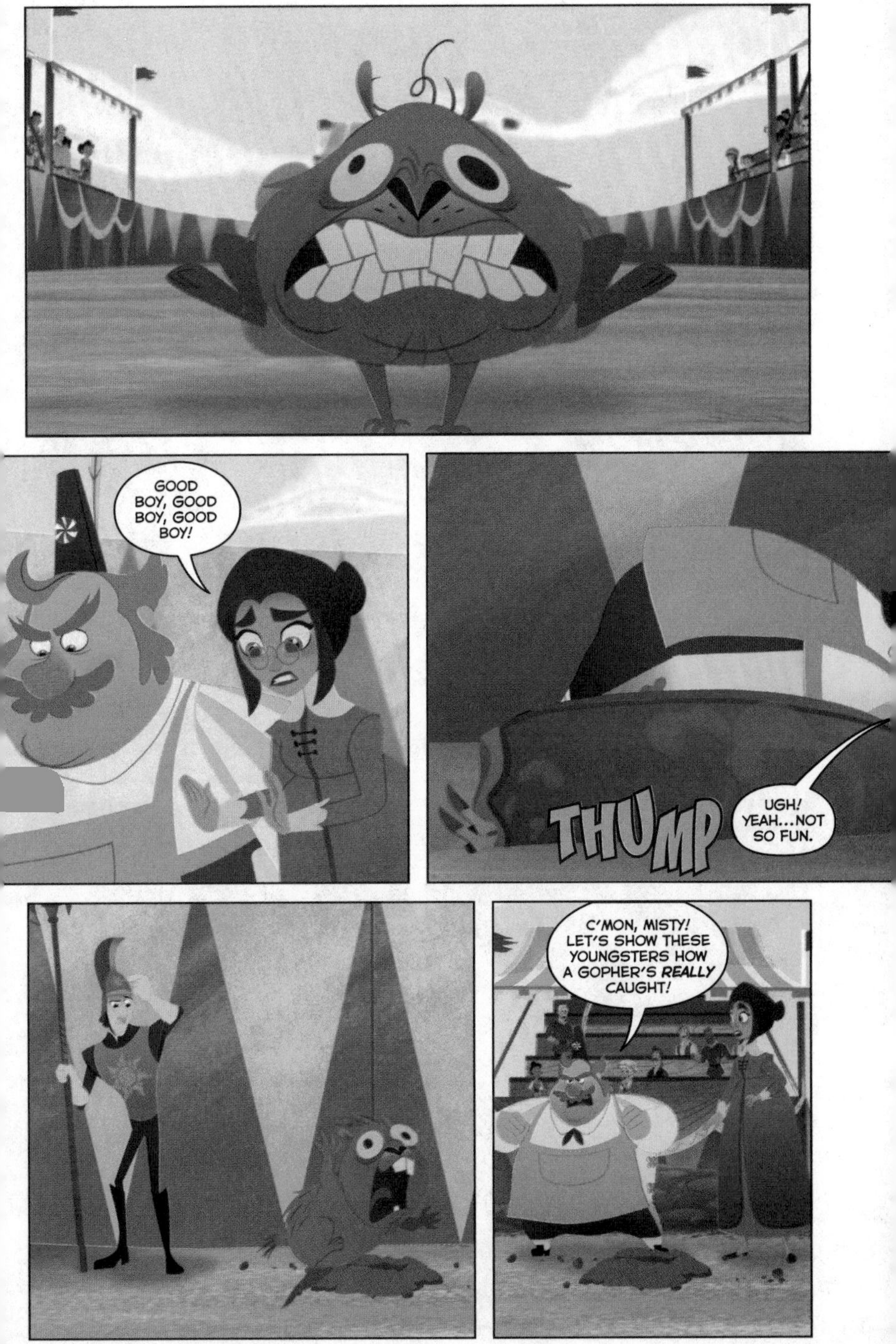
GOOD BOY, GOOD BOY, GOOD BOY!
THUMP
UGH! YEAH...NOT SO FUN.
C'MON, MISTY! LET'S SHOW THESE YOUNGSTERS HOW A GOPHER'S *REALLY* CAUGHT!

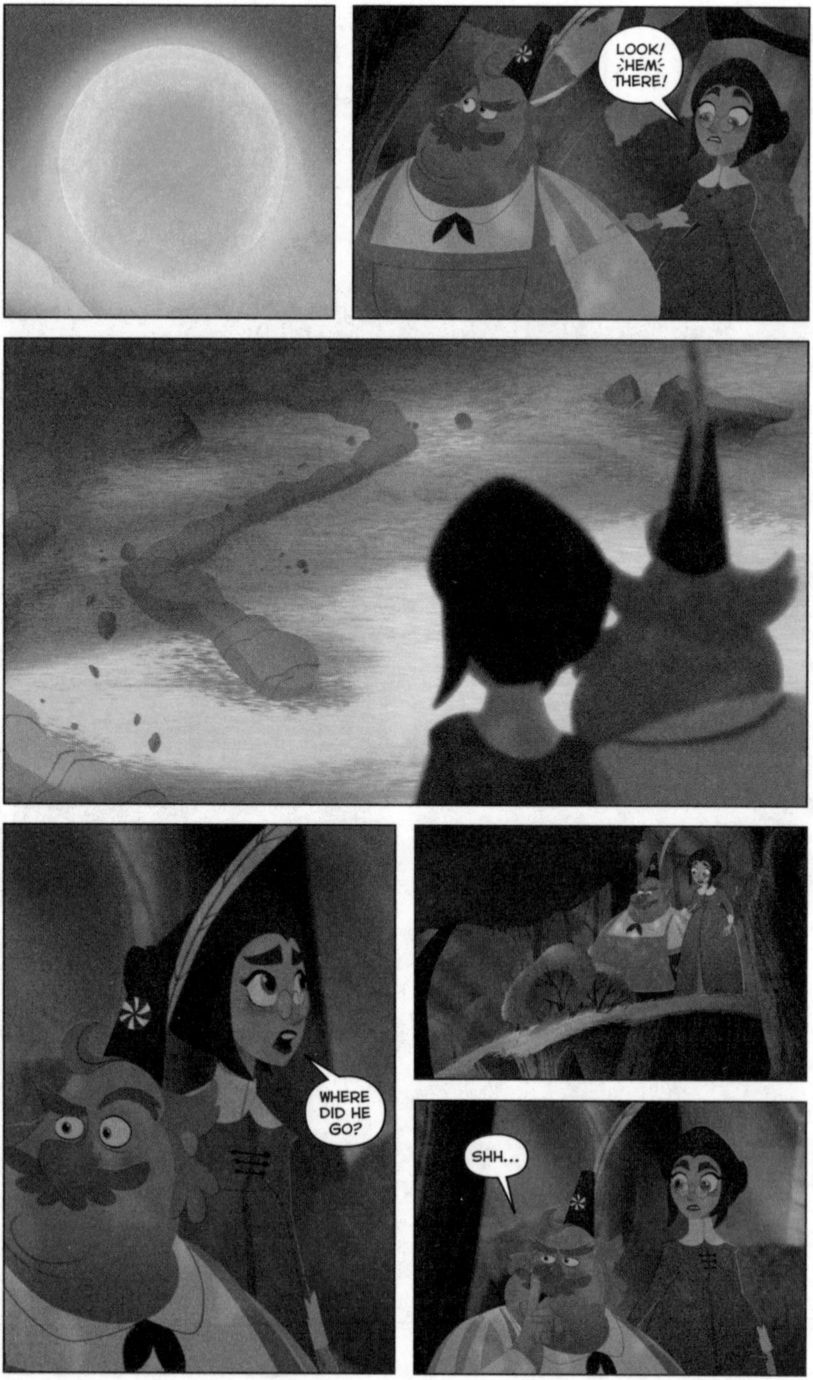
LOOK! THEM THERE!
WHERE DID HE GO?
SHH...

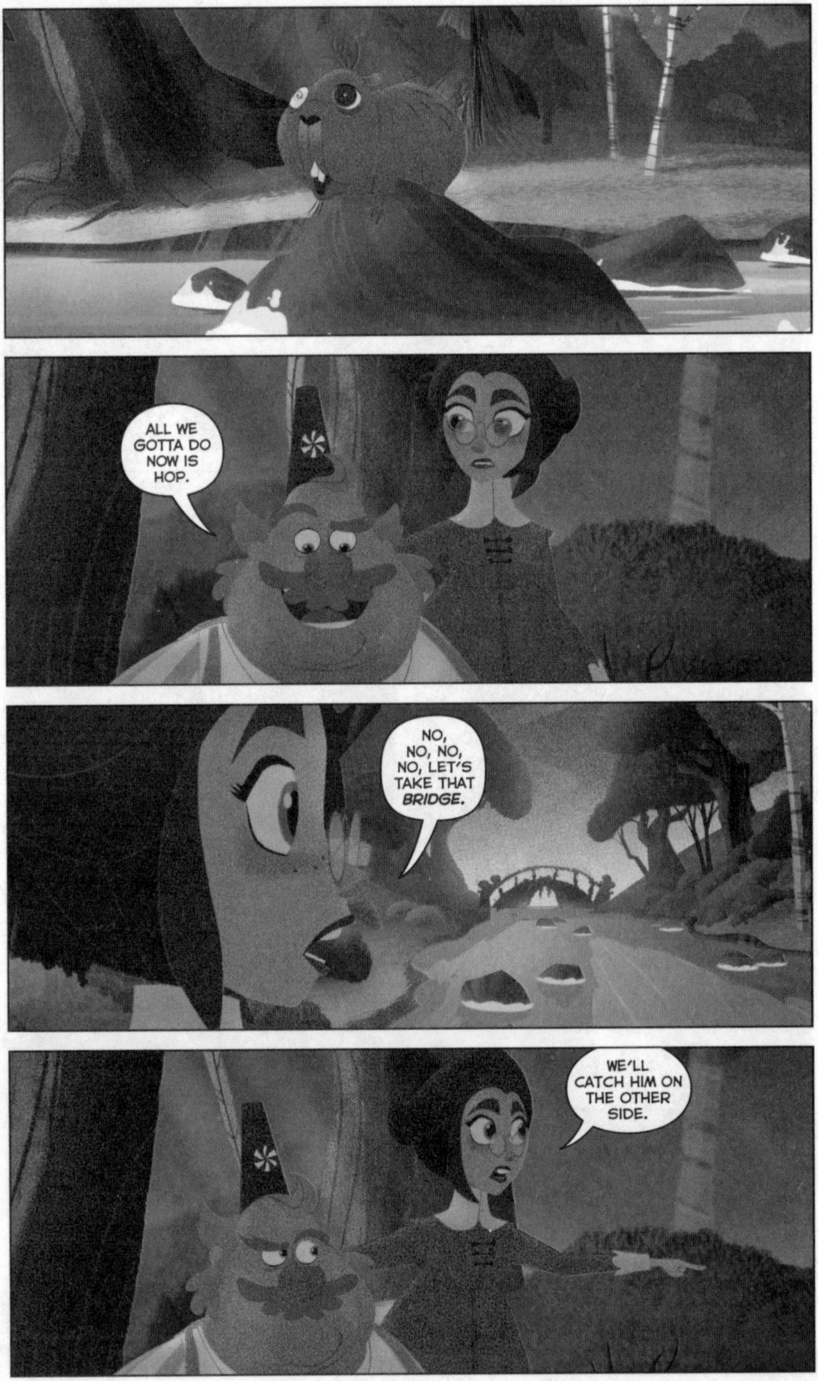
ALL WE GOTTA DO NOW IS HOP.
NO, NO, NO, NO, LET'S TAKE THAT *BRIDGE*.
WE'LL CATCH HIM ON THE OTHER SIDE.

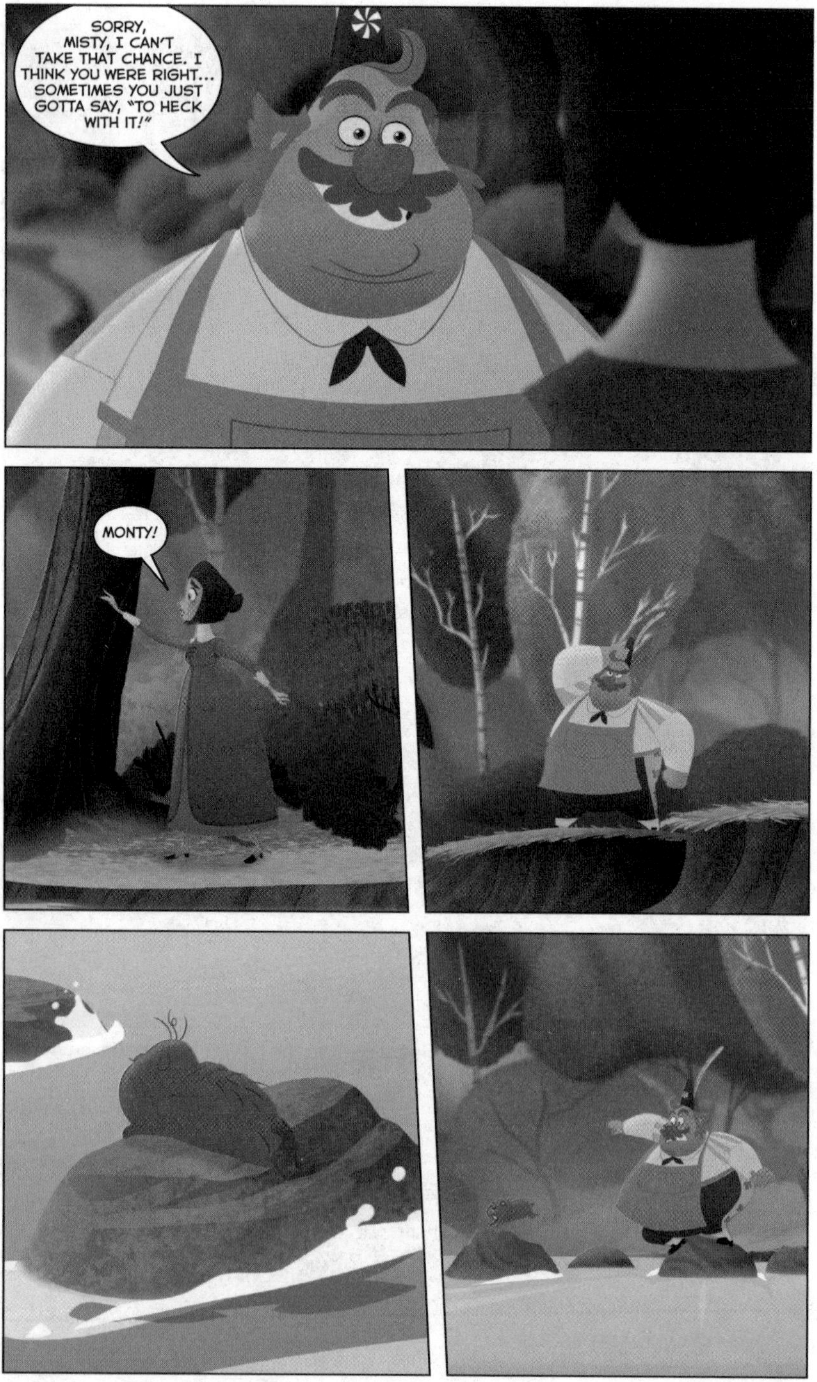
SORRY, MISTY, I CAN'T TAKE THAT CHANCE. I THINK YOU WERE RIGHT... SOMETIMES YOU JUST GOTTA SAY, "TO HECK WITH IT!"
MONTY!

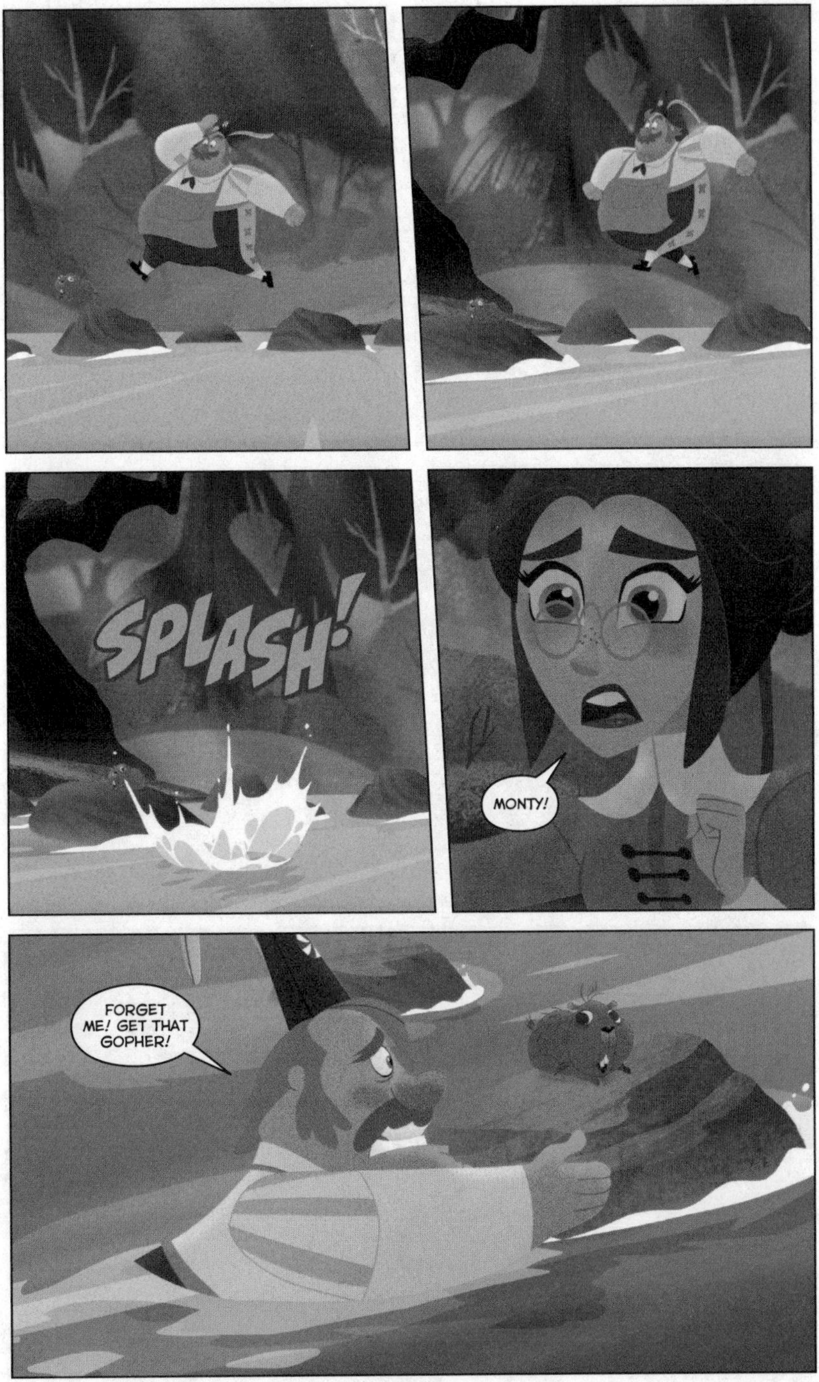
SPLASH!
MONTY!
FORGET ME! GET THAT GOPHER!

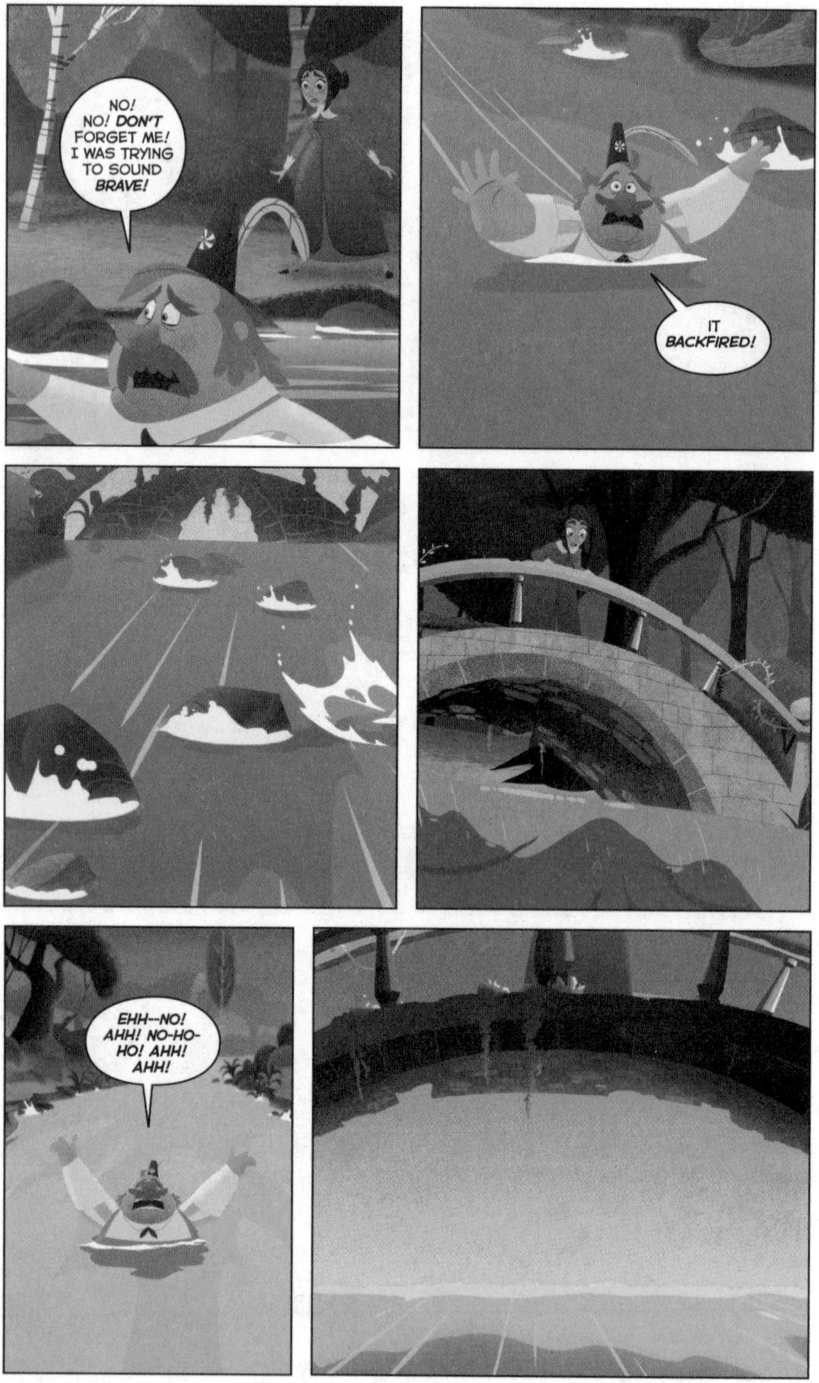
NO!
NO! DON'T FORGET ME! I WAS TRYING TO SOUND BRAVE!
IT BACKFIRED!
EHH--NO! AHH! NO-HO-HO! AHH! AHH!

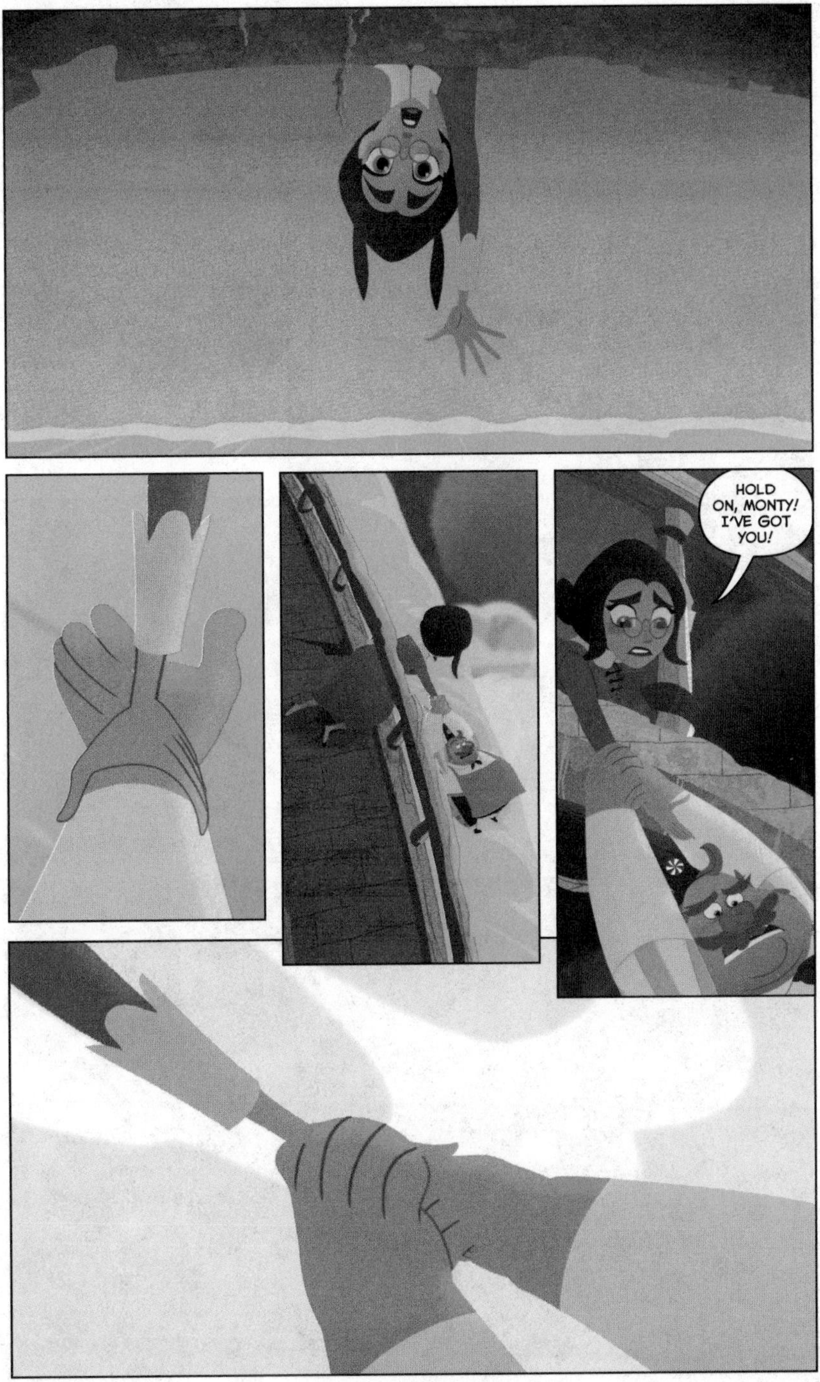
HOLD ON, MONTY! I'VE GOT YOU!

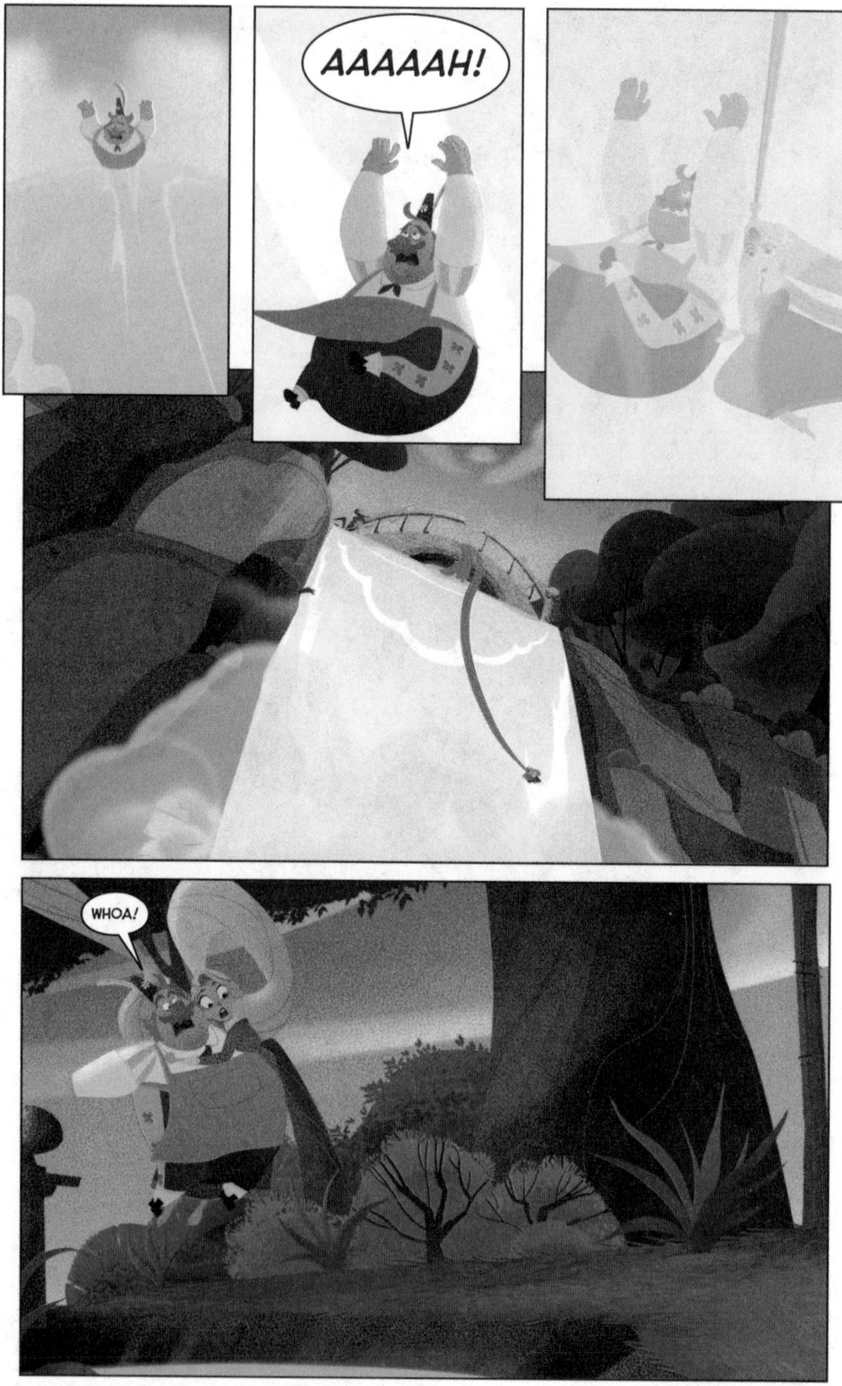
AAAAAH!
WHOA!

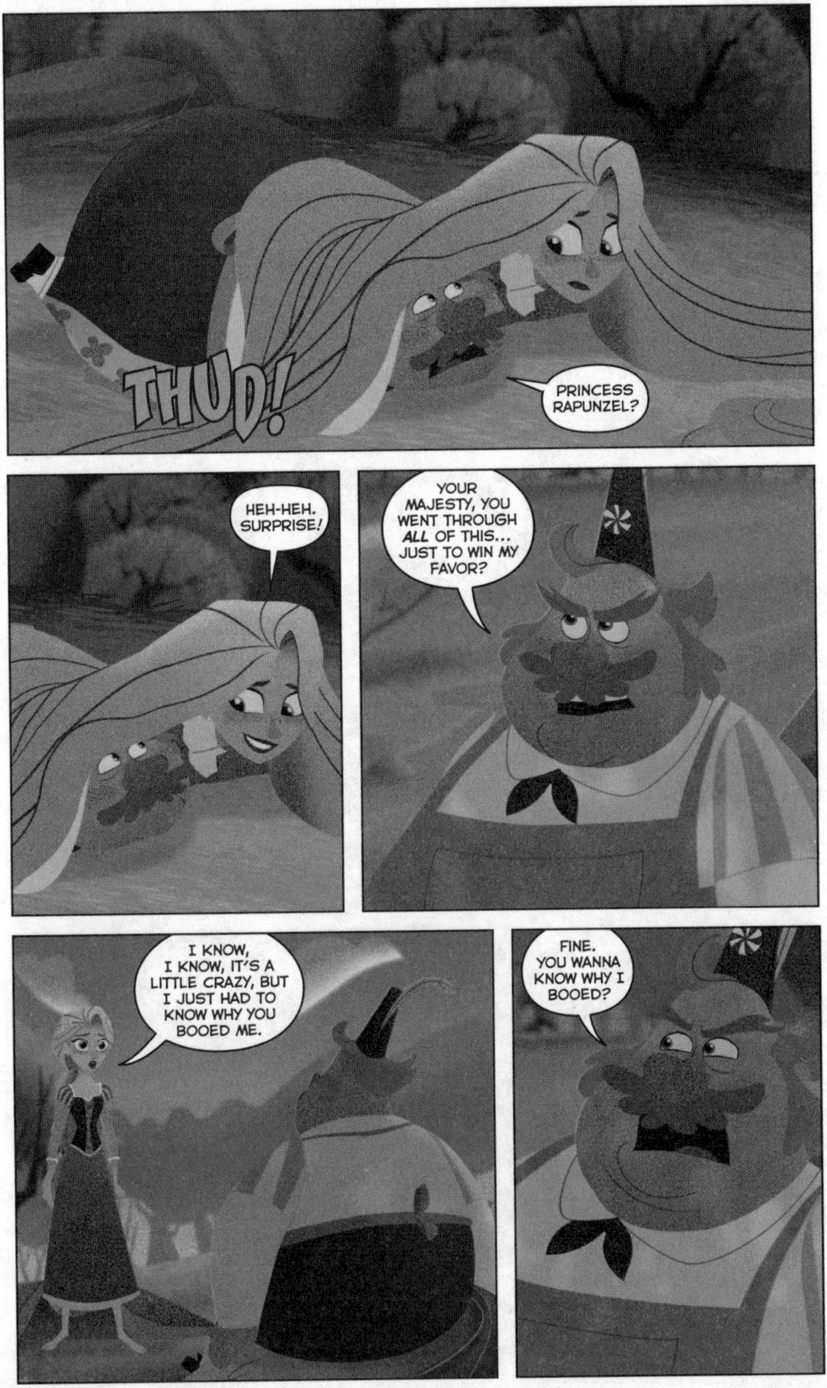
THUD!
PRINCESS RAPUNZEL?
HEH-HEH. SURPRISE!
YOUR MAJESTY, YOU WENT THROUGH *ALL* OF THIS... JUST TO WIN MY FAVOR?
I KNOW, I KNOW, IT'S A LITTLE CRAZY, BUT I JUST HAD TO KNOW WHY YOU BOOED ME.
FINE. YOU WANNA KNOW WHY I BOOED?

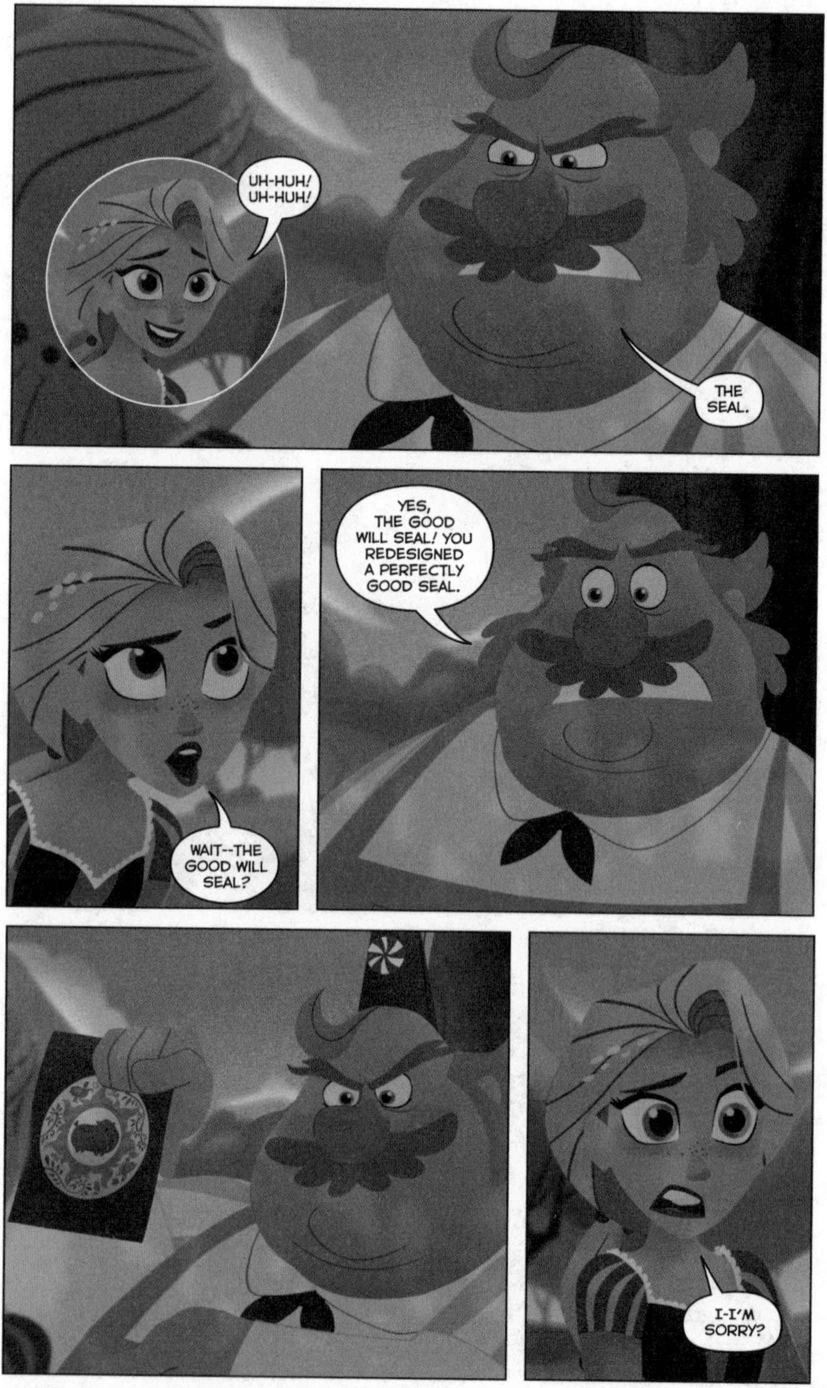
UH-HUH! UH-HUH!
THE SEAL.
WAIT--THE GOOD WILL SEAL?
YES, THE GOOD WILL SEAL! YOU REDESIGNED A PERFECTLY GOOD SEAL.
I-I'M SORRY?

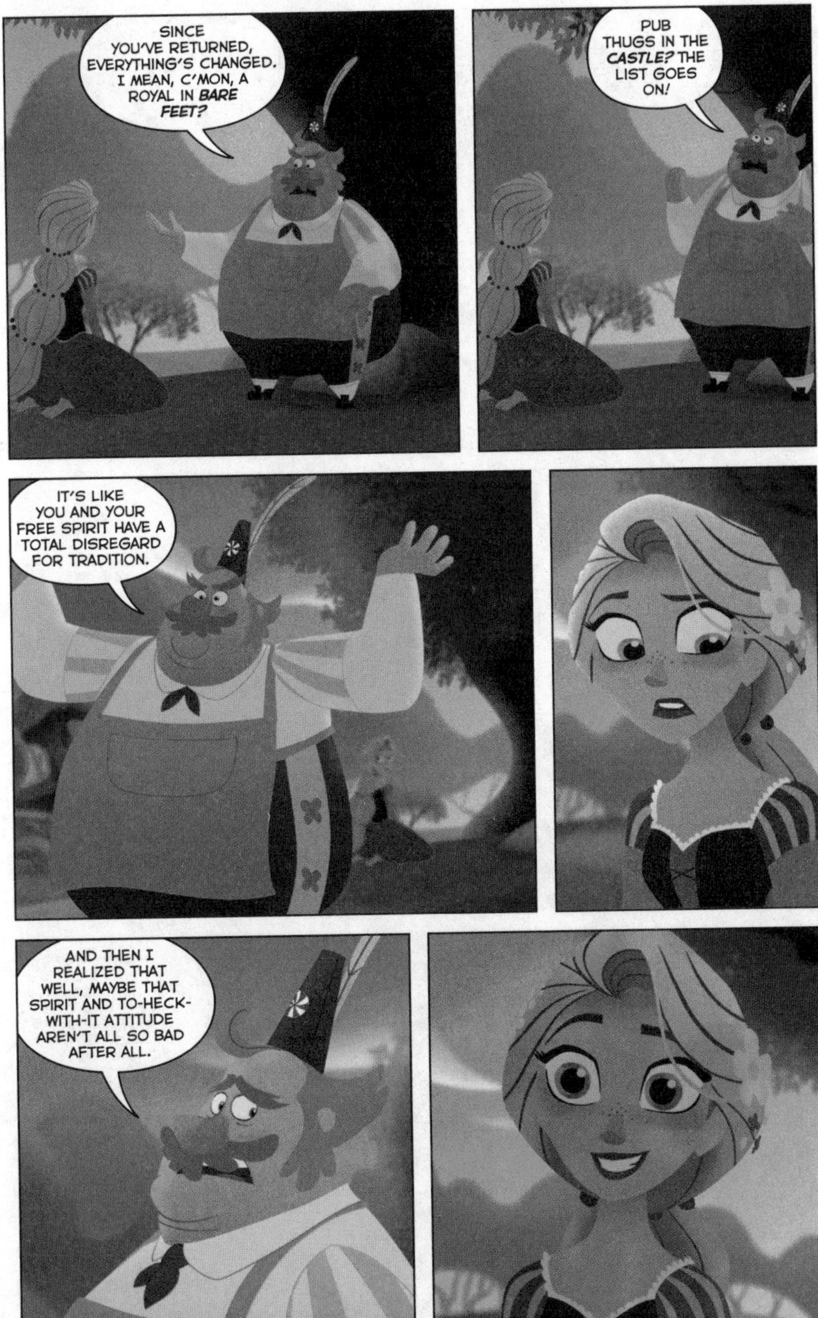
SINCE YOU'VE RETURNED, EVERYTHING'S CHANGED. I MEAN, C'MON, A ROYAL IN BARE FEET?
PUB THUGS IN THE CASTLE? THE LIST GOES ON!
IT'S LIKE YOU AND YOUR FREE SPIRIT HAVE A TOTAL DISREGARD FOR TRADITION.
AND THEN I REALIZED THAT WELL, MAYBE THAT SPIRIT AND TO-HECK-WITH-IT ATTITUDE AREN'T ALL SO BAD AFTER ALL.

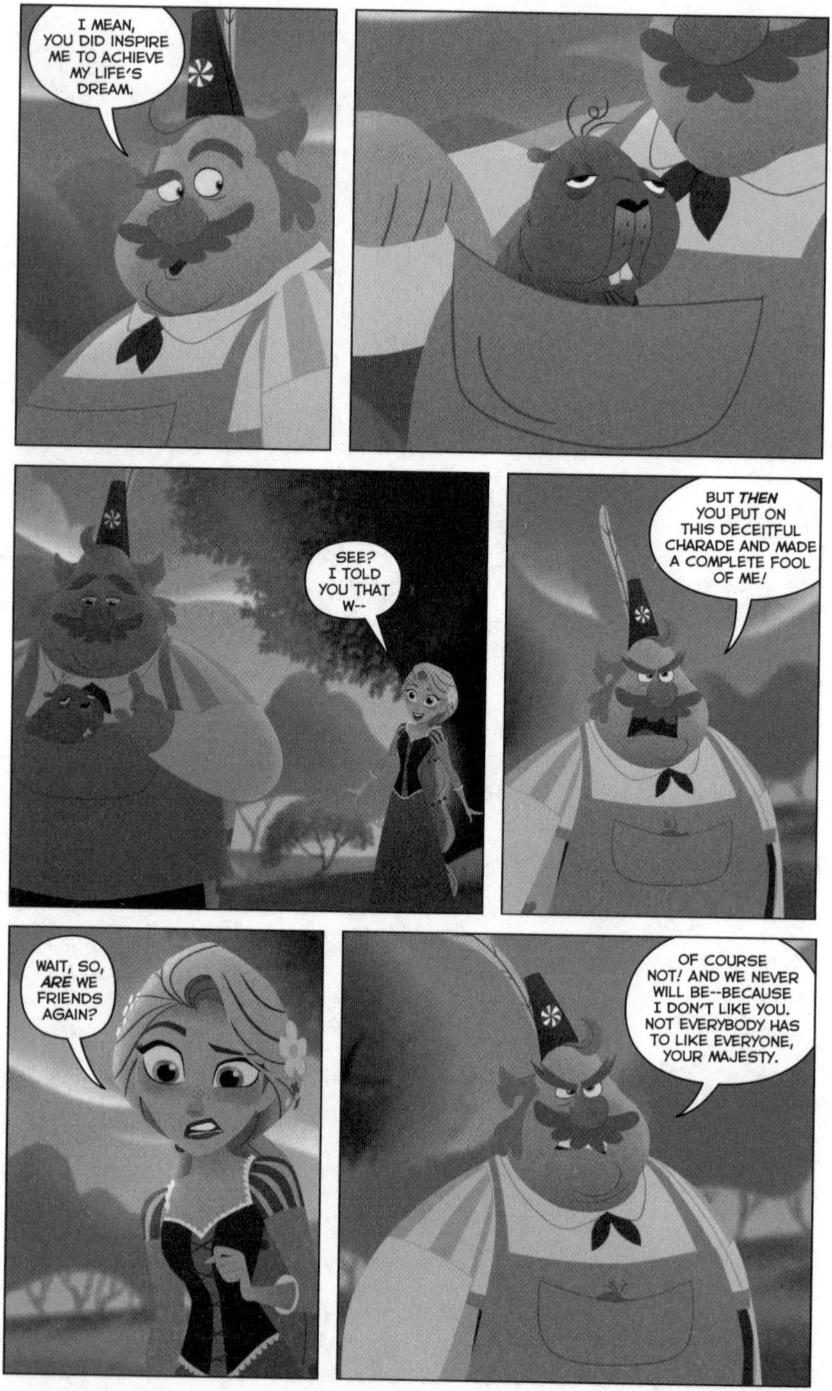
I MEAN, YOU DID INSPIRE ME TO ACHIEVE MY LIFE'S DREAM.
SEE? I TOLD YOU THAT W--
BUT *THEN* YOU PUT ON THIS DECEITFUL CHARADE AND MADE A COMPLETE FOOL OF ME!
WAIT, SO, *ARE* WE FRIENDS AGAIN?
OF COURSE NOT! AND WE NEVER WILL BE--BECAUSE I DON'T LIKE YOU. NOT EVERYBODY HAS TO LIKE EVERYONE, YOUR MAJESTY.

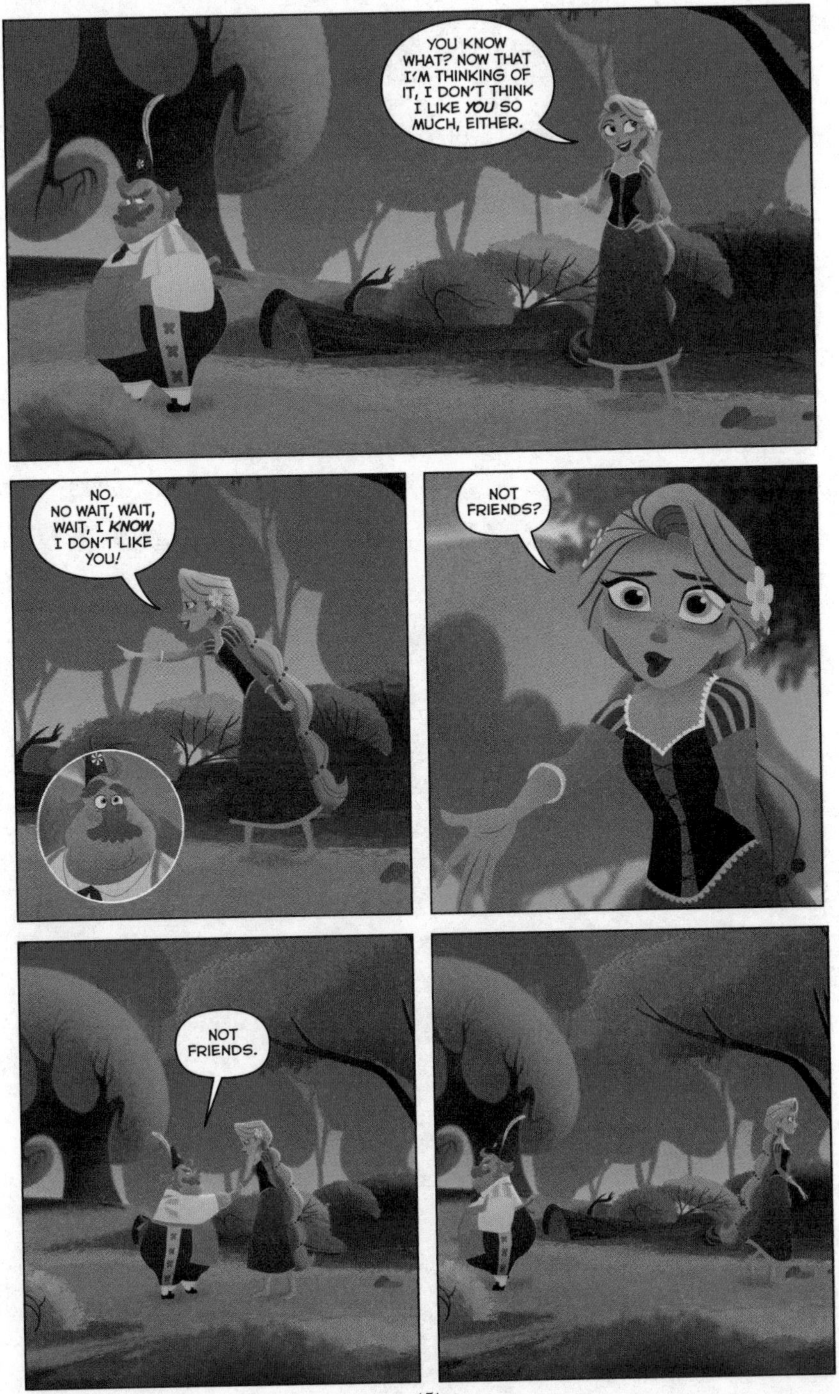
YOU KNOW WHAT? NOW THAT I'M THINKING OF IT, I DON'T THINK I LIKE *YOU* SO MUCH, EITHER.
NO, NO WAIT, WAIT, WAIT, I *KNOW* I DON'T LIKE YOU!
NOT FRIENDS?
NOT FRIENDS.

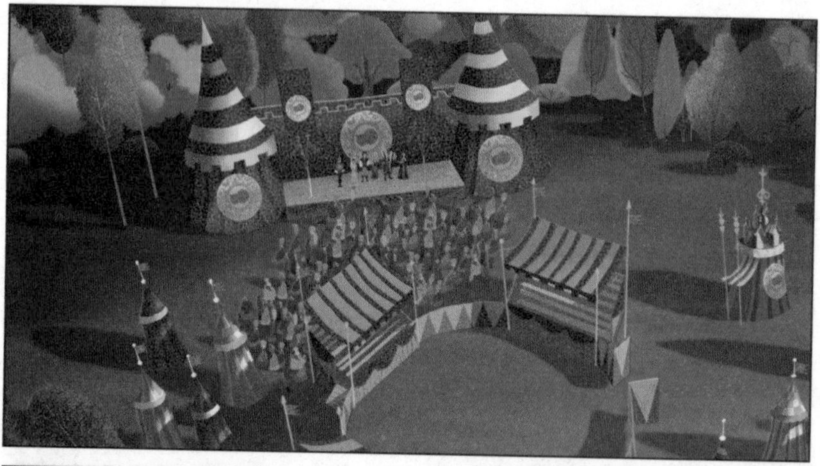

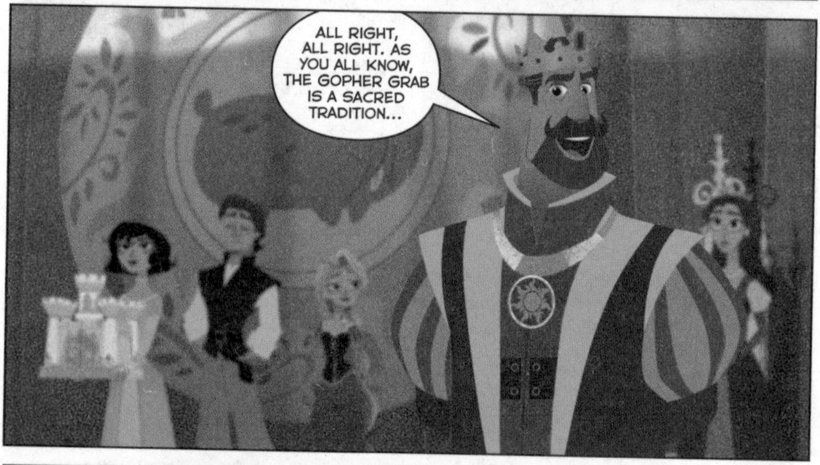
ALL RIGHT, ALL RIGHT. AS YOU ALL KNOW, THE GOPHER GRAB IS A SACRED TRADITION...

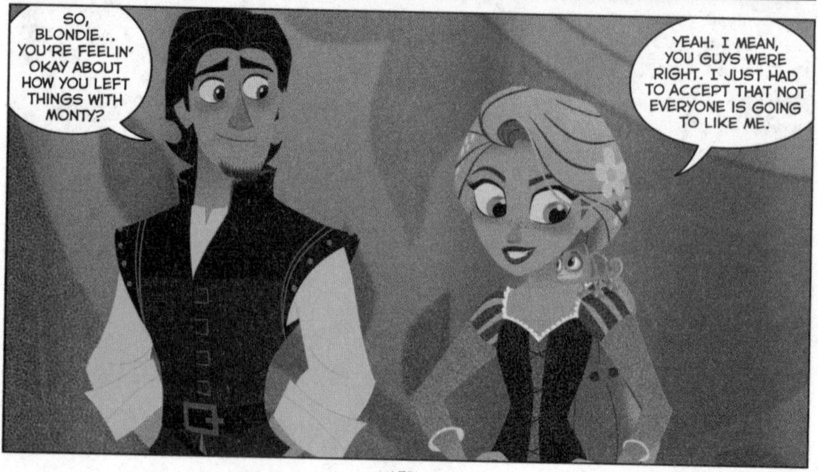
SO, BLONDIE... YOU'RE FEELIN' OKAY ABOUT HOW YOU LEFT THINGS WITH MONTY?
YEAH. I MEAN, YOU GUYS WERE RIGHT. I JUST HAD TO ACCEPT THAT NOT EVERYONE IS GOING TO LIKE ME.

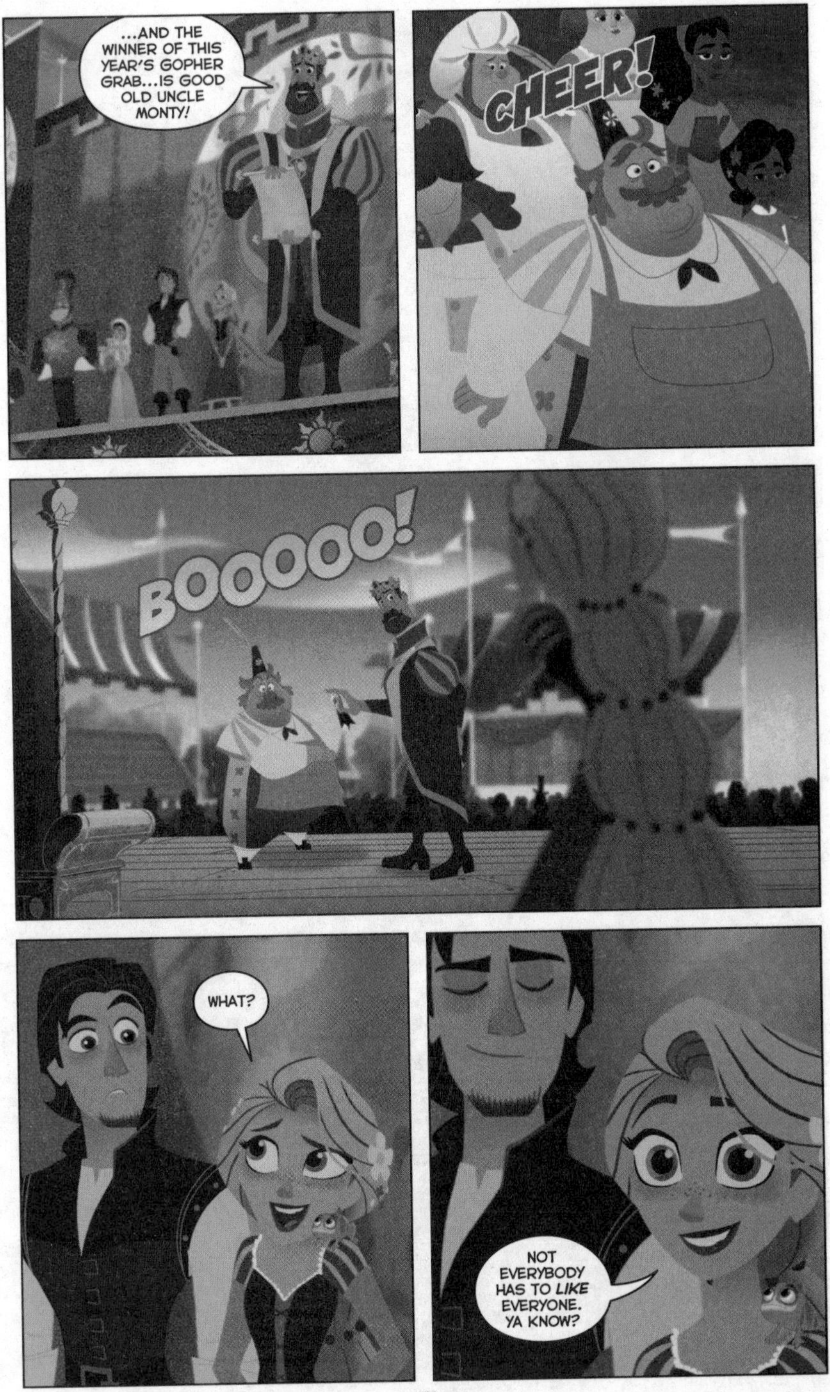
...AND THE WINNER OF THIS YEAR'S GOPHER GRAB...IS GOOD OLD UNCLE MONTY!
CHEER!
BOOOOO!
WHAT?
NOT EVERYBODY HAS TO *LIKE* EVERYONE. YA KNOW?

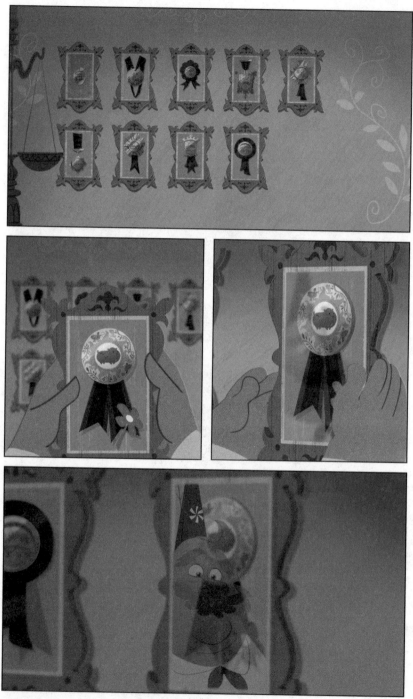

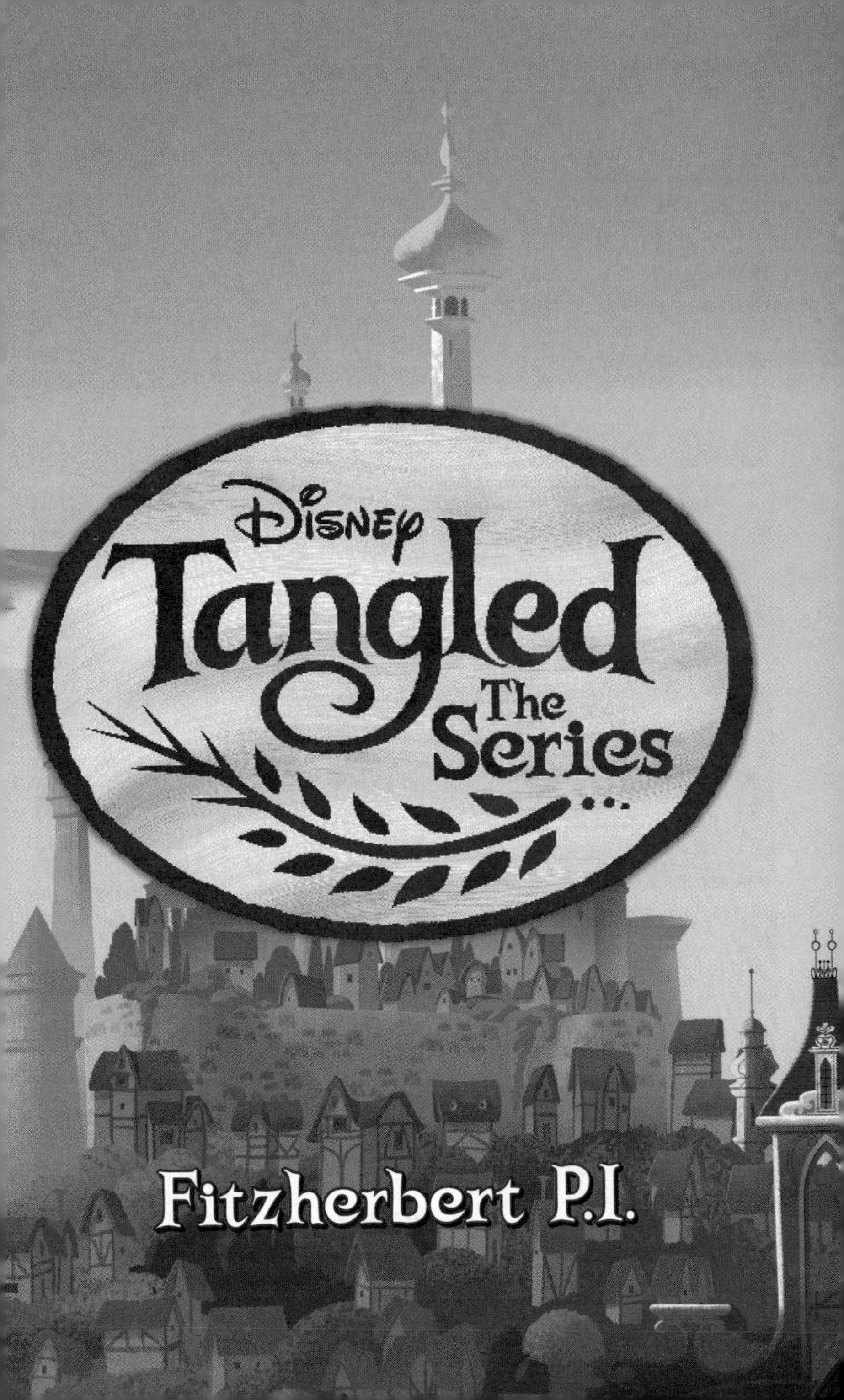
Disney
Tangled
The Series

Fitzherbert P.I.

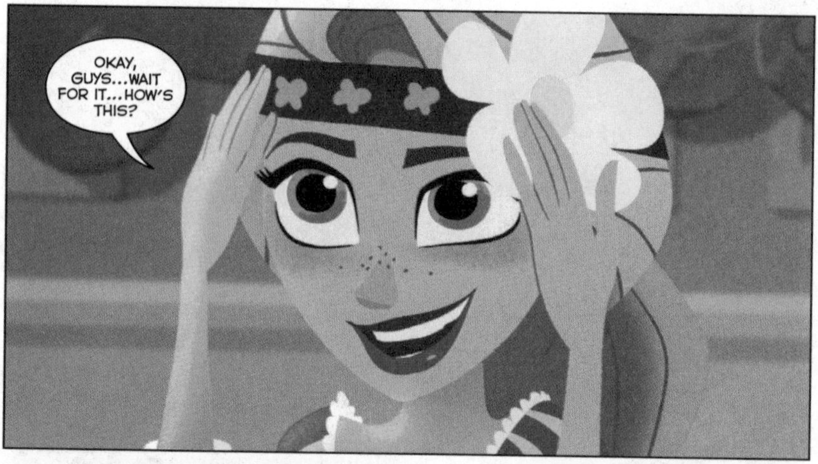
OKAY, GUYS...WAIT FOR IT...HOW'S THIS?

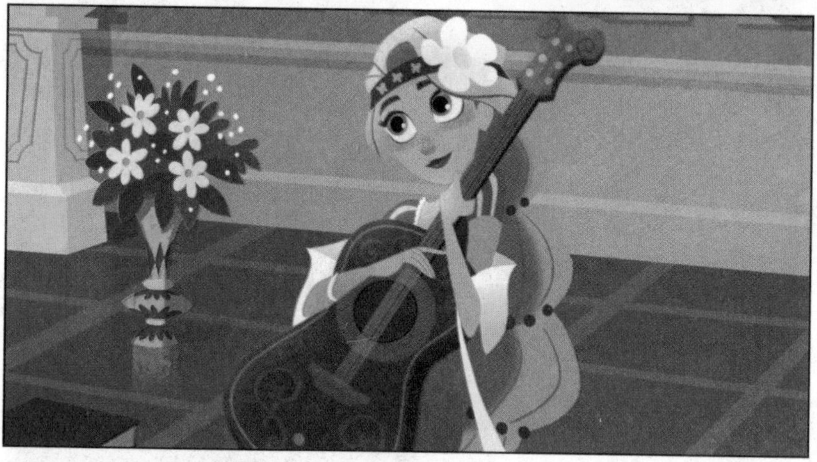

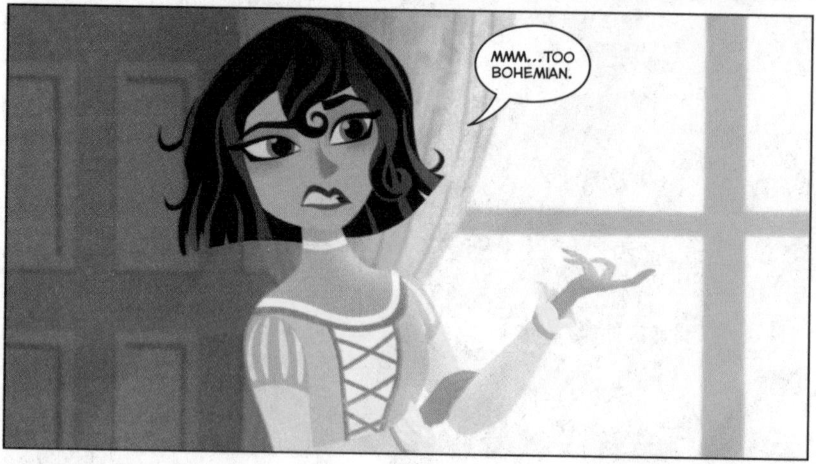
MMM...TOO BOHEMIAN.

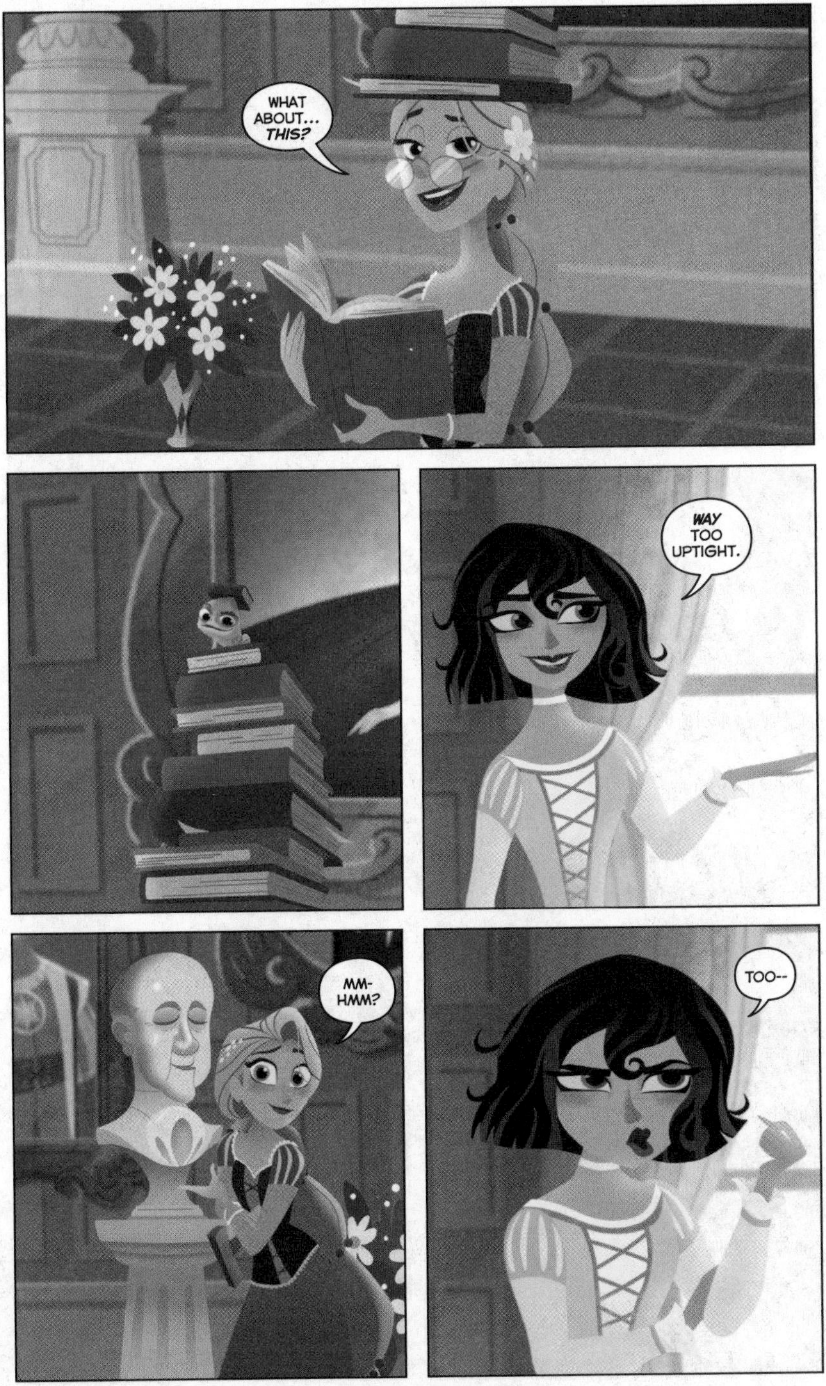
WHAT ABOUT... THIS?
WAY TOO UPTIGHT.
MM-HMM?
TOO--

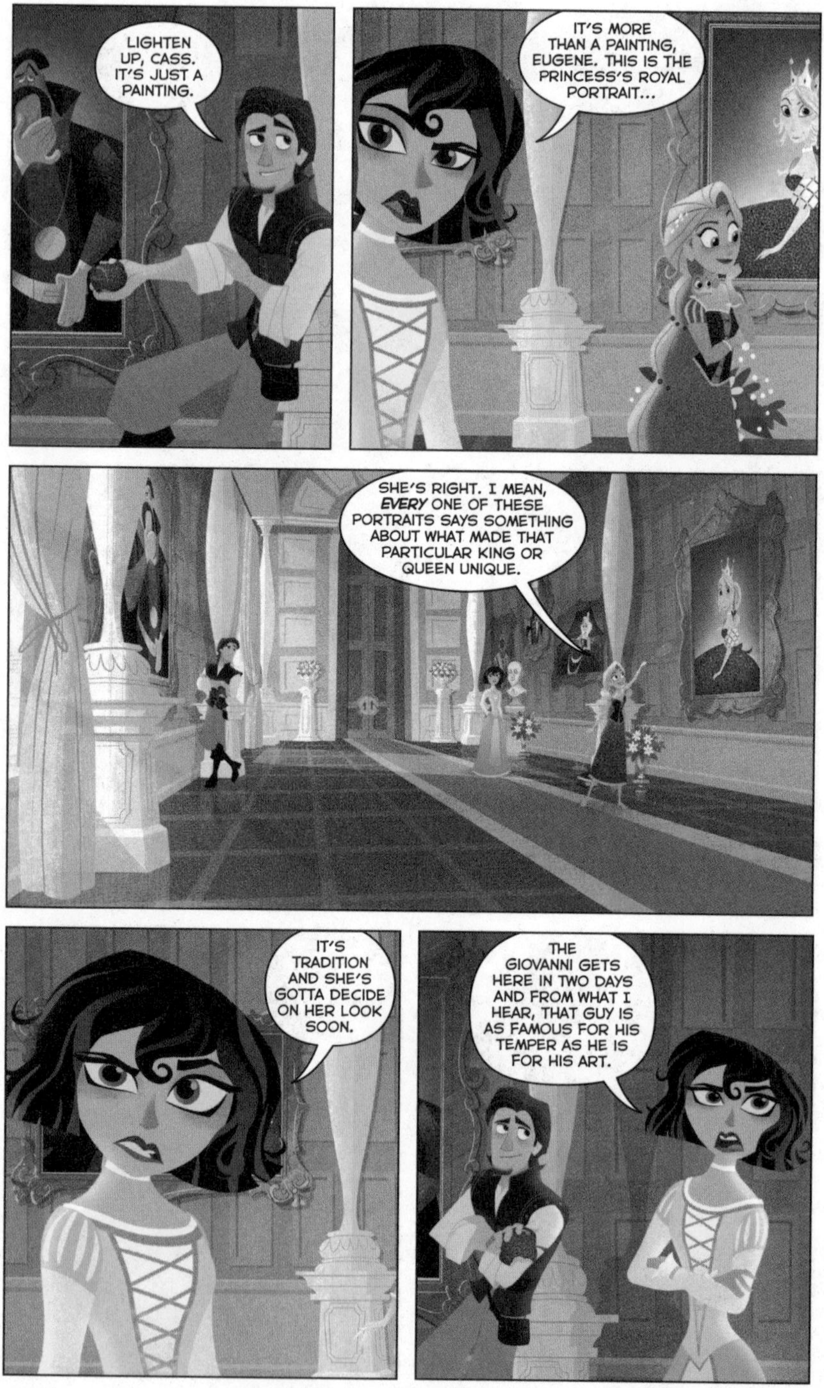

LIGHTEN UP, CASS. IT'S JUST A PAINTING.
IT'S MORE THAN A PAINTING, EUGENE. THIS IS THE PRINCESS'S ROYAL PORTRAIT...
SHE'S RIGHT. I MEAN, *EVERY* ONE OF THESE PORTRAITS SAYS SOMETHING ABOUT WHAT MADE THAT PARTICULAR KING OR QUEEN UNIQUE.
IT'S TRADITION AND SHE'S GOTTA DECIDE ON HER LOOK SOON.
THE GIOVANNI GETS HERE IN TWO DAYS AND FROM WHAT I HEAR, THAT GUY IS AS FAMOUS FOR HIS TEMPER AS HE IS FOR HIS ART.

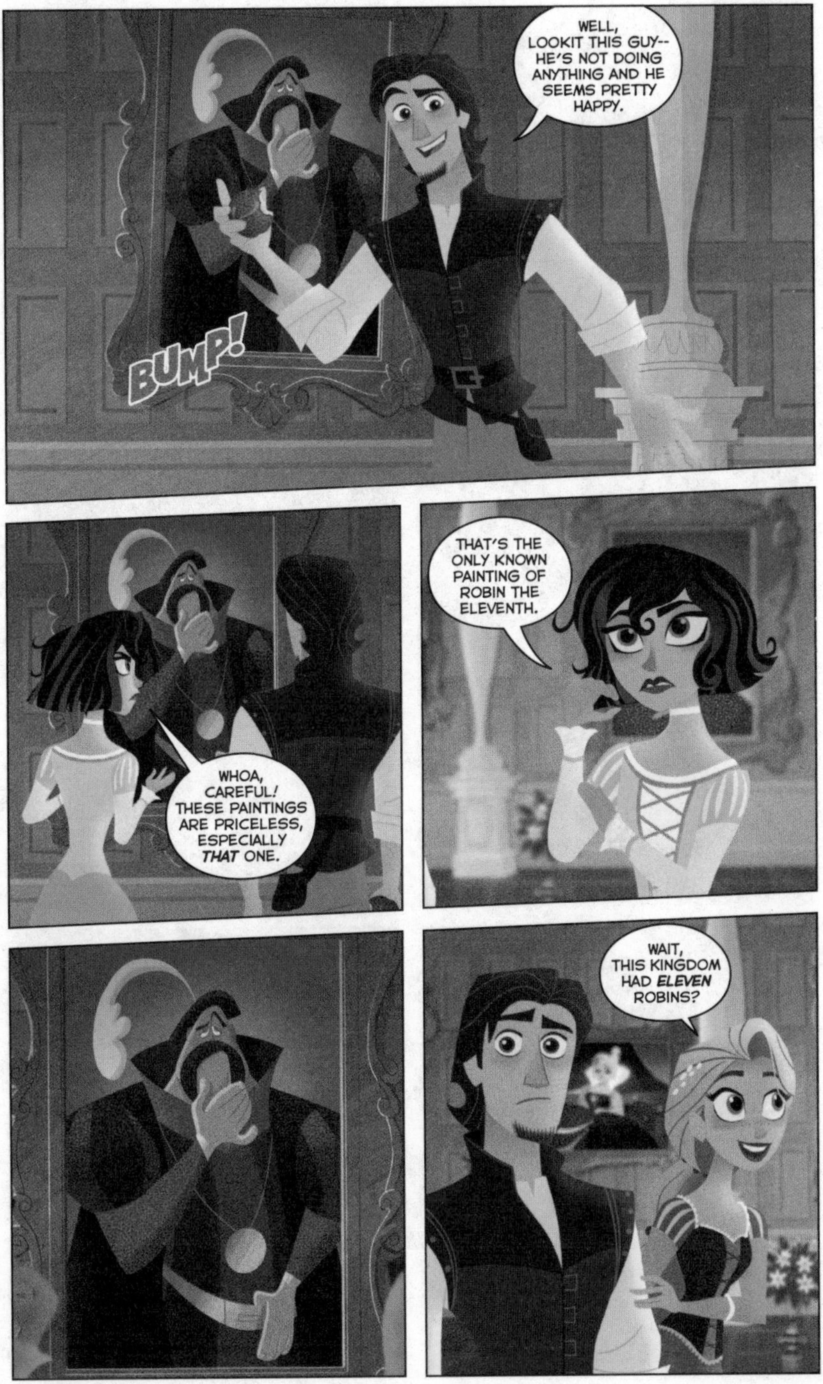
WELL, LOOKIT THIS GUY-- HE'S NOT DOING ANYTHING AND HE SEEMS PRETTY HAPPY.
BUMP!
WHOA, CAREFUL! THESE PAINTINGS ARE PRICELESS, ESPECIALLY *THAT* ONE.
THAT'S THE ONLY KNOWN PAINTING OF ROBIN THE ELEVENTH.
WAIT, THIS KINGDOM HAD *ELEVEN* ROBINS?

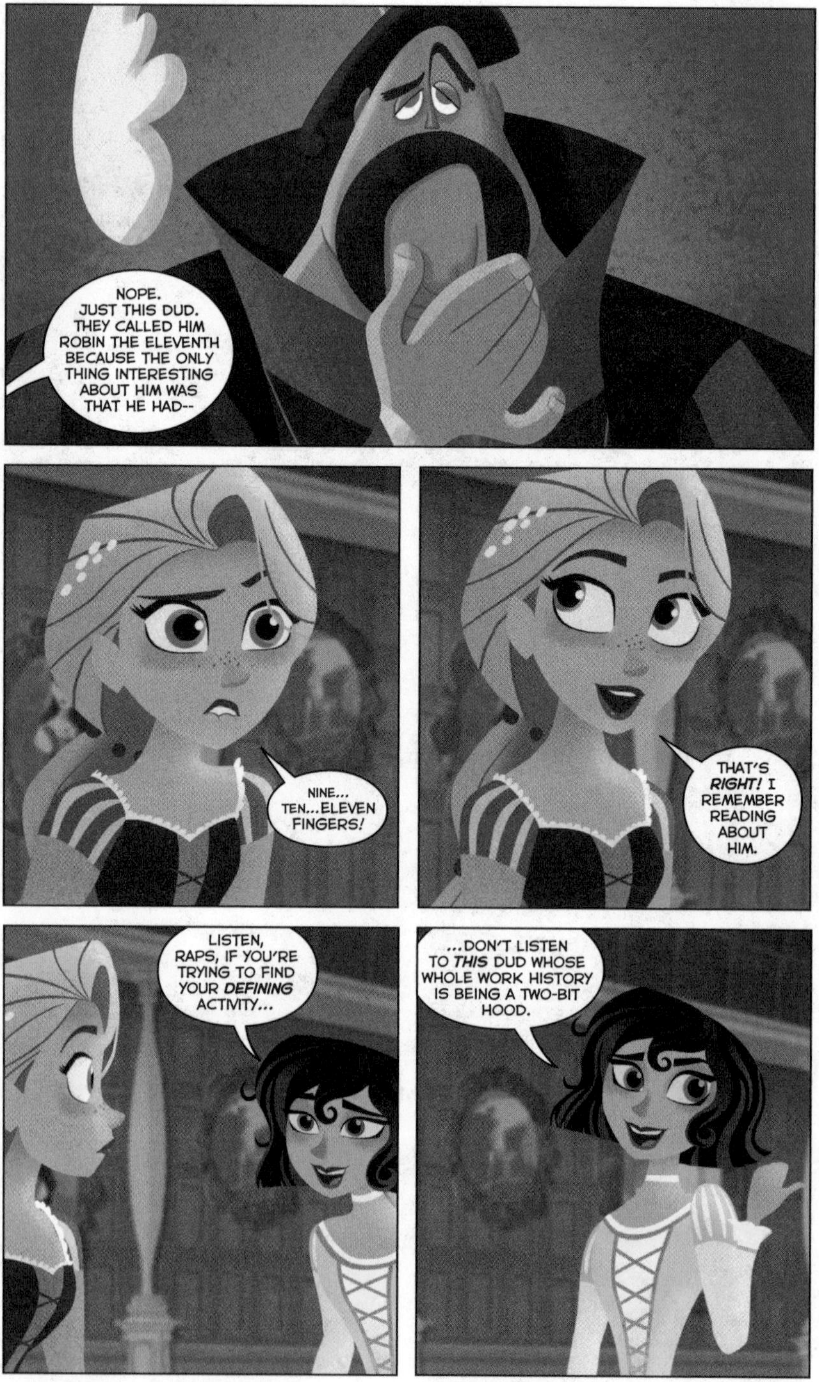
NOPE. JUST THIS DUD. THEY CALLED HIM ROBIN THE ELEVENTH BECAUSE THE ONLY THING INTERESTING ABOUT HIM WAS THAT HE HAD--
NINE... TEN...ELEVEN FINGERS!
THAT'S *RIGHT!* I REMEMBER READING ABOUT HIM.
LISTEN, RAPS, IF YOU'RE TRYING TO FIND YOUR *DEFINING* ACTIVITY...
...DON'T LISTEN TO *THIS* DUD WHOSE WHOLE WORK HISTORY IS BEING A TWO-BIT HOOD.

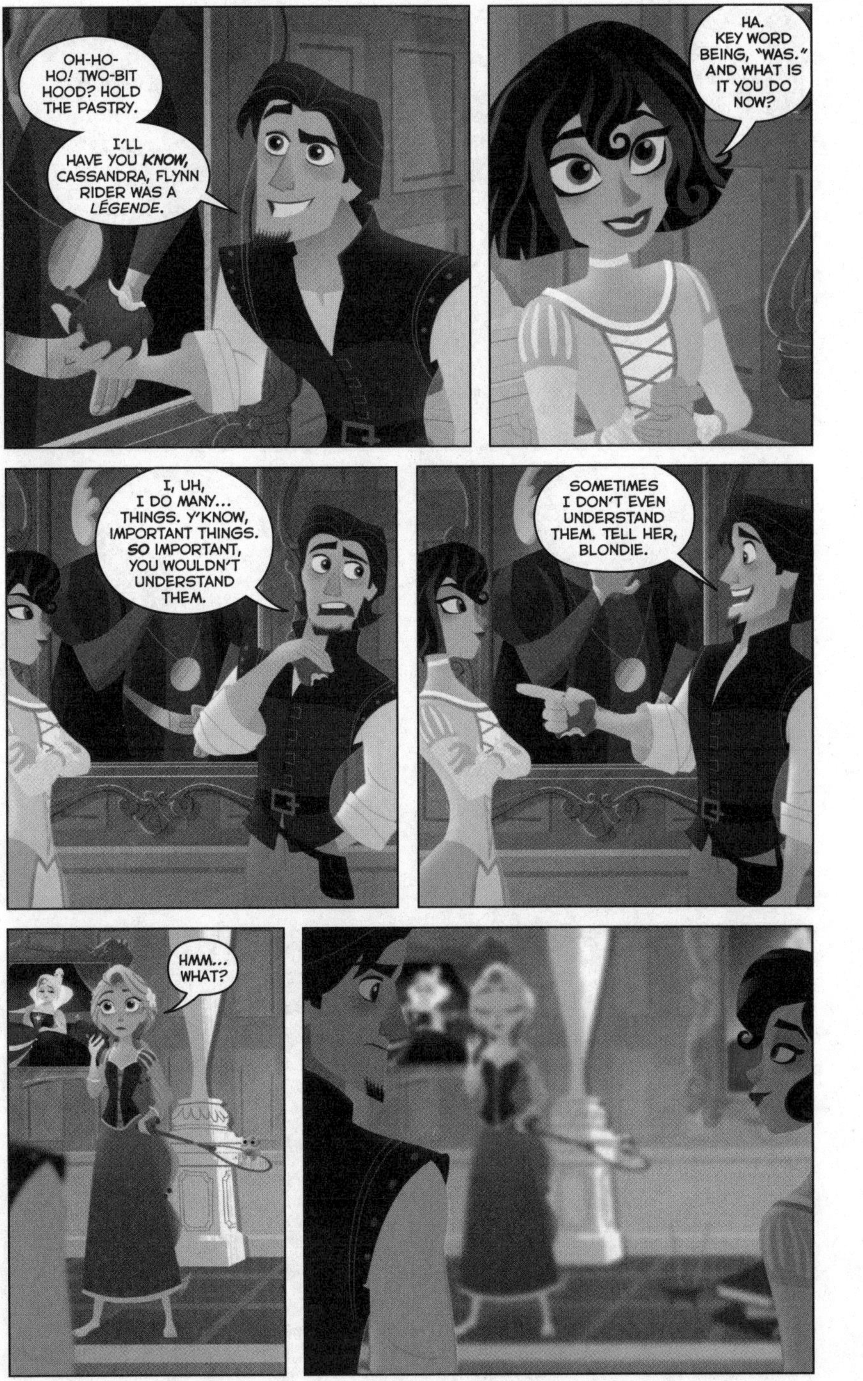
OH-HO-HO! TWO-BIT HOOD? HOLD THE PASTRY.
I'LL HAVE YOU *KNOW,* CASSANDRA, FLYNN RIDER WAS A *LÉGENDE*.
HA. KEY WORD BEING, "WAS." AND WHAT IS IT YOU DO NOW?
I, UH, I DO MANY... THINGS. Y'KNOW, IMPORTANT THINGS. **SO** IMPORTANT, YOU WOULDN'T UNDERSTAND THEM.
SOMETIMES I DON'T EVEN UNDERSTAND THEM. TELL HER, BLONDIE.
HMM... WHAT?

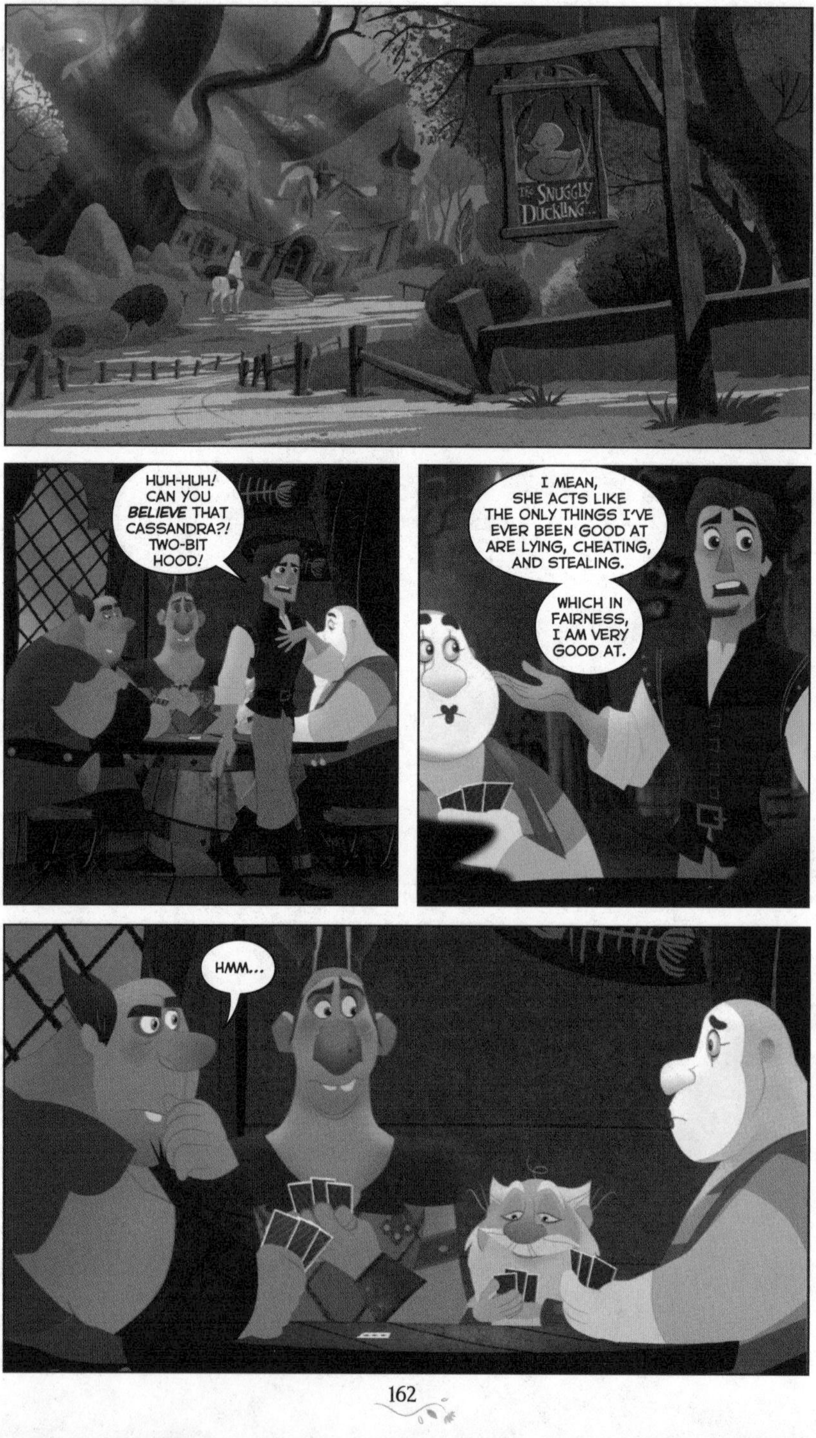
The SNUGGLY DUCKLING
HUH-HUH! CAN YOU *BELIEVE* THAT CASSANDRA?! TWO-BIT HOOD!
I MEAN, SHE ACTS LIKE THE ONLY THINGS I'VE EVER BEEN GOOD AT ARE LYING, CHEATING, AND STEALING.
WHICH IN FAIRNESS, I AM VERY GOOD AT.
HMM...

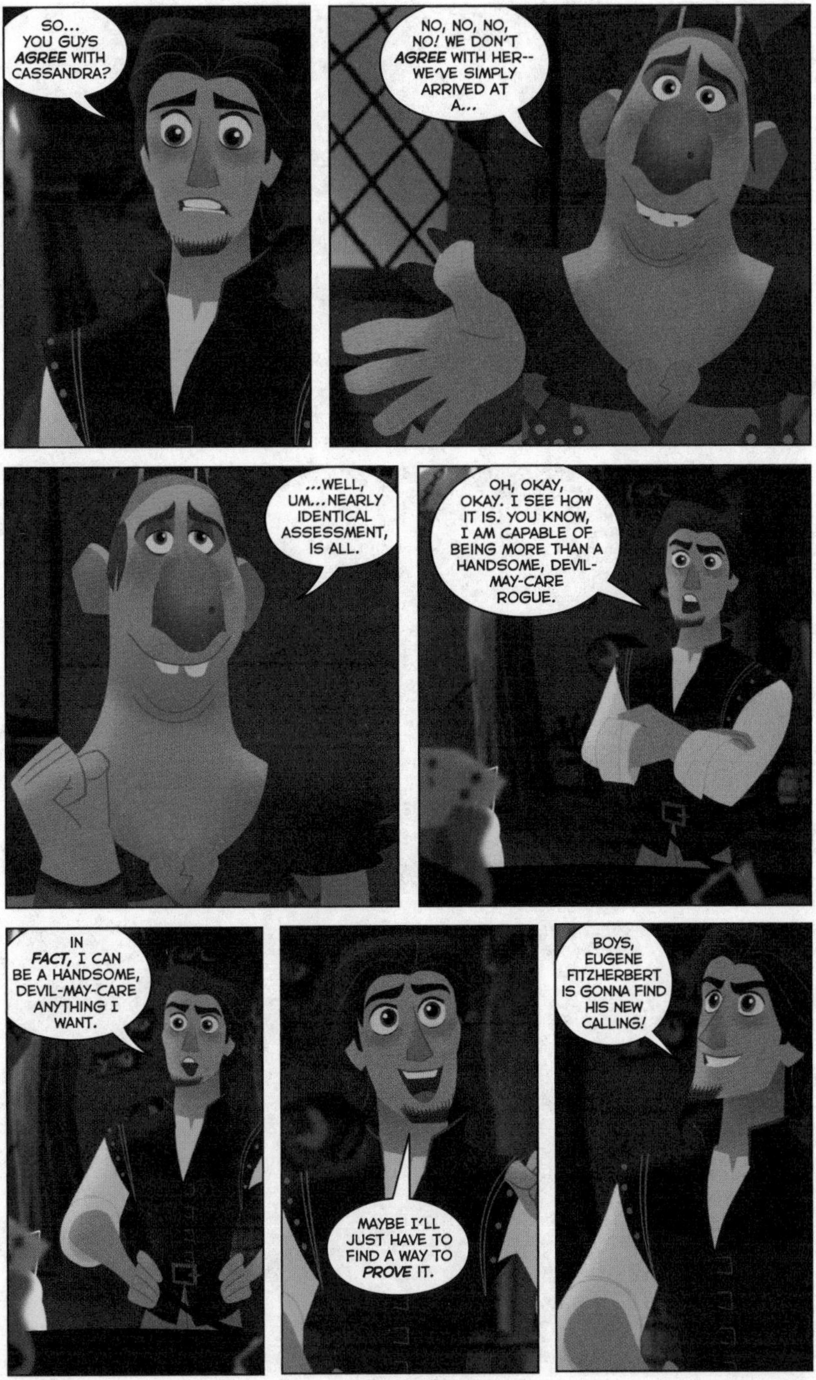
SO... YOU GUYS AGREE WITH CASSANDRA?
NO, NO, NO, NO! WE DON'T AGREE WITH HER-- WE'VE SIMPLY ARRIVED AT A...
...WELL, UM...NEARLY IDENTICAL ASSESSMENT, IS ALL.
OH, OKAY, OKAY. I SEE HOW IT IS. YOU KNOW, I AM CAPABLE OF BEING MORE THAN A HANDSOME, DEVIL-MAY-CARE ROGUE.
IN FACT, I CAN BE A HANDSOME, DEVIL-MAY-CARE ANYTHING I WANT.
MAYBE I'LL JUST HAVE TO FIND A WAY TO PROVE IT.
BOYS, EUGENE FITZHERBERT IS GONNA FIND HIS NEW CALLING!

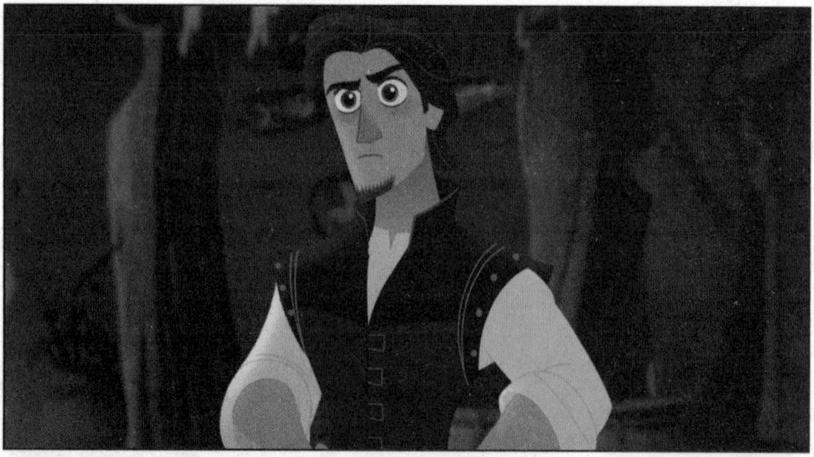

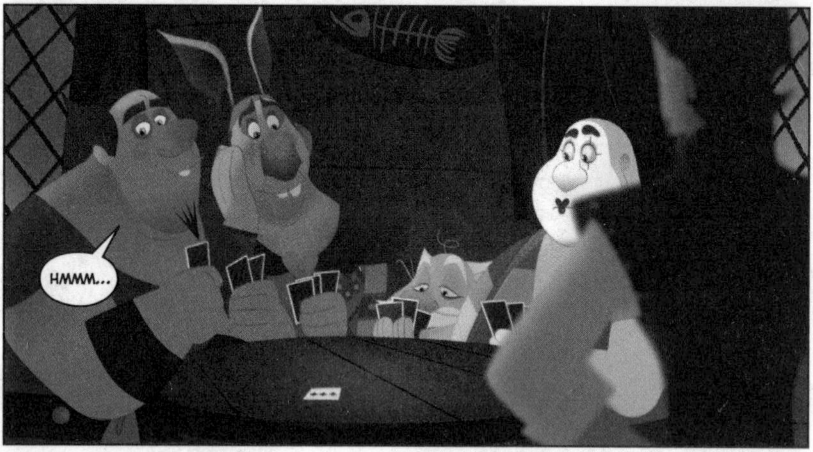
HMMM...

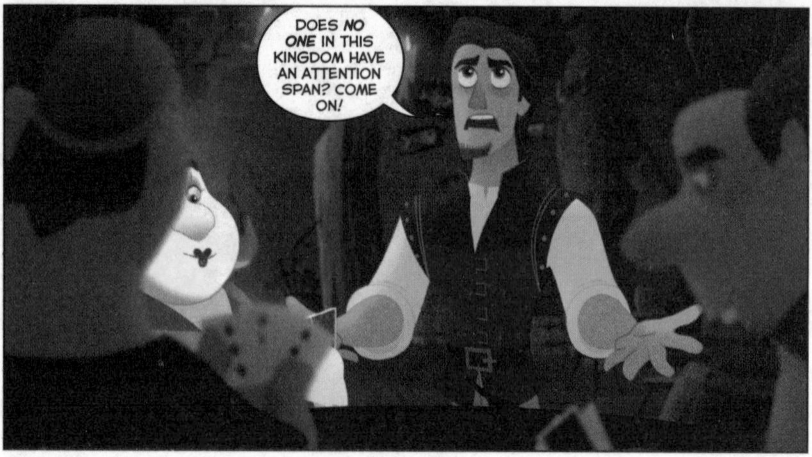
DOES *NO ONE* IN THIS KINGDOM HAVE AN ATTENTION SPAN? COME ON!

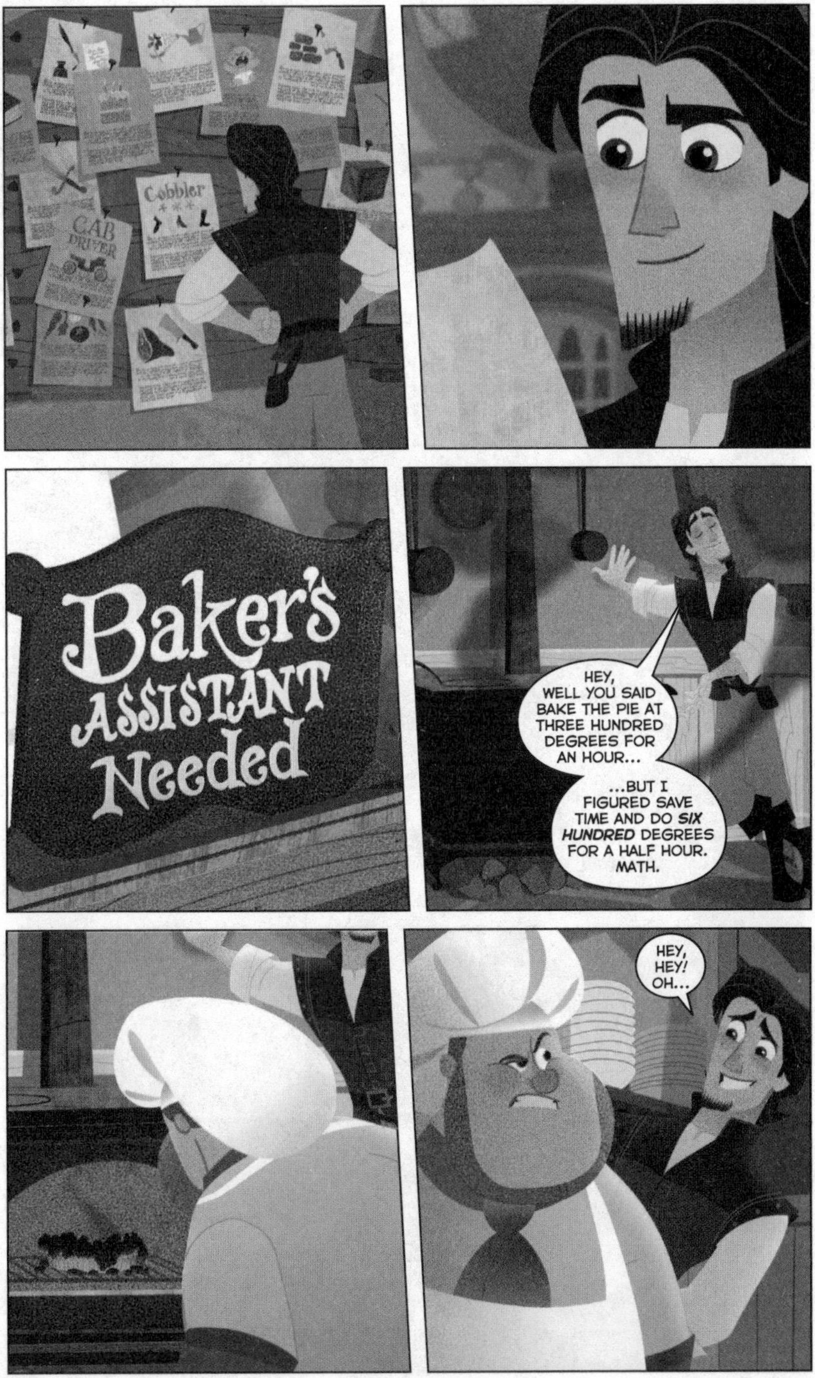
Cobbler
CAB DRIVER
Baker's ASSISTANT Needed
HEY, WELL YOU SAID BAKE THE PIE AT THREE HUNDRED DEGREES FOR AN HOUR...
...BUT I FIGURED SAVE TIME AND DO *SIX HUNDRED* DEGREES FOR A HALF HOUR. MATH.
HEY, HEY! OH...

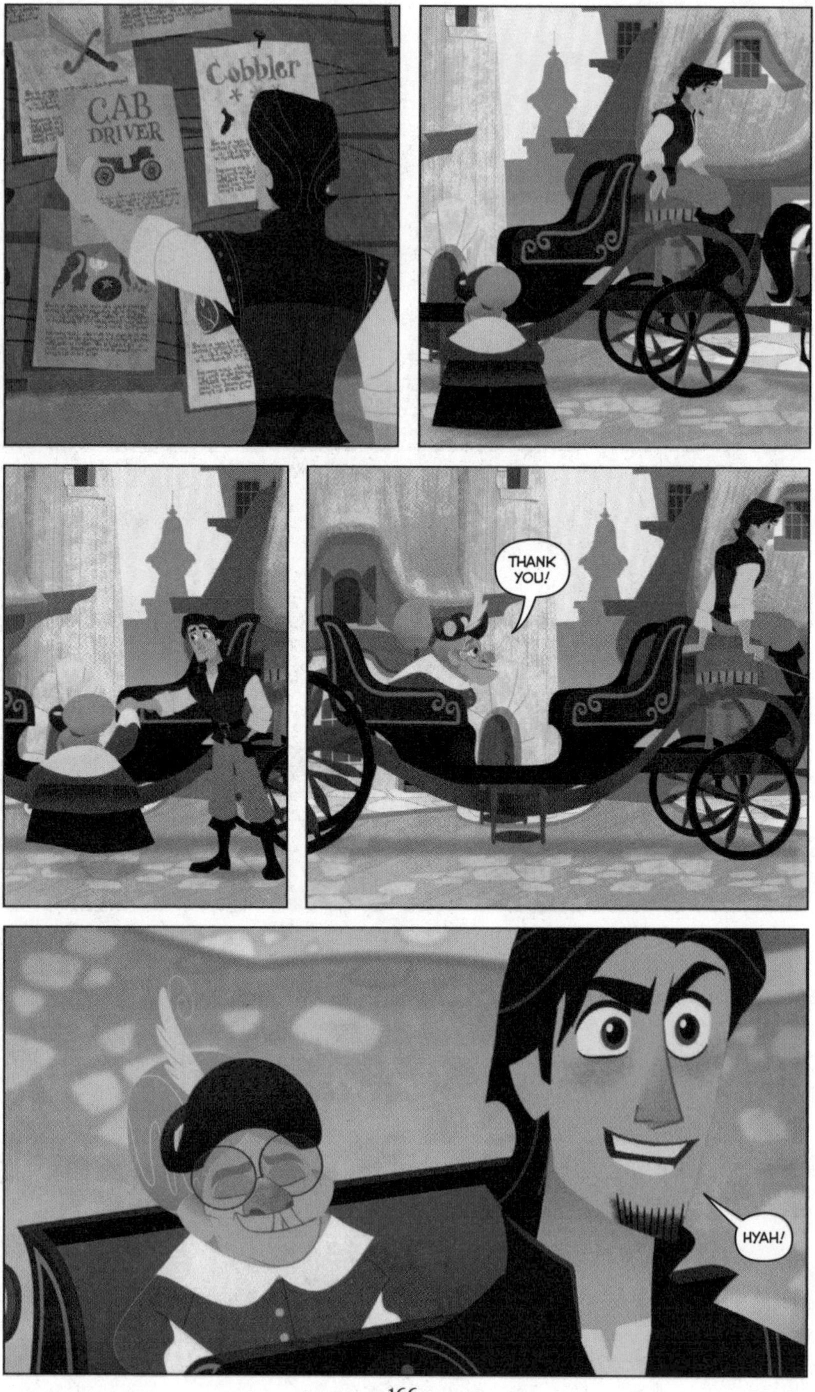
CAB DRIVER
Cobbler
THANK YOU!
HYAH!

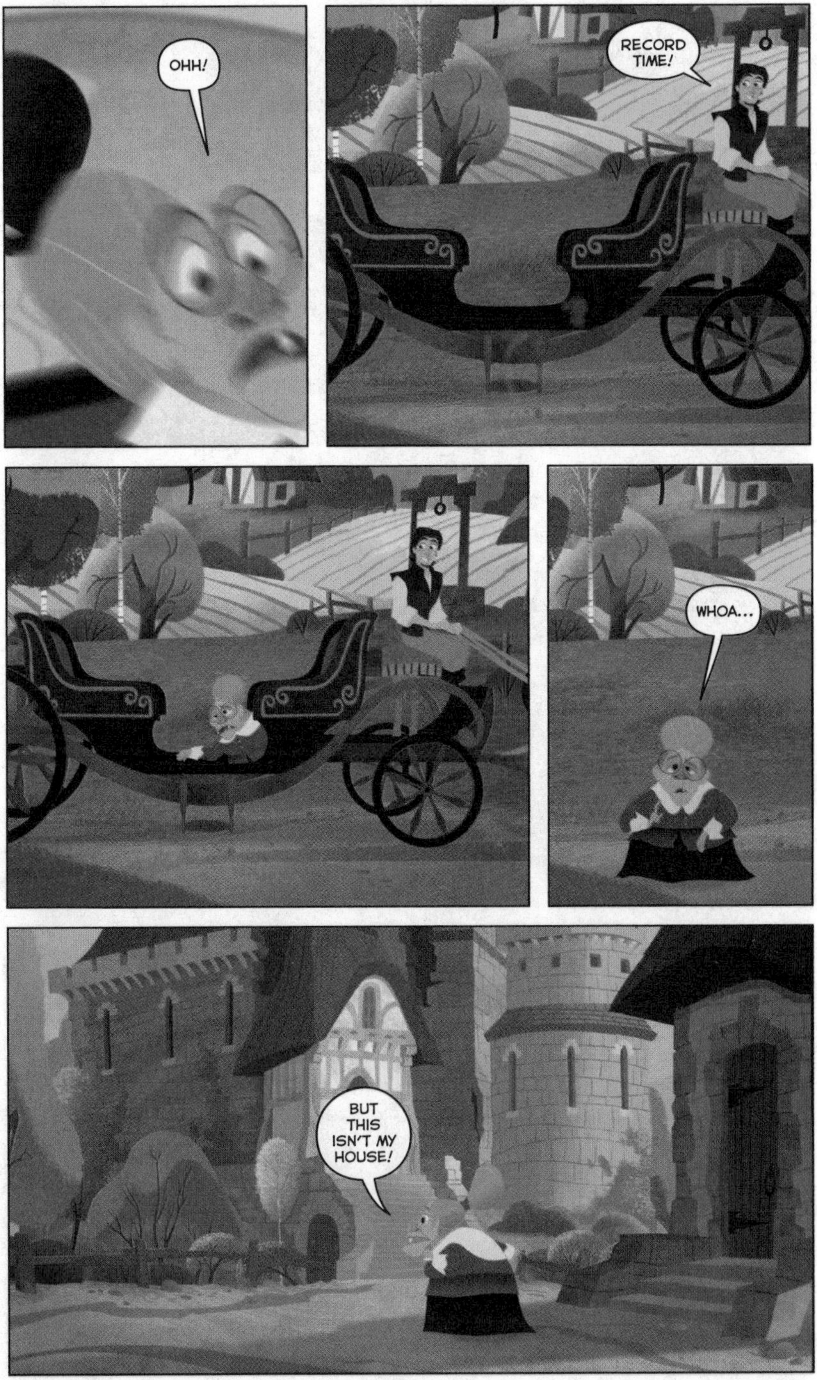
OHH!
RECORD TIME!
WHOA...
BUT THIS ISN'T MY HOUSE!

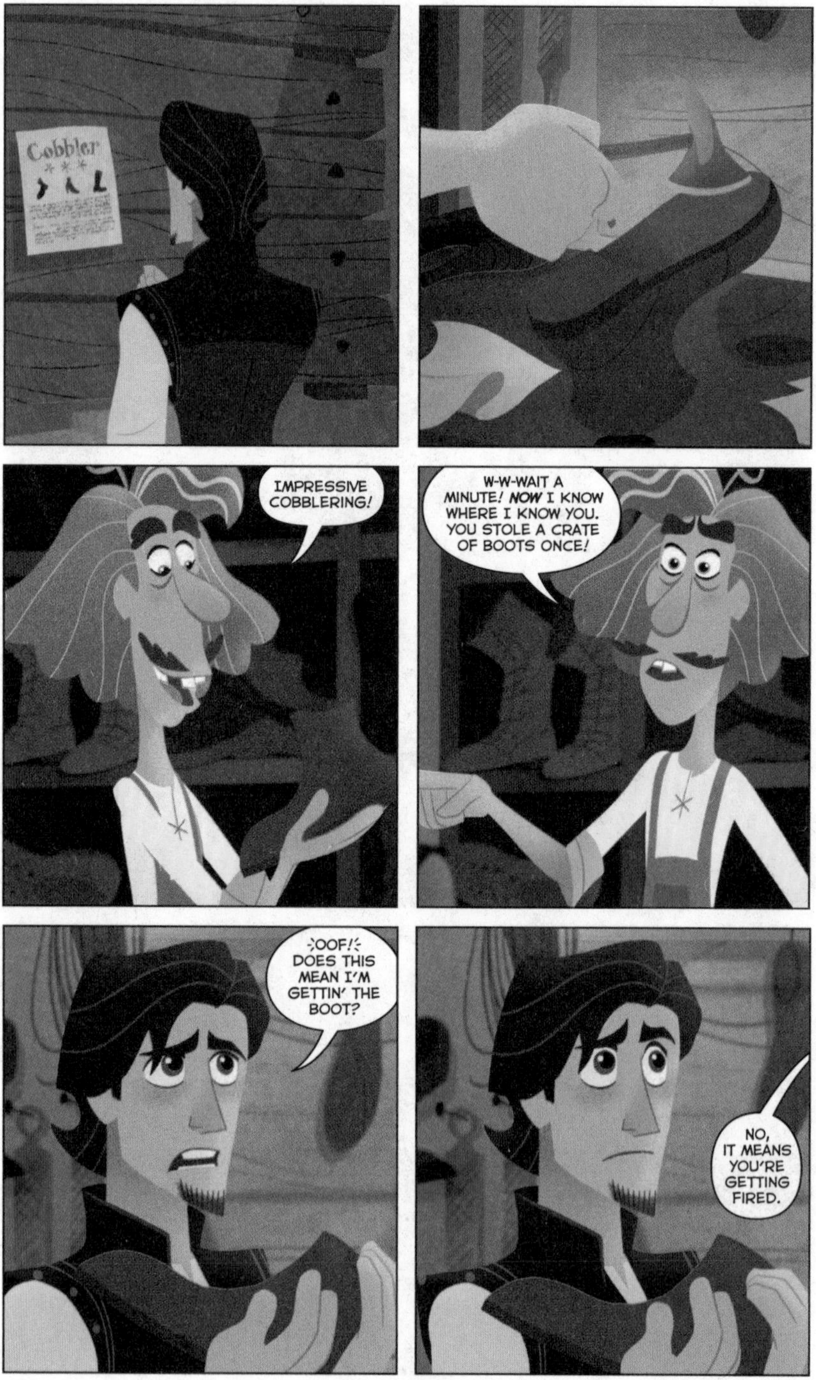
Cobbler
IMPRESSIVE COBBLERING!
W-W-WAIT A MINUTE! *NOW* I KNOW WHERE I KNOW YOU. YOU STOLE A CRATE OF BOOTS ONCE!
OOF! DOES THIS MEAN I'M GETTIN' THE BOOT?
NO, IT MEANS YOU'RE GETTING FIRED.

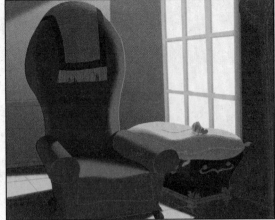

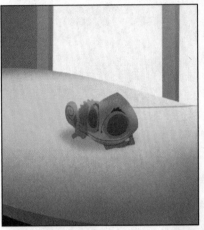

WHO KNEW HAVING A JOB WOULD BE SO MUCH *WORK*. ⸱SIGH⸱ I MEAN, WHAT WITH ALL THOSE *RULES* AND *RESPONSIBILITIES?*

YOU SHOULD'VE *HEARD* SOME OF THE GUYS I WORKED FOR.

IT'S LIKE, HEY BUDDY, WHO DIED AND MADE *YOU* BOSS?!

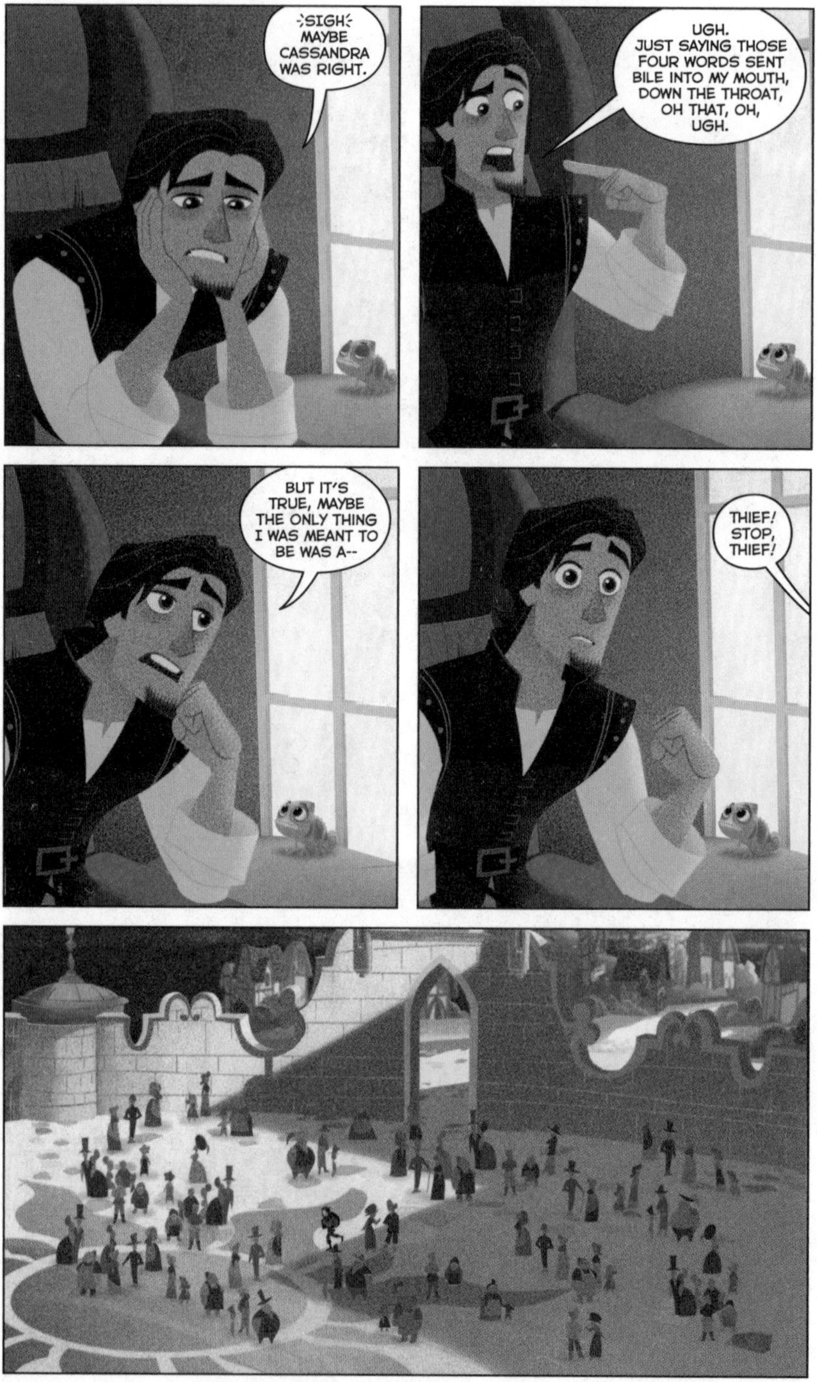

-SIGH-
MAYBE CASSANDRA WAS RIGHT.
UGH. JUST SAYING THOSE FOUR WORDS SENT BILE INTO MY MOUTH, DOWN THE THROAT, OH THAT, OH, UGH.
BUT IT'S TRUE, MAYBE THE ONLY THING I WAS MEANT TO BE WAS A--
THIEF! STOP, THIEF!

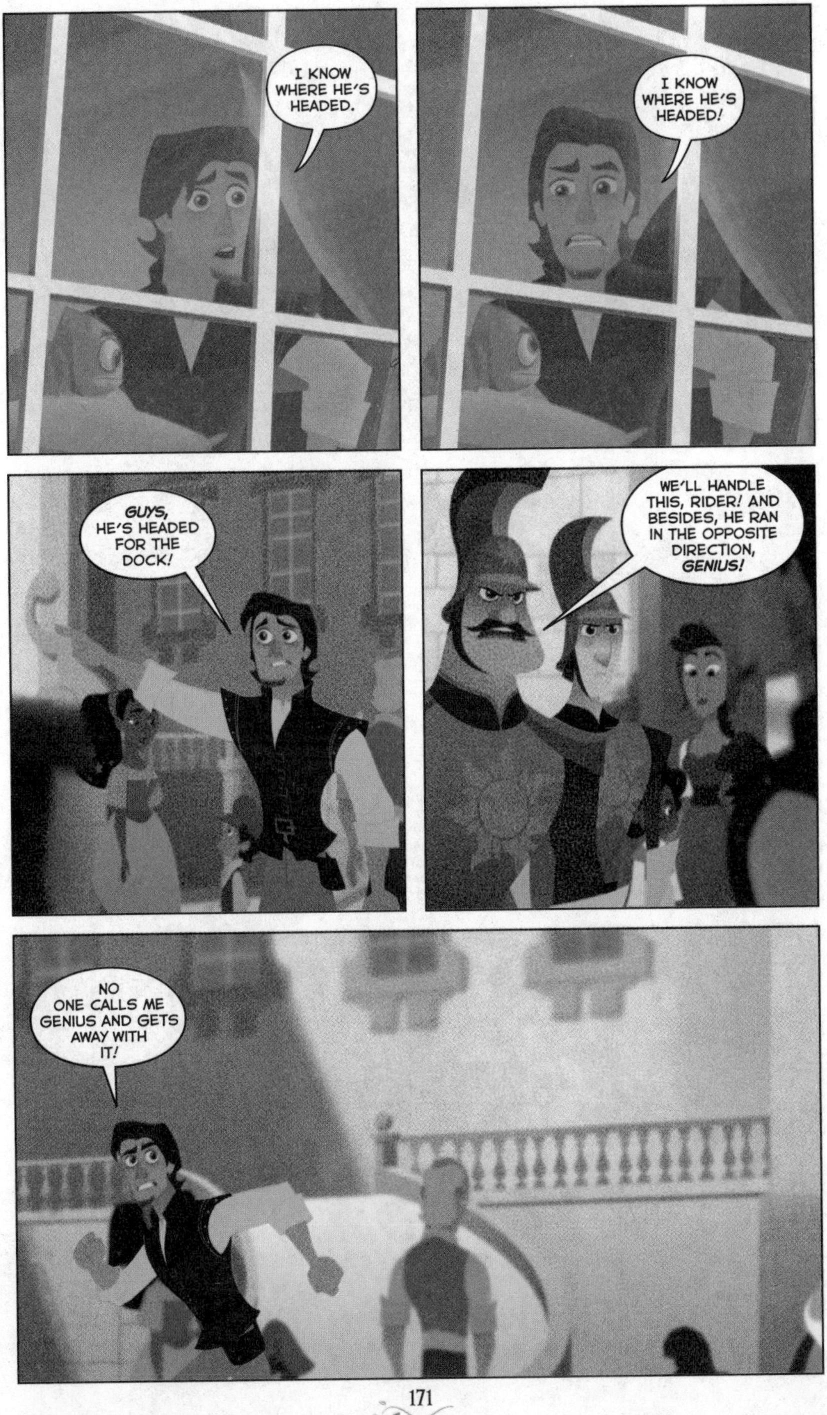
I KNOW WHERE HE'S HEADED.
I KNOW WHERE HE'S HEADED!
GUYS, HE'S HEADED FOR THE DOCK!
WE'LL HANDLE THIS, RIDER! AND BESIDES, HE RAN IN THE OPPOSITE DIRECTION, ***GENIUS!***
NO ONE CALLS ME GENIUS AND GETS AWAY WITH IT!

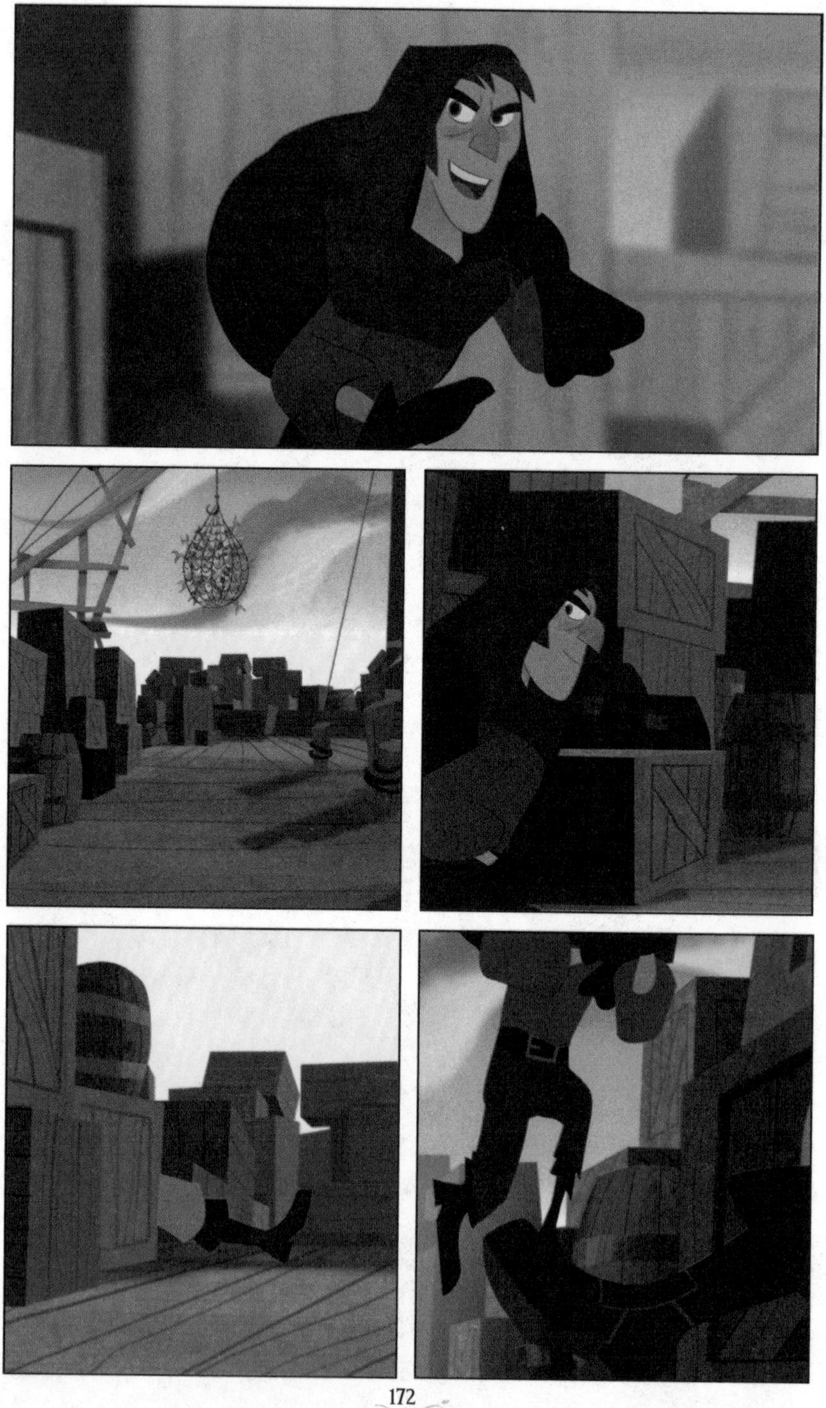

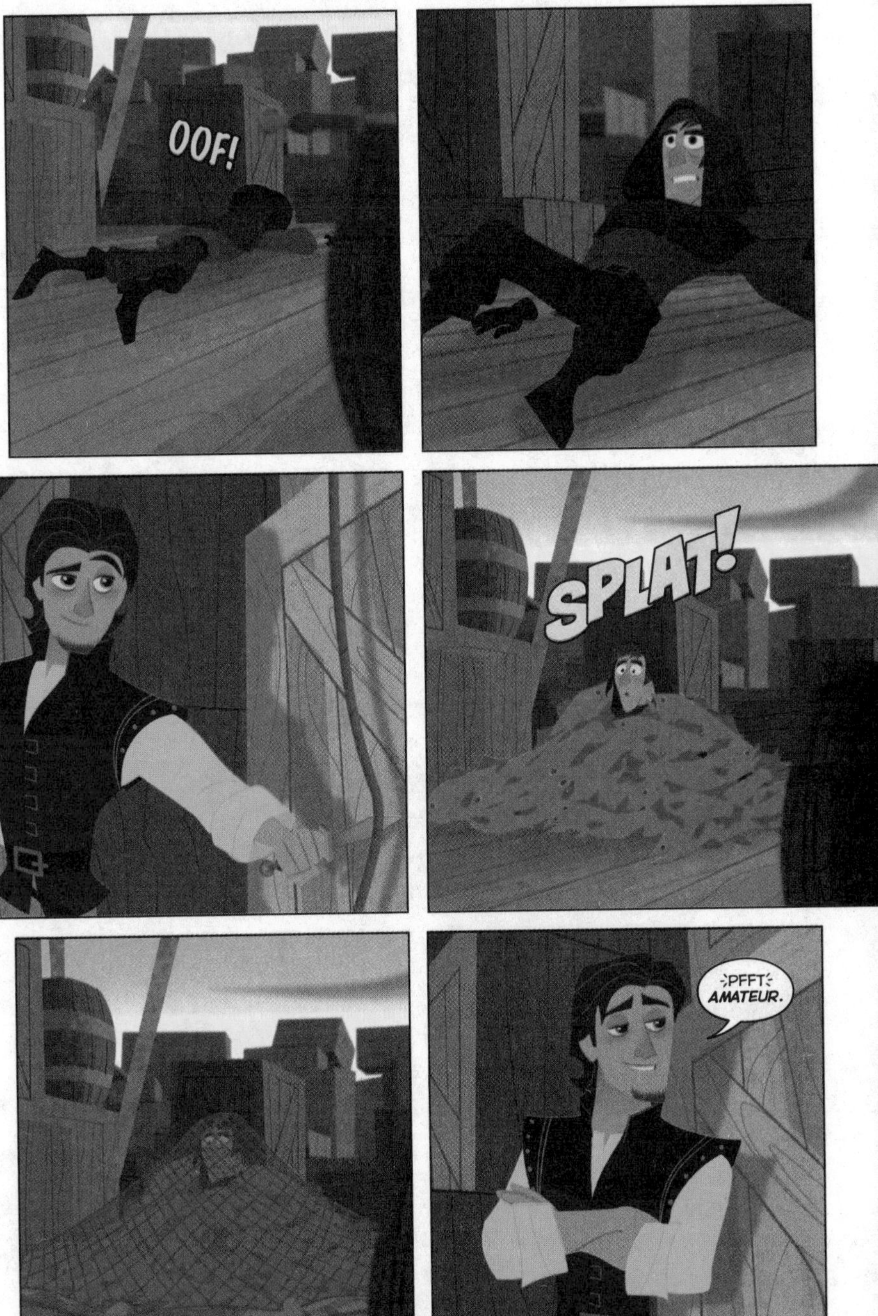
OOF!
SPLAT!
PFFT.
AMATEUR.

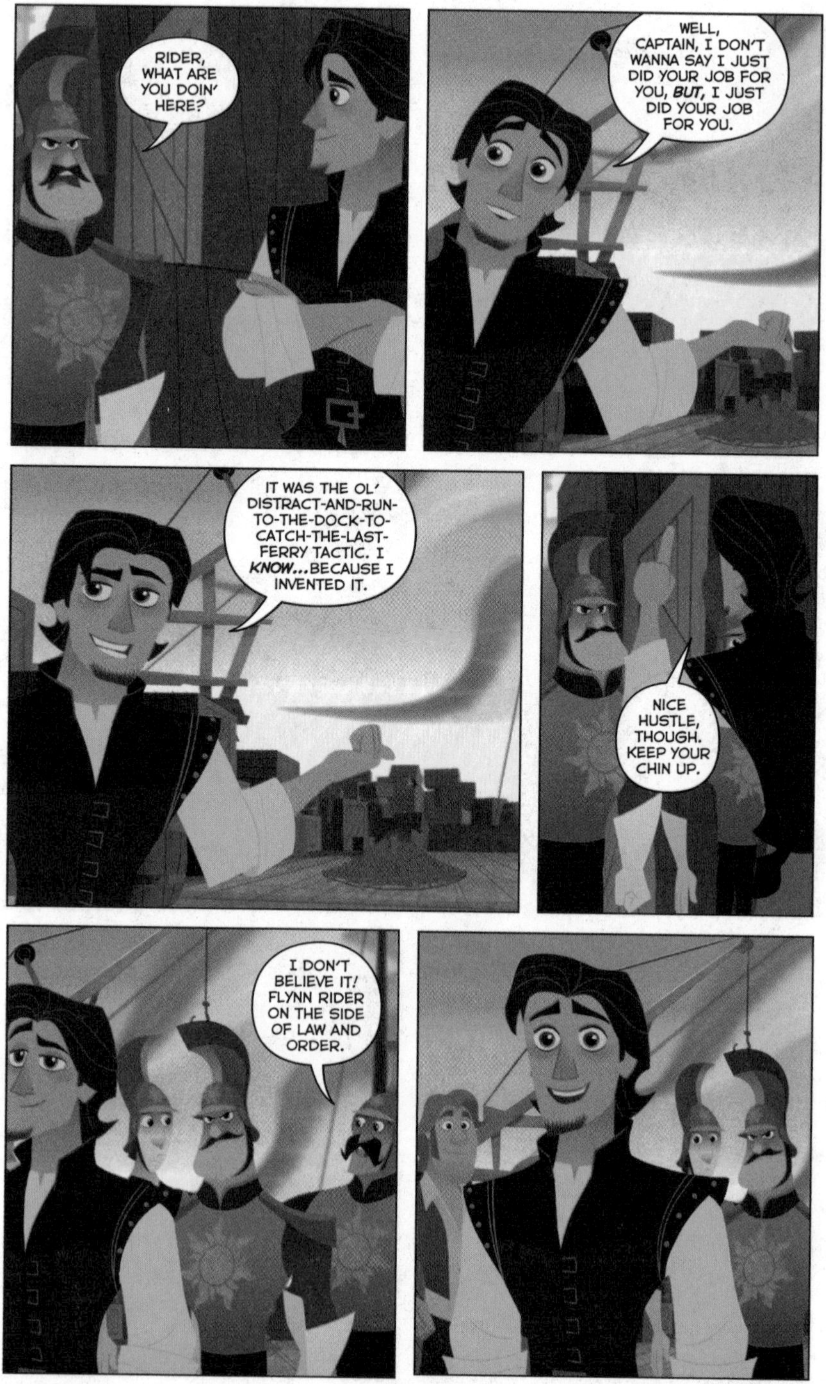
RIDER, WHAT ARE YOU DOIN' HERE?
WELL, CAPTAIN, I DON'T WANNA SAY I JUST DID YOUR JOB FOR YOU, *BUT,* I JUST DID YOUR JOB FOR YOU.
IT WAS THE OL' DISTRACT-AND-RUN-TO-THE-DOCK-TO-CATCH-THE-LAST-FERRY TACTIC. I *KNOW*...BECAUSE I INVENTED IT.
NICE HUSTLE, THOUGH. KEEP YOUR CHIN UP.
I DON'T BELIEVE IT! FLYNN RIDER ON THE SIDE OF LAW AND ORDER.

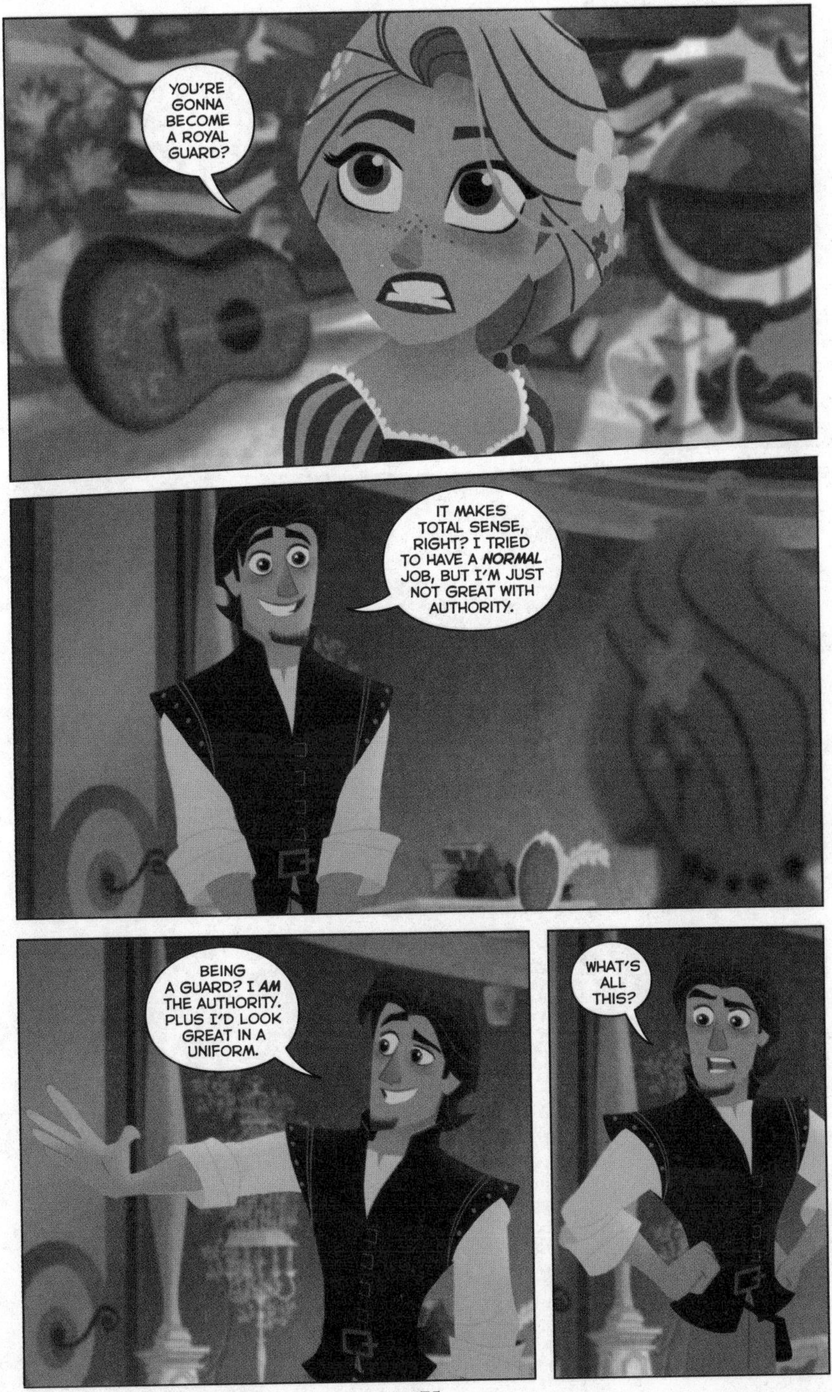
YOU'RE GONNA BECOME A ROYAL GUARD?
IT MAKES TOTAL SENSE, RIGHT? I TRIED TO HAVE A ***NORMAL*** JOB, BUT I'M JUST NOT GREAT WITH AUTHORITY.
BEING A GUARD? I ***AM*** THE AUTHORITY. PLUS I'D LOOK GREAT IN A UNIFORM.
WHAT'S ALL THIS?

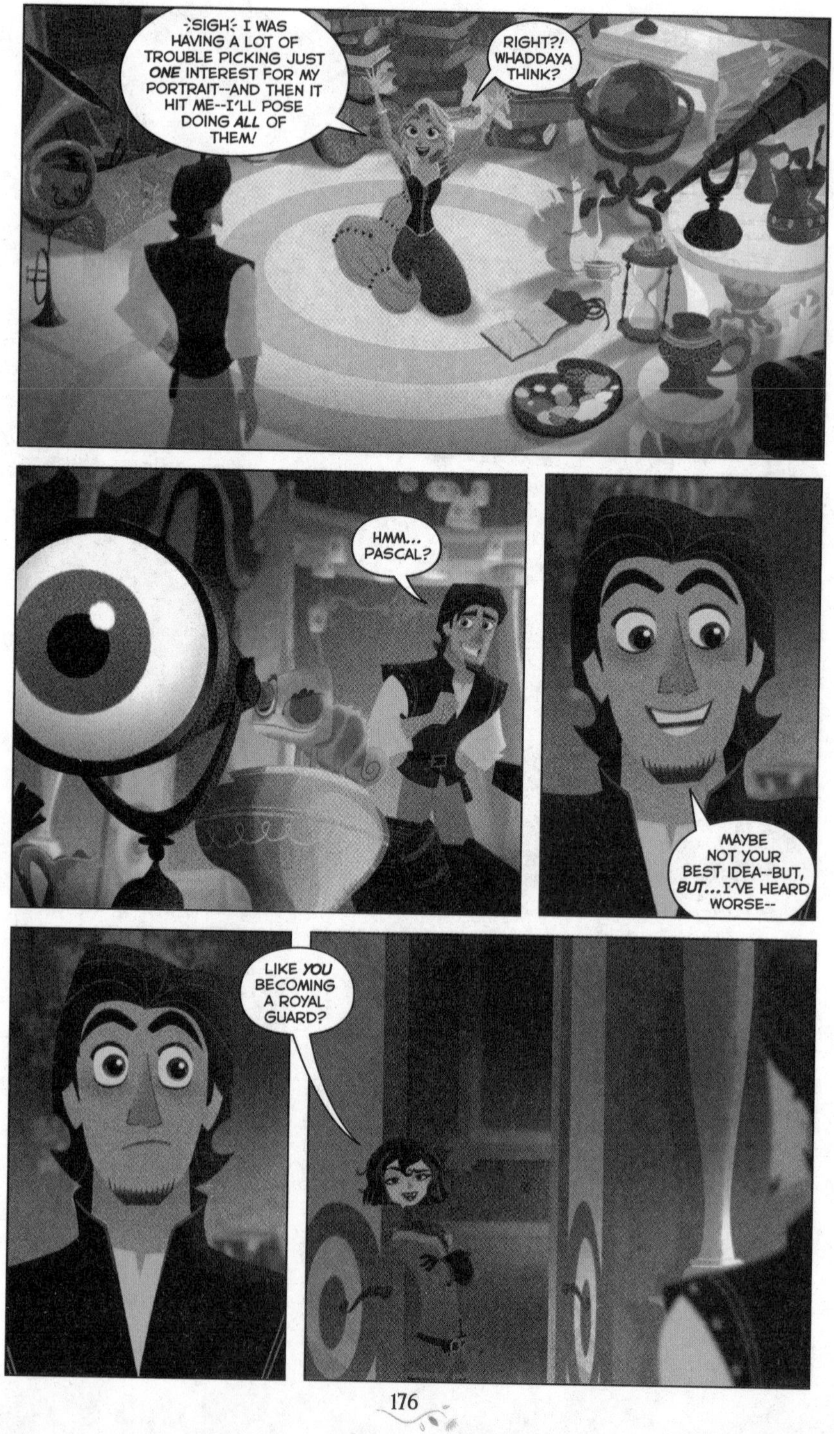
SIGH I WAS HAVING A LOT OF TROUBLE PICKING JUST ***ONE*** INTEREST FOR MY PORTRAIT--AND THEN IT HIT ME--I'LL POSE DOING ***ALL*** OF THEM!
RIGHT?! WHADDAYA THINK?
HMM... PASCAL?
MAYBE NOT YOUR BEST IDEA--BUT, ***BUT...*** I'VE HEARD WORSE--
LIKE ***YOU*** BECOMING A ROYAL GUARD?

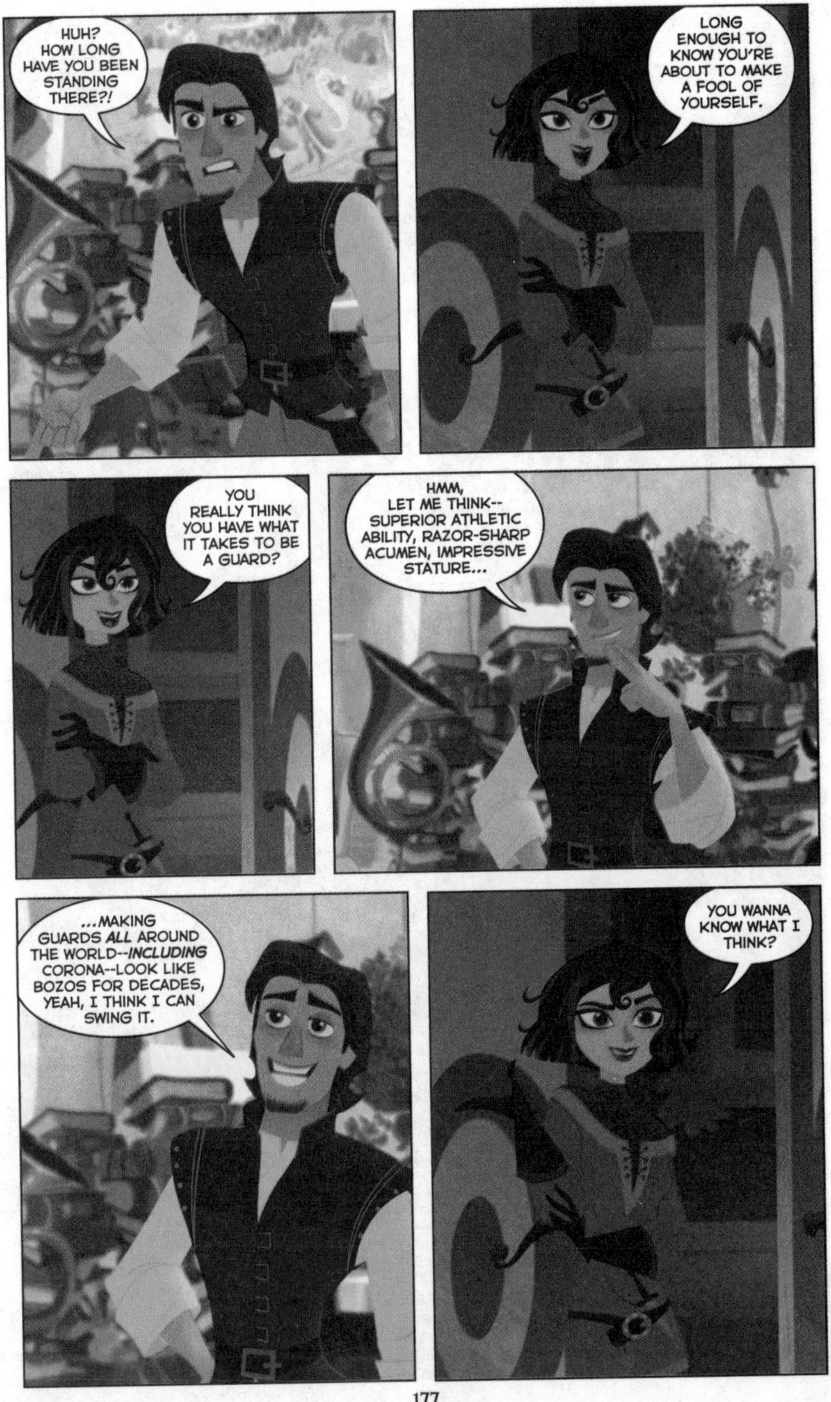
HUH? HOW LONG HAVE YOU BEEN STANDING THERE?!
LONG ENOUGH TO KNOW YOU'RE ABOUT TO MAKE A FOOL OF YOURSELF.
YOU REALLY THINK YOU HAVE WHAT IT TAKES TO BE A GUARD?
HMM, LET ME THINK--SUPERIOR ATHLETIC ABILITY, RAZOR-SHARP ACUMEN, IMPRESSIVE STATURE...
...MAKING GUARDS ALL AROUND THE WORLD--INCLUDING CORONA--LOOK LIKE BOZOS FOR DECADES, YEAH, I THINK I CAN SWING IT.
YOU WANNA KNOW WHAT I THINK?

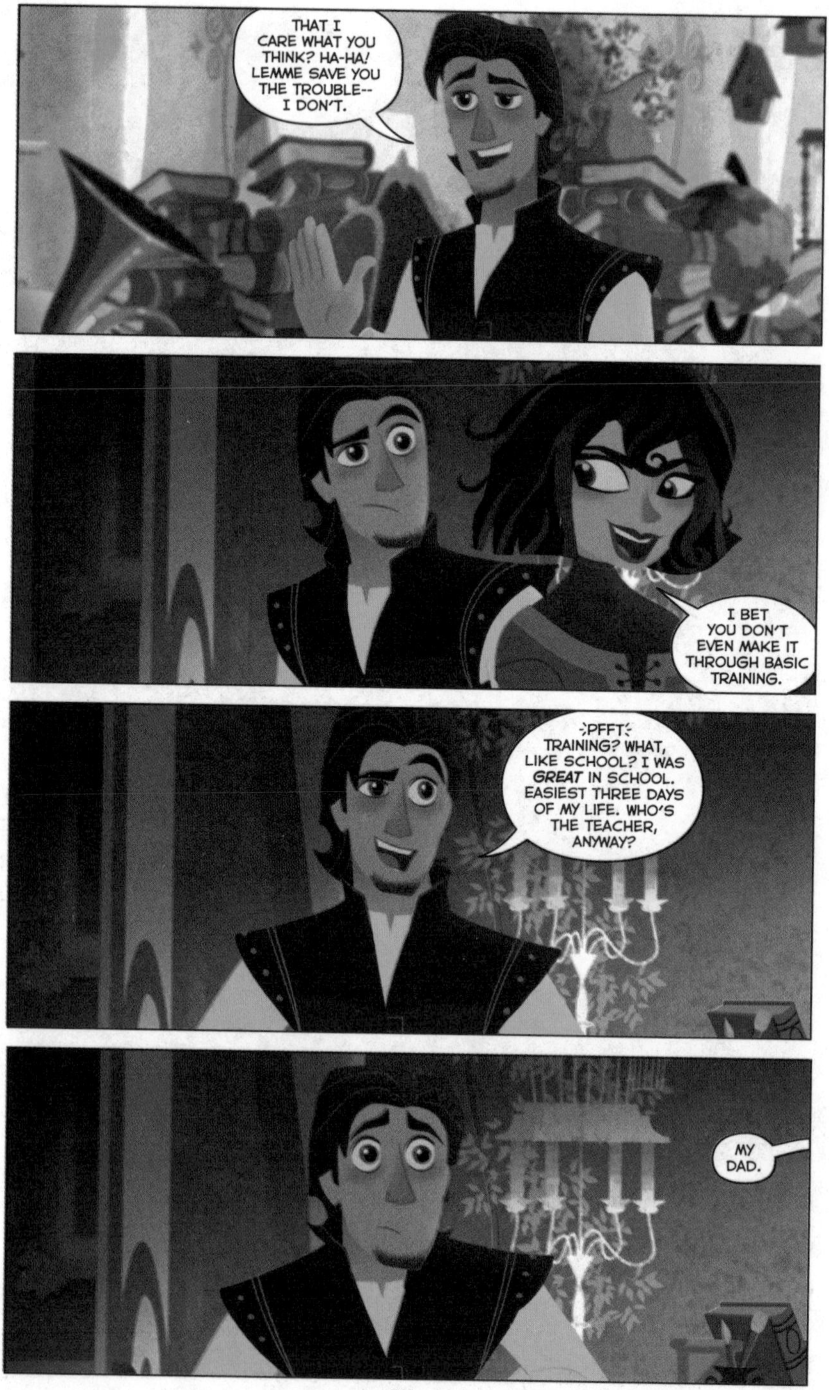
THAT I CARE WHAT YOU THINK? HA-HA! LEMME SAVE YOU THE TROUBLE-- I DON'T.
I BET YOU DON'T EVEN MAKE IT THROUGH BASIC TRAINING.
PFFT
TRAINING? WHAT, LIKE SCHOOL? I WAS *GREAT* IN SCHOOL. EASIEST THREE DAYS OF MY LIFE. WHO'S THE TEACHER, ANYWAY?
MY DAD.

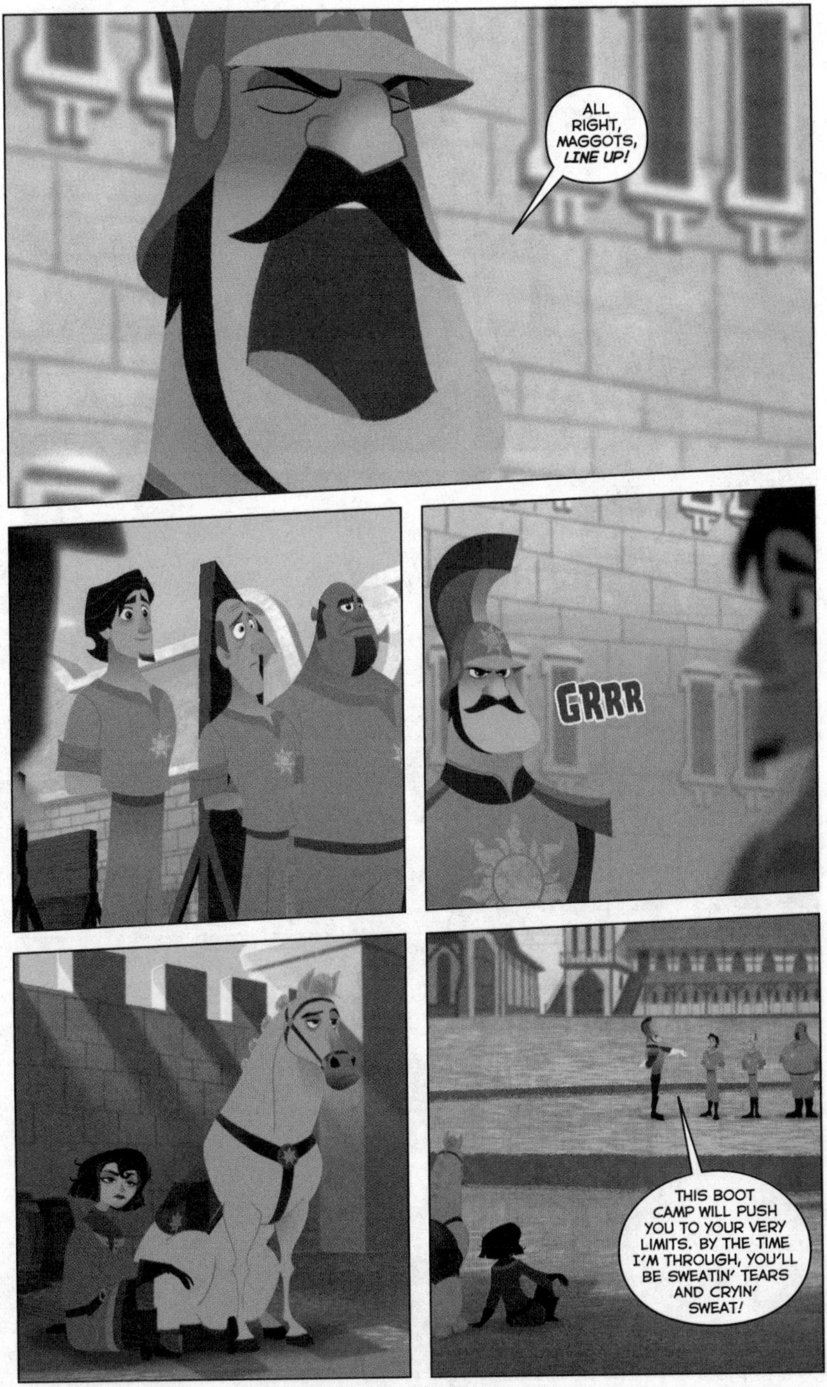
ALL RIGHT, MAGGOTS, *LINE UP!*
GRRR
THIS BOOT CAMP WILL PUSH YOU TO YOUR VERY LIMITS. BY THE TIME I'M THROUGH, YOU'LL BE SWEATIN' TEARS AND CRYIN' SWEAT!

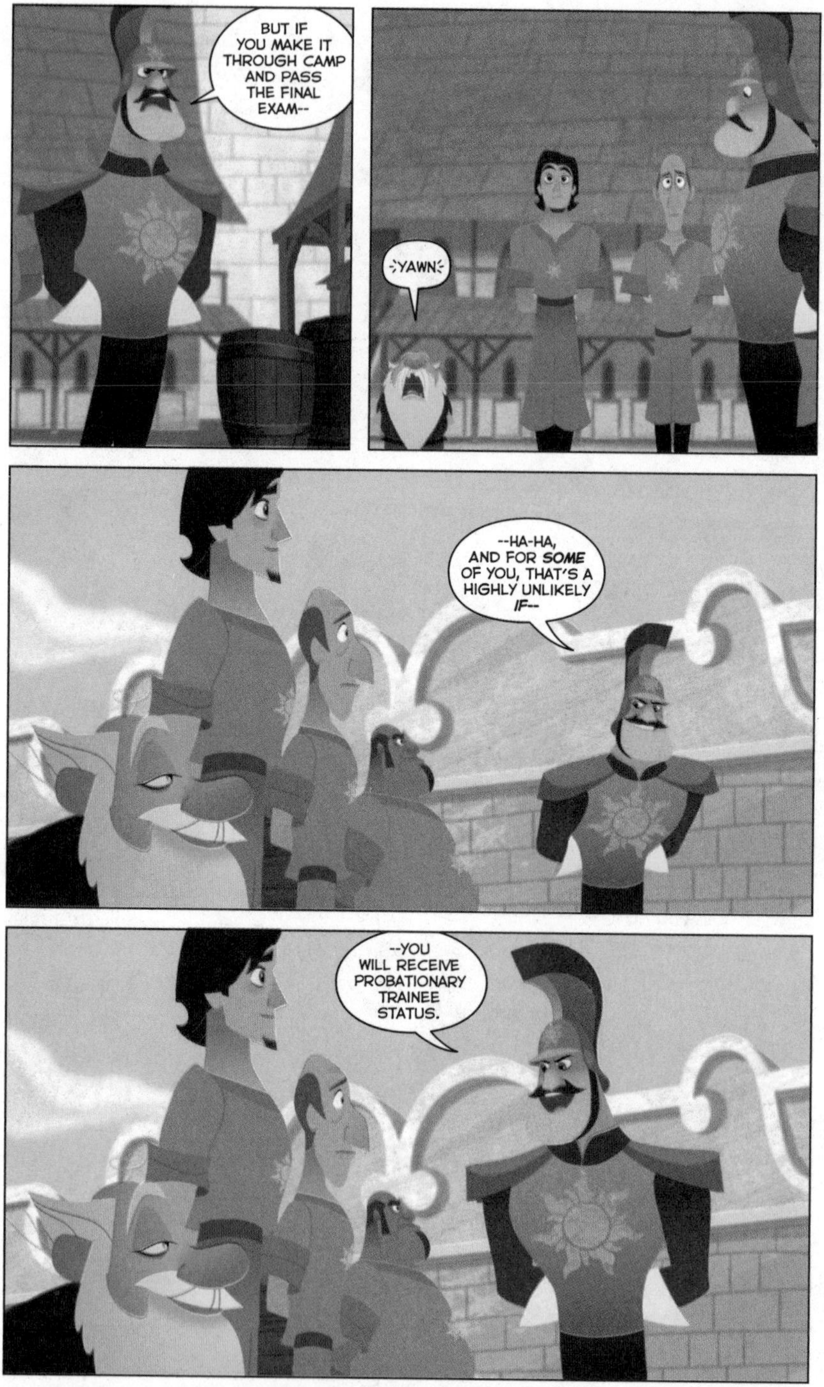
BUT IF YOU MAKE IT THROUGH CAMP AND PASS THE FINAL EXAM--
YAWN
--HA-HA, AND FOR *SOME* OF YOU, THAT'S A HIGHLY UNLIKELY *IF*--
--YOU WILL RECEIVE PROBATIONARY TRAINEE STATUS.

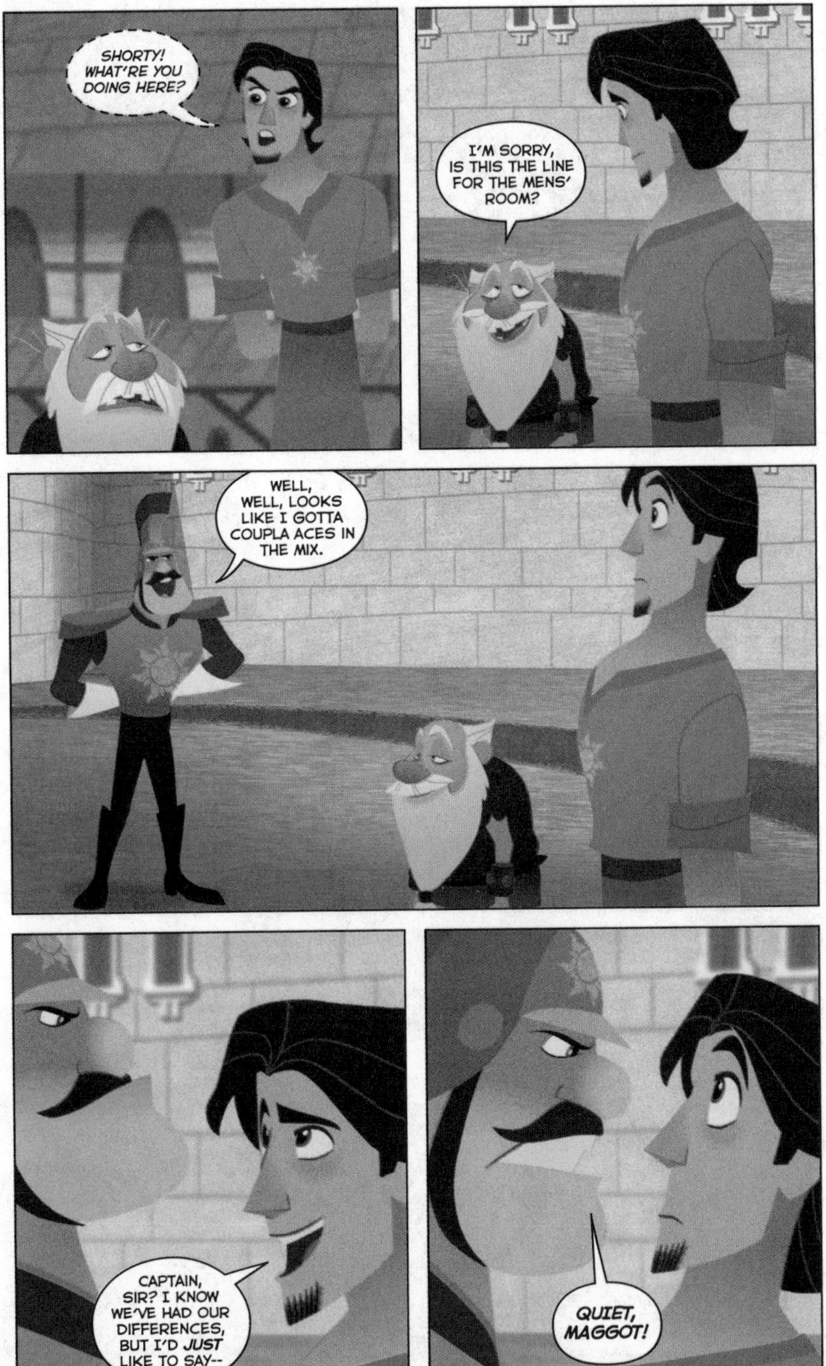
SHORTY! WHAT'RE YOU DOING HERE?
I'M SORRY, IS THIS THE LINE FOR THE MENS' ROOM?
WELL, WELL, LOOKS LIKE I GOTTA COUPLA ACES IN THE MIX.
CAPTAIN, SIR? I KNOW WE'VE HAD OUR DIFFERENCES, BUT I'D *JUST* LIKE TO SAY--
QUIET, MAGGOT!

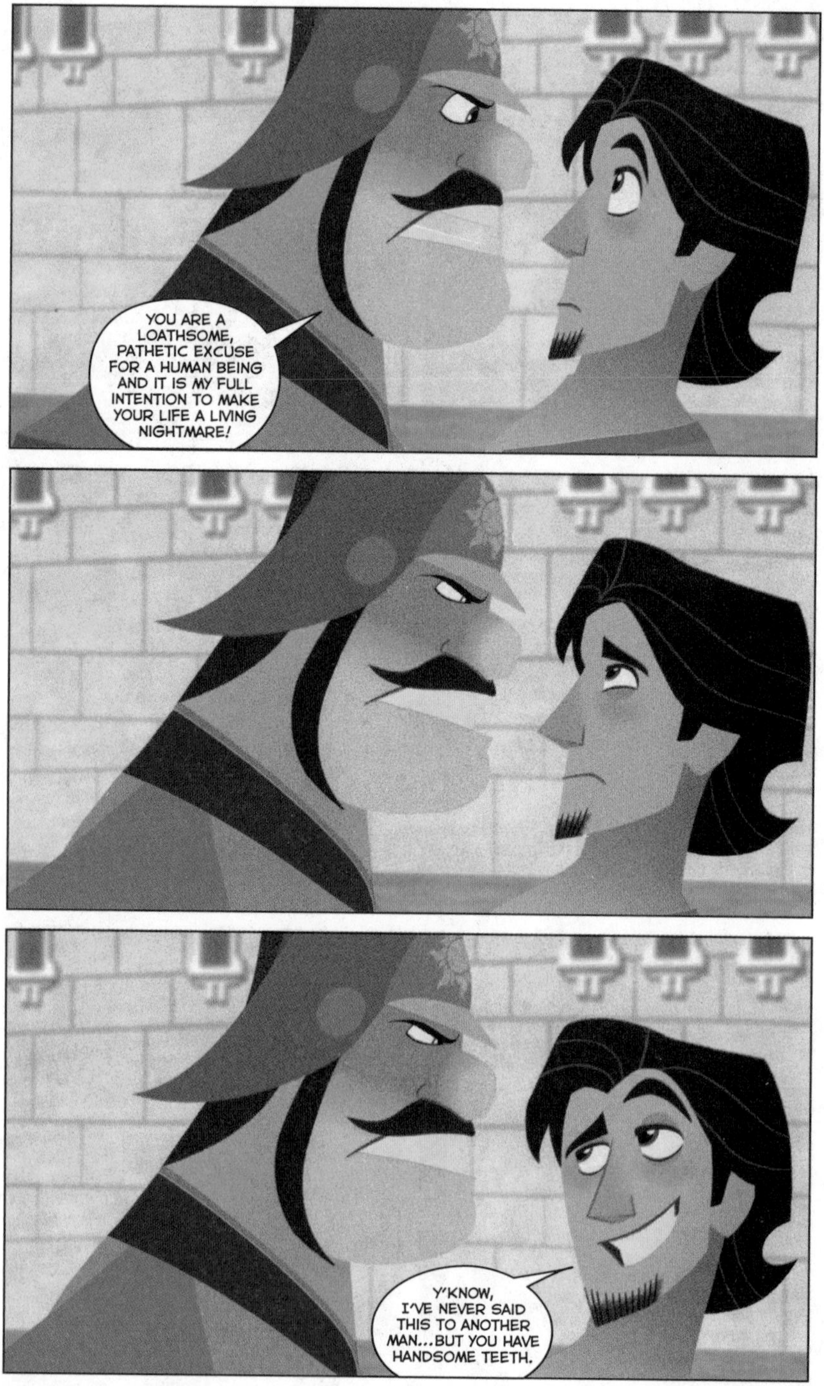
YOU ARE A LOATHSOME, PATHETIC EXCUSE FOR A HUMAN BEING AND IT IS MY FULL INTENTION TO MAKE YOUR LIFE A LIVING NIGHTMARE!
Y'KNOW, I'VE NEVER SAID THIS TO ANOTHER MAN...BUT YOU HAVE HANDSOME TEETH.

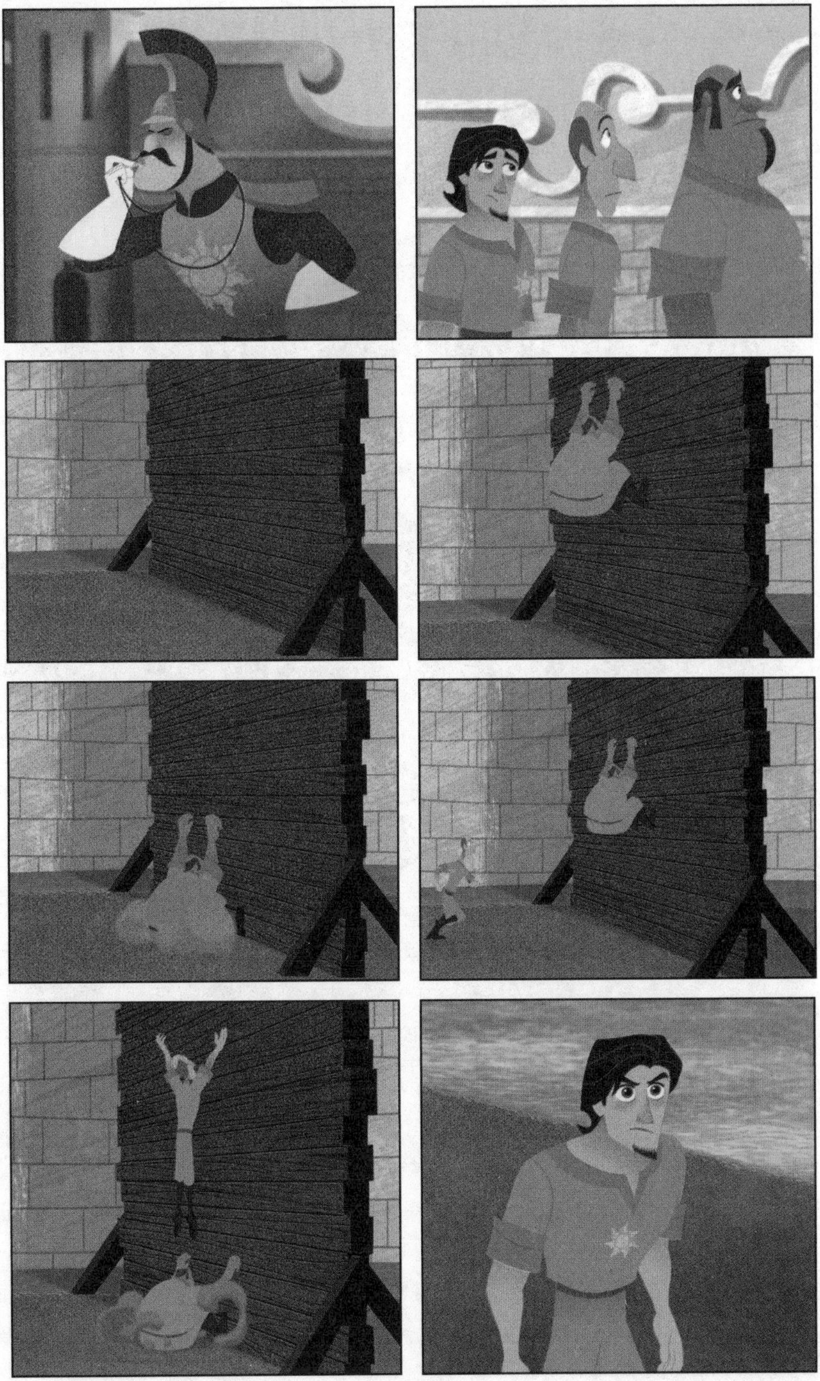

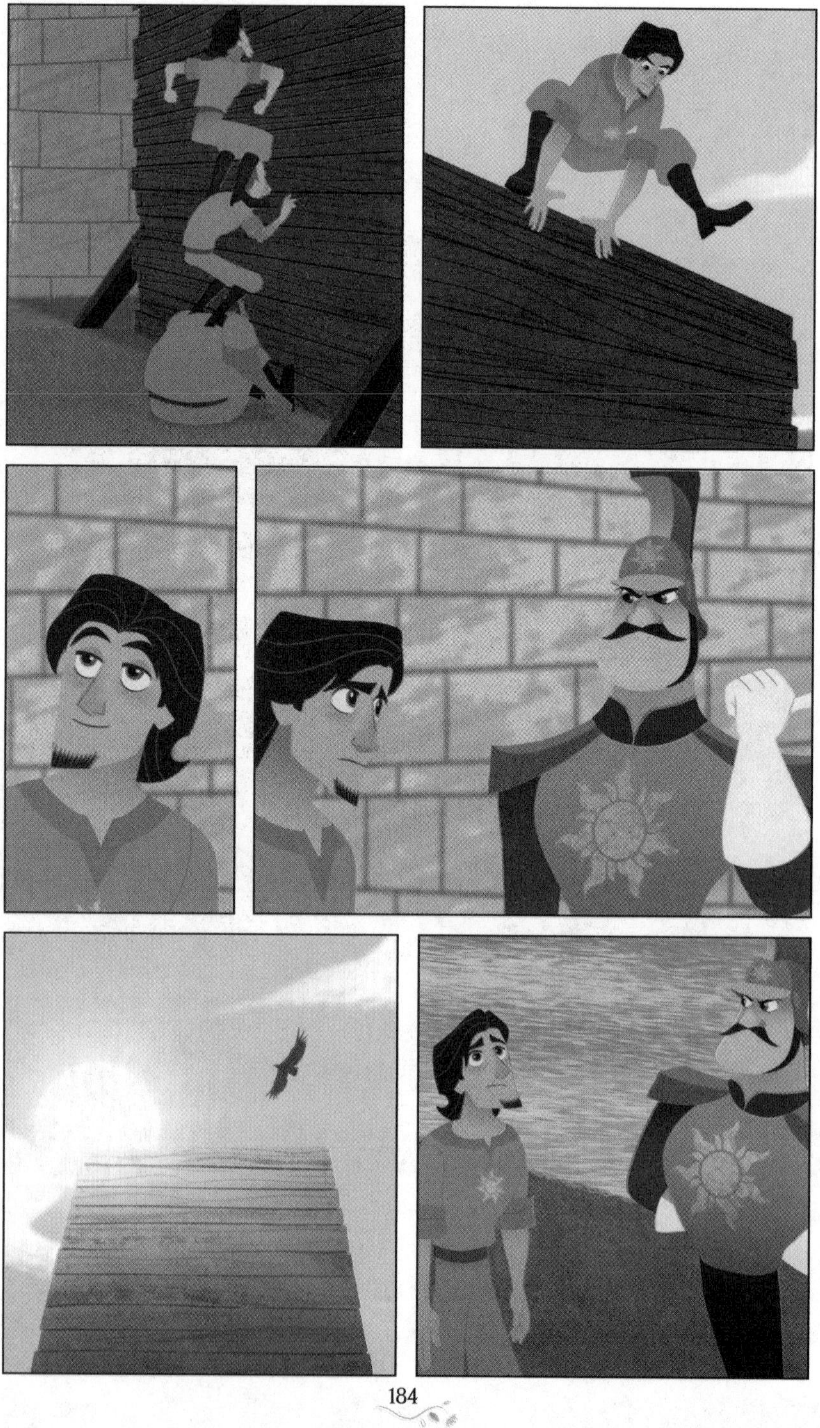

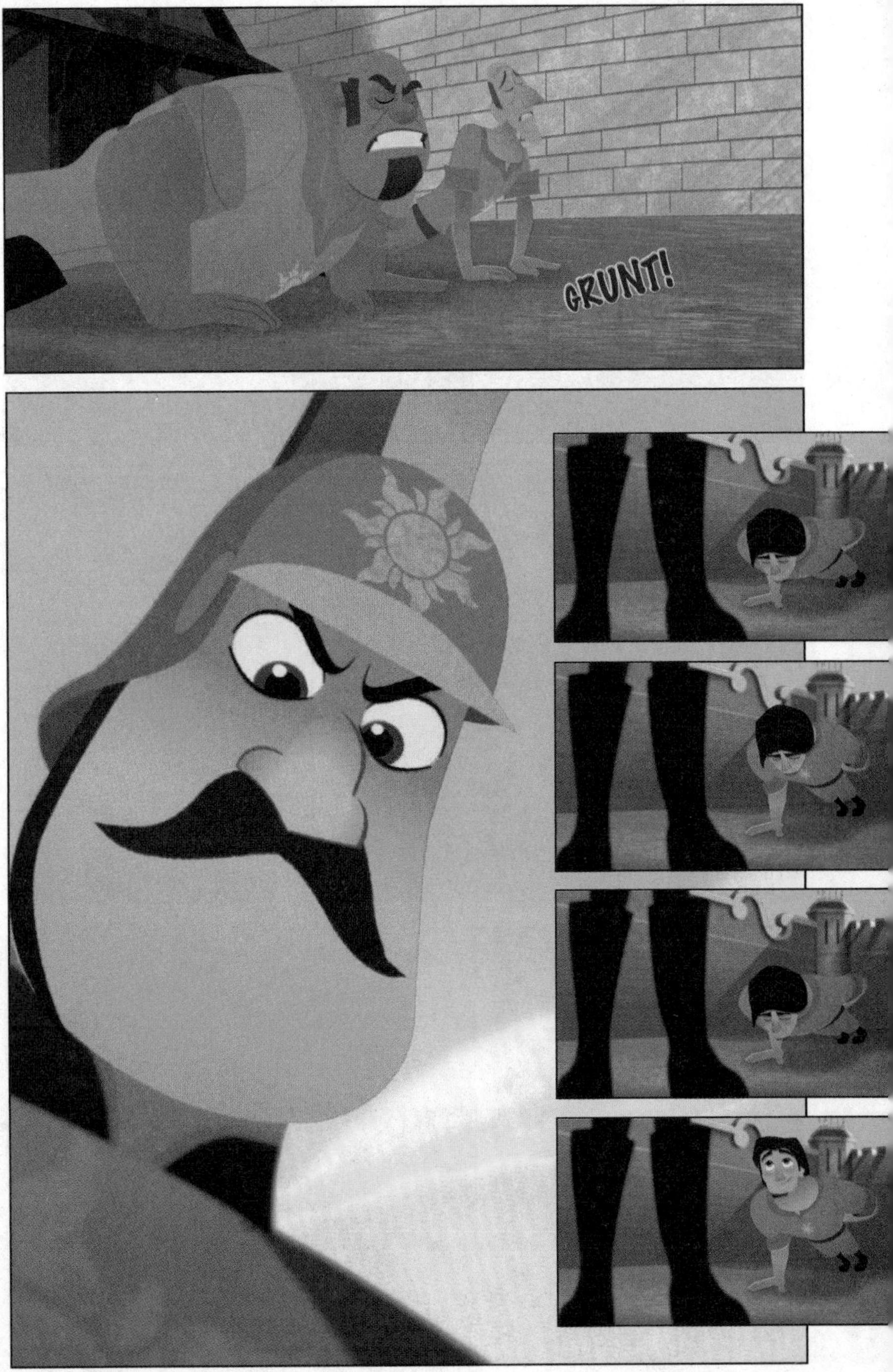
GRUNT!

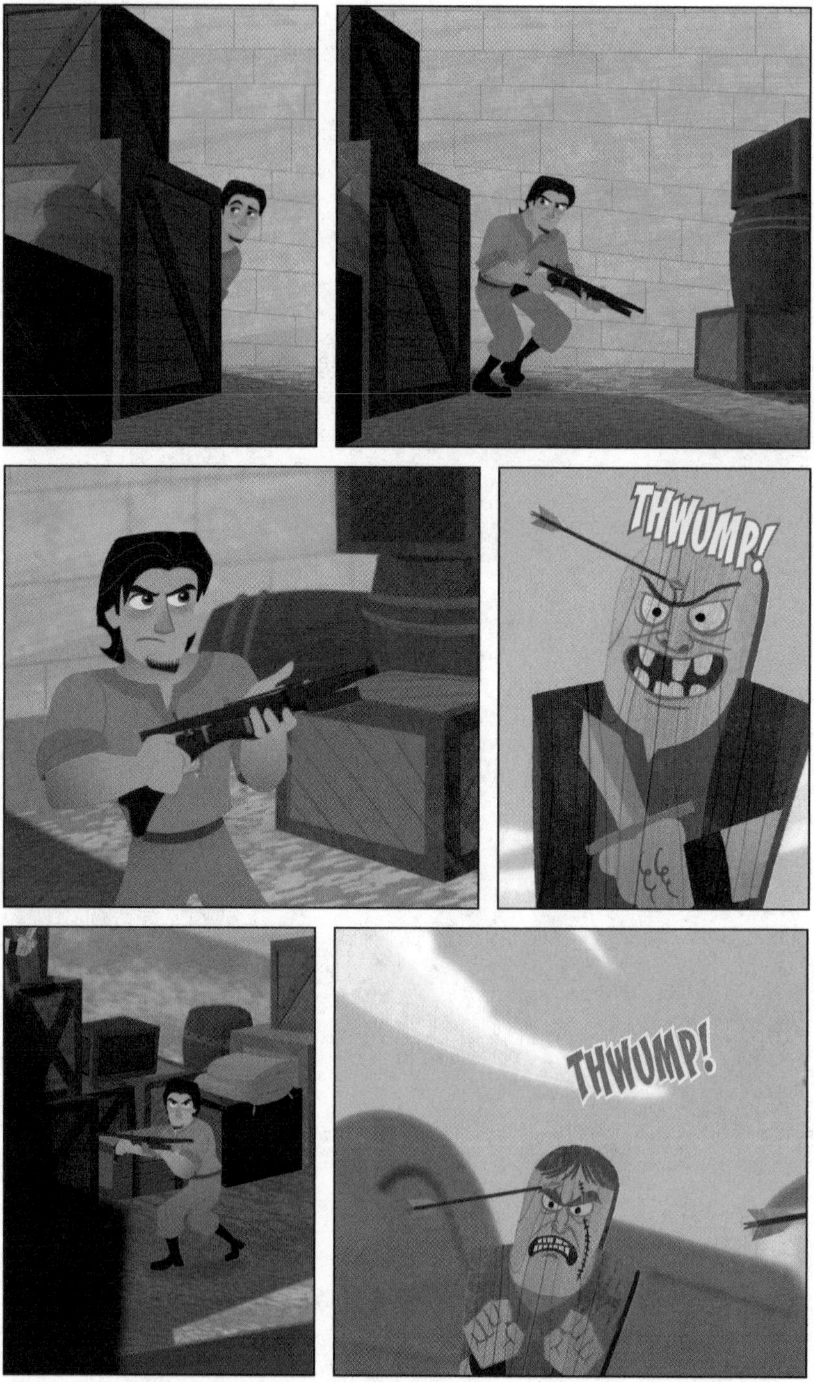
THWUMP!
THWUMP!

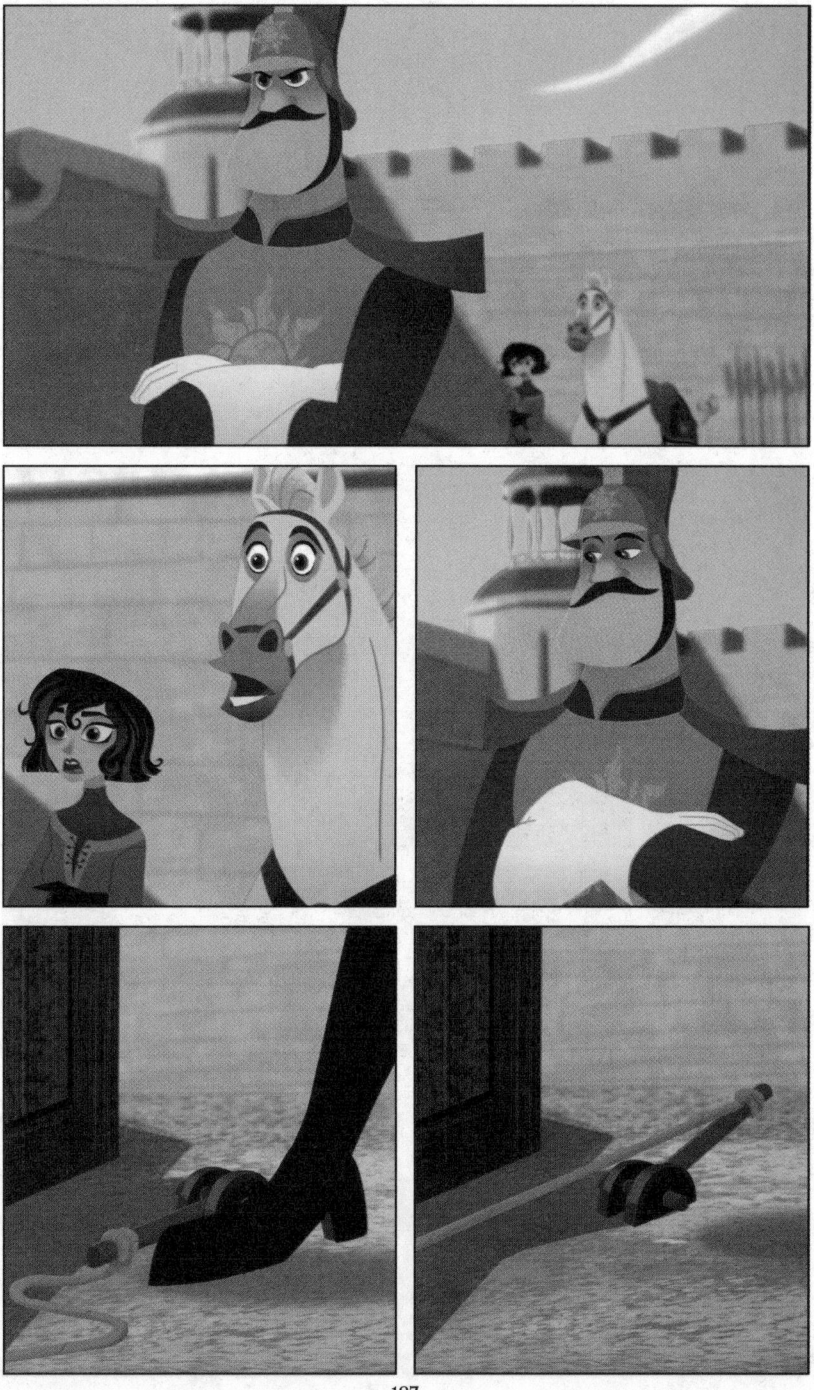

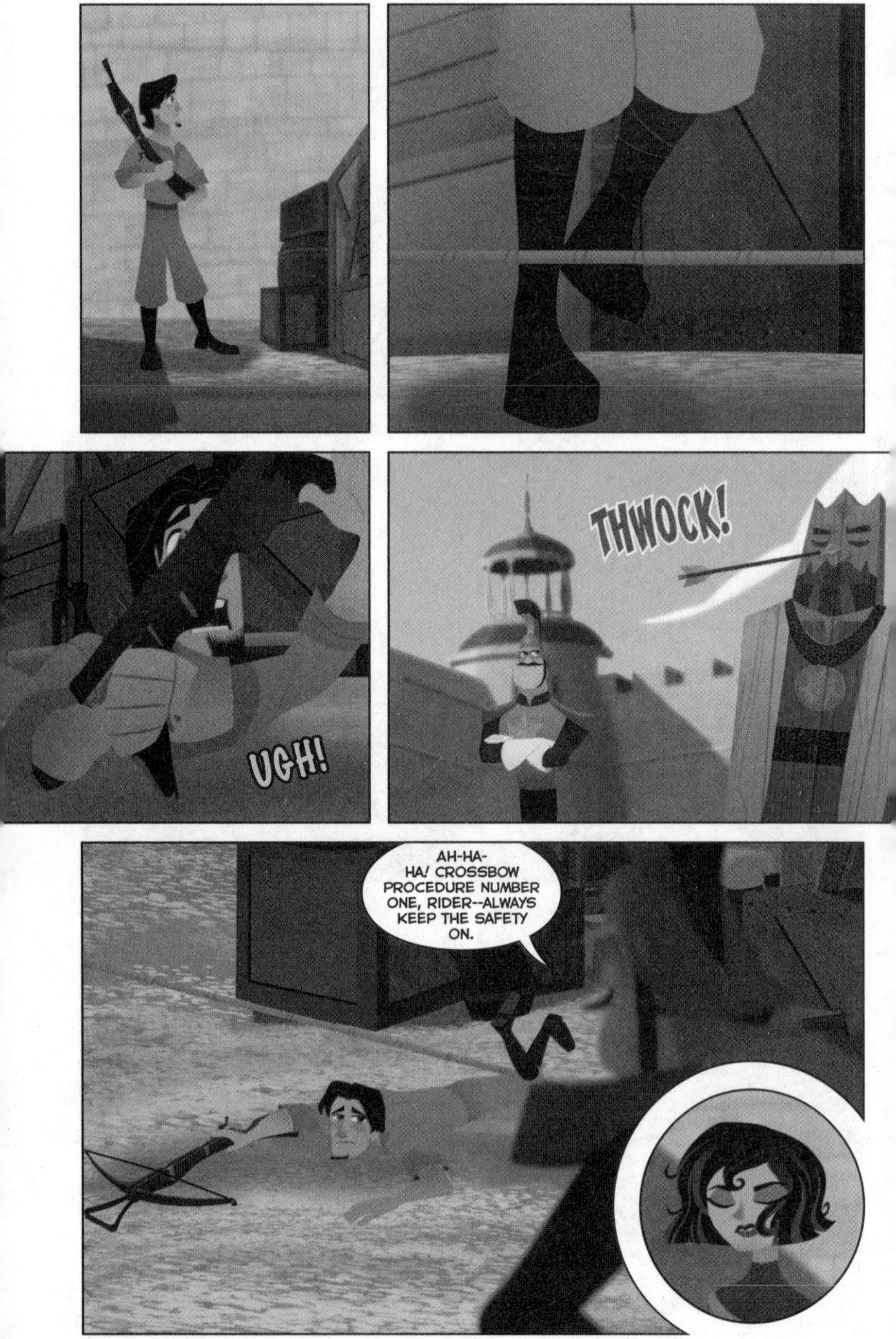
UGH!
THWOCK!
AH-HA-HA! CROSSBOW PROCEDURE NUMBER ONE, RIDER--ALWAYS KEEP THE SAFETY ON.

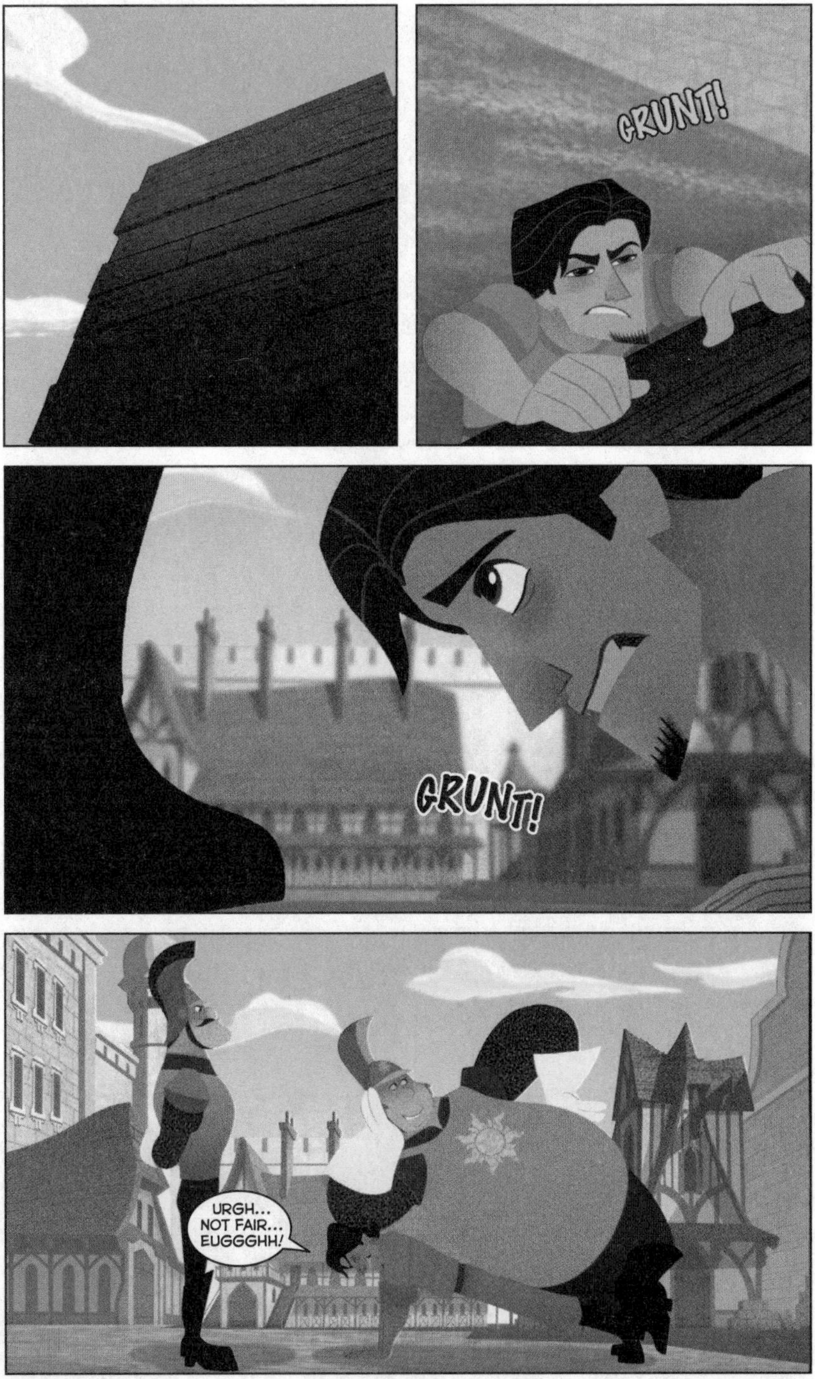
GRUNT!
GRUNT!
URGH... NOT FAIR... EUGGGHH!

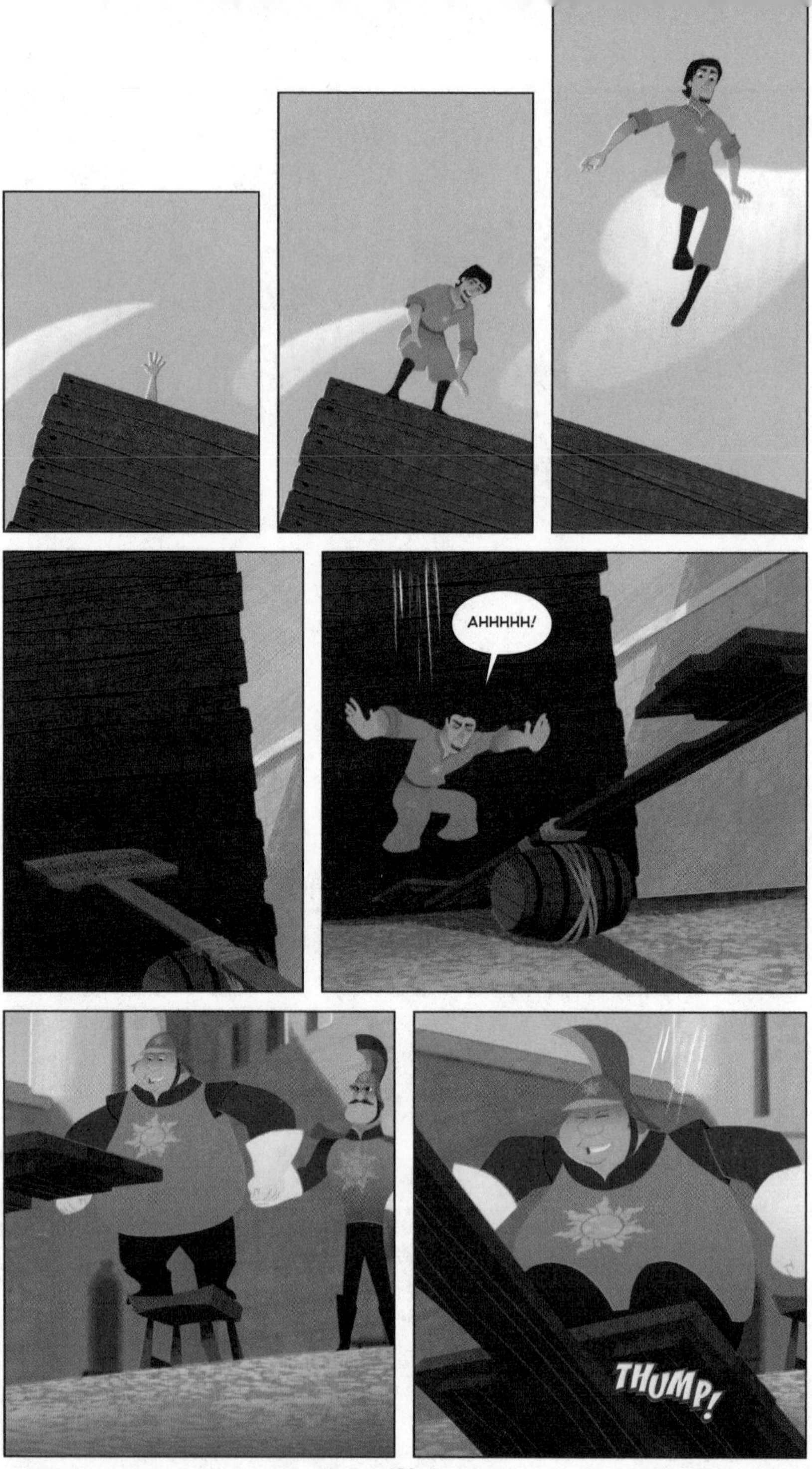
AHHHHH!
THUMP!

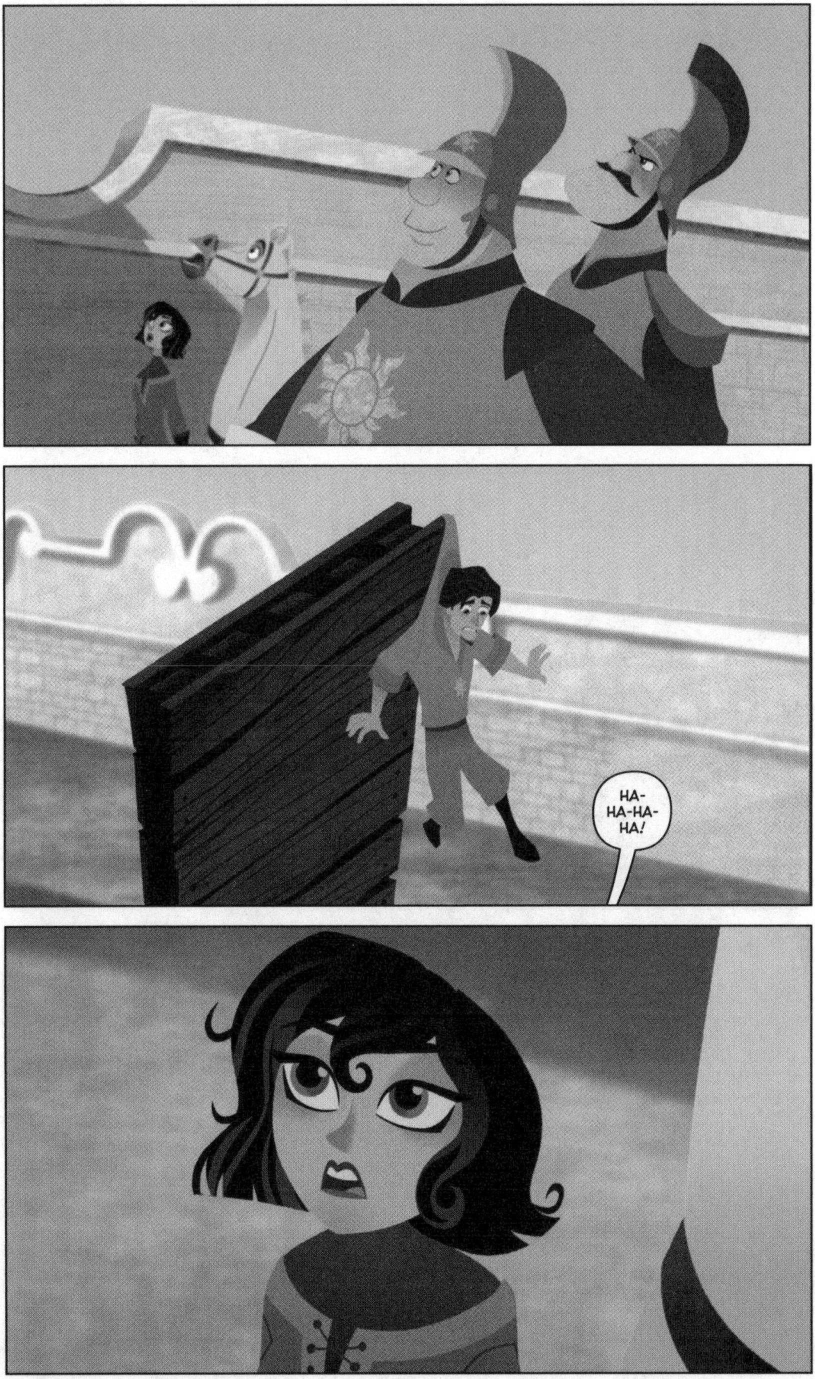
HA-HA-HA-HA!

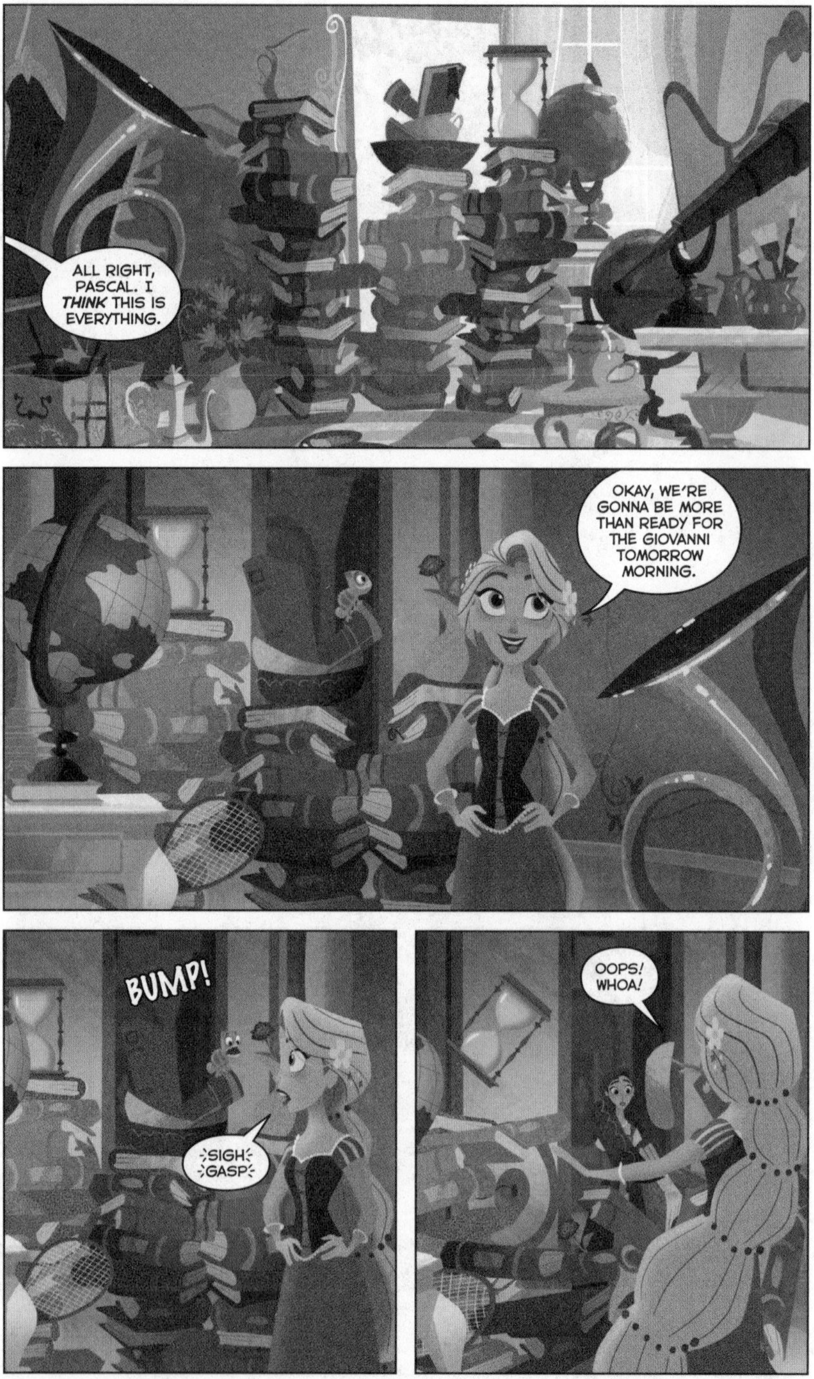
ALL RIGHT, PASCAL. I *THINK* THIS IS EVERYTHING.
OKAY, WE'RE GONNA BE MORE THAN READY FOR THE GIOVANNI TOMORROW MORNING.
BUMP!
SIGH GASP
OOPS! WHOA!

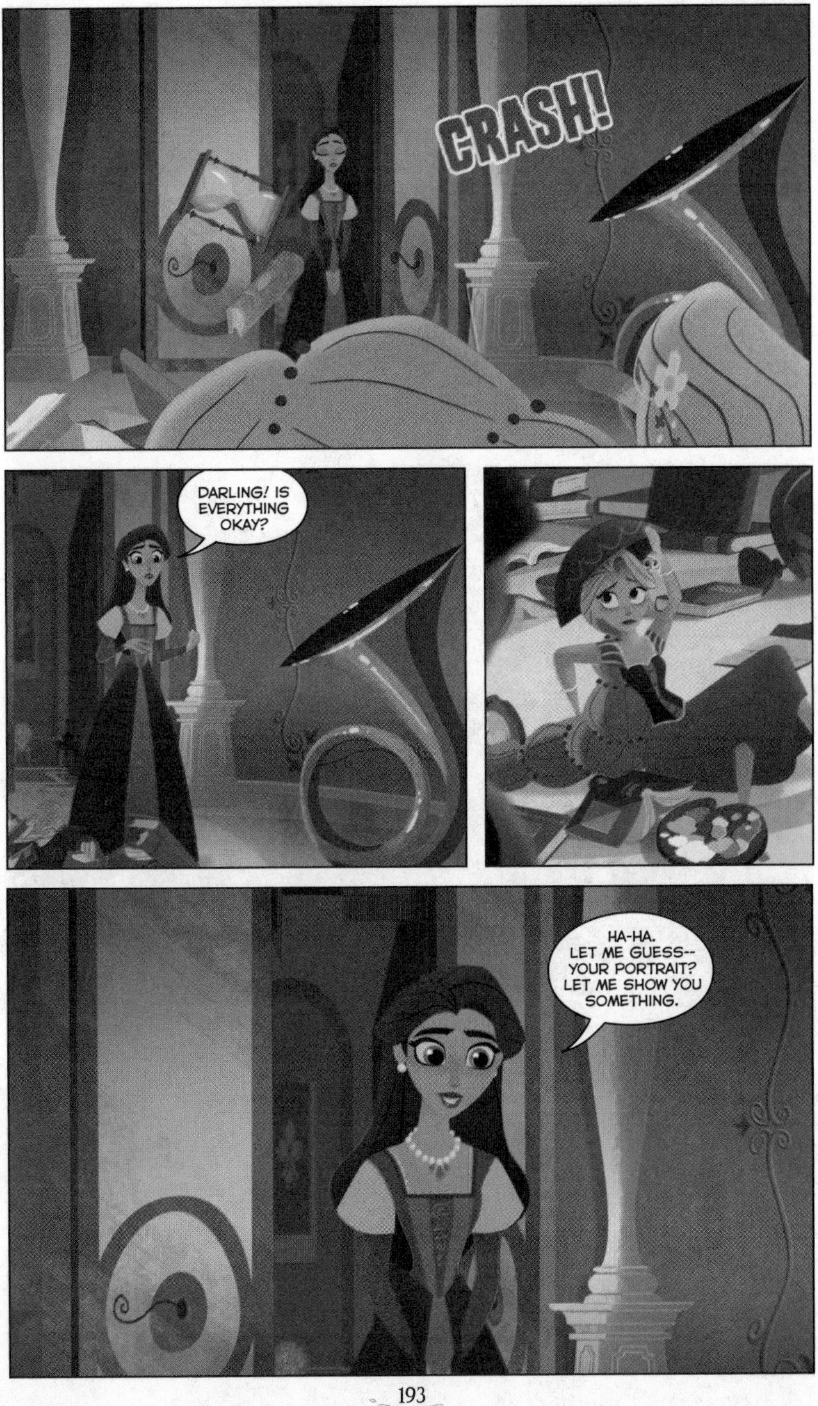
CRASH!
DARLING! IS EVERYTHING OKAY?
HA-HA. LET ME GUESS-- YOUR PORTRAIT? LET ME SHOW YOU SOMETHING.

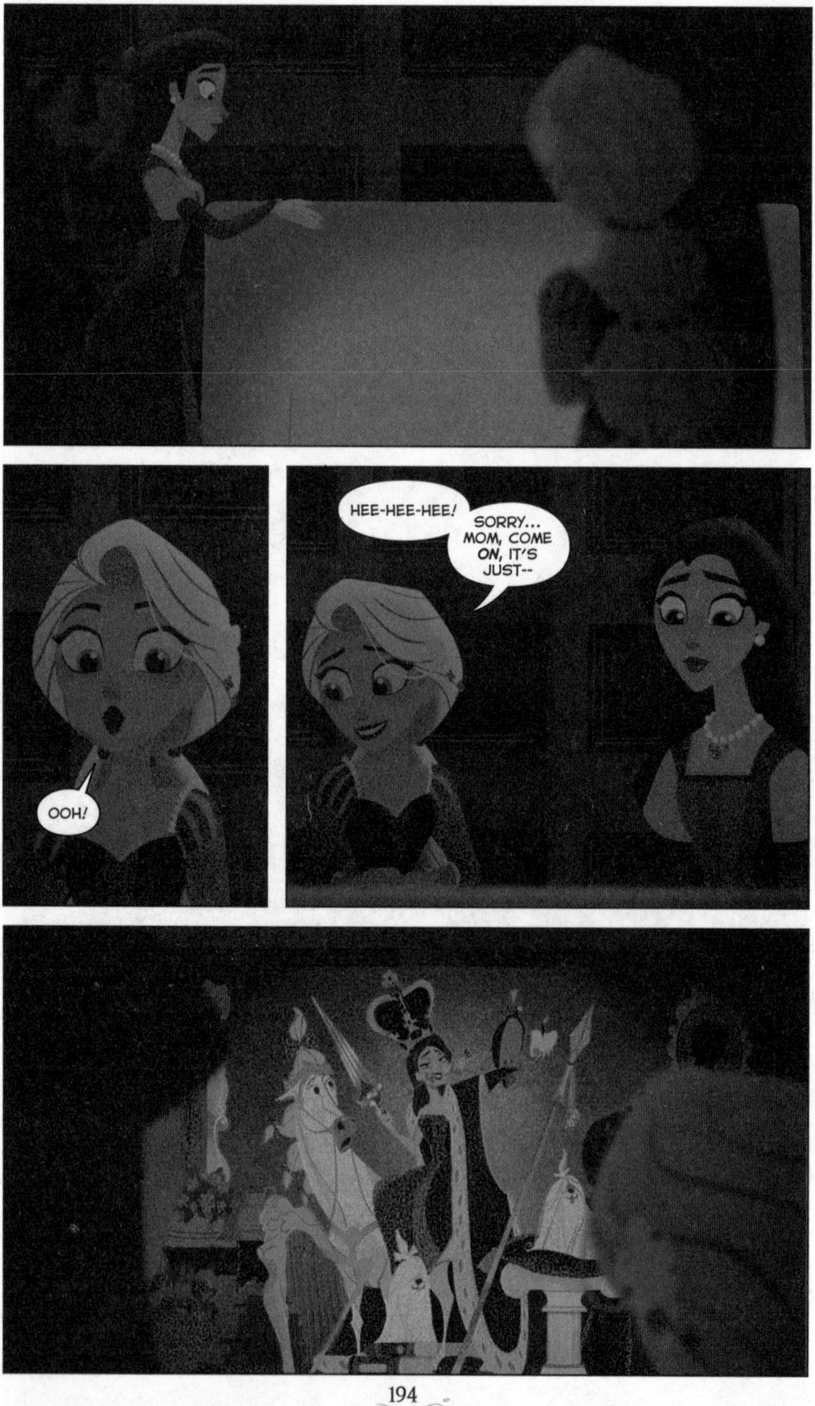
OOH!
HEE-HEE-HEE!
SORRY... MOM, COME ON, IT'S JUST--

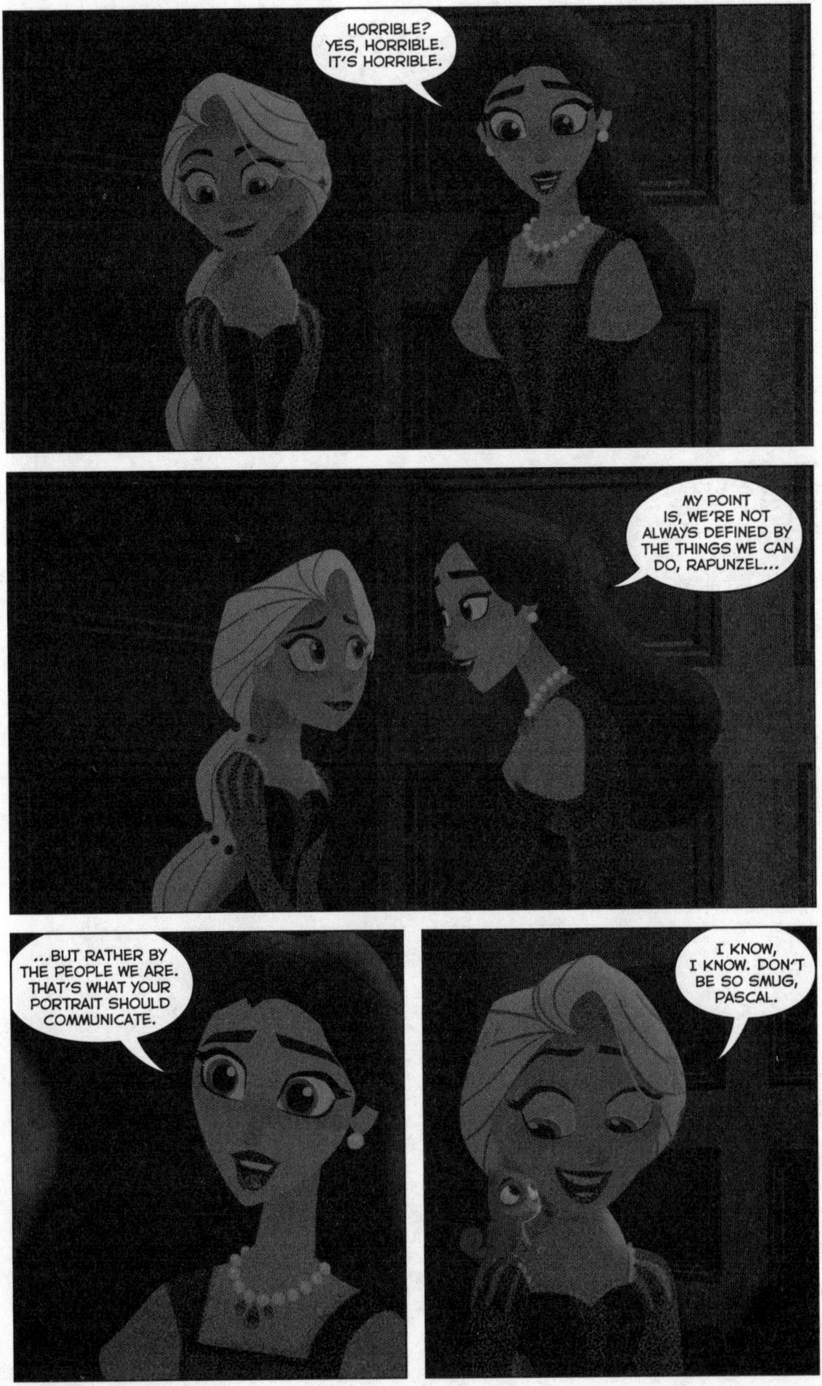
HORRIBLE? YES, HORRIBLE. IT'S HORRIBLE.
MY POINT IS, WE'RE NOT ALWAYS DEFINED BY THE THINGS WE CAN DO, RAPUNZEL...
...BUT RATHER BY THE PEOPLE WE ARE. THAT'S WHAT YOUR PORTRAIT SHOULD COMMUNICATE.
I KNOW, I KNOW. DON'T BE SO SMUG, PASCAL.

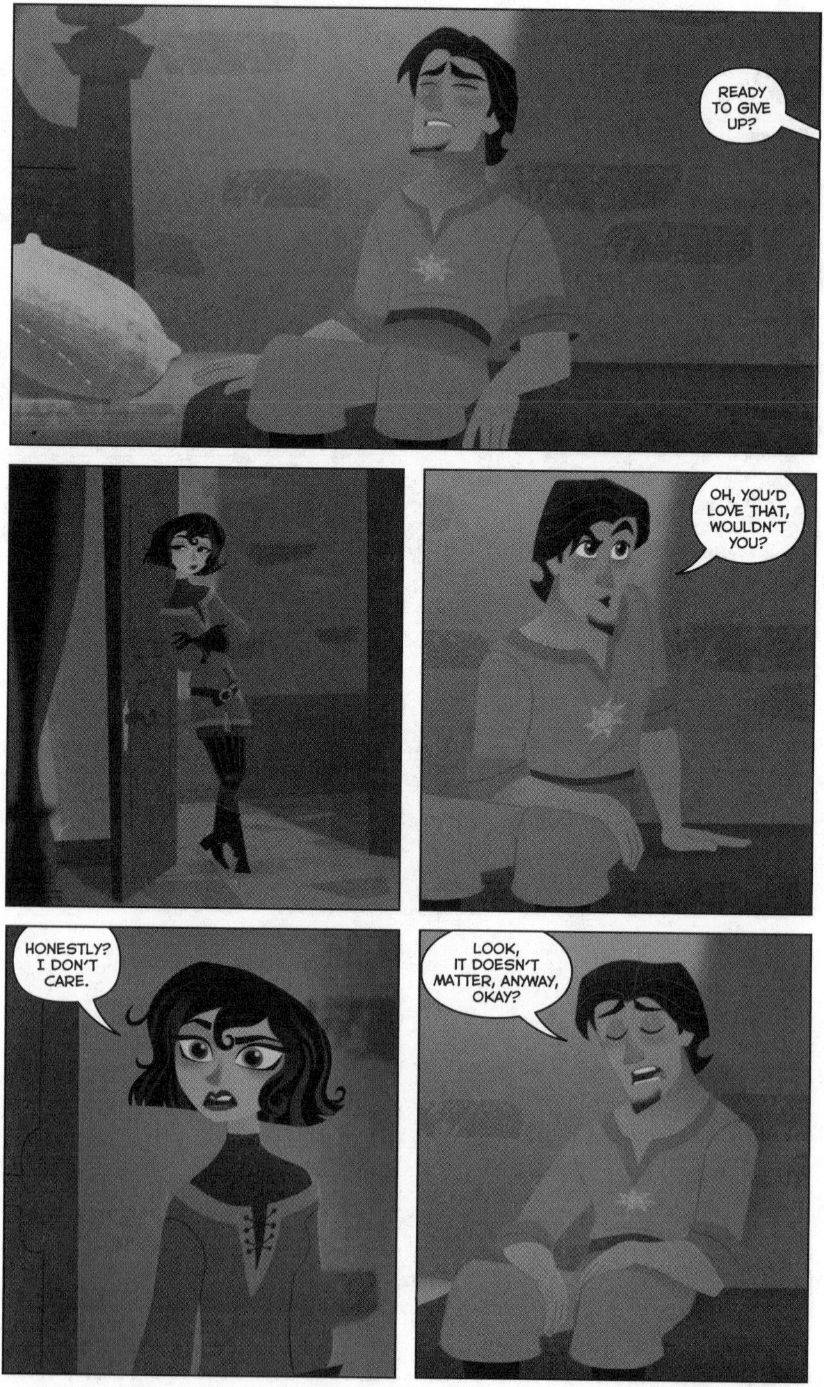
READY TO GIVE UP?
OH, YOU'D LOVE THAT, WOULDN'T YOU?
HONESTLY? I DON'T CARE.
LOOK, IT DOESN'T MATTER, ANYWAY, OKAY?

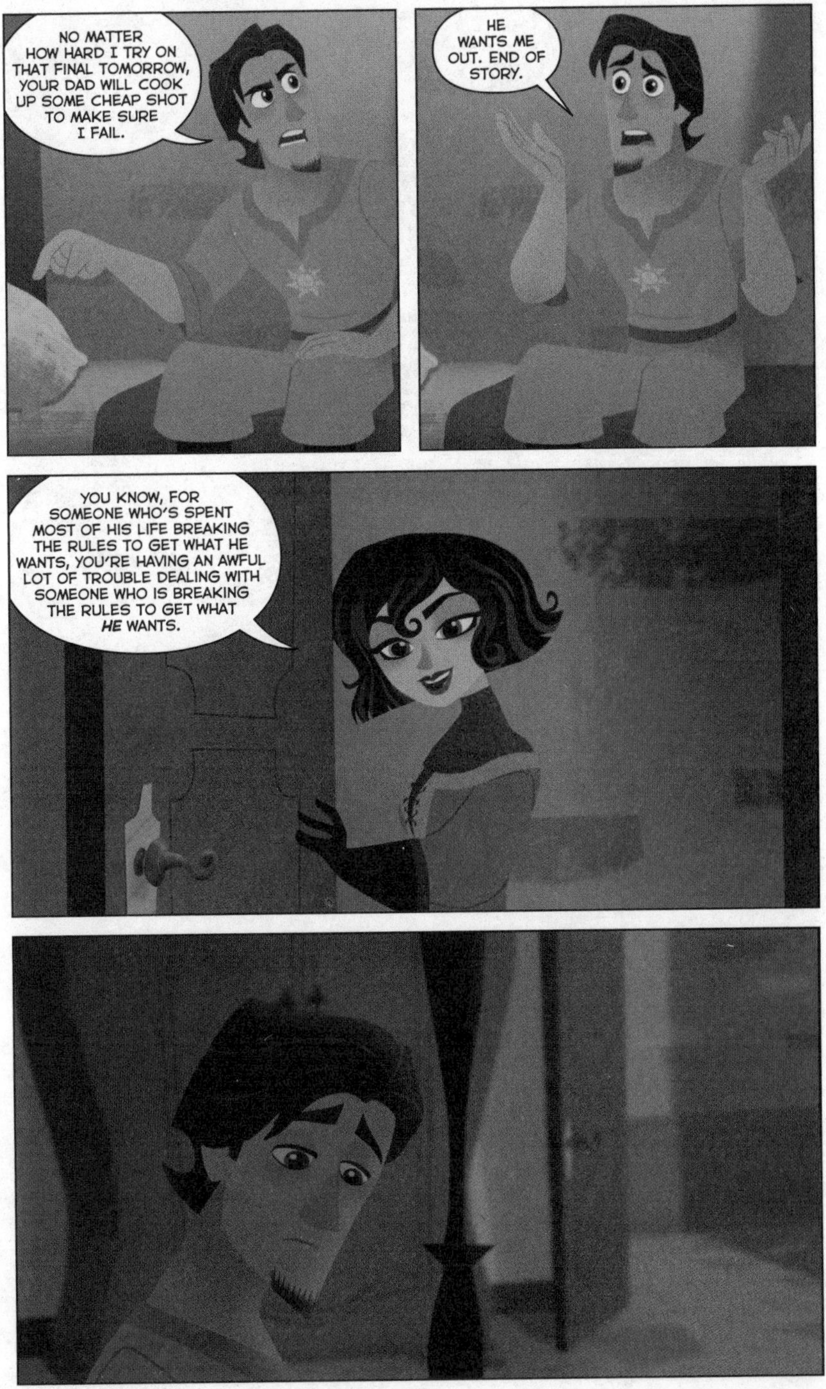
NO MATTER HOW HARD I TRY ON THAT FINAL TOMORROW, YOUR DAD WILL COOK UP SOME CHEAP SHOT TO MAKE SURE I FAIL.
HE WANTS ME OUT. END OF STORY.
YOU KNOW, FOR SOMEONE WHO'S SPENT MOST OF HIS LIFE BREAKING THE RULES TO GET WHAT HE WANTS, YOU'RE HAVING AN AWFUL LOT OF TROUBLE DEALING WITH SOMEONE WHO IS BREAKING THE RULES TO GET WHAT *HE* WANTS.

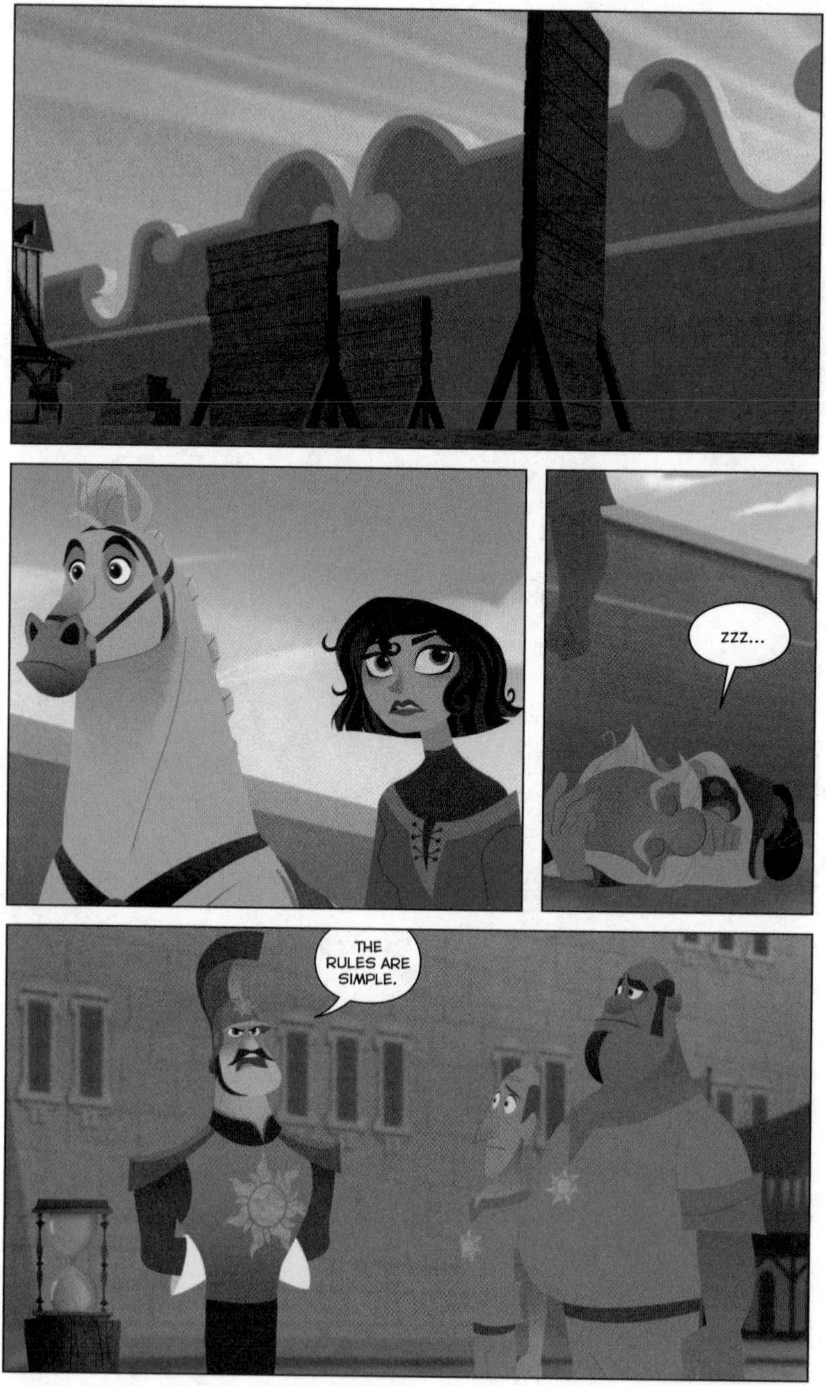
ZZZ...
THE RULES ARE SIMPLE.

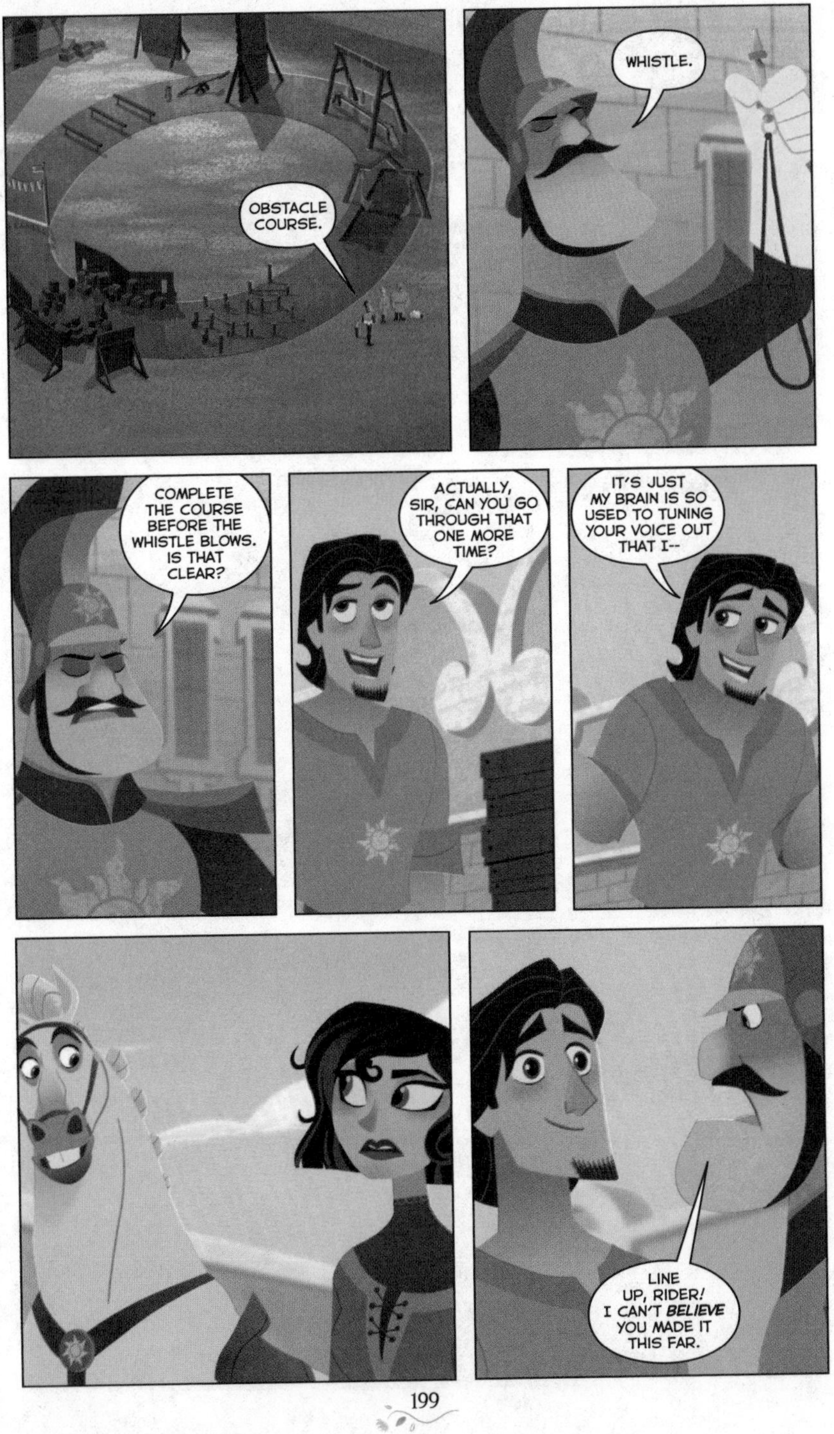
OBSTACLE COURSE.
WHISTLE.
COMPLETE THE COURSE BEFORE THE WHISTLE BLOWS. IS THAT CLEAR?
ACTUALLY, SIR, CAN YOU GO THROUGH THAT ONE MORE TIME?
IT'S JUST MY BRAIN IS SO USED TO TUNING YOUR VOICE OUT THAT I--
LINE UP, RIDER! I CAN'T *BELIEVE* YOU MADE IT THIS FAR.

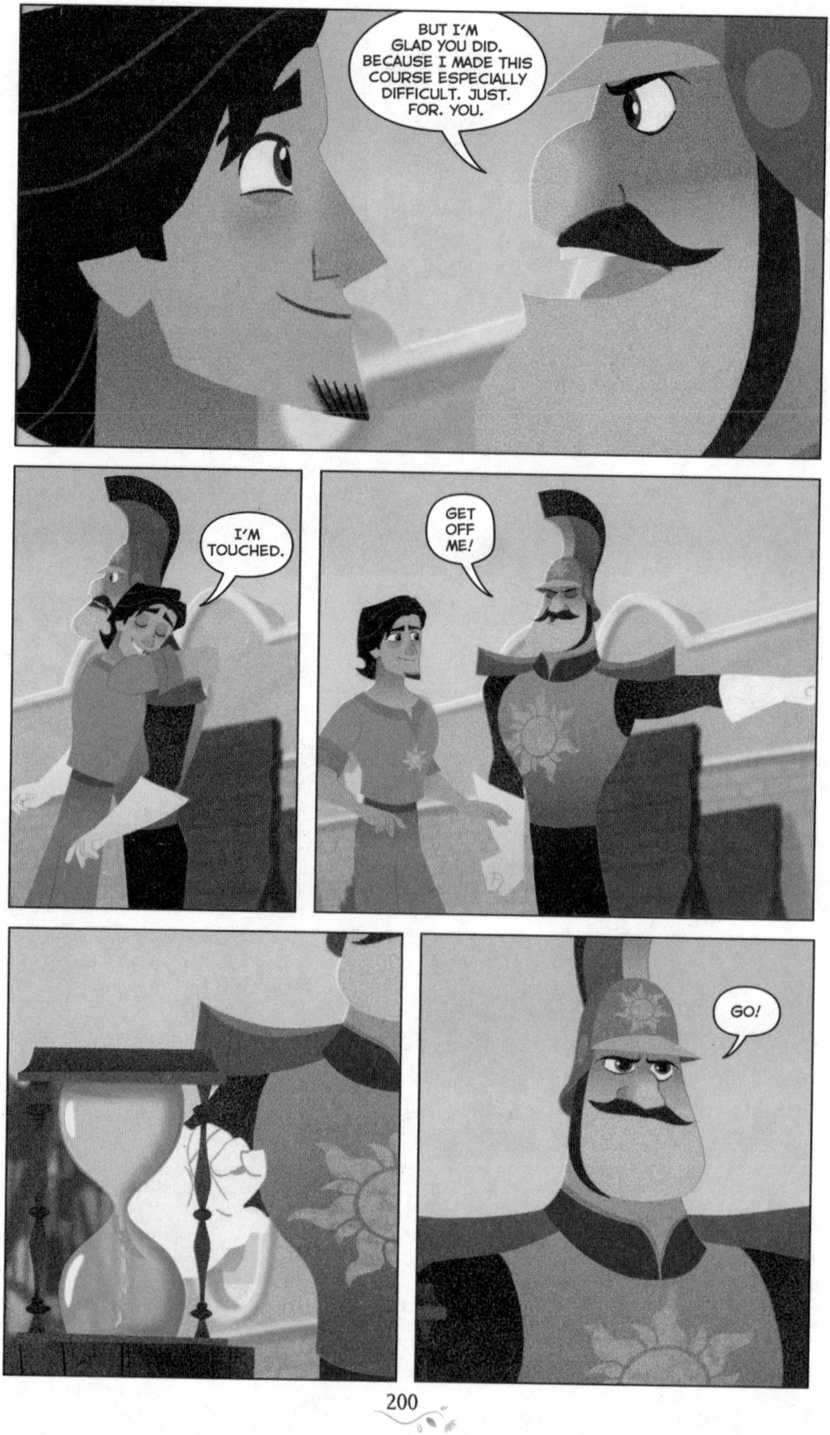
BUT I'M GLAD YOU DID. BECAUSE I MADE THIS COURSE ESPECIALLY DIFFICULT. JUST. FOR. YOU.
I'M TOUCHED.
GET OFF ME!
GO!

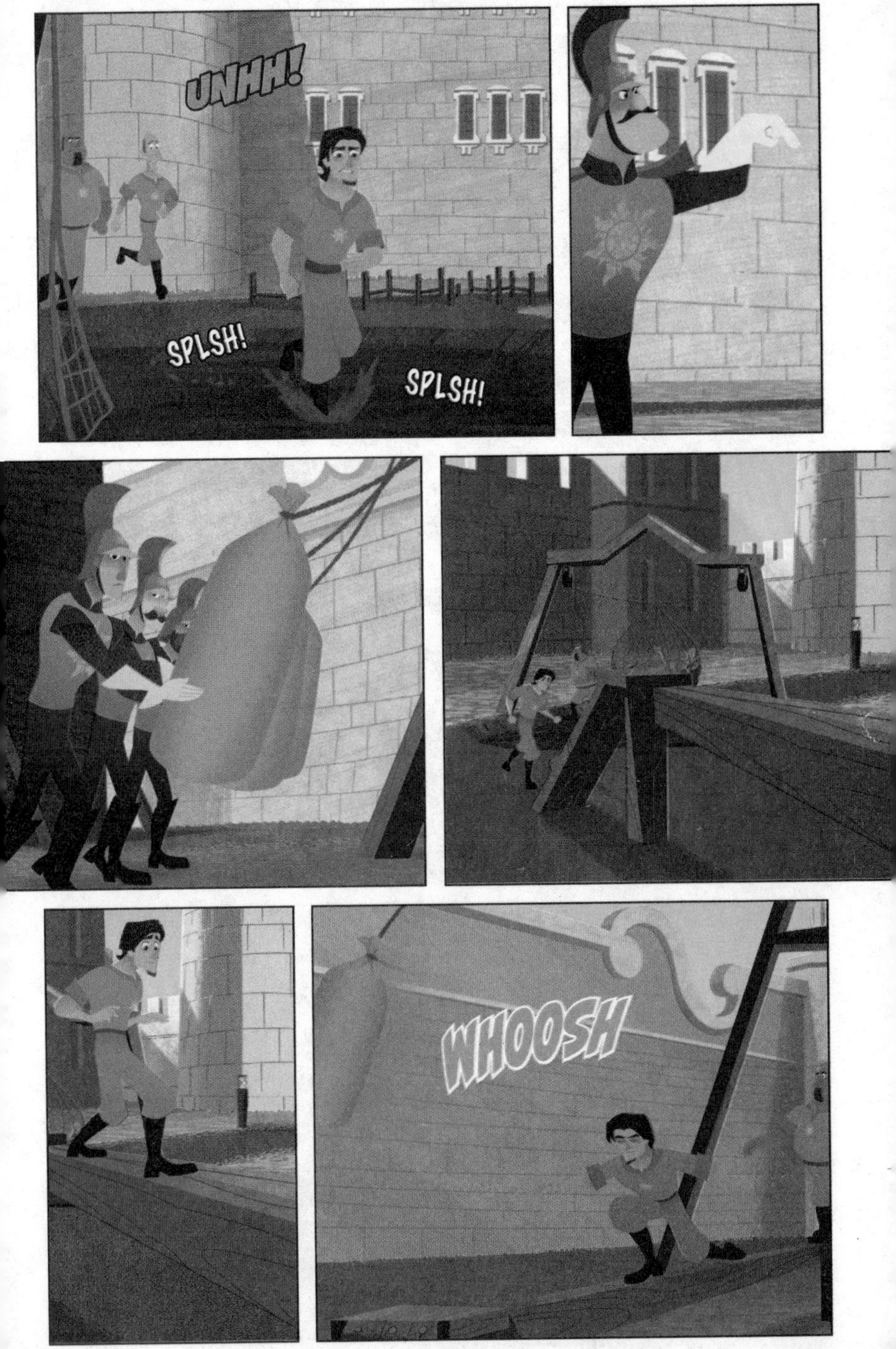
UNHH!
SPLSH!
SPLSH!
WHOOSH

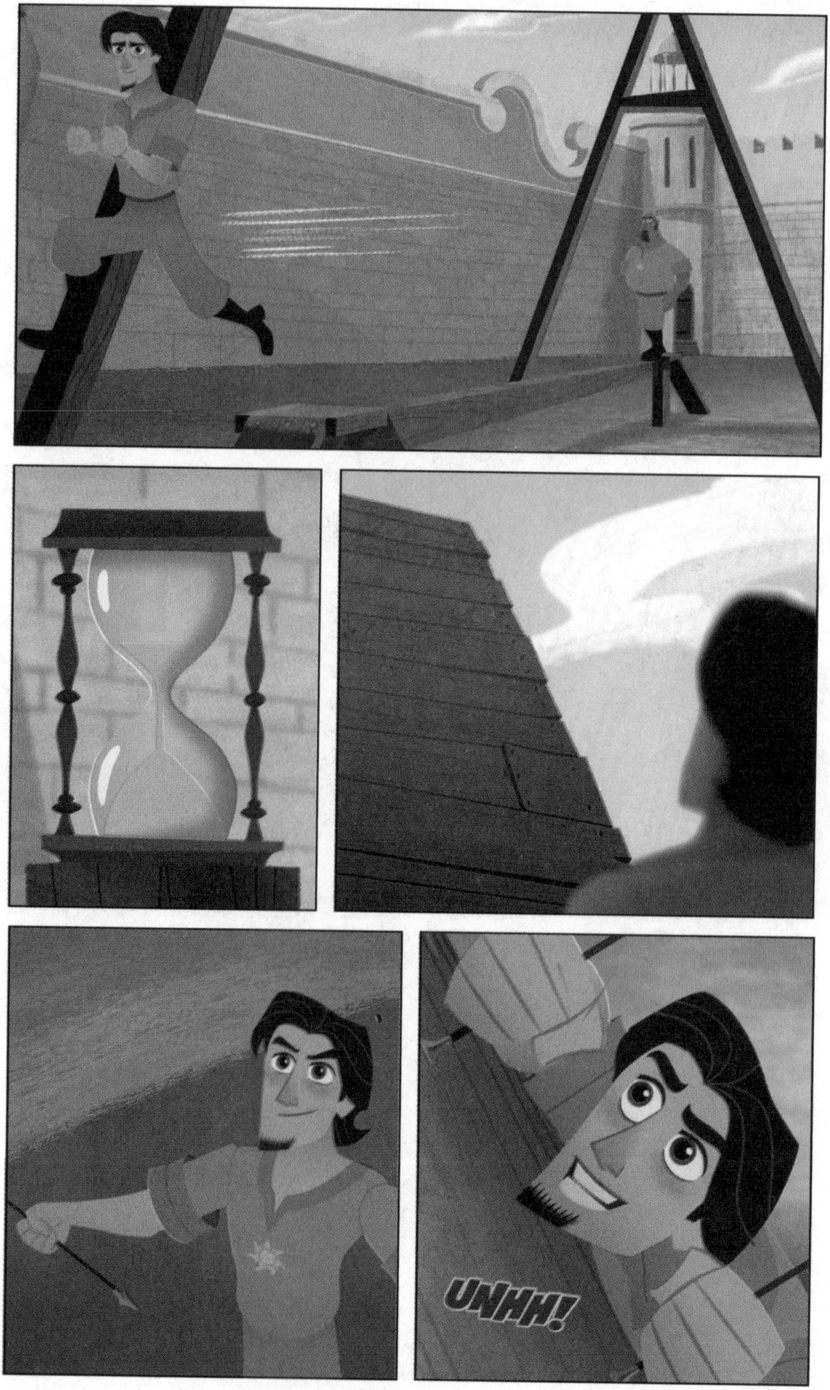
UNHH!

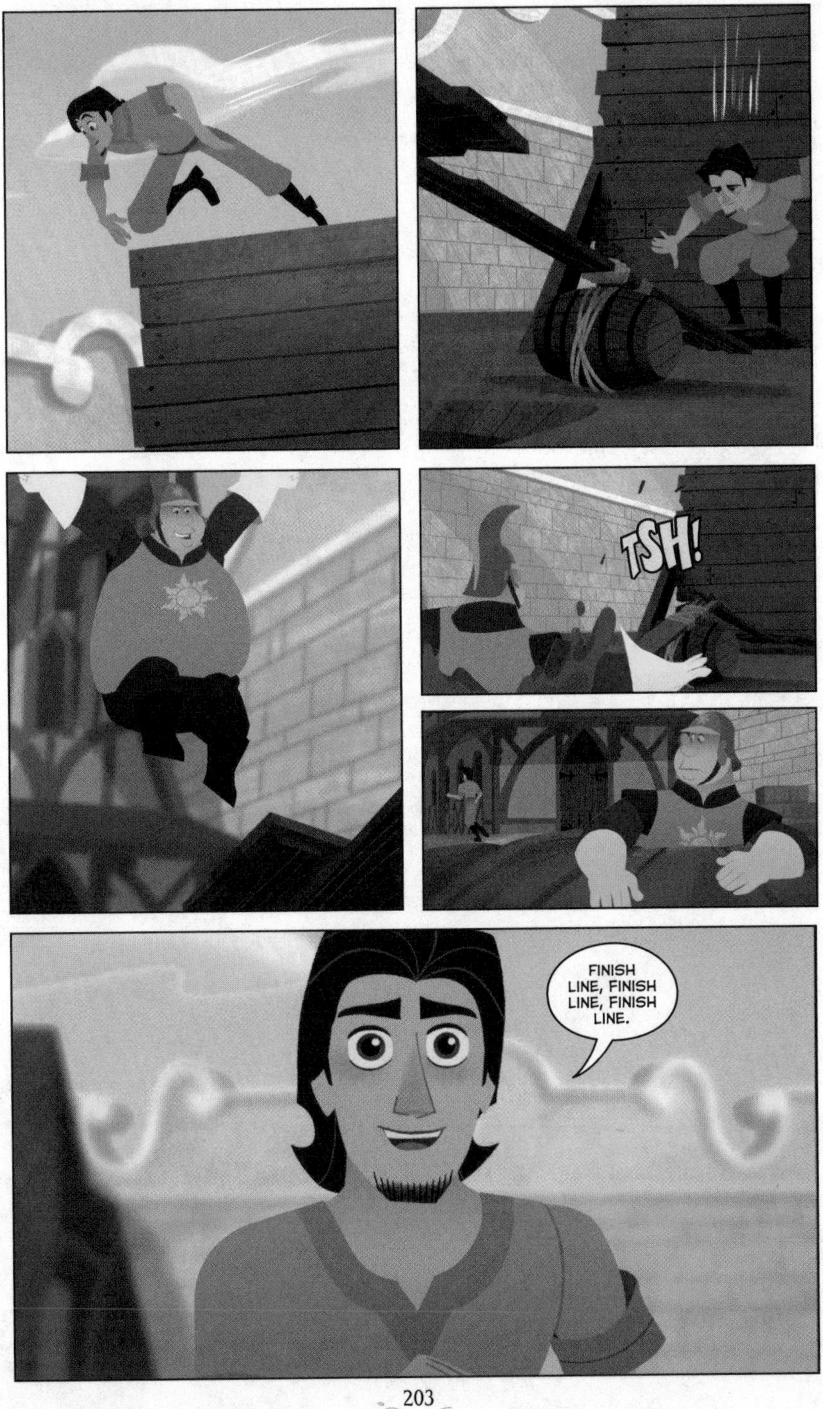
TSH!
FINISH LINE, FINISH LINE, FINISH LINE.

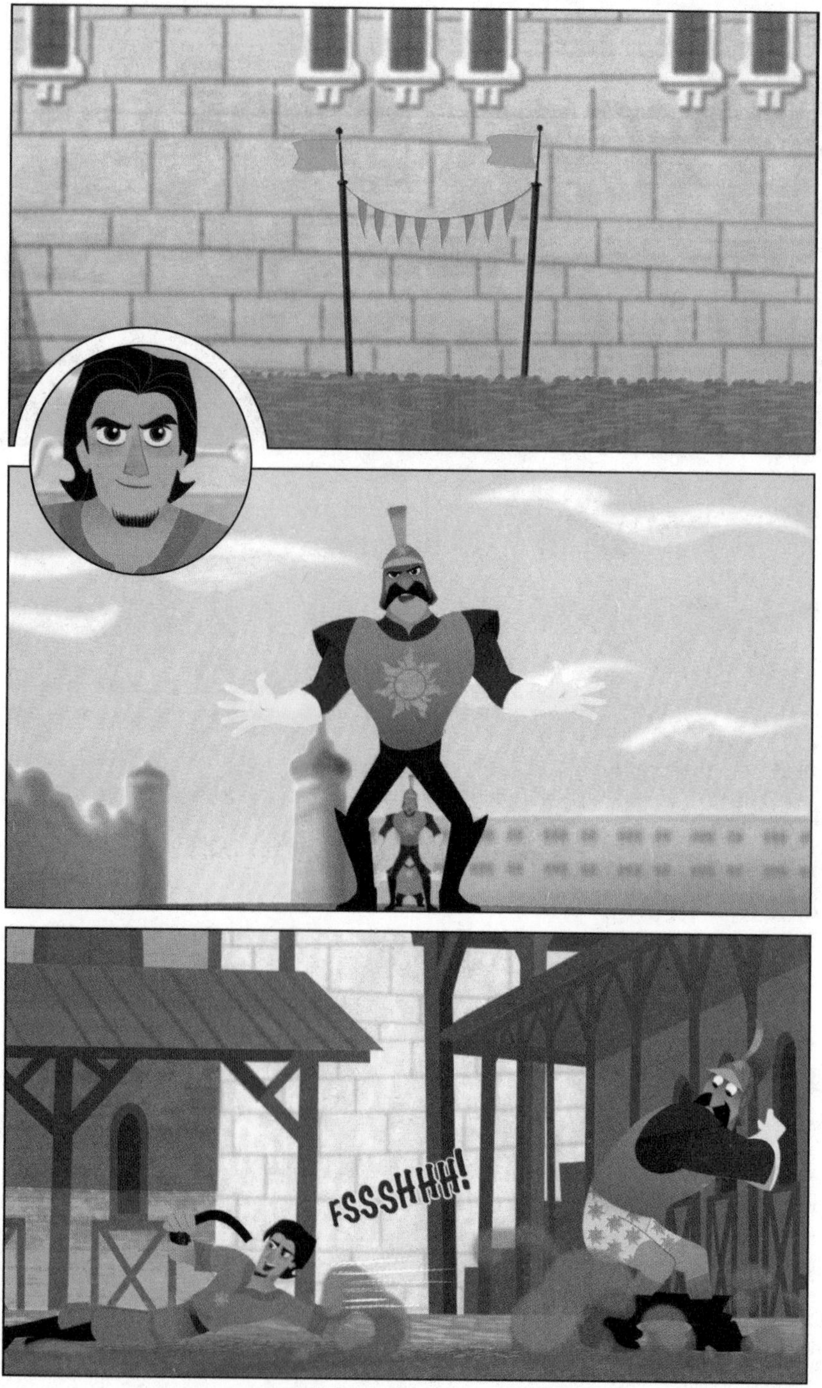
FSSSHHH!

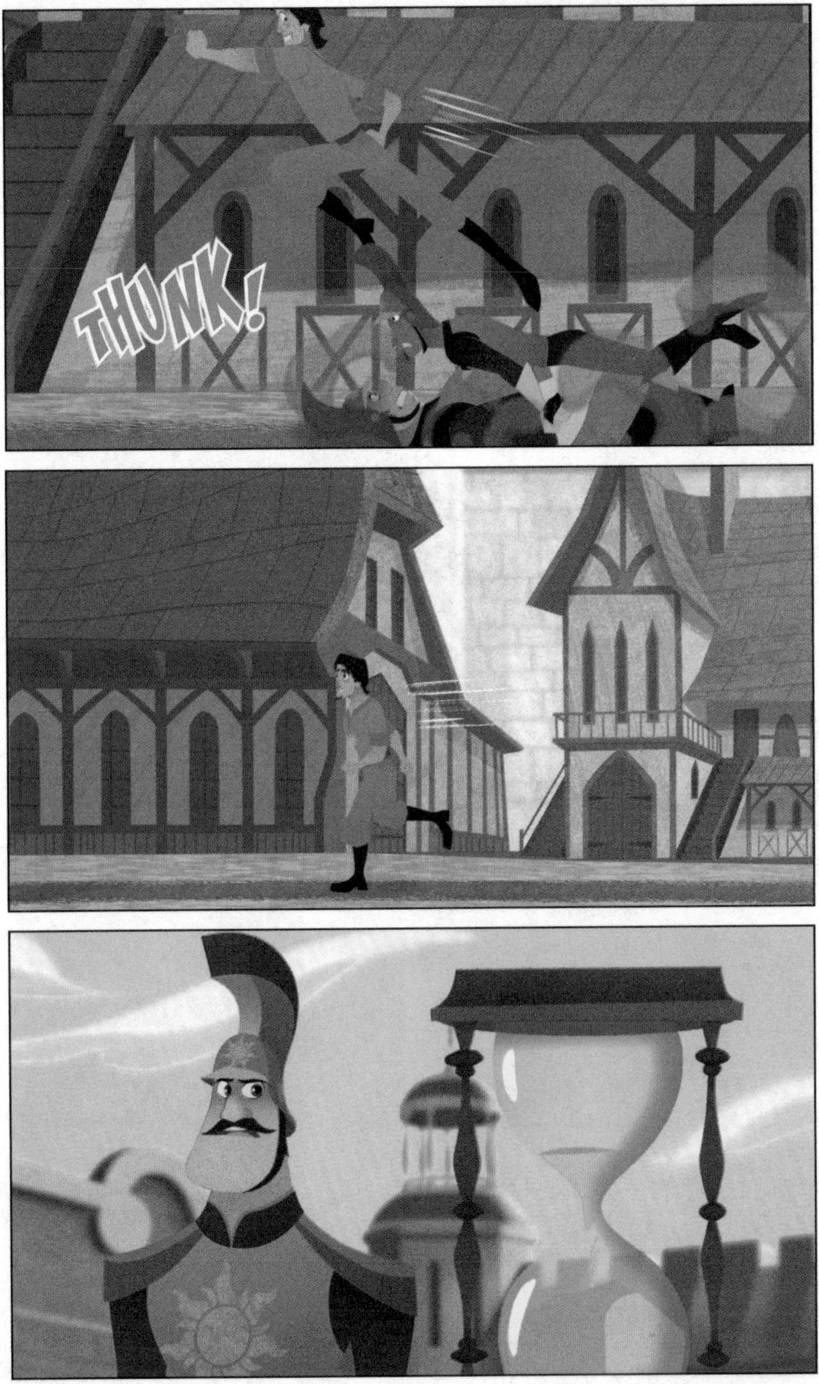
THUNK!

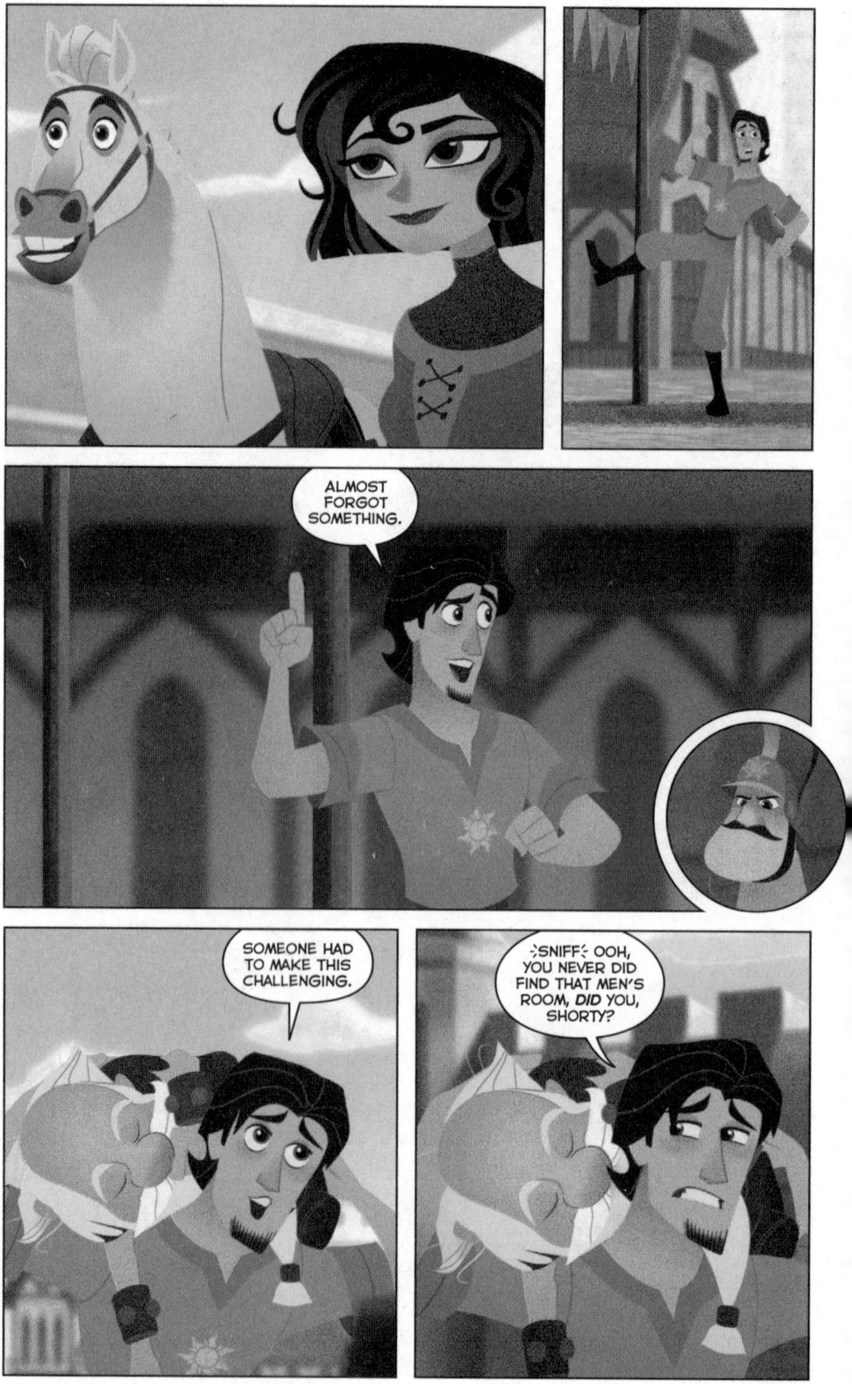
ALMOST FORGOT SOMETHING.
SOMEONE HAD TO MAKE THIS CHALLENGING.
⁘SNIFF⁘ OOH, YOU NEVER DID FIND THAT MEN'S ROOM, *DID* YOU, SHORTY?

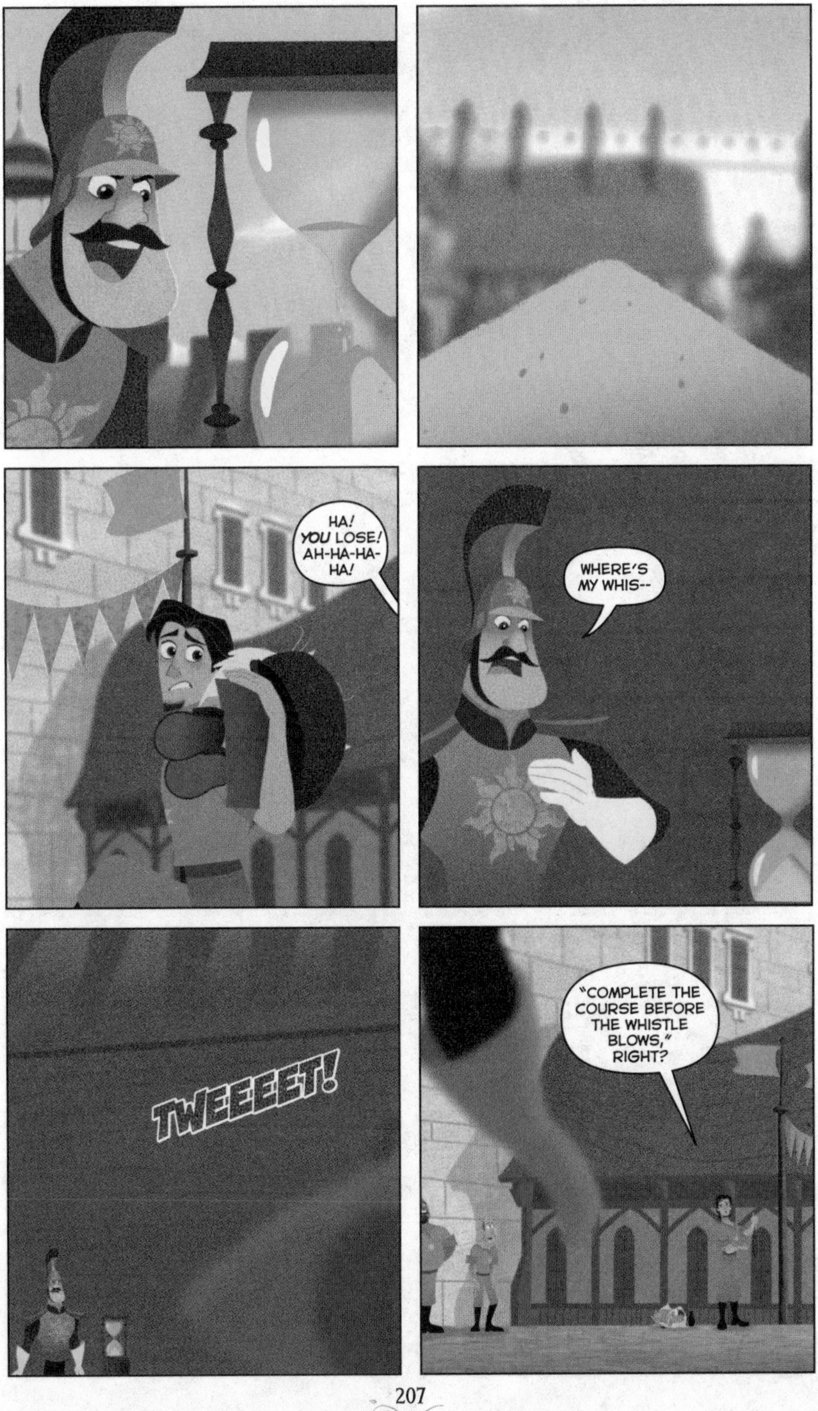
HA! YOU LOSE! AH-HA-HA-HA!
WHERE'S MY WHIS--
TWEEEET!
"COMPLETE THE COURSE BEFORE THE WHISTLE BLOWS," RIGHT?

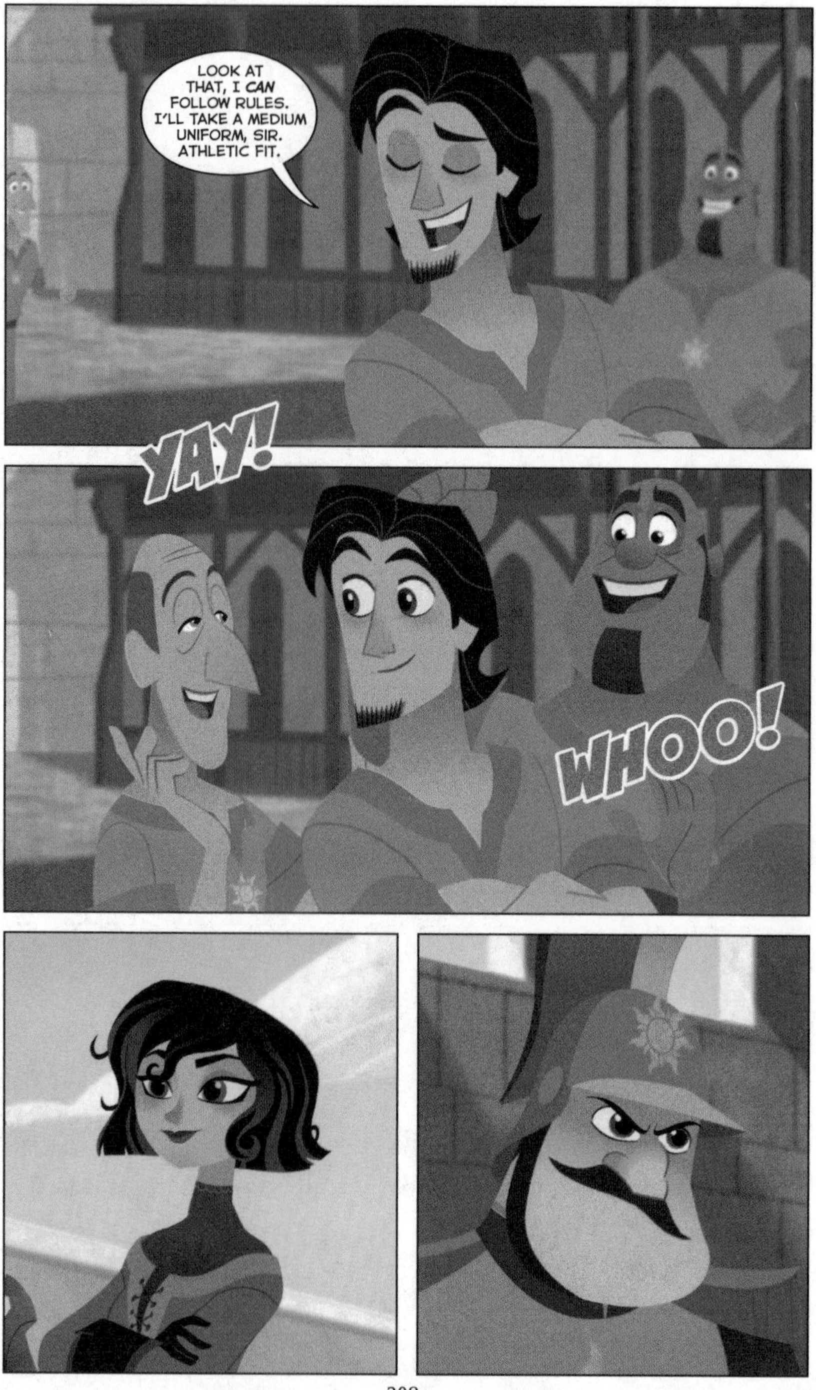
LOOK AT THAT, I *CAN* FOLLOW RULES. I'LL TAKE A MEDIUM UNIFORM, SIR. ATHLETIC FIT.
YAY!
WHOO!

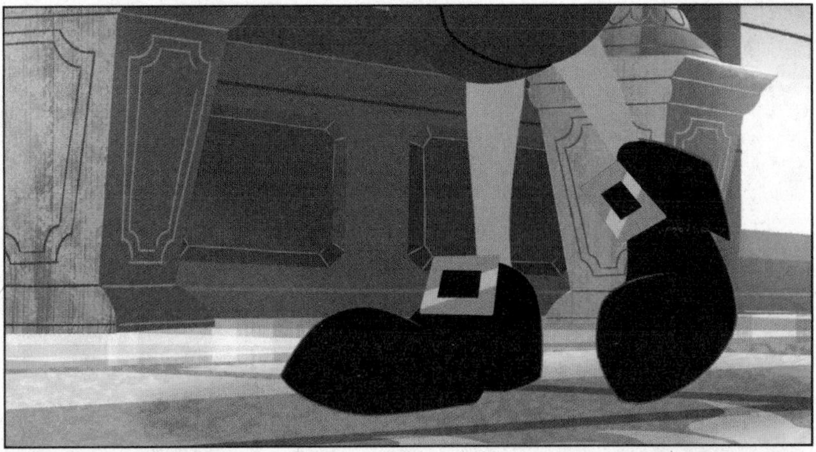

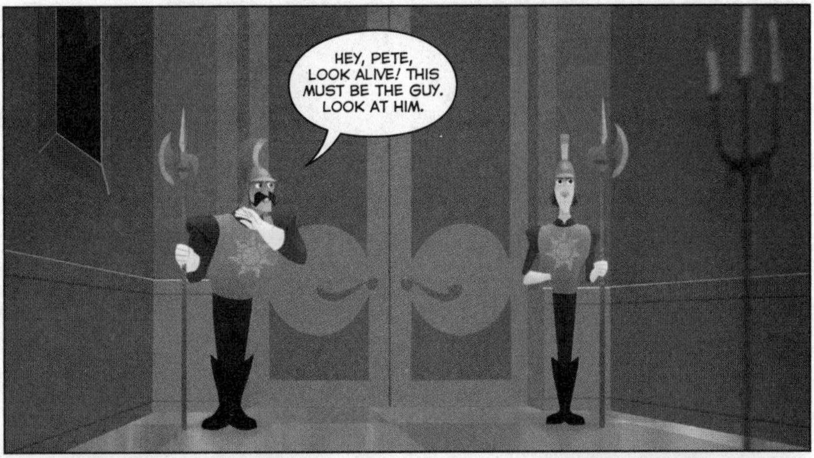
HEY, PETE, LOOK ALIVE! THIS MUST BE THE GUY. LOOK AT HIM.

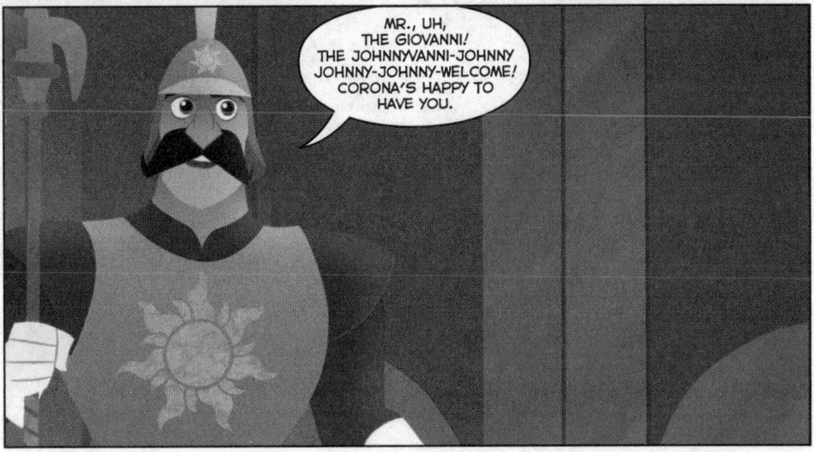
MR., UH, THE GIOVANNI! THE JOHNNYVANNI-JOHNNY JOHNNY-JOHNNY-WELCOME! CORONA'S HAPPY TO HAVE YOU.

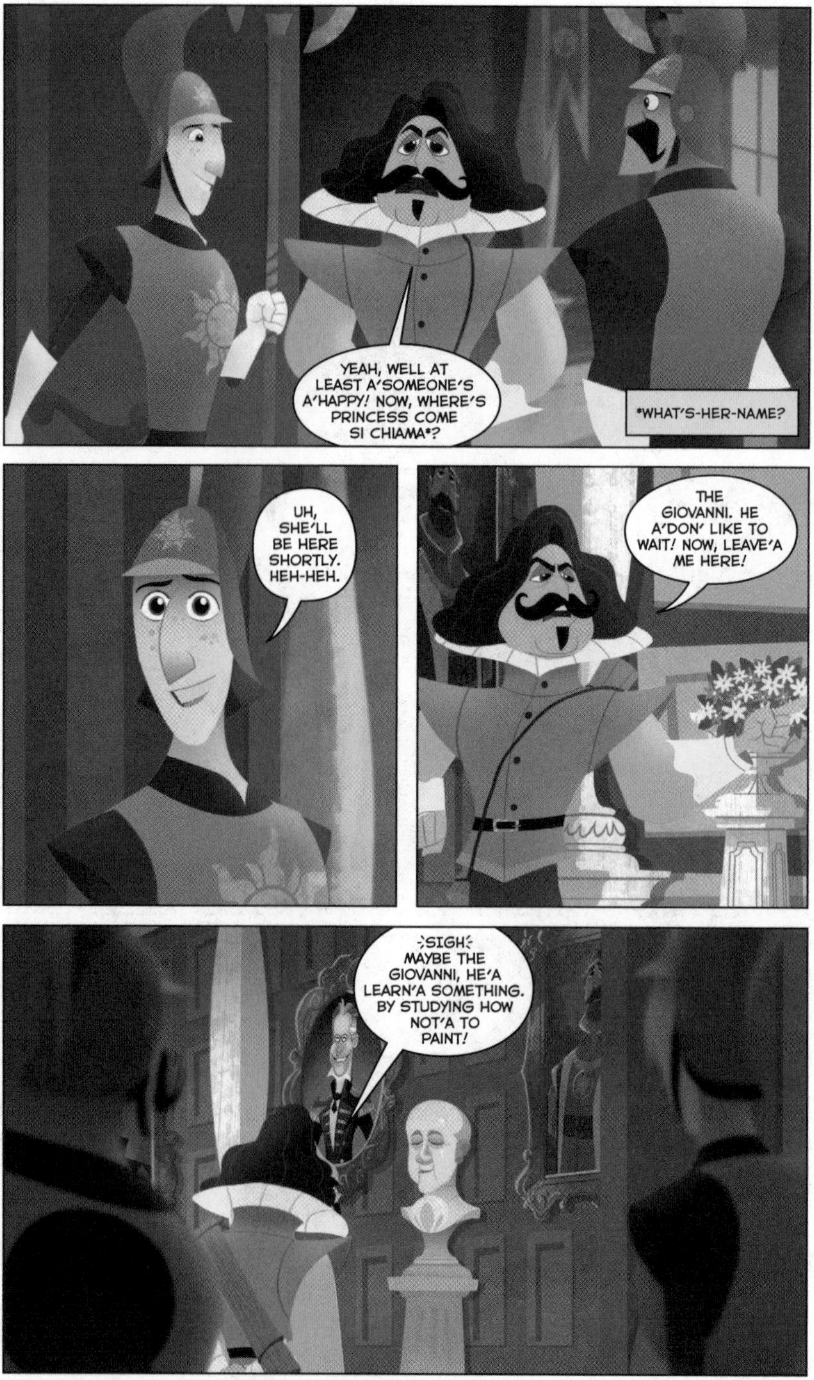
YEAH, WELL AT LEAST A'SOMEONE'S A'HAPPY! NOW, WHERE'S PRINCESS COME SI CHIAMA*?
*WHAT'S-HER-NAME?
UH, SHE'LL BE HERE SHORTLY. HEH-HEH.
THE GIOVANNI. HE A'DON' LIKE TO WAIT! NOW, LEAVE'A ME HERE!
-SIGH- MAYBE THE GIOVANNI, HE'A LEARN'A SOMETHING. BY STUDYING HOW NOT'A TO PAINT!

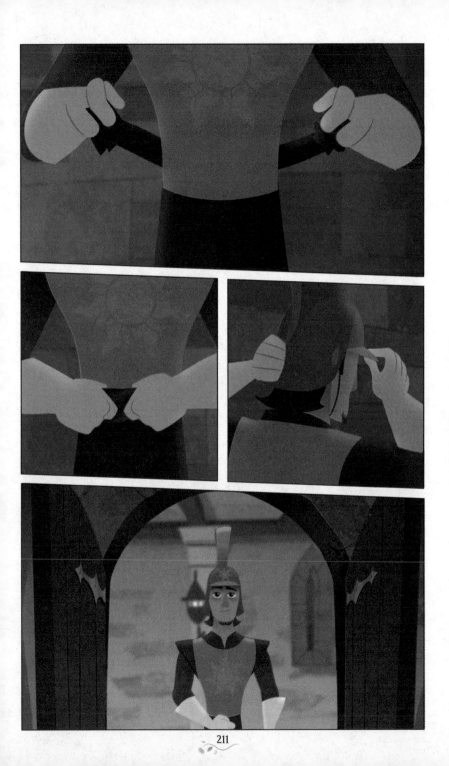

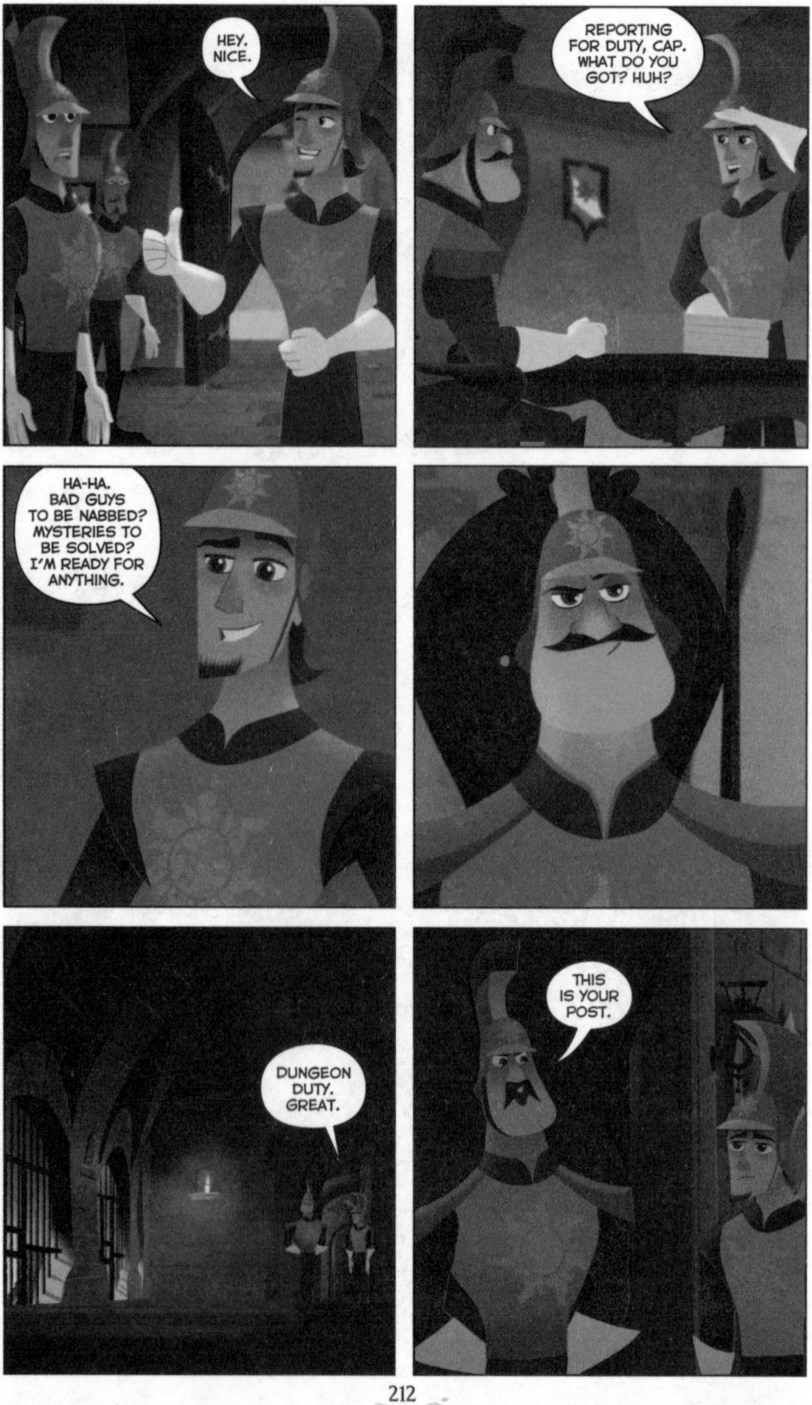
HEY. NICE.
REPORTING FOR DUTY, CAP. WHAT DO YOU GOT? HUH?
HA-HA. BAD GUYS TO BE NABBED? MYSTERIES TO BE SOLVED? I'M READY FOR ANYTHING.
DUNGEON DUTY. GREAT.
THIS IS YOUR POST.

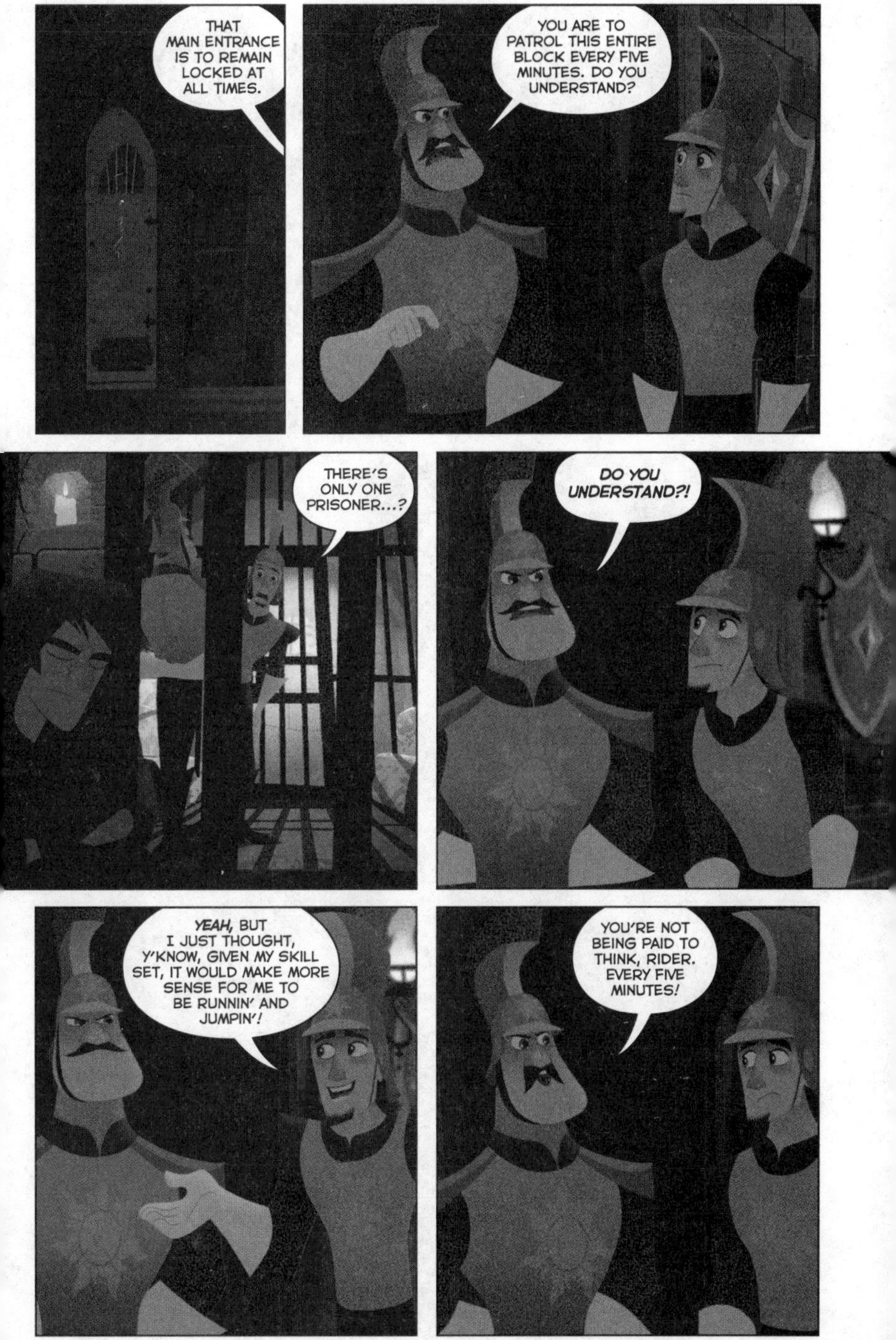
THAT MAIN ENTRANCE IS TO REMAIN LOCKED AT ALL TIMES.
YOU ARE TO PATROL THIS ENTIRE BLOCK EVERY FIVE MINUTES. DO YOU UNDERSTAND?
THERE'S ONLY ONE PRISONER...?
DO YOU UNDERSTAND?!
YEAH, BUT I JUST THOUGHT, Y'KNOW, GIVEN MY SKILL SET, IT WOULD MAKE MORE SENSE FOR ME TO BE RUNNIN' AND JUMPIN'!
YOU'RE NOT BEING PAID TO THINK, RIDER. EVERY FIVE MINUTES!

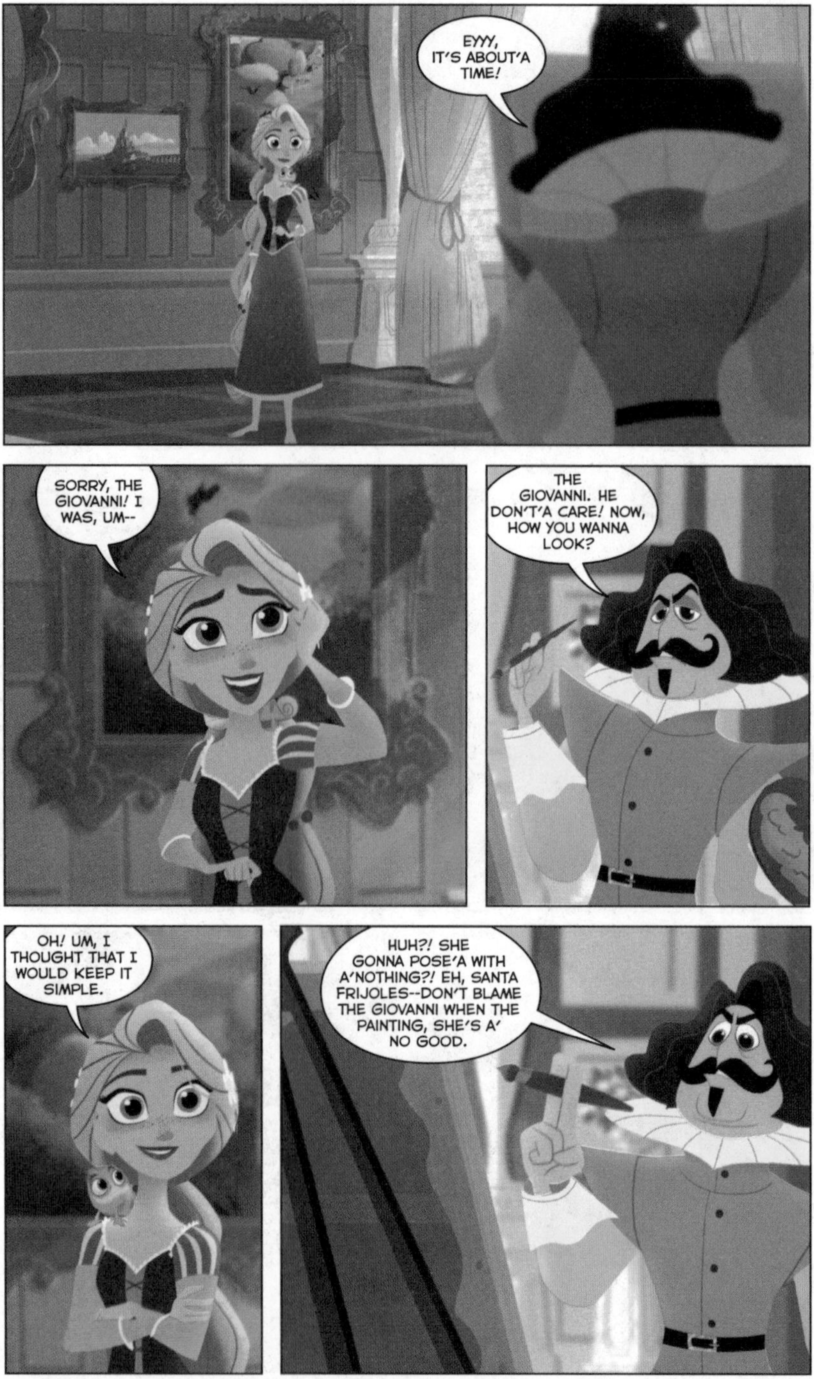
EYYY, IT'S ABOUT'A TIME!
SORRY, THE GIOVANNI! I WAS, UM--
THE GIOVANNI. HE DON'T'A CARE! NOW, HOW YOU WANNA LOOK?
OH! UM, I THOUGHT THAT I WOULD KEEP IT SIMPLE.
HUH?! SHE GONNA POSE'A WITH A'NOTHING?! EH, SANTA FRIJOLES--DON'T BLAME THE GIOVANNI WHEN THE PAINTING, SHE'S A' NO GOOD.

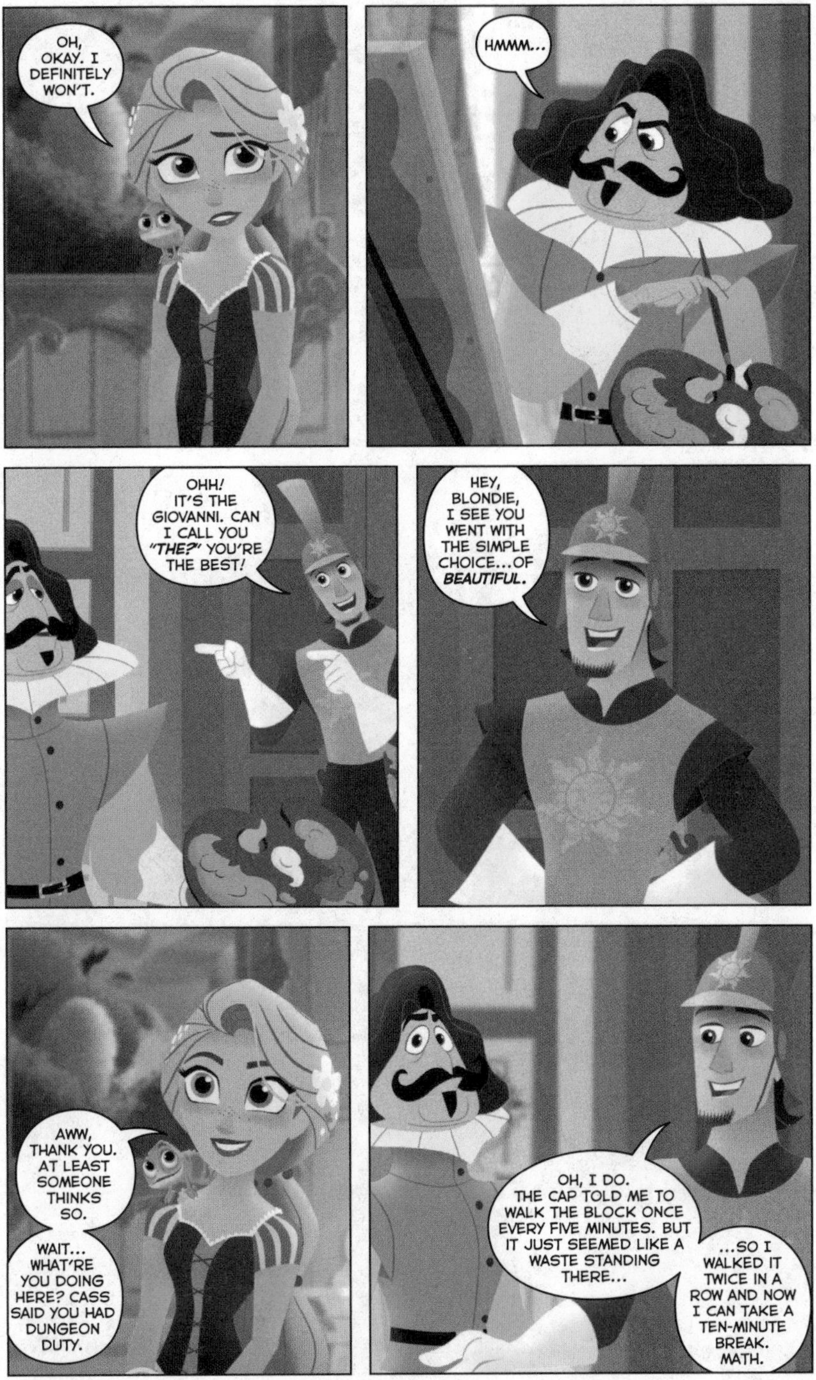
OH, OKAY. I DEFINITELY WON'T.
HMMM...
OHH! IT'S THE GIOVANNI. CAN I CALL YOU *"THE?"* YOU'RE THE BEST!
HEY, BLONDIE, I SEE YOU WENT WITH THE SIMPLE CHOICE...OF ***BEAUTIFUL.***
AWW, THANK YOU. AT LEAST SOMEONE THINKS SO.
WAIT... WHAT'RE YOU DOING HERE? CASS SAID YOU HAD DUNGEON DUTY.
OH, I DO. THE CAP TOLD ME TO WALK THE BLOCK ONCE EVERY FIVE MINUTES. BUT IT JUST SEEMED LIKE A WASTE STANDING THERE...
...SO I WALKED IT TWICE IN A ROW AND NOW I CAN TAKE A TEN-MINUTE BREAK. MATH.

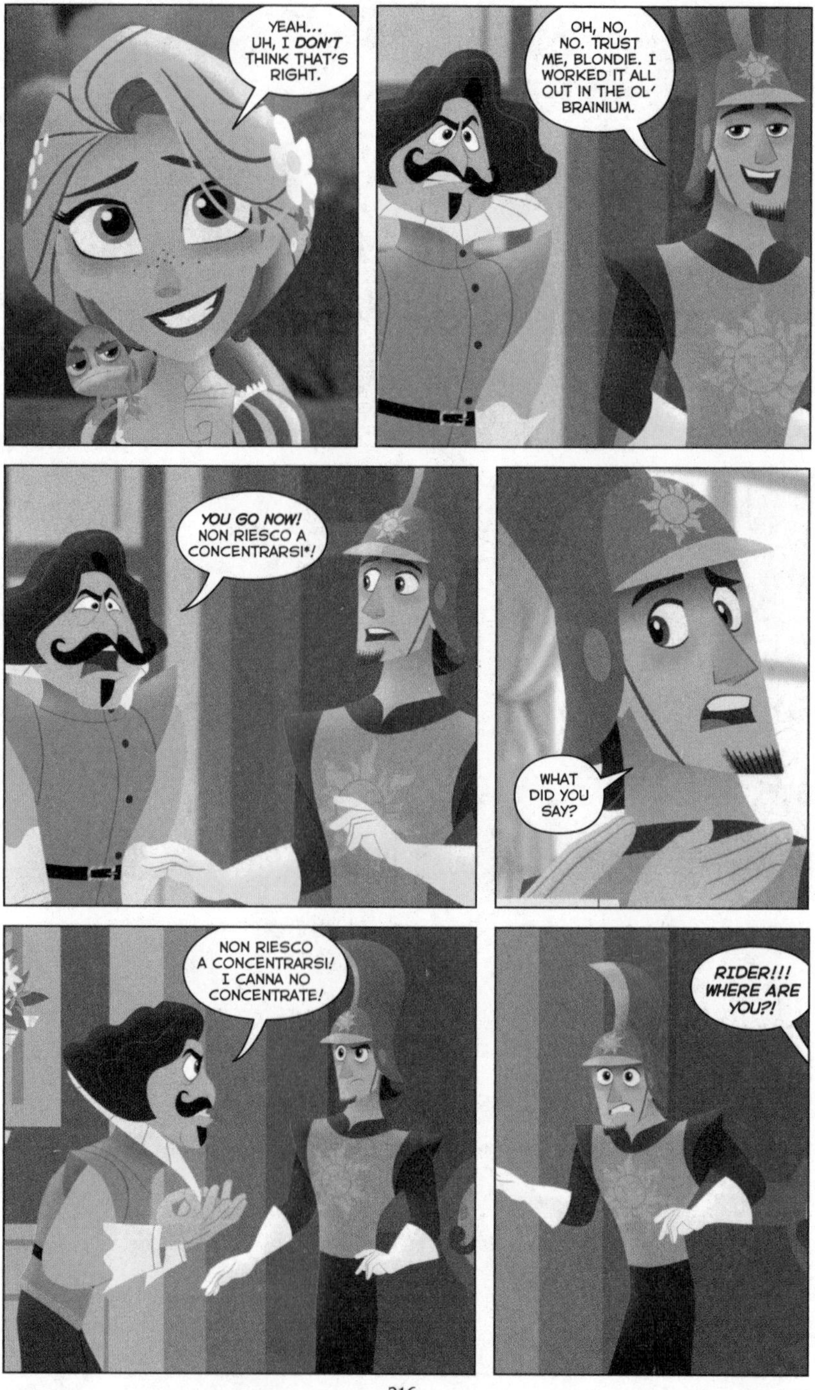
YEAH... UH, I *DON'T* THINK THAT'S RIGHT.
OH, NO, NO. TRUST ME, BLONDIE. I WORKED IT ALL OUT IN THE OL' BRAINIUM.
YOU GO NOW! NON RIESCO A CONCENTRARSI*!
WHAT DID YOU SAY?
NON RIESCO A CONCENTRARSI! I CANNA NO CONCENTRATE!
RIDER!!! WHERE ARE YOU?!

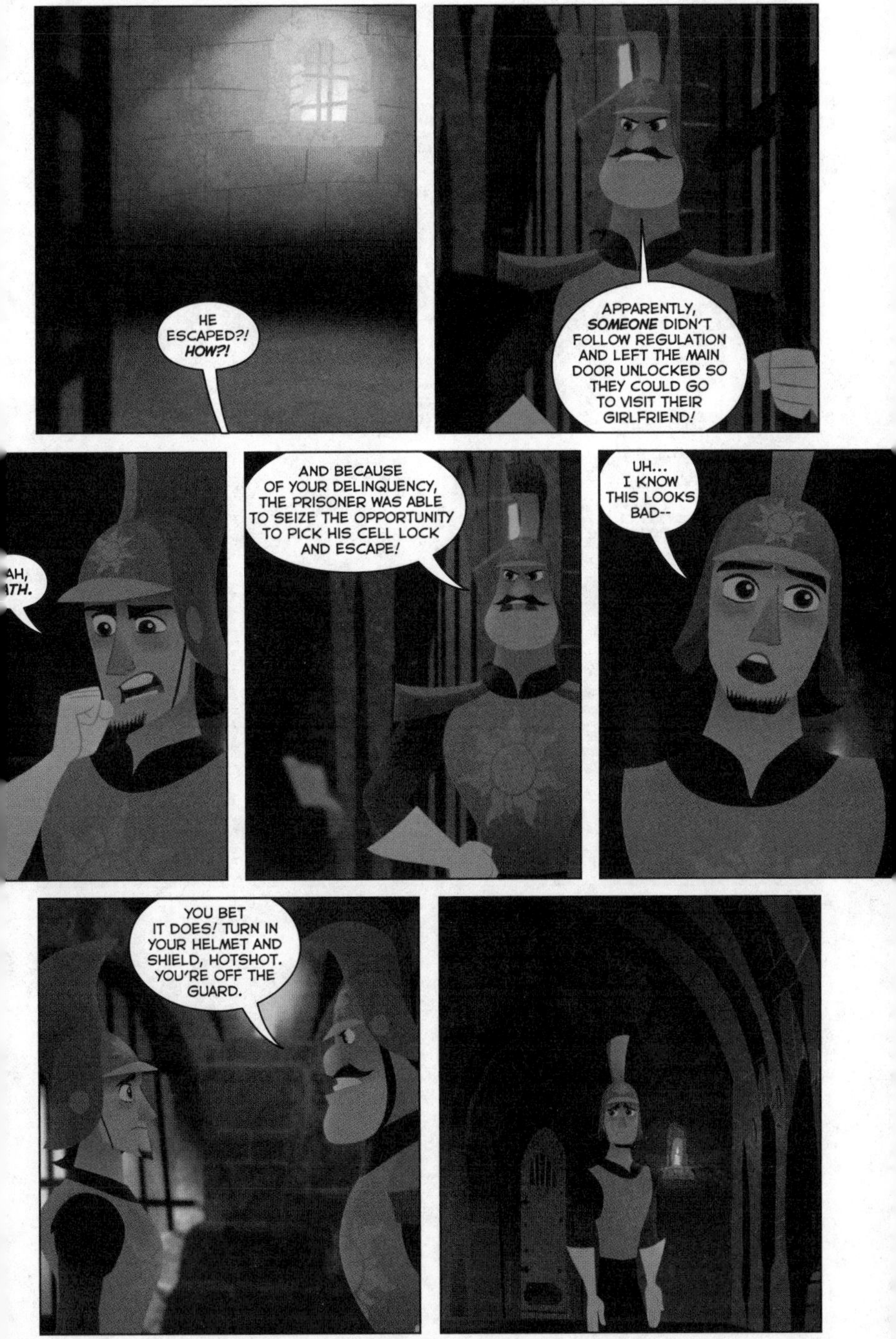
HE ESCAPED?! *HOW?!*
APPARENTLY, *SOMEONE* DIDN'T FOLLOW REGULATION AND LEFT THE MAIN DOOR UNLOCKED SO THEY COULD GO TO VISIT THEIR GIRLFRIEND!
AND BECAUSE OF YOUR DELINQUENCY, THE PRISONER WAS ABLE TO SEIZE THE OPPORTUNITY TO PICK HIS CELL LOCK AND ESCAPE!
UH... I KNOW THIS LOOKS BAD--
YOU BET IT DOES! TURN IN YOUR HELMET AND SHIELD, HOTSHOT. YOU'RE OFF THE GUARD.

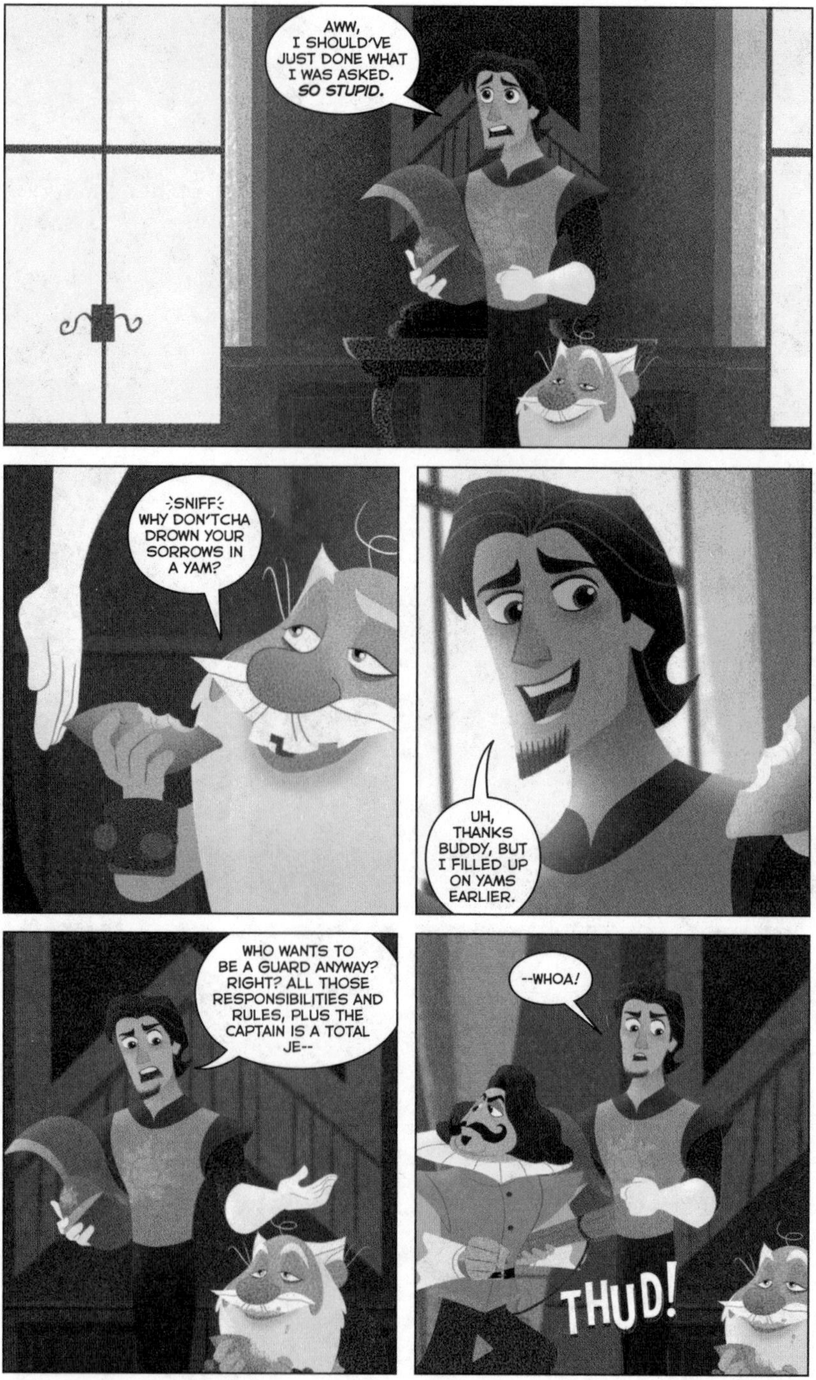
AWW, I SHOULD'VE JUST DONE WHAT I WAS ASKED. SO STUPID.
SNIFF WHY DON'TCHA DROWN YOUR SORROWS IN A YAM?
UH, THANKS BUDDY, BUT I FILLED UP ON YAMS EARLIER.
WHO WANTS TO BE A GUARD ANYWAY? RIGHT? ALL THOSE RESPONSIBILITIES AND RULES, PLUS THE CAPTAIN IS A TOTAL JE--
--WHOA!
THUD!

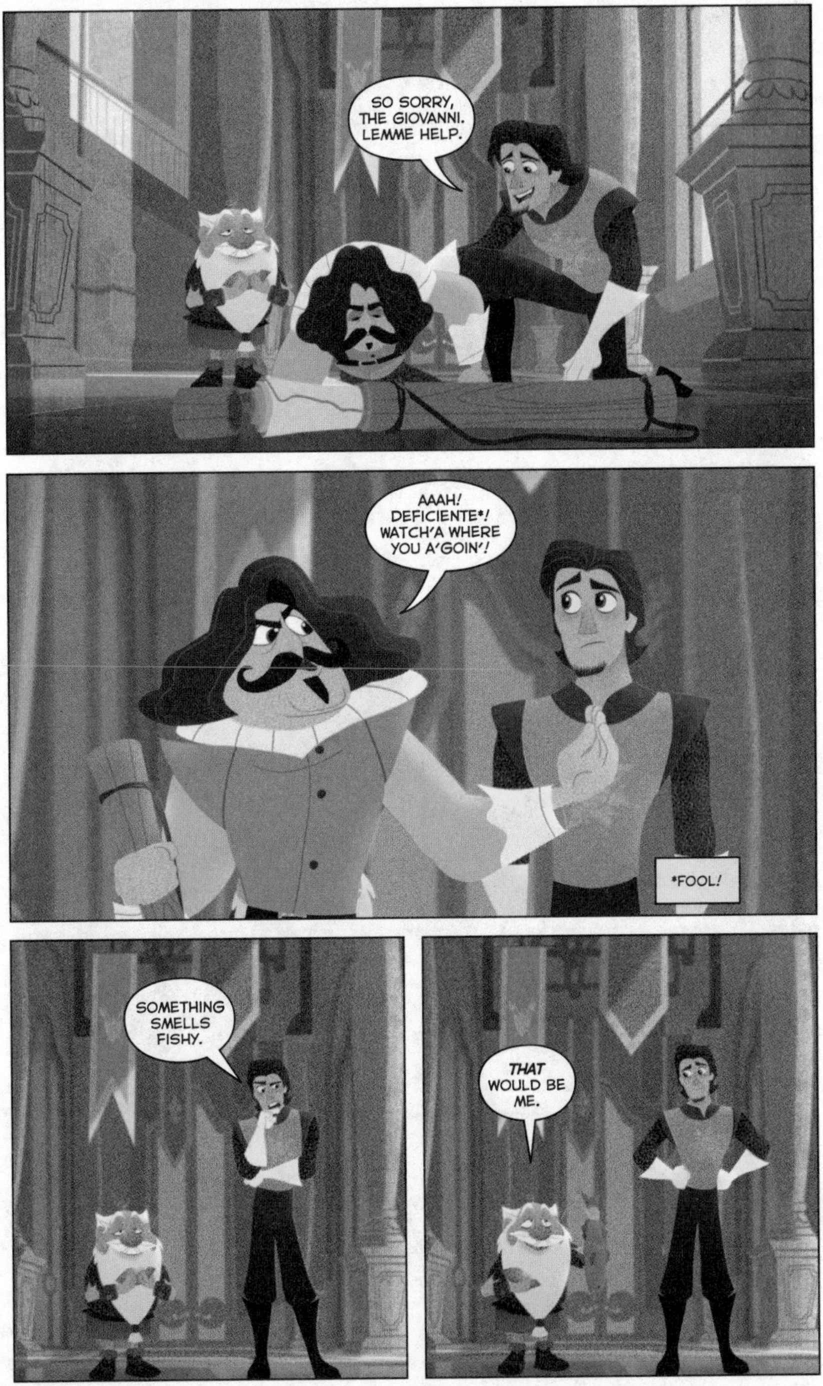
SO SORRY, THE GIOVANNI. LEMME HELP.
AAAH! DEFICIENTE*! WATCH'A WHERE YOU A'GOIN'!
*FOOL!
SOMETHING SMELLS FISHY.
THAT WOULD BE ME.

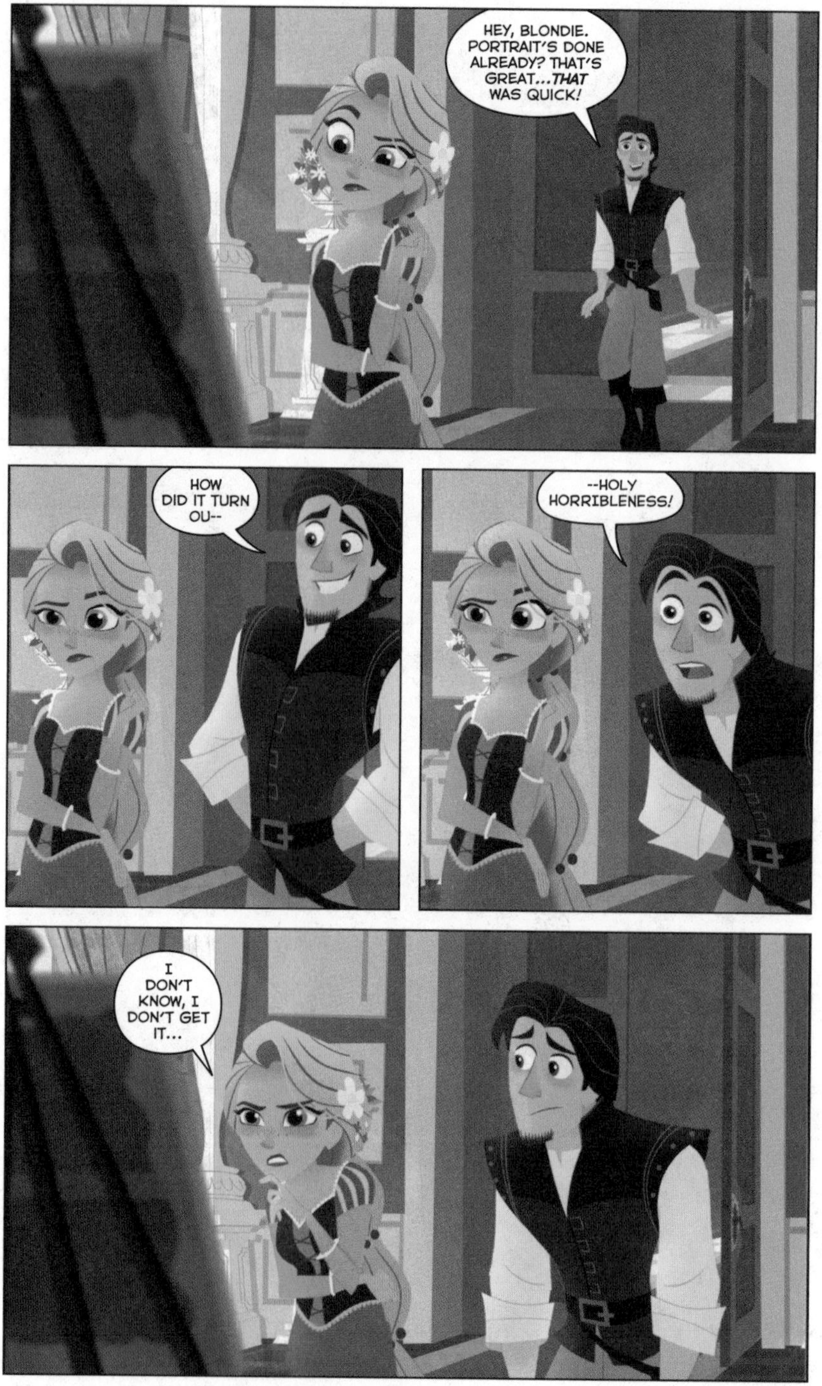
HEY, BLONDIE. PORTRAIT'S DONE ALREADY? THAT'S GREAT...*THAT* WAS QUICK!
HOW DID IT TURN OU--
--HOLY HORRIBLENESS!
I DON'T KNOW, I DON'T GET IT...

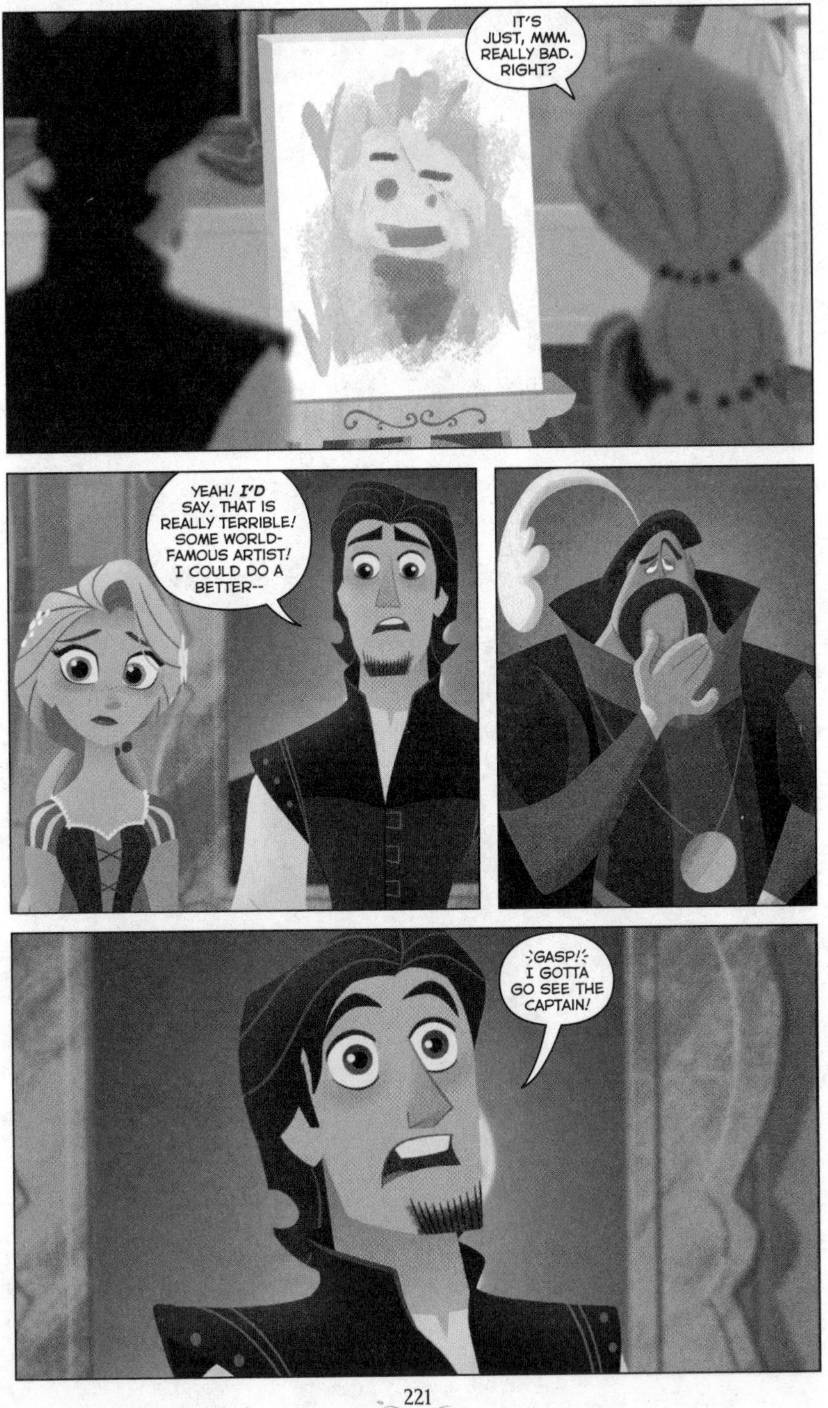
IT'S JUST, MMM. REALLY BAD. RIGHT?
YEAH! I'D SAY. THAT IS REALLY TERRIBLE! SOME WORLD-FAMOUS ARTIST! I COULD DO A BETTER--
GASP! I GOTTA GO SEE THE CAPTAIN!

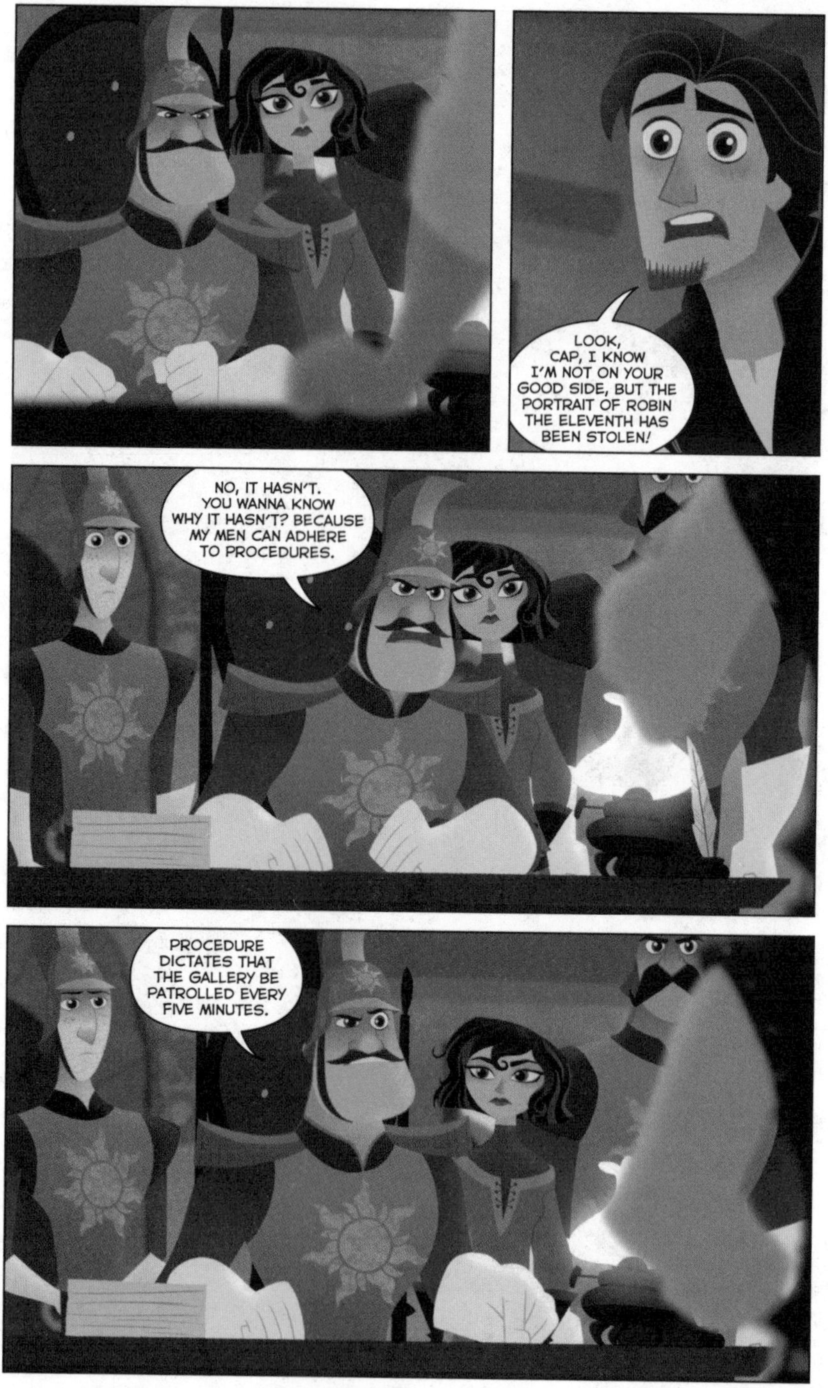
LOOK, CAP, I KNOW I'M NOT ON YOUR GOOD SIDE, BUT THE PORTRAIT OF ROBIN THE ELEVENTH HAS BEEN STOLEN!
NO, IT HASN'T. YOU WANNA KNOW WHY IT HASN'T? BECAUSE MY MEN CAN ADHERE TO PROCEDURES.
PROCEDURE DICTATES THAT THE GALLERY BE PATROLLED EVERY FIVE MINUTES.

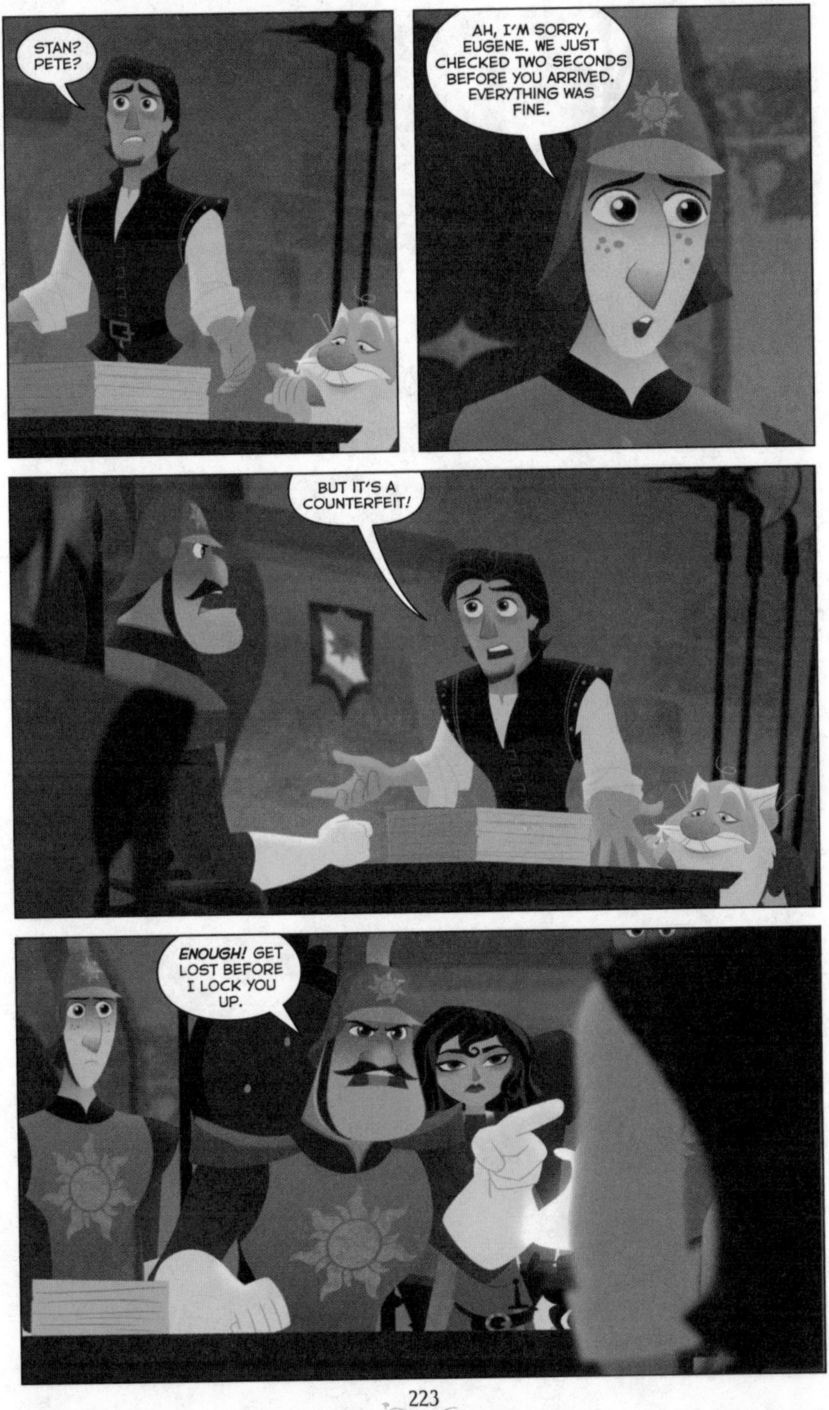

STAN? PETE?
AH, I'M SORRY, EUGENE. WE JUST CHECKED TWO SECONDS BEFORE YOU ARRIVED. EVERYTHING WAS FINE.
BUT IT'S A COUNTERFEIT!
ENOUGH! GET LOST BEFORE I LOCK YOU UP.

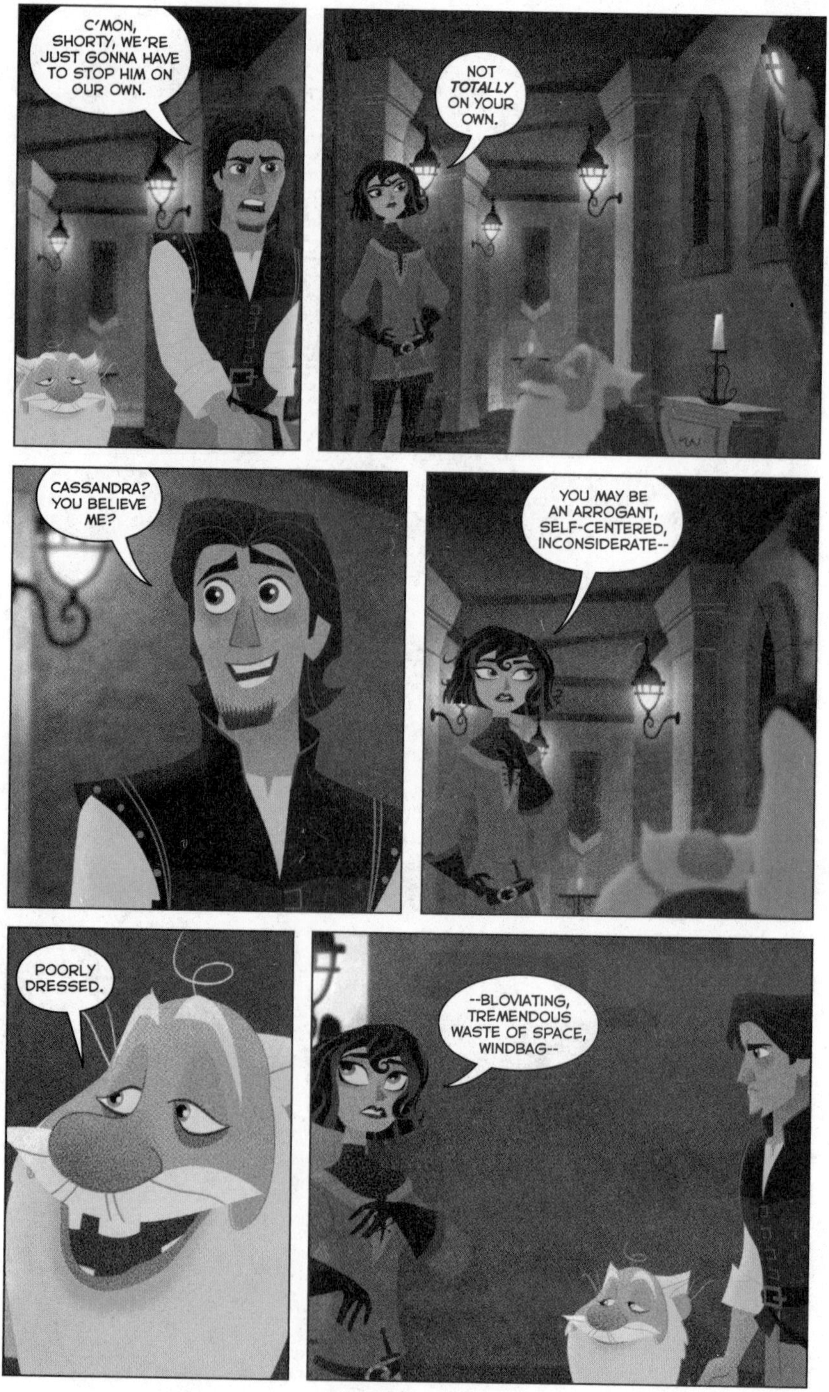
C'MON, SHORTY, WE'RE JUST GONNA HAVE TO STOP HIM ON OUR OWN.
NOT *TOTALLY* ON YOUR OWN.
CASSANDRA? YOU BELIEVE ME?
YOU MAY BE AN ARROGANT, SELF-CENTERED, INCONSIDERATE--
POORLY DRESSED.
--BLOVIATING, TREMENDOUS WASTE OF SPACE, WINDBAG--

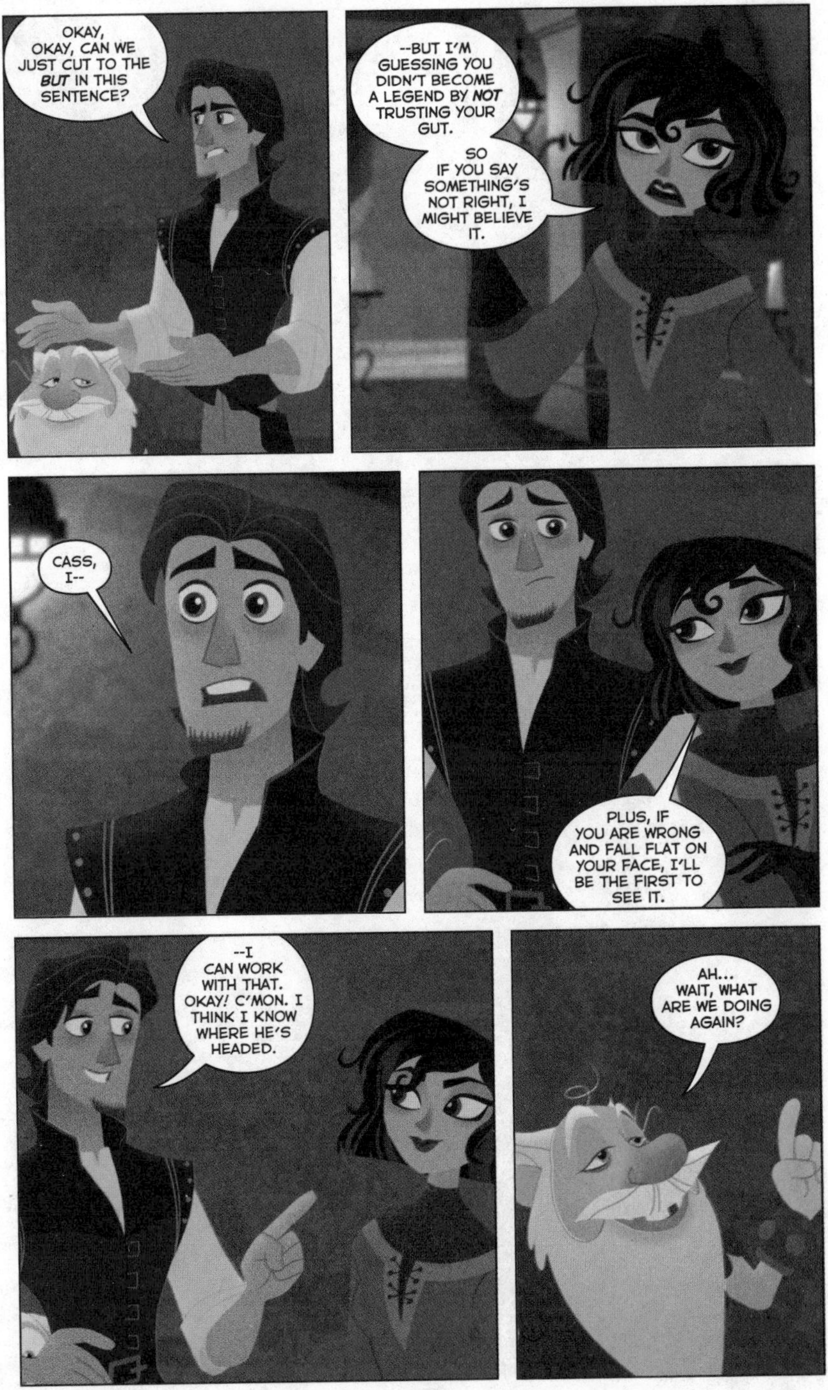
OKAY, OKAY, CAN WE JUST CUT TO THE *BUT* IN THIS SENTENCE?
--BUT I'M GUESSING YOU DIDN'T BECOME A LEGEND BY *NOT* TRUSTING YOUR GUT.
SO IF YOU SAY SOMETHING'S NOT RIGHT, I MIGHT BELIEVE IT.
CASS, I--
PLUS, IF YOU ARE WRONG AND FALL FLAT ON YOUR FACE, I'LL BE THE FIRST TO SEE IT.
--I CAN WORK WITH THAT. OKAY! C'MON. I THINK I KNOW WHERE HE'S HEADED.
AH... WAIT, WHAT ARE WE DOING AGAIN?

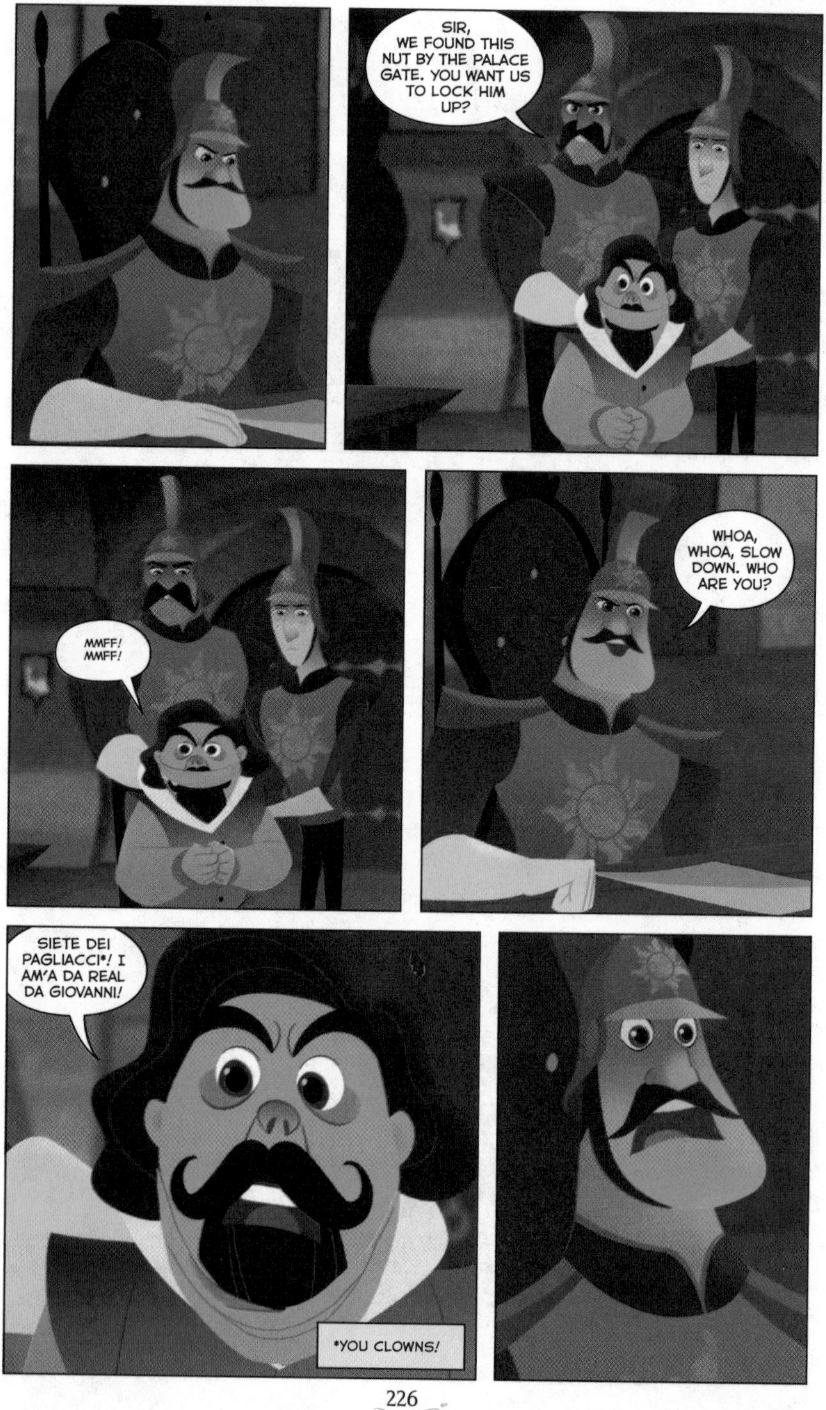
SIR, WE FOUND THIS NUT BY THE PALACE GATE. YOU WANT US TO LOCK HIM UP?
MMFF! MMFF!
WHOA, WHOA, SLOW DOWN. WHO ARE YOU?
SIETE DEI PAGLIACCI*! I AM'A DA REAL DA GIOVANNI!
*YOU CLOWNS!

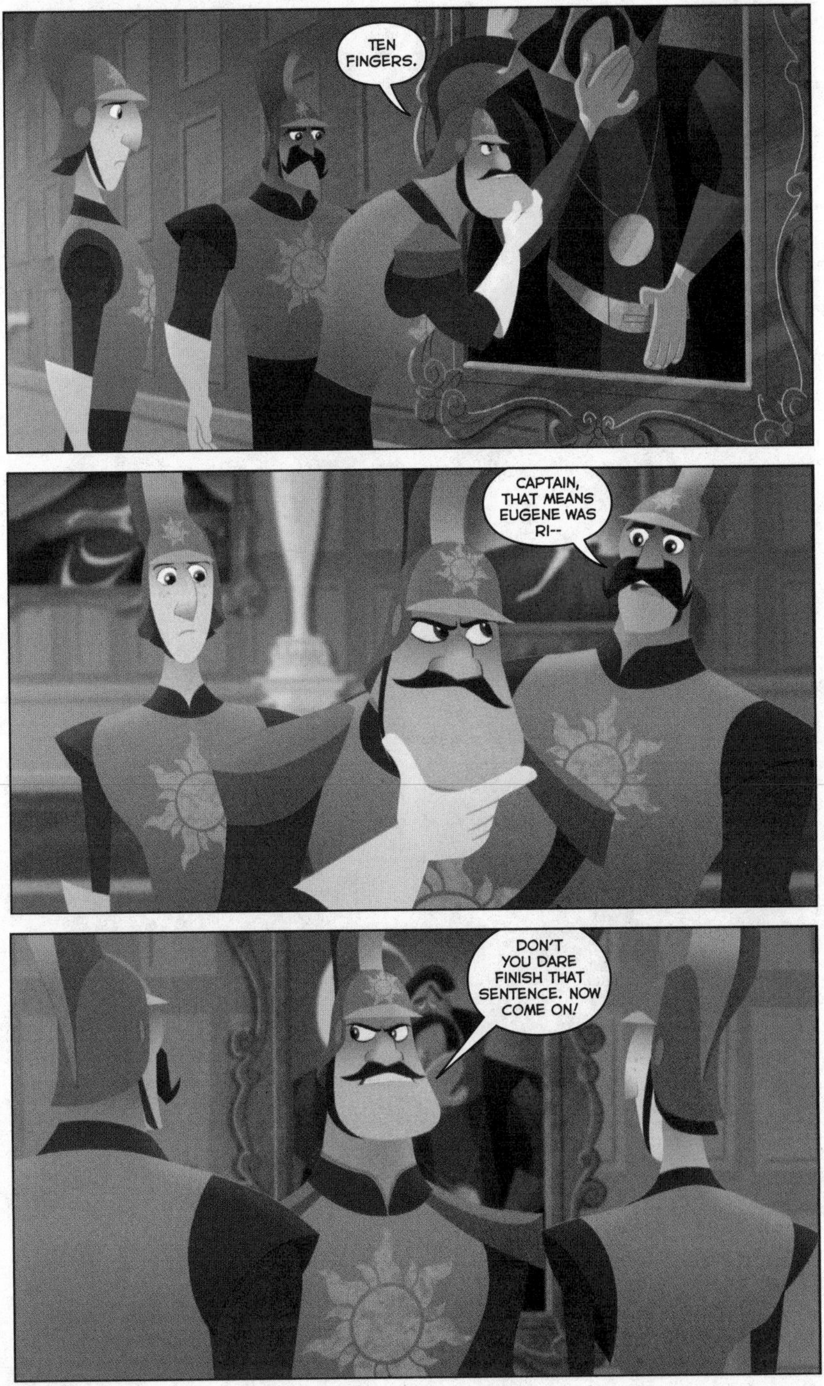
TEN FINGERS.
CAPTAIN, THAT MEANS EUGENE WAS RI--
DON'T YOU DARE FINISH THAT SENTENCE. NOW COME ON!

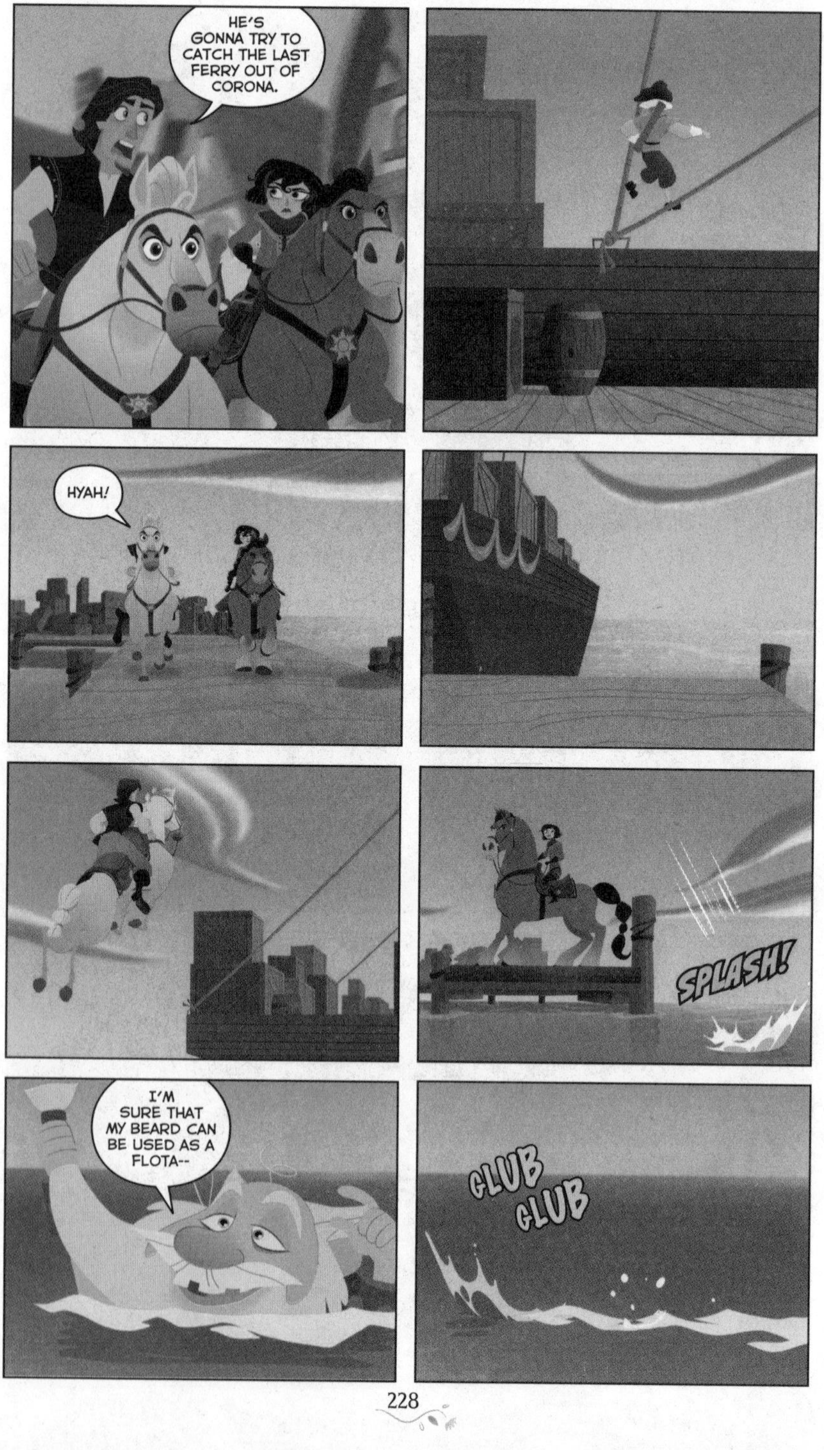
HE'S GONNA TRY TO CATCH THE LAST FERRY OUT OF CORONA.
HYAH!
SPLASH!
I'M SURE THAT MY BEARD CAN BE USED AS A FLOTA--
GLUB GLUB

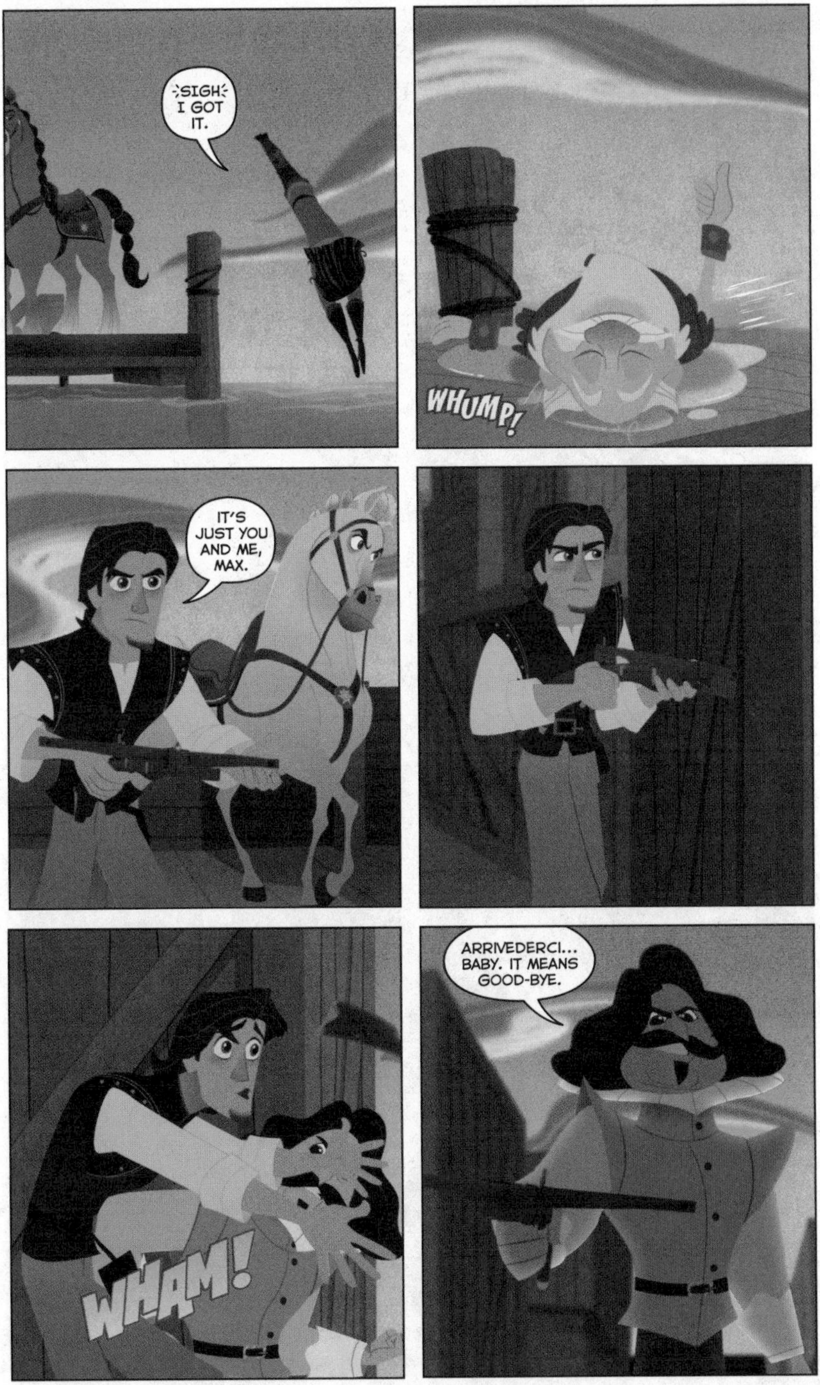
SIGH
I GOT IT.
WHUMP!
IT'S JUST YOU AND ME, MAX.
WHAM!
ARRIVEDERCI... BABY. IT MEANS GOOD-BYE.

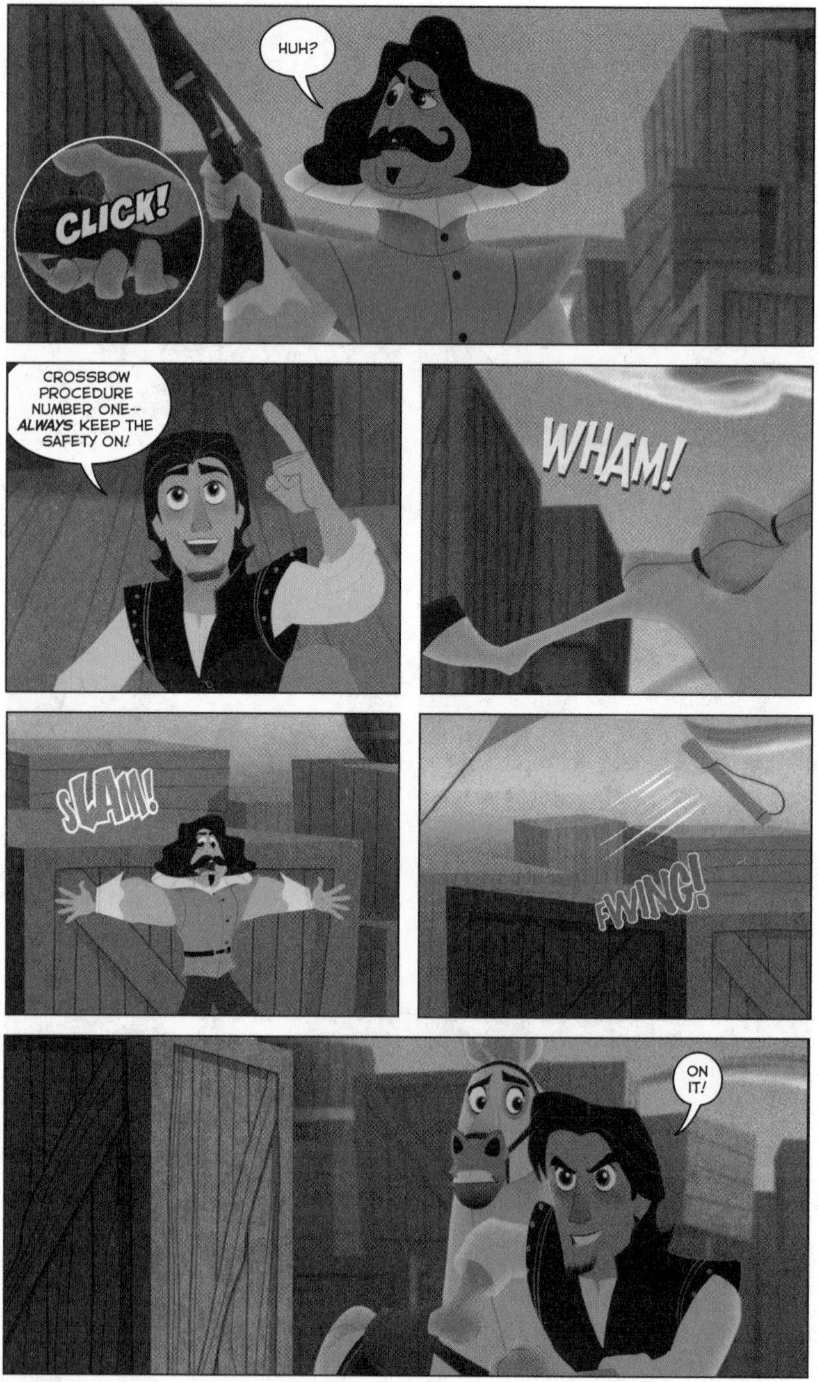
HUH?
CLICK!
CROSSBOW PROCEDURE NUMBER ONE-- ALWAYS KEEP THE SAFETY ON!
WHAM!
SLAM!
FWING!
ON IT!

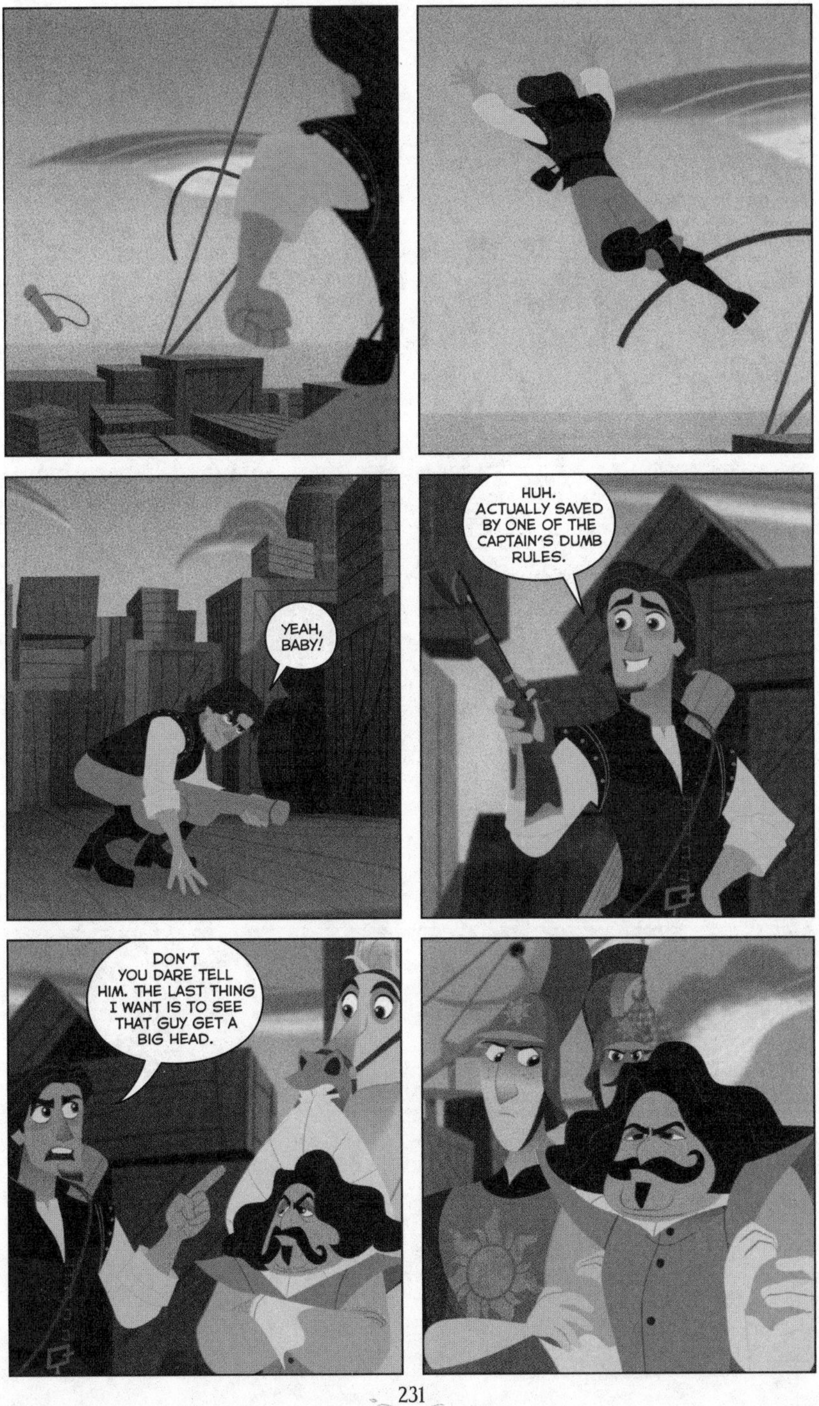
YEAH, BABY!
HUH. ACTUALLY SAVED BY ONE OF THE CAPTAIN'S DUMB RULES.
DON'T YOU DARE TELL HIM. THE LAST THING I WANT IS TO SEE THAT GUY GET A BIG HEAD.

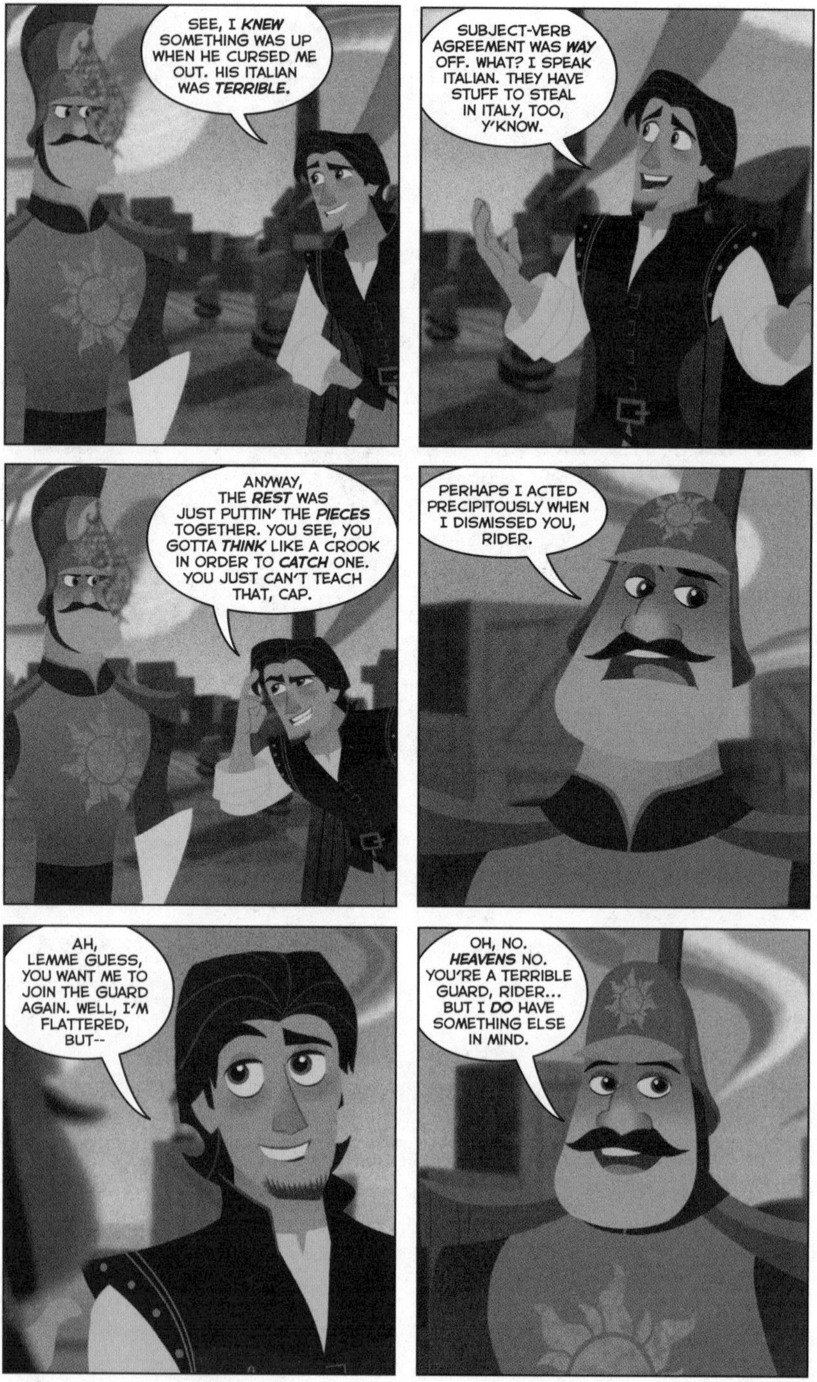
SEE, I KNEW SOMETHING WAS UP WHEN HE CURSED ME OUT. HIS ITALIAN WAS TERRIBLE.
SUBJECT-VERB AGREEMENT WAS WAY OFF. WHAT? I SPEAK ITALIAN. THEY HAVE STUFF TO STEAL IN ITALY, TOO, Y'KNOW.
ANYWAY, THE REST WAS JUST PUTTIN' THE PIECES TOGETHER. YOU SEE, YOU GOTTA THINK LIKE A CROOK IN ORDER TO CATCH ONE. YOU JUST CAN'T TEACH THAT, CAP.
PERHAPS I ACTED PRECIPITOUSLY WHEN I DISMISSED YOU, RIDER.
AH, LEMME GUESS, YOU WANT ME TO JOIN THE GUARD AGAIN. WELL, I'M FLATTERED, BUT--
OH, NO. HEAVENS NO. YOU'RE A TERRIBLE GUARD, RIDER... BUT I DO HAVE SOMETHING ELSE IN MIND.

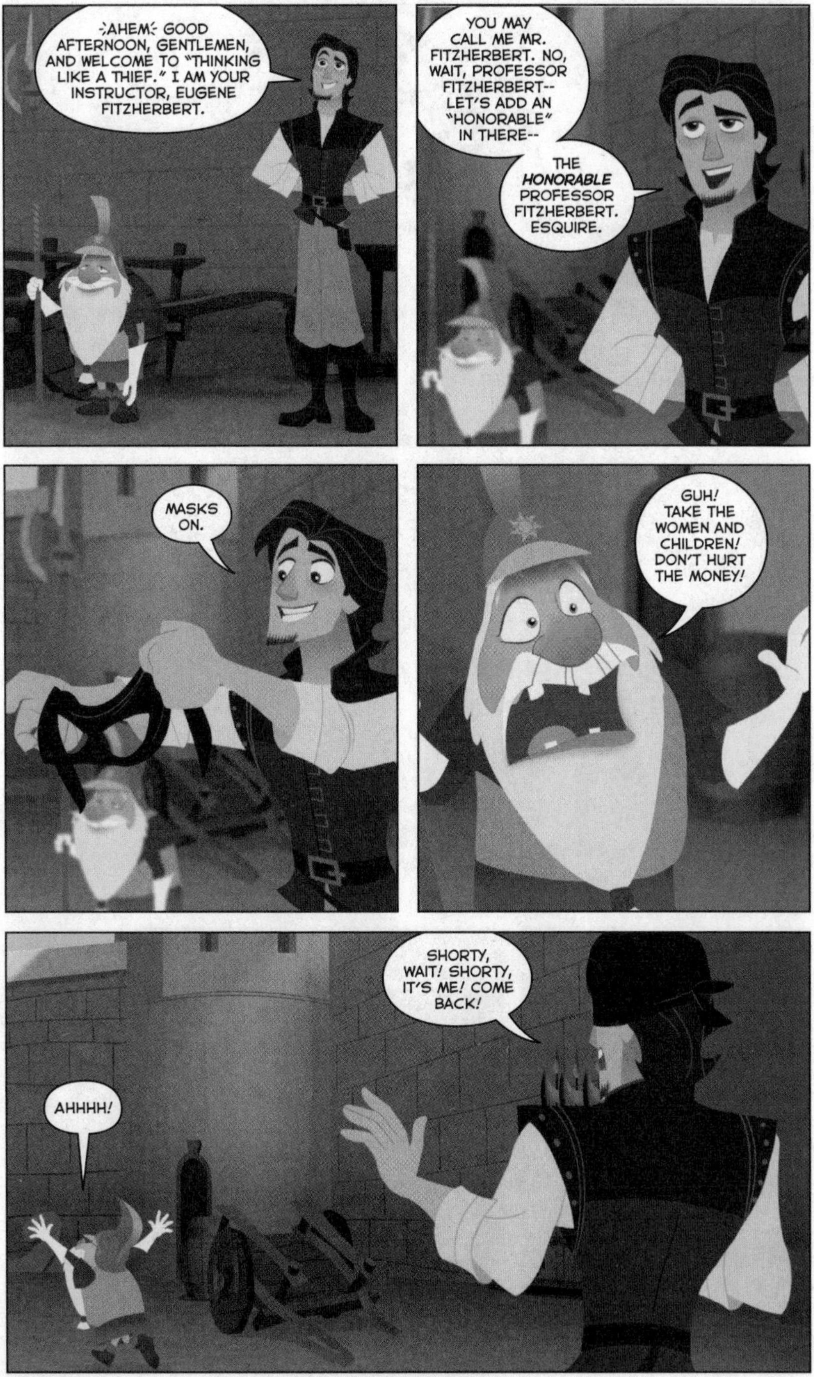
-AHEM- GOOD AFTERNOON, GENTLEMEN, AND WELCOME TO "THINKING LIKE A THIEF." I AM YOUR INSTRUCTOR, EUGENE FITZHERBERT.
YOU MAY CALL ME MR. FITZHERBERT. NO, WAIT, PROFESSOR FITZHERBERT-- LET'S ADD AN "HONORABLE" IN THERE--
THE *HONORABLE* PROFESSOR FITZHERBERT. ESQUIRE.
MASKS ON.
GUH! TAKE THE WOMEN AND CHILDREN! DON'T HURT THE MONEY!
SHORTY, WAIT! SHORTY, IT'S ME! COME BACK!
AHHHH!

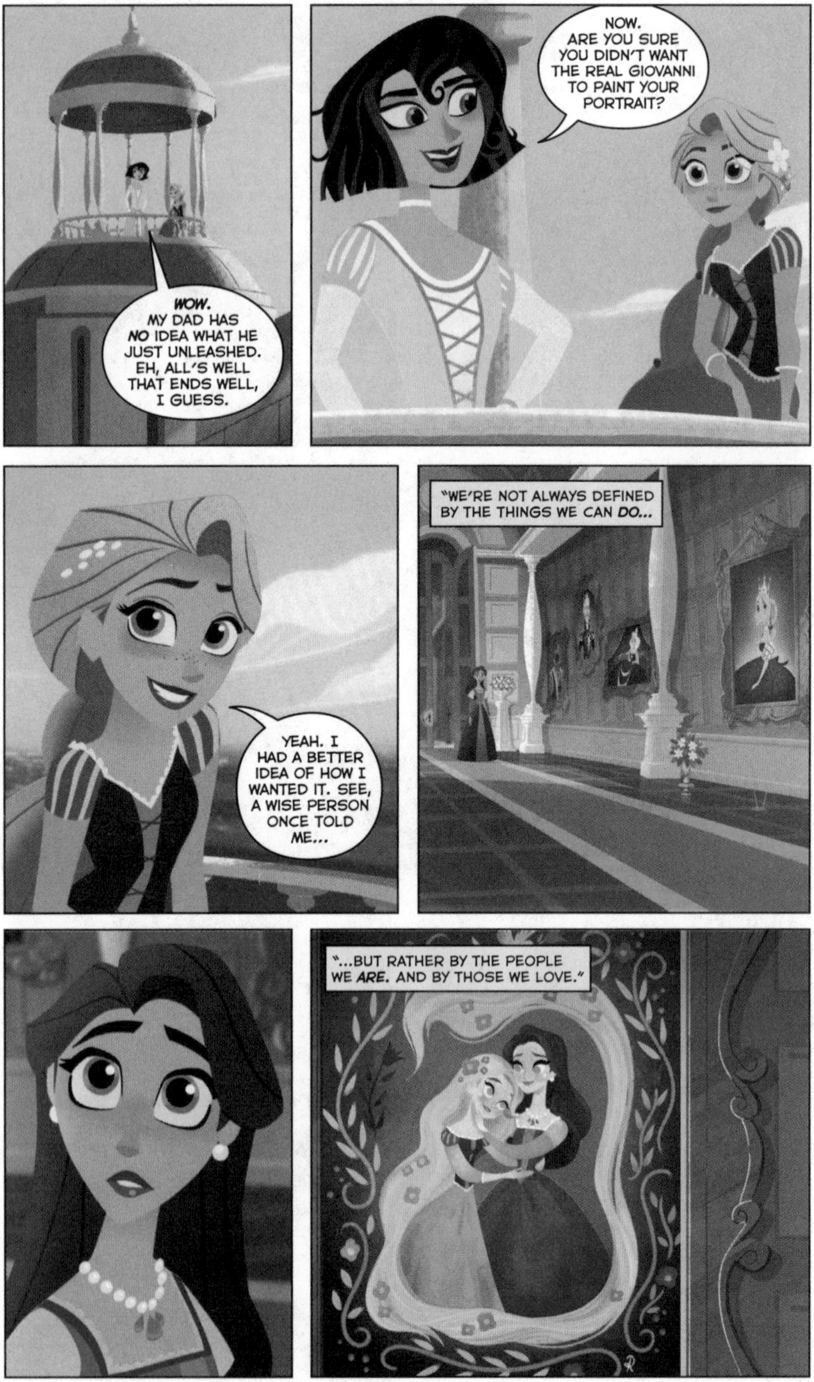
WOW. MY DAD HAS NO IDEA WHAT HE JUST UNLEASHED. EH, ALL'S WELL THAT ENDS WELL, I GUESS.
NOW. ARE YOU SURE YOU DIDN'T WANT THE REAL GIOVANNI TO PAINT YOUR PORTRAIT?
YEAH. I HAD A BETTER IDEA OF HOW I WANTED IT. SEE, A WISE PERSON ONCE TOLD ME...
"WE'RE NOT ALWAYS DEFINED BY THE THINGS WE CAN DO...
"...BUT RATHER BY THE PEOPLE WE ARE. AND BY THOSE WE LOVE."